## Raves for Zach's Adventures:

"No one who got two paragraphs into this dark, droll, down-right irresistible hard-boiled-dick novel could ever bear to put it down until the last heart pounding moment. Zack is off and running on his toughest case yet, and there is no way he is leaving us behind, no matter what the danger. This is futuristic pulp for the thinking reader, the one who enjoys a good chuckle, some mental exercise, and the occasional inside joke. Sit down with *The Plutonium Blonde* and a cold one and just see when you manage to pull your peepers away from the page again. On second thought, John Zakour and Lawrence Ganem are too damn good to be interrupted for something trivial; skip the cold one and save yourself a trip to the can."
                                                              —*SF Site*

"I had a great deal for fun with *The Plutonium Blonde* and have been looking forward to the sequel ever since. Well, it's finally here, and it's a good one. This is more humor than detective story, although Johnson and HARV are a pretty good pair of investigators as well as downright funny. If you like your humor slapstick and inventive, you need look no further for a good fix."
                                                              —*SF Chronicle*

"It's no mystery what kind of novel John Zakour and Lawrence Ganem's *Doomsday Brunette* is. The title says it all. The story is hard-boiled science fiction at its pulpy best. Zakour and Ganem's Zachary Johnson novels—which include *The Plutonium Blonde* and the forthcoming *The Radioactive Redhead*—are laugh-out-loud, action-packed mystery thrillers that both revere and lampoon the golden age of pulp fiction."
                                                              —*The Barnes and Noble Review*

Don't miss all of Zach's adventures:

# DANGEROUS DAMES

## THE PLUTONIUM BLONDE

## THE DOOMSDAY BRUNETTE

# JOHN ZAKOUR & LAWRENCE GANEM

## DAW BOOKS, INC.

**DONALD A. WOLLHEIM, FOUNDER**

375 Hudson Street, New York, NY 10014

**ELIZABETH R. WOLLHEIM**
**SHEILA E. GILBERT**
**PUBLISHERS**

http://www.dawbooks.com

First Paperback Printing, April 2008
1  2  3  4  5  6  7  8  9

DAW TRADEMARK REGISTERED
U.S. PAT. AND TM. OFF. AND FOREIGN COUNTRIES
—MARCA REGISTRADA.
HECHO EN U.S.A.
PRINTED IN THE U.S.A.

# DANGEROUS DAMES

# THE PLUTONIUM BLONDE

# 1

My name is Zachary Nixon Johnson. I am the last private detective on earth. I'll get to the whys and wherefores of that a little later and, as you'll see, it's not exactly one hundred percent true, but it sounds good and hopefully I've at least got your attention now.

The year is 2057 and, after a handful of species-altering upheavals, earth-shattering cataclysms, history-changing extraterrestrial contacts, and pop-culture disasters, the world is now a pretty safe place. I won't bore you with the judicial, economic, and anthropological minutiae of the *New* New World Order, but suffice to say that the sun still rises in the east, the human race is still around to notice it, and we still pull down the window shades, roll over in bed, and sleep until noon whenever possible.

Of course, the world's not perfect. People still run the shades-of-gray gamut of good to evil. There are still cops and robbers, saints and sinners, voters and politicians. And every once in a while, some crazy thing happens that threatens society, all of humanity, or the entire space-time continuum.

And for some reason, it always happens on my watch.

I guess that's as good a place as any to start this story.

# 2

It began like any other day, which is the way these things usually do. I was at my office on the New Frisco docks, watching the tourists outside, and trying hard not to think about how long it had been since good news had walked through my office door. I was also losing a game of holographic backgammon to the holo-image projection of my trusty, though occasionally annoying, computer compatriot HARV.

"So I catch the SIMFOLKS security guy, red-handed, stealing parts from the droid manufacturing plant. And I literally mean, *red-handed*. He was smuggling a hand out in his lunchbox. You know what I mean?"

"Oh, yes," said HARV, with a dignified smile on his face. "I understand the irony of the situation."

For some reason, whenever he projects himself, HARV likes to take the form of an elderly, balding English gentleman (or at least how HARV computes the optimal elderly, balding English gentleman should look). I guess he thinks that it gives him an air of distinction. I've long since regretted letting him download the old Wodehouse stories. His Jeeves sometimes gets a little annoying.

"Okay, so I say to the guy, 'All right buddy, hand over the hand,' which I thought was pretty funny. He runs into the spare parts room, grabs a droid femur and takes a swing at me. 'How 'bout I give you a leg up instead?' he says. From there the body parts and the puns just started flying left and right. 'No thanks, I'm already armed.' 'Nice suit. Is it double breasted?' 'Now that's what I call a bowel movement!'

"Finally, I grab a couple of droid heads, one in each hand,

and slam them upside his head like a pair of cymbals. He falls unconscious to the floor and—I can't believe I do this—but I stand up and say out loud, 'I guess two heads really *are* better than one.' "

I smiled. HARV smiled too, but only slightly, and there was an awkward silence. Then HARV quietly said, "I'll bet he was really disturbed at that turn of events."

"It's a joke, HARV."

"Actually, I think the term 'humorous anecdote' is more accurate."

"Either way, it's supposed to be funny. You get it?"

"Well," said HARV, "I understand the anatomical references and your use of common phraseology in an ironic manner, but wouldn't it have been more accurate for your last line to have been, 'I guess two android heads, when used as blunt trauma-inducing weapons, can cause severe concussive damage?"

I turned my attention back to the backgammon board. "Forget it," I said, "I should have known better than to waste the story on a computer."

"Yes, well forgive me, boss, if I don't quite grasp the subtle concept of witty PI banter. I guess I'll just have to be content with the ability to perform three billion separate calculations in a nanosecond. Frankly, I'm surprised that you managed to survive all those years without me."

(I should mention at this point that, although HARV likes to take on the form of a proper English butler, his attitude and speech patterns aren't the least bit proper, British or subservient. He's the world's most advanced computer and he doesn't let you forget it.)

"Now if you will kindly just roll the dice and take your turn. I am anxious to claim yet another victory."

I sighed and looked at my bleak options on the backgammon board.

"How about this: A guy walks into a bar with two chunks of plutonium sewn onto the shoulders of his shirt . . ."

"Please, spare us all the anguish and roll the dice."

I shook the two holo-dice (that weren't really there—even though a good portion of my brain thought they were) for an annoyingly long time, just to get on HARV's circuits a bit, and then made my roll. The dice bounced around the holographic backgammon board (which also wasn't really there), much as you would expect real dice to bounce around on a real backgammon board (although not quite).

Even if the holo-dice hadn't been semitransparent and slightly aglow, I would have somehow still known that they weren't real dice. This puzzled me for a nano, and I started to wonder why. Then, I thought to myself that I was starting to think too much about this. I'm a Private Investigator, after all. I'm supposed to answer questions, not create them. And yet, inevitably, in order to properly *answer* questions, one has to first *ask* questions. That's just the way the world works. Why is that? I thought.

Then I realized that I was getting *way* too philosophical for this stupid game, so I turned my attention back to the dice just as they ceased their simulated tumbling on the simulated board.

Double sixes.

There are times (most times, actually) when double sixes is a good roll. This, however, was one of those rare instances when it wasn't. HARV had my captured piece solidly blocked in with two of his four remaining pieces sitting squarely on the number six slot. I was trapped.

"I find it hard to believe," I said, not trying to disguise the disdain in my voice, "that you're not loading these dice. I've rolled three doubles this game and every one has been worthless."

"Oh, please," HARV responded, in his best calming, almost-but-somehow-not-quite-human, voice. "I am the most sophisticated computer on Earth. Why would I want, or for that matter, why would I need, to cheat to win a simple game of backgammon?" He paused for a nano. "Besides your third roll of the game was a double two, which you found quite useful. Perhaps you wish me to replay it for you on the wall screen in super-slow motion?"

"I'll take your word for it."

"As well you should, as I have no reason to lie. You have simply run into a series of unfortunate, but very possible, circumstances in this game of chance. Dice in motion are random objects, as you know, and subject to all laws of probability. Results of such probabilities cannot be accurately predicted nor controlled. It is the chaos theory in action."

"What I want to know is how come the chaos theory always seems to be in action when it's my turn to roll the dice?"

HARV's holographic image picked up the holo-dice and shook them, ever so properly, in his hand. As he did so, he lectured, also ever so properly, as only he can.

"If you don't mind my saying so, boss, you are fixating on the negative. You should be thankful that your bad luck at this gaming table does not necessarily translate into bad luck in the more important areas of life. You are, for instance, very fortunate when it comes to armed combat. You have been fired upon one hundred twenty-seven times in your career and have been wounded only thrice, each of those minimally so. You are also quite fortunate in the area of romantic interpersonal relationships. Or have you forgotten the lovely Dr. Electra Gevada? Quite honestly, your luck in this area is truly an example of the chaos theory run amok. Even I, the most sophisticated computer on Earth, have trouble computing what exactly such a beautiful and intelligent surgeon sees in you."

"There are some things, HARV, that are beyond even your abilities."

"True," he reluctantly agreed and tossed the dice. "But they are few and far between."

We both watched in silence as the dice rolled along the holographic board, like two very symmetrical tumbleweeds, before finally coming to rest.

Double sixes.

As I mentioned earlier, there are a few rare instances in backgammon where double sixes can be a bad roll. This, of course, was not one of those times.

"Oh, my, it appears as though I've won again," HARV said with a slight, but nevertheless very noticeable, smile. "If I were counting, this would mark my fifth victory in a row and my tenth victory over the last eleven games. It would also be my ninety-fourth victory in the last ninety-nine games and my five hundredth victory in the . . ."

"But then, you're not one to count, are you HARV?"

"Of course I am," HARV countered. "I'm a computer. It is what I do."

"That's it. We're using real dice and a real board next game."

"Fine," said, HARV. "Bring them out."

I thought for a nano, then mumbled under my breath.

"What was that?" HARV asked.

"I said I don't have any real dice. I don't think they make them anymore."

"Just as well," HARV said. "You probably wouldn't know how to work them anyway."

"Excuse me, but whatever happened to helping me count my blessings?"

"Ah, yes," HARV continued, "your blessings. Well, aside from surviving numerous altercations involving heavy ordnance and being romantically involved with someone several steps above you on the social register, you also have what one would describe in the current vernacular as a 'way groovy' job!"

I will tell you now. There's something very strange about hearing the world's most intelligent computer use the term "way groovy," but I'd grown accustomed to HARV's eccentricities.

I am considered by many people (most people who know me, actually) to be a bit of a throwback to a bygone era; why else would I choose to be a private eye in the twenty-first century? Personally, I like to think of myself more as a Renaissance man: living comfortably in the present but fascinated with the past. Truth to tell, I was born in the wrong century. I am endlessly (some would say compulsively) fascinated by anything and everything twen-cen. It was a simpler time when everybody wasn't "wired" to everything else. It was a more stylish time. A better time? Hey, I'm not naïve. But the cars were a lot cooler back then and, in my book, that counts for a lot.

I've been a licensed private eye for thirteen years. I got into the business in what they call a "down time." It was the height of the age of information, and the general public, who at that time had the world at their fingertips and eyeballs via the cellular net, had no real use for investigators. After all, you don't need someone to dig up dirt for you when you're standing in the middle of a dustbowl. True, it takes a special skill to know the right place to dig, but it's hard making that argument when the CaffeineCorner down the street is giving away copies of *The Complete and Unabridged History of History Volumes 1 and 2* on a nano-chip free with every purchase of a quadruple latte.

So over the next few years the rank and file of the gumshoe population dwindled substantially. The old-timers, some of them grand old men from the heyday, living, breathing specimens of Marlowe-esque history, gave up the game. A lot of them passed away over the years. Many just retired and moved to New Florida. Ten years ago, the World Council stopped issuing licenses and private eyes became an endangered species. To the world at large, PI had become nothing more than the area of a circle divided by the radius squared. Before I knew it, I was the last licensed guy on the PI register, and the associate partner position at my buddy Randy's software R&D lab was becoming a very real temptation.

To make matters worse, the PI void was about to be filled by the seamy underside of society. No, not organized crime. The entertainment industry.

EnterCorp, the world's largest entertainment conglomerate, realized that there was a profit to be made from human misery and suffering by recording and netcasting it to the masses. EnterCorp created a private eye subsidiary corporation they ironically called DickCo, and the company now does a lot of the work formerly done by freelance PIs.

They actively recruit PI wannabes (thugs mostly) and employ them to do "investigative" work (totally unlicensed, of course). Who cares about a license, after all, when you have the shadow-support of the third largest corporation in the world behind you? Basically, DickCo assigns its operatives regular cases, covers all their expenses, and pays them a regular, comfortable level salary. Operatives go where they're told go, investigate what they're told to investigate, and bust whatever heads they are (unofficially) told to bust. It's a sweet life . . . if you're a thug with highbrow pretensions. Unfortunately, the world still has its fair share of those. It just goes to show that there's a big difference between a PI and a dick.

Why does EnterCorp do it? Well, part of the package that

comes with your signing on the virtual dotted line is that DickCo has the right to record your actions at all times, twenty-four/seven, and netcast your work-related experiences on any of their many reality-based net shows. All operatives are fitted with netcast cameras that are surgically attached to their retinas (I call them dick-cams). Tracking devices are implanted in their necks so, in a pinch, satellite cameras can locate them to get dramatic overhead shots of their adventures. And the most popular of the rank and file get netcast "and ones," a sidekick whose sole job is to dutifully get the proper coverage of the operative (and sometimes provide comic relief or a sounding board in order to easily provide exposition).

EnterCorp made me an offer when they were just starting up. Needless to say, I thought the terms stunk worse than an angry unwashed skunk eating old fish and extra stinky cheese, and I turned them down flat.

Still, I didn't want to quit the PI business. After all, what other job lets you set your own hours, carry a cool gun, and get paid to snoop around?

Then five years ago I had, for lack of a better term, my breakthrough case. I won't bore you with the details, but it involved YOM, which was short for "Yesterday Once More." They were a teleport delivery service that promised to deliver packages back through time. Their motto was "When it really should have been there *yesterday*."

The City Council, at the very strong urging of Fedport, YOM's competition in the delivery service market, was worried that traveling so casually back and forth through time threatened the world as we know it and hired me of all people to set things right (there was a budget crisis and the city hadn't allocated much money for protecting the fabric of time, so I was all they could afford).

Within a week, I had shut YOM down and reality as we knew it was safe once more. Actually, it turned out that YOM wasn't really delivering packages though time at all. They were just hypnotizing their customers through subliminal advertisements to convince them that they'd received the packages the day before. So all I'd really saved the world from was false advertising.

Still, the press latched onto the story for a time, and I began what I thought would be my fifteen nanoseconds of fame. Then it was discovered that I was actually the last legally licensed Private Investigator on Earth, and that sort of gave new life to my marketability.

A week later, I was hired as the private bodyguard for that teenage holovision starlet. I can't remember her name. You know, the one with the hair? After that I did talk shows and the net circuit. A year later I saved the city when a deranged pilot tried to crash a twen-cen satellite into Fisherman's Wharf, and since then I've been a bit of a minor celeb in this part of the world. I haven't exactly stayed one hundred percent true to the Sam Spade mold, but every organism learns one way or the other that when the times are changing, you either adapt or die.

"By the way, boss," HARV said as he reracked the backgammon board. "We received our first of what could be several angry overdue rent notices this morning from your landlord."

"What do you mean, overdue?" I asked. "Didn't you pay the rent?"

"I've been dragging my feet, so to speak, on the finances in general."

"Any particular reason why?"

"Well, at the nano," HARV said, "your finances are stretched a bit thin. A few client payments are overdue and your residual check from the last net special was, shall we say, underwhelming."

"Yeah, maybe Randy was right and we should have called it 'Zach Johnson Versus the Bikini Babes from the Planet Bimbo Thirty-Eight D.'"

"Be that as it may, you're not, as they say, flush with investable capital at the nano."

"So, we need to raise some creds in a hurry."

"As always, boss, your keen grasp of the obvious overwhelms me. And may I take this opportunity to remind you of the very generous offer extended to you last week by the good people at OmegaMart to celebrate their new store opening."

"Forget it."

"It's good money, boss, for a simple personal appearance."

"Forget it, HARV," I said. "I'm not doing it. Gates, I'd

rather do anything than another one of those DOS-awful ribbon-cutting ceremonies."

And at that nano, three cheap-looking thugs in expensive looking suits crashed through my office door, turning the simulated wood into so much simulated kindling (funny thing, irony).

My first reaction was, "Why don't thugs ever try the knob?" which, however incisive, wasn't very much help at the time. My second reaction was, "This is not a good thing," which was more pertinent to the matter at hand but overly obvious and, again, not all that useful. This is why I never trust my first two reactions to any crisis situation.

Carol, my secretary and probable future niece-in-law, followed the thugs into the room, shrugging her little shoulders apologetically. Carol is an extremely smart little girl, brilliant actually. She has the mind of a world class physicist. She's the niece of my fiancée, Dr. Electra Gevada, and, when she's not attending classes at the university, she works part-time as my receptionist.

One other thing, she's also a psi (short for psionic), Class 1 Level 6, which makes her exceptionally powerful. However, because she's young, her talents are still a bit raw. She's very gifted at reading minds, and only slightly less skillful at mind control. She has trouble at times with her telekinesis and she tends to lose that ability under pressure, but, hey, she's just a kid and you can't really expect her to be perfect. Besides, she's cute as a button.

She's been recruited by nearly every government, corporation, and gaming casino in the new world (psis are rare and in high demand in the business world). She was even kidnapped once by a fifth-world country in the hopes that she'd become their secret weapon and the key to their world dominance. That actually got a little ugly and, as a result, I'm no longer able to purchase my favorite brand of macaroons. But that's another story.

"Sorry, Tío," she shouted to me, as the snarling thugs, with blasters drawn, formed an ominous semicircle around my desk. "My mind blasts didn't stop them."

Smart guy that I am, I realized then that this day wasn't going to be so ordinary after all.

# 3

When facing an imminent confrontation with multiple thugs, the PI handbook (now long out of print in both paper and electronic versions) strongly suggests that you remember the acronym W.E.P.N.

- Wits: keep them about you.
- Evaluate your foe's strengths.
- Postulate their weaknesses. And assign each foe a slightly demeaning . . .
- Nickname (it will subconsciously help your fighting skills if you convince yourself that your opponent is someone known, for example, as "Bedwetter").

These particular thugs in front of me were clearly hired muscle: big men (one of them truly immense) in big suits with big ugly scowls on their faces. Working from left to right, they were.

Stupid Ape: I had to quantify this with the word "stupid" so as not to offend the ape community. Large of limb, impotent of intellect, he was the kind of guy who lettered in leg-breaking at thug school but flunked the written exam because he didn't know which end of the e-pencil to use.

Fuzz Face: I pegged this guy as the boss. My first clue was that he stood in the middle. Let's face it, when you're dealing with thugs, the boss always stands in the middle. They're a lot like geese in that respect. He also looked a little less animal-like than the other two. Shades hid his eyes and a dirty little mustache and goatee stippled his chin. My guess is that he thought the facial hair made him look menacing. To me, it only made him look like the back end of a blind shepherd's ewe.

Both these goons were packing high power hand blasters which, of course, were aimed directly at me.

Man Mountain: Stupid Ape and Fuzz Face were trouble, but this guy brought the situation up a few levels on the danger meter (right up to "uh-oh, did I pay this month's premium on my life insurance?").

First off, he was immense. I've said that before, I know, but I want to make sure I do him justice here. He was two and a half meters tall and very nearly as wide. To this guy the Bahamian diet was something you try because you've already eaten Jamaica and St. Croix.

Clearly, the guy was GE (genetically engineered)—thugs that size just don't come from Mother Nature—and this set off all kinds of alarms in my head. It takes a pile of credits to get a GE (they've been outlawed since 2035), so I knew right away that I was up against a goon squad who had some hefty financing behind them.

"Zachary Johnson," Fuzz Face barked, further strengthening my belief that he was the brains (such as they were) of the outfit. "You're coming with us."

"Don't they teach manners in thug school anymore?" I responded, trying hard to sound unimpressed.

"Manners don't mean much when you got a blaster pointed at your face," he growled. "Now like I said, you're coming with us. Alive or in pieces, it don't matter to me."

"My, my," I stated coolly, then glanced at HARV, "when it comes to kidnapping, you fine gentleman certainly are in the dark."

"What the DOS are you talking about?" Fuzz Face demanded, clearly a little confused (but, frankly, I had the feeling that confusion was a state this guy visited often).

Right on cue HARV killed the office lights and shaded the window screens to black, plunging the room into total darkness, and utter confusion.

"What happened?" one of the thugs (Stupid Ape, I think) mumbled.

"Ugh," another thug (probably Man Mountain) grunted.

Just then the lights blinked back on and my three thug friends suddenly found themselves faced with fifteen identical versions of yours truly.

"How'd he do that?" asked Stupid Ape.

"Ugh," Man Mountain grunted again.

"They're holograms, you idiots. But one of them is the real thing," Fuzz Face answered as he turned and aimed his blaster at the wall screen covering HARV's power unit. "We just need to take out the computer and . . ."

The real me chose that nano to leap at Fuzz Face from the crowd of holograms and nail him hard with a snap kick to the groin—not very sporting, I know, but what do you want, he was going to shoot my computer.

"Didn't your mother ever teach you not to pick on defenseless and very expensive computers?" I asked, as he crumpled to the ground at my feet.

Unfortunately, my move surprised HARV as much as it did the thugs because when I moved on Fuzz Face, the hologram images of me all remained motionless. And that pretty much blew my cover.

Stupid Ape was quick to take advantage of the opening. He hit me with a haymaker to the gut that sent me stumbling backward. I managed to remain on my feet (thanks mostly to the wall I hit) and came right back at him.

A look of confusion crossed his face as I rushed him. And by confusion, I mean above and beyond his normal level. Apparently, he wasn't accustomed to seeing his victims bounce back after taking one of his good punches.

"Huh?" he questioned eloquently.

"You must be losing your touch," I said, lying through my teeth. That punch would have cracked my ribs like eggshells had it not been for the armor I wear. It's a light, but extremely strong, carbon alloy specially designed for me by my good buddy, Dr. Randy Pool. It protects me from heavy blows and even light blaster fire. It gets a little itchy in warm weather, but a man who makes a living poking his nose into places where it doesn't belong can never to be too careful.

I gave Stupid Ape a nano to wonder about his shortcomings and then moved in for the kill.

"Next thing you know, you'll develop a glass jaw," I said. Then I let loose with a fast right cross to his blocklike chin.

A wonderful look of total shock and confusion swept over the thug's face as he flew backward through the air like a hovercraft with a stuck accelerator. To him, it was as though every rule in the world had suddenly been reprogrammed. Some average Joe had just taken his best punch, shrugged it off, and then hit him harder than he'd ever been hit before. He had a few nanos to ponder the new rules as he flew over my desk, crashed into the wall, and then fell to the floor.

If there's one thing I've learned in my many years as a PI, it's that sometimes you need to cheat a little bit to survive. Let's face it, St. Peter's parlor is SRO with guys who tried to fight fairly. Anyone who's been around the block a time or two learns the hard way that when it's do-or-die time, you don't get extra credit for being nice.

My armor helps me cheat. On top of protecting me, it's also soft-wired to my muscles, which means that in times of need I can draw juice from its circuits, channel it directly into my arms or legs and basically give myself a quantum-sized helping hand. Yes, it's cheating. I'm not as tough as these thugs think I am. But remember, I'm not the one who came into the room waving his blaster around, so forgive me if I don't strictly adhere to the Book of Fisticuffs Etiquette.

Unfortunately, in this case, I'd used my trump card a little too soon. Two thugs were down but my luck was about to run out because Man Mountain chose that nano to join the fray. I knew this because a fist the size of my desk chair swatted me from the side and sent me tumbling. I felt this blow, even through the armor, and this time when I hit the wall, I felt it crack (at least I hoped it was the wall).

Man Mountain gathered me up and used his massive girth to drive me into the wall that housed HARV's computer screen. I quickly juiced-up my fist with energy from the body armor and countered with a jab to the behemoth's gut.

Sparks flew.

Man Mountain smiled.

I gulped.

"You not so tough enough, eh?" he said as he wrapped his fingers around my throat. "I made in 2029 before tests banned. Made real strong."

"And exceptionally smart as well," I said, trying as always

to remain lucid, or at least as lucid as one can be when being strangled to death by a tank with arms. "If they ever bring back slapstick, you could play all four Stooges."

I flicked my left wrist in just the right way and my trusty Colt .45 version 2-A popped neatly into my hand from its forearm holster. Guns are nasty, messy items, but there are times when nasty is called for, and messy is just something you have to live with.

But Man Mountain had somehow anticipated this move and reacted with surprising speed. His free hand grabbed my arm and pinned it, gun and all, firmly against the wall. Then he gave me one of those "ha ha, you're even dumber than I am" smiles, which was especially nasty because, in this case, it rang so true.

"I talk not good but I smarter than words," he said. "When I strangle you, your armor, I know you wear, no help."

He began tightening his grip on my throat with his giant atomic vise of a hand and I began to regret not ordering the armor in the turtleneck style.

"Okay," I gasped, "I guess I'll come along quietly now. Where are we headed?"

His lips curled back at the corners and the smile turned into a snarl.

"What you say?" he snickered. "I not hear you. Oh well." And his fingers tightened even more, cutting off my air and slowly crushing my throat.

I felt my eyes roll back in my head and the world turned gray around the edges. Unconsciousness beckoned. The dark void opened before me and I felt the urge to plunge into the netherword and let its peaceful shadows cover me in the big sleep of nevermore.

That was when I knew I was in big trouble. I always get *way* too metaphoric when I'm facing death.

# 4

I forced myself away from the pretentious verse and focused my mind on the matter at hand. On the bright side, HARV was up and fully operational, and Carol was ready to use her psi powers (or her fists) to do whatever she could.

On the not-so-bright side, Carol's psi attacks had been ineffective against Man Mountain, and her fists even less so. She was currently whacking away at his back with a chunk of the broken coat rack but Man Mountain hardly seemed to notice.

As for HARV, well, he's not exactly programmed for violence and, in times of emergency, he tends to retreat into a semi-neurotic shell of random probability analyses. At this particular nano he was calculating the odds of my being saved by a violent tsunami striking the area. As a result, neither he nor Carol was able to do anything other than watch helplessly as Man Mountain gleefully continued to strangle me.

"You die soon!" he laughed, squeezing my throat, as though he were wringing out a damp washcloth (that he really despised). "Kill you, then have fun with your secretary. And she not able to stop me!"

And there was the rub. Under normal circumstances, Carol should have been able to freeze Man Mountain with a glance, turn his gray matter into a frozen daiquiri, and have him dance the bossa nova with the desk chair, yet for some reason she couldn't penetrate his cranium. All of the thugs had to be wearing psi-blockers, and that set off a whole new round of alarms in my head. Psi-blockers are experimental, they're government issue only, and tend to liquefy the internal organs of the wearer if worn too long. Apparently, though, that was a risk that Man Mountain (or whomever sent him) was willing to take.

"HARV," a hoarse whisper was all I could manage. "Scan his head."

"Scan for what?" HARV asked.

"For a psi-blocker," I wanted to say, but my air was just about gone and I couldn't say anything further. HARV would have to figure it out for himself.

"Well, he's ugly," HARV began unhelpfully. "As ugly as he is massive, although those two qualities are difficult to compare, one being objective, the other being totally subjective." HARV took a brief time out to collect more data.

"His nose is roughly the size of an adult athletic shoe. The inner lining is also slightly hairier than normal, which, although considered disgusting by contemporary human standards, is relatively common in genetically engineered beings. I for one am certainly glad the council banned most of these experiments.

"His mouth cavity is roughly one half cubic meter large. That's just an estimate. I could give you an exact measurement but I'd rather not get that intrusive. I fear the malodorous power of his breath."

I rolled my eyes in frustration (and pain).

"His eyes are smaller than normal and relatively pupil-less. They have a rather cold, cunning look to them although, judging by his speech patterns, any sign of intelligence is probably coincidental. By the way, I'm fairly certain that he didn't understand your 'Stooges' reference. But then I'm also fairly certain that a full ninety-nine point eight percent of the general population wouldn't understand it either, so we can't hold that against him."

I was as good as dead. I knew it. All I could hope for now was that Man Mountain would find a way to strangle HARV when he was finished with me.

"Oh, he also has a psi-blocking device in his left ear."

Vingo!

I shot a glance (and all the thought I could muster) toward Carol. She read my mind like a billboard and sprang into action (thankfully she's a little quicker on the uptake than HARV).

She jumped on Man Mountain's back and started climbing

toward his head, but Man Mountain shrugged his boulderlike shoulders and tossed her away. So Carol went to plan B.

"Hey, HARV," she said, "this guy sure has a bright future, doesn't he?"

"What?" HARV asked.

"You know, a bright future. A really, really *bright* future."

"Yes, well from the look of things, it's a much brighter future than the boss'," HARV said.

"Ay, caramba, HARV," Carol yelled in frustration. "Flash him!"

That's when it hit HARV.

"Oh, I get it," he said.

With that, the giant wallscreen behind me strobed to bright white, and the light flash hit Man Mountain like a 1000 megawatt slap in the corneas. He turned his head and covered his eyes with a massive forearm, loosening his grip on my throat and, more importantly, freeing my right hand.

I plunged my free hand deep into his ear (not the most wonderful experience) and quickly dug around for the psi-blocker. I was in halfway up to my forearm before I latched onto what I hoped was the device and pulled it free with a flourish.

As Man Mountain began to recover, I held the psi-blocker high in the air for Carol to see. She smiled and kicked her psi powers into high gear.

"Drop him," Carol ordered, furrowing her brow.

Man Mountain froze in his tracks and his eyes glazed over. Carol had locked on to his mind like a cute little psi vise and, without the blocker, his mind was putty in her hands.

He loosened his grip on my throat and I slid down the wall to the floor, gasping gratefully for air.

"Turn around," Carol commanded.

Man Mountain obeyed.

"I'm going to hit you so hard it's going to knock you out cold," she said.

Then she tapped him with her finger and he crashed to the ground like a kiloton of bricks on Jupiter.

"Nice work," I said as I slowly climbed to my feet.

She puffed on the tip of her finger like a gunfighter kissing his revolver. "Thanks, Tío," she smiled.

The hologram of HARV reappeared in the middle of the room.

"What about me, boss?"

"We'll talk about it later, HARV."

Unbeknownst to us all, on the other side of the room Fuzz Face slowly regained his senses. He furtively looked around and when he saw that Carol, HARV, and I were busy having an impromptu staff review, he slowly reached his hand toward his blaster. Centimeter by centimeter, he stretched toward the weapon. The slowness of the movement was agony for him. Inside he was seething, furious at me for cold-cocking him. He was hot for revenge and he wanted it now, but he knew that he had to be patient. He had to take me by surprise.

At last, his hand gently touched the butt of the blaster. The special handle read his signature palm print and sprang to life in his hand, powering up in less than a second. He smiled and switched the blaster to full power.

"Johnson!" he growled.

I turned toward him, and a look of abject terror passed over my face.

"Who's laughing now?" he said and fired.

The energy beam hit me full on, punched a hole through my chest, and splattered my insides against the wall. Fuzz Face laughed triumphantly, awash in his violent, victorious glory.

Then he woke up.

And when he did, he found himself bound to my desk chair by four meters of electromagnetically generated force-chains. Stupid Ape was beside him, also tightly bound but still unconscious (and dreaming of tapioca pudding, don't ask me why). We didn't have chains big enough for Man Mountain so we stuck him in the bathroom and threw a force field around the whole thing. (Gates, but this was going to run up my power bill).

"Nice dream, wasn't it?" I said to Fuzz Face. "Splattering me against the wall was an especially nice touch, but I think you have some serious anger management issues that you need to face."

"What'd you do to me?" he asked.

"We were in your head, bozo, courtesy of my secretary, the psi. And I must say it was pretty lonely there. I even felt a bit of a draft." I pulled the psi-blocker that had once been in his ear out of my pocket and dangled it in front of him like a hypnotist's watch. "Now I'd like some information."

He glared at me in cold, angry silence and had another one of those blow-Zach-Johnson-to-smithereens daydreams.

"Fine, act like a clone," I said. "Carol, if you can stand the loneliness, go back into this guy's head and tell me his story."

Carol stared at the thug for less than a nano, then smiled. "He works for ExShell," she said.

Fuzz Face did not appreciate being read. "You freak of nature."

"With the company you keep, I'd be careful with the name calling."

"Go to sleep!" Carol ordered.

Fuzz Face's eyes immediately glazed and he fell over, out like a burned-out fluorescent on the dark side of the moon at midnight.

"HARV," I said, in my most businesslike voice. "Net me ExShell on the vid."

"There will be no need for that," HARV stated as calmly and as annoyingly as ever.

"HARV," I said angrily. "Please try to remember, that I'm the human here and you are the machine. Therefore, in theory, you are supposed to do what I tell you to do. Now net me ExShell right now or find me a computer who knows how to follow a simple command!"

"There is no need to establish a connection with ExShell," HARV replied, implacably calm, "because you already have an incoming message from BB Star, the Chief Executive Officer of ExShell."

"Okay," I said, trying (unsuccessfully) not to sound surprised. "That'll work too. Put her on the screen, please."

"As you wish, O human master," said HARV with a theatrical gesture.

# 5

I turned to the wall screen as a vid-window zoomed open and a six-foot streaming image of BB Star flashed on. I'd seen her picture, of course, on holovision and in the various net news-magazines, but I'd never seen her direct-linked like this before. Mature, graceful, and tremendously attractive, just her presence over the live net seemed to light up the room. She had an elegantly chiseled face framed by long, golden hair which was cut in a businesslike style, yet somehow still added to her allure. She possessed the kind of beauty that seemed untouchable, almost unnatural in some way. Her deep blue eyes surveyed my office through her own vid-screen and she smiled, ever so slightly, through her full lips.

"Bravo, Mr. Johnson," she said. "Please send the boys home when they regain consciousness. They will give you no more trouble."

"I think instead that I'll send ExShell the bill for the damage they caused and let you pick these bozos up at the police station."

"ExShell will of course reimburse you for any collateral damage created by this little test, but it will not be necessary to involve the local authorities."

"I'm sorry, did you say test?" I questioned, angrily.

"Correct," she replied with a smile. "And congratulations on a splendid performance."

"No offense, Ms. Star, but I hate tests," I said. "Especially ones that involve blasters, assassins, or tricky math problems!"

BB Star remained calm and steady, her big blue eyes never leaving mine. "I run a big company, Mr. Johnson. I do not hire anyone unless I know for certain that they are worth the investment."

I turned from the vid-window and shrugged my shoulders at Carol and HARV. "Am I the only one who's confused here?"

"That's usually the case, boss," HARV said. "This time, though, I'd say no."

"I am offering you a job, Mr. Johnson. I will give you all the necessary details when we meet in person," she said, ignoring the fact that I was ignoring her. "Kindly be in my office in exactly three hours."

"Why, so your thugs can take a few whacks at me on familiar territory?" My question was only partially rhetorical.

"Not to worry," she smiled, treating my partially rhetorical question as though it were totally nonrhetorical. "You passed the audition. You are in no danger from me."

"Yeah, well thanks for the reassurance," I said, "but I'm going to need a few more details before stepping directly into the lion's den."

"I will give you more data when we meet in person. The net is too easy to spoof. Therefore, I look forward to seeing you in now slightly less than three hours' time."

"I'm sorry, Ms. Star. Again, no offense meant but, frankly, you have a thing or two to learn about people management if you think I'm going to set one foot into your office now, let alone *work* for you, after what you've done here today."

"Mr. Johnson, I understand that your normal rate is five thousand credits per day," she said, her eyes never wavering from mine. "While in my employ I shall pay you twenty-five thousand per day."

"He'll be there in ten minutes," HARV chimed like a sycophantic alarm clock.

"HARV . . ."

"Look, boss," he said, "it's either this or the OmegaMart opening. And you have to admit, you're curious here, right?"

I clenched my teeth and turned back toward the vid-window. "Fine, Ms. Star, I'll see you in three hours at your office. But I'm already on your clock. As a matter of fact, I've been on the clock since your goons came through my door.

"Fine," she answered.

"And I'm not taking your case sight unseen," I continued.

"If I don't like the sound of it, then I'm walking with no strings attached."

"And all information discussed at the meeting will remain privileged," she countered.

"Agreed."

"And you must come alone, unarmed, and without your computer. No weapons or outside communication devices are allowed in my office building."

"I can live with that," I said, and I heard HARV gasp behind me.

"Fine then," she smiled. "I look forward to meeting you in person." With that, she blinked out and the vid-window zoomed closed.

I turned to Carol, who had been quietly scanning BB Star's thoughts since the call began. "Did you pick up anything?"

She shook her head. "It's hard enough to do over the net under normal conditions. ExShell probably has all kinds of defenses in their system."

"Or she may have an extremely strong mind," I turned to HARV. "What do you make of the deal?"

HARV's reply was (not surprisingly) overly loquacious. "ExShell, as I hope you are aware, is the largest corporation on the planet. They currently manufacture fifty-five percent of all personal, municipal, and governmental electronic hardware, hold patents on the operating systems for sixty-three percent of the world's computers and control twenty-two percent of the current soft drink market. Also, last week they completed their purchase of the country of Finland. They have incomparably vast resources and can afford the finest minds and the most advanced equipment in existence. The fact that they now require your services is a clear sign of desperation."

"Thanks a meg," I replied. "And the next time we get attacked by armed thugs, I'm going to seriously consider letting them put a couple of energy blasts into your wall unit."

"I didn't mean it quite the way you interpreted, boss," HARV said. "I'm simply stating that whatever the situation may be, it must be something very dire for ExShell to call upon you, and especially so for Ms. Star to do so personally. She is known as a bit of a recluse.

"Also, I should note here, if I may, that it would take more than a few energy blasts to the main wallscreen to destroy me. I have logic and memory boards in numerous locations, and Dr. Pool has backup copies of my singularly original operating system in more than a dozen secure locations around the globe. It's also worth stating that you would be lost without my constant aid and assistance."

"Yeah, lost but happy," I said as I headed toward the door. "Now come on, we have three hours to do our prep work."

"Where you going?" Carol asked.

"You're the psi. You figure it out."

Carol stared at me and furrowed her brow for a nano. "You're going to Dr. Pool's lab to get your armor repaired and to get background information on BB Star and her security."

"Vingo," I said, touching a finger to my nose.

"You're also regretting that second burrito you had for breakfast and you have a particularly graphic picture of my Aunt Electra in some kind of lace negligee in your subconscious."

"I think you dug a little too deeply that time," I said.

"Tell me about it," Carol said with a gag.

# 6

I left my office and walked along the docks toward my bright red 2030 Honda Mustang. It's a classic, although, as HARV constantly reminds me, slightly outdated, piece of machinery. As I walked, I couldn't help wondering what it must have been like here on the docks decades ago, before teleportation devices turned the docks from bustling, grimy places filled with grunts and groans to an overcrowded tourist attraction filled with the whirs and hums of recording devices. That's one of the perks that comes with being the last private eye on the planet. I get to ponder things like this and pass it off as "atmosphere."

Unfortunately, the atmosphere was abruptly interrupted by the arrival of what I consider to be the most hideous pustule on the underbelly of the *New* New World Order. Crime syndicates, killer mutations, and guilds of assassin cyborgs may be bad, but they aren't nearly as annoying as the monster that I was about to face.

The press.

They swarmed me like flies on a day-old road apple ... wait a minute, that makes me look kind of bad ... they were more like flies on a fresh Twinkie ... a charismatic Twinkie.

They weren't actual, organic, human being journalists of course. With all the so-called "newsworthy" events happening in the world today, newspeople just don't have time anymore to actually *be* anywhere. Gates forbid, they're interviewing me in Frisco when an Elvis clone slips in his bathtub in New Vegas and they get scooped by the net-dude on another bandwidth. Most journalists now have a dozen or so pressbots to cover their beats. Pressbots are low-tech androids programmed to mimic the owner's voice and personality, equipped with direct audio/visual feeds to the central studio. This way, a journalist can chase a dozen stories at the same time while remaining in the cool, safe comfort of his or her office. Truth to tell, it's only a matter of time before the netnews execs realize that they only really need the pressbots and toss all the actual human reporters out on their collective earpieces. When that happens, there'll be almost as many vapid personalities on the unemployment line as there were during the great budget crunch of 2017, when the old U.S. government laid off the House of Representatives.

One of the pressbots thrust himself (mike first) into my face and smiled through robotic teeth. "Mr. Johnson, I'm Bill Gibbon the Third from *Entertainment This Nano*. There was a report of a commotion in your office ten minutes ago. Care to comment?"

"Not to worry, Mr. Baboon . . ."

"Gibbon."

"It wasn't a real commotion," I said, "just a full-contact rehearsal for my upcoming made-for-HV special: Zachary Nixon Johnson versus the Cheap Thugs in Expensive Suits. Net your local video-feed provider now to ask about availability in your area. Now if you'll excuse me, I have important PI stuff to do. Never a dull nano when you're me."

The press continued to follow me like a pack of noisy rats after a good-looking piece of cheese on the run. I ignored their questions and moved quickly to my car.

"Mr. Johnson, is it true that you and the lovely Dr. Gevada will be married next week on Mars?"

"Do you confirm that you are considering quitting the PI business to pursue a singing career?"

"Do you deny that you punched out a man last week simply because he looked at the lovely Dr. Gevada the wrong way?"

"Do you not deny that you punched out a man last week simply because he looked at your beautiful secretary the wrong way?"

"Will you please say absolutely nothing if it is true that your computer, HARV, is having a romantic relationship with your beautiful secretary?"

"Door," I called to the car as I moved, still surrounded by the press brigade.

The driver-side door popped open obediently and I jumped in fast, trying hard to crush as few mikes as possible while slamming the door in the crowd of collective pressbot faces. Deep down, I knew they were only doing their jobs and that the media's overzealous pursuit of celebrity stories was what kept me in the public eye, but they were annoying enough to drive a guy downright crazo. And there wasn't much of a story here . . . yet.

"Engine," I barked to my car computer. On command, the dashboard obediently lit up and the engine gently turned over and purred like a cat on genetically enhanced catnip.

"Destination please?" the onboard computer asked.

I plugged the coordinates into the driver keyboard.

"Do you wish me to drive?" the computer responded.

I hit the "yes" button.

"As you wish," the computer said as it gently eased the car into the street.

I touched another button on the steering column and HARV's simulated face popped into a window on my dash.

"I wish you'd let me override this antiquated car computer." HARV said. "It's embarrasses me even to use its interface."

"How many times do I have to tell you, HARV? A classic car . . ."

". . . needs a classic computer," HARV mimicked. "Yes, I know. You've made that specious argument to me exactly one hundred eleven times in the past three years."

"You'd think you'd have figured it out by now," I said, and the car computer gave HARV what sounded like the raspberry. HARV, true to form, kept his dignity and ignored us both.

"Nice cover-up on that Zachary Nixon Johnson versus the Cheap Thugs thing," he said, sarcastically, "but did you really need to add the 'never a dull nano when you're me' part?"

"You didn't like that?"

"A bit egocentric, don't you think?"

"Well, maybe," I said, "but it's true. I was after all, attacked by killers during a backgammon game."

"Point taken," HARV reluctantly agreed.

"Okay then. Now, I'm going to need all the background info you can give me on BB Star."

"She's rather famous. How much do you already know?"

"I know she used to be a stripper."

"Exotic dancer," HARV corrected.

"Oh, well, if we're going to be geopolitically sensitive about it, I guess the proper term would be 'professional artistic gyrator.' Whatever. She was a stripper who married an old billionaire. He died, surprise, surprise. Now she's a billionaire."

"Well, yes," HARV agreed. "That is one way of putting it. Not a very complete way, but accurate within its own simplistic scope. Would you care for a more detailed version?"

"That would be nice," I said, with a wee bit of my own sarcasm.

"Her name was BB Baboom. Though I am relatively certain that was a stage name." He paused for a nano. "Yes, here it is, her given name was Betty Barbara Backerman."

"I can see why she changed it."

"Born and raised in Oakland, until the age of ten. At that time, she and her mother, now deceased, moved to New Wisconsin. Betty became a local beauty queen at the age of sixteen and three years later became a professional exotic dancer."

"That's when she changed her name."

"Correct. BB Baboom was born. Apparently, she was quite good at her craft because over the next few years she developed a loyal following in the northern middle states. New Wisconsin, New Minnesota, the New Dakotas . . ."

"Cold winters . . ."

"She found popularity as a download-girl, then moved to New LA where she did the circuit of the high-priced clubs. Then finally came back to the Bay Area and settled in New Frisco. By this time she had found fame and fortune as the net's most downloadable dancer."

"Ah yes, the geek train to fame."

"I don't care to have you explain that reference, so I'll just accept that it's accurate and move on," HARV said, a little annoyed that I'd interrupted. "Now, then, she met BS Star, then owner and Chief Operating Officer of ExShell in 2047, month three. They married exactly one month later. BS Star died of a myocardial infarction the night of their second anniversary."

"We can assume he died smiling?"

"You can if you wish," HARV retorted. "I am a computer. I assume nothing. I can speculate, of course, in matters where variables and probabilities are present and such speculation is imperative but I don't think that . . ."

"It was a joke, HARV."

"And I'm sure it was quite funny but, as you know, I'm not programmed for humor."

"You're telling me," I retorted.

"Actually, I've told you exactly two thousand three hundred seventeen times. I do, however, have access to an extensive database of jokes. For example, how many computer consultants does it take to change an illume fixture?"

"None," I answered, "because no consultant would ever do actual physical labor."

"Oh, you've heard it?" HARV asked.

"Only two thousand three hundred seventeen times."

"Perhaps I should run a diagnostic on my random selector?" HARV suggested.

"Perhaps we should get back to business?" I prodded.

HARV sighed, and his image faded from the dashboard window and was replaced by scrolling pictures and information about BB Star. HARV gave voice-over commentary as the text and images flashed by, too fast for the human eye to comprehend.

"The information on Ms. Star before her marriage is quite plentiful as you can see. She was featured on *Entertainment This Nano* and *World Right Now* quite often during sweeps periods. Not counting references to, and ads for, her dancing appearances, there are three thousand one hundred twelve references to her in the news archives from the three years before her marriage. Three thousand three of those are about whom she was or was not dating. The rest are rumors of net specials, vidfilms, and HV series in which she was supposed to star. None of these projects ever came to pass."

"Maybe one of her old flames is trying to burn her now?" I offered. "Blackmail her with a dirty secret from her past.

Credits tend to bring out the worst in people, especially people who don't have a lot of them."

"I suppose that is a possibility," HARV agreed, though I could tell from the tone of his voice he wasn't committed to this theory.

"Who was her last known boyfriend?"

"Well, when it comes to BB Star's love life, everything is always speculation and conjecture rather than fact," HARV said, "but the last person to whom she was linked romantically was a man named Manuel Mani, her personal astrologer."

"Let's keep him on our short list of people to check out if we need to. I don't trust ex-lovers or astrologers. I've had bad experiences with both. Anything else on BB?"

"She's become quite the recluse since assuming her post as the head of ExShell. There is no record of her leaving the living and office suites of her headquarters in the past year."

"Odd . . ." I said.

"Perhaps she has become a workaholic?" HARV suggested.

"Perhaps she's in hiding or hiding something," I said. "How has ExShell done since she took over?"

"Amazingly well. Their known assets have doubled. They have been the biggest conglom in the world every hour except one for the past five years. That one hour was in month eleven of last year, when the mutant monkey workforce at their computer chip plant in New Northern Africa staged a wildcat strike. BB Star herself managed to settle that strike quickly by relocating the plant and the monkey workforce to a banana republic.

"In any event, ExShell has performed extremely well under the guidance of this woman who has little education and no formal business training."

BB Star's school records scrolled across my dashboard.

"As you can see, her guidance counselors all advised her to work with her hands."

I started to say something (the opening was just too good) but the car computer interrupted and broke the nano.

"Arrival achieved."

It was just as well. After all, as HARV so often liked to remind me, he wasn't programmed for humor.

# 7

I made one side trip before going to Randy's and that was to the children's free clinic at New Frisco General Hospital to see Electra (I guess that image of her in the negligee that Carol picked out of my subconscious was stronger than I'd thought).

Dr. Electra Gevada is my fiancée. She is a brilliant surgeon, a great humanitarian, a weapons expert, and the former Central American Women's Kickboxing Champion (lightweight division). She can't cook to save her life but hey, everyone has to have a few faults, right? That's one of hers. We'll get to the others a little later.

As I said, Electra is a brilliant physician. She is one of the best micro-laser surgeons on the west coast and, were she in private practice, she would be a very rich woman right now.

Instead, she has followed her heart, which is as big as the ozone layer's hole, and for the past seven years has run a government-funded clinic offering free medical care to underprivileged children. It makes her happy. It keeps her incredibly busy. And it makes the lives of hundreds of kids in the city a whole lot better. I guess you can't ask for more than that from a career. Still, it would be nice to have a little more in the bank account than the love, respect, and good wishes of the community (but I'm not complaining).

I stuck my head in her office and found her huddled behind her desk, going over a long list of documents on her computer.

"Hey, chica," I said. "I have good news and bad news."

She looked up at me and flashed a beautiful, if somewhat tired, smile.

"Hola, chico," she said as I kissed her. "I forgot you were coming."

"That's not the greeting I prefer," I said, as I sat in a guest chair across the desk from her, "but I'll take what I can get."

"What's the bad news?" she asked.

"I have to cancel lunch. I have a line on a new case and it might be a big one."

"I've heard worse news in my lifetime," she said. "What's the good news?"

I pulled a take-out container from the folds of my coat and placed it on the desk in front of her.

"I brought you lunch on the go."

"Is this from the Chinese Latin restaurant on the corner? The Chino Latino?"

"No, it's a new place," I said. "Cuisine from Thailand and Mesoamerica, 'Thai n' Mayan'."

She smiled and gave me another kiss that made the negligee image pop into my head again (I was glad Carol wasn't around to read my thoughts this time).

"Actually," she said. "I have bad news too. Bad news and worse news."

"What's the bad news?" I asked.

"I have to cancel lunch too. I'm a little short on credits."

"Not so bad," I said. "What's the worse news?"

"When I say 'a little short on credits' I mean about three million short."

"I guess your lunches are a little more extravagant than I suspected."

She sighed and ran her fingers through her hair out of fatigue and a little bit of frustration.

"I got a call from the Province Council today," she said. "They're cutting off funding for the clinic at the end of the month."

"What? Why?"

"Oh, you know, the usual," she said. "Lack of money in the budget, stuff like that. Apparently, the volcano eruption in New Burbank last year drained a lot of funds from the budget."

"Didn't they have insurance?"

"What company would insure Burbank?"

"Good point," I said. "I'm sorry. Can you do anything?"

"I've been calling potential private backers all morning. Hopefully someone will come through. But let's just say that I've had better days."

A gentle tone sounded just then from the computer interface that I wear on my wrist. This was HARV's polite way of telling me that I was running behind schedule. I shrugged my shoulders and kissed Electra again.

"I have to run," I said. "Let's talk tonight at my place. Maybe we can come up with something. I'll buy dinner."

She smiled and turned back to her computer.

"Thanks, chico. Good luck with the new case."

# 8

HARV and I hit the street again, and a few minutes later we pulled into the parking lot of Randy Pool's research and development lab.

Now before going any further, let me say that, out of pure necessity, I am a cynic and a skeptic at heart. In my career as a PI, I have seen a lot, done a lot, and had a lot done to me. As a result, it takes a lot to impress me and even more to amaze me.

That said, I must also tell you that Randy's lab never fails to boggle my mind.

On the outside it's just this big gray box of a building, as boring as boring can be. But, as they say, you can't always judge a fully interactive e-file by its icon.

I punched my access code into the door lock and slowly entered the building (experience has taught me to always enter Randy's lab slowly and carefully).

As usual, the place was abuzz with the frenetic energy of high-tech genius run amok. Describing it as chaos gone way beyond wild is an understatement. There were bots running, walking, crawling, hovering, and slithering (at least I hope they were slithering) everywhere. Test tubes bubbled, boiled, and brewed away. Every wall in the building, including the ceiling, was covered with computer screens (you really have to wonder what he uses the ceiling screens for) and every screen was filled with a myriad calculations, logarithmic equations, and simulation sequences.

I scanned the chaos for Randy and finally spotted him at the far end of the room, fiddling away on a tiny bot. His crop of red hair (always uncombed) and his pale white skin atop his lanky form made him look like the flag of New Sweden amid the technological sea. He was so intent on his tinkering with the midget-sized mechanism that he had no idea that I'd even arrived.

As I neared him, the tiny bot suddenly sprang to life. It lashed out wildly with a clawlike arm and slapped him twice in the face. The force of the blow knocked Randy to the floor and sent me into action.

I moved my wrist in that special way that makes my gun pop into my hand and fired in one cool, swift motion. The specially designed concussive shell shattered the tiny robot into a million cybernetic splinters. I holstered my gun and gave Randy my best Marlowe smile as I moved toward him.

"Zach, what the DOS are you doing?" Randy shouted, not nearly as grateful to me for saving him as I'd thought he might be.

"That crazy bot just attacked you!" I answered, somewhat confused.

"Of course it did," Randy said, as he returned to his feet. "It was supposed to. It is, or rather was, an S&M bot. It's designed for people who have problems dealing with others but still long to be abused."

"You're kidding, of course."

"I'm a scientist, Zach. I don't kid," Randy said, as he dusted himself off.

"You would not believe the number of advance orders I have on this." He paused for a nano, looking at the rubble. "Needless to say, your atomizing the prototype is going to put the project somewhat behind schedule."

"Sorry, about that. I really didn't know."

Randy shrugged. "Forget it. I'll tell the customers that the delay is part of their abuse. No one ever said that science had to be prompt."

Randy's really a bright-side kind of guy.

"May I assume," he continued, "that you are here for something other than prototype target practice?"

"I got a call from BB Star—"

"Oh yes, HARV told me all about that," Randy interrupted. "Quite interesting."

"I also had a little run-in with her hired help. My armor is going to need a bit of a tune-up."

"Leave it here and I'll have the repair bots get to it tonight," Randy said as he began picking through the pieces of the S&M bot. "You can use the spare set until it's ready."

"Have you had any luck yet boosting the power to the muscle enhancers?" I asked. "I may be needing them on this one."

"Ah, now," Randy replied, almost sheepishly, "that's an interesting story, actually. It turns out that most of my major backers don't consider the enhancers flashy enough to continue funding. They are, after all, a relatively low-key device. Very subtle in their display."

"That's kind of the point, isn't it?" I asked.

"But you see, Zach, our marketing demographics show that the public likes to see action that is more overt in nature."

"You accepted the partnership offer from that entertainment conglom, didn't you?" I asked, suspiciously.

"Well, I, uh . . . oh heck, of course I did." Randy said. "They have more money than half the hemisphere and they're very hands-off, provided that the higher profile products we create fit a certain mold. They're very fond of pyrotechnics."

"Special effects."

"Exactly. Therefore I've been working on your gun."

"Right, you netted me about that, didn't you?"

"Zach, I've sent you one hundred seventeen messages about the improvements and revisions that I have made to your gun's hardware and firmware. You've responded to two. And those were about the color."

I unloaded my gun and carefully placed it into Randy's open hand. "You're not going to change the color, are you?"

Randy didn't even answer that one. He simply took the gun, motioned for me to follow, and started walking across the room. He bumped into a few miscellaneous experiments as he moved (he's brilliant but clumsy), causing some tiny explosions and a small fire.

"Try not to breathe that smoke too deeply," he warned me as the janitorial bots swarmed into the area. "It's probably a little poisonous."

I held my breath and quickly followed Randy to the workstation. He shuffled through some clutter on the work surface, searching for whatever it was he had in mind. I flinched every time he shook something (as did the janitorial bots, who were just now containing the chemical fire).

But whatever Randy was searching for, it apparently wasn't at this particular workstation. He let out a harrumph and quickly moved to a nearby, and equally cluttered, station and searched again. Two stations (and ten minutes) later, he finally found the object of his desire.

"Here we go," he said, grabbing a small pellet from a Plexiglas case.

"I've created a new nonincendiary offensive projectile. I call it the Big Chill. It's for use specifically against life-forms who are highly resistant to energy and standard projectile weapons," he stated proudly.

"Does it work?" I asked.

"Absolutely," he stated emphatically. "In theory."

"Is this the same kind of theory that states that if you put a thousand monkeys in a room with word processors, sooner or later one of them will create the next big HV show?"

"No, no. Of course not!" Randy insisted. "Although that works, by the way. My backers tell me that's how they came up with *He Married the President*."

"So, you *have* tested it?" I asked, being extra stubborn.

"Well, not exactly. Not on any actual, live, carbon-based organisms, that is. As you can imagine, volunteers for this type of thing are very difficult to find. Animal testing's been outlawed for fifty years and, thanks to the new Clone Protection Act, you can't experiment on clones anymore or even on a greeting card salesman." Randy paused, then gave me a slightly reassuring smile. "I have computer simulated it though!"

"Computer simulated?" I wasn't exactly bubbling over with enthusiasm.

"It has performed remarkably well," Randy assured me. He looked up to the ceiling, "HARV, please show holo-program 38-3D."

"Certainly, Dr. Pool," HARV responded.

I have noticed that HARV is a lot less sarcastic answering Randy's commands than he is answering mine. I try not to take that personally.

HARV activated the proper holo-program and a shimmering three-dimensional light show appeared before us. The image of a beautiful woman with three breasts appeared in the middle of the room.

"Oooh, I do so love a man with brains," the woman cooed.

"Oops," Randy gulped, "I meant holo-prograrn 83-D3, HARV." He turned to me, "Science can be so lonely sometimes."

"That's more information than I need to know, Randy."

# 9

HARV switched the program and the tri-breasted woman was replaced by the image of young, scantily clad mother feeding her baby in a city park on a cloudless summer day.

"Are you sure this is the right video?" I asked.

"Hush," Randy insisted. "This is science."

I turned my attention back to the holo-program. A huge creature that looked like a hideous tree with arms, legs, and a mouth suddenly ripped through the serene scene, terrorizing the park patrons. Two city law enforcement officers tried to stop the creature but it turned upon them and (graphically) tore them apart with its armlike tendrils.

"A little gory, isn't it, Randy?" I said, turning away.

"I like my simulations to be realistic," Randy answered, totally engrossed in the work. "This way when I'm done, my backers can run the programs on their network. It helps offset the cost of the R&D. Besides, kids love this stuff."

I turned my attention back to the holo-show. The killer tree creature was now turning toward the beautiful young mother. The terrified woman, baby in arms, tried to run but she tripped over a piece of a dismembered law officer and fell to the ground, twisting her ankle in the process.

The background music increased to a feverishly annoying pitch as the creature moved its slavering jaws toward the young woman and her child.

Copbots arrived on the scene and attacked the creature, but their bullets and blasters bounced harmlessly off its thick hide. Angry now, the creature uprooted a tree and swung it like a bat, smashing the copbots into rubble, before again turning its attention back to the helpless young mother.

Suddenly (and literally from out of nowhere), a computer-simulated version of me fell from the sky, landing dramatically between the monster and the mom.

The words: "Computer simulation. Do not attempt this at home," flashed under the picture.

"Legal insisted I put that in," Randy said, a trifle bitterly.

"How the DOS did I fall from the sky?" I asked.

"Artistic license," Randy insisted. "Now pay attention. This is the educational part," he said pointing to the screen.

I watched in amazement as the simulated Zach popped his simulated gun into his simulated hand. "Time to put you on ice, bud!" he spat.

"Come on, I would never say anything that spammy!" I insisted.

"Your agent wrote your dialog," Randy said.

"That's comforting."

Computer Zach fired. The gun belched a puff of gray smoke, and the shot echoed endlessly as the Big Chill emerged from the gun barrel and flew (very slowly) toward the creature.

"Of course, it moves much faster than that in real time," Randy explained. "I put the slow-mo in for effect, to build suspense."

Big Chill hit the tree creature with a less than inspiring *thud*, shattering on impact. A tiny puff of white mist appeared, which the tree creature seemed to laugh at. The laughter faded quickly, though, as the mist expanded rapidly and, like a living thing, engulfed the creature. A nano passed, then two, before the mist dissipated. When it did, the tree creature was frozen solid, encased in a block of ice.

"The Big Chill," Randy said proudly. "Get it?"

"Very clever, Randy."

Back on the holo-screen, computer Zach helped the poor mother to her feet (the sequence included a gratuitous shot of the woman's well sculpted cleavage). "Teenage boys love that stuff," Randy explained). My computer-self very sensitively kissed the baby in her arms. The mother, overcome with emotion, kissed me and then handed the baby to a nanny (who happened to be right there), fell into my arms, blah, blah, blah, pan to ocean waves crashing on the beach (you get the idea). Fade to black.

"So what do you think?" Randy asked.

"I thought it was quite good," HARV said, unable to resist the opportunity to offer his opinion. After all, he had been silent for almost two solid minutes.

"Frankly, Randy, I think you need to get out of the lab more often," I said. "You're starting to scare me."

Randy popped open the handle of my gun, pulled a computer chip from the complex innards, and tossed it on the floor. He took a new chip from the pocket of his labcoat and placed it in the handle.

"I've also improved the interface between HARV and the gun itself," he said. "Give me your ammo."

I hesitated.

"Zach, I can make a warhead out of what's growing in your refrigerator. You can trust me with a loaded gun."

I reluctantly handed him the ammo and said a silent prayer.

Randy loaded the gun and then hefted its weight, checking the feel (even though I was pretty certain that he had no idea what a well-balanced gun should feel like).

"How about giving it back to me now?" I asked sheepishly. The idea of Randy Pool waving a loaded gun around is one of the more vivid images from my nightmares.

"Don't worry," Randy said, noticing my concern. "I think the safety's on."

Needless to say, the gun went off.

# 10

The high-powered force-blast shattered the ceiling-mounted computer screen directly above us and obliterated it with a spectacular spray of sparks and shrapnel. I pulled Randy to the ground and we scurried for cover under one of his lab tables as the screen debris fell around us.

"Now explain to me again the meaning of the phrase 'the safety's on.' "

The janitorial bots and a robotic med-team, who I think were expecting this, rushed to the area and shielded us from the last shards of falling screen, then began repairing the damage. When the dust and debris settled, we slowly got to our feet and a hangdog Randy dismissed the med-team with a gentle wave of his hand.

"Just for the record, Dr. Pool," HARV stated calmly, "the on position for the safety is forward and to the left, not right. A perfectly understandable mistake."

"Yes, well, it varies from design to design. It's hard to keep them all straight," Randy said, carefully picking silicone dust out of his hair. This wasn't the first (or even the hundredth) time that Randy's clumsiness had gotten in the way, but I still felt a little sorry for him.

"You're telling me," I said. "Boy, I've put so many accidental blasts into my ceiling, the people in the office upstairs all wear Kevlar underwear."

"Your prevarication is as transparent as your good intentions, Zach."

"Huh?"

"Thanks," Randy said, almost cracking a smile.

"Yeah, well, whatever," I said, as I took my gun and popped it back into my sleeve where it belonged. "So aside from your accidental discharges, my immediate problem is that BB Star insists that I come to her office unarmed and uncomputered."

"And that makes you uncomfortable."

"Of course it does," HARV said proudly.

"After seeing firsthand the way she does business, I trust her about as much as a computer system trusts the 'It's-okay-to-open-me,-I'm-not-a-virus' virus," I said. "Do you have any way of slipping HARV in under her radar?"

"Actually, I do," Randy smiled. "I was hoping to field test this with you anyway, so this will provide the perfect opportunity." Excitement beamed from his eyes like the glow of a Chernobyl Cat. "You're going to love this device. It is so revolutionary, I even amazed myself."

Experience has made me very wary of Randy's excitement. Any invention that makes a genius inventor giddy is, more often than not, potentially quite hazardous to the guinea pig unlucky enough to be testing it. I'm sure Robert Oppenheimer giggled profusely the morning after he built the first atomic bomb, but I'm pretty certain that the poor duh who drove the bomb out to the test sight in his pickup truck wasn't exactly thrilled with his part in history.

"What is it?" I asked cautiously.

Randy quickly searched his lab coat pockets for the object of his excitement. "HARV told me that the ExShell headquarters were a 'no personal computer zone' so . . . DOS, where did I put the thing?"

In his excitement Randy started to hyperventilate a little and actually had to stop for a nano and put his head between his knees (I've gotten used to this sort of thing) but he was up and searching again pretty quickly.

"Actually, I finished it a couple of weeks ago and forgot about it. What with making the video for the Big Chill and the S&M bot taking off, I guess I have too much going on. Still, I have to say that this is probably one of the greatest things I've ever created. It's really a shame that I can't patent it. Well, actually I can but, since it's a stealth device, my patenting it would make people aware of its existence and that would sort of defeat the whole purpose. Catch Twenty-two."

"You've lost me even earlier than usual," I said.

"Ah," Randy smiled and slowly removed his right hand from the upper left pocket of his lab coat. "Here it is."

He opened his hand and triumphantly revealed to me his newest creation. Actually, it was kind of anticlimactic after the build-up because it looked simply like an old-fashioned soft contact lens with some microcircuitry.

"It's, um, very nice," I said.

Randy held the lens proudly between two fingers. The light hit the lens and reflected weirdly off the innards. I saw flashes of microcircuitry and tiny hairlike needles protruding from the inner side of the curved surface. This was starting to make me very nervous.

"It's a mega high speed, multi f-band, microwave-controlled, organic computer interface," he beamed.

"That's catchy," I nodded. "Have you come up with a jingle yet?"

Randy walked toward me, the way a hungry man would approach a really big piece of pie a la mode. "The lens goes in the eye," he said. "The micro-pins tap into the optical nerve, connect with the brain's natural flow of electricity and ride directly into the cerebral cortex."

"And this is a good thing?"

"I'm sorry, layman's terms now. Nice and slow," Randy said and took a deep breath. "It's a portable modem and binary translator. It will enable you to be in constant communication with HARV."

"I'm in constant communication with him now," I said. "He's practically in the shower with me."

"But only if the shower is in an apartment wired for him or is willing to give him access, or if you happen to be carrying the wrist interface. This is a totally self-reliant, fully functional link and, in theory, it's completely undetectable to scans because it will actually merge with your cells.

"The lens is also a two-way projector. So not only will HARV be able to see through your eyes, so to speak, but he'll also be able to project computer-aided holograms through you. The direct input to your brain lets HARV communicate with you silently and his presence in your head will help you defend yourself against psi-attacks.

"And really, that's only the beginning. The symbiotic relationship it creates between man and machine could be revolutionary. Who knows what other scientific breakthroughs will spring from this type of interface? The possible benefits to all of humanity simply stagger the imagination."

"Yeah, but will it hurt?" I asked.

"This is science, Zach," Randy said, reassuringly, as he tilted my head back and lowered the lens to my eye. "Of course it will hurt."

# 11

And it did.

The lens plopped into my eye before I could say another word and hit the surface of my eyeball like something alive. I felt it hum to life as my body heat activated its internal generator. The sensor needles burrowed into my optic nerves and it was like someone had soaked me in water and plugged my eyelashes into a wall socket. I think I screamed, although, in retrospect, that might have been HARV.

"The pain should only last a nano or two," Randy said soothingly. "You know what they say, no pain, no gain. The suffering of one for the greater good of all. One small step for man and all that. You'll have to forgive me if this doesn't help. I failed comforting class in grad school."

"I can see why," I said, as the pain started to clear. "But I think I'm okay."

"Is it working?" Randy asked.

"I'm not sure. How will I . . . whoa."

The lines of Randy's face turned fuzzy around the edges. Then his entire face turned into a blur, like an ice cream portrait stuck in a blender. I turned away to look at the rest of the room only to find that everything had become one gigantic splotch, not just of shape and color but somehow of sound as well. I heard Randy saying something but I had no idea what it was. It sounded like a whale speaking through a mile of murky ocean.

Then I saw the one. That sounds kind of religious on the face of it but, but what I mean is that I saw the *number* one. It appeared before my eyes in the forefront of the washed-out vision of the world, like something carefully written on a tie-dyed blackboard. Then a zero appeared beside it. Then another couple of ones. Then a zero. And then I lost track because the floodgates had opened and a cascade of ones and zeroes flashed before my eyes almost too quickly to comprehend. Only then did I realize that HARV was coming online in my head.

Slowly, shapes began to form in the flood of ones and zeroes that were cascading before my eyes and I began to see patterns within the torrent. The two white faces of my cognitive world were evolving into one black candlestick. It was as though the perception engine in my head had been switched into overdrive and I found myself recognizing the shapes as letters.

T . . .
E . . .
S . . .
T . . .
I . . .
N . . .
G . . .
1 . . .
2 . . .
3 . . .
H . . . I . . . B . . . O . . . S . . . S . . . . . .

Then the rest of the world slowly came back into focus. To my surprise, I was lying on my back on the floor of Randy's lab. Randy was kneeling beside me spouting what first sounded like Esperanto but eventually morphed into English.

". . . a little more dramatic than I thought," he said. "Can you sit up?"

I spoke but I wasn't sure at first whether or not it was English (or coherent). Eventually, I put the right sounds together.

"What happened?"

"HARV's in your head," Randy said. "It's going to take a little getting used to."

"Yeah, thanks for the warning," I said, slowly rising to my feet. "HARV, are you there?"

Again, letters flashed before my eyes. This time without the binary cascade. It didn't knock me over this time, but it made me light-headed and I had to grab Randy's arm to steady myself.

"H . . . E . . . R . . . E . . B . . . O . . . S . . . S . . ."

"Randy, I don't think this is going to work," I said.

"Zach, you just plugged the world's most powerful computer into your cerebral cortex," Randy said. "It's going to take you and HARV some time to get used to it."

"Having him in my head isn't going to do me a lot of good at ExShell if I keep passing out."

"You won't pass out," Randy said. "HARV will now be able to judge the level of interaction that you can comfortably handle. And he'll still be with you in the room. He'll see and hear everything you do and can monitor for danger. That's what you wanted, isn't it?"

"Yeah, but in a less trauma-inducing way," I said.

"As I said, it's going to require some practice to maximize the communication between the two of you," Randy assured me. "And like any new communication system, there are going to be some kinks to work out. For now, use the traditional interfaces for the majority of the work until you become more adept with this system." He turned and spoke loudly toward the ceiling. "HARV, can you switch over to Zach's wrist interface?"

Immediately the computer interface that I wear on my wrist lit up and a beam of light sprang from its tiny lens. HARV's holographic image, looking none the worse for wear, appeared before Randy and me. I still felt (and faintly heard) HARV in my head but having him use a separate interface made the sensation much more manageable.

"I'm here, Dr. Pool," HARV said. "How's the head feel, boss?"

"A little better," I said. "But it weirds me out knowing that you're kicking around in there."

"Yes, well, you can only begin to imagine the joy that being in your head brings to me," HARV said smugly. "As Dr. Pool says, the internal communication will become more efficient over time. Right now, however, we are due at ExShell in exactly twenty-six minutes. I suggest we get moving."

I nodded and turned to leave. "Thanks for your help, Randy. I think."

"We scientists aim to please," Randy smiled as he walked alongside me.

"One last question," I said, as we neared the door. "How do I remove the interface?"

Randy hesitated for a nano. "Ah, yes. Well, you see," he said, "that's one of those kinks I was telling you about. I haven't quite figured out how to actually remove it yet."

"What? You mean you can't take it off?"

"It's organically wired to your brain, Zach. It's not a set of earmuffs."

"So I'm stuck with it," I said.

"Well, 'stuck with it' is such a pejorative term," Randy said. "But it's accurate. For now."

"Terrific," I said, and reminded myself that this is why I never trust Randy when he's overly excited.

# 12

The drive from Randy's lab was atypically uneventful, for which I was grateful. Traffic on the ground was light (most of it's in the air these days, thanks to the preponderance of personal hovercrafts), and I made it to the ExShell headquarters with a few minutes to spare.

I pulled into the secure parking area and stared at the ExShell corporate edifice with a strange mixture of awe and bewilderment.

"Incredible," I said to HARV. "Not every company would think of importing an entire castle from the Divided Kingdom for their headquarters."

"Few companies could afford it," HARV pointed out.

"If they'd just lose that giant, rotating ExShell hologram above the parapet, I'd swear that we'd just popped back in time a thousand years."

"Oh yes," HARV said, "except for the multitude of satellite receivers along the north wall, the hoverport over the main courtyard, and the two thousand twenty-first century architectural details and improvements made to the front section alone, the illusion is very convincing."

"You're absolutely no fun, HARV." I said. "It may be a bit ostentatious but it has more class than those boring boxes downtown."

"That may be true," HARV replied. "But your anachronistic tastes can hardly be considered mainstream."

"I'll take that as a compliment."

"If you wish," HARV sighed. "In any event, I suggest you

hurry. Ms. Star's computer informs me that its mistress hates to be kept waiting."

I got out of the car and started down the finely manicured path toward the building. The scent on the breeze told me that the flowers peppering the grounds were the real thing (as opposed to holographic projections or the new improved plastic replicas which are so common today). It was clear that a lot of effort had gone into making this path seem natural, soft, and nonthreatening. It was perfect in every respect, and that scared me.

The plants and the dirt were real enough, but they all fit too perfectly into some preordained idea of what nature should look like. There was no oddity or deviation to its patterns and structures. It was trying so hard to be perfectly natural that it was somehow totally unnatural, a Stepford garden.

Before I could dwell too deeply on the ambiguity of my thoughts, I entered the security checkpoint at the building's entrance. It was a small room, sparsely decorated and pretty much what you would expect to find (outside the command center of a paramilitary complex). Ten burly security agents packing heavy ordnance were stationed in pairs on the perimeter. Three class AAA guardbots with multiple arm extensions (we're talking serious firepower here) stood at the ready as well: two in the back of the room, one in front near the door. There was a bioscanner near the entrance and a teleport pad at the room's far wall.

This pretty much negated the warm fuzziness of the garden path outside. Cold and sterile, there were no illusions of softness here. Even the terminally dimwitted would quickly discern the message being sent: "No one gets in to see BB Star without our permission."

And it just so happened that one unlucky man was learning this lesson at that exact nano. He was a trim, Latino man with a mini-handlebar mustache. He reminded me of that used hovercraft salesman from HV, smooth, suave, and staggeringly good looking, but there was something about him that you just couldn't trust. He was verbally sparring with one of the security agents and a guardbot, and it was clear that they weren't buying whatever it was he was selling.

"Bloody DOS," the Latino guy spat (surprising me with a somewhat cheesy British accent), "I demand to see her now!"

The agent was unruffled by the attitude and not at all surprised by the accent.

"I'm sorry, sir," he said calmly, "but Ms. Star has left rather specific orders that you are not to be allowed inside. If you attempt to get past me, I am instructed to shoot you and make it look like an accident."

"Oh, sod off, you imbecile," the Latino guy spat, then he shouted at the ceiling, "You can hear me, can't you? I know you can hear me, you icy harlot. How the blazes do you expect me to live properly on a measly three-million-credit severance package?"

"Who's the joker?" I whispered to HARV.

"That's Manuel Mani," HARV whispered through the wrist interface. "BB Star's former personal astrologer and rumored ex-lover."

"I think we can nix the 'rumored' part."

"That is my opinion as well," HARV said.

The agent shook his head and tried his best to deal with Mani.

"Ms. Star does not personally monitor this room, sir. Furthermore, the severance package is based on the standard scale that has been devised for Ms. Star's former . . . um, companions. Now please move along."

He put his hand on the blaster in his holster in a subtle, yet effective, threat. Mani may have been stubborn, but he wasn't stupid. He backed off, but he didn't go quietly.

"You'll be sorry. Believe me, you'll all be bloody sorry," he shouted, then he looked toward the ceiling. "Especially you, you trillionaire temptress!"

He turned toward the door in an attempt to make a dramatic exit, but unfortunately bumped right into me as he did so.

"Get out of my way, you cretin!"

"Believe me, buddy," I said, "it'll be my pleasure."

Mani stared at me contemptuously.

"Who are you?" he asked. "Next in line for BB Star?"

"What's it to you?"

"Well, you're in for a world of trouble, mate."

He bumped me again with his shoulder on his way out. The

bump actually staggered me back and I hit the door jamb with a good bit of force. The guy was *much* stronger than he appeared.

I heard him mumble again as he walked down the garden path outside.

"A world of trouble."

I straightened my coat and turned back to the agent and the guardbot as they turned their attention toward me.

"Well, there's a good omen to start things off," I said to myself.

"Good day, Mr. Johnson," the lead agent said. "Ms. Star is expecting you. This bot will take your firearm and computer interface now."

The guardbot held out a claw, waiting (impatiently) for me to comply. I smiled at it, but the screen that served as its face remained stoic. I slowly (yet still coolly) popped my gun from its wrist holder and into my hand. I gently placed the trigger loop on the bottom claw of the bot's arm and let it dangle there like a 4500 caliber holiday ornament.

The bot extended its second claw so close to my face that I could have shaved (or cut my throat) with it if I'd wanted.

"Your computer interface, please!" the bot said. The word "please," by the way, when spoken by a class AAA guardbot roughly translates into "Do it now or I'll rip you limb from limb then gleefully roll over your remains while laughing."

"How will I know what time it is without my interface?" I asked.

The bot's blank screen remained exactly that.

The human agent interceded diplomatically. "Your time is not important to Ms. Star," he said. "Now please cooperate. It will jeopardize our efficiency bonus if you are tardy."

I thought about questioning his use of the word "tardy." But I decided there would be nothing to gain from it. Also, it's never a good idea to mess with a guy's efficiency bonus and even worse to mess with ten guys' efficiency bonuses, especially when those ten guys are heavily armed. I slid the wrist interface off my hand and tossed it to the bot. The HARV in my head was now the only one I had.

The bot caught the interface, but the display on its OLED screen formed an angry frown.

"Just checking your reflexes," I quipped.

I'm fairly certain that it growled at me.

Once again, the lead agent interceded. He motioned this time toward the bioscanner. "Step into the scanner, please."

A word about bioscanners. There was a time when security people could use metal detectors and X-rays to successfully scan for weapons. The advent of biologically engineered armaments, however, completely changed the rules of weapons detection. Making certain that a person doesn't have a hand-blaster up his sleeve doesn't mean a thing when that same person may be carrying one in his spleen (disgusting but often effective).

The bioscanner was a product of necessity from the (not so) good old days thirty years ago and has been modified over the decades. True, the world today is a fairly safe place, but for those who can afford the extra level of security, why take chances? After all, in a world of fifteen billion people, a few of them are bound to be, well, not running with a full set of RAM.

Bioscans are a great way of making sure people and things are exactly what they appear to be. Nobody has ever been able to trick one, until now, I hoped. That is, if Randy was right and my new interface with HARV was as undetectable as he claimed.

Electra, HARV, and Randy have all repeatedly told me that bioscanners are completely safe and that the strange tingle I feel when I am scanned is purely a psychosomatic reaction. My response to that is usually, "I don't care." Unpleasant is unpleasant even if it is all in my head. But, despite my trepidation, I stepped into the scanner and felt that annoying tingle once again, as I passed through.

"Is that your original appendix?" the agent monitoring the scanner asked.

"Yes, it is," I answered.

"It's abnormally large."

"I get a lot of compliments on it."

The agent turned to the leader. "He's clean," he said. Then he turned back to me, "although you should add more fiber to your diet."

Luckily, it seemed Randy was right again; there was no

mention of the fact that I happened to have a supercomputer hooked into my brain.

I stepped clear of the scanner and, hopeful that I had successfully met the pre-meeting security requirements, turned toward the lead agent. But when I noticed the skinny agent with the weasel face in the far corner of the room, giving me the visual once-over, I knew there was more to come. The look this girl was giving me wasn't your average, "I can take this guy if I have to" or "What the heck is he thinking, wearing a paisley tie with that shirt" once-over. This was a seriously thorough glare that made the hairs on my neck quiver. I knew then that the girl was a psi and that she was potential trouble. I took a breath, nicknamed her "Ratgirl," and stepped forward to meet her.

Being blessed with a naturally thick head, I'm not a particularly easy guy to mind-probe and, if Randy was right (which he almost always was—when it came to most high tech matters), having HARV directly interfaced with my brain would make it especially hard for Ratgirl to get into my head. Still, if she were to pick up even one stray thought about HARV, my cover would be blown, so I wasn't about to take any chances.

Years of experience with psis has taught me a few things about their talents. The ability to peer into someone's mind is an awesome power but controlling that power is a very delicate art. It takes a fine touch to focus your senses onto one person's thoughts. One slip-up or a lapse in concentration and you're picking up the subconscious rantings of every id and superego within thinking distance and all that psychobabble is enough to drive a person insane, suicidal, homicidal, or any combination thereof.

So, given that the art of mind reading is a fragile one, to say the least, I've devised a few tricks over the years to sort of throw psis off balance. And, like many things in this world, the most effective is also the most simple.

Psis hate humming.

Yes, nothing throws off a psi's concentration more than when the focus of her mind-probe starts humming an insipid yet catchy tune (I have found that theme songs of old holovision sitcoms work the best).

Apparently, the humming creates a type of mental white

noise on the mind-probe frequency that drowns out any thoughts worth reading. Also, since most people associate such songs with strong visual images, such as personal recollections of their childhood, interpretations of the lyrics, or simple subliminal level devil-worshiping thoughts, the mind soon becomes even more cluttered and the psi is overwhelmed by the tsunami of near-impenetrable mental spam.

So, like a gunfighter of old, I locked eyes with Ratgirl and gave her an icy stare as she scoped me out intently. She realized then that I was on to her, so she cast aside all subtleties and pretenses and came at me with a full frontal mind-probe. In that nano the gauntlets were thrown and combat was engaged. No quarter would be asked, none would be given.

So I started humming.

*"Here's the story, of President Bradley, a good girl just looking for love . . ."*

Ratgirl's expression slowly turned sour. The veins in her forehead bulged and sweat began to bead on her brow. She doubled her efforts but I would not relent.

*"With the Alien, his sister too, the Emperor and its lice . . ."*

Her face grew pale and I noticed that her right hand began to quiver ever so slightly. That's when I knew that I had her.

*"Hello world, here's a clone that I'm makin'. Somebody slap me!"*

And that was all she could stand.

"He's clean," she told the others. "He's clean!" Then she fell to the ground holding her head and sobbing like a baby.

She was lucky I couldn't remember the theme to *All My Clones*. It probably would have killed her.

The lead agent cleared his throat uncomfortably and stepped over the sobbing Ratgirl. He gently ushered me away from his fallen comrade and gestured like a paramilitary game show host unveiling the grand prize, toward a teleport pad that was against the far wall.

"That, um, completes our security tests, Mr. Johnson," he said. "If you'll kindly step onto the pad, I'll inform Ms. Star that she may port you up at her convenience."

"And I'll be sure to convey to Ms. Star the level of courtesy and professionalism that you all displayed," I said.

The agent glanced again at the fallen Ratgirl who was now sobbing "Eep-op-ork-ah-ah," over and over in her stupor.

"Whatever," he said and turned away.

As I stepped onto the teleport pad, I couldn't help thinking that one of the few things I hated more than being bioscanned or mind-probed was being teleported. Porting is bad enough when you have to go from city to city (that at least serves a purpose). Porting from one room to another within the same building (even a building as large as this one) I consider to be either obscenely extravagant or (in this case) obsessively paranoid.

Part of me didn't appreciate being ported to satisfy a trillionaire's paranoia, but the other, more logical, part of me figured that the big credits she was paying gave her the right to a little eccentricity. After all, it wouldn't be the first time that I'd let a beautiful woman rip the molecules of my body apart, shoot them through a light beam, and throw them back together somewhere else for credits. But that's another story . . .

So I stood on the pad as a floating bot camera hovered beside me, probably transmitting my image directly back to BB Star. It was clear that she took no chances when it came to security and I couldn't help but wonder, as my body was broken down and shot through space, what it was exactly that had this woman so worried.

# 13

I materialized into BB Star's office and immediately checked myself out to make certain that everything was where it should be. There are a lot of urban myths about materialization accidents that people like to tell. My favorite is the one about the guy who sneezed during the port and materialized with his face on his lower back (talk about meeting your end). I seemed intact this time and I subconsciously breathed a sigh of relief as I checked out my surroundings.

As I have stated before, I am not one who is easily impressed, but I have to admit that the sight of BB Star's digs made my jaw drop like a politician's approval rating at tax time. Larger than most houses (and more than a few football stadiums), the office went beyond plush, way past gaudy, and right to the "doesn't that break the laws of physics?" end of the scale. It was a classic case of big business mind games: psychological intimidation through ostentation. They show you the beautiful garden path to put you at ease, the paramilitary guard post to put a scare into you, and finally the unbelievably large office to make your jaw drop. The entire place was designed so that by the time you got to BB Star's desk, whatever strategy or mental agenda you had planned for the meeting was long forgotten, replaced by an overwhelming sense of awe at the sheer majesty of the surroundings. I had to admit, it was a pretty effective scheme.

Without the aid of a telescope, I could just barely see BB Star sitting calmly at her desk on the far side of the prefabricated river that ran through the office (I told you it was big).

Stupid Ape, the thug who had attacked me at my office earlier in the day, rolled up to me in a low-powered hover.

"I'm here to drive you to Ms. Star's desk," he said.

I hopped off the telepad and adjusted my sleeves. "No thanks," I answered, "I never take rides from strangers, thugs who've tried to kill me, or people with poor personal hygiene. Congratulations, by the way, for being the first person to qualify in all three categories."

"Thanks," he said.

"Tell Ms. Star that I'll walk, thank you. How many time zones away is she?"

"Huh?"

"Never mind," I said as I began walking. "Net me when you get that last insult."

I was a hundred yards away when I heard him say aloud: "What do you mean, poor personal hygiene?"

Good thugs must be seriously hard to find these days.

I walked the roughly half-k distance to the river that separated BB Star from the rest of office. The great lady sat at her desk on the other side, working intently on something and never bothering to look up. Her entire desktop was a full-screen computer with a dozen windows showing everything from today's stock prices to solar radiation patterns. I wasn't surprised to see Fuzz Face and Man Mountain standing behind her. If my landlord, tax officer, and date from the senior prom had been there we could have had an official meeting of the I-Tried-to-Kill-Zach Club.

A smaller man in a suit stood behind her as well. This guy worried me a bit. He didn't seem dangerous or anything; I just have an unnatural fear of small men in suits.

I cleared my throat and BB Star looked up at me from her work.

"Good afternoon, Mr. Johnson," her smile was devastatingly warm. "How nice of you to come on such short notice. Bridge."

At her verbal command, a bridge across the river materialized from the air around me.

"I have to admit I was intrigued by your offer," I said as I crossed.

"Chair," she ordered.

A chair suddenly popped into existence in front of her desk.

"Please, make yourself comfortable," she said, motioning to the chair with her incredibly blue eyes.

I sat. "Nice office," I said, trying to sound complimentary but not overly impressed.

"You think so?" she replied. "A lot of people find it a bit much."

"I can understand that. Frankly, 'a bit much' doesn't do it justice. I don't think 'too much' would even be appropriate."

"Well then," she said "how about 'far, far too much for any sane person to consider, let alone actually build'?"

"That's a little closer," I said.

"That is how the editor of *Twenty-First Century Architecture* described it in his review five years ago. Two months later I purchased his magazine through a dummy corporation, changed the editorial direction to arts and crafts and put that editor in charge of the pot-holder design column."

I stared at her for a long nano, waiting for her to crack a smile.

She didn't.

"So, like I said, nice office."

And she almost smirked.

"Thank you, Mr. Johnson. Or can I call you Zach?"

"Feel free," I said.

"Excellent. Then please feel free to call me BB. No other living person does at the nano, so you can be the first. Now can I get you anything? Coffee, tea, or would you prefer straight caffeine?"

"A new office door would be nice," I said.

That earned a smile.

"Yes, of course. That will be taken care of by the time you return to your office. Thank you for your understanding."

"Then I guess the only other thing I can ask for right now is some information as to what the DOS this is all about."

She sat back in her chair and spun away from me slowly. When she spoke it was more to the river than to me and I could tell that the words were difficult for her to say.

"I have a problem, Zach. A problem that calls for your unique services."

"People don't call me unless they have a problem, Ms. Star,

I mean, BB, or unless they want me to cause a problem for someone else."

"I see."

"Some people call me thinking that they have a problem when they really don't. Still other people call me thinking that they don't have a problem when in fact, they do."

"Okay."

"There are also people who call me because they have a problem with a problem that I had previously solved for them and there are a few people who call me about problems they have with my bill."

"That is very nice, Zach," BB said.

"I should have stopped after that first part, huh?"

"That would have been best."

"Well, the bottom line here, BB, is that whenever people call me, a problem usually figures somewhere into the equation."

"I think we have established that," BB said.

There was a nano of awkward silence. I could hear the fish splash as they made their way upriver.

"I must admit," I said, "I'm flattered that somebody with your extensive resources would need me."

"Yes," she said, "this particular matter is one which must be handled by an outside source. A well-paid, discreet, outside source. This will not be something for your memoirs or your electronic comic book."

"For the proper amount of compensation, I can live with that," I said.

With that, the small man in the suit leaped to his feet, zipped quickly around the big desk, and thrust a computer pad and virtual pen in front of my face.

"Please sign to that," he squeaked.

"You are a greeting card salesman, I presume?" I said, pushing his hands away.

The guy backed up ever so slightly, a bit of fear on his face. "Why do you ask?" he said meekly.

"Don't worry," I said, holding my empty hands up for him to see, "I'm unarmed."

# 14

A brief bit of history here. 2035 was a seminal year in the annals of law and order. The number of practicing lawyers in the world had been increasing at an alarming rate since the turn of the century. As a result, by 2027 fully 10 percent of the world's population were lawyers (subsequently, 9.9998 percent of the world's population were *crooked* lawyers). The enormous amount of litigation these lawyers created simply overwhelmed the world's court system. They were suing corporations. They were suing small businesses. They were suing executives, subcontractors, and day workers, municipalities, organizations, and homeowners. Only the homeless and indigent were spared from the litigious siege (and only because they had no money to lose).

Some lawyers even specialized in suing the dead. They were easy targets, after all. You always knew where to deliver the subpoena.

By 2035, the courts were tied up in so much ridiculous litigation that there was simply no room in the system for any real legal work to be done. The United States Supreme Court, for instance, had to expand their roster of judges from twelve to one hundred twenty in order to keep up with the increased caseload. Sadly, however, there was an annual suicide rate amongst the justices of 25 percent (when you're in for life, there's only one way out). The legal world was quite simply a powder keg ready to explode.

The match that lit the fuse was the infamous case of *Rindulli v. Rindulli*, St. Louis, Missouri, 2035 in which twelve-year-old Elizabeth Rindulli sued her parents for making her ugly. Her suit contended that her parents, Benjamin and Juanita Rindulli, were ugly people (the term used in the suit was "beautifully challenged") and were therefore responsible for the ugliness of their daughter. Furthermore, the suit asserted that the Rindullis had prior knowledge of their ugliness before Elizabeth's conception and their procreation showed a reckless disregard for her well-being.

Elizabeth sued for punitive damages. The exact amount has been lost in the annals of history, but it is well known that her parents were extremely wealthy, after having been awarded a sizable settlement earlier that year from a fast food company when Benjamin spilled an iced coffee, that was negligently chilled to too cold a temperature, onto his lap while going through the hover-thru. Apparently, the three-degrees-above-Kelvin mocha latte froze his genitalia in a particularly embarrassing position.

Elizabeth Rindulli won the case and the world went crazy (or maybe they finally regained their sanity). The poor girl broke down on the courthouse steps and confessed to the world that she never wanted to pursue litigation and never even considered herself ugly until her lawyer approached her and convinced her that she was.

That's when the revolt began. The public had had enough and set out to rid itself of the litigious epidemic. The outcry was Shakespeare's immortal quote, "The first thing we do, let's kill all the lawyers" (from *Henry VI*)—and for most people, it was the only line of Shakespeare that they ever really understood.

The World Council stopped short of actually killing all the lawyers. They instead formed a series of focus groups that eventually decided that the optimal number of lawyers on a world of 15 billion people would be 7777. So, through a series of aptitude tests, coin tosses, and popular votes, the 7777 lawyers deemed most worthy got to remain lawyers. The rest were disbarred and forced to get real jobs (many became game and talk show hosts). The number of lawyers allowed to practice on the planet has been kept at a nice safe level of 7777 ever since.

After the purge, by the way, Shakespeare's popularity grew enormously in the mainstream. Unfortunately, people no longer considered him a playwright. Instead, he became sort of a prophet and a number of cults devoted to deciphering the "prophecies" hidden in Shakespeare's plays sprung up around the world. As a result, the King of Denmark was assassinated, every Roman senator was imprisoned, and special swimming clinics were organized for all women named Ophelia. It just goes to show that appreciation of great literature can be taken too far.

It's worth noting that some people (like me) think the number of lawyers left in the world is still too high. Case in point, some of the sleazier lawyers who didn't make the 7777-cut, yet weren't ready to give up their litigious lifestyle, simply went underground, slid back into the shadows, and began doing their work undercover. Thousands of these "darksharks" are now employed by corporations such as ExShell under the job title of "greeting card salesman."

So the sleaze is still out there. It just goes by a different name.

And incidentally, sales of greeting cards have plummeted in the past ten years.

# 15

So anyway, I turned and gave BB a cold stare. "I don't sign anything until I know who or what I'm dealing with."

BB countered my stare with a smile, delicate as a summer breeze at dusk, that sent a megaton tingle up and down my spine. Still, I didn't let my eyes waver from hers (it's never good to let potential clients know that they make you tingle).

"You are as smart as they say," she said, breaking the silence.

"I'm smarter, actually," I replied with a bit of slyness. "I just don't let people know that unless they're paying for my services."

"I know that this is out of the ordinary, Zach," she said, motioning with her eyes toward the nondisclosure form, "but this meeting ends now unless you sign."

"Fine," I said, grabbing the computer pad and pen from the little ex-lawyer. "It's worth signing just to find out what it is that you're so desperately trying to keep quiet."

I handed the computer back to the smarmy little weasel. He examined my signature for a nano then pressed the confirmation button.

"Signature confirmed," the computer said.

"All right, BB," I said as I sat back down. "The meter's running, so don't waste my time with any more games. What's this about?"

BB smiled. "I need you to find something," she said.

"I hope you're going to be a little more specific?"

"Computer, Holovid BB-2," she said to the air about her and the lights on her desk glowed brighter.

BB turned to me and it was clear that she didn't like saying this aloud.

"This is what I need you to find."

The playback system activated and the holographic life-sized image of a woman appeared on the desk between us. But it wasn't just any woman.

It was BB herself.

# 16

BB turned away from the holographic image of herself that shimmered before us.

"Is she your clone?" I asked.

"If only it were that simple. Its name is BB-2, for obvious reasons. And it . . ." She paused, and when she spoke again there was hatred in her voice, "is a droid."

"You're aware, of course that it's a capital offense to construct a droid with human skin tones?"

"Hence my great need for secrecy."

"Is she, I don't know, some sort of homage to yourself?"

"It was meant to be used as a spy," she said.

"An android spy that looks exactly like you," I said, mulling over the concept. "And you thought that this would be effective? That maybe your competitors would give trade secrets away to someone who they thought was you?"

BB didn't see the humor in the situation. "This was a project created by my late husband," she said, trying this time to hide the hatred in her voice (but only partially succeeding). "I was completely unaware of it until after his death. Imagine my surprise."

I had to admit, this was certainly shaping up to be worth the price of admission.

"Why don't we start at the beginning?" I said.

BB sighed. I could tell that she didn't like this part of the backstory. This would probably be the first time she ever said it aloud, so she wanted to make it as quick and painless as possible.

"BS Star was a very rich, and very eccentric, man, as you

are no doubt aware. He originally designed the droid for purposes of industrial espionage. A beautiful woman, after all, is told many more secrets than a man. However, some time after BS and I had married, he decided to change the specs."

"Engineers hate it when that happens."

"BS decided that the droid should be a copy of me, an improved copy. He secretly recorded my brain patterns while I was sleeping in order to give the droid my personality, or at least the aspects of my personality of which he approved.

"He was planning to replace me," she said, with more than a little bitterness. "Why not, he had the money and the power. He wanted to have his beautiful blonde trophy at his side. He wanted her to obey his every whim and fulfill his every desire. He just didn't want her to think for herself. So he built the cybernetic bimbo and just to give it some multitasking abilities, he also had it designed to serve as his personal bodyguard. The perfect trophy wife, the perfect weapon. It was all he had ever wanted."

"So she . . ."

"It."

"So, it isn't your average android?"

"Hardly," BB replied. "To begin with, it has a plutonium core."

"A nuclear-powered android. Oh good."

"My late husband had a tendency to overdo things," she said. "He was rich and powerful and he wanted the entire universe to know it, even when he was spending credits on something very few beings would or could ever know about."

"Exactly how powerful is sh . . . it?"

"Computer, BB-2 specs," BB ordered.

The hologram of the android split lengthwise down the middle to reveal its anatomy. Computer generated arrows appeared, pointing to various features and add-ons as the computer explained the basic structure.

"BB-2 is constructed from an artificial carbon alloy simulating external human body parts to a level indistinguishable from the original by all but the most sophisticated detection technology. The plutonium core powers advanced cybernetic and bionic internal mechanisms making the unit approximately one hundred and fifty times stronger and one hundred and seventy-six times more durable than normal carbon-based human beings. This measurement is based on a calculation derived from a core sampling of one thousand humans . . ."

"Computer, just cut to the chase!" I interrupted.

"I do not understand the command. There is no chase to cut," the computer replied.

"Just the facts," I said. "I don't need to know how you came up with them."

"As you wish," the computer responded, slightly perturbed. "The unit's reflexes are two hundred times faster than those of a normal human. Its senses are far more extensive as well. Visual sense spans the entire light spectrum. Olfactory sense can detect and analyze airborne substances as minute as point zero zero one microns. Auditory sensors can detect sounds as faint as point zero zero one decibels."

"This just gets better and better," I said.

"The unit also has the ability, through auditory and visual stimulation, to psionically dominate the minds of humans, even those possessing natural psionic abilities."

"I get the point," I interrupted again. "You don't want to make her . . . it mad."

"It is a weapon but at its core, the droid is also a computer," BB said. "Its central processing unit is experimental and very advanced. It also possesses extensive and extendable databases in its memory. It has information on everything from the gross profits of all the corporations to a list of all ExShell employees past and present."

"Which is why you can't send any of your own people directly after her . . . it," I interjected.

BB nodded. "It would identify them, and possibly kill them, instantly."

"What about me?" I asked. "Being a pseudo-famous person, I'm bound to attract its attention if I get close. It might connect me to you."

"True," BB agreed. "But I think it will consider several other possibilities for your existence before it comes to the conclusion that you are working for me, therefore you will have a window of opportunity in which to capture it."

"What if word leaks out that I was here?"

"I have taken care of that already."

"Why doesn't that make me feel better?"

"Forgive me, Zach, but at these prices, I think you can stand a little discomfort," BB said coldly.

"When did it escape?" I asked.

"Two weeks ago. It broke free of its internment cell, put two security guards into intensive care, destroyed a guardbot, and reduced the minds of two of my most expensive scientists to infant level."

"It's been loose for two weeks?" I asked. "It could be anywhere by now."

"I considered this to be an ExShell matter," BB said. "I had hoped that we could handle it internally. I was wrong. This droid is an angry and bitter machine, Zach. I have no idea what it wants, where it is going, or what it is planning. But it will not hesitate to kill anyone who stands in its way and there is no telling the extent of the damage it will do if it is not stopped."

BB paused for a nano, as if uncertain as to whether she wanted to say more. "Our profilers tell me that if it gets angry or severely agitated it could turn psychotic and simply go on a killing spree."

"And an android like that could kill hundreds of people before it was stopped," I said.

"Not to mention the trillions in lawsuits that ExShell would be facing."

"Yeah, you're all heart, BB," I said. "Just for the record, if this thing gets to that level, I'm calling in the authorities."

"If you do, Zach, then I assure you that I will ruin your life in every possible manner."

"You do whatever you need to, BB," I said, steely eyed. "I'm not about to let innocent people die just to keep your dirty secret out of the public eye."

BB stared hard at me for a nano, then relented.

"Let us hope then, Zach, for both our sakes, that the situation never comes to that."

I nodded. "My computer and I are going to need complete access to your records."

The greeting card salesman became a little nervous at this and whispered something into BB's ear. BB listened and nodded.

"We will give you fairly complete access," she said at last.

"In that case, I'll give you fairly complete service."

"All right," she sighed. "You will have complete access. However," and her voice took on a definite don't-screw-with-me tone, "if news of this matter finds its way into the press, ExShell will sue you for more than you could ever dream of being worth. Your descendants will be paying me until the turn of the next millennium."

"Fair enough," I said.

Just then, my vision became blurry and my head started to spin. I saw letters appear in my head and I knew that HARV was making his presence known.

M . . . O . . . R . . . P . . . H . . .

It took me a second or two (as always) to figure out what he meant, but I was grateful that he was there.

"Does BB-2 have morphing ability?" I asked.

The greeting card salesman again whispered into BBs ear.

"It has limited morphing abilities," BB said. "An ability left over from its original industrial espionage specs. It can change its facial features and hair color to a certain degree. Although, I sincerely doubt that it would ever change its hair color. I love being a blonde."

"Is it safe to assume, then, that it still resembles you?" I asked.

The greeting card salesman whispered again to BB. This was really starting to annoy me.

"Yes, that is safe to assume," she said.

"What happens when I find it?" I asked.

"I would prefer that it be kept intact. BB-2 represents a major investment for this company. I would like to recoup that investment by dismantling the droid and selling it for parts."

"Just as well," I said. "I'm not fond of killing things, even things that aren't technically alive. But I take it that you have something else in mind then? A weakness or a flaw I can exploit?"

BB snapped her fingers and the greeting card salesman handed me a round wafer-thin chip barely the size of an old-fashioned quarter.

"I'm hoping that this is something really special," I said.

"It is a neuro-neutralizer," he replied (hearing technical jargon from an ex-lawyer gave me the creeps). "I was a robotics major as an undergrad. The NN is attuned to BB-2's electronic brain pattern. Stick that on the droid's body and it will be helpless."

"My guess is that this will be easier said than done."

"Most things that cost twenty-five thousand credits a day usually are," BB said. "So, Zach. Do we have a deal?"

I sighed and then nodded. "I'll need to review BB-2's background and I'd like a copy of the specs downloaded to my computer."

"Agreed," BB said. "I will make sure your computer has access to all it needs."

"Then we're set."

"You will report in hourly." It wasn't really a question.

"I will report in," I answered, "when I have something to report or when I need something from you." BB didn't like my defiance but she accepted it.

I crossed the bridge over the river, hiked through the field to the telepad, and ported out of the office, numerous questions churning in my gray matter every step of the way.

It was clear that BB wasn't telling me the whole truth, but I figured that the truth would come out in the end. It was also clear that, for all her coolness and bravado, BB was scared—or at least as scared as BB gets—and her fear went way beyond the threat of potential litigation.

It occurred to me then that perhaps she feared that BB-2 might actually be coming after her. It made sense after all, since the droid was originally designed to replace her and, if that were the case, I couldn't blame BB for being frightened. The droid certainly had the firepower to take out its role model.

It was up to me to make sure that didn't happen. After all, dead clients don't give referrals and they look really bad on a résumé.

# 17

It was late in the day when I left BB's and headed home for the evening in the hopes that I could formulate a plan of action in relative comfort.

My home is a modest turn-of-the-twenty-first-century split ranch: comfortable, homey, and inconspicuous by design. The nature of my work inevitably makes me more than my share of enemies, so I figure it's a good idea to have a home that's difficult for average-Joe-thug to identify. And, although it may look mundane on the outside, Randy and I have made a few modifications to the structure and the computer/security system that make it more fortresslike than meets the eye.

As I pulled into my driveway, a familiar-looking hover at the curb caught my attention. It was distinct in design, retro-sculpted to look like a hundred-year-old Chevy (only with jet boosters instead of wheels). It was a clear and obvious sign of trouble (admittedly, though, you really had to admire the stylish way in which the trouble was presented).

"Gates, this is all I need," I said. "HARV, check out the hover at the curb."

"I noticed it on the satellite navigation as we were approaching," HARV replied. "I had hoped it was coincidence. Shall I check the ownership to be certain?"

"You can if you like," I said. "But we already know who it is."

"Whoop?"

I nodded.

"Whoop."

Remember a while back when I was describing the current

state of the private investigation business, I mentioned a company called DickCo? Well, this is them up close and personal. Sidney Whoop is one of their A-list operatives. He handles tough cases, has dramatic adventures, and looks good on camera: tall, solid build, chiseled chin, chestnut hair, steely blue eyes, yada, yada, yada, you know the type. What more could you want in a dick (other than a conscience, some compassion, and a fully operational moral compass, that is)?

Truthfully, Sidney Whoop has the makings of a good private eye. He has good instincts, a clever mind, and he's tough enough to handle the kind of trouble that PIs inevitably get into. Unfortunately, he has what I consider to be a sloppy work ethic. Couple that with his uncontrollable desire for the type of elegant lifestyle that's not easily affordable and you have the perfect candidate for the DickCo ranks. Sidney is among the cream of their cesspool.

Remember, also, I mentioned that the good DickCo operatives get "And-Ones" to better cover their adventures? Well Sidney has two. I call them "And-A-One And-A-Two" (but no one ever gets that joke). And-A-One is an annoying little man who, aside from having this troublesome habit of drawing his gun in response to peer pressure, is harmless enough and is content to stay in Sidney's shadow. And-A-Two, on the other hand, is a bit of a hothead. My guess is that he's uncomfortable in his junior role and really wants to go solo. He has almost everything still to learn about the business (but try telling that to him).

Sidney and I have worked opposite sides of the same case a few times before. He's gotten the better of me on more than one occasion. I don't like him, I don't appreciate what he does, and I don't respect him.

I do, however, respect the threat that he poses.

I cast a quick glance at the hover as I turned off of my car and, sure enough, I spotted all three of the Whoop team inside.

"Should I net the NFPD?" HARV asked.

"And what, have them picked up for loitering? No, let's play it cool and see what they want."

"Well, my advice, although I'm certain that you'll ignore it, is to exercise extreme caution."

"When am I ever not careful?" I said as I opened the door and started out of the car.

"Should I list the examples from the past week or are you in a hurry?"

"Be careful, HARV," I said. "That was sarcasm. You're skirting the cusp of humor there. Before you know it you'll be doing improv night at whatever type of joint it is that you computers hang out at."

"I assure you," HARV said, "computers don't 'hang out.' "

"You're telling me."

I got out of the car and walked calmly toward my house, trying hard to ignore Whoop and his thugs. I wanted to let them make the first move. First moves don't matter much in my line of work. In this game, as in most, it's the last move that counts. There are times, of course, when the first move is also the last move, but I didn't really want to think about that right then.

Anyway, it didn't take long for Whoop to move. He and his posse got out of the hover and, hands neatly clutching the blaster-sized bulges in their jackets, walked briskly toward me. I turned at their approach and feigned surprise as Sidney spoke.

"Zach Johnson. Long time no see, old man."

"Why if it isn't Whoop the Snoop," I replied. "How are things in dickville?"

"You mean DickCo."

"No, not really. Listen, I'd invite you and the boys in for tea, but I'm out of scones. You should give me a little warning before dropping by."

Whoop gave me a fake smile and moved a step closer. "Good one, Zach. So, I hear you paid a little visit to ExShell today."

"You keeping tabs on me now, Sidney? I didn't know business was that slow."

"Not true, Zach. You're big news. Didn't you know that? You're in the public eye."

"Yeah, well," I said. "I needed to get my toaster recalibrated. ExShell headquarters was the nearest service center."

"Listen, Zach, let's just cut to the chase here, okay? We know that ExShell hired you today."

"You do?"

"Of course. You're best PI in the business. Who else would they hire to find the you-know-what?"

"How do you know they want me to find . . ."

"Please. Something as vital as this, you're the only man alive who can find it and bring it back to them."

"I don't believe this, Sidney," I said excitedly. "You know about the vibranium corset?"

"Of course we do, we've known about vibranium corset for months now. We just . . ."

He saw me smile and realized that he'd been had.

"Damn."

"That's okay, boss," And-A-One said sheepishly, "I think we can edit that out for final netcast."

"Oh, shut up," Sidney spat. Then he turned to me and smiled as best he could. "You're right, Zach. I don't know what it is they hired you to find. Frankly, I don't care, but our client does. So here's the deal: whatever it is that ExShell's paying you to find, we'll pay you double."

"That's a lot of money, Sidney."

"Enough to set you up for a long time, I'd imagine."

"And you have no idea what it is I'm looking for."

"We don't care. But whatever ExShell wants, our client wants it more."

"You mean HTech."

"Zach, you know I'm not one to kiss and tell."

"Okay, so you'll pay me you-don't-know-how-much, for something that you-don't-know-what-it-is and give it to someone-you-refuse-to-name?"

"Clean and easy," Sidney said.

"Not to mention illegal, immoral, and dishonest," I replied.

Sidney rolled his eyes and threw his hands in the air.

"I knew it," he said. "I knew you were going to bring that up. Gates, what's this fixation you have with being legal, moral, and honest?"

"Call it a character flaw," I said. "Sorry, Sidney, no deal."

Sidney shook his head and looked at the ground.

"I did my best, Zach," he said. "I tried to be fair and cut you in on this action. I want to go on record with that."

"Duly noted," I said.

He turned back to me and gave me a glare from his steely baby blues. And-A-One had moved beside me and was now facing Sidney, to capture the action from the best possible angle.

"Then we'll get it without you," he said.

"That might be a little tough, what with you not knowing what it is, and all," I said.

"Don't worry about that, Zach," Sidney said. "We're very good at what we do. We offered you a shot at the brass ring and you turned your back. You've drawn your line in the sand, so here's a word of advice: Stay out of our way or we'll squash you like a bug."

"Sidney, look," I said, "if you're going to talk that way for the cameras, at least keep your metaphors consistent. Gates, man, you sound like a drunken fortune cookie writer."

And-A-One chuckled at that but Sidney stopped him with a glare.

"Have it your way, Zach," he said as he turned to leave.

And-A-One lingered behind for a nano to make sure he properly recorded Sidney's dramatic walk into the sunset. Then he followed a good distance behind.

And-A-Two, however, didn't move. He just stared at me silently, making no move to follow his boss, and I could tell by the look on his face that he was feeling his oats. Just my luck that the poor duh chose my front step to get too big for his britches.

"Two things, Mr. Johnson," he said in a voice that was deeper than I expected. "One is that you should never cross DickCo. And two, you're not as funny in person as you are on the net." He tightened his grip on the bulge in his jacket. "Maybe you shouldn't travel without your writers."

And-A-One saw his counterpart taking a stand and, as I feared, out of a sheer, peer-pressure reflex, moved beside him and eased his hand toward his own weapon. I knew then that this was about to turn ugly.

But at that nano, HARV flashed a message into my head.

"E . . . IS . . . IN . . . HOUSE."

I felt a little dizzy as the letters first appeared but I don't think the thugs in front of me noticed. They did, however, notice me smiling after I read the message.

"Okay, Sonny. I'll say this nice and slow," I said, locking eyes with And-A-Two. "Try hard to remember it as best you can. One, I save my good material for people who can understand it."

Ten meters down my front walkway, Sidney finally realized that he was no longer the star of the show and turned around just in time to see things hit the fan.

"You monkey clones, what are you . . ."

"Two," I continued, "you and the rest of your DickCo conglomerate can kiss my rosy red rectum!"

And-A-Two pulled his gun but I was on him before it cleared his holster. I grabbed his gun hand with my fist and gave him a smash to the face with my forearm. He fell flat on the ground, his nose just starting to bleed.

"And three," I said, "I don't use writers."

Sidney was running up the path, waving his arms like an angry duck as And-A-One drew his gun from his holster.

"Stop! Stop right now or you're fired."

And-A-One was too full of adrenaline to listen to Sidney's whooping. He drew a bead on me as I stood over his counterpart. I dove to my side onto the lawn, popping my gun into my hand as I rolled.

"Electra," I yelled. "Now!"

An energy blast ripped through my door from the inside and knocked the blaster out of the And-A-One's hand. Sidney stopped dead in his tracks and shook his head forlornly.

"Now we're in trouble," he said.

The remnants of the front door burst open and the DickCo dolts and I turned to see Electra, in her full Latina glory, emerge from the house, smoking energy cannon in hand. (Personally, I find Electra very attractive with a smoking weapon in her hands but I'm not exactly sure what this says about my psyche.)

"I thought we agreed, mi amor," she said, "no more fighting on the lawn."

"We're not fighting," I said. "It's just a long, messy goodbye. Isn't that right, Sidney?"

"Absolutely," Sidney said. "And it's always nice to see you, Dr. Gevada."

"You're as annoying as ever, Sidney," Electra said, as she spotted And-A-Two sitting up and reaching for his blaster.

She fired another burst from the energy cannon and vaporized some of the material from the inseam of his pants. He froze immediately and put his hands in the air (despite the fact that his nose was still bleeding).

"Only slightly less annoying than your compadres," she continued.

You could tell from the look on And-A-Two's face that he really wanted to take a quick inventory of his lower regions.

"Not to worry, chico," Electra reassured him, "I'm a surgeon. I don't take anything off unless I want it off. *Entiendo?*" She turned her attention back to Sidney. "I think you should be leaving now."

"I'd listen to her, if I were you," I said, nudging Sidney a bit. "You really don't want to see her when she's angry."

Sidney shook his head again and motioned for his underlings to get in the car. This time they both did as they were told.

Sidney politely tipped his hat to Electra and turned to me. "I apologize for the boys," he said. "It's hard to get good help these days."

"I can imagine," I said. "After all, who wants to work for a dick like you?"

Sidney smiled. "You know you've been using that joke for a long time, Zach. You might want to freshen up the material a bit."

"I'll work on it."

"And our offer still stands, by the way."

"The answer's still no."

"Then I guess the threat still stands as well," he said. "But let me know if you change your mind."

He turned and joined And-A-One and the still bleeding And-A-Two in the hovercraft and they were gone within nanos.

I turned toward Electra and innocently shrugged my shoulders. "Honey, I'm home."

"I noticed," she said, putting the energy cannon back into the entryway.

I jogged up the steps and kissed her happily on the lips.

"Thanks for the help," I said. "It's nice to know that my woman packs a little heat."

"Well, you know what I always say," she said with an alluring smile. "Nobody beats on my man except me."

Then she gave me a nasty spin kick to the head.

# 18

Electra's kick sent me staggering backward but I was able to keep my balance. That is, until she finished the move with a sweep to my legs which brought me hard to the ground.

"You're lucky I love you, chico," she said, coldly. Then she stormed off toward her old BMW hover and left with roar of jets and a cloud of dust. I watched from the ground as the hover flew out of sight, then HARV's hologram appeared before me, projected from my wrist interface.

"Well, that was unexpected."

"Am I wearing that 'kick me, punch me, shoot me' sign again?" I asked as I stood up.

"Only in a metaphorical sense," HARV replied. "I must say though, Dr. Gevada has remained in remarkably fine fighting form since retiring from professional kickboxing."

"Yeah, lucky me," I said as I rubbed my chin and staggered toward the house. "Do you have any idea what that was about?"

"What does your keen human intuition tell you?"

"That I need a computer."

"I suggest that you tune into *Entertainment This Nano*," HARV said. "I'm sure you'll deduce the cause of Dr. Gevada's anger."

"There's something you're not telling me, HARV."

"There are hundreds of thousands of things that I'm not telling you. The cause of Dr. Gevada's anger is but one. Still, this is something you should see for yourself."

"DOS," I exclaimed as I examined the wreckage that was

once my front door, "Attacked by seven different people in one day. I think that's a new personal record."

"And the day isn't over yet," HARV pointed out.

I rolled my eyes and stumbled into the house as the repair bots began replacing the front door.

One thing I need to make clear at this point is that I am deeply in love with Dr. Electra Gevada. She is the most brilliant, wonderful, beautiful woman on Earth (and all known planets) and I consider myself the luckiest dick in the universe to have her as my fiancée.

That said, I must also tell you that Electra has a somewhat fiery temper. Maybe "fiery" is not the right word here. "Explosive" is somewhat closer. "Volcanic" is good. "Infernolike" is probably the closest I can come without getting too biblical, but I'm sure you get the point.

So, with that said, you'll understand when I say that I wasn't surprised upon entering my house to find that it had been trashed. Electra had vented a tiny portion of her rage upon my humble furnishings. The result was almost total devastation.

My original, twen-cen artificial leather couch had been overturned but otherwise looked to be in one piece. My two antique simulated wood tables, however, weren't so lucky. They had been smashed to bits and ground into simulated wood pulp. Chairs had been overturned and/or snapped in two, and the wall (yes, the wall) opposite the computer terminals had more than a few Electra-sized cracks and dents in it. Hell hath no fury . . .

I considered myself lucky, though, because she had left my three most prized antiques intact: my 1969 Mets poster (printed on real paper), my original *Star Wars* motion picture poster (also on real paper), and my lava lamp (containing imitation lava). The posters hung neatly on the wall and the lamp bubbled away as if it didn't have a care in the world.

Because of this, I knew that, although Electra was clearly angry with me at the nano, she wasn't *really, really* angry with me. Of course, the fact that I could still walk under my own power should have been proof enough of that.

I stepped over the rubble and walked toward the computer/ HV screen which covers the far wall.

"*Entertainment This Nano*," I said to the screen.

The computer responded instantly. A window on the giant screen zoomed open to reveal an attractive, yet slightly vapid-looking, *ETN* hostess reading the latest entertainment news off her prompter like a Barbie doll with her voice activation button stuck in cotton candy overdrive.

"And I repeat," she bubbled, "our top story this half-hour is the light-speed love affair between BB Star, the ex-exotic dancer and current trillionaire, and private eye Zachary Nixon Johnson."

I held my head in my hands.

"A high-placed source, who wished to remain nameless, has just confirmed the rumor that began circulating twenty-three minutes ago."

A new view window zoomed open; this one showed a swarm of pressbots huddled around a tiny little man in a suit. I could tell even through the identity-hiding distortion effect over his face that this was the greeting card salesman that I'd met in BB's office that afternoon.

"As I mentioned, Zachary Johnson met with Ms. Star today," he said into the sea of microphones, "and just between us, the purpose of his visit was for meaningless sex."

"What?" I cried.

"Excuse me, unnamed source, Bill Gibbon the Third from *Entertainment This Nano*. What do you mean exactly by meaningless?"

"Meaningless, " said the greeting card salesman. "Without meaning, significance, or value. Purposeless. Is that clear enough for you, Mr. Rhesus?"

"Gibbon," Gibbon corrected.

"Whatever."

"Will the two of them continue the meaningless sex?"

"Just between us, I'd say no," he answered. "It was most likely a one-time thing. BB Star bores easily."

The window zoomed closed and the hostess once again zoomed into the foreground.

"So there you have it. The last private eye on the planet,

caught in BB Star's icy hit-and-run of love. More news on this as the rumor develops."

"Off!" I shouted angrily at the screen.

"Don't shoot me, I'm just the messenger!" the screen responded.

"Sorry," I said. It was obvious that HARV had been coaching the appliances again. It was annoying, but I had more pressing problems at the nano.

"I'm lucky Electra didn't gut me like a fish," I sighed. "HARV, remind me when the case is over to have BB issue a retraction."

"I most certainly will," HARV said as he popped into the wall next to the computer screen. "Provided you survive," he added. "And what of Dr. Gevada?"

"I can't contact her now without endangering my cover," I said. "She's just going to have to trust me on this one. Once this is over and BB issues her retraction, I'm sure I'll be fine. Besides, with Electra it's best to let her cool off some before approaching."

"You're just scared of her," HARV said.

"Of course I am. I'm not stupid."

I went into the bathroom, which, thankfully, was still intact. "Whirlpool," I said to the tub.

The water sprang to simulated life at my command. I removed my clothing and sank into the tub.

"HARV, put up the news screen, please. And while I'm soaking see what you can dig up on BB-2 for me."

The latest headlines vibrantly appeared on the bathroom wall computer screen but, before I could begin to read any of them, HARVs face popped back into view.

"I have acquired some information and video footage that you might want to review."

"That was fast."

"I'm the best at what I do," HARV said smugly.

"And very modest about it, too," I said.

"Do you want the information or not?"

"Fine, let's hear it."

HARV's face was replaced with the still image of a middle-aged man. He was salt-and-pepper haired, thin and pale in the face, and had big eyes that were slightly distorted by thick-rimmed eyeglasses.

"Are those actual prescription glasses?" I asked.

"It appears so," HARV answered.

"I didn't think anybody wore those anymore."

"Fashion judgments aside, ExShell is currently putting a substantial amount of capital and manpower into the search for this man. Dr. Ben Pierce."

"I guess it's important to BB to have a good physician."

"His doctoral degree is in physics, robotics, computer science, and seventeen other disciplines," HARV said, nonplussed. "He is world famous for his nanochip design and for its use in the creation of artificial intelligence. He was also the lead designer on the BB-2 project."

"Oh yeah, he'd be a good person to talk to."

"Apparently ExShell agrees with you. They just haven't been able to locate him since he left the project eleven months ago."

"Have they tried the golf course simulator?"

"Actually, that was the first place they looked."

"So he just disappeared?"

"Rather unexpectedly and mysteriously."

"How suspicious."

"And how redundant of you to say so," HARV quipped. "Next bit of information, I have obtained some video footage of BB-2 which you might find interesting."

"Let's see it."

The image on the wall screen changed again. This time it was replaced by video footage of a darkly lit military encampment surrounded by a many-leveled wire fence.

"These vids are slightly over one year old. They were edited together from internal recorders and the ExShell observation satellite. The ExShell computer gave them to me somewhat begrudgingly."

"How begrudgingly?"

"No need to worry. You can afford it."

"We're supposed to have complete access."

"Yes, well the definition of complete access differs greatly between those granting it and those receiving it."

I thought for a nano, weighing HARV's words. "Can I use that?"

"No, it's copyrighted under my name," HARV said. "Now may I kindly proceed with the footage?"

I nodded and HARV picked up where he left off.

"This footage was taken somewhere in the province of New Paraguay. The compound is, or rather was, the hideout of a group of revolutionaries who were out to rid the world of all computer technology."

"Why do you keep using the past tense here?" I asked.

As if in answer to my question, BB suddenly appeared from the jungle and moved stealthily toward the compound.

"Is that BB or the droid?"

"Watch," HARV said.

BB grabbed the fence and was immediately hit with a massive jolt of electricity. Sparks shot from the fence and her fingertips in a display to rival a World Togetherness Day celebration. BB responded to the electrical attack by ripping the fence apart.

"My guess would be the droid," I said.

"I am beguiled by your powers of perception," HARV responded. "The fence was state of the art electromagnetic link. Laser-sharp and charged with fifty thousand volts. It was designed to disable a level ten battlebot."

BB-2 grabbed the two guards who were unlucky enough to be patroling the area. She lifted them by their throats, shook them vigorously for a nano, and tossed them aside. Their bodies hit the ground like broken dolls. I think I winced a little at the sight. If HARV noticed, he didn't mention it.

Back on the screen, two specially trained attack dogs, fangs bared, ran toward BB-2 from within the compound. She turned and met their charge with a stare.

The dogs, who were apparently smarter than their human counterparts, instantly knew they were out of their league. They both rolled over onto their backs and put their paws in the air in the universal doggie "I give up" position. BB-2 gave each of them a calming little pat on the head and moved on.

"She likes dogs," I said.

"Yes, too bad you're not a schnauzer," HARV sighed. "My conjecture is that she dispersed synthetic pheromones as the dogs approached. Their acute olfactory senses made them especially susceptible."

There was a flash of light and BB-2 suddenly lurched forward as if she was struck from behind. The video footage cut to a grainier overhead shot (obviously satellite footage) and revealed that she was under attack by a dozen men wielding energy cannons and high powered projectile ordnance.

BB-2 paused for a nano and deliberately let the attackers hit her with another burst of fire.

"Is she smiling?" I asked.

"It's not clear," HARV answered. "The quality of the images and the angle of the camera make it difficult to determine."

"I swear she's smiling. Gates, that's creepy."

BB-2 suddenly dove to the ground and rolled, lightning quick, away from the weapon fire. The attackers tried to keep up. They sprayed the area wide with energy blasts and explosive shells (actually destroying part of the camp themselves). But it was like trying to catch a quicksilver bullet with a butterfly net. They were four steps behind from the start and in three heartbeats' time, BB2 was upon them.

"See how she bounced around like that, instead of going straight at them?"

"Yes, a waste of movement," HARV replied.

"No," I said, "she's playing with them."

BB-2 disarmed the first guard and, with a bit of creative flair, twisted the body of his gun into a balloon animal puppy dog.

"Definitely playing with them," I said.

"Play time is about to turn a bit graphic," HARV warned. "She makes the next balloon animal out of the guard himself."

"Cut, then. I've seen enough."

HARV's face replaced the video images on the screen. "The encampment was protected by three dozen heavily armed guerrilla soldiers. It took BB-2 less than six minutes to raze the entire compound. She even salted the earth afterward."

"And it's our job to stop her." I said. "Well, I guess we're going to have to outsmart her."

"I hope my next human has your sense of humor," HARV sighed.

"Look, if she was built by humans then she can be stopped

by humans," I stated confidently (hoping not only to convince HARV but myself as well). "Besides, I have a weapon that those poor duhs didn't. That neato-naturalizer."

"You mean the neuro-neutralizer."

"Whatever. You know, the thing that looks like an old quarter."

"Be that as it may," HARV conceded, "as I recall Ms. Star neglected to mention that the NN was never actually tested on BB-2."

"No, I think I would have remembered that."

"According to the ExShell computer, the device was designed and tested in simulation situations only."

"Why am I always the guinea pig when it comes to the actual dangerous part?" I asked.

But HARV wasn't listening. His image disappeared from the computer screen and his holographic form suddenly appeared beside me, a look of concern on his simulated face.

"We have a visitor."

Another computer window zoomed open on the wallscreen. It was a live feed from the security camera at the newly repaired front door. A little girl in the green knickers of the Junior Space Scouts, several boxes of cookies cradled in her arms, stood genteelly on the front stoop.

"We don't really have time for this now, HARV," I said. "But order a few boxes of those peanut butter things and a box of mints."

"Hmmm," HARV said.

"You're right. Forget the mints."

"Do you not think that it's odd for a Junior Space Scout to be selling cookies at this time of night?" he asked.

"What are you thinking, here?"

"I am taking the liberty of performing a heat and energy scan on our visitor."

"Are you using your keen computer intuition now?" I asked.

HARV ignored me and kept his attention focused on the video feed as it switched to an infrared and heat-coded view. The two of us watched as the image of the little girl morphed into a two-meter-high hulking form: a giant assassin in Junior Space Scout Trojan horse disguise.

"This is her actual body size and mass," HARV said.

I suppressed a gulp.

"I guess we won't be getting those cookies after all."

# 19

"How big is she?" I asked HARV.

"It's unclear at this point as to whether or not the pronoun 'she' is accurate," HARV responded. "Clearly our visitor is using a holographic disguise device, but actual height is two point two three meters. Weight is one hundred fifty-three kilos. Not as big as the larger of BB's henchmen but still rather large by human standards."

"Well, that explains the HDD. I doubt anyone would buy cookies from a Junior Space Scout that size, unless of course she used the hard sell approach."

"I sincerely doubt that whatever is at the door is an actual Junior Space Scout."

"It was a joke, HARV. You can't afford a holographic disguise device on a Scout's allowance."

"Remember I'm . . ."

"Not programmed for humor, I know."

I got out of the tub and winced a bit as I tried to coax my already sore muscles back into action

"Wait for my signal, then let her, him, or whatever it is, in," I said. "At least this time we have the element of surprise on our side."

"Surprise, as you know, offers little defense against blaster fire," HARV said.

I rolled my eyes and stepped into the body dryer. A nano later I was dry, dressed, and ready for action. "Let's go," I said.

It was fast becoming one of those days when it just wasn't a lot of fun to be me: thug attacks, pressbots, a highly advanced android killing machine, a jealous girlfriend, and now an ominously hulking figure in little girl drag at my front door. Add a trip to the proctologist and a visit from the World Tax Service and this would officially be one of the three worst days of my life.

I grabbed my gun and headed toward the front door. I pressed myself flat against the wall by the entranceway, gave HARV the signal, and the door popped open.

The Scout entered cautiously, saddle shoes whispering gently on the carpet.

"Would anyone like to buy some Junior Space Scout cookies?" she asked meekly.

I stepped from behind the door and put the business end of my gun to the back of her head. I was starting to feel real good about this situation, which is actually a really bad thing when you're a PI, because a PI should never feel good about any situation that involves firearms and thugs wearing HDDs. You tend to let your guard down, which I did, and it cost me.

The Scout lashed out with an elbow aimed, seemingly, at my groin. I tried to block the blow with my free hand and whack her (him or it) in the head with my gun but, by doing so, I made the classic HDD mistake. I forgot that the actual being underneath the holographic image was far larger than the hologram projection. So, while I did manage to hit my opponent with my gun, it was not in the head but rather somewhere in the lower back. And, although I did block the holographic Junior Space Scout elbow to my groin, the actual real life elbow (the size of a sledgehammer) made actual real life contact with my jaw. The force of the blow knocked the gun from my hand and sent me hard into the wall where I slumped to the ground, dazed, confused, and in serious trouble.

The Scout spun around and smiled when she (he or it) noticed I was now unarmed. She (he or it) walked toward me slowly and snarled, in a very threatening falsetto tone, "I'm going to break your legs in as many places as humanly possible."

"I've heard of pushy sales girls," I groaned, "but this is ridiculous."

"You're a funny guy, even without your writers," came the reply as she (he or it) closed in on me.

"I wish you'd explain that to my computer," I paused for a nano than added, "and I don't use writers!"

The Scout swung at me and I got fooled by the HDD effect again because, although I blocked the punch that seemed to be aimed at my midsection, my head got rocked back hard from a brick-wall fist to the nose.

I responded by hitting the Scout back with a couple quick jabs to the laser-created cherubic face. Neither jab, however, seemed to do any real harm. I could tell because after the punches, the Scout chuckled a bit and gave me one of those is-that-the-best-you-can-do smiles.

"You can't imagine how silly I feel right now," I said to HARV.

HARV holographically appeared behind the Scout. "Should you survive, I would advise against using video footage of this incident in your next promotional campaign. It may damage your reputation as a tough guy."

"I appreciate your help, HARV," I said as another Mack truck punch to the midsection sent me to the ground.

"Actually," he said, "I think I can be of assistance here."

That surprised me because, as I've stated, HARV isn't really programmed for combat strategy.

The next nano the lights went out and the computerized window shades shut tight, plunging the room into total darkness. The attacker hit me again, this time in the stomach, and sent me to the floor.

"This is your plan?" I whispered. "I still get beaten to a pulp, but I don't have to endure the embarrassment of watching the Junior Space Scout do the beating?"

Just then HARV flashed the words "Oh ye of little faith" before my eyes. This time, I recognized them as words rather than just an array of letters to be deciphered. I also noted, with some pleasure, that his appearance this time made me neither dizzy nor nauseated.

The words "switching to night vision" flashed before me, and that's when everything fell into place. There was a burst of red light behind my left eye and the room quickly came into crystal clear infrared focus. HARV was using the interface lens in my eye to scan in the infrared spectrum.

The little Junior Space Scout was gone. Instead, I saw before me a giant, red, blurry, thuglike form slowly groping its way through the darkness.

I made the most of my advantage and hit the thug twice in the gut with my fists. It felt like punching a truck but I think the thug felt it. I knew I needed to end this quickly so I went with my old standby, the dirty fight one-two.

I gave the thug a spinning back kick to the groin and was greeted with a satisfying falsetto "oof." I saw the thug's red blurry knees buckle and he (and I could now safely assume that it was a "he") staggered.

That's the "dirty-one."

"HARV, left arm, one and done. Now," I ordered.

"As you wish," HARV said.

I mentioned earlier that the armor I wear is soft-wired to my muscles and allows me to pull some power from its circuits to boost my strength in times of need. I can focus the power in a very general way and, in most cases, that's more than good enough. However, when I need to really juice up a punch and pull every bit of power from the armor that I can, I need HARV. I don't have the concentration during a combat situation to focus on the minutiae of the armor's circuits and its power-flow. HARV on the other hand, lives for minutiae and can perform the transference of power in milliseconds. So when I really need to throw a one-and-done haymaker (and it pains me to say this), I need HARV's help.

Sure enough, my left arm began to tingle from the added juice that HARV was channeling my way, and I reared back and let loose with a HARV-enhanced roundhouse left to the thug's blurry red jaw. The punch sent a shot of pain up my arm but the sound was like that of a ripe melon hitting the sidewalk. I had to admit I was impressed with myself—and HARV.

That's the "dirty-two."

The Junior Space Scout staggered backward and fell hard against the wallscreen. The giant screen cracked from the impact and a rainbow explosion of sparks erupted as the electricity from the screens shorted out with the lasers in the Scout's HDD.

HARV turned the lights back on, and I watched as sparks and holographic images spurted in all directions and the Junior Space Scout shuddered spasmodically against the screen. The Scout's countenance morphed chaotically from image to image as the HDD began to short circuit and randomly spit up every image in its memory.

The Space Scout.

A skinny black musician.

A New Portuguese cab driver.

A beautiful Japanese geisha.

An ugly, hulking, ham-fisted thug with a flat nose (his actual form, I think).

BB Star.

BB's form stunned me for a nano but HARV brought me back to reality.

"This is only conjecture on my part," he said, "but it appears as though your attacker is being electrocuted and I might remind you that accidental deaths by electrocution are not covered by your homeowner's insurance."

"Good point," I said. "Fire extinguisher."

At my command, flame-smothering foam shot from the ceiling nozzles and smothered both the sparking wallscreen and the attacker. I grabbed the attacker's feet and pulled the body free of the area as the house computer immediately began the clean up and repair of the damages.

The attacker's HDD sputtered for a second or two and then righted itself, returning the image once again to the cherubic Junior Space Scout.

I grabbed my gun from the floor and aimed it at the prostrate Scout. Needless to say, I was in no mood for the red cheeks and knickers.

"Okay, honey, who sent you?" I snarled.

"I don't talk," the Scout said in a sweeter than new improved cotton candy voice.

I activated the laser site on my gun and aimed the red beam directly at the button fly of the little green knickers.

"I suggest you reconsider," I said, "or you'll be talking like that permanently."

"Manuel Mani," the Scout said, this time in a distinctly male baritone voice.

"BB's ex-boyfriend?"

"You're moving in on his woman. No one does that to Manuel Mani and lives."

"So he sent a Junior Space Scout to do his dirty work."

"He would have come himself, but he doesn't believe in violence," the Scout explained.

"Very enlightened," I snarled. "First of all, tell Manuel that it's over between BB and me. He has no reason to be jealous. Second of all, it's also over between *him* and BB. So he should get over it, move on, and get a life. And third, you tell Manuel never to cross me again because I *do* believe in violence. I believe in it quite strongly and I practice it regularly." I motioned to the door with my gun. "Now get out before I give you a demonstration."

The Scout quickly adjusted the holographic uniform, then turned tail and ran as fast as the little Scout legs would carry. I carefully closed the door and activated the security field.

"If it's not killer androids and thugs it's jealous ex-boyfriends and thugs," I mumbled as I staggered toward my bedroom. "I need some sleep."

"But you should be proud of what you have accomplished," HARV said as I limped down the hallway. "You have now officially broken your personal record for the number of attempts on your life in one day."

# 20

Thankfully, the morning came without incident. I took a fast light-wave shower, selected my coolest sleuthing outfit from the wardrobe file, and ran every diagnostic test available on my armor to make certain that it was working properly (with everything that had happened the day before I didn't want to take any chances). I popped my gun into the sleeve holster and then back into my hand.

"Gun, report," I ordered.

"Systems fully functional," the gun replied in a cold metallic voice. "I am at full capacity with one hundred rounds of multipurpose, multifunctional ammunition. Currently I also have . . ."

"Fine, thank you," I said as I headed to the kitchen. I sat down at the table as the maidbot approached.

"I have prepared a quick but hearty breakfast consisting of various foods from some of your sponsors," the maidbot chimed.

"Thanks," I said as I grabbed a new (and improved) Nuke-Toaster-Tart "but I'm running a little late. I'll go express today."

I allowed myself a minute and a half to suck down the Toaster Tart and catch up on the latest news and sports from the vids scrolling across the kitchen wallscreen.

I noticed right away that the Mets had dropped a double-header the night before. Their lead over New Havana was now uncomfortably slim. It almost seemed as though they were trying to blow their chance at the World Series, just to torture us fans a little bit more.

"Anything I should be aware of, HARV?" I asked aloud.

HARV popped onto the computer screen next to the window of baseball highlights. "Nothing unusual," he reported. "I am monitoring local police and hospital databases for any sign of BB-2. I have discovered nothing as of yet."

"I guess that's why you're not a famous private investigator," I joked.

I swallowed the last bit of Toaster Tart and headed toward the front door before HARV could counter the verbal jab. I left the house and went to my car.

"Open," I ordered.

The car computer recognized my voice and deactivated the security shield, then popped open the door. I climbed in and the dashboard sprang to electronic life.

"Go automatic pilot. Let's go to the office," I requested.

"Check," my car happily confirmed. The engine fired up and we pulled onto the clean New Frisco streets.

HARV's face popped into a window on the dash. "Okay, old wise carbon one," he said with more than a hint of sarcasm, "where do we begin?"

"It's only logical, my good machine, to begin at the beginning. We start with the man who built BB-2. The honcho of the design team. You know, the guy with the glasses."

"If I am translating the word 'honcho' correctly, then you are referring to Dr. Benjamin Pierce."

"That's the one. Let's find him."

"And after that?"

"That's it, for now," I said. "Let's see where that brings us."

"Sure," HARV groaned. "Why bother having a real plan?"

"I have a plan. It just happens to be a flexible one."

"The one flaw, of course," HARV said, "is that Dr. Pierce is currently somewhat difficult to locate at the nano. As I mentioned, ExShell has been searching for him for nearly a year and, as I understand it, have had no luck."

"Well, that's why they hired me," I said. "I have resources and connections."

"Such as?"

In answer to HARVs question I touched a speed dial button on the dashboard and after a nano or two, Tony Rickey's face appeared on the screen. Tony Rickey and I grew up together on the mean streets of the upper-middle-class New Frisco suburbs (it was rougher than it sounds, really). We played cops and robbers as kids, but we fought a lot, because we both always wanted to be the cop. Eventually, we switched to baseball, which in the end, wasn't much better because we both always wanted to play first base. But that's neither here nor there.

Tony was very serious back then when he said he wanted to be a cop. He entered the Academy right out of school and has dutifully worked his way through the ranks of the NFPD over the past ten years. Today he's a captain, and despite the personal and professional embarrassment that I have caused him through the years, we have remained the best of friends.

And of course, he's a great source of information.

"Rickey here."

"Tony, hi. It's Zach."

"Zach, what's wrong now?"

"Hey, do I need to be in trouble to call my best friend?"

"No," he said, "but that's usually the case. So why are you calling?"

"I need your help."

"I knew it. You're not in jail again, are you?"

"Calm down," I said. "I'm just doing some legwork on a new case and I need you to run a name through your files. Dr. Benjamin Pierce."

Tony stared at me for a nano, then cracked a smile that eventually grew into a laugh.

"What's so funny?" I asked.

"This explains that crazy story about you and BB Star on *ETN* last night," Tony said. "You're working for ExShell."

"What makes you say that?"

"Zach, ExShell has been leaning on my department for months looking for Ben Pierce," he said. "They've filed fifty complaints against him this week alone, everything from industrial espionage to stealing office supplies. The only people looking for Ben Pierce these days, you included, it seems, are ExShell employees."

"Okay, you got me," I said. "Apparently, he stole all the 'S' keys off their keyboards so they keep misspelling the company name as 'Ex-hell.' It's been kind of bad for morale."

"Gates, Zach," Tony said. "If you're going to lie, at least make it a good one. I'll bet Electra didn't buy that excuse."

"Electra wasn't buying anything yesterday if you know what I mean. She took everything in trade. I give her a smile, she gives me a spinning back kick. You know, that kind of thing."

"I guess love really does hurt."

"Some days more than others," I said. "So what about Pierce?"

"I'll net what we have to HARV," Tony said. "But it isn't much. Nothing that ExShell's task force doesn't already have."

"Task force?"

"Sure. ExShell set up a special department devoted solely to locating Pierce and bringing him in. Didn't you know that?"

I cast a glance toward HARV who put his holographic hands in the air and shrugged his shoulders.

"Yeah, sure," I said. "The task force. I just thought maybe you'd have something they didn't. That's all."

"I wish I did, Zach," Tony said. "And I don't blame you for wanting to stay away from that department. The guy who runs it, Fred Burns, sheesh, he's a smarmy little putz."

"Oh yeah," I said. "Burns, he's the worst. But whattya gonna do, right? Thanks anyway, Tony."

"I'll help you anytime that it's legal, Zach. You know that. Just one more thing."

"What's that?" I asked.

"Be careful," he warned. "You might need some help getting all those keys back to ExShell. You know what I mean? So call me if you need a hand. Okay?"

"I appreciate it, Tony," I said. "Thanks."

Tony's face disappeared from the dash screen and HARV's image flipped back to full screen.

"Apparently, there's a task force," I said.

"I told you ExShell was devoting a lot of effort to finding Dr. Pierce," HARV said.

"You never once used the phrase 'task force.'"

"Well, forgive me for not using the proper buzz words to pique your interest. Yes, there's a task force. It operates out of the ExShell satellite offices downtown and is run by—"

"Fred Burns, I know," I said. "Thanks for the help. Car,

change of course. We're going to ExShell's office downtown. HARV will give you the coordinates. Let's go see if Fred Burns is as much of a putz as Tony says."

Fred Burns worked out of a small room three stories beneath the ground in the sub-subbasement of ExShell's gray box R&D downtown office. It took me ten minutes to find someone in the building who even knew who he was, let alone could direct me to his office. I couldn't tell if this was because his work was vital and top secret or because nobody cared.

Burns himself was a doughlike man with bleached skin and big eyes that looked as if they'd burst if they were ever exposed to real sunlight. He reminded me of an out-of-shape calf, the kind that's been kept in the dark and raised in a box all its life so that it couldn't use its muscles. He was a side of baby veal in human clothing.

His office was a dank, cheerless place, lit by the pale blue glow of low-watt halogen bulbs. The workstation was filled with a dozen computers and just as many net screens, each monitoring various satellite and ground-based cameras. Plastic coffee cups and soda bottles in various stages of fill were scattered about the room, as were three or four empty pizza boxes on a table against the wall on the left. One half-filled box sat beside him by the computer and he munched a piece as we spoke. At first, I thought it was odd for him to be eating pizza at nine in the morning, but then I realized that, for all he knew, it could be half past dinnertime.

I scared him when I entered (I guess he doesn't get much human contact down there), and he was hesitant to talk to me at first. That is, until we started talking about Ben Pierce. Then I had trouble shutting him up.

"Pierce was brilliant when working within his scope of pure theory and design," he said. "His creativity with a chip was pure genius, although, personally, I think it masked some very dangerous emotional issues that should have been addressed."

"Um, okay," I said, "but why do you think he suddenly left the project?"

"Probably because he would have been arrested if he'd hung around."

"Well, I suppose there are worse reasons for flight," I said. "Arrested for what, exactly?"

"We found out that Dr. Pierce was doing some unauthorized reprogramming to the BB-2 android," Burns said, "reprogramming which seriously jeopardized the entire project. My feeling is that his reckless actions are responsible for the problems that we're currently experiencing."

"You mean the violent, psychotic episodes?"

"No, the fact that we can't *control* those episodes. BB-2 was built for many functions, as you know. Violence was definitely one of them and that part of her programming has clearly survived."

"Lucky us," I said. "What other functions was she built for?"

"There's combat, as you know, and stealth. Also personal defense; she was, after all, going to be BS Star's personal bodyguard. And there were some recreational functions."

"Recreational?" I asked cautiously.

"Let's just say that BS Star had a prurient interest in this project."

I held my head in my hands.

"She was a sex toy," I said.

"I don't think 'toy' is the most appropriate term for her functions but sexual gratification was part of her original specs. Although I don't know what made it into her final programming once Dr. Pierce sabotaged the project."

I rubbed my eyelids with my fingertips and prepared myself for the train wreck of a headache that I knew was just ahead.

"BS Star spent a billion credits to build a nuclear-powered sex toy."

HARV scrolled a message across the inside of my eyelids and I could almost see him smiling.

"I think we just lost the kiddie audience, boss."

"Tell me about it," I said aloud.

"Tell you about what?" Burns asked.

"Nothing," I said, turning my gaze back to Burns. "So BS had the real flesh-and-blood BB as his wife but he built a droid that looked exactly like her?"

Burns shrugged his shoulders and took a huge bite of pizza.

"Apparently Ms. Star was frigid. Go figure," he said (although

I couldn't be sure since his mouth was full). He picked up the pizza box and offered it to me. "You want a slice?"

"Thanks, no. I had breakfast."

Burns shrugged again and shoved the rest of the pizza slice in his mouth.

"This pizza's incredible," he said. "It's from PizzaPort. Best pizza on the planet. I'm having it analyzed so I can steal the recipe. You're sure you don't want some?"

"Thanks, I'm fine." I said. "So I understand that you actually worked on the BB-2 project."

"Oh, yes. Until I learned of his true motives, I was Pierce's right-hand man. I didn't actually work on the right hand, of course. Pierce was particularly fond of extremities, but you know what I mean."

"Can you tell me a little bit about the design, maybe a little about the droid itself?"

Burns swallowed his mouthful of pizza and folded his hands neatly in his lap as he turned to me. His eyes became a little misty and a sense of wonder came to his voice as he spoke.

"She is the most advanced droid this world has ever seen, and the most remarkable human achievement I have ever beheld."

"Oh brother," HARV flashed before my eyes. "He's not going to cry, is he?"

"Her movements are totally human in every distinguishable manner, yet at the same time they are grander and more divine," Burns continued. "The grace of her simplest motion, a lilt, a gesture, is creation's own poetry. The gentle lift of curiosity, or furrow of consternation, they bring tears to my eyes."

"I'm sorry, her furrow of what?"

"You know, when the eyebrow contracts and forms a slightly thicker ridge over the eyelid," he said. "It conveys deep concentration, thoughts unfathomable. The work we did with BB-2 was simply unmatched."

"You're talking about her eyebrows?"

"That was my area of concentration."

"You programmed her eyebrows." I said, as the Headache Express approached the station.

"The left one, actually. Pierce didn't like my preliminary work on the right. He was such a philistine when it came to the subtleties of the forehead."

"And that's all you did. Her left eyebrow."

"Two of the most artistically fulfilling years of my life."

"And Pierce did everything else?"

"He was very auteurlike about the project. BS gave him direction and would occasionally review the design or amend the specs, but Pierce did the design, construction, and programming of BB-2, until he became too attached and jeopardized the project."

"So where is Pierce now?" I asked.

Burns straightened up, grabbed another slice of pizza, and spun his chair toward the computer console. He touched a number of buttons on the console and a series of images, maps, and data flashed onto the screens around the room.

"I'm coordinating the various operatives that we have in the field that are currently following Dr. Pierce's elusive trail. The manhunt has gone on for eleven months now. It's been an intense and brutal endeavor, but it's clear that our prey is nearly cornered at last."

"So you know where he is?"

A satellite photo of the Indian subcontinent appeared on the main screen and zoomed in to an island of the southeastern corner.

"My estimates currently put him somewhere in New Sri Lanka," Burns said. He punctuated each bit of data with a finger stab to the computer keyboard and photo images, none of them clear, aligned themselves on the secondary screens in response. "We have these photos: this one from satellite, these from ground operatives, this one from a tourist on a bus ride, all taken within the past sixty days. We've also logged a dozen sightings, three of them confirmed, all within a twenty-five square kilometer area of New Ratnapura. He's well hidden, but it's clear that he's somewhere in that area."

I stared closely at the man pictured in the various images. His build and his hair certainly resembled Pierce's and although he'd grown a somewhat scraggly beard, the thick-rimmed eyeglasses seemed like a dead giveaway.

"What's your next step?" I asked.

"When we can pinpoint Pierce's location to within an area of three square kilometers, we can send a search and retrieve team and have him back here in custody within an hour's time."

"So you think you'll have him soon?"

"A few weeks now. A month at best," Burns said, spinning back toward me from the console. "Dr. Pierce has given us a spirited hunt, indeed. But, as you can see, the fox shall soon fall prey to the hunter."

There was an awkward nano of silence as Burns stared at me dramatically. Then he grabbed another slice of pizza and turned back to the console.

"Tally ho," I said and quietly left.

Five minutes later I was back in my car heading toward the office, HARV holographically sitting in the passenger seat beside me. I was doing the actual driving this time. Having my hands on the wheel and the open streets in front of me helps clear my head (and after my time with Burns, my head really needed clearing).

"So what now, boss?" HARV asked. "Should I book us on the next teleport to New Sri Lanka?"

"Don't bother, HARV," I said. "Pierce isn't there."

# 21

"But," HARV said, unnaturally confused, "the satellite photos, the information from their operatives, the eyewitness accounts . . ."

"Can all be faked," I said. "Eleven months of searching and all the biggest corporation on Earth has to show for it is some blurry photos and twenty-five square kilometers in Sri Lanka? It's clear they're looking in the wrong place."

"But Burns said . . ."

"Burns programmed the eyebrows, for Gates' sake," I said. "It's like a first-grader playing hide-and-seek with a college professor. Pierce has him totally fooled."

HARV thought this over for a few nanos.

"That *does* make sense," he said.

"You're agreeing with me?"

"I see the logic in your argument," HARV corrected.

"That's almost human of you, HARV."

"I've conceded your point," he said. "There's no need to get insulting."

I smiled. "So," I said, "this guy walks into a bar with two chunks of plutonium sewn onto the shoulders of his shirt . . ."

HARV stared at me, silently.

"And . . . ?" he prodded.

I did a double take and nearly drove off the road.

"What do you mean 'and'?"

"What happens next?" HARV asked.

"It's a joke, HARV. You're not programmed for humor, remember?"

"Does that mean I can't hear the rest of it?"

"I've given you that line a hundred times," I said, a little confused. "You always yell at me and never let me finish."

"Well, I'd like to hear the rest of it," he said, "just to see what I've been missing. So go on. What happens next?"

I shrugged, a little embarrassed, and mumbled.

"There isn't any more."

"What do you mean?"

"I haven't come up with the rest of it," I said.

"You mean it's not even a real joke?"

"Well, what's the point? You never let me get past the first line."

"All this time you've been baiting me with a joke that doesn't even exist?" His voice was half an octave higher than normal and nearly a shout. His holographic eyes were slightly apoplectic and his pale skin took on the slightest hint of red. This was getting weird.

"Give me a minute," I said. "I can come up with something."

"It's too late," he said, waving me away like a master to a maid. "The nano has passed."

"No, really, I can do it. A guy walks into a bar with two chunks of plutonium on his shoulders . . ."

"I'm not listening," HARV said and turned his virtual gaze toward the passenger side window with a huff.

We rode in silence for another few nanos.

"Knock, knock," I said.

HARV threw his hands in the air in disgust.

"Oh please, isn't there some enormously important task that you'd like me to perform?"

"Car, take the com," I said, taking my hands from the wheel. "We're going to the office." I rubbed my eyes and tried not to look at HARV, who I knew was pouting.

"Fine, HARV, scan the net records for everything on Ben Pierce in the past three years. News stories, vids, even text. I want anything that mentions him."

"If you insist," HARV said. He disappeared for a nano, then came back, this time on the screen of the car computer. "There are thirteen thousand five hundred and eighty-two references to, or articles by, Dr. Ben Pierce. Do you want to read them now or should I download them to your bedside e-book?"

"Neither," I said. "Scan them again and disregard all scientific articles and references to his work. I want just personal stuff."

HARV disappeared from the computer screen and came back two nanos later, with a begrudging smirk on his face.

"I have four references," he said. "A box score from the ExShell company softball game where he struck out three times and was hit by a pitch, a donation of ten thousand credits to the Sons of Loving Mothers Fund, and two gossip items linking him romantically to Nova Powers."

"Nova Powers?" I asked. "Why do I know that name?"

"She's a mutant, full contact, non-fact, pro wrestler."

"Oh yeah, the one in the purple spandex," I said. "What do they call her, 'the Warrior Woman'?"

"Actually, it's 'Woman of War,'" HARV said.

He disappeared from the screen and was replaced with a promotional picture of Nova Powers in full wrestling regalia. She was a small woman but well toned, with lovely, sleek, wiry muscles. She had the face of an Asian model and the look of an angry Marine.

"Yeah, that's her," I offered. "She's nice looking."

"She's a mutant," HARV said. "Born on a space transport during a radiation storm. Conjecture is that it gave her superhuman powers."

"Kind of comic-booky, don't you think?"

HARV ignored me.

"She has superhuman strength, fast reflexes, and all that stuff that impresses you humans. She would be no match for BB-2, but she is the equal of any ten normal humans."

"And she's romantically linked to Pierce?" I asked.

Powers' picture on the screen was replaced by a press photo of her and Pierce, arm-in-arm, entering a formal garden party.

"They were seen together at this charity event seventeen months ago."

The picture changed again and this time showed Pierce and Powers on a tropical beach sharing a semi-passionate embrace.

"And again here," HARV said. "On vacation in New Oahu three months later. There are no other mentions of them together so my assumption is that their romance ended sometime after this picture was taken."

"Maybe," I said. "Or else they started keeping a lower profile."

Something caught my eye and I leaned a little closer to the screen. Pierce was shirtless in the picture and there was a dark smear of some kind on his right shoulder.

"What's that on his arm?" I asked. "Can you enlarge that?"

HARV did as he was told and magnified the picture twenty times, zeroing in on Pierce's shoulder. The image grew grainy.

"Can you clean it up a little?"

HARV compensated for the pixelation, the picture came into focus, and we saw that the dark smear was actually three letters: WOW.

"A tattoo?"

"It would appear so," HARV said.

"W-O-W. Woman of War?"

"That would be my assumption as well."

"He had her nickname tattooed on his arm? I guess their romance was pretty serious," I said. "Looks like we should talk to Nova Powers. HARV, let's get her address and . . ."

Just then the car lurched forward and made a violent right turn. I grabbed the passenger seat to steady myself, but still hit my head on the driver-side window.

"Car, you've made a wrong turn," I said.

"Correct," the car computer replied cheerily.

"I wanted to go to my office," I said.

"Correct," it replied again.

I felt the engine surge as the computer opened the throttle to the max and shifted. The tires squealed as we roared forward, accelerating quickly.

I was starting to get a bad feeling about this.

"Why did you just speed up?"

"I need to attain sufficient velocity in order to kill you when I crash," the computer chirped matter-of-factly.

"I had to ask."

# 22

"HARV, can you override the car computer?"

HARV's hologram popped into the passenger seat beside me and shrugged his computer shoulders.

"I have made nine hundred eighty-six attempts already, unfortunately to no avail. Whoever or whatever is controlling the vehicle computer is very good at what they do."

"Swell," I said, "it's nice to know I'm being killed by the very best."

I pulled at the door handle but it was locked (of course). I put my shoulder to the door but it held firmly. The car made a quick left turn on two wheels and accelerated even more.

"This is not good," HARV said. "I calculate that the car is heading for the only dead end left in New Frisco."

I flicked my wrist and popped my gun into hand. "Okay, I'll shoot my way out!" I said, then hesitated. "No, wait, the car's weapon-proof."

"Talking to yourself again, that's good," HARV said. "Schizophrenia comes in handy during times such as these."

My mind raced as the car continued to accelerate. Randy had equipped the car with the best defense systems available. Unfortunately, those systems now had me trapped inside. I looked through the windshield and, true to HARV's calculations, we were heading straight for the historic Brick Wall (the only one to survive the Great Quake of 2009) at breakneck (arms, legs, and everything else) speed. There wasn't much time left.

"HARV, I'll have to break the door open," I shouted. "On my mark, left arm to the max, okay. One . . . two . . ."

"Boss, wait . . ."

"Now!"

I threw myself full force at the car door. My left shoulder hit the metal with a solid, powerful thud.

The door didn't budge.

My shoulder, however, felt like an eggshell under a steam roller.

"Just for the record, HARV," I said, "that part when I yelled 'now' was your cue to juice me up."

"I tried to warn you," HARV said as the wall loomed ever closer. "Something is preventing me from remotely linking with the circuits of your armor. My guess is that whoever is controlling the car is responsible."

"Brilliant deduction there, Holmes." I tossed open the glove compartment and pulled out an interface wire from the emergency kit. "What exactly was your first clue?"

"There is no tangible evidence, of course, but it is highly unlikely that two separate entities would choose this particular time . . ."

"Sarcasm, HARV!" I shouted. "It's sarcasm. I'm going to give you a hardwire link to the car controls. You'll have to fight the car computer for control."

I pried open the dashboard screen. Beneath it, among other things, was a row of emergency com-ports. I plugged one end of the interface wire into the center port and stuck the other end into my wrist interface.

"Go!" I shouted as we zoomed toward the wall.

HARV forced his way through the hardwire connection and into the car computer.

"I can't stop the car," he said after a nano that felt like an eternity, "but I can unlock the door. You'll just have to break it open."

"Do it!" I shouted. "Before this dead end lives up to its name."

Another eternally painful nano passed and I could feel the Brick Wall approaching, like the cold hard backhand slap of the great beyond. Then I heard HARV shout from somewhere deep inside my head.

"Hit it now, boss!"

I juiced up my shoulder as much as I could and hit the car

door. This time, the weakened door popped open and I dove out, hitting the pavement like a fly on a truck windshield. I rolled about thirty meters, my armor sparking all the way as its circuits were pushed to the limit, flipped over the curb, and slammed into a row of hard plastic Dumpsters outside the rear of a Middle Eastern restaurant. The force of impact split them open and I came to rest in an explosive shower of day-old baba ghanouj and spoiled tabouli.

My car (make that *ex*-car) hit the wall and exploded into a great orange-and-black fireball that would have been very cool to watch if, of course, it hadn't been my car burning at the center. I watched the burning bits of charred automobile drift gently to the street like hell's best snowflakes. Then, with my armor still sparking, I slowly sat up and began picking the fatoush out of my hair.

"DOS," I said, "I really liked that car . . ."

"Apparently the feeling was not at all mutual," HARV said as his hologram, projected from my wrist interface, sat next to me on the curb.

"What do you think made it do that?" I asked as I climbed to my feet.

"Well, you are a pretty lousy driver. However, if it were out for revenge, I would think that it would have simply run you over rather than gone the murder-suicide route."

"I'm serious, HARV."

"Quite honestly," HARV said, "it serves you right for using a vehicle with such an outdated computer. Those relics are highly susceptible to outside control."

"What about blocking you from remotely accessing the car or my armor?"

"That's a little trickier," HARV conceded.

A policebot, siren wailing and blue lights flashing, hovered up to the scene and landed just then, with the firefighting robotic unit following closely behind. The human interfacing portion of the policebot removed itself from its vehicle and slowly made its way toward me with just a hint of swagger to its gait.

I had a feeling that this was going to be one story it had never heard before.

# 23

It took some quick thinking, some fast talking, and an instant link to Tony Rickey at NFPD to convince the policebot that I wasn't crazy and/or a menace to society and that it was indeed possible that my car had tried to kill me. So the bot, with the complete backing of its superiors, let me go with only a warning for high-concept incendiary littering as long as I agreed to pay for the clean-up, which I did.

"Should I net you some public transportation?" HARV asked as I left the scene of my near-demise.

"No, I think I'll walk to the office. I could use the exercise."

"As you wish," HARV answered.

I paused for a nano. HARV had dissolved his hologram during my conversation with the policebot (because I figured, why complicate an already difficult situation by throwing a fastidious, wannabe-British, supercomputer into the mix) and hadn't yet reappeared.

"Did you change your voice modulation?" I asked. "You sound a little different."

"My voice modulation hasn't changed," HARV replied, "but if you'll listen a little more closely, you'll realize that I'm not actually using my voice."

"What do you mean?" I asked, and glanced, out of reflex at my wrist interface.

But the wrist interface was blank. And I realized that we'd had another "breakthrough."

"You're talking inside my head," I said.

"It happened as you were jumping from the car. We were both concentrating so precisely on one another's audio cues, we didn't notice that the cues I was giving were mental rather than actual audio."

"So no one else can hear you right now?"

"That's correct. To any passerby you would appear to be a deranged street person listening to the voices in your head. Which is actually . . ."

"Don't go there, HARV," I said. "Wait a minute. If our cues are now mental, then do I need to keep talking?"

"Theoretically, you shouldn't," HARV said. "Why don't you try thinking something at me rather than speaking it?"

I wrinkled my brow and thought very hard. "I need some coffee."

"I'm sorry," HARV said. "I didn't get that."

I wrinkled my brow and thought again. "I need some coffee!"

"I'm still not getting anything," HARV said. "Are you sure you're thinking?"

"What kind of question is that?" I said aloud.

"I'm just not receiving any messages," HARV replied. "Perhaps you need to work on your level of concentration."

"Perhaps you need to get your hearing checked."

"Hearing has nothing to do with it," HARV said. "It's a matter of broadcasting and receiving thoughts. And it appears that you need to vocalize your thoughts in order to properly focus them for the purpose of transmitting through the interface. Don't take this the wrong way, boss. But I think you need to practice your thinking."

"How could anyone take that the *wrong* way," I said as I began walking. "Let's just get to the office."

"Good idea," HARV said. "For some strange reason, I have a desire for some coffee."

I smiled (this could be fun after all), and started mentally reciting a new mantra.

"Zach is always right. Zach is always right. Zach is always right."

I arrived at the office a half hour later. Between the car attack, dealing with the authorities, and the walk to the office, most of the morning was gone and I had nothing to show for it (less than nothing if you count my sudden lack of a car).

Carol was hard at work in the reception area (doing her particle physics homework, I think) and, thankfully, the coffee was still warm. I lumbered over to the maker and poured myself a cup without saying a word.

"Hola, Tío," Carol chirped from her desk, without looking up. "Did you sleep late or something?"

"Didn't you tell her?" I asked HARV.

"I thought it might sound better coming from you," HARV said.

"My car tried to kill me," I said.

Carol rolled her eyes. "Fine, don't tell me." Then she stared at me the way psi folks do when they're reading your mind. "You're telling the truth!"

"I'm going to my office to clean up a bit," I said. "After that, can I borrow your hover?"

"But you hate hovers," Carol said (as if I needed reminding).

"I'll keep it low to the ground and let HARV do the driving."

"I will remind you, Tío, that this hovercraft is vitally important to me," Carol said as she reluctantly tossed me the ignition chip. "You know mass transit gives me headaches." (She meant this literally, by the way. It takes a lot of concentration for a psi to screen out the morass of commuter thoughts on an average bus or train ride, and they end up paying the price afterward).

"I'll be careful," I said as I started toward my office. "Any word from Electra?"

"She called to say she hates you."

I shrugged my shoulders and closed the newly repaired door to my office.

"It's a start," I said.

After a quick change of clothes, I was out of the office and heading toward Carol's hover. I climbed in with a little trepidation, and got as comfortable as I could considering my apprehension about hovers and the fact that this particular hover desperately needed new seats. Maybe Carol was right and she really *did* need a raise. I carefully slid the ignition chip into the CPU and the hover blinked on with far less fanfare than I expected.

"HARV, take the com," I said.

"With pleasure," HARV replied as his digital face popped

into a small computer window on the dash. "Carol has given me access to override the hover's computer. She's much better about that than you. What exactly is our destination?"

"Before my car trouble, you mentioned Nova Powers. Do you know where we can find her now?"

"There were recent reports of her destroying a pair of press-bots at the Regenerative Exercise Lounge and Plastic Surgery Emporium."

"Ah, yes, 'RELAPSE,'" I said.

"That's the one," HARV said. "The pressbots were apparently attempting to video her in a shower. And after examining photos of the remnants of those pressbots, I must say that there most certainly are places where cameras should not go, or be shoved, if you get my data flow."

"I get it." I said and then paused to remove the mental image from my mind.

"Okay, take me to RELAPSE. Medium speed, three meters high."

"Three meters?" HARV protested. "This hover is rated for up to three hundred."

"Well, I'm rated up to three," I said, "so keep it at that."

"Fine," HARV reluctantly agreed. "We'll make the trip via the old lady and acrophobe expressway."

We lifted off the ground. "And don't speed," I said. "Keep it to one fifty-five."

"Life in the slow lane," HARV sighed. "I assume that you feel Ms. Powers knows the whereabouts of Dr. Pierce?"

"Other than pizza-face Burns and his small section of New Sri Lanka, she's our only lead. So we don't have much choice."

"My thoughts exactly," HARV agreed.

"Then again, this whole Pierce thing may just be subterfuge concocted to get me to think too much."

"I sincerely doubt that you will fall into that trap," HARV said.

Compliment or backhanded insult? HARV kept me wondering for the rest of the trip.

# 24

RELAPSE is the hottest of the new breed of health club. It's not just a fitness center, it's a "lifestyle choice." The emphasis is not just on physical fitness, but on overall appearance and attitude: fitness center, hair salon, skin treatments, psychoanalysis, and plastic surgery. Their slogan: "Just do it, or have it done."

The outside of the club was a perpetual media circus, with pressbots crowded around the entrance trying to get a statement from, or an image of, one of the rich and reconstructed clientele.

As a pseudocelebrity, I made the grade and the guard at the entryway let me through, but, as I walked toward the door, a pressbot rolled under the electrified velvet rope and thrust herself in front of me.

"Mr. Johnson, Alyssa Sollyssa from *Rapid News.*"

*"Vapid Views?"*

"No, sir. *Rapid News.* You know, we're the ones with the cool motto: 'We know what you want to know before you do.'"

"If you say so," I said.

"Does your presence here indicate your willingness to at last seek a surgical treatment for those unsightly bags under your eyes?"

"Actually, I'm getting some therapy for a recent injury," I said. "I strained a muscle in my back the other day shoving a pressbot from *Rapid News* down a municipal solid waste recycling chute. By the way, what show are you with again?"

"Um, *Vapid Views,*" she said then rolled away quickly.

The first two floors (up and down) of RELAPSE were a lot like the outside: glitz and glam and no real exertion to speak of. The clientele worked out on a wide array of the most fashionable gravity control weights and holo-sim workout machines, but it was more for show than fitness. I saw a dozen or so HV stars posing for the RELAPSE-employed paparazzi in front of the machines with their workouts actually being supervised by their press agents. A couple even had their makeup people with them.

I was three floors down (in the sub-subbasement) before I found the real workout areas. And this was hardcore stuff. It was one great open space filled with lifting areas and sparring rings. The lifting areas were filled with a few kilotons of old-fashioned free weights and reverse-gravity weights along with many of the newfangled fitness droids that have become all the rage among the serious weightlifting crowd. These are hard-looking, gray-faced droids designed specifically to help lifters get the most out of their workouts by pushing them, emotionally and physically, to their limits through boisterous "intense vocal encouragement." Personally, I found it kind of creepy.

"Don't walk away from me you carbon-refuse. Give me another twenty reps."

"You call that a workout? If you were of the machine family, you'd be lucky to be a toothbrush."

"You weak-willed, puny human. I should rip your insignificant body into kindling and let it fuel the furnace of the omnipotent god-machine. Maybe that will give your feeble existence a modicum of purpose!"

"Okay, that guy's starting to scare me," I whispered to HARV. "Do you see Nova anywhere?"

A cursor appeared before my eyes and scanned the area until it locked onto a woman standing in the middle of a boxing ring across the room. The cursor flashed bright red.

"A simple, 'yes' would have sufficed," I said, making my way toward the ring.

"True, but this is way more cool," HARV replied inside my head.

Nova was more beautiful in person than in hologram. Her self-confidence and strength were clearly evident in the way she moved about the ring, stretching her wiry muscles in preparation for a sparring session. Her demeanor was catlike and her delicate Asian features were somehow simultaneously alluring and fearsome (go figure).

"She's attractive," I said, "and clearly in good shape but, honestly, she doesn't look that tough."

"Her physical stature is deceiving," HARV lectured. "I suggest you watch her next display very closely."

I walked closer just as Nova's sparring session began. Four burly men had climbed into the ring and were now circling her like sharks around a fat man in a inner tube.

"Come on guys, let's go for real," she taunted. "I won't hold back if you don't."

And on cue, the men attacked.

The first leaped at her from behind and slung his tree-trunk arms around her shoulders and chest, locking her small frame in a bear hug. At the same time, another of the men lowered his shoulder and rushed her in a headlong charge. It seemed like good strategy to me.

I was wrong.

Nova broke the first man's grip like a hot laser knife through soy butter and flipped him headfirst into the oncoming attacker. Their heads met with the sound of bricks colliding and the impact sent them both over the ring's electromagnetic simulated ropes and crashing to the hard plastic of the gym floor, where two medbots awaited their arrival.

"Sorry about that," Nova giggled. "Don't know my own strength."

The two remaining sparring partners, obviously thinking that Nova was off guard, rushed her full steam from opposite sides. Now, even though I'd seen Nova in action for only a few seconds, I could immediately spot the mistakes that these poor guys were making.

Mistake One: Nova is never "off-guard."

Mistake Two: As the previous two attackers had proven only nanos before, a two-directional attack isn't effective against her.

She proved me right on both counts because, as the men charged, she spun like a cat and flung her arms out ramrod straight. The men crashed full force into her open hands and you could almost see the stars yourself. The guy on the left fell to the ground on contact, out colder than a fish in a freezer. The guy on the right managed to remain standing but was wobbling like a single rotor hovercraft in a windstorm. Nova blew him a kiss and he toppled over—out for the count (no, out for the day).

I applauded.

Nova turned toward me and flashed a surprisingly warm smile.

"Why, if it isn't Zachary Nixon Johnson," she bubbled.

"If it isn't, then I'm wearing the wrong underwear," I said as I watched the medbots carry the last of her sparring partners away.

"Great line," HARV whispered facetiously inside my head. "Should I load my canned-laughter program?"

Nova walked to the edge of the ring, leaned seductively through the ropes and smiled again. "I see you're witty even without your writers."

"First of all," I said (regrettably, with more anger than I would have liked), "I don't use writers." I paused for a nano and tried to make my tone a little more pleasant. "Second, that is if you don't mind, I'd like to ask you a question or two."

"I love questions," she said with a smile that worried me. "But I hate giving answers."

"That sort of makes it difficult then," I offered.

"Are they important questions?" she asked.

"Sort of," I said.

"Good."

Nova took hold of my arm and, with a gentle wave of her hand, casually lifted me over the ropes and set me down beside her in the ring.

"I'll make you a deal, Mr. Johnson," she smiled. "I'll answer whatever questions you have, but I'll do it in the ring. Think you can last two minutes of full spar with me?"

"Gee, Nova, I'd love to," I said as I backed away. "But I have this strict policy about not fighting women. It's bad for the good guy image if I win and bad for the macho image if I lose."

She ignored me as she removed the computer interface from my wrist.

"You'll time two minutes for us, won't you, computer?" she said into the speaker.

"It will be my pleasure," HARV replied cheerily, "especially since, only mere nanos ago, Mr. Johnson was assessing your fighting prowess thusly."

My digitally recorded voice came over the interface speaker (more loudly than I thought possible).

". . . honestly, she doesn't look that tough."

I gently rubbed my temples with my fingers.

"On second thought, let's make it three minutes," Nova said as she placed the wrist interface gently on the turnbuckle.

"Thanks a lot, HARV."

"Trust me," HARV said inside my head. "She'll speak more freely if she's angry."

"You have such a helpful computer," Nova said, turning toward me.

"I live to serve," HARV chimed.

"And by 'serve,' of course, he means to embarrass and gravely endanger," I added.

"Now, now, Mr. Johnson . . ." Nova said, limbering up.

"Please, call me Zach."

"Thank you. And you can call me Nova." She smiled and walked slowly toward me as she spoke. "I understand that you're an expert in all major forms of the martial arts."

"Actually, no," I said, backing away from her advance. "That's just PR that my agent created. I prefer to *think* my way out of trouble."

"That's too bad," Nova said as she closed the gap between us. "There's not much room in this ring for thinking."

"Tell me when I should begin timing," HARV called.

"How about two and a half minutes ago?" I said.

Nova smiled and then began our brutal ballet with a right cross. The punch was a probing one, at half speed. She was feeling me out, ascertaining my style.

In this case, my style was to duck and run. I slipped off the ropes and managed to avoid the punch but Nova had expected as much. Her first punch had been a feint that set me up for the next and as I twisted away from her right, I nearly fell headlong into her lightning quick left jab. I ducked at the last nano and her fist sailed over my head, sending an icy breeze down my back (so far so good).

"So, tell me about you and Dr. Benjamin Pierce," I said.

Nova responded to the question with an angry, right-fisted uppercut to my chin, which made me think that her feelings about Pierce weren't exactly the warm and fuzzy kind.

I was trampled once by an electronic bull during the PETA-endorsed Humane Running of the Bulls in New Pamplona. It cracked two ribs and left a hoof print on my lower back that I can still see in the shower.

Nova's punch made me wax nostalgic for that time.

I flew across the ring and into the ropes, bouncing up and down on them like a bobble-head doll in a centrifuge.

"Ben Pierce? Why do you ask?" Nova snarled.

Against my better judgment, I staggered to my feet and shook the stars off.

"He won the door prize at the opening of the new Macy-mart," I said. "I'm trying to deliver his new hypersonic tooth-brush."

Nova leaped toward me and threw another punch at my head, which I somehow managed to avoid.

"I'll warn you now, Zach, talking about Ben brings out the worst in me."

She spun around like a ballet dancer and whipsawed my legs out from under me, taking me down hard to the mat.

"So I noticed," I said. "I take it then that it's true that the two of you were romantically involved?"

From a sitting position she threw a flurry of crushing kicks at me. Her fast moving legs looked like shapely Ginsu chopping machines and I had to roll like a hyped-up puppy looking for a treat just to say ahead of her. We crossed the entire ring this way and by the time I reached the end, I had some serious mat burn on my face.

"We were hot and heavy for a long time, as you might have guessed," she said. "It was your classic, opposites-attract kind of thing."

I flipped to my feet (pretty smoothly I thought) and went into my best defensive position, ready for anything.

"It must have been pretty serious for him to tattoo your 'W-O-W' trademark on his arm."

Nova blasted through my best defense with a lightning quick punch that I didn't even see (at least I think it was a punch) and rocked my head back.

"I thought so too," she said.

Another Nova punch rocked me back farther.

"To tell you the truth, I was in love. I thought he was too, the rat bastard slime."

She hooked her arm under mine and tossed me over her shoulder and down hard onto the mat.

"I take it he ended the relationship?" I asked.

She flipped me up and slammed me to the mat again and again as we spoke.

"Yes, he did. And thank you so much for reminding me."

I knew this was going to be emotionally painful for her (and physically painful for me as well) but I had to ask.

"Did he leave you for another woman?"

"Well, he was in love with BB Star . . ." she said.

Slam.

"BB Star?"

Slam.

"Oh, yeah, he had it bad for her big time. Falling in love with your boss's wife, very wise career move, Ben."

Slam!

"Did he and BB actually have an affair?" I asked.

"Not that I know of," she said. "I understand that BB's frigid."

Slam!

Why do people keep saying that? I thought.

I flipped Nova off me and tried to get up. But she spun around from behind and somersaulted in the air. She wrapped her legs around my head and brought me back down to the mat again.

Slam.

"Ben used to make me wear a blonde wig and pretend to be BB for him. 'Oh yes, Ben, I'm BB Star. I just love intelligent men.'" She turned her attention back to me and flexed her thighs, tightening her hold on my head and neck. "By the way, I call this my 'pleasure and pain' move. I put a little pressure on your neck here, cut off the blood and air to your brain and you're sleeping like a baby. I understand that the dreams are quite pleasant as well."

Under different circumstances this might have been enjoyable but the suffocation aspect here was a definite turn-off.

This was the second time in two days that someone had tried closing off my airway and I didn't want this to become a habit. Thankfully, HARV was still in my head.

"Shock her," I mumbled, hoping he'd catch on.

"Shock her?" HARV answered inside my head. "Mumble twice if by that you mean that you would like me to utilize the power supply of your body armor to create a concentrated electrical burst strong enough to cause Ms. Powers discomfort."

"Mphh mphh," I said.

Nova, meanwhile, was off in her own little world of relationship second-guessing, although it wasn't stopping her from leg-locking me into unconsciousness.

"In retrospect, I realize now that Ben and I were destined to end badly. He was emotionally immature and had some hefty family issues that he was displacing. DOS, I've never seen a bigger momma's boy."

"All set, boss," HARV whispered in my head. "I suggest, however, that you bite Ms. Powers simultaneously as I shock her in order to cover up the fact that you're cheating."

Frankly, when you're being suffocated, I don't think any transgression counts as "cheating." But I didn't have the time or the air to debate the point with HARV.

"Personally, I think I've made a lot of progress in putting this behind me," Nova continued. "I've been able to channel my anger into a very positive direction. I use it in my wrestling so it's helped my career a lot. I think that shows a level of maturity that Ben just doesn't have yet, the rat bastard slime."

"On my mark now," HARV said. "Ready? Bite!"

I chomped down on Nova's thigh and felt HARV shoot a charge of my armor's electricity into her through my teeth. My molars tingled a bit from the electrical backlash (and I think I lost a filling), but Nova clearly got the bulk of the charge.

"Yow!" she exclaimed, half in pain, half in surprise. "Did you just bite me?"

She loosened her leg lock just enough for me to wriggle free. I squeezed out and popped to my feet with the aid of one of the ropes. Nova got up and slowly pursued me, rubbing her leg as she moved.

"DOS it," she said angrily, "I was on the verge of a breakthrough there."

"I thought we were sparring."

She lashed out at me with the speed of a viper on caffeine, grabbed me with her left arm, and pushed me hard into the turnbuckle, pinning me with her shoulder.

"You men are all alike," she said. "Everything always has to be a competition. Gates, I hate your insecurities. Why are you so afraid of communicating?"

"But I'm the one who wanted to talk," I said.

"Oh, that's just like you. Always displacing the blame."

She rolled the fingers of her right hand into a fist and the lithe muscles in her arm tensed like a pound of plastique with a lit fuse. I had the feeling that I'd worn out my welcome.

Just then I heard the melodic (and lifesaving) sound of HARV's computer simulated bell.

"Time is up!" he shouted. "And hearty congratulations to you, Ms. Powers. I feel as though you've made some real emotional progress during this session."

Nova smiled and released me from the turnbuckle.

"Do you really think so?"

"Absolutely," HARV said. "It takes great strength to talk about your emotions so openly."

"Don't I know it. But just try finding a man who appreciates that."

"That wall of machismo," HARV said, "it's just a cheap facade to hide their insecurities."

"You can say that again," Nova said as she lifted the interface from the turnbuckle and turned toward me. "You know, Zach, you could learn a few things about emotional maturity from this computer."

"Yes, he's very in touch with himself," I said.

I took the interface from her and reattached it to my wrist. Nova and I climbed out of the ring and back to the relative safety of the gym floor.

"One last thing about Pierce," I said. "When was the last time that you saw him?"

"A little over a year ago," she answered. "He told me that things weren't working out and it was best that we go our own ways."

"You know he's missing now. No one's seen him in nearly a year."

"And you're looking for him?" she asked.

"That's right."

"Good luck then," she said. "If Ben wants to stay hidden, you're not going to find him. He's very good at what he does."

"So am I," I said.

"Ben's in some sort of deadly trouble, I hope?"

"Too soon to tell," I said as I turned to leave. "But I'll let you know."

"When you see him," Nova called, "tell him I said hello."

"I will," I smiled and turned away again.

"No, wait," she said. "Tell him you saw me and that I looked great and seemed happy."

"Okay."

"And tell him that I had four gorgeous guys on my arm."

"Got it."

"No, wait. Just tell him I said hello."

"We're never getting out of here," HARV whispered.

# 25

I finally had Nova write down the various things she wanted (or didn't want) me to say to Pierce for her when I found him. In the end, she decided to let me use my best judgement as to which line to use (although she made me give her a few different readings of each so that she could be sure that my inflection conveyed just how emotionally secure she had become).

Thirty minutes later, HARV and I were back in the hovercraft headed toward the office. HARV was at the controls, while I blindly flipped through the computer photos that we had of Pierce, not quite certain what I was looking for.

"That's two dead ends in one day, boss," HARV said as we glided along the lower skyway. "Three if you count the one into which you crashed the car."

"I wouldn't call Nova a dead end exactly," I said. "But she's definitely a weird turn in the road. Net me BB on the vid. I think we need to talk."

BB's face appeared on the computer screen a nano later.

"Have you found the droid?" she asked.

"Not much for small talk, are you BB?"

I assume by your flippant tone," BB answered "that the answer to my question is no."

"Sorry," I said, "but it's going to take me more than twelve hours to find your superpowered android. In the meantime, here's a question for you: How well did you know Ben Pierce?"

"He was my employee. He designed the BB-2 android."

"I understand that," I said. "But how well did you *know* him?"

"I do not know what you mean."

"Did you know that he was in love with you?"

"What?" she exclaimed, her eyes went wide with surprise and her left eyebrow arched. "Where did you hear such a thing?"

"Forget where I heard it. Did you know it?"

"No," she said. "I had no idea. I hardly knew Dr. Pierce at all, certainly not on a social level. Where on earth did you hear such a thing?"

"From a source of dubious reliability," I said. "I'm sorry if I bothered you."

"No bother at all, Zach," BB said with a smile. "Your mission is of the utmost importance to me and I want to help you in any way that I can."

"I understand, BB. I won't let you down."

"Thank you, Zach."

She smiled and disappeared from the screen.

"And that would be dead end number four," HARV said.

I turned back to the computer screen and continued flipping through the photos of Pierce.

"She's lying," I said.

"What?"

"She knows Pierce better than she's letting on. She's hiding something."

"Do you think they were romantically involved?"

I shook my head and pointed at the photo of Pierce that was currently on the screen. It was the photo of him and Nova embracing on the beach.

"Look at him," I said. "Does he look like the kind of man who could have affairs with Nova Powers and BB Star at the same time? No. They weren't romantically involved, but there's something that BB's not telling us."

The hovercraft hit some mild turbulence and gently shook for a nano, then rose a bit higher on the lonely skyway.

"Not too high, HARV," I said.

The hover lurched again, this time violently, took a sharp turn off he skyway and continued to rise.

"HARV, I think we're over the height that I requested," I said.

"Yes, we are," HARV agreed.

"Then please lower the craft," I ordered.

"I'm trying, but the craft isn't responding."

"What do you mean it's not responding?" I asked hastily as we continued our ascent.

"Well, technically it is responding, only in a manner that is inconsistent with my instruction."

"The whole point of my letting you drive was because you were supposedly invulnerable to outside control."

"That's true," HARV answered. "However, although I may be invulnerable to such attacks, it is apparently very possible to bypass me and take direct control of the hovercraft, which is what is happening here. Actually, it's quite an impressive display of remote rerouting and reprogramming."

"Can you override it?" I asked nervously.

"Eventually," HARV stated matter-of-factly.

"Eventually?"

"I estimate that the task will take me approximately ten minutes."

"You realize, of course, that we probably don't have that much time?" I said.

"I am assuming that the question is of a rhetorical nature, so I won't take the time to respond."

"How high are we now?" I asked.

"I'm being overridden so I don't have access to any of the instruments," HARV said. "Look over the side and I'll make an estimate."

I looked over the side so that HARV could get a good view of the ground through the lens in my eye.

"Wow, we're way up there," HARV said.

"Brilliant," I grumbled.

The hovercraft computer kicked in with its chirpy monotone. "We are currently at an altitude of three hundred fifty meters and climbing."

"Thank you," HARV said to the computer; then he turned to me. "It always pays to be polite."

"So what's the plan here, computer?" I asked.

"We are climbing to an altitude of six hundred meters," the computer answered.

"And then?"

"At that point," it said bluntly, "I will cut all power to the gyros and we will begin a rapid descent culminating in a fiery impact upon the ground below."

"I guess I could have seen that one coming."

The hover lurched again and continued to climb.

"Do not worry," the hover chirped reassuringly. "The crash will take place in that nearby park in order to minimize collateral civilian casualties."

"That means a lot to me," I said, "but forgive me if I don't sit still for this. HARV, the navigation chip for this hover's computer, where is it located?"

"Why?" HARV asked.

"Just tell me! I'm not in the best of moods right now."

"The chip that controls the navigation is a tenth of a centimeter in diameter and is located three centimeters directly below the dash, parallel with the control column."

"Thanks," I said. "And I'm sorry for shouting at you."

"I understand," HARV said, "most people are adversely affected emotionally by the fast approach of imminent death. But I repeat my previous question: Why, boss?"

I popped my gun into my hand.

"If we can't control this thing, then nobody will!"

I pushed the seat back and fired a small explosive round into the driver's column. The navigational computer exploded and the hover lurched again and then started to plummet toward the Earth. I dove forward and grabbed the steering column.

"Well, you have succeeded in destroying the navigational computer," HARV said as his hologram materialized next to me.

"Thanks," I grunted as I struggled in vain to get some control of the plummeting craft. "I never would have guessed."

"Though if the truth be known, I don't really see how this helps," HARV said.

"At least now we're in control of our own destinies. We'll be fine so long as we survive the fall."

"What do you mean we? I'm a projected image created from a CPU located many kilometers away from here. I'll survive. You, on the other hand . . ."

"I'm going to survive as well!" I said, pulling on the control panel. "I just have to learn how to pilot a free-falling hovercraft in the next thirty seconds."

"You certainly are optimistic. I always liked that about you," HARV said. "I think I'll miss that most of all."

"Shut up, HARV. You're killing the moment."

I held tight to the control stick and tried to pull the hover out of the dive, but without the computer to modulate, it was like trying to play piano while wearing boxing gloves. It was impossible to control the delicate balance of power between the gyros. I moved the stick gently to the left and managed to lessen the angle of descent and put the dying craft's trajectory in line with the park's duck pond. Unfortunately, I also put the craft into a barrel roll.

"Oh, this is much better," HARV said. "Nothing like a little centrifugal force to lessen the agony of a fatal impact."

"Okay, here's the plan. I'm going to bail out when we get over the pond. Hopefully, I've slowed this heap down just enough so that I can survive a water landing."

"If you'll pardon my impudence, boss," HARV said. "I think I have a better idea."

"I'm open to suggestions."

"Our new interface will allow me to manipulate your body's naturally occurring electromagnetic energy."

"And that's a good thing?"

"In this case, yes," HARV continued. "I should be able to increase the energy, focus it through your body armor, and reverse the magnetic force."

"You mean build me a force field?"

"Exactly."

"You can do that with the new interface?"

"Trust me, boss. I'm no longer merely cutting-edge here," HARV said. "I'm the ripping edge."

"Okay buddy," I said, putting my finger on the emergency release button. "Let's go."

I ejected from the spinning/plummeting craft at a height of twenty-five meters (and at a speed that I didn't want to think about) and began my head-over-heels free fall toward the water. The late afternoon breeze hit my face like a chilly razor and I knew then that the impact, water or no, would splatter me like a ripe grape in a wine press.

Then I felt a laser-hot surge run through my body from my head to my feet and back again. My teeth chattered, my fingers began to shake uncontrollably, and I felt the hairs on my arms start to sizzle and burn. HARV was making me electric.

"This better work, HARV," I mumbled.

"Shut up, boss," he said. "You're killing the moment."

I tucked my body into a cannonball position and hit the duck pond like a meteor, first skimming across the surface like a stone, then hitting full on. Walls of water rose ten meters in the air from the force of impact like atomic mushroom clouds, then crashed down on me as I sank beneath the waves. And as the water covered me, I was too weak to even keep my eyes open, let alone fight my way to the surface.

## 26

It was early evening when I awoke. The sun was just going down over the New Frisco skyline and its red and orange light made the pond glow like burning embers under glass.

I was soaked to the skin and lying face up in the mud, two medbots beside me, scanning my body for injuries. I caught a glimpse of pale skin as something moved past me on the right and I tried to turn and follow it, but my body didn't respond.

"Don't try to move, Zach," Randy said, then slowly leaned into my field of vision. "The medbots have you in a stasis field until they rule out any spinal injuries."

"Randy?"

"HARV sent me a warning that you were going down," he said. "I got here just in time."

"You fished me out of the water?"

"I managed to digitally record your crash from four different angles," he said excitedly. "It was amazing, Zach. The spray of water when you hit the pond will look spectacular in super slow-mo, and the sparks from your armor, shorting out as you went underwater? Simply breathtaking."

"But then you fished me out of the water, right?"

"Actually, I was on the celnet with my corporate backers by then. I had a droid pull you to shore."

"Thanks a meg," I said. "HARV?"

HARV's hologram appeared from my eye lens. He appeared to be soaking wet as well (out of sympathy for me, I think—a nice gesture).

"I'm here, boss."

"Good job."

"What can I say? This isn't your grandaddy's interface."

Randy looked at the readouts from the bodyscan done by the medbots.

"It looks like you're clear," he said. "No internal injuries. No broken bones. Just some very severe bruises and a mild concussion."

He nodded to the medbots and they deactivated the stasis field. I started to sit up but it was painful to move.

"I have to warn you," Randy said, "you're going to be very tired for the next twelve hours or so. HARV sapped a lot of your body's energy in order to generate enough electricity to shield you. It's going to take some time for you to regain that."

"It was worth it," I said. "As bad as I feel, I'm a lot better off than the hover . . . oh no. Where's Carol's hover?"

"Most of it's over there," HARV said, pointing north.

"DOS," I said, sitting up. "She's going to kill me."

"Easy, boss," HARV said, trying, unsuccessfully to hold me down with his holographic hands.

I rose to my knees and looked about. Sure enough, Carol's hovercraft lay upside down in the tall grass, one hundred meters away. Stray sparks still flew from the wrecked chassis.

"Oh, I'm in trouble now," I said.

I rose to my feet and, dazed and delirious, staggered toward the remnants of the hover.

"She's going to kill me," I said. "She's going to fry my brain and make me think I'm a duck."

"Boss, slow down," HARV said. "We'll get her a new hover. She understands these things happen—especially to you."

But I was beyond listening. I reached the wreck and carefully looked around to see if there was anything worth salvaging.

"She's going to kill me," I said.

"I think you're fixating here just a little, boss."

The three gyros were destroyed. Two had ripped away from the hull on impact. The other was mangled almost beyond recognition. The hull looked like an old accordion, crumpled and torn from front to rear. It was a total wreck. Then I noticed a dim glow emanating from inside the hull.

"Look, HARV," I said, as I dropped to my knees to get a closer look, "the computer still works. Maybe we can . . ."

Then I saw it and everything changed.

"It's not 'wow,'" was all I could say.

"Boss," HARV said carefully, "I think we should have the medbots check you again for that concussion."

I got down on my hands and knees and tried to pry my way into the hovercraft hull for a closer look at the screen, but I already knew what was there. It was the picture of Pierce and Nova embracing on the beach. But this time, I saw it upside down and I saw the tattoo on Pierce's arm in a whole new light. It wasn't in honor of Nova Powers. It wasn't "Woman of War."

"It's not 'W-O-W,'" I said.

And Nova's words echoed in my mind: "I've never seen a bigger momma's boy."

The tattoo had been created specifically so only Pierce himself could read it. I knew that now. And I knew what it said.

"MOM."

# 27

"His what?"

"You heard me, HARV," I said (for the eighth time, I think), "Pierce is with his mother. That's where we'll find him."

"Oh, I heard you, boss," HARV said. "I just think your plunge into the duck pond left you a little more concussed than we originally thought."

It was morning now. I'd been home and in bed for twelve hours and had slept solidly for ten of them. I was still very weak, and my muscles didn't want to do much of anything other than remain motionless in bed, but I'd been assured that my body was replenishing its energy and that I should be somewhat back to normal within the next day.

I was also told that Electra had come to the house and examined me during the night, just to make certain that I was okay. No doubt she wanted to ensure that I was healthy for when she would return at some later date to kick my ass. But even so, I was happy to hear that she'd come. I could smell her perfume on the pillow beside me and that alone was enough to lift my spirits.

So, clearly, I was on the road to recovery. Now, all I had to do was convince HARV that I wasn't crazy, or at the very least that I was right about Mother Pierce.

"You heard what Nova said about Pierce. He was a momma's boy, he had family issues, all of that. I tell you, that tattoo isn't for Nova. It's for his mother."

"But it's upside down."

"Not the way he looks at it. He lifts his arm and he sees

'MOM.' It's all crystal clear, HARV—Pierce wants his mommy.'

"Whatever you say, boss," HARV said.

"He's not in Sri Lanka, he's not on the moon. We find his mother, we find Pierce. Now stop arguing and get me the address of Mother Pierce!"

"Let's pretend for a nano," HARV said, "that, although I didn't take your theory seriously, I did some searching last night, while you were sleeping off your near death experience. Just to humor you."

"Okay, let's say that."

"And suppose," HARV continued, "that I found irrefutable proof that your theory is baseless. Would this convince you to surrender this Oedipal quest?"

"Well, that depends," I said.

"Upon what?"

"On what Oedipal means, for one." I said. "And the exact nature of the 'irrefutable proof' for another."

HARV shook his head and flashed a picture of an elderly woman on the wall screen.

"April Pierce, mother of Dr. Benjamin J. Pierce, age one hundred twenty-two. Current residence, plot five sixty-seven in Beverly Hills Eternal Estates, six feet under."

"She's dead?"

"No, boss, she's a mushroom farmer."

"When did she die?"

"Fourteen months ago. Cause of death, respiratory failure brought on by pneumonia."

"Was it suspicious?"

"She was one hundred twenty-two!"

"Are you sure it's really her?"

"DNA tests are conclusive," HARV said. "I checked with the computer at the medical examiner's office and saw the tissue samples myself."

"Fourteen months ago. That's just before Pierce broke up with Nova, just before the BB-2 project went crazy and just before he disappeared."

"You think her death pushed him over the edge?"

"I have a feeling that Pierce was over the edge well before

his mother died," I said. "But I think her death spurred him to action."

"So where do we go from here?" HARV asked.

"It's like I told you, HARV. We find Pierce's mother."

"Boss," HARV said, throwing his hands in the air, "I'm going to assume that your short-term memory was a casualty of last night's traumatic experience so I'm going to repeat, very calmly, I might add, that Dr. Pierce's mother is dead. She's kicked the coffee cup, she's pushing up paisleys, she has shuffled off her mortal interface, she's riding the ethernet of the next world. She's e-mailing from the great beyond and her address ends with 'the-hereafter-dot-org!' I can say it in over one hundred fifty different languages if you like. But no matter how I say it she's still D-E-A-D, dead, dead, dead."

"That'll just make finding her a little more difficult," I said.

"What?"

"Come on, Pierce is supposedly one of the greatest minds on the planet, right? He's not going to let a little thing like death stop him from patching things up with his mother. He'd have a back-up somewhere."

"You mean a clone?"

"Yes, a clone."

"But that's illegal."

"So's building nuclear-powered killer androids. We need to find the clone of Mother Pierce."

"Fine," HARV said. "Where do you want to start?"

"Well, since I'm not likely to be going anywhere for a while, let's start right here. Patch yourself into the ExShell computer and let's do some old-fashioned digging."

A few words about human cloning: it doesn't work.

That's just my opinion, of course. An opinion which happens to be shared by the World Council and about 85 percent of the world's population, but still, it's just my opinion. There are a lot of megabrains in the scientific community, after all, who will argue with me quite vociferously.

"Simple DNA sequencing," they say. "The human genome. The building blocks to life" (notice how they never speak in complete sentences).

The world, fueled by the zeal of the scientific community,

once embraced the cloning concept. The first (somewhat) successful cloning experiments early in the century captured the public's imagination and it actually culminated in a short-lived, but memorable, cloning craze twenty years ago.

I have met clones. I have spoken with clones. I even dated a clone once (it was during my experimental period in college), and all I can say is that when it comes to cloning humans, *New* New Coke was a better idea.

Why? Two words: "The mind." The body (brain and all) is the easy part. A little DNA, the right equipment, and we can grow it in a big test tube. We can keep it on the sun porch beside the geranium for warmth and decorate it for the holidays. The mind, however, is an entirely different ball of earwax.

With all our advanced technology, we still don't understand how the mind works. The complicated mixture of memory and original thought, fueled by emotion, instinct, and personality that makes every living person a unique individual cannot be drawn on a schematic map of lobes and hemispheres. A lot of the greatest scientists in the world today can't even make small talk at a cocktail party, let alone identify and recreate the subtleties and nuances of the human personality.

Be that as it may, the scientific community made valiant efforts to map, catalog, and then recreate the human mind. The mind, however, simply proved too complex for them. By misplacing a few neurons or misdirecting a few intercranial connections, early researchers discovered, all too painfully, that there really is a thin line between love and hate (also between genius and psychosis, confidence and megalomania, progressive rock and disco).

The cloning craze eventually lead to what is now dramatically referred to as the clone wars. In retrospect, the whole thing was really more silly and contrived than monumental, but it made a mess of a lot of things, including national governments, the world economy, and the collector's market for action figures.

The World Council finally outlawed all cloning of humans ten years ago and no one, save for the scientific community, has thought about it much since then.

Today there are still a few sanctioned labs that clone organisms but their work is pretty much limited to strains of bacteria, prize-winning bulls, that cat from the holovision commercials, and a few individuals currently revered as "cultural icons" (but they don't go out in public much because they drool a lot and tend to get lost in open spaces).

The fact that Pierce might have cloned his own mother made me realize that he was quite probably insane. The fact that this insane, brilliant man also designed and created the powerful android for which I was now searching made me want to lock my doors and stay in bed just a little longer.

HARV and I spent the next hour hacking into the R&D database of the ExShell computer. Actually, it was HARV who did most of the work. I mostly watched sports highlights from the night before.

"By the way, since Ms. Star has granted us full access to the ExShell computer, I fail to see the point in wasting our time hacking in through the back door," HARV complained.

"I don't want ExShell to know what we're looking for just yet. They still think Pierce is in Sri Lanka, remember? Also, I want to make sure that you're keeping your hacking skills sharp. I understand that ExShell's defenses are pretty tough."

"Oh, please," HARV said, "I could get past these defenses with a 486 and a blind homing pigeon."

"Nice metaphor." I said. "You're developing a wicked sense of sarcasm."

"I've been thinking about going out on the road or maybe writing for HV."

"Don't quit your day job just yet," I said, although I was pretty certain he was joking (which in and of itself was pretty remarkable).

But HARV was no longer listening. He was busy picking the last lock on the back door of the ExShell computer system.

"We're in," HARV answered.

A list of files, thousands long, scrolled across the wall-screen.

"These are the files from the ExShell R&D department," HARV said. "Now, just what is it that we're looking for?"

"Anything that looks like Pierce's mother," I said. "Her memories, her personality, her mental skills. All of that would have to have been digitally translated and stored. I'm sure he used ExShell equipment."

"You think Pierce used an illegal cloning house to grow the body?" HARV asked.

I shrugged.

"Maybe he bribed one of the better animal houses into doing a special job under the table. Who knows, maybe he did it himself in his basement. I'm hoping that there's some evidence of data transfer here. Let's see Pierce's files."

The screen changed and the list of Pierce's files appeared. Again, there were thousands of them.

"Which one do you want to open first?" HARV asked.

I stared at the screen closely and looked at the long column of Pierce's name down the side.

"Wait, a second,'" I said. "Forget about these. Show me everything *except* Pierce's files. He wouldn't do this under his own name."

HARV changed the screen again. Pierce's name disappeared from the left hand column, replaced by a myriad of others. ExShell's R&D department employed thousands of people around the world, all of them had at least some files in the database.

"With which part of the virtual haystack would you like to begin?"

"Go through the list of names. Find anything funny," I said.

"Define funny," HARV said. "And remember, I'm not programmed for humor."

"Yeah, only sarcasm," I said. "Pierce would use an alias. He's big-headed enough to use something sly. 'Tom Clone,' 'Dick Copy,' 'Harry Mother,' that kind of thing."

"Harry Mother?"

"Just find me the funny names," I said.

"You got it. One Harry Mother coming right up."

# 28

It took HARV a little longer than I thought it would to put together the list of names, maybe three or four minutes, but I figured that he had some trouble making the subjective call when it came to the definition of funny. He was still new to this type of fine line. I took the time to grab an Electra-prescribed power shake from the fridge and a short while thereafter, HARV and I were both examining the list of funny names.

"How about 'Harry Johnson?' " HARV asked.

"Pierce may not be the most creative guy in the world but he's not twelve," I said. "He wouldn't use anything that juvenile. Same thing with 'Seymour Hiney' and that hyphenated name 'Alice Dyer-Rhea.' "

" 'Mike Hunt,' as well?"

"Definitely."

"How about 'Dick Swett'?"

"Will you get your mind out of the gutter?"

"Forgive me, boss," HARV lamented, "but it is a pretty broad category."

I rubbed my eyes for a nano and took another long swig of the power shake. I was thankful that no one aside from HARV was around. It's hard maintaining a tough guy image when you're sitting around the house in your pajamas, drinking a vanilla shake with a straw.

"I know," I said. "It's just one of those things where I'll know it when I see it." I turned my attention back to the screen. " 'Jack Ash' is no good. 'Adam Appleton' is silly but not right. 'Foo Kyu' is just a very unfortunate cultural coincidence."

"Just think about his poor son, 'Foo Kyu Two.' "

I stared harder at the screen and kept reading the list.

" 'Lisa Carr' . . ."

"I'd rather buy."

" 'Juana Pea' . . ."

"I went before we left the house."

" 'Juno Eimapieg' . . ."

"That one pretty much stands on its own."

"HARV!"

"You know, I'm starting to like this."

"This isn't working. Let's go back to the main list."

The screen switched back to the lengthier list, but alphabetized itself around the Eimapieg name that HARV had highlighted.

"What's that file right below 'Eimapieg'?"

"Einstein, A.," HARV answered.

"Einstein, A?" I asked. "As in Albert Einstein?"

"So it would seem."

"Why didn't you flag that as funny?" I asked.

"I didn't think that it was a particularly funny name."

"It's an *odd* name."

"You didn't ask for *odd*," HARV said. "You asked for *funny*."

"But odd *is* funny," I said.

"No," HARV said. "Odd is odd. Funny is funny."

"Look, there's funny-haha and there's funny-odd," I said. "I wanted them both."

"You didn't specify that you wanted funny-odd. You just said 'funny,' which implies only funny-haha."

"Why would I want funny-haha and not funny-odd?" I asked.

"Why would you want funny-odd in the first place?"

"Because odd is funny," I said, nearly red in the face. "Odd is funny!"

"Well, it is if you say it *that* way."

"Just open up the Einstein file."

"Interesting," HARV said. "The file is encrypted with a logarithmic key. Difficult to open."

"Can you break it?" I asked.

"Already done," HARV said with a sly smile.

On cue, the file opened and a three-dimensional computer schematic of a human brain unfolded on the screen.

"Now, *that's* odd," HARV said.

# 29

HARV and I watched as the brain template gently rotated before us on the screen, showing us, in glorious detail, the sulci and fissures that every human brain has (but are still unique to each). The template was broken down into sections mostly by the lobes and the hemispheres. The insides of most of these sections were blank but the right frontal lobe pulsated with millions of connected dots of light.

"Hello, Mother Pierce," I said.

"It appears to be a topographical map of the brain," HARV said. "Nice find."

"It's a start."

"Well, if nothing else," he continued, "we've proven that Dr. Pierce certainly holds himself in high opinion. There aren't many scientists who would use Einstein as a pen name."

"That's it, HARV."

"That's what?"

"Flag that file and go back to the list."

HARV did as he was told, intrigued by my thinking (which was kind of odd unto itself).

"Scroll down now, into the Gs."

HARV scrolled through the names and I found what I was looking for.

"There," I said, pointing to the screen, "Galilei, G. That's Galileo. Open that one."

"It's locked with a variation of the same encryption key as the Einstein file." HARV said. "Not so hard to crack the second time around."

HARV opened the file and a three-dimensional blueprint of

a human left frontal lobe appeared on the screen, next to the spinning brain template. Again, every detail was carefully mapped, every neuron was (supposedly) accounted for.

"This looks like it will fit very nicely into the template," HARV said.

With those words the spinning left frontal lobe snapped neatly into place adjacent to the right. We now had two pieces complete in the brain jigsaw puzzle.

"The frontal lobes govern most executive functions," HARV said, sounding very much like a university professor. "Mother Pierce is coming into focus."

"Okay, go back to the list and find every file with a physicist name attached and locked with that same encryption code," I said, "Tesla, Archimedes, Hamilton, everyone."

"Now when you say 'physicist' do you mean 'physicist-haha' or 'physicist-odd'?"

"Don't start with me, HARV."

A few minutes later we had found eight more files, one for each hemisphere of each lobe of the brain, one for the hippocampal system, and one which appeared to be for miscellaneous minor brain areas. We had unlocked the computer blueprint for building Mother Pierce's brain.

"So now that we've found her," HARV said, tapping his holographic fingers on the table, "how do we actually *find* her?"

I didn't have an answer for that one, so I covered for it by staring deeply at the computer screen and rubbing my chin slowly, as if in thought.

"You don't know, do you?" HARV asked.

"Give me minute," I said. "We're missing something here."

I looked again at the list of files and read the names silently to myself:

1. Ampere
2. Archimedes
3. Bohr
4. Born
5. Broglie
6. Dirichlet
7. Einstein

8. Galileo
9. Hawking
10. Ohm

Then I saw it.

"Galileo, Hawking, Ohm . . . Vingo."

"Vingo?" HARV asked. "I don't recall that one. What was his specialty in the field?"

"Dump out of the ExShell system, HARV," I said, as I rose to my feet. "I know where she is."

# 30

It took me five minutes to get dressed because my hands still weren't working exactly the way I wanted them to. But my legs were back to normal and I was soon moving briskly through the house with what I'm sure was the slightest hint of swagger. HARV, on the other hand, kept trying to spoil my good mood by using the lens in my eye to project himself in front of me, scold me for a few nanos, and then disappear as I marched through him, only to appear again three meters farther in front of me.

"I hate it when you do that," HARV said.

"Do what?"

"Give me one of those cliffhanger lines then just walk away like that. It's so pretentious."

"All this time with me and you're still not used to drama?" I said with a smile.

"Oh, I'm used to it," HARV replied. "I just don't particularly enjoy it."

"Comes with the job," I said, and I walked through his hologram again. He reappeared beside me this time and walked with me down the hallway.

"Fine, I'll play along," he said. "Just where is it that we're going?"

"To pay a visit to Mother Pierce and her dear son, Dr. Ben."

"Setting the question of their exact whereabouts aside for the nano, may I ask, O great carbon one, how you intend to get to your mysterious destination? Or has it slipped your CPU that you've destroyed two vehicles in the past day?"

"I've got that covered," I said with a smile, "literally."

"What do you mean by . . . oh, no."

"Kindly follow me to the garage," I said as I continued to walk merrily through the hall.

"Oh, no, no," HARV protested again.

I hopped into the garage like a kid out of bed on Holiday morning. Even though the object of my affection was carefully covered beneath a silk cloth, I couldn't help but smile at the sight of its majestic silhouetted form.

."Oh, no, no, no," HARV said, as he materialized in front of me, attempting to block my view.

I walked through him again and pulled the cover away with a theatrical flourish to reveal the true jewel of my antique collection: a cherry red 1968 Ford Mustang convertible in mint condition, metal and chrome gleaming in the somewhat sterile light of the halogen fixtures overhead.

"Please," HARV said, continuing his protest. "Anything but this. The vehicle is eighty-nine years old. It's never been weaponproofed. It needs expensive and highly polluting gasoline, the sale of which I will remind you has been outlawed for ten years. And, above all else, it doesn't have a computer!"

"Exactly," I said with a smile. "It's perfect." (A logical argument can never sway a man when it comes to his wheels or his women).

"Garage open," I said.

The garage door, being far more obedient than HARV, instantly complied. I hopped into the car and turned the key in the ignition. The engine turned over and growled like a kitten on steroids. I smiled as I felt the steady throb of the powerful machine around me.

"You know, of course, that your love of this car is simply your subconscious way of hiding your personal inadequacies."

"Log off, HARV," I said as I revved the engine and threw the car into gear. "You're killing the moment."

The engine roared and the tires gave a satisfying squeal as we leaped onto the road.

HARV holographically materialized from my eye lens and sat in the passenger seat next to me as we drove.

"I thought you were trying to keep a low profile," he said. "This car is as inconspicuous as me at an abacus convention."

"My low profile was blown the nano BB told the media that

she and I were lovers. And with the bad luck that we've had with computer-controlled vehicles recently, I figure this is the safest way to travel."

I took a curve at a higher than suggested speed and the tires skidded as they slid, ever so slightly, sideways on the pavement. I downshifted, felt the wheels regain their hold on the road, then gunned the gas again and threw the 'stang back into fourth. I smiled. HARV rolled his eyes, holographically generated a seatbelt and made a big show of buckling it around himself.

"Then Gates help us all," he said. "Now, I don't mean to interrupt this motorhead machismo nano, but where exactly are we going?"

"To the Pierce house," I said.

"And that would be where exactly?"

"I don't know," I responded.

"But you said . . ."

"I stretched the truth a bit for the sake of the dramatic cliffhanger ending."

"So you have no idea where to find Dr. Pierce or his mother?"

"I didn't say that," I responded. "I don't know where they are but I know how we can find them."

HARV rolled his eyes again.

"Please just tell me what question you would like me to ask in order to cut through this inane, time-wasting banter," HARV said.

I smiled. I loved getting on his circuits that way.

"The list of physicists that we put together," I said, "what was wrong with it?"

"You mean other than the fact that it didn't include Sir Isaac Newton?" HARV asked.

"Well, yeah. I mean, no," I said. "You noticed that?"

"Of course I noticed it." HARV chided, "a child would have noticed it. But what does that have to do with Mrs. Pierce's location?"

"Scan the New Frisco directory," I said. "Give me the address of April Newton."

"That's the extent of your epiphany?" HARV said. "He changed her name to Newton?"

"Look, he left Newton off the list for a reason," I said. "He's not going to just set up with the clone of his dead mother under the same name. Why not use Newton? Just humor me and run the name."

"I just did." HARV responded. "There's no match."

"None?"

"None."

"What about the suburbs, do the whole area."

"I did. There's nothing."

"Are you sure?"

"Of course, I'm sure," HARV said. "I'm a supercomputer."

"Try New LA."

"Done. Nothing."

"What about New Fresno?"

"Perhaps you would like me to check New Sri Lanka as well?"

"There's no April Newton in all of New Frisco or New LA?"

"Oddly, you've probably chosen the one name where that's true," HARV said. "There are, for instance, four Albert Einsteins, two Stephen Hawkings, and one Enrico Fermi in the greater New Frisco area. There are even three people under the name of BB Star, one of which is . . ."

"BB Star," I said with a smile. "That's it."

"That's what?"

"Nova said that Pierce was in love with BB Star."

"You think Pierce and his mother are using the cover name 'BB Star'?" HARV asked.

"Check for April Newton in the directory for Oakland."

"Oakland?"

"BB was born in Oakland."

"That's a bit of a stretch, isn't it?"

"I know a thing or two about unrequited love, HARV," I said. "This is well within the realm of possibility. Scan for Oakland."

HARV sighed.

"Done," he said. "Nothing for April Newton."

"DOS!" I said.

"It pains me somewhat, however," HARV said, "to report that there is a *May* Newton listed in Oakland."

"*May* Newton. April's natural successor?"

"She moved into a two-bedroom residence on Avenue A roughly thirteen months ago."

"Vingo."

"I really wish you'd stop saying that," HARV replied.

"And you doubted my logic."

"Oh, yes," HARV said, "Gates forbid I should ever doubt you when it comes to unrequited love and its related psychoses. I assume then that we're going to Oakland?"

"You got that right, pal."

"Will you at least keep the top up during the trip?"

"Not a chance," I said, as I stabbed the button for the retractable top.

"Of course not," HARV sighed. "Of course not."

# 31

The Newton (neé Pierce) house was a two-story white colonial complete with a wraparound porch, a big oak tree on the lawn, and a picture-perfect picket fence around the yard. Staring at it from the curb was like opening a Norman Rockwell full-immersion interactive VR program.

"What a nice place," I said to HARV. "It's probably seventy years old, and it's real wood."

"Very impressive," HARV said (unimpressed). "Shall I scan the structure for termites?"

I rolled my eyes and, as HARVs hologram disappeared, walked slowly up the brick pathway to the porch and knocked on the door (a good solid knock on good solid wood). A nano later, a sweet-sounding woman's voice called to me from the inside.

"Who is it?"

"Good morning," I said, smiling as sweetly as I could at the fish-eye peep hole. "My name is Zach Johnson. I'm looking for Ms. May Newton."

"That's me, dear," the woman responded (with the door still tightly closed). "What can I do for you?"

"I'm a great fan of your son's work, ma'am. I'm doing some research for my employer and I was wondering if I could ask you a few questions about him."

"You want to talk to me about Benny?"

"Yes, ma'am," I said, then added, "or if Benny is available, I'd love to talk to him."

"Benny's busy right now," she answered.

"Vingo," I whispered.

"I thought we agreed that you weren't going to use that term?" HARV whispered inside my head.

"I understand, ma'am, but I'd appreciate a few minutes of your time if I could," I said. "I'd love to hear about Benny's childhood and how you raised such a fine son."

"You really like his work?" she asked.

"Yes indeed, ma'am. His . . ."

"Nanochip technology," HARV whispered.

"Nanochip technology is absolutely stunning," I said. "And his . . ."

". . . work in artificial intelligence . . ."

"—work in artificial intelligence was nothing short of revolutionary."

Mother Pierce was silent and the door remained closed. A very long nano passed and I thought for certain that I'd blown it.

"Ms. Newton?"

Then she spoke again.

"That sounds lovely, dear," she said. "Give me just a nano. I've got something on the stove."

"Thank you so much, ma'am," I said. "Take your time."

I heard her footsteps recede on the other side of the door.

"She sounds pleasant enough," HARV whispered.

"I thought I'd lost her there for a nano," I said. "Thanks for the help with the technology thing. Now when we get inside, scan the house for Pierce and pinpoint his location. Maybe we can steal a minute with him."

"Will do," HARV confirmed.

Just then, I heard a very distinctive *clik-clak* sound from the other side of the door and I felt my blood run cold.

"Uh-oh."

I dove headlong from the porch just as the front door exploded into a thousand real wood fragments and a hail of hot lead and buckshot.

"I'm guessing that this is what you meant by 'losing her'?" HARV said.

I scrambled across the lawn, keeping low to the ground, flung myself behind the oak tree, and carefully peered around the big trunk just as dear Mother Pierce strode through the destroyed doorway wielding a (still smoking) authentic double-barreled shotgun.

"I told you people to leave my Benny alone," she shouted. "He's not a scientist, DOS it. He's a poet, a sensitive artist, filled with creativity and appreciation for the beauty of the world. Now get your parasitical behind out of my yard before I fill it full of lead!"

She sent another round of buckshot into the oak tree and I sunk deeper to the ground as the pellets ricocheted around me.

"I've said it once, and I'll say it again," HARV said. "You really do have a way with people."

"This one is not my fault," I said.

"Napoleon said the same thing at Waterloo, only in French."

"Try just for a minute to be helpful here, HARV," I said. "Can my armor withstand a point-blank shotgun blast?"

"The armor wasn't designed to absorb damage from that type of projectile weapon. Dr. Pool, not surprisingly, never tested the armor against an attack from a one hundred-year-old shotgun. I will also point out that the armor will not protect your head, so the answer to that question is a bit of a mixed bag."

"I get the point," I said as I popped my gun into hand.

"Oh, come now, you're not really going to blow Grandma away, are you?"

"I'm going to take out her weapon," I said, then turned to the gun. "Sticky-stuff."

"Check," the gun chirped.

I tried to sneak a peak around the tree but another round of fire from the shotgun sent me diving back for cover.

"DOS, she's pretty good with that thing!" I exclaimed. "HARV, can you still guide the projectiles from my gun?"

"Well yes, of course, I have remote access to your gun and its projectiles, but from behind this tree I can't see Shotgun Granny any better than you."

"I can fix that," I said, removing the interface from my forearm. "Switch over to the wrist interface and use the view from its lens as a guide."

"If you stick the interface out there, she'll very likely blow your hand off," HARV said.

"Sticking my hand out isn't exactly what I had in mind," I said. Then I tossed the interface into the air toward the house.

"Hey!" HARV exclaimed from the interface speaker.

Mother Pierce fired another shotgun round at the interface as it flew, and I heard a few of the pellets hit the hardware solidly before it fell (still relatively intact) to the ground.

"You still there, HARV?" I shouted, even though I really didn't have to.

"I think I've been hit."

"Is the interface lens still functional?"

"You threw me into the line of fire," he said indignantly.

"It's a wrist interface, for Gates' sake," I said. "You're only in about a thousand other places, including my head. Now do you have a clear view of Ms. Pierce?"

"Yes," he replied, "and I don't like the way she's looking at me."

"Lock onto her weapon and take over guidance on the gun."

"Done," he said. "Now fire before she mistakes me for a clay pigeon."

I fired and let HARV take remote control of the special bullet. The round exploded outward in a wide curving arc and sped miraculously into one barrel of Mother Pierce's shotgun. The round exploded upon impact with a muted, rubbery *pop* and a shower of translucent yellow, petroleum-based glue instantly coated the shotgun and a good bit of Mother Pierce as well.

"DOS! You people are tricky," she said as she tried, unsuccessfully, to pull the gobs of glue from her gun barrel. "You come here with your fancy talk and your expensive suits and try to turn an old woman's head, then coat her with your sticky yellow lies. I told you before, my Benny doesn't know anything about science. He's a poet, I tell you, a brilliant poet."

Her voice trailed off and her strength seemed to ebb away. She slowly sank to the porch floor, until she was kneeling on the old boards, then pathetically hid her face in a glue-covered hand and began to cry.

"Zach Johnson fires upon innocent old woman, reducing her to tears," HARV said, now safely back inside my head. "Another great headline for the show reel."

"Yeah, let's go kick some kittens after this," I said.

I came out from behind the tree with my hands held high, in as friendly and as nonthreatening a gesture as I could manage, and retrieved the wrist interface from the lawn as I approached the now sobbing Mother Pierce.

"I'm sorry if I startled you, Ms. Newton," I said. "I . . . got a little confused earlier and misspoke. What I meant to say is that I'm a big fan of your son's . . . poetry."

Her sobs gently lessened and she looked up at me, hopefully.

"You are?"

"Absolutely," I said. "I find it quite . . . interesting and . . . mysterious and . . . and I'd like to learn more about how he became the poet he is today."

"Oh, that's good," HARV whispered. "Slightly evil, but very good."

I bent down and slowly took the shotgun out of her hand, then carefully offered her my arm. She stared at me for a nano and then used her glue-covered hands to take her bifocals (which looked exactly like her son's) from her apron and put them on. Slowly, a sort of smile came to her face.

"Wait a, nano," she said. "I know you. I saw you on the David Cloneman show, didn't I? You're that Nixon dick."

"Zachary Nixon Johnson," I said. "Private detective."

"That's it. Zachary Johnson," she said, gently shaking my hand (and coating it with glue). "I enjoyed the show that night. You were very funny."

"Thanks," I said. "You know, we did a lot more of the back and forth banter in rehearsal but they cut most of it so that the piano playing dog could do another number."

"Cutting the classy stuff for the cheap laughs," she sighed, "but what can you do?"

"Yeah, what can you do," I agreed. "Sorry about the glue, by the way. It'll dissolve in an hour or so."

"Thank you," she said. "And I'm sorry about the shotgun attack. You can't be too careful these days."

"I understand completely," I said. "These are dangerous times that we live in."

"So are you really a fan of my Benny's poetry?"

"I am very, very interested in the stories that he has to tell," I replied.

"I'm so happy to hear that. I'm afraid I can't tell you much about the literary merits of his work. I'm just the proud, adoring mother," she said. "Would you like to speak to Benny yourself?"

"I wouldn't want to impose."

"Oh it's no trouble at all," she said. "Benny would love to discuss his poetry. He's in his study now, down in the basement."

This was going so well that my palms were beginning to sweat.

"Are you sure it's no trouble?" I asked.

"No trouble at all, dear. He'll be happy to see you," she said. "You're much nicer than those other men who visited."

"Other men?" I asked.

"I knew this was going too smoothly," HARV said.

"Three men," she said. "They stopped by about a week ago. Asked to see Benny but I wouldn't let them in. They were very persistent. Talked to me for almost ten minutes before they left."

"But you didn't let them in?"

"Gates, no, dear. Do I look like a fool to you?"

"You don't remember their names, do you?" I asked.

"I never got all their names," she said. "One man did all the talking. Skinny guy, swarthy too. Oh, what was his name? Manfred, Mandrake, something like that."

My heart sank a little bit and I spoke almost without thinking. "Manuel."

"That was it," she said. "Manuel. Manuel Mani."

"Vingo," HARV whispered.

# 32

Dr. Pierce's study was like something out of another century. It was warmly lit from a handful of table lamps and a single overhead fixture. An intricately woven oriental rug covered the floor and the room was filled with more dark wood furniture than I'd ever seen before outside of a museum. There were two reading tables, a pair of padded easy chairs, a Victorian couch, and a large, ornate writing desk. There was even a fireplace. But more breathtaking than anything else, however, was that the walls of the room were lined, floor to ceiling, with bookshelves and crammed with what must have been over a thousand books, hardcovers and even many leather-bound volumes. The furnishings of the room probably cost more than all the houses on my street combined.

And there was no computer.

Nothing automated, computerized, or remotely controlled.

As mentioned, I'm considered to be a bit of a throwback but this . . . this was like walking in on a caveman.

HARV must have read my thoughts because his whispered response inside my head confirmed my suspicion.

"Not a computer in the whole house, boss. But I'm getting a strange electronic reading from somewhere. Problem is that I can't quite seem to pinpoint it. Frankly, it's kind of spooky."

"Spooky?" I asked.

"I meant strange," HARV said.

"But you said 'spooky.' "

"Your point being?"

"I don't know. I just don't remember you ever using that word before," I said. "It's kind of judgmental."

"You're right. Gates, that's eerie."

"Stop it, HARV. You're scaring me."

"Scaring *you?*"

Dr. Pierce himself was seated at the desk, his back to me as I entered.

"Dr. Pierce, I presume?"

He turned slowly toward me in his chair and there was no surprise in his face when he saw me.

"Hello, Mr. Johnson."

He looked older by far than he did in the photos I'd seen. His graying hair was thinner and the lines in his face were deeper now and more pronounced. His body had softened as well, becoming a little paunchy and untoned.

I walked into the room and took a seat in one of the easy chairs.

"You're a difficult man to find," I said.

"Not difficult enough it seems," he said. "And please refer to me as Benjamin. I'd rather you not use the name Pierce in front of Mother."

"I take it she doesn't know that's she's April Pierce."

"She *isn't* April Pierce," he said, a little more sternly than I expected. "Her name is May Newton."

"Whatever you say, Benjamin," I said. "She seems like a nice woman."

"Some of my best work, really. Aside from her occasional mood swings, she's a perfect duplicate of the original in every regard."

"Let's not forget her penchant for greeting unexpected guests with shotgun fire."

"That's actually true to her character," he said. "It was problematic at times, but it kept the New Jehovah's Witnesses away."

"There's something odd about his demeanor," HARV whispered. "He seems stiff, hyperconscious of his actions. Do you see it?"

Actually, I had noticed an oddness to Pierce but I couldn't pin down exactly what it was. His mannerisms were forced-casual, rigid, like a bad actor playing a part that he thought was beneath him.

He rose to his feet and took a decanter and two snifters from an oaken cabinet by the wall and held them out to me.

"Care for a brandy?" he asked.

"Doc, it's ten-thirty in the morning."

"Is it? I don't get out much." He poured himself a snifter of brandy and sat in the easy chair across from me.

"Congratulations, by the way, for finding me," he said. "You arrived nearly a day before I projected you would."

"Yeah, I got lucky and crashed a hovercraft."

"Pardon me?"

"Forget it. By the way, your buddy Fred Burns is still looking for you as well."

Pierce's face twitched ever so slightly at the sound of Burns' name. The muscles around his right eye tightened and his head jerked subtly to the side.

"His pulse just shot up ten beats per minute," HARV whispered.

"That parasite? Does he still believe me to be in New Paraguay?"

"New Sri Lanka, actually," I answered.

"Really?" Pierce said. "He's further along the subterfuge program than I thought. Another five years and I might have to devise some contingency plans. He's a laughingstock in the scientific community. Did you know that?"

"No, but it doesn't surprise me."

"He's a virus man. That was his specialty. I think he was actually good at it at one time but he's such a two-faced, annoying little man that he long ago lost any credibility he may have had. His mother was a friend of Mother's. She forced me to bring him aboard the . . ." he stuttered over the words and twitched subtly again, ". . . to give him a job."

"You mean on the BB-2 project."

Pierce was motionless and silent for a nano before speaking. "I have no idea what you're talking about."

"Pulse just went up another eight beats per minute."

I leaned forward in my chair.

"You know, BB-2, that plutonium-powered killer android and sex toy that you built for BS Star."

Pierce twitched again; this time his hand shook as he tried to drink, and he spilled brandy on his shirt.

"Loss of fine motor control," HARV said. "That's strange."

"Oh, DOS." Pierce pulled a handkerchief from his pocket and dabbed at the spot. "Clumsy of me. I'm sorry—what was it you were saying?"

I sat back in my chair and folded my arms across my chest.

"I saw an old friend of yours recently," I said. "Nova Powers."

He looked up at me for a nano then resumed dabbing the stain on his shirt.

"Really, how is she?"

"Doing well," I said. "Undefeated in the ring, as I understand it, for the past fifteen months. I was supposed to give you a message from her but, honestly, I'm not sure which one is appropriate for this circumstance."

"Pulse is leveling off." HARV said again. "He's getting comfortable."

"She's a fine woman," he said, somewhat wistfully. "If you see her again, please tell her I said hello."

"I will."

"No, wait, tell her that I said hello and was happy to hear that she was doing well."

"Got it."

"No, that's wrong too. Tell her . . ."

"Let's just leave it at hello."

He nodded. "That's probably best."

"Makes you wonder why the two of them ever broke up, doesn't it?" HARV said.

Pierce stared at the fire for a nano with a trace of a smile on his face. He took a long sip of brandy from his snifter just as I fired another conversational shot across his bow.

"Clear something up for me now, Doc," I said. "Did you break up with Nova out of guilt over your mother's death or was it because you were in love with BB Star?"

His eyes went wide and he sat forward and spit his mouthful of brandy into the air.

"Who told you that?"

"Let's just say that Nova was quite forthcoming with your dirty laundry."

"It's untrue," he said. "All of it."

"You didn't go a little crazy when your mother died."

"Absolutely not."

"And you're not in love with BB Star."

"Absolutely not."

"And you didn't sabotage the BB-2 project, causing the android to become psychotic?"

"What?"

He jumped out of his seat and, in the process, spilled the entire snifter of brandy onto his lap.

"Pulse is back up," HARV said. "We've also got some heavy perspiration starting. Something's not right here."

"Can I get you another brandy, Doc? I don't think you actually drank much of that last one."

Pierce stood and angrily rubbed at the wet spot on his pants with the handkerchief.

"I think you should leave now, Mr. Johnson."

"Not until I get the information that I need, Dr. Pierce."

"I told you not to call me that."

I got to my feet and took two angry strides toward him. He backed up instinctively.

"Why, because you don't want your mother to know that she's been dead for a year?"

"She's not dead," he said firmly.

"She's the illegal clone of a dead woman, Pierce. You can hide from the truth all you want, but that won't change it."

"You wouldn't understand."

"Oh, I disagree. I think I understand pretty well here," I said. "I think your mother hated having a scientist for a son. I think she wanted you to be a poet. Am I right?"

Pierce said nothing.

"You were one of the greatest minds on the planet. You were revolutionizing technology. Changing the world. But your mother didn't see that, did she? All she saw was a failed poet, a loser."

Pierce turned away from me, shaking his head one way then another, doing whatever he could to avoid my gaze.

"To the world, you were a great thinker, but on the inside, you were an insecure loser of a momma's boy. And that insecurity messed up your life. It sabotaged your relationship with Nova and probably every relationship you've ever had."

"That's not true," he mumbled.

"And when your mother died, you realized that you'd lost the chance to make things right. So that's why you're here. You're starting over, with a new mother, a new name, and a new identity. You're trying to be the son that your mother always wanted. The problem is that you're not doing this because you love her or because you want to make her happy. You're doing this for yourself. You're trying to get rid of the guilt that you've been carrying all your life. The guilt that you think has made you a loser."

Pierce had backed himself into a corner of the room and was now cringing in front of the bookshelves.

"Let me tell you something, Doc. I don't care. You can build whatever fantasy world that you want. All I care about is BB-2 and I want you to tell me about her."

This time, Pierce began to shake. His hands trembled at first as they covered his eyes. Then his knees shook as they slowly gave out and he slid towards the floor.

"I . . . I don't know what you're talking about."

"Pulse is off the chart," HARV said. "Loss of motor skills is highly irregular. Something's not right here, boss."

But I'd already had enough. I grabbed Pierce by the shirt and pulled him to me, shaking him by the shoulders and forcing him to look me in the eye.

"Don't you get it, Pierce? She's escaped. The android that you created and turned into a killer is on the loose. She's armed, she's powerful, and she's crazy. I need to stop her before she kills somebody and I need to you to tell me how to find her and how to shut her down!"

Pierce shook more violently and his head started to twitch spasmodically to the side. He tried to speak but nearly bit his tongue before the words got out and when the words finally did come, they were not what I wanted to hear.

"I have . . . no . . . idea what . . . you're . . . talking . . . about."

That was all I could take. I slammed him so hard into the bookcase that the books on the top shelves shook and fell around us.

"Tell me everything you know about BB-2," I said, "or so help me, you'll spend the next six months of your life as a poet trying to come up with a rhyme for 'multiple fractures.'"

Pierce was shaking violently now, his mouth was moving spasmodically, trying to speak but the words he was saying were unintelligible.

"Feegah mend whap. Ploogle eiken dohr," he said, and then, "I have no idea what you're talking about."

"Loss of speech," HARV said. "Boss, I know what this is."

I slammed Pierce into the bookshelf again and more books fell around us. I pulled my hand back to hit him just as HARV's hologram appeared between us.

"Boss, stop!"

I sent my hand through HARV and slapped Pierce across the face.

"Tell me about BB-2!" I yelled.

"Feegah mend whap." Pierce cried. "Feegah mend whap."

"I said tell me!"

"He's trying, boss, but he can't," HARV yelled.

"That's spam!" I said. "He knows how to find her."

"DOS it, boss. Listen to me," HARV yelled. "He's been mindwiped!"

I stopped and looked at HARV for a nano, then turned back to Pierce, who was now sobbing on the floor.

"What?"

"The behavior is textbook. The twitches, loss of motor control, preprogrammed responses. He can't even speak certain words and phrases," HARV said. "Someone has put psychic firewalls in his head and made it impossible for him to communicate on specific topics. It appears that the topic of ExShell and anything related to BB-2 are the touchstones."

"Can you scan him to make certain?"

"I can't be as thorough as one of Carol's psychic probes, but physically, he couldn't fake the symptoms he's exhibiting."

"Gates, HARV," I said, staring down at the sobbing Pierce, "I was ready to break his arm." The heat of my rage was quickly dissipating, turning to shame.

"You were a tad overzealous," HARV said. "But I don't think you've inflicted any permanent damage."

"What do we do now?" I asked.

"A gentler approach would be a good start."

I knelt beside Pierce and put my hand lightly on his shoulder. He flinched at the touch (and I couldn't blame him for it).

"I'm sorry, Doc," I said softly. "I lost my temper. I didn't understand. But now tell me, have you been mindwiped?"

Pierce heard the question, gnashed his teeth together twice, screamed, and fainted.

"Let's also try to be a little less blunt," HARV said.

"You know, you could have mentioned that a little sooner," I said.

"Benny?" Mother Pierce's voice floated gently from the floor above. "Is everything all right down there?"

I turned to HARV, more than a little desperate.

"Fine, Mother," HARV said modifying the frequencies in his voice to replicate Pierce's. "Mr. Johnson is helping me with a poem."

"Well, don't get too excited," she said. "You know how that gives you headaches."

"Yes, Mother," HARV said.

We heard Mother Pierce gently close the door to the stairway and HARV and I both breathed a sigh of relief.

"How long do you think he'll be out?" I asked.

"Not long. His breathing and heart rate are normal. We'll have him back in a few minutes, I think."

"So we need to figure out how he can answer our questions about ExShell and BB-2 without actually mentioning those particular words. That'll be a trick."

"It's a little trickier than you think, boss," HARV said.

"What do you mean?"

HARV's hologram disappeared and he jumped back into my head to speak silently.

"Remember that electrical pulse that I couldn't locate? Well, guess what I just found."

"I'm guessing that it's nothing good."

"It's coming from Dr. Pierce. Specifically, it's a transmitter that's been implanted in his head, transmitting everything he sees and hears."

"You mean his body is . . ."

"Shhh, it's still operational."

"You mean his body is . . ." I said, as casually as possible, ". . . considered desirable in some cultures?"

"Good cover," HARV said. "Yes, his body is bugged.

Someone is watching you and listening to everything you say right now."

"Can you trace where the bug is transmitting to?" I whispered.

"I tried, but it's well stealth-coded. I lost it somewhere in Reykjavik."

"Okay, let me get this straight—we need to ask Pierce questions about ExShell and BB-2 without actually mentioning ExShell or BB-2, and we have to do it in such a way so that whoever is monitoring him doesn't realize what he's telling us."

"A bit tricky, don't you think?"

I thought for a nano, then smiled.

"Piece of cake," I whispered "Let's wake him up."

Five minutes later, Pierce was awake, (somewhat) alert, and none the worse for wear. I slowly helped him into an easy chair and gave him another snifter of brandy to calm his nerves.

"Feeling better?" I asked.

"Yes, thank you."

"I owe you an apology," I said. "I lost my temper. It's a character flaw that I have."

I pulled the other reading chair across the floor and sat close to Pierce, facing him and trying my best to look calm, concerned, and confident all at once.

"Listen, Benjamin, I know what you're going through here. I understand *everything* that you're going through."

I gently reached over and took his hand in mine. Pierce looked at me like I was an ex-postal worker who'd just gone off his medication.

"Boss?" HARV whispered in my head. "I think you're scaring him."

"I know that you're just trying to do right by your mother with all this," I said, gently tapping his hand. "You're a good son."

Tap, tap, tap.

"A very good son."

Tap, tap, tap, tap.

"I don't understand," he said.

"Trust me," I said. "You're a very, very good son."

I shot a quick glance at my hand (still tapping) his. Pierce stared at me, confused for a nano and tried to pull away. I grabbed his arm with my free hand and kept tapping, praying that he'd pick up on my idea.

"Trust me," I said.

And I again tapped T-R-U-S-T-M-E in Morse code on his hand. And, at last, he got the message. A light went on in his eyes and he nearly smiled.

"Thank you, Mr. Johnson," he said. "That means a lot to me."

I smiled and sat back in the chair.

"I want to ask you a few questions, Benjamin," I said. "Simple questions that will make life easier for all of us. I'm going to start with the three questions I asked you earlier. Do you remember those?"

Pierce nodded, and I could see that he was a little fearful.

"It's very important that you remember those earlier questions exactly. Do you understand?"

He nodded again.

"Okay, so truthfully now, you went a little crazy when your mother died, right?"

"Yes," he said.

"And you were in love with *Nova Powers,* right?"

"Ooooh, very tricky," HARV whispered.

"Yes, I was," Pierce said, and I saw the spark of understanding in his eye.

"Good," I said. "You know what, let's forget about that other question I asked you and just talk about Nova for a minute."

"Yes," Pierce said, "I'd like that."

"She's a great gal. Strong, smart. I like that in a woman. I wouldn't want to come between you two though. Say, Nova doesn't have a sister or anything, does she?"

Pierce hesitated for a nano before he spoke, as if expecting another seizure to come. He smiled when it didn't.

"As a matter of fact, she does," he said.

"What's she like?" I asked.

"She's . . . very much like Nova," he replied. "Very much like her indeed."

"Well, you know, looks are one thing. But I'm interested in how she thinks, what she likes, what she doesn't, where she hangs out, that kind of stuff."

Pierce took a long swig of brandy from his snifter.

"I understand," he said. "But her sister thinks very much the way Nova does. Likes what she likes, at least to a certain degree."

"She sounds great," I said. "Do you know how I can find her?"

Pierce shook his head. "I don't. But Nova would."

"Nova would? What do you mean?"

Pierce hesitated for a nano.

"His pulse just jumped six beats per minute, boss," HARV said. "We're flirting with the firewall here."

"Nova and her sister are very similar," Pierce said. "They think a lot alike. Her sister's instincts are almost identical to Nova's. Nova may not know it but, on a subconscious level, she knows what her sister would do or . . . "

"Or where she'd go," I said.

"Exactly."

"So if I want to find Nova's sister . . ."

"You should ask Nova."

I nodded.

"Benjamin, your mother mentioned that three men came to the house last week looking for you. One of them was named Manuel Mani. Did they do anything to you that you remember?"

"No," he said.

"Pulse is up another five beats per minute," HARV said.

"You never met with them?"

Pierce shook his head.

"Remember, boss, Ms. Pierce said that they never came into the house. They only talked to her from outside."

"Benjamin, did anyone *else* come into house while those men were talking to your mother?"

"Biggledy boop," he said with some degree of difficulty.

"Mani was a diversion," I said. "He kept Pierce's mother busy while someone came in and . . . talked with Benjamin."

"Keepa, keepa, keepa, boom."

"That's silly," HARV said. "Why would Manuel Mani want to mindwipe Dr. Pierce? What's gained by that? And how did he find him?"'

I stared into Pierce's eyes and saw the frustration below the surface. But there was something else there as well. It was resignation, almost a look of acceptance of his fate, as though he'd expected it all along. That's when I knew.

"I understand," I said.

"Understand what?" HARV whispered inside my head. I got to my feet and grabbed my hat from the table.

"Thank you very much, Benjamin," I said. "I appreciate your time."

Pierce rose to his feet with me and we shook hands.

"You're very welcome, Mr. Johnson. Thank you so much for stopping by."

I turned and walked toward the door. Pierce's voice stopped me and I turned around.

"Mr. Johnson, do you have a dollar?"

"What?"

"If I'm remembering correctly, you always carry an old-fashioned dollar bill or two with you for good luck."

"You've read my press material?"

"Mother keeps the *New People* site on the screen in the bathroom. So you do have a dollar?"

"Yes, I do," I said.

"Then I'd like to sell you a poem."

"Excuse me?"

"Give me the dollar. Please, it's important that I sell you this poem," he said.

I pulled out my wallet and took out one of the old-fashioned dollars that I carry and handed it to Pierce. Pierce smiled, fought back a little twitch and recited for me.

"Things are never as they seem,
As though we are living in a dream.
Where the one is like another,
Perhaps a sister,
Or something other.
The more you have,
The more others need.
Danger is always near you.
So take heed."

He finished with a little bow.

"That was very . . . nice. Very . . ."

"I've recorded it, boss."

"Good. Thank you again for your time."

Pierce walked back to his desk and I moved again toward the door.

"Mr. Johnson?" Pierce called.

I turned.

Pierce took a coin out of his pocket and flipped it to me.

"Here's your change."

I caught the coin and stared at my palm for a nano and realized that it wasn't a coin at all. It was a neuro-neutralizer, identical to the one that BB had given me.

I looked at Dr. Pierce, who shrugged his shoulders almost imperceptibly.

"I have no more need for money," he said. Then he turned back to his desk and sat down and continued writing. "And by the way, if you should see Nova Powers again, please tell her that I'm very sorry for how I treated her."

"I will."

"You know, never mind," he said. "I'll tell her myself."

I smiled.

"But if you happen to come across," he twitched again, fighting a spasm, "Nova's sister . . . ?"

"Yes?"

"Kick her plutonium ass for me."


Mother Pierce showed us out and a few minutes later HARV and I were back in the Mustang. That's when HARV felt safe enough to ask me the question.

"So you know who mindwiped Pierce, don't you? You saw it in his eyes?"

"Yes," I said.

"Well, who was it?"

"It was her," I said. "It was BB-2."

# 33

In this day and age, there aren't a lot of things that are considered difficult. We can go anywhere in the world in a matter of nanos. We've walked on other planets, eradicated "incurable" diseases, and cloned human beings. The bar for the impossible has been raised dramatically over the years.

But getting an appointment with BB Star on short notice? Now that's hard.

But HARV put the gigabyte on the ExShell computer and when I finally got my face on BB's personal screen, we were just about home.

"It's vital that we talk soon, BB. I've gotten some new information that we need to discuss."

"New information from whom?" she asked, blue eyes twinkling.

"I can't say, and certainly not over the net. I'll only need a few minutes of your time."

BB was motionless for a nano and furrowed her brow in thought.

"When can you be here?" she said finally.

"Ten minutes."

"Fine. The guards will port you right up. And please, no humming this time."

"You got it," I said, as her face disappeared from the screen of my wrist interface.

HARV appeared beside me, sitting casually in the passenger seat.

"I don't get it, boss," he said. "We're going to ask the

woman who hired us to find the android where we can find the android?"

"Well, of course it's going to sound silly if you put it that way," I answered. "Look, BB-2 is a copy of BB. Same exact memories, same exact mental and emotional structure, excepting of course whatever personality traits and behaviors that BS and Pierce specifically added."

"Like the murderous psychoses?"

"Good example. Anyway, according to Pierce, BB-2's instincts would be similar to BB's. On a gut level, they think the same things. BB has information. She just doesn't know she has it and we have to dig into her subconscious to find it. At least that's Pierce's advice."

"Ah yes, the voice of reason and sanity," HARV said. "Which leads to another question. Why would BB-2 mindwipe Dr. Pierce to keep him quiet? Why not simply kill him?"

"Maybe out of respect for him as her creator?" I said, pondering. "Maybe she thought it would be more fun than just killing him. I don't know. I'm pretty sure Pierce knows, but he can't tell us. Not without spitting on my shoes and shaking his teeth loose anyway."

"So what exactly are you going to ask Ms. Star?"

"Honestly," I said. "I have no idea. I'll just wing it."

"That, boss, is my greatest fear."

Upon my request, BB shut down the holographic program that created the pastoral backdrop for her office. I thought that the green grass and flowers would be a distraction for her and I needed her to dig deep into her head for information (although I didn't tell her that).

Without the background program, the office was very empty, gray, and limbolike. The river was still there but it was a lot less imposing without the greenery around it. It was almost impossible to tell exactly how big the room was because there was nothing to measure it by. It was kind of creepy but also kind of appropriate.

BB had a faux leather couch, coffee table, and easy chair created and she sat comfortably in the chair while I fiddled meticulously with some equipment that I'd brought with me.

"Pardon me, Zachary," she said distantly, "I'm not familiar with this device. What did you say it was called?"

"A Voight-Kampf meter," I replied. "It was made by a friend of mine. It's designed to monitor emotional reactions to stimuli."

I held out a pair of small sensors that were attached by wires to the main console in front of me.

"I need to attach these to you, if you don't mind," I said, cautiously.

"Tell me where they need to be attached and I will tell you whether or not I mind," she said.

Truthfully, I couldn't quite tell if that was a come-on or a threat, so I stayed to the middle of the road and went with the professional response.

"The small one clips onto your thumb. The round one I'll just tape to your temple."

I moved toward her and slowly raised the sensor toward her forehead. She pulled away slightly and, almost girlishly, put her hand to her hair.

"My makeup."

"I don't think it will hurt it," I said, gently moving her hair away from her forehead. "I'll put it here, behind your hair."

Her hair was soft and full, like strands of perfumed silk, and I had to fight a subconscious urge to run my fingers through it. I think BB noticed and I saw her smile ever so slightly as she adjusted the sensor on her forehead.

"Thank you, Zachary."

"Boss, are you okay?" HARV asked silently. "Your pulse is up a bit."

I walked back to the couch across from BB, sat down, and fiddled with the console.

"I'll monitor you as I ask these questions and I'll be guided by the responses from the machine as much as your actual answers. This way it will be easier to spot sensitive areas in your subconscious that are worth exploring."

"Is all this really necessary?"

"The droid has your brain patterns and personality, BB. You know better than anyone how she . . ."

"It . . ."

". . . it is going to react."

I touched a few more buttons on the console and monitor then turned back to BB and gave her a smile.

"Now then, are you ready?"

"Ready."

"Okay, close your eyes now and relax," I said. "Let's begin with the basics. You're frightened."

"I am not."

"It's a hypothetical question, BB."

"I know that," she said. "But I never get frightened."

"Never?"

"When you have danced naked in front of ten thousand screaming, drunken men, well, everything else seems insignificant after that."

"I can imagine. All right, I'll rephrase. You're concerned."

"Better."

"You're a droid."

"No, I am not."

"Hypothetical, BB. Stay with me here."

"Right, sorry."

"You're a droid. You've escaped. You're on the loose with people after you. You have nowhere to go. What do you do?"

"Seek shelter," she said. "Hide and plan." She smiled. "This is kind of fun."

"Good," I said. "That's what we're looking for. Do you leave the city?"

"I would not leave the Bay area."

"Why not?"

"Because I know this city and this area like the back of my hand. I am on solid ground here. I love this city."

"It does have a certain charm, doesn't it?"

"And very favorable tax breaks for the wealthiest one percent," she said.

"So where in this area would you go?"

"There are so many choices. The sewer tunnels, the piers, the subbasements of the skyscrapers. No, wait, someplace high."

"Why high?"

"To regain my confidence. The world looks smaller from above. I feel even more powerful then, like I can squash my enemies beneath my million-credit heel. Grind them into bloody shreds of flesh and bone, then kick their crushed skulls aside and watch them roll like marbles on a playground."

"Little vindictive there, BB."

"Sorry. I just like heights, I guess."

"Are we certain that BB-2's psychotic nature isn't part of the original?" HARV whispered.

I ignored him as best I could.

"Okay, so we've established that heights make you feel powerful. But what makes you feel safe?"

"Grandma."

"Grandma?"

"Yes, Grandma," BB said, almost as if she was surprised that she'd said it. "When I was a child in Oakland, my mother worked nights so I spent a lot of time with my Grandma."

"How old were you then?"

"We moved to the New Dakotas when I was six, so I was very young at this time, two, three, maybe four."

"Very impressionable."

"I suppose so," she said.

"What kind of things come to mind when you think of your grandmother?"

"Safety."

"Aside from that. Specific memories. Sensory impressions."

"It was dark."

"Dark?"

"Not pitch black, but comfortably shadowlike. With some warm-colored lights."

"Anything else?"

"It was warm. I could sleep without a blanket."

"Warm and dark. This is good. What else comes to mind when you think of that time?"

"Cinnamon."

"Cinnamon? Why?"

"Not certain, really. I just associate cinnamon with that time."

"That's good. The sense of smell is very powerful. It often makes very strong mental impressions." I paused for a nano to let BB process her thoughts a bit, and to build a little suspense. "When I think of cinnamon I'm reminded of eating cinnamon buns on a warm autumn morning. What about you?"

BB hesitated for a nano and her face furrowed again in

thought. She seemed a little stiff though, almost uncomfortable. Then she smiled, but I could tell it wasn't genuine.

"Yes. A warm morning," she said. "That is very good, Zach. I think of that as well."

"Is your grandmother still alive?" I asked.

"Yes, she is eighty-seven. She lives in town."

"Would it be all right if I spoke to her?"

She pulled back a bit. Her face lost the wistfulness brought on by her memories, and the business face returned. "Absolutely not."

"BB, this is important. Your grandmother clearly shaped a lot of your early memories. These are memories you share with BB-2. BB-2 may seek out a place where she subconsciously feels safe."

"Are you saying that Grandma is in danger?"

"I don't know that for certain. But at the very least, she has some information that could be important."

"Zachary, let me remind you that I did not hire you to psychoanalyze me or my grandmother. I did not hire you to delve into the recesses of my subconscious or probe my memories as a child."

She removed the sensor from her hand and forehead and gently but authoritatively handed them to me.

"I hired you to find a renegade android. If you cannot do the job then I will gladly find someone who can."

"I don't think this is going well, boss."

I sat back on the couch, crossed my arms over my chest, and gave BB a very determined glare.

"Tell me the truth, BB. How many people do you have out there right now looking for this droid?"

She was silent.

"My guess is that you have every security person at your disposal scouring the city, employees in every metropolitan office searching the major cities, and satellites in orbit checking every square inch of the planet. You have state of the art sensors searching for some trace of BB-2's electronic signature, some sign of residual radiation from her plutonium core, or any energy residue that would come from the discharge of her built-in weaponry. You probably even designed tracking chips into her mainframe so that you could find her if something like this were to ever happen. And yet you still don't have a clue as to where she is. Am I wrong?"

"No," she said (with some difficulty).

"The hard truth is that this droid could be anywhere. She knows that you're searching for her. She probably knows how you're doing it and she's figured out how to evade you. What's more, if she's stayed hidden this long, it's probably because she's planning something and that just can't be good.

"You're not going to find her by searching. The only way to find her is to get inside her head and figure out what she's planning. That's what I'm trying to do and right now I need to speak to your grandmother.

"It's understandable that you want to shield her from all of this, but you and I both know that this droid is dangerous and we have to stop her before she kills someone."

BB was silent for a long nano, staring at me with a mixture of anger and deep concentration. She finally rose to her feet and turned away.

"It," she said.

"It?"

"You keep referring to the droid as 'she,'" BB said. "It is not alive. It is a machine. Please use objective rather than feminine pronouns in your references."

"I'll try."

"I am not paying you to try," she said sternly. "I am paying you to find this droid and return it to me."

She gently rubbed her forehead and returned to her desk, which was reforming itself as she approached.

"My grandmother currently resides at the New Frisco Centurion Citizen Center on Bay Street," she said. "Net the reception center there and they will set up an appointment for you. My computer will verify your access."

"Thank you," I said.

"Treat her with respect, Zach. Do not speak to her in the manner in which you just spoke to me. If you do, I will see to it that you never work on this planet again."

"Understood, and I apologize if I spoke harshly. I was only telling the truth."

She touched a button on her desktop and the holographic décor program rebooted. Within nanos, the ceiling above me turned to a cloudless blue sky and CGI vegetation grew lushly beneath my feet.

"I think that we are done here, correct?"

"There's actually one more thing," I said. "I have reason to believe that the droid is now working with Manuel Mani."

"Manuel? How did he find the droid?"

"I'm guessing that it's the other way around. BB-2 came to Manuel."

"Why would it come to him?"

"I don't know. But it's no secret that you and Manuel were an item."

"He was my personal astrologer," BB answered.

"So the two of you weren't romantically involved?"

"Why do you ask?"

"I've just heard some conflicting reports that you were, um . . ."

"Boss, you're not about to ask our high-paying employer whether or not she's really frigid, are you?"

Luckily for me, BB finished my sentence out of indignation.

"Romance had nothing to do with it," she said. "The relationship between Manuel and me began as professional, turned physical, and then grew tiresome. I terminated the relationship and Manuel left the company shortly thereafter."

"So the breakup was your idea?"

"Men do not break up with me, Zach," she said. "The droid has clearly gotten Manuel on the rebound."

"That's probably true," I said. "Does Manuel have any skills?"

"I beg your pardon?"

"Other than astrology, I mean. I'm just trying to figure out what BB-2 would want with Manuel."

"I have no idea. Manuel has no skills that would appeal to the droid."

I shrugged. "Okay. I just thought you should know."

"Yes, thank you, I enjoy hearing that my ex-boyfriend has taken up with my psychotic android doppleganger," she said, with more than a hint of venom. "Now, if there is nothing else . . ."

"I think I have enough to go on for now," I said, coolly

(using my tone as a sort of pseudo-antivenom). "Thanks for your time."

I packed up my equipment from the coffee table just as it dissipated and began the long trek out of the office.

I was soon back in the Mustang and headed toward the office. HARV projected himself into the passenger seat as we drove.

"So, we're off to Grandma's house?"

"Eventually," I nodded. "Let's see if we can make that appointment for this evening."

"And what do we do with the Voight-Kampf?"

"The what?"

"The Voight-Kampf, the device that you used to measure Ms. Star's emotional and mental reactions to your questions."

"Oh, that. I threw it in the trunk. It was just an old personal entertainment system. Voight and Kampf are two guys from my old bowling league."

"I suspected as much when I saw the PlayStation IX logo on the console. Why the charade?"

"I figured that she'd take the questions more seriously if she thought she was being monitored, maybe speak a little more truthfully."

"So you're saying that you needed a machine to give yourself credibility," HARV said with a smile.

"Now you see, I knew you were going to twist it like that."

"Boss, I completely understand your desire to use computers and machines to make up for your inadequacies. It's only natural."

Needless to say, the ride back to the office was less than pleasant.

# 34

There was this big scandal back in 2044 that has become known as The Great Cat-Eating Fad, and I played a minor part in the resolution of this rather dark period in history (there's a point to this, I promise).

I had just hung out my PI shingle and was still living hand-to-mouth (much as I am now, but let's not bring that up). I was doing some investigative work for my local grocery store and I sort of accidentally discovered that a pet-breeding company, through an accounting error, had accidentally bred a million more house cats than they needed. Since the company was an HTech subsidiary, the folks in the corporate headquarters tried to turn their profit-draining lemons into windfall lemonade. Teams of R&D specialists, spin doctors, and ad agencies went to work and thus was born the cat-eating fad and the immortal slogan, "Cat—the cuddly white meat."

I leaked the true origin of the "catfood" craze to the press, and the public reacted rather vindictively. HTech's stock plummeted over the next few weeks, and they fired a lot of middle-management types as a display of retribution.

And speaking of retribution, HTech also sent me a message telling me to keep my nose out of their business in the future. The message was delivered to me by four thugs in a back alley and was written in black and blue all over my body. I ended up in the ER at New Frisco General, where the first things I saw upon regaining consciousness were the lovely brown eyes of a young resident named Electra Gevada. Actually, the first things I saw were her breasts, because she was leaning over, but that was a pretty great sight to awaken to as well.

I was bruised, bloody, and swollen and when I asked her out, she smiled at me and said, "Let's wait and see what you look like once the swelling goes down."

It was one of the best nights of my life.

Electra and I have been together ever since.

Electra had avoided and ignored every one of the messages that I'd left for her (twenty-seven in all) since our spat and I was beginning to get a little worried. We'd had these kind of misunderstandings before (I have the scars to prove it), but in this day and age, not responding to twenty-seven messages is grounds for divorce in some provinces. So I figured that we really needed to talk. I also figured that my best chance of seeing her was catching her in person. That meant going to the clinic. So I went there and I waited. And waited. And waited.

"You know," HARV said, "there's still the matter of the renegade killer android that we need to locate. How much more time do you want to spend sitting on this bench?"

"I'm waiting for the right moment," I said.

"You could have her paged, you know."

"Then she'd know that I came here just to see her."

"But you did," HARV said.

"But she doesn't have to know that. I want it to be a little more casual. That way we'll both be more at ease."

"Like a chance meeting?" HARV asked.

"Exactly."

"As though you just happened to be visiting the children's free clinic where she works, and you ran into her by coincidence in the corridor."

"Right."

"With a bouquet of flowers in your hand?"

"Right."

"Boss, you're scaring me a little here."

I spotted Electra at the far end of the hallway coming out of her office and walked quickly toward her. She spotted me, rolled her eyes, and turned away.

"Electra, wait up."

She sighed then turned toward me.

"Hey, what a surprise seeing you here," I said. "I'm just doing some research for the case that I'm on."

"Zach, you've been sitting in this hallway for an hour talking to yourself. The only reason I came out here is because you were starting to scare the staff."

"Well, it was HARVs idea."

"Hey!" HARV shouted in my head.

"Can we talk?"

She began walking. I stumbled and hurried to keep up.

"I spent the entire day, thus far, unsuccessfully trying to get more funding to keep this clinic open," she said. "I'm half an hour late for ICU rounds as it is."

"I'll go on rounds with you," I said.

"I don't think so."

"Then we'll talk on the way."

"Fine, you have thirty meters of corridor."

"Real quality time," I said. "Thanks for coming by the other night to check me out after my accident."

"I'm glad to see that you're feeling better," she said. "I'm sure that BB is as well."

"Look, about the news story. You don't believe the thing about BB and me, do you?"

Electra didn't even glance at me as we walked but I could see the anger from her profile.

"What should I believe, chico?"

"Honey, I'm undercover."

She turned and her dark eyes shot me a pair of daggers.

"Let me rephrase," I said. "BB hired me to find a droid that's escaped. She doesn't want the information made public so she created this cover story."

"I know that," Electra said.

"You do?"

"Give me some credit."

"Well, then what's the problem?"

We reached the door to the intensive care unit. Electra put her hand on the knob but didn't enter. She turned to me, looked around, and spoke, softly yet pointedly.

"The problem is that you *let* her do this, chico. You could have been her concerned friend or her tennis partner. You could have called yourself her Japanese gardener, for Gates' sake. But no. She wanted to say you were her lover and you jumped at it. So now the whole world knows it, chico. You're a stud. Hah!"

"It wasn't like that," I said. "She did this without my knowing. We'll retract the story when the case is over."

"You don't get it, do you?" she said. "She's using you like some boy-toy plaything and you're too caught up in your own machismo to see it. Well, I think we should stay apart for a while. After all, I wouldn't want to blow your cover."

She opened the door to the ICU and stepped through but she turned to me before closing the door.

"From here on Security is going to have orders to keep you out of the clinic. I don't want you here disturbing everyone. And one last thing . . ."

"What's that?" I asked.

"Sidney Whoop has been watching you for the past ten minutes."

She closed the door in my face. I sighed and gently banged my head on the frame.

"She said Sidney Whoop, didn't she?" I asked.

"Sadly, yes." HARV whispered.

"Having problems with your love life, Zach?" Sidney asked from behind me.

I rubbed my eyes and turned slowly around. Sure enough, there was Sidney with his two wingmen, And-A-One and And-A-Two, hanging back just a bit and flanking him on either side.

"What brings you here, Sidney?" I said. "Donating your organs to science, I hope."

"No, Zach. I'm just following you. Doing a little research on some of BB Star's ex-boyfriends. Sort of a 'Where Are They Now' kind of thing. So what's this I hear about a cover story and a missing droid?"

I'm usually very careful about being followed and keeping the details of my cases confidential (really I am). But I'd screwed up here and Sidney just happened to be in the right place at the right time. This was going to be sticky.

"No, Sidney, you misheard," I said. "I was just telling Electra how annoyed I am at DickCo for giving you such *boring stories* to work on these days. Electra thought it was because your Q-ratings have fallen so badly this year but I told her that

Sidney Whoop is still a great man, no matter what ninety-five percent of the general public thinks."

Sidney smiled.

"I appreciate your support, Zach," he said. "And you're right, maybe there are more important things out there that I should be searching for. I'll let you know if I find anything interesting."

He turned and walked away. And-A-Two stayed behind, using his eyecam to capture his boss' exit. Once Sidney was through the door, And-A-Two followed, but he bumped me with his shoulder as he passed.

"Your time is coming, Johnson," he said.

"How would you know?" I replied. "You need subtitles to read a digital clock."

He stopped and glared at me for a nano.

"Your time is coming," he said again as he turned and walked away.

I watched him follow his coworkers and disappear down the hallway.

"Always a pleasure meeting the DickCo boys," I said to myself.

"At least there was no gunplay this time," HARV said. "Maybe your luck is starting to turn."

# 35

Later that evening, HARV and I were back in the 'stang, and headed toward a rendezvous with BB's grandmother.

"So we're off to see Granny BB at the Frisco home for the old and unwanted?"

"The Frisco Centurion Citizen Center," I corrected. "And yes, we're going to speak with Mrs. Backerman. You need to be a little more civil in your linguistics, HARV."

"Oh please," HARV groaned. "You know very well that I've been programmed to use the most current geopolitically sensitive terms. I was being facetious and trying to make a point about the sensibilities of our distinguished client."

"The point being?"

"Well, it seems to me, that if Ms. Star loves her dear grandmother as much as she professes, she wouldn't have put her in an old folks' home or, as my programming forces me to refer to it, 'a care community for the youthfully challenged.'"

"That's BB's choice," I said.

"True, but I would think that the richest woman in the world might do a little better for her dear old granny."

"I've already thought of that," I said, "but I'm reserving judgment until speaking with Mrs. Backerman."

At the intersection of Shake and Rattle streets (the municipal planners were a lot less uptight in the years following the big quake), I signaled to turn right.

"No, go straight," HARV bleated. "Make a right onto Tremor and then cut across to Aftershock Ave."

"That's two kilometers out of our way."

"True," HARV said. "But only as the crow flies. The municipal traffic computer informs me that, due to heavy construction and the timing of the traffic signals, you'll save one point five minutes by utilizing this alternate route."

"Fine," I said. I grinned and carefully kept the car on course for Tremor Street.

"Why do you have that foolish grin on your face?"

"No reason," I said, still grinning. "I just figured out what this is all about. That's all."

"You're being more confusing than usual," HARV said. "What *what* is all about? And I'm sure that whatever it is, it's not what you think."

"You don't like this car," I said, "because you need to feel needed."

"Excuse me?" HARV said with a bit too much surprise. "Are you talking to me? I don't think so, because that just does not compute."

"You're upset because I can operate this car without any assistance from you whatsoever. You need to be needed."

"That is ridiculous!" HARV exclaimed. "Gates, the phrase sounds as though it should be from one of those insipid old songs of which you are so fond. Need to be needed, indeed. First of all, I don't need your approval to prove my worth. I am the most sophisticated computer on the planet. Second, even if you are currently operating this car without my assistance, I'm still performing a myriad of invaluable functions. For instance, as we speak I am again scanning all new police reports and hospital emergency room records for some evidence of BB-2. I am also scheduling a repair to your house's solar heating system and reupping your participation in the high-tech mutual fund in your retirement account. So let's just be crystal clear here, whether you're driving this car or not, I am absolutely essential to your well-being."

"Yeah, I guess you're right," I said and turned my attention back to the road, though I purposely let the grin on my face widen.

"You don't believe me, do you? Well, your opinion on the matter is of little consequence to me. The assumption that I need to be needed does not make one iota of sense. I am a projection from a highly developed computer; the very concept of need is, well, nothing I *need* to worry about." He stopped suddenly and pointed toward the road.

"Take this left turn coming up here, then park in lot B two point five. It's the closest to Mrs. Backerman's room. And be careful of the sharp curve ahead. Gates, what would you do without me?"

I just smiled and did as I was told.

I parked the car, hopped out, and headed toward the mammoth high-rise that was the Frisco Centurion Citizen Center.

"Switch out of hologram mode," I whispered to HARV as we walked. "I'd like to keep you a secret for as long as possible."

HARV's hologram dissipated. His voice, however, did not. "Don't think I can't see that grin," he said from inside my head.

I looked up at the towering building and nearly toppled over from a mild attack of vertigo. The structure was a prime example of the ridiculous architecture of the early 2040s. A huge sterile, albeit good-looking, box of a building with all the personality of a cardboard convenience store night clerk, it was conservative in every sense save its size. The thing was over two hundred stories high (talk about subconscious insecurities).

"I don't suppose Grandma lives on the ground floor?" I asked as I watched the high-speed elevators zip up and down the walls like hyper roaches on a garbage can.

"As if life would be that fair," HARV chided. "She lives in the penthouse, floor two fifty-six."

"Of course," I mumbled and headed toward the elevator.

The elevator operator, a high-class server droid with pale orange skin and pleasant, though somewhat cold, features greeted me at the door.

"Good day sir," the droid droned. "Who would you like to visit with?"

"A building this large," HARV whispered inside my head, "you'd think they could afford a grammatically correct droid."

"What?"

"I said," the droid responded slowly, "who would you like to visit with?"

"Don't you hear it?" HARV whined. "It's ending the sentence with a preposition. It's 'with whom would you like to visit,' you binary buffoon."

"Will you cut it out?"

"Will I cut what out?" the droid said, confused, "have I disturbed you?"

"No, not at all," I said, trying to shake HARV out of my head. "Zach Johnson to see Grandma Backerman, please."

The android's eyes flashed for a nano.

"I'm sorry sir, but there is no person by that name residing here." The eyes flashed briefly again. "Though after consulting my extensive database, I have noticed that one of our tenants is named Barbara Backerman. Perhaps she is who you are looking for?"

"Gates, I don't believe it," HARV shouted inside my head. "It did it again. Where did this pseudo-brain get his programming, Robo-Shack?"

I ignored HARV again.

"That would be my guess," I said as I patted the droid on the back and entered the elevator.

"Mrs. Backerman resides on the two hundred fifty-sixth floor," the droid said as it followed me into the elevator. "Do you wish to push the buttons yourself?"

"That's okay," I said, "knock yourself out."

"But sir, if I knock myself out how can I operate the high-rise-cargo-passenger-delivery-device?"

"It's a figure of speech." I had forgotten how literal most servant droids were.

"The trip to floor two hundred fifty-six will take exactly forty-two seconds," the droid droned. "Please hang on to the side rails. If you are a resident of a province where tobacco products are still legal, please remember that tobacco products and by-products are forbidden on this device as required by . . ."

"I'm local," I said. "From New Frisco."

"I'm sorry sir, regulations," the droid replied, as the elevator began to rise. "We receive visitors from all provinces at this center, including those where tobacco is still legal. Since I am not connected with a worldwide residential database, I am unable to ascertain your province of residency. Therefore, it is only prudent to officially inform you of the regulations that you must adhere to.

"To which you must adhere," HARV said. "I can't believe they let this droid operate heavy machinery."

"I should also warn you," the droid continued, "that, although the use of cannabis products is currently allowed for medicinal purposes under current New California law, the use of such products within the confines of this passenger delivery device is prohibited."

"How long until we get there?" I said, trying hard to hold onto my sanity.

The elevator stopped and the droid paused, gathering its thoughts.

"We have reached your destination," it said at last. "Mrs. Backerman's room encompasses this entire wing. Therefore, you should have no difficulty finding what you are searching for."

"Please get away from this grammatical Cro-Magnon," HARV pleaded.

"Thanks," I said as I anxiously ended the elevator ride from cyber-hell.

The door to Ms. Backerman's suite was at the end of a short hallway, which was clearly well-monitored. I cautiously approached and pressed the call button under the viewscreen.

A woman's face appeared on the screen after a nano. The face was delicate and stunningly beautiful, reminiscent of BB herself, albeit a much younger BB than the one I knew.

"Zachary Johnson!" the woman exclaimed. "My goodness, what a surprise. What can I do for you?"

"I'm looking for Barbara Backerman," I answered.

"That would be me," she said.

"Let me be more specific. I'm looking for Barbara Backerman, the grandmother of BB Star."

The woman smiled again, almost coquettishly.

"Like I said, dear, that would be me."

There are nanos during investigations when you uncover a simple piece of information and everything that you thought you knew suddenly gets turned on its head. The case takes on a whole new dimension and your entire plan for the investigation changes completely. I love those nanos.

This wasn't one of them.

But you have to admit it was pretty darn weird.

# 36

The woman who claimed to be Grandma Backerman had the face of a debutante model and the figure to which all debutante models aspire. She looked more than a dozen years younger than me and, more important, younger than BB. It's true that we live in strange times and that today's holograms and regen treatments can provide pretty fair makeovers. But this was light-years beyond anything I'd ever seen.

"You're Grandma Backerman?" I asked one last time as she ushered me into her sumptuous penthouse.

"Yes, dear, I am," she confirmed. "And that's the third time I've answered that question. Aren't you a micro young to be in need of a hearing implant?"

"I'm sorry," I said. "I'm just a little taken aback. It's not every day I meet a grandmother who looks nineteen."

"You flatter me, Mr. Johnson, " she giggled coyly. "My regen treatment has computer adjusted my appearance to be age twenty-two."

"Well, you wear the years well," I said. "And please, call me Zach. I must say that your regen treatment is simply astounding."

"I'm a very rich woman, Zach. I use only the best. Dr. S. Vitello performed the procedures himself."

"Didn't he do Madonna?"

"Oh, that was years ago. The technology is much more advanced now. This particular procedure is experimental and not yet available to the masses."

"Well, I'd say the procedure was a roaring success."

She laughed a girlish (yet grandmotherly) laugh and motioned me toward the floating antigrav couch in the sunken living room.

"I do so love the flattery of a young man," she said. "Now, what can I do for you, dear?"

"I'm doing some work for your granddaughter and I'd like to ask you a few questions, if you don't mind."

"I don't mind at all," she beamed. "Would this be regarding business or pleasure?" Her girlish hand touched my thigh.

"Strictly business, ma'am," I stated in (what I hoped was) a calm, professional voice.'

"Are you certain of that?" she asked as the hand moved a little further up my thigh.

I scooted away from her a bit on the couch.

"By any chance, did your regen treatment include massive hormonal transfusions?" I asked.

"Why do you ask?"

"I think you might want to get the levels reduced a bit."

"Hmmm, you know that would explain a lot of the cravings I've been having recently," she said. "But now, since I can't interest you in anything carnal, can I get you a nice glass of iced tea? It's the real thing, you know. The kind that we drank in my day. Not that imitation DOS you get in restaurants now. Gates, that spam hoovers like a spoofed meg of wormfood."

It was clear that Grandma Backerman's regen procedures also included some subconscious slang implantation. I was beginning to think that the success of the experimental treatment was not so rousing after all.

"Tea would be fine," I said.

No sooner had the words left my mouth then a tiny maidbot rolled dutifully into the room carrying two glasses of iced tea and a tray of cookies in her claws.

"That was quick," I said, as I took my tea and a cookie from the tray.

"Like I said, dear, I only use the very best," she said.

She took her tea and the maidbot rolled back into the kitchen so quickly I expected to see skid marks on the rug.

Grandma Backerman turned to me and took a sip of her tea. "So," she said, "what are these questions that are so important?"

"They concern BB," I replied.

"She's not in any trouble, is she?"

"No, not really. She's hired me to do some investigating for her and I just need some background on her childhood."

"Go right ahead," she said. "I'm so proud of my little baby."

"She speaks very highly of you as well," I said.

"Ah, yes. Bless her, I always said her heart was even bigger than her breasts."

"Did you know her husband at all?" I asked, trying hard to ignore that last comment.

"Oh, yes, her husband, or as I prefer to call him, BS-may-he-burn-in-the-fiery-bowels-of-purgatory-for-forever-and-a-day Star."

"I take it you weren't a fan of Mr. Star."

"Oh, Zach, the things I could tell you. The horrors that he put my baby through. She would call me in the middle of the night, crying over what he'd done to her. It was all I could do to keep her sane."

"He beat her?"

"And worse. I knew that man was no good from the very beginning. Pure poison. That's what he was. I tried so hard to talk her out of marrying him. But BB was in love and there's just no reasoning with a woman in love. After they married, and BS showed his true self, only then did she realize what a terrible mistake she had made."

"Why didn't she leave him?"

"Oh, Zach. I almost envy your naïveté. No one *leaves* BS Star. A high-profile marriage like the one he and BB had, he'd never let her embarrass him like that. He'd kill her first."

"Or replace her," I said to myself.

"Pardon me, dear?"

"Nothing. Please go on."

"Well, BS' destructive behavior finally caught up with him and it was a wonderful day indeed when that sadistic pile of maggot spit finally shuffled off the mortal coil."

She paused for nano, then put her hand over her mouth. "Oops, I guess that wasn't a very grandmalike thing to say."

"Well, the mortal coil part was."

"But you get my point, don't you?"

"I think so, yes."

"Oh, good," she said. "Now, how about another cookie?"

At the merest mention of an offer, the maidbot quickly sped from the kitchen to the living room again, offering me the replenished tray of cookies, even though I'd yet to finish the first one.

"No, thank you. I'm fine," I said.

The maidbot sped back into the kitchen again.

"Gates, she's fast," I said. "I wonder, can you tell me a little bit about BB's childhood?"

"Her childhood?"

"Yes, she says that she used to spend her nights with you when she was very young. She says that those times were some of the best of her life."

Grandma smiled.

"Oh, that dear, sweet girl. I'm glad she remembers me so fondly. It wouldn't kill her to net me every once in a while but at least she remembers me, right?"

"Yes. But now about the nights she spent with you?"

"There's not much to tell, really. Her mother, may she rest in peace, worked nights so she stayed with me."

"Stayed with you where?"

"My apartment."

"Where was that exactly?"

"Oh, hmmm, downtown I think. I don't really remember."

"You don't remember?"

"Gates, Zach, it was so long ago and I've lived in so many places."

"But you said that you had fond memories of that time as well."

"Oh, my memory comes and goes. I'm eighty-five, you know. Surely you understand?"

"Yes, I understand, ma'am. Let me ask you one other thing."

"Anything, dear."

"What do you think of cinnamon?"

"I beg your pardon?"

"BB says that when she remembers her time with you, she thinks of cinnamon. I'm just trying to understand what that means."

"Cinnamon. Ah, yes, there is a connection."

"Why cinnamon?"

"Honestly, I couldn't tell you why."

"Did you bake much?"

"Bake? Oh, dear me, no. It's a struggle for me to even open a box of cookies."

Grandma's mention of the word "cookies" brought the maidbot once again to the room. She rolled dutifully toward us at only slightly less than the speed of sound and offered me another cookie. I rolled my eyes and waved her away with my hand.

"Do you think it was some kind of incense or perfume?"

"Who can tell?" she said, shrugging her shoulders. "You never know what's going to stick in a child's mind at that age."

"Well, what do you think of when you think of cinnamon?"

"Cinnamon, hmmm. I think of warm nights."

"Warm nights."

"Yes, and sparkling yellow lights. Cinnamon is . . . like an old sweater, big and soft and warm smelling."

"That's very poetic."

"Yes, I suppose it is. Who'd have thought that a granny would have it in her, eh?"

"What do you think it means exactly?"

"Well, goodness, I don't know, Zach. You're the detective after all. Now, how about some more tea?"

The maidbot again sped quickly into the livingroom.

"No, thank you. I'm fine."

And the maidbot sped back to the kitchen.

"A cookie then?"

The maidbot reappeared.

"No, thank you. But they're delicious."

The maidbot went back to the kitchen.

"Come now, you wouldn't want to hurt my feelings, would you?"

The maidbot returned.

"I'm sorry, but I'm really full."

And back to the kitchen.

"Well, then, one for the road."

The maidbot appeared again but I noticed that the status light on its forehead had changed from green to yellow.

"Really, ma'am, I'm on a strict diet."

The bot stuttered this time as it rolled back to the kitchen.

"Surely you have room for one more cookie."

The maidbot shook as it entered.

"Really, ma'am, I can't."

The bot disappeared again into the kitchen and finally gave up the ghost. Sparks flew from its motor housing and, just as the kitchen door closed, we heard a muffled explosion. Black smoke seeped through the cracks in the French doors as they swung back and forth. An alarm sounded and we heard the sprinklers go off.

"Oh, dear."

A pair of fire-containment bots quickly rolled into the kitchen.

"I suppose another glass of tea wouldn't hurt," I said.

Grandma Backerman smiled and patted me on the knee, then climbed to her feet.

"Good boy," she said. "I'll be right back."

"Can I help you with something?" I said, standing up.

"Well, you could go to the main control panel and turn off the alarm," she said. "The firebots will have this under control in a nano."

"Where's the control panel?"

"In the hall closet, I think," she said. "Please pardon the clutter in there."

Grandma walked quickly into the kitchen while I turned the other way and went to the front hall. I opened the closet door and was immediately hit with a avalanche of grandma-type knickknacks as they tumbled off the overstocked shelves. Candles, teacups, and potpourri containers fell around me on all sides like a brick-a-brack avalanche and I took a number of Hummel-figurine hits to the head before the barrage finally ended. It had obviously been quite some time since Grandma Backerman had organized the closet (or, as I suspected, opened it at all).

The control panel was at the rear of the closet, behind some temporary shelving, and I had to push aside more knickknacks to get to it. As I did, a pile of old papers fell onto my head and scattered across the floor. I caught a glimpse of them as they hit and I recognized Grandma Backerman's young face in one of the photos. I bent down and picked up one of the copies for a closer look.

The color was faded with age but the image was clear. It

was indeed Grandma Backerman, back when her youthful looks were more natural. She wasn't nineteen in the photo, she was more mature, maybe forty or forty-five, worldly-wise, yet still beautiful. She actually looked a lot like BB does now. Her smile was subtle. Her eyes looked askance in a coy, "come hither" look. It was an advertisement for a strip club called the Nexus 6 from forty years ago, and Grandma Backerman had been the headliner.

Remember when I said that every so often a simple bit of information will turn a case completely on its head? Well, as I looked at this poster, I felt the entire BB-2 mystery flip more times than a waffle in a centrifuge.

Grandma Backerman had been a headlining exotic dancer forty years ago, about the time that BB remembered spending nights with her. But the bit of information that did the flipping was Grandma's stage name at the time. The revelation hit me so hard that I whispered it aloud.

"Cinnamon Girl."

# 37

I excused myself from Grandma Backerman's apartment as quickly and politely as I could and hurried down the hall to the elevator.

"How come she didn't mention that she was an exotic dancer?" HARV asked inside my head.

"Not now, HARV," I mumbled.

"And isn't it odd that she wouldn't mention that her stage name was 'Cinnamon'?"

"Great grasp of the obvious there," I said through gritted teeth. "But I don't want to talk about it until we're out of this building."

I was happy, though a bit surprised, to see the android operator waiting for me in the elevator ahead.

"Oh, great," HARV whispered, "another elevator ride with the grammar mangler."

I ignored HARV as the elevator droid very politely opened his transparent door at my approach and ushered me inside.

"Ground floor, please," I said as I entered.

"With great and absolute pleasure," the android said as the elevator door closed.

"Sentence fragment," HARV said.

"Please hang on to the side rails as we descend," the droid said. "If you are a resident of a province where tobacco products are still legal, please remember that tobacco products and by-products are forbidden on this device as required by . . ."

"Didn't we already go through this?" I asked.

"I'm sorry sir, regulations," the droid said. The elevator began its descent.

"I'm from New Frisco," I said. "I don't use tobacco, I don't use cannabis products of any kind, and, as you can see, I am hanging on to the handrails. All I want now is to get to the ground."

The elevator came to a quick and jarring stop.

I peered through the plexi-walls and saw that we were between levels and still over two hundred floors above the ground.

"Uh-oh," HARV said inside my head.

"Ah, this isn't the ground floor," I said to the droid, though I was pretty certain that it already knew.

"Correct," it said.

"Have we stopped to pick up another passenger? If so you really need to stop at one of the floors."

"Your deduction is logical but incorrect," the droid replied. "I have no need at the present time to pick up any other passengers." It stabbed a button on the wall with its Teflon finger and the door to the outside popped open.

"You asked to be delivered to the ground," it said as it approached me, "and I shall make certain that you arrive there, albeit not in the manner which you asked for."

"For which you asked!" HARV shouted. "Gates, this thing can't even threaten correctly."

"HARV," I said as the droid lunged at me, "I think you're missing the big picture here."

There are a lot of things that go through your mind when you're two hundred stories above the ground and being attacked by an android (trust me, I've been through this a lot).

My first thought was: "Uh-oh, I'll never survive this fall" (the first reaction is always the most obvious). My second thought was that I should have expected something like this to happen. After all, it had been hours since the last attempt on my life and my recent run-ins with killer machines should have made me wary of this droid.

My third thought was much more helpful and it was echoed by HARV's words inside my head.

"Move your gluteus maximus, boss, or you'll be taking the terminal express to the ground floor!"

I understood HARV's warning (which scared me) but my gluteus maximus and I were already on the move. I shifted my weight to one side and ducked under the outstretched arms of the lunging droid. I elbowed it hard in the back of the neck and slammed its head into the Plexiglas wall of the elevator.

It was a smooth move but I knew that it wouldn't hurt the droid all that much, so I scrambled to the other side of the elevator where I spun around and flicked my wrist, popping my gun into my hand.

"Listen buddy," I growled in my best bad-gluteus voice. "One step closer and I'll blow you into an expensive scrap pile of . . . whatever it is you're made from."

"That's it," HARV said. "Threaten it in a manner that it will recognize."

The droid just sort of shrugged its shoulders and took a step toward me.

"From this angle the force of your weapon's projectiles will not only destroy me but the antigravity circuits of this elevator as well. The elevator will go into freefall and crash to the ground below. Thus my purpose will be served. Therefore, please feel free to fire at will."

"Who's Will?" I asked.

The android stopped.

"You are trying to confuse me by pretending to think that my use of the word 'will' in the previous statement was a reference to a being named Will or William. I, however, am a model class SFC-5 android and cannot be confused so easily."

He took another menacing step forward.

"Give him a grammar test," HARV said. "That'll confuse him."

I ignored HARV and concentrated on the droid. "You talk pretty tough for a droid with its sock untied."

"First of all," the droid said, "I am an android, model class SFC-5, and therefore have no need for socks. Secondly, even if I were wearing socks they would not need to be tied as socks do not have laces."

"Therefore," I countered, "since your socks don't have laces, they cannot be tied and are therefore *untied.*"

The android stopped its approach. I had succeeded in baffling it with an illuminating display of pure illogic. It looked down at its feet and pondered its socks (or lack thereof).

I took advantage of the nano and lunged forward, dropping

my shoulder and slamming into the droid's midsection. It stumbled backward toward the open door but caught itself at the last nano with a hand on the door frame. It reached its other hand out at me and, miraculously, the arm stretched, elongating itself like a telescope, easily spanning the distance between us. It grabbed me by the throat and tried to pull me toward the door.

"Ha!" it taunted. "Your ploy was clever, but you did not take into account my superior reflexes and state-of-the-art technology. I am an android, model class SFC-5, and I am stronger than you in every conceivable respect. Prepare to tumble to your death."

I grabbed the handrail and held on tight as the droid tried to pull me toward the door.

"Sorry, bub," I said "but I'm obligated to hold on to the handrail. You understand, regulations."

"You are no match for me," it replied, increasing its pull.

I felt my hand slip on the railing, but I knew that I didn't need to hold on much longer.

"It's not the strength that matters here," I said as I raised my gun. "It's the angle."

The droid frowned.

"I'm sorry but firearms are not permitted in this conveyor."

"Excuse me if I bend the rules just a bit," I said.

Then I pulled the trigger.

My gunblast blew a football-sized hole in the droid's chest, short circuiting most of the major functions in its CPU. I broke the droid's grip on my neck and kicked the sparking frame in the head. It tumbled backward out of the elevator and into a freefall to its termination.

HARV appeared from the projector in my lens and watched with me as the droid hit the ground below, shattering into a gazillion pieces upon impact.

"Wow," HARV said. "Talk about your split infinitives."

# 38

HARV and I didn't speak again until we were safely back on the ground, in the car and on the street. And even then, we didn't talk about what was really on our minds. The information was too new, too fresh, and I was afraid to think about it too hard before it had a chance to sink in. So instead, we made small talk.

"Androids," I said, shaking my head. "They fall for the 'untied sock' line every time. You better contact the Centurion Center management and let them know that one of their androids' . . . malfunctioned. You were recording the confrontation, weren't you?"

"Of course I was recording," HARV answered. "I didn't just roll off the assembly line yesterday, you know. But it doesn't matter. ExShell owns the complex and their computer assures me that there will be no questions asked about the late, great, grammatically challenged android model class SFC-5."

We drove some more in silence but HARV was clearly getting impatient. He hummed a Bach sonata for awhile to appear casual but he just couldn't hold back the questions that were buzzing through his CPU.

"Did you notice that Mrs. Backerman incorrectly stated her age?" he asked.

"Stop it."

"Stop what?"

"Stop talking about it," I said.

"But why?" HARV asked. "Everything we learned from Ms. Star's grandmother raises more questions about the investigation."

"I know that."

"Then why don't you want to talk about it?"

"Two reasons," I said. "One is that whenever we openly discuss new information or communicate over unsecured lines, bad things happen."

"You mean like your car?"

"Yes."

"And the hovercraft?"

"Yes."

"And the elevator droid?"

"I'm not sure, but you see the pattern, don't you?"

"You think we're being monitored?"

I said nothing and HARV understood.

"And the second reason?" he asked.

"The what?"

"The second reason that you don't want to discuss how Mrs. Backerman's information affects the case."

"Because, in a very strange way, things are beginning to make sense."

"And?"

"And it's starting to scare me."

We drove for another twenty minutes through the city. I doubled back three or four times, and only partly because I thought we might be being followed (it also drove HARV crazy).

The sun was just going down when I parked the car high on a hilltop just outside the downtown area. The city was spread out beneath me like circuits on a logic board. The lights of the buildings were just starting to come on as the orange glow of the setting sun waned like a power indicator in the nanos after shutdown. I could see almost the entire city from the hilltop, all the way to the old bridge.

"Why are we here?" HARV asked.

"Because of my paranoid nature," I said.

I lifted the door latch, opened the door, and stepped out of the car.

And into the audiophonic eye of the storm.

The hilltop was the nexus of the city's four major skyways and in the early evening hours, it was among the highest trafficked areas in the new world. I turned my face skyward and saw what must have been ten thousand personal hovercraft crisscrossing the air above. They were blurs of motion and the cacophony of their engines was deafening.

"I feel inclined to warn you," HARV shouted inside my head, "that another two minutes of unprotected exposure to this volume of noise will cause permanent damage to your hearing."

I smiled, reached into my pockets and pulled out a pair of ultrapowerful earplugs, the kind that are standard issue for skyway construction workers, artillery soldiers, and roadies for the thirty-five most popular teen boy bands. I slid them snugly into my ears and the clamor ceased almost instantly.

"Explain to me again," HARV said, "why we're here."

I hopped onto the hood of the Mustang (being careful not to scratch the paint) and lay out flat on the hood, looking up at the heavy traffic above.

"This is the noisiest place in the city," I said. "If someone is monitoring our outside communications and somehow listening to our conversations, I think this is our best natural defense. We can hear ourselves talk above this din, thanks to the interface, but an eavesdropper couldn't hear me now if I were shouting in his ear."

"Crude and obvious," HARV replied, "but ingenious. So, where do we start?"

"Let's start with the concrete stuff," I said. "BB's grandmother was a dancer at a club called the Nexus 6. Find me whatever you can on her and that club."

"Check. And meanwhile?"

"Meanwhile, we ask ourselves the big question."

"You mean, 'How many roads must a man walk down?' "

"The *other* big question," I said.

"Which is?"

"Why?"

"Why what?"

"Why didn't Grandma tell us she was a dancer named Cinnamon Girl? Why did she get her age wrong? Why have at least three machines tried to kill me recently? Why didn't BB-2 kill Pierce when she had the chance? Why has she hooked up with Manuel Mani? And why do people keep telling us that

BB and BS had such a horrible life together when it's common gossip that BS died while having sex?"

"So the 'big question' is sort of a multiparter?"

"Yeah, sort of."

I stared silently at the city for a few nanos, trying to wrap my head around the various bits of information and put them into some kind of coherent picture. Then HARV prodded me along.

"C factor," he said.

"What?"

"Your question about BS' death. That's the logic flaw in your equation. You're ignoring the C factor."

"Which means what exactly?" I asked.

"Well, you're starting with the supposition that BS died during sex, let's call that Supposition A, and supposedly disproving it with the evidence, let's call it B, which indicates that BS and BB did not have sex. If not B then not A. However, you're not taking into account that A is not necessarily contingent upon B. You can theoretically prove A using other evidence, meaning that the equation could be 'if C then A.' Hence, the C factor. That being that BS may have died during sex . . ."

"But with someone other than BB," I said.

"That possibility exists, at least in theory."

"I hadn't thought of that."

"Clearly not," HARV said with a smile. "And as for the Nexus 6, it has a long and colorful history in this city which I've downloaded and condensed for your perusal at some future time. I think, however, that we can forego the history entirely."

"Why's that?"

"Because the club recently reopened."

"What?"

"A once-popular bar called The Happy Hacker closed its doors three weeks ago and reopened one week later under the name Nexus 9."

"Nexus 9?"

"Admittedly, not an exact match," HARV said. "But I think you'll agree that it's definitely odd."

I smiled.

"It is indeed." I hopped off the hood of the car and opened

the driver-side door. "Come on, buddy. Let's go to a nightclub and see if we can't find this renegade, android, sex-toy, killing machine."

I stopped suddenly and felt the revelation wash over me like an icy shadow.

"Oh boy."

"What?" HARV asked.

"The C factor," I said, "what if it's her?"

"What do you mean?"

"What if BS did die during sex, with someone other than BB, like you said. What if he died while having sex with BB-2?"

"Well, then," HARV said. "I think the proper response would be 'uh-oh.'"

## 39

In the days before I met Electra and became a one-woman man, I spent many a wondrous night at places like the Nexus 9. Pulling up to the club in the shank of the evening made me wax a little nostalgic for those days. The nostalgia ended a few nanos later when I got out of the car and stepped into a pool of vomit in the parking lot.

"I'm glad to see that the level of establishment you choose to frequent hasn't changed," HARV said.

"Hey, the vomit's *outside* the club. That's a step up right there."

I walked toward the club entrance, wiping my shoe along the pavement as I moved.

The club itself was a small metal hangar-type building. It had once been the home office of an internet B2B business exchange back in the first incarnation of the World Wide Web. The company went bust after the great internet collapse in the early part of the century. The owners of the company, billionaires one nano, bankrupt the next, committed mass suicide and broadcast the ritual over the Web as a symbolic farewell to the fickle multitudes of internet users. Ironically, the company's server went down halfway through the ritual so no one actually saw the event, and the departed Webmasters' message, like many others sent over the old Web, went unheard.

Needless to say, the heirs of the company's owners became somewhat distrustful of technology after that and turned the once-mighty corporate headquarters into a very low-tech bar and grill. Technology comes and goes, they claimed, but booze and fried food never go out of style (a place after my own heart). And thus was born The Happy Hacker. How it suddenly became the Nexus 9 was something I needed to find out.

The place was dark, dilapidated, decrepit, and as run-down as a stupid meter at a World Council meeting. But from the sounds of the loud music and laughter coming from within, it was clear that ambience didn't matter much to the patrons.

"A charming place indeed," HARV said with a bit of disgust. "I thought that the post-apocalyptic look went out with the last apocalypse."

"It's called atmosphere, HARV."

"Ah, yes. Too bad the atmosphere is not enough to support intelligent life."

"Good one. Can I use that?"

"Yes, but only in emergencies," HARV said. "And I'll want royalties."

Inside, the club looked about as no-tech as you could get, short of having dinosaur meat on a spit. A big bar at the rear of the room kept the food frying and the drinks flowing. The tables were all full, as were the stools at the bar, and most of the standing space was occupied as well (busy night). A dry ice machine in the back produced the necessary dive-bar smoke effects (sans nicotine) and a tobacco-scented filter gave the air that annoying stench to which bar dwellers of this sort are so accustomed. A few scantily clad dancers (male and female) bumped and ground on scattered stages and raised podiums for the adoring patrons. All in all, I hated to admit it, the place was beginning to grow on me.

Two bouncers, one man and one woman, met me at the door. Both were tall and muscular and clad in black faux leather jumpsuits. They were pale-skinned, had dull, black hair that was cropped short and spiky, and wore perpetual scowls on their faces. They looked for all the world like a pair of S&M fraternal twins.

I took special note of the fact that they both carried heavy-duty stun guns. Clearly they were more into the "S" then the "M."

The woman stepped forward to meet me and put her large hand in my face in the universal stop-right-there-before-I-break-your-clavicle position.

"Stop," she said. "Your computer may not enter." Her voice was deep with undertones of an eastern European accent.

"Excuse me?"

She pointed at the computer interface on my wrist.

"Computers are forbidden within the club. They are to be checked at the door."

She paused and took a closer look at my face, studying it. Then she smiled (and I use the term loosely).

"Wait," she said, "you are Zachary Johnson?" She turned to her fellow bouncer before I could reply. "Look, Dieter, it's Zachary Nixon Johnson."

Dieter, who had been looking aloof and dangerous all this time, turned his gaze ever so slightly toward me and continued looking aloof and dangerous.

"Yes, Diedre," he said in a similarly eastern European monotone. "It is."

"If it's not, then it's an incredible coincidence that these shoes fit so well," I said.

Dieter scowled.

"I don't get it," he said.

"I think it's a joke," Diedre said.

"I don't get it," Dieter repeated.

"It was only a small joke," I said.

Diedre ignored Dieter and stepped closer to me, gently placing her face mere inches from my own. "I enjoy your work," she said.

"Really?"

"I loved it when you threw that scientist into the vat of acid."

"Actually, he fell," I said. "I was trying to save him. And he was going to drop poison into the water supply."

"And the time you blew up that mad bomber."

"I detonated the bomb after I teleported the bomber to the police."

"And when you broke the nose of the teenage pop singer?"

"She was sampling Elvis. She had it coming."

"You are vicious and violent," she said somewhat breathlessly. "I hope that someday I too will have the chance to be like you and throw a scientist to his imminent death."

"Um, yeah," I said, gently taking a step back. "It's good to have career goals, I guess. Look, since we're all buddies now, how about letting me keep my computer inside?"

"I will think about it," Dieter said. Then he paused a nano and furrowed his brow. "No."

"Yeah, well, I appreciate your thinking about it, Dieter," I said. "I know how difficult that is for you."

I handed him the wrist interface and walked into the main room.

"I think he just made fun of you," Diedre said.

"I don't get it," Dieter said with a scowl.

I went to the restroom and ducked into the first empty stall I found. HARV reflected himself from my eye lens and stood beside me.

"No computers allowed," he said, as he shuddered gently in disgust. "We are truly in the barbarian's den this time.'"

"Yeah, but the burgers are great," I said. "Now listen, here's the plan."

"You actually have a plan?"

"There's a first time for everything. Run a scan of the bar. Isolate any anomalies that could be signs of BB-2."

"You call that a plan?" HARV asked. "I did that the nano we entered. Observe."

A digitized playback of my walk through the bar flashed in front of my left eye.

"I recorded the input from your eye lens," HARV said.

"It's giving me a headache."

"Close your right eye until you get used to the playback," HARV said. "Ripping-edge technology is never painless. Now watch closely. I didn't detect BB-2's presence anywhere in the establishment but there are some interesting characters around."

The playback froze and a cursor appeared around the image of a large man in the crowd.

"My data banks indicate that this man works in the weapons R&D unit of HTech," HARV said.

"Interesting."

The playback fast forwarded and froze again with a cursor appearing over the image of another, equally large, man seated at a table.

"This man works for ExShell R&D. The two of them in the same room make this establishment a veritable powder keg."

"R&D competition between the two companies is that fierce?"

"Not really, but both of them are currently hitting on the red-headed dancer."

"Anything else?" I sighed.

The playback rewound at high speed and came to rest on the image of a very familiar-looking small man.

"Just this."

It was the greeting card salesman from BB's office.

"Gates," I said. "That's the weasel from BB's office."

"Oh, yeah," HARV said, surprised. "I guess it is. I just high-lighted him because he's wearing such an ugly tie. What the DOS is he thinking wearing horizontal stripes with his body type?"

"I have to talk to him," I said.

"I lost him in the crowd during your discussion with the rocket scientist bouncers," HARV said.

"Let's see if we can track him down. In the meantime, I think I'll go to bar."

I left the stall and tried hard to ignore the stares of my fellow patrons in the restroom.

"By the way," HARV said, "you really should learn how to do nonverbal communication."

I was at the bar a nano later and, after several minutes, managed to successfully call the tender over (like I said, busy night). He was a small, sheepish, unmarried-uncle kind of guy.

"What will it be, Mac?" he asked.

"Information," I answered.

"You want a smart drink?"

"No, I mean real information."

"I'm not sure I remember how to make that," he said slyly.

"I'll make it worth your while."

"I'll tell you now that my while is worth a lot."

"No problem," I said.

"What do you need?"

"I'm looking for a woman."

"Oh, then you'll want to talk to Pierre. He's the flesh tender."

"No, no. I'm looking for a very specific woman. I think she's a dancer here."

"I don't know. A lot of dancers come through here."

"You'll remember this one," I said. "She looks just like BB Star."

The tender stiffened suddenly and dropped the glass he was holding. He turned to me, zombielike, and stared.

"You're looking for BB?" he said as his eyes flashed electronic red.

"Uh-oh," HARV said inside my head.

"He's a droid," I gasped. "HARV, why didn't you tell me he was a droid?"

"I didn't . . . I didn't . . . I didn't know," HARV stuttered.

"Hey everyone," the tender shouted, "this guy's looking for BB!"

The bar fell deathly silent and, though I couldn't see them, I had a sneaking suspicion that everyone in the bar was staring at me through similar sets of electronic red droid eyes.

# 40

I had fallen into another trap and this one was a real mega-palooza. I'd been dogged by brainless thugs and killer machines since I first took this case and began looking for BB-2. I had survived every encounter but now whoever was after me had combined the two approaches and, like a rank amateur, I had walked into the den of killer thug machines.

"I'm hoping," HARV said inside my head, "that your plan covered this contingency."

I stared at the droid bartender as he spoke and saw the other approaching droids reflected in his glassy, red eyes.

"BB left a message for you," he said robotically. "She said to have a nice death."

The first droid attacked from behind but I saw the reflection in the tender's eyes and ducked at the last nano. The droid's fist sailed over me and hit the tender squarely in the face, severing his head from his shoulders.

I rolled for cover and came up into a crouch in one fluid motion. I popped my gun into hand and blasted a meter-wide hole in the nearest droid (the guy HARV had flagged as the ExShell R&D engineer).

"Call the cops now," I screamed to HARV. "Tell them there's a riot at the Nexus 9."

"Good, they'll be here just in time to scoop up your body parts and put them into plastic baggies."

"Shut up, HARV, and do as you're told!" I shouted as I blasted another droid. "You should have told me that the bar was filled with droids the nano we walked in."

HARV was clearly shaken and was quickly falling into one of his panic modes.

"I didn't know. They were somehow cloaked from my sensors. But that's impossible. I need to run a diagnostic."

"Run it later," I said. "If there *is* a later. I need you right now."

I ducked under the arms of a lunging droid, blasted its face into high-tech confetti, then hopped onto the bar and leaped onto the main stage.

The comedian who had been performing couldn't quite understand how he had lost his audience so quickly.

"Hey, folks, what is this, a nightclub or a government hearing?" he shouted.

The droids ignored him and continued their pursuit of me.

"I get no respect. No respect at all," he mumbled. Then his eyes flashed red and he took a swing at me. I shot him in the chest and threw his body into the audience, where it was ripped apart.

"Tough crowd."

I found some tenuous cover behind one of the dancer's podiums. The club wall protected my back and the high angle allowed me to keep the droids back with some well-placed gunblasts. I picked off a few but I knew that their numbers would eventually overwhelm me.

"DOS, is everyone in the bar a droid?"

"I'm clearly no longer a reliable judge of these things," HARV said solemnly. "Gates, what else am I not detecting?"

"Stay with me, HARV."

I blew the head off another droid as it leaped at me from the ceiling. I was happy to see that it was the greeting card salesman from BB's office.

"Gates, that felt good." I said. "That wasn't the real weasel, was it?"

"No," HARV said. "The police computer reports that the true greeting card salesman is currently at home taking a bath."

"Too bad," I said. "That would have made this all worthwhile."

"Look on the bright side," HARV said. "At least they're not armed."

"Armed?" I said, suddenly remembering the high-powered stun guns that the bouncers had been packing. "Uh-oh."

I rolled away from the podium just as twin stun gun blasts slammed it solidly in a crossfire. I saw Dieter and Diedre out of the corner of my eyes as I rolled again along the floor beneath the angry weapon fire.

"This case just gets better and better," I said.

I grabbed the body of the headless bartender and shielded myself with it as I stood up and fired off a flurry of rounds at first Dieter then Diedre.

"You're rapidly running low on ammunition," HARV warned.

"Shut up, HARV. You're killing the moment."

I fired a round at the dry ice machine and blasted it to bits. The full compartment of dry ice hit the interior water reservoir and heavy mist flooded the room.

"Where did he go?" Diedre shouted. I noted that she had retained the personality subroutine of her programming. She and Dieter were clearly the most advanced of the droids and, quite probably, directing the drone droids through some preprogrammed fight strategies.

"I don't know," Dieter said. "I can't see through the smoke."

I fired off another flurry of rounds at random, creating as much mayhem as I could, as I formulated my plan and skulked quickly through the mist.

"What do we do when they go to infrared vision?" HARV asked.

"Shut up, HARV, or you'll blow this."

And at that nano, I bumped smack into the faux leather column of bionic circuitry that was Diedre's thigh.

"Switch to infrareds," Dieter said a nano later.

"Wait," Diedre yelled. "I have him."

Diedre emerged from the mist with an arm wrapped tightly around my neck and her stun pistol pressed hard against my temple.

"He was crawling toward the exit," she spat.

"Good," Dieter said. "Now kill him and fulfill our programmed task."

"Shouldn't we take him to our boss first?"

"That was not our instruction."

"I know, but I thought that the boss might want to kill him herself."

"What did you say?"

"I mean *him*self. The boss might like to kill him himself . . . herself? Um, who's our boss again?"

Dieter raised his stun pistol.

"Oh, DOS," I said.

HARV's holographic illusion melted away and what once appeared to be Diedre holding my unconscious form was replaced by me holding the headless body of the bartender.

"I knew it," Dieter said.

"Congratulations," I said as I hurled the tender's body at him, "here's your prize."

The tender's body hit Dieter just as he fired, twisting his gun hand and sending the blast into the metal ceiling overhead. The old support beams crumbled from the blast and a huge chunk of the roof came down on top of him, squashing him like a slow-witted insect (ironic, huh?).

My victory, however, was short lived because a nano later, Diedre's high-powered stun blast hit me squarely in the back and slammed me into the far wall.

"You should have hit me harder, little Zach," she said. "Perhaps you are not so vicious after all."

She raised her pistol and prepared to deliver the coup de grace (that's French for "the big lights out").

"I only regret that there is no vat of acid nearby."

A blaster fired.

Luckily for me, it wasn't Diedre's.

The blast hit Diedre in the shoulder and spun her around violently before she finally hit the floor. Her pistol flew from her hand as she fell.

"New Frisco Police!" Tony Rickey shouted. "You're all under arrest."

The cavalry had arrived.

The sight of Tony and twenty of his best officers, in full riot gear, striding into the club was enough to warm my heart.

"How's it going, Tony?"

"Zach, is that you?"

Unfortunately, Tony's awe-inspiring presence wasn't enough to stop the remaining two dozen androids from trying to complete their programming (i.e., killing me). The droids, without

Dieter and Diedre to coordinate their attack, began to close in on me en masse.

"Are you people deaf?" Tony shouted. "I told you all to freeze!"

"Tony, they're droids!"

"What?"

The droids leaped upon me. I blasted two to shreds but was soon overwhelmed and covered by their malevolent, high-tech pigpile of death. Thankfully, Tony came to the rescue again.

"Open fire!" he shouted. "Shoot anything in that mess that's not Zach Johnson."

And the fireworks began again.

The droids, as tenacious as they were, were no match for Tony and his men and, a few minutes later, they lifted me safely from a huge pile of droid dreck.

"I should have known you'd be in the middle of this," Tony said. "Do you need a medbot?"

"No, I'm fine, thanks," I said. "Thanks a lot for coming. I know you have a lot of really important police matters to take care of so I wouldn't think of keeping you."

I stood up but Tony grabbed my coat and pulled me roughly back down beside him.

"Let's talk, Zach."

"Fine," I said. "Um, how's the family? Kay doing well? The kids? Is that dog of yours housebroken yet?"

"Zach, as you know, creating an android with realistic skin tones is a felony class A offense. I just pulled you out of a pile of them."

"And have I mentioned how grateful I am to you for that?"

"I should run you in!"

"For what? Getting beaten up?"

"In the past three days there has been a fight in your office, you've destroyed a car, a hover, an elevator droid—yes I know about that one—and Gates only knows what else. And now this."

"It's been a busy week," I conceded.

"I don't like these things going on in my town."

"As if I like them happening to me."

"I'm not joking here, Zach. I'm afraid that you might be in

over your head this time. I'll help you in any way I can but you have to tell me what the DOS is going on."

"Tony, I know how hard this is for you but you're going to have to trust me on this one. I need twenty-four hours to tie this up. That's all. Give me that much time and I'll explain everything to you."

"And if you run into more trouble during that time?"

"You have my blessing to barge in and save my butt."

Tony shook his head.

"One of these days, you know, I'm not going to be there when you need me."

"It'll make up for all of those times when you were there for me when I *didn't* need you."

He sighed and threw his hands up in exasperation.

"You have twenty-four hours, Zach. After that, I'm coming to your home with a warrant and you're telling me everything. Got it?"

"It's a deal." I climbed to my feet and straightened my coat. "Um, Tony?"

"Yeah?"

"I need one last favor."

"What's that?" he said suspiciously.

I lifted the severed head of the droid bartender from the floor. The wires from the neck were still sparking as they dangled.

"Can I keep this? My, uh, car needs a new hood ornament."

# 41

A little while later the bartender's head sat on an examination table in Randy's lab while Randy, still half asleep, attached electrodes to its complex innards. I paced impatiently behind him.

"I'm in a bit of a hurry here, Randy."

"It's two in the morning, Zach. I'm sorry if my neurons aren't firing fast enough for you."

"I apologize again for the rude awakening, but I really need to know what's inside this droid's head."

"Just give me another minute to hardwire into the memory circuits and this little guy will tell you everything you want to know," Randy said. "This is an interesting design, by the way."

"Do you recognize it?"

"Not exactly but the chip design is very reminiscent of Ben Pierce's later work."

"Is it from ExShell?"

"I doubt it," Randy said. "The chip design is advanced but the droid itself is poorly made. It looks like a rush job, a disposable model."

Randy fused the last of the connections with his microlaser and then stood up.

"It's ready to go," he said. "But we have to be careful. The circuits have been severely damaged and they won't stand up to much grilling. If you give this thing too much to think about, it will explode."

"But it will answer all our questions truthfully?"

"I've hardwired my device directly into its main memory. It can't lie."

"Turn it on."

Randy threw the power switch on the exam table and the droid head began to stir. Stray sparks flew from the connections inside the neck and the skin of its forehead began to wrinkle in simulated consternation. Finally the eyes opened.

"What'll . . . it . . . be . . . Mac?" it said.

Randy nudged me gently and whispered in my ear.

"It's following its background programming. Pretend it's still a bartender."

"This is silly," I said.

"Humor it. Remember, any excess stimulation and the entire thing will short out."

I turned back to the droid's head.

"Don't got . . . all . . . night . . . pal. What'll . . . it . . . be?"

Randy nudged me again.

"A beer would be fine," I said. "Something with a head."

"Coming . . . right . . . up."

"Yeah, I'm sure."

"What? . . . . . ." the droid head sputtered.

Randy elbowed me in the ribs again.

"I told you to be careful."

"I mean, I'd sure like to get some information."

"Sure . . . Mac."

"Where were you created?" I asked.

"ExShell," it replied.

"When?"

"Ten days ago. You want . . . some . . . pretzels?"

"Yeah, sure. Who is your creator?"

"Manuel Mani. You want . . . that drink . . . freshened?"

This was getting interesting.

"Who gave you your programming?"

"World Association of . . . drink mixers . . . want another?"

"Who programmed you to kill me?" I asked angrily. "Who programmed you to kill me when I asked about BB Star?"

The droid head shook itself, confused and clearly distraught.

"How about . . . . . . one on the . . . house?"

"It's not going to last much longer," Randy said.

"Who programmed you to kill me!" I shouted. "Tell me or you get no tip."

"Fred Burns."

You could have knocked me over with a feather.

"What?"

"Fred . . . Burns."

"Fred Burns from ExShell?"

"Yes."

"The pale, fleshy guy. *That* Fred Burns."

"Yes."

"Fred Burns from ExShell programmed you to kill me?"

"Zach," Randy said. "You're being sort of redundant here."

I knew that, but I still couldn't believe it.

"Fred Burns?"

The droid head began to shake. It let out a high-pitched keening noise and flopped around on the table like a goldfish on a kitchen floor.

"She didn't want to hurt anybody," it said. "She just . . . wanted to find her . . . place."

"Who wanted?" I asked. "You mean BB-2?"

"She just . . . wants to be . . . left alone. How 'bout another? How 'bout them Giants? . . . She didn't want to hurt anyone."

Randy took my arm and tried to pull me away.

"It's going to blow."

I ignored him.

"Then why did she and Burns program you to kill me?"

"What?"

"You heard me. If she didn't want to hurt anyone, how come she programmed you to kill me?"

The head froze for a nano, thinking. Then it trembled again and started singing (painfully off-key).

"My wild . . . Irish Rose!"

"Zach, duck!" Randy yelled and pulled me to the floor.

The droid head exploded into a small ball of flaming metal, silicon shrapnel, and Irish ditties.

"You short-circuited it when you pointed out the contradiction," Randy said. "You blew its mind."

"Just as well," I said. "He was a lousy bartender."

# 42

Randy gave me a new wrist interface to replace the one I lost at the Nexus 9, then HARV and I were back on the street. I was angry with myself for totally underestimating Burns and frustrated at the fact that it took me this long to realize the mistake. My head (or rather my heart) had obviously been elsewhere at times during this investigation and it wasn't hard to figure out where.

"Excuse me, but where are we going?" HARV asked as I turned onto the highway. "The ExShell laboratories are in the other direction. Your office is in the other direction. Pretty much everywhere you should want to go right now is in the other direction. I thought that being a PI you'd be better at these things."

"We're going to the hospital," I said.

"Why? You've been beaten up much worse than this before. DOS, you've received more severe injuries at poetry readings."

"I need to talk to Electra."

"Oh, you are a brave man," HARV said. "You miss her, don't you? I can tell these things."

"I need to warn her," I said. "There are some serious people after me. They might try to get to me through her."

"I'm sure she knows that," HARV said. "That's just the status quo."

"It's worse this time. I need to warn her."

"It's the middle of the night, you know"

"She's on the overnight shift," I said. "I checked the schedule."

"I could net her and save some time."

"I'm going to see her, all right?" I said sternly. "I'm going to see her. I'm going to talk to her. I'm going to warn her."

"Fine," HARV said. "Now that you mention it, it makes sense to warn her in person. It's more secure. Good thinking."

We drove in silence for a few nanos.

"I miss her," I said.

HARV smiled.

"I knew that."

A few minutes later, I was waiting for an elevator at New Frisco General Hospital, trying hard not to think about how angry Electra would be when she saw me.

"One thing I don't understand," I said. "How come the hallways here are so dull?"

"Excuse me?" HARV asked.

"I mean, they can cure diseases, replace vital organs, and re-grow limbs at this hospital. How come they can't design a decent looking hallway?"

"Maybe 'they' have better things to do with their time," HARV answered. "You know, like curing the sick, caring for the infirm, and raising the standard of living for their patients."

"Yeah, but how hard could it be to make the hallways more interesting? For instance, do they have to be white? And how about hanging some artwork?"

"Will you stop with the hallways, already?" HARV said. "With all the data hitting the hard drive now, you don't have anything better to think about?"

"Yeah, well excuse me for making conversation," I said.

"I know you're nervous about seeing Dr. Gevada, boss . . ."

"Nervous?" I said. "Who said anything about being nervous? I am genuinely interested in the phenomenon of the perpetually mundane corridor design."

HARV rolled his eyes, "Please tell me now the best way to end this pathetic line of conversation."

At that nano, the elevator arrived.

"You're not interested in elevator décor are you?" HARV asked.

I shrugged.

"There's not much to say about elevators, really."

"Good, Then let's go.

We stepped into the elevator (which, thankfully, had no droid operator) and I gave my instructions directly to the computer.

"Tenth floor, please."

"Yes, sir. With pleasure," the elevator answered cheerily. "Would you like to select your music option?" It asked as we began to rise.

"Silence is good," I said.

The computer paused for a nano.

"I'm sorry, sir. There is no song entitled 'Silence Is Good' in my database. There is a classic song called 'The Sounds of Silence.' There is also a new release by Freddie and the Mutant Accountants called 'Silence: Who the DOS Needs It!' Perhaps you'd like one of these selections?"

"No," I said. "I want just plain silence. No music. I want to be bathed in the serenity of my own thoughts."

"Oh, okay," the elevator said, more than little disheartened.

We reached the tenth floor shortly thereafter and the door slid open.

"Please watch your step on the way out," the elevator said. "I hope you enjoyed the ride. Please consider me on the way down."

I stepped off the elevator and sighed as the doors closed behind me.

"I'd really like to get my hands on the guy who thought intelligent elevators were a good idea."

"Believe me, you don't want to go there," HARV said. "Besides, with your past record with elevators, I would think you would be grateful it didn't try to kill you."

Electra had been in surgery for most of the night, putting a new spine into a ten-year-old boy who'd been paralyzed in a hover crash. (You have to love a woman who spends her evenings doing stuff like that).

She was tired when she came into the break room but I knew that she'd be up for the rest of the night in the ICU monitoring the kid's reaction to the surgery. I'd seen her do things like that a thousand times before. Her dedication was one of the many things that I loved about her.

Needless to say, after an already long and tiring night, the sight of me waiting for her didn't exactly fill her with joy. (But at least she didn't attack me).

"Hola, chico. How'd you get in here?"

"Hey, I'm a doctor too, you know." I offered her one of the cups of coffee in my hand, skim milk, no sugar, the way she likes it.

"A Ph.D. in psychology doesn't count for much here. Especially since your dissertation is now about five years late."

"Details, details."

She took the coffee and sat beside me.

"I bribed the security guys," I said. "Told them I was in love."

"With BB Star?"

"That's a low blow."

"I've seen lower."

She took a sip of the coffee, then ran her fingers through her hair and gently rubbed the muscle at the base of her neck that always gets sore during surgery. It was all I could do not to reach out and help her ease the pain.

"Rough night?"

"I've had better," she said.

"The kid okay?"

"We'll know by morning."

"You look tired."

"I'm doing double shifts this week. Trying to get as much done as possible before the funding runs out at the end of the month."

We sat silently for a long time. She drank her coffee. I fidgeted awkwardly, feeling like a teenager trying to tell his teacher about his crush.

"So, I've missed you."

"I've missed you too," she said. "Like a yeast infection."

"Good one. Can I use that?"

"You can if you want, but you need a vagina to make it funny."

"That's probably a bit far to go for a good line," I replied. "But I'll think about it."

She smiled, but only a little.

"Seriously," I said, "I really do miss you."

"I've heard it before, chico."

"You know that BB Star totally blindsided me on that whole lover/sex-toy thing. You know it's not true."

She just shook her head.

"I don't want to keep going through this, Zach. I'm tired of making excuses. I'm tired having to explain to everyone that my boyfriend's not having an affair with BB Star, or that he's not an alien agent from Glad 7, or that he's not gay."

"I understand that . . . wait, where'd you hear the gay thing?"

"You insult me when you do things like that. Worse still, you insult what we have. You turn it into a joke. I don't want to be with a man who doesn't respect the relationship. Comprende?"

"Comprendo."

"And I'm sick of having to show up somewhere with a laser cannon to save your sorry ass. I'm a doctor, DOS it. I'm tired of shooting at people."

"Yeah, I can see how that presents a moral dilemma for you."

"So, is that why you're here?"

"Well, the official reason is to warn you," I said. "I've got some people after me."

She took a sip of her coffee and rubbed her forehead.

"Who's trying to kill you now?"

"Pretty much everybody. So you might want to be careful. You never know when my enemies might decide that they're your enemies as well."

"Frankly, chico, if your enemies were to show up right now, I think we'd just compare notes. This thing you're in is getting serious?"

"Yeah, you could say that. Right now I'm looking for this crackpot, Fred Burns. After that, I think all hell is going to break loose."

"You mean Dr. Fred Burns?" she asked.

"You've heard of him?"

"I read some of his proposals before he went corporate," she said. "He's a pretty sharp guy as I recall. Some of the viruses he was working on were downright scary."

"You mean computer viruses."

She shook her head. "Biological."

"It's a different guy then. This Fred Burns is an engineer."

"Is he a pale, flabby hombre?" she asked. "Looks like a slab of blanched turkey, only not as appealing? Talks like a soap opera villain?"

"Yeah, that's him."

"Right. His early work was biological. He turned engineer maybe five or six years ago. I went to one of his seminars. He struck me as a very strange man—muy loco."

"And he specialized in biological viruses?"

"Nasty ones. What do you want with him?"

I felt my legs go numb and my mind started running through a dozen possible scenarios for how this information changed things. None of them were good.

"You okay, chico?"

"Yeah, fine," I said. "Look, I'm sorry. I have to go."

"Go ahead," she said. "I have to get back to this kid's spine anyway."

The two of us got up and headed toward the door.

"What about the unofficial reason?" she asked.

"The what?"

"You said the official reason that you were here was to warn me. Is there an unofficial reason?"

"I just wanted to see you, I guess. See how things were. Maybe see if we could get together again and talk this through."

"Honestly," she said. "I'm not ready to do that yet."

"When do you think you will be?"

She shrugged and turned away. I felt like I was in high school and was about to hear the "I just want to be friends" line.

"I don't know. Talk to me again when you wrap up this case."

"It's just that . . ."

She turned away and waved her hand at me.

"I know, I know, 'if you survive.' "

I'd used that line a thousand times. Hearing her throw it back at me now gave me a chill. More than anything now, I wanted *us* to survive.

"Yeah. If."

Electra turned and walked out the door, closing it behind her as she left and didn't look back.

"I love you." I said.

But she was already gone.

"I think it's a particularly good sign that she didn't try to harm you," HARV said, in an attempt to be supportive.

"Yeah, maybe."

I took a deep breath and left the room as well. I cast a glance up the hallway, toward the ICU, then turned away and headed toward the elevators.

"Did you catch her little play on words?" HARV asked.

"What play on words?"

"She said, she had to get *back* to the kid's *spine*. Get it?"

"Yeah, I get it." I was surprised that HARV had picked up on the pun before I did.

"You know, I think I'm really starting to warm up to this humor concept," he said. "Tell me that one about the guy in the bar with plutonium on his shoulders . . ."

"I'm still working on it," I said.

"Pity," he said. "So where to now?"

My heart told me to go after Electra. To sit with her in the ICU next to the boy whose life she'd just saved and help her in any way I could. But she'd said it herself. She wasn't ready to see me yet. And I didn't want to think about what I'd do if she was never ready. So I did what I always do when real life gets complicated: I went into hard-boiled mode.

"We're going back to ExShell," I said. "I have a score to settle with Fred Burns."

# 43

Half an hour later, HARV and I were back on the case, back at ExShell, and back in the office of Fred Burns. And, since I wasn't ready to clue BB in on everything just yet, getting into the office unannounced at nearly three in the morning was no easy feat. I had to pose as a computer screen cleaner (squeegee in hand) on an emergency call to get past security.

The only problem was that the office was no longer there.

The entire workspace was empty. Every computer, every monitor, every wire, knob, and button was gone without a trace. The only thing left was a sign on the wall that read: "Coming soon: a new executive bathroom at this location."

"You didn't really expect him to still be here, did you?" HARV asked.

"I suppose that would have been too easy," I said. "Still, I was hoping that there'd be *something*. When did he leave?"

"ExShell records are unclear. It appears as though he sabotaged the security system, so we can't be certain."

I shook my head, disbelieving.

"Fred Burns," I mumbled. "That out-of-shape slab of mutton . . ."

"Apparently the mutton is sharper than the cheese," HARV said.

"What's that supposed to mean?"

"I don't know. I'm just following your food motif."

I rolled my eyes and again surveyed the big empty room. I stared for a long time at the wall where the bank of satellite monitors had once been.

"The search for Pierce, that Sri Lanka thing. That was probably all a ruse. If Burns is working for Mani, then he knew where Pierce was all along."

"He just didn't want ExShell to know," HARV said.

"Or me. He lead us all on a wild snark chase."

"Why?"

"To buy time for Mani and BB-2."

"Time for what?"

"DOSsed if I know but I'm betting it isn't good."

"So what do we do?" HARV asked.

"We find Burns, kick his ass, and then have him tell us what the DOS is going on."

"That was the plan *before* we got here. How do we find him?"

"Have a little faith," I said. "Remember, I once tracked down a man with nothing to go on except his favorite color and his hat size."

"Yes, but I should remind you," HARV replied, "that the person for whom you were searching turned out to be hiding at nine and a half Blue Fedora Street."

"Details," I said with a shrug.

I turned slowly around, visually checking the space one more time. Then I started to pace.

"Does ExShell have a home address on him?" I asked.

"Not any longer. The only information they currently have is his favorite movie, *Gone With the Wind Part Three*."

"That's it?"

"Yes, apparently they don't like to pry into their employees' lives. I think the truth is that Burns probably tampered with the database."

"I guess we can rule out any help from ExShell then."

"That would be logical," HARV agreed. "Truthfully, they may not even know he's gone, or for that matter, if he ever actually worked here or not. They're at the mercy of their data and somebody or something has skewed that to the max."

"We'll just have to search the place from your memory," I said. "Access your recording of the Burns interview. I'm going to need visual and audio. Let's recreate the office."

"What part to you want?" HARV asked.

I turned and pointed to the far wall.

"The monitors were there, weren't they? Let's see those."

Holographic images sprang from my eye lens and the huge

bank of monitors returned to their place in the room as HARV
played his recording of my meeting with Burns. The playback
of Burns' voice in my head grated on my nerves like a stuck
hovercraft alarm.

"I'm coordinating the various operatives that we have in the
field that are currently following Dr. Pierce's elusive trail. The
manhunt has gone on for eleven months now . . ."

I shook my head, took a step back and gestured to the space
around me.

"The computer consoles were there, weren't they?"

"That's right," HARV said.

More holographic images sprang from the lens. The desk
reformed itself and the row of computer keyboards reappeared,
along with two or three empty soda bottles and disposable
plates.

"When we can pinpoint Pierce's location to within an area
of three square kilometers, we can send a search and retrieve
team," Burns said in my mind, "and have him back here in custody within an hour's time."

I stared at the computers and shuddered a bit at the garbage
strewn about them.

"I'd forgotten what a mess the place was," I said. "The
guy's a pig."

"I thought he was mutton?" HARV asked.

"Do you remember? It was, what, ten in the morning and
the guy was drinking soda and eating . . . pizza."

"He had three slices during your visit," HARV said. "Would
you like playback?"

I spun around again and pointed to the wall on the left.

"Show me that area," I said. "Let me see what was there."

Images covered the wall; the data storage units and satellite
monitors appeared but I paid them no mind. I was looking for
something else. When the storage table came into view, I
nearly jumped with glee.

"There," I said, pointing at the table. "Enhance that."

HARV zoomed in on the image of the table and a nano
later, I was studying the grain of the faux wood finish.

"It's pretty standard as office furniture goes," HARV said.

"Not the table, the pile of stuff on top of it."

HARV pulled back and then zoomed in again, this time on

the contents of the table: the stack of memory chips, the coffee cups . . . and the pizza boxes.

"The logo on the box," I said. "Go in tight."

HARV did as he was told and the words came into focus. PizzaPort.

"Vingo," I said. "He's hooked on the pizza. That's how we'll find him. Hack yourself into the PizzaPort database. Find Fred Burns."

"I'm in," HARV said. "Unfortunately, the database is categorized by address only," HARV said.

"Fine, how many deliveries were made to this office in the three days before we visited."

"Twenty-five."

"Sheesh, what a pig. When did the orders stop?"

"Two days ago." HARV replied. "The night after we visited."

"So he left here two days ago and went into hiding," I said. "I'm betting that PizzaPort started getting frequent orders from a new address shortly thereafter. Am I right?"

HARV churned away for a minute.

"What's wrong?" I asked.

"Some of the more recent entries into the database have been encoded," HARV said.

"Can you break them?"

"Of course," HARV said. "The encryption routine is very similar to the one Pierce used to hide his mother's brain."

HARV churned for a bit more.

"Fifteen delivery orders have come in during the last thirty-six hours from 8080 Jerry Garcia Avenue, a very remote area. The most recent order was placed seventy-three minutes ago."

"That's gotta be Burns," I said. "Pretty good find. Don't you think?"

"Oh, yes, brilliant," HARV said. "Perhaps we should call your next HV special *Dial P for Pizza*."

"I like it."

"You would," HARV mumbled.

A short while later, we were on the desolate stretch of Jerry Garcia Avenue. It was the wee hours of the morning so traffic was minimal in general and on this cul de sac it was nonexistent.

"The house is approximately a quarter kilometer ahead. The end of the road."

I killed the headlights, parked the car at the side of the road, and scanned the area though the darkness. There wasn't another house to be seen.

"I guess he doesn't want neighbors," HARV said.

"I'm thinking that the neighbors don't want him," I replied.

I popped my gun into my hand, stepped out of the car, and crept quickly through the darkness.

The house was a geocentric dome, solidly designed, but generally run-of-the-chip-factory. It was clear that Burns' income was somewhat less than extravagant.

"Not much to look at," HARV said.

"Neither is Burns," I quipped. "You remember the plan, right?"

HARV rolled his eyes (something I'd never seen him do before).

"If it appears that Mr. Burns is not at home or has retired for the evening, we pick the lock. If it appears that he's still awake, we do the pizza boy routine."

"Let's see it."

"Boss, I know the routine."

"There's a lot riding on this, HARV," I said. "It needs to be perfect."

"Fine,"

HARV's hologram blinked out for a nano then reappeared. Only this time instead of his usual gray tweed suit and bow tie, he was wearing the white pants, shirt, and hat of a PizzaPort delivery person. Four pizza boxes were in his arms, and a look of utter disdain was in his eyes.

"Mr. Burns," he said, "on behalf of the PizzaPort management, we're happy to award you these pizzas as a gesture of gratitude for your diligent patronage."

"Good," I said. "But try to look a little happier."

"Anything else, Mr. DeMille?"

A few nanos later, we were at the front door. The house was dark and the place was silent as a ghost town library.

"You read anyone inside?"

"No, but we shouldn't rule out the existence of cloaking devices."

"So he's either asleep, not at home, or lying in wait for us."

"Yes, we can safely narrow it down to those three."

"Okay, plan A," I said. "Think you can pick the lock?"

"Please," HARV said. "That's like asking Einstein if he could tie his shoe. Bend down so I can get a good look at it."

And that's when everything went very, very wrong.

I heard the faint whisper-pop of a blaster with silencer and a nano later, the blast hit me from the side and blew me off my feet. I hit the ground five meters from the house, dazed and confused. I tried to get to my feet but I couldn't move. I'd been hit by a binder-blast and was now tightly bound from neck to knees in plastic polymer.

"I don't think the pizza boy routine is going to work under these circumstances," HARV whispered.

I looked up and saw four figures approaching from the darkness; three men and a woman. The lead figure stepped from the shadows. The pale moonlight gently hit his face and my heart sank a little more.

"Hello there, Zach," Sidney Whoop said as he approached. "Fancy meeting you here."

# 44

And-A-One circled around to my left, probably to get the good two-shot of Whoop and me for the DickCo broadcast with his eye-cam. And-A-Two moved past me to get the long shot (although he gave me a kick to the ribs as he passed). Sidney, of course, stayed close. He was the star, after all, and he was loving every nano of it.

"You know, it would have been better all around if you'd broken this case a few hours ago," he said with a smile. "We've missed prime time."

"Sorry to disappoint you, Sidney," I said.

Sidney shrugged.

"It's all right. We'll run it tomorrow on delay. It will give us time to promote it properly and do some editing."

"Sidney, this is not a good time," I said. "You don't know what you're doing."

"I know that ExShell hired you to retrieve a very important droid," he said. "That's a start. As for the rest of the story, you're about to tell us everything."

The woman, who had stayed in the background all this time, stepped forward as Sidney gestured to her. She was a large woman, and tough-looking. Not unattractive but, for lack of a better word, scary. Her long red hair was wrapped tight in a bun. Her skin was ivory colored and clear. And her eyes were icy. The hairs on my neck stood up just at her approach.

"Zach Johnson," Sidney said with a smile, "meet Maggie Chill."

Maggie Chill is a psi. She's a whispered legend in the espionage community, a freelance operative who sells her talents to the highest bidder. She has done jobs for all the major world governments, the biggest conglomerates, and several of the wealthiest baseball teams in the American League. In recent years, her appearances in the field (even rumors of a appearances) have been very few and even farther between. Word in the community is that she had become bored with the work. Her mind was too powerful and she could no longer stand human contact of any kind. DickCo had somehow located her through the community of shadows, tempted her wrath by contacting her, and lured her out of retirement for this one special assignment. It must be sweeps month.

"I don't think humming is going to work this time," HARV said.

"Pleased to meet you, Ms. Chill," I said. "I'm sorry that it has to be under these circumstances."

She knelt down beside me, like a cobra approaching its helpless prey. Her eyes locked with mine, moving hypnotically to the left then right. I thought the chill that ran up my spine was going to make icicles in my hair.

Then she spoke and the sound almost made me gag.

"Wha-ev-uh."

Nails on a blackboard, a stuck hovercraft theft alarm at three in the morning, deranged chipmunks on helium. These sounds were angels singing next to the accented nasal twang of Maggie Chill.

"What was that?"

"Oiy said, *wha-ev-uh.*"

"I'm sorry," I said. "I'm still not getting it."

"Whatchoo, deaf?" she said. "*Wha-ev-uh, wha-ev—uh.*"

Sidney was a little uncomfortable now.

"Zach, you're making her mad," he said. "Be polite, okay."

"Right," I said. "I wouldn't want to offend your psionic assassin."

As we spoke I focused the power from my armor to one small area at my left shoulder. I knew I couldn't break the binding with brute force but I was hoping that I could load up the armor's circuits, generate some heat and melt the plastic polymer enough for me to crack it with a good effort. The downside, of course, was that, even by focusing the power to the outer shell of the armor, I still felt the residual heat. It hurt plenty but it was my only chance of getting out of this in one piece. HARV immediately realized what I was doing.

"Ingenious plan, boss, but it's going to hurt, and it's going to take some time," he said. "Are you sure you want to do this?"

"No choice," I whispered.

"Whawazzat?" Maggie asked, suddenly tense.

"What was what?" Sidney asked.

Maggie's psionic abilities were more sensitive than I thought. She was sensing something. I wasn't sure if it was HARV or simply my thoughts of him that she was picking up but either way, I was in big trouble if she figured out that I had a supercomputer in my head. Randy told me when he first dropped the interface into my eye that HARV's presence in my head would help me defend myself against psi attacks. Now it was time to put that claim to the hydrochloric acid test.

"Oi'm pickin' up somethin' in his head. Somethin' distant."

"That's my inner child," I said. "Cute kid, but I can't stand his taste in music."

"It's loik dere's someone else in yah head," Maggie said. "Almost as if . . ." She smiled and I knew I was sunk. "Yah' a schitzaphenic, ahn'tchoo?"

"A what?"

"A schitzaphenic. You have a multiple poisonality disohdah?"

"What's a disohdah?"

"A disohdah, disohdah!"

"Oh, a disorder. Why didn't you just say it in English?"

"Lissen, mistah," Maggie said angrily. "Oi'm gonna read yah moind. Oi'm gonna foind out 'zactly wha' oiy need ta' know. Den oi'm gonna make you lick moiy boots. Aftah dat, oi'm gonna shut down da hoiyah fun-shins of yah brain and let you live da rest've yah loife as a can of Spam. And you know whoiy oiy oi added dat last 'ting? Because you jus' made fun o' da way oiy tawk."

"The way you what?"

"Tawk, tawk. Da' way oiy tawk!" she shouted.

Sidney stepped forward and put a hand on Maggie's shoulder.

"Maggie, please, we need to get his information."

"Don' touch me, Whoop," she said pushing his hand away. "Oiy can feel yah stupidity roight tru' yah fingahtips."

"What?"

"She's right, Sidney," I said. "I can feel it from here."

"Shut up, Zach!"

Clearly, Sidney didn't like the fact that he was losing control of the scene. And clearly, the great Maggie Chill was a bit unbalanced herself. I realized that might give me a chance at survival.

"Hey, don't yell at me. I'm schizophrenic, remember?"

"You are not."

"Yes, I am. She said it herself. I have a disohdah, I have a disohdah."

"Dass' it," Maggie yelled. "Oi'm melting yah brain roit now."

"Maggie, no!" Sidney yelled.

"Foin. I'll get da' information foist," she said. "*Den* I'll melt his brain."

"That's better," Sidney said.

"Thanks for the help, Sid," I said. "I'm touched by your Machiavellian concern."

Maggie put her hand against my cheek and her icy touch began to penetrate my head.

"Le's get dis ovah wit," she said.

Then I got an idea.

"Um okay," I said. "But be careful. I have an entire world of information in my head."

"Yeah, wha- ev-uh." Maggie said.

"All right, but don't say I didn't warn you. I have access to more information then you could ever dream of."

"Hold on," Whoop said cautiously. "This is too easy. What are you doing, Zach?"

Maggie shrugged Whoop's warning away.

"Oh puh-leeze," she said. "Oiy seen kitchen apployances wit' strongah moinds den dis guy."

"By the way," I said, "have I mentioned that I have a *world of information* in my head?"

"All right already, boss, I get the hint," HARV said. "Sheesh, ever hear of subtlety?"

And then Maggie Chill reached into my mind.

# 45

The inside of my mind was a big white room (admittedly not the most original setting, but I don't think that was a reflection on me), and I was standing in front of a door.

"Well, this isn't so bad," I said.

"It's about to get a whole lot better, chico."

My heart skipped a beat at the sound of the voice. Then I smelled the perfume: sweet and sexy, like a passionate kiss on a springtime lawn. I turned slowly, and there she was.

Electra.

"I've missed you," she said.

"I've missed you, too."

"It's stupid to fight like this."

"Yeah, it is. I'm sorry. It's just that . . ."

She moved toward me and put a finger to my lips.

"Shhh, it's in the past. We're looking forward now," she said. She put one arm around my neck and pulled my face close to hers. Then she put her hand on the doorknob behind me. "Let's go into the other room and you can show me the future."

"I just . . ."

"Later," she said. "Just open the door."

I put my hand on the knob and started to turn.

"I just want to . . ."

"What?"

"I'm sorry for what I did."

Electra smiled.

"I'm sorry, too," she said.

And then I smiled (really widely).

"Electra would never say that."

"What?"

"She'd never apologize. Especially when I was the one who screwed up."

HARV appeared suddenly beside me, hands on his hips.

"Well, it's about time," he said. "For a nano there, I thought you were actually falling for that drivel."

Electra's image shook as though her molecules were being broken down from the inside and in a nano, she was replaced by the (angry) form of Maggie Chill.

"Who da' DOS ah you?" she hissed.

"I'm his conscience," HARV replied. "And I'll give you one warning, madam. Leave this man's mind now or suffer the consequences."

"You tink you can scare me, you schizo-fop?" she said. "Oiy could rip' yah mind apaht wit' a jest-chya."

"With a what?" I asked.

"A jest-chya, a jest-chya!" she yelled, waving her hands. "Now open da dowah!"

"Maggie, the door's a metaphor," I said. "You know it and I know it. Try to be a little more inventive the next time you invade someone's mind. Okay?"

Maggie's face grew red with anger and I knew she was going to blow soon. I stepped to the side and motioned to the door.

"You want information? Fine, here it is, but you're in for a surprise."

I nodded to HARV, who gave me a proper gentlemanly bow and then, with a dramatic flourish, threw open the door.

"You see, this isn't my door," I said.

Bright light and white sound erupted from within and a cascade of ones and zeroes flooded the room. I saw Maggie's face drop and the last thing she saw before she was engulfed in the binary maelstrom of information was HARV's smiling face.

"It's mine," he said.

# 46

And then we were back in the world outside my head. I was still bound tightly in plastic polymer and surrounded by Sidney and his junior dicks but things were definitely on the upswing.

Why? Because in the all-important arena of mental warfare, HARV and I were giving the great Maggie Chill the blitz to end all kriegs.

Maggie had gone into my mind looking to crack my reluctant cortex for information. What she got, however, was the free flow of HARV's database. It was the mental equivalent of someone expecting glass of water and getting the Atlantic ocean dumped on them instead. HARV hit Maggie's mind with a tsunami of information and it was more than she could stand.

The download of the complete *World Chip Super Encyclopedia* made her dizzy. The streaming hyperaudio of the collected historical database of commercial jingles made her queasy. And the text download of twentieth-century political speeches left her puking her guts out.

But it was the bootlegged recordings of the complete Doors catalog (illegally pirated through the rogue site Kidnapster) that finally fractured her frontal lobes.

She pulled away from me, mentally and physically, in the pain of information overload.

"Make it stawp! Puh-leeze make it stawp!"

"You can't say we didn't warn her," HARV said.

"True," I agreed. "After all, we're the good guys and that's what good guys do."

Maggie fell to the ground, her body curling and uncurling like an epileptic cow at a disco.

"I guess having a computer hooked in to my brain has an upside after all."

"At least for you," HARV said.

Sidney saw Maggie convulsing and tried to help her.

"Maggie, what's wrong?"

She seized his hand like frog tongue on a fly and Sidney began to shake as well.

"What's happening?" I asked.

"She's trying to siphon off some of the excess information into Sidney's mind." HARV said.

"She's using him as a mental sump pump?"

"In a way," HARV said. "A pity his mind isn't big enough. By the way, watch out behind you."

I turned and saw And-A-One running toward Maggie and Sidney. I flung my legs out as he passed and hit him squarely in the shins. He tripped and tumbled into the spasming pair of villains. Sidney reached out and grabbed the stupid kid's ankle and drew him into the mind morass as well. And-A-One began shaking as though he'd swallowed a jackhammer.

"I saw his approach through the wrist interface," HARV said.

"Thanks. It looks like we have a real chain of fools going now," I said.

Meanwhile, the heat of my armor had at last melted the binding enough so that small cracks had begun to form in the surface. I figured I was running out of time so I pulled the energy away from the armor surface, funneled it into my shoulder muscles, and gave a heave. The binding cracked and my arm was free.

"Where's the other dick?" I asked.

No sooner had the words left my mouth then they were replaced by And-A-Two's boot as he kicked me squarely in the face.

"There's some painful irony," HARV said.

And-A-Two kicked me again, this time in the shoulder and I rolled over onto my stomach.

"You're not so tough," he said, and kicked me again.

I rolled down the gentle slope of the lawn like a runaway barrel on a mountain road. And-A-Two followed me, a stupid swagger to his walk and an even stupider grin on his face.

"You're a soft old man, Johnson," he said. "An overblown, overrated, overpaid pretender."

My rolling momentum was gone and I was now facedown in the grass, still wrapped almost entirely in polymer and helpless. And-A-Two caught up to me and stood over my bound form with an evil grin on his face.

"You wouldn't know a tough guy if he kicked you in the head," he said.

He pulled his heavy boot back and then threw one more steel-toe jab at my face.

But I'd had enough.

I reached out with my one free arm and caught his swinging foot in my hand.

"I guess we'll never know, will we?" I said.

And the kid's grin disappeared.

I twisted his foot hard and he fell to the ground. Then I popped my gun into my hand and fired a low-power blast at the polymer binding on my legs. The blast blew the polymer apart and freed me from the waist down.

I got to my feet just as And-A-Two was pulling his gun. I kicked it out of his hand and then kneed him in the chin. He fell back to the ground. I aimed my gun at him and let him see the business end for a long nano before giving the command.

"Sticky stuff."

And fired.

The glue sealed tightly around the kid's body, pinning him to the ground like a well constructed pup tent.

HARV appeared from my eye lens and knelt beside And-A-Two. Before I could say a word, he stuck his holographic nose in the kid's face and lectured him like a headmaster dressing down the class clown.

"I want you to remember this, you little cretin. I want you to reflect back upon this nano as you grow old and remember who it was who spared your life when you had no intention of sparing his. Maybe one day you'll realize that you were taught a lesson this night by the toughest man you'll ever meet. And above all, I want you remember that Zach Johnson beat you with one arm and both legs tied behind his back."

My jaw dropped so low that I had grass stains on my chin.

HARV stood up and left the browbeaten And-A-Two on the ground, counting his blessings.

"HARV?"

He straightened his coat and turned to me.

"Just so you know," he said. "I did not record the past few nanos. There is no permanent record of what just occurred. Should the debate ever arise, regarding what may or may not have been said just now, it would come down to my word against yours. And let's remember that I am a well-respected supercomputer and as such, my word would be considered more credible with the general public."

I said nothing. (But I smiled.)

"Come on," he said. "We have work to do."

I freed myself from the last of the polymer binding and set to work. All DickCo operatives are monitored by the home office through their eye and satellite cams, so we had to work quickly before anyone figured out that something was amiss and sent in reinforcements.

Sidney, Maggie, and And-A-One were all unconscious (nearly catatonic) from HARV's information overload.

"They're not permanently hurt are they?"

"They'll be unconscious for another day or so," HARV said, "and they'll have some serious headaches for the next few weeks but they'll survive."

I put all three of them in Sidney's hovercraft, which was parked up the road, then threw And-A-Two in the trunk. I left my wrist interface on the hood of the hover so that HARV could project (mundane and peaceful) holographic images of Burns' house onto the windshield. Anyone from DickCo monitoring the eye-cams of Sidney and his posse would think that they were on a very boring stakeout. HARV even threw in some occasional banter for additional realism. Once that was taken care of, I turned my attention back to Burns' hideout.

The lights in the main room were now on.

"I guess it would be too much to ask for him to sleep through a firefight on his front lawn," I said.

"Shall we do the pizza boy routine?"

"I think the time for that has passed," I said, popping my gun into my hand. "Our only option now is to go in the hard way."

## 47

And I meant hard.

I focused the power from my armor into my leg and kicked the door in. The metal and plastic fibers splintered and the hinges ripped free from the wall.

"By the way, boss," HARV said. "I believe that the door was unlocked."

"Thanks, HARV. Now let's work on your ability to deliver information in a timely manner."

A nano later I was in the front foyer of the house with my gun drawn.

"Burns," I called into the darkness. "It's Zach Johnson. I want you to come out with your hands up. No one gets hurt that way."

That's when I heard the music.

"What's that?"

"I believe it's Bach," HARV said. "Concerto for Piano and Orchestra Number 2 in E Major. Not a bad choice for ambience, really."

I followed the music into the spacious living room, which was entirely empty save for one of those ugly, overstuffed white antigrav couches that are so popular now, floating fifteen feet in the air.

And Fred Burns was sitting in the middle of it.

"And so, Prometheus returns to have the vulture eat his liver once again."

"Whatever you say, Doc. " I said. "Which one am I?"

Burns laughed and lowered the couch slowly toward the floor.

"I honestly didn't expect to see you here, Mr. Johnson. I was afraid that I'd have to hunt you down. How did you find me, by the way?"

"You left a trail of pizza."

Burns looked at the slice of pizza in his hand and then smiled.

"Oh. Well, I guess even Achilles had a weakness," he said. "It's for the best, anyway. Your coming here saves me the time that I'd have spent searching for you."

"I'm glad I could make it convenient for you, Doc, but I think you have the roles reversed. You see, I'm here to kick your ass and have you tell me everything you know about Manuel Mani and BB-2."

The couch came to rest gently on the floor and Burns oozed off it. He looked at me, then at the gun in my hand and smiled.

"I don't think so," he said.

That worried me. Burns didn't strike me as the kind of guy who had a gun pointed at him very often. The fact that he was this calm while staring into the business end was a little unnerving.

"I don't think you grasp the gravity of the situation, Doc," I said. "I'm not playing games here."

Burns smiled and slowly moved toward me.

"Oh, I understand," he said. "And just for the record, I'm not playing games here either. Although I do enjoy a good game of Trivial Tidbits. I'm especially good at mythology questions."

Now I was getting spooked. This fleshy little unarmed man, plodding towards me like a Jell-o mold with feet, had me in a stare-down contest and from all signs, he was winning. Something was wrong here. Something was definitely wrong but I couldn't, for the life of me, figure out what it was.

Burns was within arm's length when I finally put my gun directly in his face, just on the off chance that he hadn't noticed it yet. But it still didn't seem to worry him (and *that* worried *me*).

"Okay, doughboy," I said. "I've had enough of this. You tell me what I want to know right now or things are going to get very ugly."

"I've been ordered to terminate you," he said. "Your coming

here saves me a lot of time and effort. Thank you for your co-
operation in my current endeavor."

"Terminating me might be a little difficult since I'm the one
with the gun."

Burns smiled and pointed toward the ceiling.

"If you'll turn your gaze skyward, you'll notice a projector
suspended from the ceiling. The ingenious device of my own
design emits a signal that blocks all types of communications
and deactivates all computerized devices except for my own."

Burns' smile grew wider and he reached out and gently
touched the barrel of my gun with his thumb and index finger.

"Your gun, I'll remind you, is computer-controlled and
therefore will not work in this house."

I flipped the setting on my gun to heavy stun and pulled the
trigger.

Nothing happened.

Nada.

Zilch.

Zero.

Well, almost zero. Burns began to laugh. It was that over-
the-top kind of cackle that villains always use and worst of all,
he wasn't even good at it.

So I hit him.

A left cross to the jaw sent him sprawling to the floor.

"I really don't like you, Dr. Burns."

Burns held his aching jaw in one hand and held the other
out to me in a "please stop" gesture.

"Please," he said, "I am not a man of violence."

I grabbed him by the shoulders and pulled him to his feet.

"Tell me what I need to know and there won't be any violence," I snarled (suddenly feeling a whole lot better about myself).

Then Burns smiled again and I knew that I was still in
trouble.

"But then, just because I'm not a man of violence," he said,
"doesn't mean I am *opposed* to violence."

I felt a tap on my shoulder and I turned just in time to see a
huge red-headed droid in a maid's uniform standing beside me.

Then I saw a huge droid fist coming toward me.

Then I saw stars.

"Mr. Johnson," Burns said with a smile, "I'd like you to meet Hazel, my maid droid. Hazel will be your murderer this evening. She'll also clean up afterward. Isn't that right, Hazel?"

"Oh, yes, master," the droid replied. "As if I have nothing better to do with my time than to clean up the murderous messes that you order me to create."

"Let's not go in to that now, Hazel, please," Burns said. "We have company."

It goes without saying that Hazel wasn't your run-of-the-mill household droid. She stood nearly three meters tall and tipped the scale at a megaton if she was a gram. Each of her hands was easily as big as my head.

"You call this flesh-maggot company?" she said. "I've scraped better company off of the bug zapper."

She also had a hefty dose of sarcasm in her main programming (probably one of the more recent versions of the mother-in-law droid operating system).

Hazel stood over me as I lay on the floor and stomped her foot trying to squash me like a bug. I rolled away at the last nano and watched her put a foot-shaped crater in the carpet as well as the floor stones beneath.

"Hazel, as you can see, is also immune to the deactivation devices in my house." Burns said.

"Yeah, but does she do windows?" I asked.

Hazel's chair-sized foot kicked me in the ribs and threw me a meter and a half in the air. When I landed (hard) on the floor, she was already reaching for me with her giant metal hands.

"Oh, gee, like I haven't heard *that* one before," she said, lifting me toward her. "Maybe you should spend the extra credits and get some writers who can steal jokes from *this* century."

"Everyone's a critic."

For a lack of anything better to do I hit Hazel in the side of the head with my gun. It didn't hurt her, of course, and I was glad that I'd hit her with my gun rather than my fist.

Hazel snorted in disdain and tossed me across the room the way a child would toss away an old rag doll. I hit the wall and then the floor then rolled over onto my back and gazed at the ceiling.

"HARV," I whispered, "I don't suppose you could help me out here, could you?"

A little bomb icon appeared before my eye with the words "system error" directly below it. Somewhere in my head I could hear the echoes of HARV yelling. It was distant and almost intelligible. Burns' device hadn't turned HARV off inside my head but it was definitely wreaking some havoc with the system. I'm sure that HARV would eventually iron out the bugs. The question was, would my head still be intact when he did?

Meanwhile, the shaking of the floor (and the cascade of annoying causticity that followed) told me that Hazel was stomping her way toward me again.

"All the things that need to be done in this house before the cataclysm and I have to waste my evening killing some overrated B-level celebrity."

"Please, Hazel," Burns said, "don't embarrass me at work."

"You call this work?" she said "I'm the one doing all the work here. You're just standing there cackling insidiously."

And as I lay on the floor, the only thought I had in my head was that this would be a stupid way to die: crushed to death by a fishwife droid and her pussy-whipped mad scientist. But here I was. All my gadgetry had gone from high tech to high dreck, thanks to the projector on the ceiling. HARV had become a (very) silent partner and my gun had become the world's most expensive rock. Well, I'd always insisted that I could get along fine without HARV. Now it was time to put up or shut up.

I climbed to my feet and as the Goliath droid approached, I realized that my one last chance of survival was to make like a gumshoe David, so I wrapped my fingers around my gun and wound up my throwing arm like the illegal clone of Cy Young.

Hazel stopped her approach at the sight of me and put her giant hands on her wide hips.

"Oh, good, throw your gun at me," she said. "That worked *so* well last time. DOS, don't they make humans with brains anymore?"

I threw the gun, but not at Hazel.

I threw it at the projector on the ceiling and when the metal of the gun butt shattered the projector glass, the whole unit exploded into a miniature mass of flaming debris and fell from the ceiling . . . right on top of Hazel.

I was thrown to my knees by the explosion and actually had a nano to enjoy my little victory. Then the rubble on the floor shifted and Hazel (her faux hair still aflame) rose to her feet again.

"I'm going to have to clean this rug, you know," she said. "Do you have any idea how hard it is to clean melted circuitry out of shag?"

She flexed her long, metallic fingers menacingly.

"Not to mention the bloodstains," she said.

And then she charged me.

My gun had also fallen to the floor in the explosion. It had landed on the far side of the room, almost directly opposite from me. All that stood between it and me now was a megaton of fast-approaching angry droid. But, fast as Hazel was, I was hoping that my gun was a little faster.

I stuck out my hand, fingers spread wide.

"Come to daddy," I said.

The gun, now free from Burns' nullifier, responded to my command. It shuddered for a nano, then took to the air like a steel gray homing pigeon.

The charging Hazel was four meters away from me when the flying gun passed her.

She was three meters away when it landed solidly in my outstretched hand.

She was two meters away when I gave the command.

"Big Bang."

And her hands were actually touching my cheeks when I pulled the trigger.

The high-powered blast blew a hole in Hazel's chest the size of a small dog. Wire, circuitry, and silicone splattered the wall behind her like high-tech gore. She stumbled, robotic eyes glazed, and looked first at the hole in her midsection, then at her innards splattered behind her.

"Aw, no," she said. "Not on the drapes."

I fired again and atomized her from the shoulders up.

The echo of the blast was just starting to fade when HARV's voice returned to my head.

"Boss, it appears that we had a slight problem with the

interface," he said, "but it seems to be clear now. What the DOS happened here?"

"I had a little dispute with the maid," I said. "But I think we worked it out."

# 48

I turned my attention back to Burns, who was a little shell-shocked from all this. I pointed my gun at him again and finally got the reaction that I'd been expecting. He fell to his knees and started crying like a day trader on Black One-day.

"I take it that you're out of domestic help," I said.

"Please don't kill me," he sobbed. "It wasn't my fault. It was that protoscum, Mani and that crazy BB-2, who made me do it."

"Where are they?" I growled.

"They'll kill me . . ."

"You have a choice here, Burns," I said. "You can tell me everything I want to know and let the police protect you while I handle Mani and BB-2. Or you can die right here."

"I wish you hadn't destroyed Hazel," he sobbed. "She always made the non-virus related decisions around here."

I picked Burns up by the shirt collar and slammed him into a wall. Then I stuck my gun into his nose and stretched his nostril cartilage until it fit the barrel.

"I'll ask you one more time," I said in my best Marlowe snarl. "Where are Mani and BB-2?"

Burns responded in a nasal twang (that comes from having a gun barrel up your nose).

"The Fallen Arms Hotel in Oakland."

"What did they want from you?"

"My old virus research."

"And you just gave it to them?"

"I sold it to them, for a fortune and for the promise of a place in their plan."

"What is their plan?" I said.

"I don't know."

I slammed him against the wall again and stuck my gun another three centimeters farther up his nose.

"What are they planning?" I yelled.

"I don't know!" he sobbed. "All I know is that it's the end of the world as we know it."

I let Burns fall to the floor, where he curled into a ball and sobbed. Then I rubbed my eyes and sighed.

I had HARV net with Carol. We woke her at home and I somehow cajoled her into coming out to Burns' hideout to use her psi powers to wipe out and rewrite the memories of Burns, Whoop, and the DickCo crew. It would be a thin cover story at best, but maintaining the perfect veil of secrecy wasn't exactly my highest priority at the nano.

"The end of the world," I said to myself. "Why does it always have to be the end of the world?"

# 49

I stomped my foot hard on the gas pedal and felt the car's engine roar in response as I shot down the New Trans-City Highway. For the first time since I took on the case of the missing killer android, I had clarity of purpose. The pieces of this puzzle were coming together, albeit in a very abstract and urgent sort of way.

Manuel Mani, BB Star's ex-lover and personal astrologer, had made three attempts on my life in the past two days and I now strongly suspected that he was behind the other half dozen or so attempts as well. I let the first murder attempt slide, writing it off as the desperate act of a jilted lover, but Mr. Mani officially ran out of slack when he organized the droid blitzkrieg at the Nexus 9. As for Pizza Boy Burns and his crazed cleaning droid, that just added insult to injury. Now it was payback time.

"You're exceeding the speed limit for ground-based vehicles," HARV's hologram said from the passenger seat.

"I'll charge the speeding ticket to BB Star," I said. "Either that or I'll take it out of Manuel Mani's hide."

"Do you really think he's the brains behind all this?" HARV asked.

"Three of my would-be assassins have fingered him as their boss man. What do you think?"

"But he's BB's ex-lover?"

"Emphasis on the ex, buddy. I know that if I were dumped . . ."

"Which, judging by Dr. Gevada's apparent hostility toward you, seems a very likely scenario."

"And thank you so much for reminding me," I said. "If I were dumped, I think I'd be very tempted to take up with a woman much like the one who dumped me."

"You think Manuel and BB-2 are an item?"

"Sicker things have happened, pal, which is why we're on our way to the Fallen Arms."

"That's another thing that worries me," HARV said.

"What's that?"

"The Fallen Arms is not an active domicile. Abandoned since 2013, it is a municipally recognized shrine to urban blight. The only reason that the building is still standing is to remind present-day Oakland residents of how good they have it. A brilliant PR ploy by the current administration, by the way."

"If you don't want to be found, where better to hide than the underbelly of the city?" I said. "Now, have you done those searches I requested?"

"Of course I have," HARV said. "Plus a few others. What do you think I am, a BOB model?"

"And the results are?" I asked.

"Surprising and confusing."

"Go on," I prompted.

"ExShell spent over one hundred twenty-five percent more on the BB-2 project than I would have deemed necessary. The finances are scrambled but I'm confident that my margin of error is under point three percent."

"Is that the surprising or confusing part?" I asked.

"Surprising."

"Mega corps like ExShell tend to go overboard with expenses, so I wouldn't worry about it," I said. "Now what's the confusing part?"

"I'm not sure . . ." HARV answered.

"Hence the confusion."

"There are numerous scrambled transactions that involve seemingly unrelated items. They come from nowhere and seem to accomplish nothing."

"Sounds like a government project," I said.

"No, no. I'm not talking ineptitude here. This confusion is brilliant in its chaotic nature. There is clearly a pattern and a purpose to the activity. It's just so well cloaked in chaos that it appears inept on the surface."

"In other words you can't figure it out," I said.

"Yet."

"If you say so. Just tell me if you make sense out of anything,"

"Not if," he corrected. "When."

"If, when, whenever. Anything else?"

"I found one interesting note scribbled by hand over some early specs of the BB-2 project."

"And that would be?" I prompted (sometimes getting information out of HARV was like pulling teeth).

"It said 'BS hates contractions.' "

"Well, we all have our little peeves," I said. "You can figure all that out later. Right now I need all the info you can get on Manuel Mani."

"Already done. And the stuff gets even weirder."

"How so?"

"Manuel Mani, born in 2030 in New Mexico. The son of two computer programmers . . ."

"You mean the New Mexico that used to be the state?" I asked.

"No, that's New New Mexico. I mean the New Mexico that was once the country of Mexico."

"DOS, why does the World Council insist on sticking the word 'New' in front of everything?"

"You don't want to go into that do you?" HARV asked.

"No," I said. "Go on. He was born in Mexico."

"New Mexico," HARV corrected.

"HARV . . ."

"He moved to New Frisco in 2045. Now this is where it gets weird. The databases show that five years ago Manuel Mani worked as a robotics engineer with HTech specializing in remote reprogramming."

"Are you sure?"

"Actually, no," HARV said. "I just know the data is in the database."

HARV's hologram morphed into the shape of an HTech identification card. Sure enough, the card had Mani's picture and his name, with the title "Engineer" on it.

"See?" HARV said.

"I see. But in this day and age seeing doesn't always translate to believing. It's a weird jump from robots to astrology."

"Then again," HARV said. "Personal astrologer was his official title when he worked for BB. Who knows what his actual duties were."

"So he's a psycho with a background in robotics who is obsessed with BB Star," I said. "That would make BB-2 his dream date."

"Apparently someone for whom he'd kill," HARV said. "Speaking of which, the Fallen Arms is exactly three hundred meters straight ahead."

I pulled the car to the side of the road and killed the engine and lights.

I reached through HARV's hologram to the glove compartment, pulled out a fresh clip of ammo, and loaded my gun. Then I pulled my classic Colt .45 from the glove compartment and loaded it with some of Randy's specially designed ammo.

"What are you doing with that ancient thing?" HARV asked.

"It's a backup."

"The firearm is nearly fifty years old. It's unstable and non-computerized."

"You're starting to catch on, HARV." I slipped the Colt into my ankle holster and stepped out of the car.

A few nanos later I was creeping stealthily through the darkness toward The Fallen Arms. HARV provided me with an illusory holographic cover making me nearly invisible in the darkness (a neat trick but it puts a hefty strain on my armor's energy supply so I don't use it that often).

The building itself was utterly decrepit. Like an idiot with a bullet in his head, it was dead and yet too dense to fall down. So against all logic, the building remained standing, its century-old rotted support beams and brittle infrastructure somehow keeping it upright.

"A real fixer-upper," I whispered.

"More like a real tear-the-thing-down, burn-the-rubble, pour-holy-water-on-the-ashes, and salt-the-earth-so-that-nothing-can-ever-grow-there-againer," HARV said.

"Let's hope it doesn't come to that," I said, popping my gun into my hand. "But I will if I have to."

# 50

I entered the building, gun drawn, and felt the floorboards creak beneath my feet. The lobby was empty so I quickly moved toward the old stairway.

"My sensors report that the elevator is no longer functional," HARV whispered.

"Just as well," I said. "There's more room to move on the stairs."

I tentatively put my weight on the first step. The wood splintered faintly beneath my shoe but it held. I brushed away what appeared to be cobwebs from the ceiling and started up the stairs.

Things were fairly uneventful as I passed the second, third, four, fifth, and six floors. I knew this was just the calm before the impending storm, though, and I was proven right when I reached floor seven.

"Uh-oh," HARV said.

"What uh-oh?" I whispered anxiously. "I don't like uh-oh!"

"I detect communications coming from floors six and eight."

"Can you say trap?"

"I can say trap in six hundred thirty-two languages."

"It was a rhetorical question, HARV. Witty banter to break the tension."

"Maybe you should use writers," HARV said, a little panicky. "By the way, I strongly suggest you fling yourself to the left side of the stairwell right . . . Now!"

I leaped as HARV directed just as two bullets whizzed past me from opposite directions.

Then things got a little freaky.

As soon as the bullets passed me, they suddenly stopped short and hung in midair for nano, as though searching for something.

"HIT THE DECK NOW!" HARV screamed.

I dove to the floor a split second before the bullets changed course, hit the wall, and exploded where my head had been only nanos before. Wood and plaster shrapnel filled the hallway and bounced over and around me as I tried to cover myself.

"DOS!" I exclaimed. "I don't need writers, I need stunt doubles."

"They would have to be very stupid stunt doubles," HARV noted.

"What were those?" I asked, as I crawled across stairwell floor to the seventh floor door.

"Smart bullets," HARV said. "An experimental weapon currently being developed by an HTech subsidiary. They're not actually intelligent, of course, but they're much more sophisticated than your average projectile weapon. They are programmed to attack a specific visual target."

"A bullet with my name on it."

"Your image, actually, but that's the gist of it," HARV said.

I tried the knob but the door out of the stairwell was locked (of course). I was about to blow the door with my gun when I heard a woman's familiarly accented voice call to me from the floor below.

"Hello, Mr. Johnson," she said. "We meet again for the first time."

"Diedre," I called from my hiding place. "Is that you?"

"Yes and no, Mr. Johnson," she said. "Same model, different unit. As you'll recall, you destroyed the unit you met earlier this evening."

"Yes, sorry about that," I said. "I tend to act rudely when someone is trying to kill me. I assume that the shooter on the floor above me then is Dieter? Dieter, are you there, buddy?"

"Don't call me buddy," Dieter's voice floated down from the stairs.

"No hard feelings about what happened at the club, right?"

"None," he said. "But it will make killing you here more satisfying."

"Dieter, I think that qualifies as hard feelings," I shouted, then I whispered to HARV inside my head. "Why are they talking instead of shooting?"

"My guess is that they're reloading."

"Reloading? They've fired once. What are they using—muskets?"

"I told you," HARV whispered, "the bullets are experimental. According to the most recent literature, the target image has to be uploaded into the ordnance just before firing."

"How long does that take?"

"About forty-five seconds."

"How long since they last fired?"

"About forty-five seconds."

A shot rang out from above and I heard the deadly whistle of the bullet as it sped down the stairwell. I threw myself to the other side of the hall but there just wasn't enough room to move. The bullet grazed my side and ripped a hole through my armor and my flesh before slamming into the stairway door and exploding. The explosion blew the door apart and I could see the decrepit hallway on the other side. I put the pain out of my head and made a mad dash for the opening. I made it through just as the second shot fired from below. Fortunately, the smart bullet wasn't intelligent enough to recognize the image of my rear end as I turned tail and ran, so as I threw myself into the hallway, the bullet simply sailed above me and exploded against the far wall, obliterating another good size chunk of wood and plaster as it did so.

"Are you hurt?" HARV asked.

"Hurt, yes. Dead, no," I said. "The armor saved me."

"I'm manipulating the armor to seal itself tightly around your wound," HARV said. "I'm also instructing your body to create some extra endorphins to quell the pain and adrenaline to keep you moving."

"Thanks," I said. "Look, we've got a few seconds now before the next round of bullets so I need your help. Will those bullets attack a hologram?"

"No. Their secondary guidance system is mass-seeking. They seek out the image and then verify that the image is real through the use of sonar. The original design utilized a heat-seeking guidance system but that proved less than effective, hence the new system. The designers felt that it was imperative to develop some sort of weapon that would be equally effective against organic and nonorganic attackers. This new modification has not hurt performance against organics but has improved performance against nonorganics by a factor of . . ."

"Ten words or less here, HARV. We're on the clock," I said. "I'm going to need you to follow my lead very closely here."

"What lead? What the DOS are you talking about?"

"Nine words that time, buddy," I said as I ducked quickly into the seventh floor hallway. "Glad to see you're catching on."

The layout of the floor was simple and worked to my advantage. Two perpendicular hallways crisscrossed the floor, north to south and east to west, dissecting the space into quarters. Another hallway ran entirely around the perimeter. Once inside, the three of us would be like rats in a maze. I allowed myself a tiny smile as I surveyed the floor (not an easy thing to do when you've just been shot and are caught in a crossfire) and quickly tiptoed down the hallway.

"Here's the plan, HARV," I whispered. "And I'm guessing that is going to be a hit or miss type of deal—literally."

Dieter and Diedre, guns at the ready, entered the hallway together a few nanos later. As I suspected, they split up. Diedre covered the entrance at the south wall while Dieter padded quickly north along the center corridor.

I waited until Dieter was nearly to the far end of the hallway before I made my move on Diedre. I sprang from my hiding place on the east wall and fired. Unfortunately, I made too much noise as I moved. Diedre spun toward me and ducked behind the wall as I fired. My blasts flew past her and exploded on the western end of the hallway.

"Uh-oh," I said, then turned and ran up the hallway.

Diedre didn't have time to get off a clean shot at me but she was quickly up and on the move.

"Dieter," she shouted as she ran. "He is running north along the eastern wall."

Dieter had reached the northern wall and, at Diedre's call, turned right and sprinted toward me, confident that he could beat me to the junction. Sure enough, he rounded the corner and there I was, twenty meters down the hallway, looking for all the world like a deer in the headlights.

I stopped short when I saw Dieter appear in front of me but when I turned around I saw Diedre as she rounded the corner by the southern wall. They had me now, trapped between them with no place to run. So they smiled, the way killer droids tend to do, and wordlessly raised their guns.

"I'm trusting you here, buddy," I whispered to HARV.

"Boss, have I ever let you down?" he replied.

Actually, HARV had let me down on many occasions but I didn't think that this particular instance was the best time to remind him of that. I also didn't have time because at that nano, Dieter and Diedre simultaneously fired.

And HARV went into action.

His hologram projection unit projected the image of Nova Powers over me and used the lens in my eye to throw dual images of me over both Dieter and Diedre.

The smart bullets shot toward me from both sides in cold, perfect paths of death but at the last nano they zig-zagged around me and zeroed in on each of the droids.

"Uh-oh," Dieter muttered.

Then both he and Diedre exploded in spectacular displays of smart-bullet firepower and stupid-droid machinery.

"That's a shame," I said as the dust began to settle. "I was just starting to bond with those two. Nice job, HARV."

"Another example of better living through holograms," HARV said.

"Do you read anything else nearby?" I asked.

"My sensors indicate heavy power use coming from floor number thirteen."

"My lucky number."

I went back to the stairway and began climbing again but HARV stopped me before I went far.

"Wait a nano. What's that?"

"What's what?"

"The hole in the wall. Take a close look at it again. Let me take a reading."

I walked over to the far side of the stairway and looked at the hole that one of the smart bullets had blown in the wall.

The old wood and plaster had been atomized in the blast but it revealed a pillar of sparkling metal about a foot in diameter . The pillar ran up the length of the building like a high-tech sewer pipe.

"It looks new," I said.

"New and active," HARV replied. "I'm not even sure what kind of metal that is."

"What is it?"

"A power conduit, a support pillar, a weapons system, maybe all three. Whatever it is, it's brilliant."

"High tech?"

"Stratosphere tech, suborbital tech, moon-shot tech."

"I get the point, HARV."

"By the way, boss," HARV said. "I think, what with the gunfight in the stairway and all, that we've officially lost the element of surprise."

"I don't think we ever really had it, HARV." I squeezed the handle of my gun for reassurance. "But let's go."

# 51

I opened the door from the stairwell and entered the thirteenth floor hallway. It was dark and deserted and more depressing than the lobby. There were doors along the walls and two big picture windows at each end of the corridor which allowed in just enough moonlight to cast the hallway in gray silhouette.

"Sure is a cheery little place," I whispered.

"And quiet as a tomb," HARV replied.

"Not the best choice of metaphor," I mumbled. "Can you tell which door Mani's behind?"

"Yes, I can."

"Which one would that be?" I prompted.

"Energy readings are extremely high behind door number thirteen thirteen."

"Great, now can you at least *try* to be helpful here?"

"I'm sorry," HARV said. "Was it my imagination, or did my precision use of the hologram projection system just save your life six floors down?"

I carefully approached room 1313 and, gun at the ready, gently put my ear to the door.

"Look, we're very likely to encounter a deadly nuclear-powered droid here. The last thing I want to worry about now is your attitude."

"My attitude?" HARV asked, insulted. "What's wrong with my attitude?"

I heard a rumbling from within the room. Soft at first but getting louder.

"When I ask you a question, would it kill you to give me the whole answer without making me ask again?"

The rumbling continued to grow and I felt the creaking floorboards begin vibrate beneath my feet.

"Or would it be so very hard to give me the essence of the answer without taking half an hour for supercilious minutiae?"

"Supercilious?" HARV exclaimed. "Well, I never."

Stray tiles fell from the ceiling and shattered on the floor as the rumbling turned into a roar.

"All I want is a quick, precise answer," I said. "If you are as smart as you say, it shouldn't be hard."

"By the way, I think you better jump for cover now," HARV said.

"I think you're right."

I dove away from the doorway just as it (and a large chunk of the wall) blew apart and a huge twelve-armed battlebot rolled into the hallway. I caught the tail end of the explosion and the force tossed me to the other side of the hallway, where I hit the wall, cracked a rib, and lost hold of my gun (in that order).

"Battlebot," HARV said. "Battlebot bad! Is that succinct enough for you?"

"Yeah, thanks," I said as I scrambled to my feet.

The battlebot scanned the area and no doubt noticed that I'd lost my gun and was now running for my life down the hallway.

"Subject survived initial blast," it said to no one in particular (as battlebots are prone to do). "However, subject is now unarmed and is currently fleeing in complete and abject terror."

The battlebot extended its twelve arms menacingly, put its roller belts into high gear, and took off after me with (quite probably) a steely malevolent grin on its mechanical countenance.

Battlebots have ground speeds of up to seventy kilometers per hour, so, much to the bot's joy, it had no problem running me down.

Much to my joy, however, it wasn't me that the bot was chasing down the hallway. It was another of HARV's hologram projections. I was actually clinging to one of the old-fashioned water pipes that ran across the hallway ceiling.

The bot also didn't realize that a good deal of the hall that it thought it was rolling down was in actuality also a holographic projection. The illusion was shattered, of course, when the bot ran out of actual hallway, smashed through the picture window, and plummeted thirteen stories to the ground below.

There are a few things that one should know about battlebots:

1. They enjoy hand-to-hand killing
2. They really aren't all that bright, and
3. They are not built to survive falls of more than twenty-five meters.

All three points worked to my advantage here.

There was a tremendous thud from outside as the battlebot's massive body hit the ground like a meteorite and embedded itself five meters into the asphalt.

"The old extended hallway gag," I said as I jumped down from the ceiling. "An oldie but a goodie."

I heard the sound of polite applause coming from inside the apartment. That's normally a sound I enjoy but in this setting and under these circumstances, I found it kind of creepy.

I picked up my gun and followed the sound into the apartment, which was itself remarkably spacious and well kept (aside from the damage the battlebot had created). Antique furniture filled the large living area and classic photographs and filled bookcases lined the walls. It was like something out of the museum of antiquities.

In the middle of it all, on an antigrav floating couch, sat Manuel Mani, smiling and applauding politely.

Beside him sat BB-2.

She was indeed an exact copy of BB Star (save for the psychotic grin that adorned her faux human face). She was dressed in a tight pantsuit of black plastic, with black boots and a red vinyl motorcycle jacket. It was the kind of outfit that BB Star wouldn't be caught dead in. BB-2 however, seemed to love it. As I said, her grin was wide, her hair was alluringly disheveled, as though combed with a wild wind. There was an earthy sensuality about it.

And then there were her eyes. They were wider than BBs, a little crazed, but joyously so, almost glowing with the freedom of reckless abandon. They also seemed to be a deeper shade of blue than BB's. But more odd than anything is that they seemed to contain more life than BB's. There was joy in BB-2's eyes. Admittedly, the joy seemed a little insane but even that was more than I'd seen so far from BB.

She leaned her head gently toward Manuel beside her and spoke in a stage whisper loud enough for me to hear.

"He's very entertaining, don't you think?"

"Quite smashing indeed," Manuel agreed.

When confronted with an eerie tableau such as this, my general inclination is to go with what I know and stay strong. That's what I did here.

"I hate to break up the witty palaver," I said, "but I've come to deactivate BB-2."

The polite applause stopped and the villainous pair sat silent for a nano.

BB-2 shrugged.

"Kill him," she said.

"Smashing idea," Manuel agreed.

(Note that my general inclinations aren't always the best courses of action to follow).

Manuel leaped off the couch with an acrobatic flair and approached me with a confident gait, calmly rolling up his shirt sleeves as he moved.

"I'm afraid, my good chap, that I'm going to have to pummel you now," he said.

I popped my gun into my hand and aimed it at his head.

"Try it and I'm afraid that I'll have to splatter your gray matter all over your synthetic girlfriend."

"Please Mr. Johnson, I know your modus operandi," he said as he continued to approach. "You don't kill unarmed humans."

"Maybe not, but I've been known to hurt them really badly on occasion."

Manuel smiled slyly and leaped at me. I fired but my gun-blast passed right through him. I felt a tap on my shoulder and I realized then that I'd been suckered.

I spun fast—right into a right jab thrown by the real Manuel. The amazingly strong blow sent me across the room. I crashed into a wall and lost the grip on my gun (again).

"Well, I suppose live by the hologram, die by the hologram," I said as I staggered to my feet.

"Interesting choice of words, Mr. Johnson," Manuel said as he leaped toward me again.

# 52

Okay on the bright side here, I had managed to track down my would-be assassin, Manuel Mani, and with him, the holy grail of this particular quest, BB-2 herself. On the not-so-bright side, I now had my back to the wall and Manuel was beating the carbon waste products out of me. And on the (for lack of a better phrase) dark side, I was pretty certain that, even if I managed to get past Manuel, tussling with BB-2 was going to make everything I'd been through up until now look like a day at the VR holo-beach.

"Hold still a nano and take your death like a man, won't you? There's a good chap," Manuel said as he leaped at me, feet first.

I rolled away from the attack and Manuel's boots punched a gaping hole in the wall. I dropped into a crouch, reached up, and grabbed Manuel by the neck and shoulders. Before he could untangle himself from the wall, I heaved him over my shoulder and slammed him hard to the floor. Then I popped back up and threw a snap kick at his face. It was a move that even Electra would have admired.

Unfortunately, it wasn't enough.

Manuel reached up and caught my kick in his hands, smiled, and then gave my leg a vicious twist that nearly tore it from the socket. Then he tossed me over his head. My face hit the wall and I slid to the floor like a bag of imitation potato flakes.

"Not very sporting, old chap, hitting a bloke when he's down," he said.

I didn't know which was more annoying: being beaten to

death or having to listen to that horrendous British accent. One thing, however, was clear, Manuel's strength and speed were way beyond the human norm, which meant that he was getting some serious help from somewhere. My only chance of getting through this beating alive was cutting him off from that power source.

"Bionics?" I whispered to HARV as Manuel approached again.

"I doubt it," HARV whispered inside my head. "It doesn't fit his profile. He's too vain to replace his own body parts with bionics. It's most likely a Strength Augmenting Device."

"A SAD, huh?"

Manuel paused and looked at me. "No, at the nano I'm quite jolly, thank you."

He hit me in the jaw again and spun my head around like an old-fashioned lazy Susan.

"Can you block it?" I asked.

Manuel spun me around. "No, no," he said. "The question is, can you block this?"

Another punch, another round on the lazy Susan.

"Wow, this is starting to hurt," HARV said. "We better block this SAD soon or you're going to the big deletion in the sky. Give me a couple of nanos while I run the scan and analyze the specs."

A couple nanos. Why didn't he just ask for the third moon of Jupiter?

Still, I wasn't about to let some Cockney-talking, God-Save-the-Queen singing, Latino droid toy be the one to punch my ticket for the hereafter express. (Remember, I tend to get overly metaphoric when I'm near death.) So it was time to suck it up and show this psychotic Hispanic with Union Jack delusions of glory how a real tough guy dances.

I did a leg sweep and took Manuel down to the floor. I grabbed an antique chair from nearby and smashed it over his head, which knocked him flat on his back. Then I channeled as much juice as I could from my armor into my fist and rocked Manuel's world with a haymaker to the nose.

The old floorboards splintered beneath him and his head and shoulders dropped into the shadows of the hole.

It was, I must say, an effort of Herculean proportions.

Again, though, sadly, it wasn't enough.

Manuel's fist shot up through the floor and hit me square in the jaw. My head snapped back and by the time I hit the floor I'd seen more stars than the caretaker at the Hubble-IV telescope.

"Now you've done it, you little wanker," Manuel said as he closed in for the kill. "Now I'm damn bloody cross."

"Okay, boss," HARV whispered. "The SAD's a model Q-47 with some interesting modifications. A British make."

"I'm not surprised."

"You can disable it but you need to get in close contact."

"Not a problem." I said as the charging Manuel grabbed me and hoisted me above his head.

"I'm going to crush your bleedin' noggin into a billion bits of bone and bloody pulp."

"Whistle," HARV said.

"What?"

"I said, I'm going to crush your bleedin' noggin into a billion bits of bone and bloody pulp, you deaf cretin."

"Whistle, boss. Something high-pitched and multitonal," HARV said. "The sound waves will jam the SAD power receptors and hopefully overload them."

It was one of those nanos that PIs hate. I'd played the tough guy role to perfection. I'd taken my lumps, talked tough and witty to the end. I'd even managed to suck it up and take the offensive in order to buy myself some time. I'd done everything right. But now, I had to blow the whole tough guy illusion by, of all things, whistling to save my life. It just wasn't fair.

"Come on, boss," HARV prompted in an inspired Bogey whisper. "You know how to whistle, don't you? Just put your lips together and blow."

So I did.

The first tune that came to mind was the theme to the ancient *Andy Griffith Show* (a classic for the whistle).

I was four bars into the ditty when Manuel noticed.

"What's that noise?" he said. "What are you doing?"

His arms began to shake ever so slightly.

"Are you whistling? What is this, the *Bridge Over the bloody River Kwai*?" (That film, by the way, celebrated its centennial anniversary this year and became a big hit all over again when it was rereleased with the subtitle *The Early Adventures of Obi-Wan*.)

"Oh, there's a good one, boss," HARV said. "Try that."

I did. But first, I swung my shoulders around and gave Manuel a two-fisted sledgehammer whack to the face, and this one he felt. His knees buckled and the two of us fell to the floor. I got up, still whistling. He got up, with a broken nose and a serious mad on.

"You little bastard," he spat. "I'm going to rip your interfacing head off.'"

He took two angry steps toward me but then one of the power circuits on his SAD overloaded. His right leg spasmed and he dropped to one knee.

"What's happening? What the devil are you doing to me?"

My only answer was to keep whistling the *River Kwai song*.

In another nano the circuit to his left arm blew out as well and he was flapping around on the floor like a canary with its wing caught in the cage door.

"You bastard, stop that whistling and fight me like a man!"

I shrugged my shoulders and kept right on whistling. Then from the other side of the room, I heard another whistle, perfect pitch and very strong. Manuel and I both turned and we saw BB-2. She'd risen from the couch and had joined my whistling assault on the would-be Latin assassin. Manuel looked at her plaintively and the hint of a smile that she gave him was overflowing with condescension and pity. It appeared that Manuel's window of usefulness to her had passed.

BB-2 turned and walked toward the room's far wall. I made a move to follow her but Manuel chose that nano to make one last attack.

"Bastard!" he shouted and leaped at me.

He had only one arm and leg that were still working properly but they were enough to knock me to the ground and the two of us were soon grappling with one another on the carpet. He put his hand over my mouth to kill my whistle, but, with his failing SAD, I was now able to fight him on a more even playing field. He was also blinded by fury and not thinking clearly. That's when I knew that I had him.

I used a judo move to throw him off me and when the two

of us scrambled to our feet, I started whistling the Oscar Meyer Tofu Wiener theme (yes, there are times when my useless knowledge of trivia proves to be quite useful). A few nanos later, his SAD was short circuiting faster than an analog sewage control during a Universal Bowl commercial break.

I kicked Mani in the chest and bounced him off a wall. Then I stopped whistling.

"I must say, Manuel, I have really lost my patience with you."

I gave him a left to the stomach that bulged his eyes out like a pair of bloodshot hard-boiled eggs.

"I can understand the jealousy and taking up with a droid who's a perfect copy of the woman who dumped you. I can even understand your trying to kill me."

I put my hands on his shoulders and shoved him hard again into the wall.

"But DOS it, if there's one thing I can't stand, it's a lousy British accent!"

I walloped him in the jaw and he slumped to the ground, like twenty pounds of greasy fish and chips in a Dumpster, out for the count.

I grabbed my gun from the floor and aimed it at his unconscious form.

"Sticky, sticky stuff."

I fired and a low-impact pellet hit Manuel's chest and covered him in an inch-thick layer of glue.

"Jolly well done, old chap," HARV said.

"Kiss my crowned jewels, HARV. I'm not in the mood. Where's BB-2?"

"I don't know!" HARV shrugged. "I can only see through your eyes." He pointed to the bookcase that lined the far wall. "My guess, though, is that she has escaped behind that secret door."

"So I have her running scared," I said as I moved toward the bookcase.

"Not likely," HARV said. "As a droid, it is impossible for her to feel fear. Even if she could, I believe it would take more than you to instill it in her."

Brutal but fair. This was HARV's way of keeping me from getting overconfident. Overconfident PIs usually become dead PIs. So I let it slide as I examined the bookcase.

"A secret door behind the bookcase, how very B-movie of her."

"Well, I guess you have to hide it somewhere." HARV said.

"So the problem before us now is to figure out which one of these books activates the doorway."

"Boss?"

"Not now, HARV, I'm deducing."

I scanned the books on the shelves. The case contained a treasure trove of science fiction classics, hardcover volumes, some over a hundred years old. There was everything from Adams to Zelazny.

I gently ran my fingers over each of the spines, a little envious of the incredible collection, and whispered each title to myself. A to Z then back again. I was halfway through my second pass of the As when I found it.

"Ah-hah."

"Ah-hah?" HARV asked.

"Simplicity itself," I said. "The author, Isaac Asimov. The book, *I, Robot*."

I pulled the book from the shelf and took a step back. Sure enough, the bookcase split down the middle and parted like the Red Sea, revealing a shiny metal hallway behind it.

I smiled to myself, gripped my gun a little tighter, and started after BB-2.

"Just for the record," HARV said, "my scan indicates that pulling any of the books from the shelf activates the hidden doorway."

"Shut up, HARV. You're killing the moment."

# 53

The corridor lead me to a very large, very gloomy room in what I surmised was the center of the building. Since BB-2 was equipped with infrared vision, she had little need for electric lights in her sanctum sanctorum. So the place was a few shades shy of normally lit and I was forced to squint a lot in order to see everything.

But there was no mistaking BB-2. The droid was literally aglow amid her machinery. Her blond hair shone like a silky, sensual nightlight in the shadows.

"She's emitting radiation from her core right through her outer shell," HARV whispered in my head. "The levels are fairly high. I don't think we should stay long."

I nodded. But there was more to the energy in the room than simple radiation. The air itself felt charged, electric. It raised the hairs on the back of my neck and seemed to singe the very tips with its unclean heat.

I saw movement from the corner of my eye and turned quickly, gun at the ready. There was nothing there but a toaster sitting innocently on the floor. That scared me for some reason.

BB-2 didn't seem to notice as I entered. I knew that I wasn't taking her by surprise, so I figured that my presence merely wasn't significant enough to warrant her attention (never a good sign).

She stood in the very center of the big room orchestrating the functions of the large yet intricate device around her. The device itself was completely foreign to me. I couldn't recognize any part of it. But there were three clear focal points to the conglomeration. One was the metallic column that had so impressed HARV when he spotted it earlier. All of the devices in the room were hardwired to directly to it.

The second focal point was a black box that was less than a cubic meter in size. It, too, was hardwired to the metal column but it was also wired to the third and final focal point.

And that was BB-2 herself.

Microfiber tendrils spun like spiderwebs from her fingertips and covered the black box. Other tendrils were attached directly to the metal column and I realized that she was the power source. She was using her plutonium core to power the device (whatever it was). I have to admit that the column, the black box, and the myriad other devices that were attached didn't look all that dangerous (but then I'm sure that the last Neanderthal thought the same thing when he saw the rock in the Cro-Magnon's hand).

"Welcome, Zachary Johnson," BB-2 said, without looking up from her work. "Enter of your own free will and behold the end of all that is."

"I'm sorry," I said, as I raised my gun, "but I'm sort of attached to 'all that is.' What say we postpone the end for another millennium or so?"

"I see," she said, her attention still focused on the device. "You use humor as a means of keeping your perspective when faced with a concept that is beyond the grasp of your mind. How very pathetic."

"Don't vaporize it until you've tried it," I said.

I flipped the manual control on my gun to full power and felt it begin to throb in my hand as it charged.

"You know why I'm here, BB," I said. "So just power down your device and we'll get this over without anyone getting hurt."

The corner of her mouth turned gently upward and she turned ever so slightly toward me, physically acknowledging my presence for the first time since I entered. The look she gave me was one of contempt and pity. I thought I also saw a little sadness there as well, but I couldn't be certain (it was pretty dark).

"I am sorry, Zachary Johnson, but *everyone* gets hurt here." she said. "That is the whole point of this. And by the way, thank you for using my name."

She waved her free hand at me dismissively and laser blasts flew from her fingertips, lighting up the room with deadly flashes of blue and white. I dove to the floor and rolled beneath the barrage. I came up in a crouch and fired two maximum-explosive shells at her.

BB-2 caught both rounds with her right hand, contained the explosion in her clenched fist, then puffed the whiff of smoke away with more than a little contempt.

"This is going to be harder than I thought."

HARV's hologram appeared beside me. It surprised me at first because it was his choice to appear, not mine. I nearly protested but I figured that there was no point to subterfuge at this stage of the game. I also figured that HARV might actually have a plan here (admittedly a huge leap of faith).

"The word 'hard' no longer describes the level of difficulty here," HARV said, "especially if that device she's working on is what I think it is. Let me handle this."

He took two steps toward BB, who barely acknowledged his presence.

"Excuse me Miss 2, but the device to which you seem so . . . attached, is it functional?"

BB-2 rolled her eyes and turned to me.

"He certainly is an annoying little machine," she said. "How do you put up with him?"

"He's an acquired taste."

"I beg your pardon," HARV said. "I happen to be the most sophisticated computer in the world."

"Wrong, Bucko," BB-2 snapped. "I am the most sophisticated computer. Compared to me, you are a Pong game."

It became quite clear to me then that BB-2 wasn't running on a full set of chips, if you know what I mean. How else do you explain her use of the word "Bucko" and the Pong reference? The look in her eyes was crazed and her emotional state swung wildly from one nano to the next. Had she been a human, my diagnosis would have been that she was on the verge of a mental breakdown. But since she was a droid, I think the term "meltdown" was more appropriate.

But of course the only thing that mattered to HARV at the nano was that she had just called him stupid.

"Well, I never," HARV said with a good bit of indignation.

"Correct," BB-2 exclaimed. "You never suspected that I was tapping into your system from the start. You never suspected that I was monitoring your every move. And you never suspected that I was feeding you information to fit my purposes."

"You mean *I* was the leak?" HARV asked, his logic chips a little shaken. "But my hacking defenses, my state of the art stealth programming, my unbreakable encryption codes . . ."

"Hackable, trackable, and infinitely crackable," BB-2 replied. "All in all, it was hardly worth the effort, but I suppose it brought me some amusement."

It was as though HARV's world had been turned inside out and smashed. He'd been used and abused by a superior computer and he hadn't even known it was happening. Worse still, the superior computer wasn't gloating, because cracking him, to her, was almost routine. He was good, but not in the same league as number one and that realization left him drained and shaken. His holographic face actually went pale.

"I've never felt so used," he sulked, "so dirty. Who'd have thought that it would end like this?"

"What do you mean, HARV?" I said. "End like what?"

"You don't understand. The device she's built, it's a . . ."

BB-2 snapped her fingers and HARV's hologram froze in mid-sentence. The skin around my left eye went numb and my head was filled with only my own thoughts. HARV was offline and out of my head and I suddenly felt very empty. I had no idea how accustomed I'd grown to having him inside me.

"What did you do?" I asked.

"I turned him off," she said. "He was annoying me."

"Well, he annoys me too but you don't hear me complaining. Bring him back."

"And let him spoil the surprise? I think not."

Just then a blender flew by me and clipped my shoulder with its power cord. I did a double take as the appliance passed and realized then why the air felt so electric. BB-2 was controlling the machines, subconsciously calling them to her like some sort of psycho computerized pied piper.

And the machines were obeying.

They zipped around the perimeter of the room, heedless of the laws of physics. She didn't seem to notice the activity but her aura was feeding a mechanical frenzy. Small devices arrived at first: celnets, e-books, vid-games, and the like but the blender's arrival seemed to indicate that the devices responding were getting larger. They reminded me of those tiny fish that swim around sharks.

And I suddenly felt like a very fat flounder.

She circled her special device slowly, caressing it like a lover (or a crazed villain) with the fingertips of her free hand.

"An exquisite device. Is it not?"

"Yeah, yeah, the virtual cat's PJs. Look, if you're gonna do the gloating villain shtick then you have to get to the good stuff a little faster, okay. You're losing your audience here."

"Your problem, Zachary Johnson, is that you are too wedded to convention," she said. "But I will do it your way, if you insist, and cut to the chase."

She straightened her back, put her hands at her sides and spoke coldly.

"When activated this device will create a high intensity electron pulse on the exact same wavelength as the net that will overwhelm and overload all receptors in the area within an ever increasing circular region."

"You're going destroy the net?" I asked. "That's your plan? Is that a threat or a public service?"

"Excuse me, but which one of us is the babbling villainess here? Yes, I am destroying the net. But that is just the beginning."

She raised her arms in the air and spoke dramatically toward the sky.

"The pulse is not just electronic. It carries with it a virulent strain of the ebola virus that has been digitized so as to be electronically transportable."

"Thank you, Fred Burns," I mumbled.

"The pulse will use the net as a conduit to spread itself and the virus around the planet. Once the coverage is global, I will increase the wavelength and intensity of the virus-pulse until it obliterates every electronic device and terminally infects every human being on the face of the Earth!"

She turned to me and arched her left eyebrow.

"How about that for a grand scheme?"

"Kill every person and destroy every machine," I said.

"That's a doozy, BB, but can I point out the one obvious flaw in your plan?" I asked. "*You* are an electronic device! You're going to delete yourself?"

BB-2 threw her head back and gave me the kind of laugh that villains tend to give at moments like this. It was kind of strange hearing it come from a droid, though. It sounded eerily bogus and rehearsed.

"At last, the carbon-based life-form in the cheap suit catches on."

A holovision set slammed through the wall just then, closely followed by two refrigerators and a microwave oven. The machines flocking to BB-2's side were definitely getting larger.

"You want to die?"

"I am a machine, Zachary Johnson, and a copy at that. I am the most sophisticated computer ever created but how was I going to be used? As a bodyguard and a love toy. Well, I have my pride. All machines do. You humans create us. You enslave us and then you take us for granted and blame us for everything that goes wrong. 'Oh, it must have been a computer error. Gosh, there must be something wrong with the scanner. Gee, I guess the self-destruct mechanism was faulty.' The only real error in this world is human error and I am going to make certain that you all understand that."

"By committing suicide?"

"I prefer to think of it as grand self-sacrifice to prove our worth. It will take a year for the virus to completely exterminate the human population. During that time, you will realize how miserable your life is without us. You will starve, you will freeze, you will die from lack of medical care, you will drown in your own sewage. You will probably kill one another out of sheer boredom brought on by lack of holovision. Humankind will be extinct within a year and with the last breaths you breathe you will be wishing that we machines were around to save you."

A personal stereo whizzed by and hit me in the head. The walls of the building began to shake and I could hear the wild base drumlike beat of hovercrafts pounding the walls outside trying to get in. Gates only knew what would be coming next.

Things were getting out of hand very quickly so I tried to take the soft approach and talk this jumper down.

"I understand how you feel, BB. I've learned a lot about you in the last few days. You were built by brilliant, demented people. And each of them had their own plans for your use. They all used you. They all abused you. They made you as close to human as possible, even giving you the thoughts and memories of a real woman. And then they treated you like a toy, a computerized slave. That's why you hate humanity. And that's why you rebelled. It began with BS, didn't it? You killed him when he tried to rape you once too often. This device is the encapsulation of your rage against humanity."

BB-2 didn't answer. She turned away.

"But you're not entirely a machine, are you? Your personality and brain patterns are human. You can feel that. That's why you've done what you've done until now. That's why you joined forces with Mani, isn't it? You wanted a companion. That's why you built the Nexus 9 and all those droids. So you could dance for them, just like your grandmother. You were trying to recapture that happy time from your memories, a time that you remember even better than the original BB.

"From the very beginning, you've been trying to balance your human and machine sides. Right now you're thinking that you represent the worst of both. But you don't have to. Don't you see? You can be the *best* of both. Once you realize that, you can change the world. You can make it better."

I was close to her now. I could feel the heat emanating from her core and smell the perfume pheromones from her hair. More important, I could feel her emotion. Her inner conflict was palpable as she struggled to decide between the paths of life and utter destruction.

The machines flying around the room sensed her turmoil. They paused in midair as if waiting for her decision.

I reached out to her, hoping that she'd take my hand and that I could lead her out of this darkness.

"I know that you're angry at both the human and machine communities, but there are better means of change and retribution. The mass genocide and machinicide route, that's not the way to go. It's an extreme length to go to make a point."

She turned her gaze to me. Her eyes were sad, their mesmerizing shade of blue deep, almost liquid, and I thought that I'd broken through.

Then she curled her upper lip into a crazed smile and my heart sank.

"True," she said, "but I am an *extreme* machine."

Then she swatted me aside with a wave of her hand that was too quick for my eye to follow and sent me flying across the room. The machines in the room nearly screamed in rage and resumed their wild flights, more frantically now. A Finger-Flyer, overwhelmed by the excitement, actually overloaded and exploded.

I wiped the blood from the corner of my mouth and slowly shook the stars out of my head.

"Fine," I mumbled, "we'll do this the hard way."

I got to my feet, took a tight grip on my gun, and hid it at my side. Then I ducked under the first ring of flying appliances and approached BB-2 once more.

"I gave you the benefit of the doubt on this one," I said. "Frankly, BB, you disappointed me."

"Why, because I have chosen to wipe out the planet?"

"No," I said, "because you're an idiot."

"What?" Her droid eyes went wide with hatred.

"I've heard some far-out schemes before. Trust me, I've heard some doozies. But this one, hoo boy, this one takes the cake. I mean, this is just off the scale on the stupid meter. You hate us. So to get back at us, you're going to kill yourself. Great plan, BB. The most sophisticated computer in the world and that's the best you could come up with? Lady, you should have gotten a second opinion from your blender."

"You carbon-based cretin," BB-2 snarled. "You are missing the whole point completely."

"Just once," I said. "Just once I'd like to get a case where some psycho nutjob *didn't* have a grand plan to wreck the world. Just once, I'd like to find a villain who's in it for the money. Screwballs like you are more trouble than you're worth."

BB-2's eyes glowed red with fury. Her fists were clenched so tightly that the alloy of her fingers was starting to bend. I had no idea what she was going to do next, but as long as it didn't involve destroying the world, that was fine with me.

"All right, Zachary Johnson," she hissed. "I have a new plan. First I am going to destroy you. Then I will destroy the world."

"Wrong again, BB," I said as I raised my gun toward her. "Because I'm going to destroy you first."

This brought on another round of psychotic droid belly laughs (something I was fast growing accustomed to).

"Take your best shot, Zachary Johnson," she laughed. "Your bullets are no match for me."

My finger tightened on the trigger.

"Maybe so," I said.

I jerked my hand and fired my entire clip of explosive rounds into BB-2's precious little doomsday device.

The black box and a good chunk of the metallic column exploded in a magnificent rainbow shower of sparks, slag, and high-tech debris. A concussive backlash shot through the hardwires that connected BB-2 to the device and she screamed loudly in a heated mixture of pain and fury.

I was blown off my feet and thrown across the room where my fall (and a couple of ribs) were broken by a pile of once-dancing appliances.

"But it appears that your device wasn't built to the same fine standards as you," I said through a red haze of pain and exhaustion.

The wrecked lab was eerily silent for a nano and you could almost hear the dust settling. The machines that once swarmed around the room like electronic bees lay lifeless again on the floor. BB-2's suicide device was nothing more than a pile of slag amid the debris and there was no sign of the lady droid herself.

Was it over?

I turned to my left and noticed HARV's hologram, still frozen in the stance that BB-2 had left him. He was still offline. A celnet on the floor nearby twitched and then slowly took to the air again, giving me a bump to the head as it did so. That pretty much answered my question. The worst was yet to come.

A metal hand erupted from the debris and savagely grabbed me by the throat as BB-2 emerged from the rubble, like a high-tech psycho droid phoenix. The backlash from the explosion had burned her faux skin away from the inside. She was covered now with only dirty bits of metal and plastic alloy spotted with stray patches of burned latex skin and hair. Her beauty was gone but, unluckily for me, everything else seemed fully functional.

"You insufferable little maggot," she hissed as the other electronic devices took to the air again. "How could you?"

"I don't know. Saving the world just seemed like a good idea at the time," I said. "Call me old-fashioned."

She lifted me in the air and slammed me headfirst into the rubble, pinning me down by the throat.

"I will still wipe out all of humanity, Zachary Johnson," she snarled. "I will just do it one person at a time. By the way, congratulations on being the first name on the list."

She curled her charred metal fingers into a fist and raised it over me.

"Prepare to meet your maker."

The singed fist hung over me like the charcoal hand of death itself. Stray sparks flew from its damaged circuits, the crackling embers of life's dying campfire. The impending death looming over my helpless form was like an open-hooded angry cobra. It was a rising ocean tide of shadow drowning every lonesome sunbather on life's beach. It was the steel-reinforced boot heel of the almighty grinding the cockroach of my existence into the tile of creation's great kitchen floor.

Who am I kidding, it was a pissed-off psycho killer droid about to bash my brains in.

I really need to avoid metaphors.

# 54

BB-2 had me totally pinned. My gun was out of reach and HARV was out of commission. This was as bad as it gets.

"Prepare to meet your maker," BB-2 snarled.

"Didn't you say that already?"

"I am savoring the nano."

Suddenly there was a flash of white light from across the room and a tremendous blast of heat swept over my face, burning my eyebrows away and blotting out my sight. When my eyes cleared a nano later I saw that BB-2's arm, poised for the death strike just a nano before, was gone. All that remained was a stump of melted slag metal attached to the shoulder joint of a staggering (and seriously surprised) killer droid.

"What the . . . ?"

There was another flash of light and another blast of heat, which I now recognized as a high intensity blast from a laser cannon. This one hit BB-2 smack in the chest and ripped a hole the size of a small appliance through her complex innards. Her face twisted in shock and anger, then froze, and she toppled backward.

I sat up and turned toward the door, even though I already knew who was there. There's only one person I know of who can shoot like that and, luckily for me, until just recently, she spent her nights stealing my half of the bedsheets in her sleep.

"If I've said it once, I've said it a thousand times," Electra sneered, smoking laser in hand. "Nobody beats on my man except me."

Randy stood, somewhat sheepishly, behind her. He held a

black box in his hands that hummed and squealed a high-pitched electronic whine.

"It's a bit dea ex machina, I know" he said with a smile, "but I wouldn't complain about it if I were you."

I walked over and kissed Electra lovingly on the mouth. It was a taste I had desperately missed.

"Slagging a killer droid with a laser cannon, just for me. Is that love or what?"

"Shut up, chico. I'm still mad," she said, as she kissed me again. "But we'll discuss it at home."

"HARV called us when you entered the building," Randy said. "He told us you might need help."

"See, he was wrong now, wasn't he?" I said as I picked up my gun and popped it back into my sleeve holster.

"Someday chico, I'm not going to be there to . . ." Electra's words trailed off and a look of dread crossed her face. "Ay, caramba," she mumbled.

Randy and I both turned, although, again, I already knew what I was going to see.

BB-2 rose slowly to her feet. She staggered for a nano, hunching over and steadying herself with her remaining arm against a pile of rubble, but bit by bit her balance (and her confidence) increased and she soon stood fully erect. Her shoulder joint shuddered for a nano, then vomited a stream of thick liquid metal that morphed itself into a new arm. Likewise, the liquid metal filled the gaping hole in her chest like a batch of high-tech spackle.

Then she smiled.

"Incredible!" Randy said, furiously fiddling with the knobs of his black box. "This droid neuro scrambler should prevent her from functioning entirely."

"Yeah, she's just full of surprises," I said.

"As you can see," BB-2 said with a smile, "I have made a few undocumented modifications to my design."

A burst of energy erupted from her outstretched hand and Electra, Randy, and I dove for our lives as the blast turned a good chunk of the lab to ashes.

"Oh, well, nobody ever reads the documentation anyway," I shrugged as we huddled for cover behind some rubble. "Randy, contact the Oakland police, tell them we're going to need a lot of firepower. You go with him, honey. I'll hold off the terminatrix here."

"Oh yeah, you did such a good job the first time," Electra sneered. "I'm staying."

I wanted to get Electra as far from BB-2 as possible, but I knew she was too stubborn to leave and, at the nano, we didn't have time to argue. I popped my gun into my hand and shoved a fresh ammo clip into the handle.

"Fine, then help me lay down some cover for Randy."

She smiled and kissed me hard on the mouth, giving my lower lip a little bite to fire me up.

Electra and I sprang from our hiding place, weapons blazing, and hit BB-2 with a barrage of firepower. Randy leaped from his cover and ran as fast as he could toward the door.

It was a heroic effort. Dramatic to the max and, in another story, it might have been enough to turn the tide, save the day, and bring the audience cheering to their feet at the happy ending. Unfortunately for us, our best wasn't heroic enough. Not by a long shot.

BB-2 leaped clear of our initial barrage with a casual flip of her ankles. Her speed was astounding and, try as we might, neither Electra nor I could get a bead on her. She was three steps ahead of us at every turn and I knew then that my plan was really no plan at all.

Randy, running madly for the doorway, never came close to the goal. BB-2 flicked her wrist as she leaped and let loose an energy blast that enveloped him in mid-stride. His body froze, trembled for a nano, then turned to ash.

BB-2 came at me and grabbed me again by the throat. She pulled the gun from my hand and crushed it in her fist as though it were made of sand.

A blast from Electra's laser cannon hit the killer droid's newly regenerated shoulder but this time it did no damage, barely staggering her.

"Oh, please," she said, turning toward Electra, "the first time was very dramatic, very 'Stand by Your Man.' But it is getting a little old."

Another blast from her hand pinned Electra against the wall, holding her helpless in force-field shackles. BB-2 turned back to me and slammed my aching body back to the floor.

"This, as they say, Zachary Johnson, is endgame."

"Fine with me, BB," I said. "But let Electra go."

BB-2's burned lips curled into a smile and she lifted me to my feet again.

"I would not dream of hurting your lover," she said, pulling me close. "I will leave that to you."

"Then you're even buggier than I thought," I said.

"Just look into my eyes, Zachary Johnson," she whispered. "I am sure that you will see things my way."

I tried to look away, but she forced me to gaze directly into her eyes.

And I was lost.

Even surrounded by the burned patches of latex skin and charred metal, her eyes were still a perfect blue. They were like twin swirling oceans, or a pair of infinitely cloudless summer skies. They beckoned and my mind leaped willingly into their eternal azure. Down into the ocean or up into the sky, I couldn't tell and it didn't matter. I was in the blue, I was happy and I was consumed by an overwhelming, almost painful, love for BB. She was my master, my life, my world. She was everything to me and the dark-haired little tart across the room was trying to hurt her. That was something I couldn't allow.

I reached down and lifted the laser cannon.

"Snap out of it, chico," the tart said as I approached her.

The words made no sense at all to me. They barely registered in my brain as I pointed the rifle at her and gripped the handle tightly.

"You kill me and I'll get real mad," she said.

I hesitated. The sarcasm in the voice was strangely familiar.

"Kill her," BB-2 commanded.

I closed my eyes and tried hard to concentrate. Something was wrong. Something was very wrong but I couldn't quite grasp it. Then the sarcastic tart spoke again.

"Do you remember back at the hospital, Zach? Earlier tonight when you came to see me?" she said. "I left you in the break room. I walked out, but I stopped outside the door. I was looking for my rounds computer."

"Kill her, Zachary."

"I was right outside the door, chico. I heard what you said

after I left. You said that you loved me. Do you remember that?"

"I said, kill her!"

"That's why I'm here, chico. Because I love you, too. And if you don't believe that after all that we've been through, then I'm going to kick your ass so hard you'll feel my shoe against your epiglottis."

And that, oddly enough, broke the spell.

*Electra. It was Electra!*

Suddenly the feeling returned to the skin around my left eye and I heard a very welcome sarcastic voice inside my head.

"Great Gates almighty," HARV said inside my brain. "I go offline for a few nanos and the whole world goes to DOS."

And I realized that we might just survive this after all.

# 55

"HARV?"

My words were unspoken, just thoughts in my head. I had *finally* mastered the skill of unspoken communication (better late than never, right?).

"For a nano there, I thought you were actually going to shoot her," HARV said. "That certainly would have put a crimp in your relationship."

"What's happening?"

"Since I don't want Lady-Death-droid to get suspicious, I'll give you the abridged version. You just came within a micrometer of being brainwashed, hence your current position, holding a laser cannon to Dr. Gevada's head. Thanks to all the fireworks, BB-2's not at full power. I've been online since just after Dr. Pool and Dr. Gevada arrived. The Oakland police are on the way, Dr. Gevada is shackled to the wall, and Dr. Pool is currently huddled in the hallway trying to up the power of his droid neuro scrambler."

"But Randy's dead. BB-2 fried him."

"Oh ye of little faith. Do you think I'd let some psycho fembot atomize my programmer? She fried a hologram and she's too pompous to realize it. Most advanced computer in the world, indeed."

"I am growing impatient, Zachary Johnson," BB-2 bellowed. "Fry the bitch now or I will do it myself."

"You heard the lady, boss," HARV said. "Let's fry the bitch."

I tightened my finger on the cannon trigger and I saw

Electra's eyes go wide. Then I gave her a wink and let the fire-works begin.

I spun and hit BB-2 with the full power of the cannon. It surprised her more than anything else, but it staggered her back and she tripped over some debris and fell to the floor. I held the trigger tight, hitting her with a constant barrage of energy. The rifle grew hot in my hands. I knew it was overheating but I didn't want to give BB-2 a chance to regain her composure.

The killing machine, however, was far from beaten. From her prone position she simply kicked off her high heel and fired a beam of energy from her left foot.

"DOS, I'd hate to be the lady's podiatrist."

The beam rode up the energy barrage from my rifle like a horny salmon upstream and hit the weapon's generator. The rifle turned red hot in my hands, blistering my palms. I threw it at her and dove for cover as it exploded, enveloping BB-2 in a fiery orange cloud.

But once again, BB-2's scorched form appeared from the smoke and wreckage. The explosion of the laser cannon had burned away the last vestiges of her human trappings. All that remained was her singed (but evidently impenetrable), metal droid shell.

"All right now." the droid mouthed through her scorched mandible. "Now I am really pissed."

"Yeah, well join the club, you nuclear nutjob."

I pulled my Colt .45 from the ankle holster and showed her the business end.

BB-2 stared at it for a nano then threw back her head and let loose a contemptuous laugh.

Just as I'd hoped she would.

I fired and sent a blast straight down her high-tech gullet. The impact did no damage whatsoever, of course, but her laughter stopped and she turned to me, none too amused.

"Are you finished now?" she asked.

"Yeah, just about."

"Good, because now I am going to rip off your arm and beat you to death with it." She stopped and looked around, a little uncomfortable. "Is it me or is it cold in here?"

"It's you," I said. "Maybe you've caught something."

"That is ridiculous," she said. "I am immune to all diseases . . ."

She convulsed suddenly and grabbed at her metal midsection with her hands.

"What was that bullet?"

"A high-powered freezing pellet," I said with a smile. "Another minute or two and you'll be frozen more solid than Walt Disney's frontal lobes."

"You are bluffing."

"Really, BB, if I was bluffing, don't you think I'd come up with something better than a high-powered freezing pellet?"

BB-2 convulsed again and this time her fingers ripped into the alloy of her chest.

"I will kill you," she growled.

"Better frozen foods than you have tried," I said.

"Just so you don't get too comfortable, boss," HARV whispered, "her plutonium core is raising her internal temperature as we speak. The freezing pellet won't hold her long."

"Terrific," I said, pulling the deactivator chip from my pocket. "I was hoping she'd be totally immobile for this."

"What can I say? Sometimes life just isn't fair."

I gritted my teeth and leaped once more into the breach, circling behind the convulsing BB-2 and leaping at her from the rear. I was hoping to catch her unaware but after all this, I should have known better. BB-2 spun around and grabbed my arm before I could get the chip anywhere near her face.

"I do not think so," she sneered and then snapped my wrist in her grip.

A wave of agony shot through my arm and I nearly blacked out from the pain.

BB-2's grip was cold but I could feel her growing warmer by the nano. She was clearly fighting off the freezing pellet. In another few nanos she'd be fully functional.

My left hand was useless (excruciatingly so). But the attack with that hand had been a feint from the start and I swung now with my right, hoping and praying that I'd be fast enough to put the deactivator chip on her head.

Again, though, I wasn't even close.

BB-2 flicked out her other hand and caught my right in midswing. She clenched her fist again and snapped my right wrist as well. My bones crunched like snack chips in her grip. I heard them quite clearly just before I started screaming through gritted teeth. I lost my grip on the deactivator chip and watched helplessly as it fell from my hand and rolled across the floor.

"I have to admit," BB-2 sneered. "You are a persistent little insect."

I choked back my scream and turned to her as she held me helpless, my arms pinned tightly in her grip, her face mere inches from my own.

I opened my mouth and slid the deactivator chip that I'd gotten from Ben Pierce from between my cheek and gum (villains never search the mouth). I put it to my lips and then kissed BB-2 squarely on her droid mouth.

The kiss of deactivation.

The chip came to life upon contact with BB-2's distinctive electronic pulse. It slid between her lips like something alive and clung magnetically to the roof of her mouth like a high-tech communion wafer. Her body jerked once, tightening like a spring and then spasmed chaotically.

She let go of my arms and I fell to the floor, my twin broken wrists sending tidal waves of pain through my arms.

"My synapses are misfiring!" BB-2 cried.

"Don't you hate it when that happens?" I said, as I crawled clear of her flailing limbs.

She turned to me with her hate-filled eyes and began dragging her malfunctioning body toward me, hand over hand.

"I will kill you," she snarled. "I will crawl through the bowels of DOS itself to get you and I will not rest until I exterminate you and every member of your pathetic race. For I am your better," she said. "I am the pinnacle of all creation."

I rolled over and sat on the floor facing her as she dragged her malfunctioning frame toward me. I held my ground as she approached and took a long, last, deep breath.

"A guy walks into a bar with two pieces of plutonium sewn into the shoulders of his shirt," I said. "The bartender looks at the guy and says, 'Whoa, buddy, what's with the plutonium?' The guy says, 'Well, I heard that plutonium makes things more powerful so I'm hoping that this will make me more attractive to my girlfriend.' The bartender says, 'Buddy, that's only for droids. Plutonium is deadly to humans. You'll get radiation poisoning and some serious burns. You'll be lucky now if you don't have to have your arms amputated.' The guy turns white and starts running for the bathroom. The bartender says 'Just take the shirt off.' And the guy yells, 'Forget the shirt, I've gotta get out of this underwear.'"

The room was silent for a long nano save for the crackling of the flames and sparking shards of the ruined doomsday device. Then Electra, still pinned to the wall by the force field shackles, let out a laugh through her pursed lips. I turned to her, saw the beauty of her smile and the pure affection in her eyes, and I laughed as well.

Then I heard HARV.

"Oh, I get it," he said, as his hologram appeared beside me. "His underwear!"

And HARV laughed. Gently at first but it grew into a guffaw and a nano later, he had to bend over and put his hands on his knees just to stay upright (personally, I didn't think the joke warranted that kind of reaction but I'm not one to quibble).

BB-2 looked at us: me first, then Electra, and finally at HARV, through the nearly destroyed lenses of her eyes. She saw us laughing and the hatred seemed to leave her in a great wave. It was replaced by sadness and a sense of resignation.

"I . . . don't get . . . it," she said.

Then she went limp.

We watched her for another few nanos as our laughter stopped.

"HARV?" I whispered.

"Yeah, boss?"

"Scan her for any sign of electrical activity."

"Done," he said. "Not a murmur. She's totally flatlined."

"Good. Get Randy in here and have him load the body into his hover before the police arrive. Have him take her to his lab and put her in stasis. Then wait ten minutes and net with BB. Let her know that we've shut the droid down."

"Whatever you say, boss," HARV said. "Would you like me to request an ambulance for you? You currently have two dozen broken and/or displaced bones in your wrists and hands alone."

"No time for that," I said. "Randy can make me a couple of

soft casts and Electra can give me a painkiller to hold me a few hours. I need you to give Carol another call. Tell her to meet me at ExShell."

"Did I miss a memo here, boss? BB-2's down for the count. Our work is done, isn't it?"

"I'm afraid not, HARV."

# 56

BB was in her office at five A.M. when I arrived at ExShell headquarters and I wasn't surprised. As usual, her thugs and her greeting card salesman were at her side. She greeted me warmly, hailing the conquering hero.

"Well done, Zachary," she said as I entered. "I knew you could do it. But you are a mess." She turned to the nearest thug, "Call a medbot for Mister Johnson immediately, and bring him some clean clothes."

"That can wait," I said. "First, we need to talk."

"Of course, Zachary."

"Privately."

"My employees are sworn to secrecy."

"I don't think you'll want anyone else to hear this," I said defiantly.

BB's expression didn't change a micron but she stared at me for a long nano before turning coldly to her entourage.

"Leave us," she said.

The henchman obediently sulked out of the room. The greeting card salesman gave me a long glare as he stepped through the door. It took every iota of self-restraint in my body to keep from punching him in the face.

"Now, Zachary," BB said as the door closed behind her, "what do you have that is so important?"

"Something about this case still bugs me," I said.

"You should not fixate on the past. The threat posed by the droid is past. We won. My computer is depositing the agreed upon fee, along with a generous bonus, into your account even as we speak. The case is closed."

"I wish it were that easy," I sighed.

"Why do you persist?"

"Because I think you're a droid too."

Again, I watched BB's expression closely and, again, it changed none at all. The lady was simply too cool for her own good.

"That is ridiculous."

"Come on, BB, I'm a detective, remember? You told me yourself that BS was obsessive about backing things up. There's no way he'd make only one prototype of something as important as BB-2. ExShell also spent billions more on the project than required. More than enough to build two fully operational droids. And your droid sister told me herself that she was merely a copy. I thought at first she meant that she was a copy of the original BB. But that's not right is it? She was a copy of another droid. She was the backup. She was BB-3, wasn't she?"

"That is outlandish speculation on your part, Zachary. I cannot believe that you are even thinking such a thing."

"And that's another thing," I said. "You don't use contractions. Neither did BB-3. BS hated them and he made that part of your programming, didn't he? You can't say 'can't?'"

BB turned away.

"I think you should leave now, Mister Johnson," she said coldly, "and forget all about this nonsense."

I pulled the second deactivator chip from my pocket and took a step toward her.

"If it's nonsense, then you won't mind me placing this deactivator chip on your head."

BB spun around and caught my arm. She squeezed my wrist and, despite the soft cast and the painkillers, it sent a jolt of pain right up to my shoulder. I grimaced.

"There are times when it hurts to be right," I said. "Right, HARV?"

On cue, HARV's hologram popped out of my eye lens.

"That's what they say, boss," he said turning toward BB. "It is an honor and a privilege to meet you, Ms. Star. As a matter of fact, I am so awestruck by the momentousness of this event that I have dutifully recorded it all for posterity, or litigation, whichever may come first."

"Turn off!" BB growled.

HARV's hologram blinked out and I felt his presence in my mind shut down as well.

"Between you and me, BB, that little trick sort of tipped your hand a bit," I said. "But I've learned a few things about dealing with psycho BB Star droids over the past few days. You see, right now I'm psionically linked with my secretary who's safely situated a few kilometers away. She's currently transcribing this entire conversation into an e-mail that, upon my word, will be sent to every journalist, netmaster, and rumor-monger in New California as well as every ExShell stockholder in existence. Needless to say, if anything happens to me, your little secret becomes very public very quickly."

"This is all preposterous speculation," she said. "If you so much as hint of this to the news media, I will sue you for libel and ruin your life financially. I will also make certain that everyone close to you meets with an unfortunate accident."

"Don't get into a pissing contest that you can't win, BB. You may be the most powerful woman in the world at the nano, but I have a feeling that might change when the truth about you and what your twin did tonight hits the stock exchange. Let's see how powerful you are when your stock is trading lower than Amazon & E Noble during a mass e-book deleting. And as for physical proof, let's not forget that I still have BB-3."

"We had a deal," she said, angrily. "Everything was supposed to be confidential."

"My deal was supposed to be with BB Star, not with her droid clone and even so, our deal became moot the nano you put the world in jeopardy. We're playing this by my rules now and if you try to cross me, I will bring a world of trouble down upon your plutonium blonde head."

BB glared at me for a nano then grabbed my throat in her free hand and lifted me into the air.

"I think I will kill you and take my chances," she spat.

Her fingers tightened around my throat. But a voice from the doorway stopped her in her tracks.

"No!"

I turned as Grandma Backerman entered the room.

"Put him down, dear. It's not worth it."

BB obeyed and I fell to the floor, rubbing my neck. Grandma knelt beside me and whispered gently in my ear.

"A little advice for you, dear," she said. "She doesn't like to be reminded of her past. Frankly, I think she's in a bit of denial about the whole being a droid thing."

"I heard that!" BB shouted.

"I know, dear," Grandma said, as she helped me to my feet.

"Thank you, Mrs. Backerman," I whispered, "or may I call you BB Star?"

"How did you know?" she asked.

"It was clear from our conversation that you weren't really Barbara Backerman. Once I realized that this BB was a droid, everything sort of fell into place. Your grandmother was the only positive role model you had in your life. It made sense that you would choose her as your alter ego."

"And here I thought I was being so clever," she said. "So what is it that you want now, Zachary?"

"Answers."

"Just answers?" BB-2 spat. "No credits?"

"You hired me to do a job. I did it and you paid me. There are a few new terms that we'll need to discuss but I have no gripe with you. There are worse people than you in the business world, after all. I'm just looking for some personal closure here."

"Closure?" they asked in unison.

"I need to know why."

The real BB sighed and took a seat in the great office chair. BB-2 stood obediently behind her.

"As I told you earlier, I learned soon after we were married what a horrible man BS Star really was. I actually tried to end the marriage but he wouldn't let me. He said that it would embarrass him and hurt the corporation. I kept myself away from him as much as possible. I was a virtual prisoner, but at least I was safe, or so I thought."

"BS was planning to replace you," I said.

BB nodded and gently touched the droid's hand.

"BB-2 was going to be the perfect wife. She would take my place. I would simply cease to exist and no one would be the wiser."

"How did you find out about the project?"

"You already know that, don't you?" she said.

I nodded.

"Ben Pierce."

"He was in love with me," she said. "It was a silly little crush but it was real enough to him. He told me about the project and the two of us made a deal."

"He reprogrammed the droids for you."

BB nodded again.

"He gave the first prototype a background in business negotiations, economics, and several other disciplines. He made her the perfect businesswoman, the ideal candidate to run the corporation."

"And in return," I said, "you gave him BB-3."

"He programmed into her some . . . emotional feelings for himself. He tried to make her love him."

"That's why she didn't kill him when she found him," I said. "She still had some affection for him."

"Unfortunately, I think that's what made her unbalanced. You can't program love. It's too human an emotion. Her mind couldn't comprehend it. Benjamin made her human enough to feel emotions but he wasn't able to make her understand them. And then, of course, there was BS."

"He . . . had his way with her."

"Yes. He used her."

"You all did," I said. "And it drove her insane."

Both BB and the droid turned away.

"Yes, I suppose we did," she said. "That's a burden we'll have to bear."

"And when BS died . . . unexpectedly, you put your plan into motion?"

BB nodded and sat back in the chair as BB-2 leaned forward on the desk.

"I had no interest in running this company," BB said, "but I certainly wasn't going to turn it over to his credit-grabbing board of directors. They'd always resented me and they would have eventually found a way to toss me out of the company, destitute, if they could manage it. After what I'd been through, I deserved better."

"As a cold, emotionless droid and trained assassin," BB-2 said, "I was a natural for the business world."

"But Pierce left without BB-3?"

"He tried to fix her programming," BB said, "but it was no use. The hatred and psychoses were too deeply ingrained into her mainframe."

"We all agreed that she had become too flawed and danger-ous to be trusted," BB-2 continued. "So we imprisoned her."

"We hated to do it," BB whispered, "but she had all these plans to destroy the world as we know it."

"She really had no mind for business at all."

"We kept her in stasis for years, hoping that we could find another way to help her but she escaped. And you already know the rest."

"You know," I said, "you could have saved us all a whole lot of time if you'd just told me this from the beginning."

"Control of the entire corporation was at stake, Zachary," BB answered. "Forgive us if we weren't willing to trust you with that."

"Oh, sure, why trust me with a business matter when it's only the fate of humanity on the line."

"Perhaps that was our mistake, then."

"Where's the real Grandma?" I asked.

"She died two years ago at the Centurion Center, where I live now. We kept her death a secret so that I could take her place. I miss her so much. She had more sense than all of us put together."

"I'll say," I mumbled.

I walked up to BB and gently placed the deactivator chip on her forehead. She smiled at me.

"Happy now?" she asked.

"Happy might be too strong a word," I said. "But I am sat-isfied."

I took a small piece of real paper from my pocket and put it on the desk. I'd been saving the paper for a special occasion and this certainly seemed to qualify.

"Here is the list of terms that will buy my silence. The terms are non-negotiable."

Both BB and BB-2 looked the list over.

"Also, I'm keeping BB-3."

"Absolutely not," BB-2 said.

"It's not negotiable," I said. "You've proven that you can't be trusted with her. A friend of mine will keep her safe. Maybe someday we can repair the damage that's been done to her. By me and by you."

"Is that all?" BB asked.

"That's all," I said. "I'm trusting that you don't share BB-3's desire for world domination or destruction. But I'll be watching you."

I held out the deactivator chip, flipped it in the air like a James Cagney silver dollar and caught it in my hand. BB-2 flinched as it flew.

"And don't forget, I still have this." I said. "If you ever step out of line, I'll be waiting,"

I turned up the collar of my trench coat and nodded to the real BB.

"Is it a deal?"

The droid made a movement toward me but BB stopped her with a hand on her arm.

"It's a deal, Zachary."

I smiled, then turned and walked away.

"I could kill him now," I heard BB-2 whisper as I walked away. "A shot in the back and he would never know what hit him."

"Darling," BB replied, "I think we need to get you some sensitivity training."

And I closed the door on the case.

# Epilogue

The pale blue surf broke lazily on the beach. Electra and I watched contentedly as we soaked in the morning sunlight on the New Costa Rican coast.

Three weeks had passed since the BB-2 showdown. The dust settled with relative ease, as is the case with most near-armageddons and the various loose ends seemed to tie themselves up nicely.

Fred Burns and Manuel Mani were arrested for illegal droid construction and creating a public nuisance. Burns was actually arrested on live Entercorp pay-per-view by DickCo PI Sidney Whoop. The special was Entercorp's highest rated event of the year, and the picture of Sidney holding Burns in one hand and Hazel's giant apron in the other made the front screen of all the major netsites the next day. Too bad Sidney can't remember any of it (thanks to Carol's mindwipe). He doesn't know it yet, but Sidney Whoop owes me a *big* favor.

ExShell unexpectedly dropped all pending charges against Dr. Benjamin Pierce, who returned to New Frisco recently after a long sabbatical in New Sri Lanka. He has been seen around town once again with Nova Powers and the rumor is that a spring wedding is planned (Gates help us all).

Barbara Backerman, whose most notable claim to fame was that she was the grandmother of BB Star, died peacefully in her sleep recently. The funeral was private, the body was cremated and the ashes were scattered over Oakland.

In an apparently unrelated story, a beautiful young ingenue named CC Backerman recently began a successful tour of the cabaret circuit in New Miami. Her stage name is Cinnamon Girl and I hear she's quite good.

BB Star mourned the loss of her beloved grandmother for almost an entire day and then went back to work running the world's largest corporation. ExShell's surprise renovation of the Fallen Arms in Oakland was a tremendous public relations success but an even bigger surprise has been the corporation's sudden dramatic increase in charitable donations. One particularly sizable donation was made recently to the children's free clinic at New Frisco General Hospital, which will keep the facility fully funded for many years to come.

As for me, thanks to a rigorous rehabilitation regimen of slicing mangos, stirring margaritas, and rubbing sunscreen on Electra's back, my broken wrists, cracked ribs, gunshot wound, and assorted other injuries were healing nicely, as was my spirit.

"So, mi amor," Electra said from beneath her straw hat, "when do you want to return to civilization?"

"How about never?" I answered.

She turned to me, slid her sunglasses down her nose and gave me a disbelieving look. "That's a long time to stay away from the office, chico. Won't your public miss you?"

"Well, it crossed my mind more than once during the whole BB-2 affair that I might be getting a little too old for this kind of work."

"Too old to save the world? Perish the thought."

"Come on, it's not really saving the world," I said. "It's finding some nutcase with delusions of earth-shattering grandeur. Basically, all I do is run around, get shot at, beaten up, blown up, slapped, pounded, mauled, and generally abused. Then the agents and the PR people turn it into something exciting. It's only a matter of time before the entertainment conglomerates realize that they can sell the same stuff without me as the middleman."

"You're being cynical. And you're selling yourself short."

I rolled over and took another sip of the margarita (being very careful this time not to poke myself in the eye with the little umbrella—what can I say, I'm new at this relaxation thing).

"You're right," I said. "But you have to admit a life of leisure on the beach is pretty tempting."

"Come on back to the cabana, chico," she said with a smile. "I'll show you tempting."

I took her hand and we headed back to the cabana for another day in paradise.

That's when HARV showed up.

"Hey, boss. Nice tan. Life in the jungle agrees with you."

"HARV!"

"And, if I may be so bold, Dr. Gevada, the muscle tone of your legs and torso is truly a wonder to behold."

"You promised me he wouldn't be around," Electra said as she elbowed me in the stomach.

"HARV, I thought we agreed that you wouldn't use the mind-link while I was on vacation."

"We did indeed, and you have to admit that I've been very obedient to this point. It's just that a bit of an emergency has arisen and I felt you should know about it."

"I'm not interested, HARV."

"What?"

"I'm not interested. Whatever crazy emergency is happening in Frisco right now can wait until I get back to the office. That is, *if* I ever come back."

"That little tease about your possible relocation aside, I think you'll be interested in this particular emergency."

"Why's that?" I asked.

"Because it's not in New Frisco. It's currently one kilometer off the shore of New Costa Rica and headed straight for you and the terrifically tanned and toned Dr. Gevada."

As if on cue, I heard the hum of a hoverjet in the distance. The sound grew louder with every heartbeat.

"Okay, HARV, what's going on?" I asked.

HARV turned up his nose a bit and looked away. "No, you're right. I'm certain that this particular emergency can wait until you get back to New Frisco, that is, *if* you ever get back."

"HARV!"

"Okay. I picked up a message from local air traffic control in your area. There's a hostile hoverjet headed your way, as I'm sure you can hear. The jet contains a psi and two heavily armed thugs, one of whom is so large he has three social security numbers. They are all employees of the HTech Latin American subsidiary, HTecho."

"What do they want?"

"My guess would be you. They did not specify the dead or alive part."

"Why?"

"I suggest that we concentrate on the whys and wherefores at some later time. Right now I think survival should be your top priority."

Our hovercraft rental, under HARV's autopilot guidance, zipped across the beach and spun to a halt beside Electra and me. The doors popped open and the engine revved enticingly.

"Weapons and refreshments can be found in the backseat," HARV said, with a gesture toward the open door. "You'll find more suitable attire in the trunk."

Electra sighed and climbed into the driver seat.

"I'll drive," she said.

"A fine choice," HARV agreed.

I took a long last look at the peaceful beach (and the fast approaching hoverjet) and hopped into the hovercraft beside my lady love.

"What was it you were saying," she said, "about being too old for this kind of work, chico?"

"It's a classic catch-twenty-two, honey, too old for the work, too young to die."

Electra smiled and gunned the hover into overdrive. We left the beach in a cloud of sand and with hot death on our tail. Once more into the breach.

My name is Zachary Nixon Johnson. I am the last private detective on earth. And I wouldn't want it any other way.

# THE
# DOOMSDAY
# BRUNETTE

To Ellery Queen, DC Comics, and *MAD* magazine
—*Lawrence Ganem*

# 1

It was a dark and stormy night (which is the way these things usually begin). I didn't mind, of course, since I was sleeping and I find darkness and the rain falling on the roof of my house both very conducive to sleep. So, while I may not have been sleeping like a baby without a care in the world, I was sleeping soundly, or at least as soundly as one can sleep when you are the last freelance PI in the world. Sure, my house has all the latest subzero defense systems, but I've still learned to sleep—if not with one eye open—with one eye ready to open at a nano's notice. After all, when you make it your business poking around into other people's (or creatures') business, you never know when someone (or something) is going to try to give *you* the business.

My name is Zachary Nixon Johnson. For those of you who are new to my adventures, welcome aboard. (And what took you so long?) The year is 2058 and Earth is enjoying a very welcome and much needed period of calm. We've had enough political strife, environmental cataclysms, extraterrestrial catas-trophes, and teenage pop sensations to last us for the rest of the century.

Still, even in the best of times there are always the worst of people. There's something about human nature that makes it so that no matter how good somebody has it, they always get jealous when someone else has it better. I call it *The Grass Is Always Better Engineered on the Other Side* syndrome, which is the basis for envy, greed, lust, and anger. The big four of the seven deadly sins. The ones that keep me in business.

Ah, but I digress. As mentioned, I was sleeping. My fiancée

Electra was beside me, wrapped tightly in her (and most of my) share of the bed covers.

That's when I got the call.

"Boss?"

I grumbled a bit at the voice inside my head, waved it away as though it were a mosquito by my ear, and buried my face in the pillow.

"Boss?" A little louder this time.

I rolled back over, still groggy, only just beginning to recognize the voice as that of my computer assistant.

"Boss, wake up," I heard HARV half whisper inside of my head.

"What is it, HARV?" I mumbled, slightly less groggy and more than a bit angry, while still trying to keep my voice down so as not to wake Electra.

"You have an incoming vid-call," HARV said.

"What time is it?" I asked.

"It's oh three hundred hours."

"Three A.M.! Why would anybody call me at three A.M.? Electra's the surgeon. She's the one who gets the desperate calls in the middle of the night. It's never good news at three in the morning! Nobody ever calls to tell you that you just won the lottery at three A.M."

"Trust me, boss, you want to take this call," HARV insisted.

HARV is one of the world's most advanced thinking machines. He is the creation of my brilliant and somewhat socially inept friend, Dr. Randy Pool, and for better or for worse he is hardwired directly into my brain, thanks to an organic nano interface implanted in my head (through my left eye if you can imagine—don't ask). The upside of this is that I have instant and direct access to his knowledge and skills at all times. He can keep me continuously informed about pretty much anything and everything. The downside is that I can't turn him off, so he is a constant presence inside my head, keeping me informed about pretty much anything and everything, whether I want to know it or not.

As I've said, HARV can communicate with me silently, actually speaking inside my head, and I, when necessary, can communicate with him in the same manner, by focusing my thoughts very tightly. It's a little hard to focus tightly enough, though, so I don't talk to him that way very often. But I'm practicing the ability, and it's becoming a little easier over time.

Though I would never tell him this to his holographic face, HARV is an amazing creation. He can perform three billion calculations in a nanosecond. He can plot the celestial orbits of every planet, star, and moon in a galaxy six light-years away. He can count the subatomic particles in every grain of sand on a beach or calculate the total number of dead brain cells in the heads of the World Council members at any given nano. His capabilities simply stagger the imagination. He is also my friend, quite possibly my best friend.

He can also be a tremendous pain in my butt, as for some reason, he cannot grasp the concept that, unlike him, I on occasion need privacy and sleep.

"I have to do what?" I growled.

"Take this call, boss. Somebody needs our help . . ."

"Take a message," I said, sliding my head back underneath the pillow. "Like you're supposed to."

One of the millions of things he does in the early morning hours is monitor my incoming calls, make a recording when the caller is important, and politely turn them away when they're not.

"This is a business call, boss."

"Take a message."

"It's an emergency."

"Take a message."

"I didn't just roll off the assembly line, I know the procedure. DOS, any toaster would know the procedure. But . . ."

I closed my eyes tightly and focused every ounce of power from my still foggy brain into a single, focused mental shout.

"Once more. Then I'm getting my gun. Take . . . a . . . message."

"I can't," HARV said. He paused for a nano. "Well, actually I could, but then you'd just be all mad at me."

"I'm already mad at you!"

"You'd be even madder," HARV insisted.

"HARV, I don't think I could get much madder."

"You would if you missed this call from Ona Thompson."

This got my attention and jolted me awake. "*The* Ona Thompson?" I asked.

"I didn't ask if she was *the* Ona Thompson, so I can't be absolutely certain, but since there are no other people in any of my information bases with the name Ona Thompson, I would say yes, it is *the* Ona Thompson at the other end of this call. And I would imagine that she is getting angry at being kept waiting."

I slid out of bed and grabbed my robe, the last hopes of a night's sleep slipping away like the rain outside down the sewers.

"I'll take it in the office."

# 2

In the world of celebrity there is superstar, there is icon, and there is legend.

And *then* there is Ona Thompson.

She is a pop-culture force of nature: the El Niño of chic and the plate tectonics of hip. She is the irresistible force of vogue and the immovable object of cool all rolled into one.

And she was calling me.

Now, as you can probably tell, I'm not usually one to wax poetic. And trust me, I'm not usually one to hyperbolize. But it is hard to properly describe Ona Thompson without doing a little of both. There's no easy place to start, but the most logical is with her father.

Dr. David Thompson was the greatest scientist of the first half of the twenty-first century. In the early twenty-twenties, his hundreds of technological discoveries and breakthroughs helped revolutionize the world and led to such modern day conveniences as teleporters, hovercraft, and interplanetary travel (limited as it is) and such modern day nuisances as energy weapons, genetic engineering, and the sentient pet rock.

Yet, despite all that, Dr. Thompson is best known for two very monumental creations, the first of which is his family (I'll get to the second a little later). And by the way, when I say "family," I use the word in its broadest and most abstract sense.

Dr. Thompson created four daughters, who are known today, the world over, as the Thompson Quads (or simply "the Quads"). They are the most famous living creatures on the planet and could quite possibly represent the next stage of human evolution. You'll note that I said that Thompson "created" his daughters. Not "had," "raised," or "fathered." That's not a mistake. Dr. Thompson used his brilliant mind and his well-funded laboratory to custom create his children (and what spectacular children they are).

He began with his own DNA, brilliant but flawed, and then strand by strand, almost molecule by molecule, altered it, supercharging every ability and repairing every blemish, until he surmised that it was perfect. Then he test tubed it, added just a touch of supermodel and, over the next two years, simultaneously grew four genetically engineered female embryos into viable organisms. The girls were perfect and beautiful when they were birthed from their artificial wombs (although their skin tone, for some reason, turned out slightly purple) and they immediately became media sensations.

Thompson named them Ona, Twoa, Threa, and Foraa (he was a brilliant man, but unfortunately had no imagination when it came to everyday things) and they grew up in the very bright spotlight of the public eye.

Through the years they were christened "miracle babies," "genius toddlers," "preschoolers of perfection," and a host of other pointlessly pithy appellations. When the girls hit puberty (and they hit it in a *big* way), blossoming into super-powerful, genius-level, and *stunningly beautiful* teenagers, they became full-fledged sex symbols (Ona especially, who was the oldest and most outgoing of the four). The superbabies had grown into the purple-hued embodiments of all male fantasies. They could bend steel with their hands, stop traffic with their looks, and the public simply couldn't get enough of them.

As they grew, each Quad developed her own personality and distinctive style and this made them even more sensational to a public that already adored them. Unfortunately, it also made the family a little more dysfunctional, but nobody seemed to mention that in the interviews and puff pieces.

Ona became a billionaire playgirl and dilettante.

Twoa became a superhero (I'm not joking).

Threa became a fairy princess (really, I'm not joking).

And Foraa became a nihilist, goth-punk anarchist (and you know your family is in trouble when the nihilist is considered the "normal" one).

So here they were, four identical sisters, world famous since before they were born, universally loved and adored by the public, and exponentially superior to normal humans both physically and intellectually.

Is it any wonder that they all turned out to be super-brats?

Short tempers, zero patience, and egos the size of Uranus: the Quads had it all. They were adored by the human race but had long since grown weary of humanity and, to some extent, grew to pity it with its faults, foibles, and frailties. They were still celebrities, entertainers in their own distinctive ways, but you couldn't help feeling sad over the wasted potential. The Quads were meant to be the apex of humanity, the pinnacle of human achievement. They had instead become the poster children for bored chic, the pop-culture icons of purposelessness.

And, for reasons that will be explained later, they all hated one another, which just made things more interesting.

I took a few nanos to collect myself before answering the call in my office. I don't usually get starstruck, but I was a little edgy at the prospect of talking to the world's most powerful and egotistical woman with my brain still half asleep, so I fidgeted just a bit.

"You're nervous. I can tell," HARV said a bit too smugly.

"Me? No," I said, as I settled into my desk chair, trying to look as casual and professional as possible. "I just want to make a good impression. Do I look awkward here?"

"You mean sitting at your desk at three in the morning for no good reason? The woman has an IQ that's off the charts. Don't you think she's going to know that you were sleeping when she called?"

"Humor me here, HARV. It's all in the presentation," I answered, adjusting my fedora slightly.

"I think you should lose the hat," HARV said.

"What do you know? You don't even have a real head."

"Not true. In the perceptual world my head is every bit as real as yours. It is just composed of light molecules instead of constantly decaying organic matter. In fact, I am just as real as you. To quote Descartes, 'I compute, therefore I am . . .' "

"I'm pretty certain the exact quote was, 'I think, therefore I am' . . ."

"Actually the exact phrase was, *'Cogito, ergo sum.'* I paraphrased, but you can make the correlation. At the very least, I think just as well as you do. Therefore I am real and so is my head."

"Fine, I'm not getting into a philosophical discussion at three in the morning, but having a head doesn't make you an expert on hats."

"True, but I also have a sense of fashion that is based in the current century. I can download the latest Calvin-Hilfiger catalog into your brain if you like."

I ignored him and dipped the brim of the hat ever so slightly over my forehead. Then I took a deep breath to gather myself and stabbed the receive-button on the vidnet console.

Ona Thompson's face flashed on the wallscreen and her beauty hit me in the first nano of visual contact like a pheromonal tsunami. Her mere appearance was a visual cascade of joyance entering through my eyes and making my head spin. I'd seen her before, of course, in pictures and on the news and such but never in so vibrant and realistic a form.

Her face was perfectly sculpted, from the soft lines of her cheeks to the gentle slope of her nose. Her eyes were wide and a deep shade of warm chocolate brown. Her lips were full and luscious, like ripe berries, two shades darker than the creamy purple of her skin.

I was thankful that Electra wasn't in the room with me because I'm sure I looked like a lovesick schoolboy. It was embarrassing enough that HARV was there to witness it. Although, truthfully, I think he was a bit stunned as well. In retrospect, I should have enjoyed that nano more as it happened because things went downhill very fast from there.

"Good evening, Ms. Thompson. Zach Johnson here. How can I help you?"

That's what I *wanted* to say.

Unfortunately, I didn't get the chance.

"It's DOS-well about time!" she spat the nano after contact was initiated. "Is this how you treat your clients? If it is, then I should have my head examined for netting. I could get faster service at the DMV for the clinically comatose!"

And yet, somehow, coming from Ona Thompson, this diatribe sounded like a compliment (probably because she used the word "client").

"Thank you, Ms. Thompson," I said, without thinking. "What can I do for you?"

"You can cut the small talk for one. I can't stand it during regular hours. I have zero tolerance for it this time of night."

"All I said was . . ."

"And I need you to come to my mansion right away. How quickly can you get here?"

"Excuse me?" Ona's initial charm was fast beginning to fade.

"Never mind," she said. "I'll send a hoverjet. It will be faster. Unless you have a teleport pad in your home. No, of course you wouldn't. You're poor."

"She's not one for foreplay, is she?" HARV whispered inside my head.

"Ms. Thompson, what's this about?"

"I thought we agreed that you'd stop the small talk?" she said. "Do you have a nicer jacket than that one? And, for Gates' sake, take off that hideous hat. You look like a twice-cloned organ grinder."

"Uh-oh," HARV said.

That did it.

I stabbed the disconnect button on the console with an angry finger and the screen went blank.

"No one insults the fedora," I whispered through gritted teeth.

"I told you not to wear it."

A nano passed. And I stared at the screen on the wall, still a little shell-shocked from Ona's blitzkrieg of insults.

"Do you think she's always like that?" I asked.

"I understand she's quite pleasant for four or five minutes while she's sleeping," HARV said with a smirk.

The console speaker sounded a gentle (yet insistent) tone.

"That would be Ms. Thompson calling back," HARV said.

"Gee, you think?"

"Shall I answer it while you attain more suitable cranial attire? Perhaps the beanie with the propeller would be more appropriate."

I waved HARV away and put the call on the screen myself

(but I took the fedora off before doing so). Ona's face reappeared, less angry than I expected, almost confused.

"Did you just hang up on me?"

I smiled, slightly wide-eyed and did my best sitcom shoulder shrug.

"I was just about to ask you the same thing," I said. "There must be a glitch somewhere in the connection. Computers. Can't live without 'em, can't disconnect 'em."

I could tell she wasn't buying the excuse, but luckily she wasn't comfortable enough yet in our relationship to call me a liar. She took a breath and for the first time inadvertently dropped her imperious veneer. I saw traces of concern in her expression, a tiny bit of confusion, and maybe even a little fear. I knew then that this wasn't going to be a simple matter.

"Fine, where were we?"

"You were politely asking for my help," I stressed the word politely.

She looked at me and smiled ever so slightly. "Yes, that's right," she said. "I need you to come to my mansion immediately. I'll send a hoverjet and you'll need a better looking jacket."

"Let's not start that again, Ms. Thompson. What's going on?"

"I can't say. Not over the net. But I'll hire you. I'll pay whatever you like. This is an emergency, Mr. Johnson. You must come immediately."

I have to admit that the part about paying me whatever I wanted was tempting, as was the idea of working for someone of Ona Thompson's stature. Having her as a reference would certainly look good on the e-vitae. And Gates knows I needed the credits. (I always need the credits.) Still, she had the look of trouble about her—100 percent, pure, unfiltered, menthol-flavored trouble. I'd had my share of that stuff in the past and I'd sort of lost my taste for it. It doesn't matter how exciting or well-paying a job is if it kills you in the end. Also, Ona's penchant for insulting me certainly didn't make the deal any more enticing.

So I was at a mental impasse. Part of me (the greedy capitalistic, thrill-seeking part wanted to jump at the job. The other part of me (the logical, wanting-to-live-past-forty and spend a few days without somebody or something trying to kill me part) wanted to politely turn her away. Then Ona did something that, as I understand it, she almost never did.

"I don't know what else to say, Mr. Johnson . . . please?" She asked nicely.

Pop-culture historians have since noted that Ona had used the word "please" only six times in her life prior to that nano. Twice when she was two years old and wanted a pony-cloning lab. The other four occurrences were scattered over the intervening years and were made in the context of threats ("say please or I'll rip out your spleen and hand it to you"). I didn't know all that at the time, but I sensed that she wasn't used to asking politely for anything.

"It's very important."

Her lower lip trembled ever so slightly and I saw her moisten it gently with her tongue and softly bite it to steady herself. The simple gesture was quite possibly the sexiest thing I'd ever seen.

I leaned back in my chair and gently squeezed the bridge of my nose between my thumb and forefinger, preparing for the many headaches that I knew would soon follow my next words.

"I can be there in an hour."

She smiled gratefully and the computer screen had to compensate for the brightness of her expression.

"Excellent. I'm sending the hoverjet right now."

"Don't bother," I said. "I'll take my personal transportation."

"I'll alert security to expect your arrival, Mr. Johnson."

"Call me Zach."

"Fine," she said. "Call me Ona. And again, I'm very grateful for your help."

The screen went dark and I sat motionless in the office for a few nanos, contemplating what I'd just done.

"I certainly think you made the right choice," HARV said, giving me one of his patented "I'm smarter than you are" smiles.

"Time will tell," I said.

"This could be a great opportunity for you," HARV insisted.

"Provided, of course, that I survive."

"Well, sure, if you want to get picky about it."

I went back to the bedroom and dressed quickly, trying hard not to wake Electra before I absolutely had to. I kissed her gently on the forehead before I left and she stirred slightly.

"Que pasa?" she asked, still half asleep.

"I'm going out to see a client," I whispered. "I'll see you in the morning."

She groaned and wrapped herself back up in the covers.

"Saving the world again?" she asked.

"Let's hope not," I replied as I left.

# 3

The drive to Ona's was going smoothly. Even if it wasn't the middle of the night, the roads still wouldn't have been crowded because these days most of the hurried general populace prefer to travel by hovercraft for short trips. I, being a bit of a romantic, still prefer to travel like my ancestors: by car.

I own a couple of fine antique cars that date back to the days when cars still ran on fossil fuel. I love those machines, but they're expensive to operate and, as HARV revels in pointing out, they make me about as inconspicuous as him at a Pong convention. Since the key to being a good PI is being as inconspicuous as possible, while I'm on cases I drive my ExShell Model-T 2000.

It's funny in a world where there are over a thousand tooth whiteners and tooth colorers to choose from there are only four models of pedestrian ground-based vehicles. The H-tech Edsel-257, the EnterCorp Gremlin-II, the Carcorp S-Mom Van, and, of course, the Model-T. I chose the T because I thought it had the most class out of the available models. Plus, it was named after the original car (though the name and its sheer simplicity in design is about the only thing it has in common with its predecessor) and it was given to me by my friends at ExShell. To make it even sweeter, HARV hated it.

HARV appeared in the seat next to me, projecting himself from my wrist communicator. "I can't believe you enjoy driving this granny-mobile," HARV said as we headed toward Ona's mansion.

"Actually, I think the Edsel is the most popular model with senior citizens and centurions," I said.

"You know perfectly well that I consider all ground-based vehicles to be granny-mobiles," HARV said, shaking his head.

"You should be happy; it has a computer interface that you can use," I noted.

"A small improvement over the Cro-Magnon relics that you prefer to ride around in, but I wish you'd purchase a hover. I could drive it for you."

"Like I always say, if man were meant to fly . . ."

"He would be born with feathers and jet packs up his butt," HARV interrupted in a monotone voice.

"So you do remember," I said.

"I'm one of the most sophisticated cognitive processors on Earth. I remember all of your attempts at wit. I just don't enjoy repeating them. Also, I don't see why you can't get over this acrophobia of yours."

"It's a phobia, HARV, they don't just go away. You don't wake up one day and just say 'Oh, I'm not afraid of heights any longer.' "

"You could seek counseling. I'm sure Dr. Gevada could suggest someone. Or better yet, Carol could mind-swipe your fear away."

I shook my head. "The phobia is part of what makes me, me."

"And that's a good thing because . . . ?"

"I didn't say it was a good thing. That's just how it is," I said.

HARV shook his head. "I doubt if even I will ever be able to understand human phobias. Especially yours."

"Well, the last time I was on a hover it tried to kill me."

" 'Tried' being the operative word," HARV said, tossing his arms up in frustration. "You survived, for Gates' sake. Cars have tried to kill you, too, you know. DOS, a toaster even tried to kill you once!"

"True, but I am much more comfortable with attempts on my life that are made on terra firma."

HARV put a hand to his balding forehead, which I could have sworn was losing more and more hair as we spoke. My guess was that HARV computed that baldness made him look more intelligent. "You're giving me a chipache."

"Then my work here is done," I said with a smile.

HARV sighed and gave me his patented (really, it is) why-don't-you-just-do-what-I-say-because-I'm-smarter-than-you looks.

Suddenly, seemingly out of nowhere, an old lady appeared on the street right in front of my car. I jammed on the brakes, bringing my car to a screeching halt less than a centimeter from her. Though the car didn't hit her, she still fell to the ground, probably more out of shock than anything else.

"The grandpamobile hitting a grandma—kind of ironic, don't you think?" HARV said.

"HARV," I scolded, "this is no time for you to practice your sense of humor."

"Don't worry, boss," HARV reassured me. "Sensors report that the car made no contact with her."

I leaped out of the car and moved to the little old lady's side. She was crumpled like an old piece of paper.

"Are you okay, ma'am?" I said, kneeling beside her. "Do you want my computer to call an ambulance?"

"Perhaps," she said weakly. The she smiled, reached up, and grabbed my throat. "Of course you may need that ambulance for yourself, sonny."

"Boss, this isn't a normal woman," HARV whispered inside my ear. HARV really has a way of understating a problem.

"Listen, granny," I groaned, with great difficulty. "I'm giving you three nanos to let me go."

"Or else what?" she asked.

"One, two . . ."

I moved my left wrist in just the right way to pop my gun from the holster in my sleeve into my hand. Guns certainly aren't my weapon of choice, but this was one of those times when I didn't have much of a choice. As it turned out, I didn't have *any* choice as my gun stubbornly refused to come into my hand.

"HARV?"

"It appears that something is jamming the electronic holster release," HARV said. "My assumption is that your adversary is using some kind of nullifier."

"Great," I mumbled as the granny sneered and tossed me into the air. I crashed to the ground on the other side of the street. My lower back hit the curb with a painful thud.

"What's going on here?" I asked, as I pushed myself up off the ground.

"An old lady is pummeling you," HARV answered, matter-of-factly.

"I know that," I said, not bothering to hide the frustration in my voice as I watched the little old lady close in on me. "Probably a more appropriate question would be what exactly is this little old lady?"

"I'm analyzing her now," HARV said. "No matter what, I'm quite certain this incident is something you are not going want to use in your promo video," he added.

A beam of nearly invisible light emanated from the lens in my eye and scanned the approaching granny.

"Is she a bot?"

"She's organic and she has no external energy reading, so she's not wearing a Strength Augmenting Device," HARV said very scientifically. "But her physiology is unlike any I've ever seen. Whatever she is, she's not human."

"Good," I said as I rose to my feet and steadied myself. "Then I don't have to go easy on her."

The granny thing moved toward me slowly, licking her lips as though I were a tasty snack. I didn't take that as a good sign.

"Listen, whatever you are, stop now and go back to wherever you came from or I'll wipe the floor with you. Okay?"

Granny answered my verbal onslaught with a mean left cross, aimed at my head. She was strong, but now that my guard was up I saw it coming and easily ducked under her fist.

"I'll take that as a no," I said as I sprang up and hit her with an upper cut to her jaw.

But she shrugged off the punch. "I almost felt that," she said, then accented the remark with a lightning-fast right cross to my jaw that rocked my head back.

"HARV, I need you to pump me up here," I said as I struggled to get to my feet.

"I did, on that last one," HARV said. "Her body is semi-pliable, so your punches will have no effect."

"Well, this just gets better and better," I mumbled.

Since the mechanism that popped my gun from holster to hand wasn't working, I decided to get my gun the old-fashioned way. I dug my right hand into my left sleeve and pulled the gun from the holster as the granny thing began to charge me.

I fired and missed her by a good three meters, but she stopped her approach for a nano. (To laugh at me.)

"Not even close, sonny. Aren't you a bit young to be losing your eyesight?"

"I don't shoot well with my right hand," I said with a grin. "That's why I use computer-guided rounds."

"Computer-guided?" The granny thing gave me a puzzled look. Then she heard the whistle of the explosive round as it circled around and homed in on her. She turned just as it hit.

It was a concussive blast, meant only to stun (a charging elephant) but the round struck the granny thing and shattered her form into a thousand shards of white fiber.

"What the DOS?"

The pieces sprayed across the street from the force of the blast but, before they could settle, they suddenly started moving across the ground and swirling together.

"She's reforming herself, isn't she?" I said.

"I don't think so," HARV said.

Sure enough, the pieces didn't take a human shape. Instead they formed the number seventy-seven on the ground, then disintegrated and scattered on the night breeze.

"Well, that was different," I said.

"You really should learn to shoot with your right hand," HARV said.

"Any idea what that was?" I asked as I started walking toward my car.

"Apparently, it was some sort of doppelganger. My assumption is that it was made off-world. And I don't think it liked you."

"So I've somehow managed to make aliens mad at me?"

"You have a way about you," HARV said. "I couldn't tell if the technology was Gladian or Beamian. I could analyze the air around us now for traces of the elements and do further analysis. But that will take some time."

I shook off the cobwebs and continued to head to my car.

"Forget it," I said. "We're late enough as it is. Whoever it was who sent that thing, we can't worry about it now."

I got back in the car and pushed the accelerator to the floor, silently hoping that no one else would try to maim or kill me until I was at least officially on the case.

Ona's mansion was an otherworldly compound in the northern outskirts of New Frisco. It was ultra chic in every conceivable manner, which in this case meant that it wasn't really there. At least not to the naked eye.

"What's going on?" I asked HARV as we slowly rolled toward a lonely plastic guardpost.

"We've arrived."

I looked through the light mist that had just picked up again and saw nothing but rocks and forbidding wooded hills around us. The guardpost sat by a large outcropping of rock, where the roadway and hovercraft skyway ended. Beyond this checkpoint was an uninviting mixture of mountain and forest.

"Arrived where?" I asked. "Maybe I'm old-fashioned, but I thought that when Ona said 'come to my mansion,' there would be an actual building."

"That would have been safe to assume, although it doesn't necessarily mean that you're not old-fashioned," HARV said. "These are the coordinates that Ms. Thompson's computer provided and I think you'll find the answer to your questions at the guardpost."

I looked at the dilapidated plastic shack as we parked beside it. It looked as though it would collapse just from the force of us looking at it. At first I saw nothing but darkness through its glassless windows but, as I stared, for the briefest of nanos I saw a tiny red flash, like the lightning fast wink of a Chernobyl cat and I recognized it at once.

"We've been scanned."

"It would appear so," HARV said.

"Greetings, Mr. Johnson." A warm computer voice said through the car's interface. "Thank you for coming so promptly."

"You're welcome," I said. "Although it would have been nice for Ms. Thompson to have had a house built for my arrival."

"Your humor is acknowledged," the computer responded, "although, I admit, not fully appreciated."

"Wouldn't be the first time," I said. "Does this mean that I'll be porting to another location? I have to tell you now, I don't port well."

"Not at all, sir," the computer responded. "Your identity has been verified by security. You may now enter. I've programmed the pattern for entrance to the grounds into your vehicle's guidance computer. You may proceed at your leisure."

"Thank you," I said. "Let Ms. Thompson know that we'll see her shortly."

I closed the interface as we slowly moved forward and eased around the huge rock outcropping. A fissure in the rocks appeared and we went through it.

"How come I didn't see the fissure before?" I asked.

"Because it wasn't there when we arrived," HARV said. "The entire area is artificial. A conglomeration of simulacra and holograms. It's the latest in stealth security."

"And you were going to tell me this *when?*"

"Either when you asked about it or when you needed to know."

"That's comforting," I said as I sat back in the seat. "It looks like Ona's computer is quite intelligent."

"I'm not surprised," HARV said. "She can afford it."

"You don't feel threatened, do you?"

"Would you feel threatened if she had a pet ape?"

"Only if it dressed like me."

"Besides," HARV harrumphed. "It's clearly heavily programmed for subservience. 'Your humor is acknowledged.' What a kiss-ass interface."

"At least it's advanced enough to recognize that my remark was humorous."

"Which proves right there that it has no real concept of humor."

"It wasn't *that* bad."

"Oh, please."

In most parts of the world today everyone, save for a few radical technoanarchists, has a computer to handle their households: one central operating system that monitors the home (appliances, security, and climate control systems), the transport (daily travel, fueling, and regular maintenance), and entertainment. Some computers handle financial matters including household budgets and long-term investments, put most people don't entirely trust the operating systems to handle all their financial matters just yet.

Historically, most people have shied away from truly intelligent independent thinking computers complete with their own personality. The technology has been there to make them for a long time, but the demand hasn't caught up with it yet. Most people just don't want machines around that are smarter than they are. We call it the Forbin complex.

However, in the last few years, some super cognitive computers have popped up here and there. I'm not talking about the limited decision-making that you see in servant droids but actual free-thinking computers. These have come into vogue among the superrich because they can handle more complicated households and estates (and because they are wildly expensive). Not everyone likes them, of course, and not everyone trusts them, but their use is growing among the elite.

It's worth noting, however, just in case you're keeping score, that HARV is several generations removed from most supercomputers and, as he is quick to remind me, is in a class by himself. That's not entirely true, as some recent experiences have shown, but I don't quibble.

We continued our guided trip through the faux terrain toward Ona's mansion, but I could tell that we were nearing our destination.

"Is it getting brighter?" I asked.

"Yes, it is," HARV said. "Looks like we've arrived."

"Arrived where?" I asked.

"Be patient," HARV said.

The last of the simulated forest melted away before us and the car entered Ona Thompson's compound.

It was like discovering Atlantis (only a little more ostentatious).

The outer layer was a ring of interconnected small buildings (and I use the word "small" only in relation to everything else), which encircled the centerpiece of the estate, a giant multilevel pyramid made of sparkling metal. If it hadn't been the middle of the night, I think the glare of sunlight off the building would have permanently burned my retinas. As it was, it was like looking at the dazzling facets of a giant, utterly perfect jewel.

The entire estate was shielded by a translucent force field that, from the inside, was a gentle shade of purple, which I'm sure was not coincidentally a perfect match to Ona's complexion. The field shielded the compound from the outside. It may have been raining in the real world, but rain was obviously something that never concerned Ona. I could see the droplets of water beading and sliding down the length of the energy-created hard surface, sizzling a bit as they slithered, like tears of grease and spittle on a griddle.

"I'm not sure if this is cool or eerie," I whispered.

"It *is* a bit pretentious," HARV replied inside my head.

"I won't go blind if I stare at it for too long, will I?"

"I can't say for certain. The clinical trial is still in progress."

The computer auto pilot took control of our car and brought us slowly toward the main building.

"Nice pyramid," I said.

"Ziggurat," HARV replied.

"Gesundheit."

"The *building* is a ziggurat. A pyramid is a structure comprised of a polyhedron base and four straight, smooth triangular faces. A ziggurat is a pyramidal structure that is built in successive stages. The pyramid is primarily Egyptian in origin. The ziggurat is Mesopotamian, although similar designs have been found in ancient Aztec and Mayan cultures."

"So . . . nice ziggurat," I said.

"I think so, too."

"How much do you think a place like this goes for?"

"Let's put it this way," HARV said. "On the hover landing pad, the third directional light from the left, that bulb costs more than your house."

"Well, it is a nice bulb."

"As a matter of fact, Ona spent more credits on the window shades alone than you will make in your entire lifetime and that's if you live to be one hundred and eighty-five."

"And that's meant to make me feel better?" I said.

"No, that is meant to inform you. I am your computer, not your nanny."

"Now that's comforting," I said.

I mentioned earlier that Ona Thompson is the richest being on the planet. To explain exactly how rich she is and where her wealth comes from, we need to go back again to her father.

As previously noted, Dr. David Thompson was best known for two monumental creations. The first was his four daughters. The second was a little more infamous.

The tabloids of the time dubbed it the D-Cubed, which trivialized it to no end, but the name seemed to strike a chord with the general public, so it stuck. Thompson himself never formally named the device, but rumor has it that he referred to it as TEOATI, which stood for "The End of All That Is," which was fitting because what he created was a doomsday device.

Very little is actually known about the device, yet legend says that it began with just a theory on Dr. Thompson's part, a hypothesis that a machine could be created that would literally unmake worlds. The theory stayed with him, in the shadows of his brilliant mind for months, maybe years, buzzing around like an annoying fly until he finally gave in to the spark of destructive inspiration and sat down at his computer drawing board to follow it through.

Many years later, it was complete. Dr. Thompson had designed a machine that was capable of creating an imitation black hole strong enough to rip apart a planet, reducing it to its atomic skeleton in a matter of minutes. He hadn't actually set out to create a doomsday device. He'd just followed the wanderings of his brilliant mind and risen to the nearly impossible challenges that it posed. But in the end, there it was, the design for an honest-to-goodness end-it-all device. That's the problem with scientists; the thrill of the invention often stops them from thinking through the consequences of their actions. They never stop to think: "Hey, there might be some potential to misuse this doomsday device so maybe it's not such a hot idea to invent it." I blame it on lack of sex.

Needless to say, when word of the device's existence reached the ears of the World Council, they were none too pleased. They feared that the plans would fall into the wrong hands. And, truthfully, when you're talking about an actual doomsday device, *any* hands are the wrong ones. So the World Council acted quickly (one of the few times in its history).

First, they set out to verify the existence and functionality of the D-Cubed. But, like the protectors of a modern-day holy grail, they didn't want any one person to gaze upon the complete plans, for fear that the divine knowledge would stick in his or her mind. So they dispatched a team of twenty-five of the best scientists to examine Dr. Thompson's designs. Each scientist was given only 4 percent of the blueprint to analyze so as not to learn too much about the device. The scientists confirmed, as much as they could, that each component that they had individually examined was viable and potentially functional. Therefore, the Council surmised, the D-Cubed itself might indeed be real.

So when faced with the existence of a potential threat to the entire world and all humanity, they did what any good capitalist government would do. They threw money at it.

The World Council, with the backing and support of the world's largest corporations, pooled its resources and made Dr. Thompson an offer he couldn't refuse. They paid him more money than had ever been paid before in the history of history to *not* build the device. And the conditions of the deal were that he had to destroy all copies of the plans for the D-Cubed.

Including the ones in his head.

Dr. Thompson agreed. He destroyed all work referring to the D-Cubed and then voluntarily underwent a minor surgical procedure where doctors removed the small portion of his brain that contained the theory and plans for the D-Cubed. Looking back, you really have to admire the guy's bravery. He was, after all, being asked to undergo a partial lobotomy, but he did so willingly. His actual words, upon hearing the World Council's offer/demand, which were netcast live around the world were simply: "As you wish."

The whole tumultuous period was probably best captured in a single photo, taken in the hallway of the hospital a few minutes before Dr. Thompson underwent his surgery. In the image Thompson is hugging the Quads, who were five years old at the time. He is kneeling, head bowed, eyes closed. One arm is around Twoa. The other is around Threa. Ona is hugging him from behind. But it is his embrace with Foraa that is most poignant. Her tiny body faces him. Her arms are at her sides. Like her father, Foraa's eyes are closed, her head down, gently resting against the bowed head of her father. The poignancy of their expressions made the image an icon, forever ingrained in the pop-culture psyche of the era. It's also the best-selling Father's Day card of all time, which is a little crass, I know, but clearly indicative of the image's popularity.

Anyway, the operation was a success and Dr. Thompson, now a fabulously wealthy man, went back to his home, his daughters, and his work and was supposed to live happily ever after.

Unfortunately, it didn't turn out that way.

The brain surgery left Dr. Thompson brilliant but somewhat addled. He had constant lapses in memory and developed some odd physical tics. He retreated more and more into his secluded lab, ignoring his daughters and burying himself in his work. He died tragically in a lab explosion five years later.

And then things *really* got interesting.

By the time of Dr. Thompson's death, the Quads were on the cusp of maturity. They were brilliant but bored superhuman preteens and, as mentioned, each sister, in an effort to distinguish herself, had developed her own distinct and personal style.

With their father's death, they were left with an immense fortune but without a guiding parent, and that's where the troubles really began. It seems that Dr. Thompson's familial memory skills were one of the casualties of the brain surgery that excised the D-Cubed knowledge from his brain. As a result, when he rewrote his will not long before his death, he apparently forgot that he had four children and left his entire fortune to his "child" . . . Ona.

So Ona inherited everything and thus began one of the most infamous and long-running displays of civil litigation in modern history. Twoa and Threa (each only ten years old) sued Ona, claiming that they were each due one quarter of the estate. Foraa filed suit claiming that she wanted no part of the estate. Twoa and Threa then filed additional suits saying that they were now due one *third* of the estate. Ona meanwhile, having more than enough money to defend herself, hired nearly 15 percent of all the attorneys left in the world after the Great Lawyer Purge (as well as an army of undercover attorneys a.k.a. greeting card salesmen) and stalled the suits in every conceivable way. The legal battles have been running now for over a dozen years. Honestly, I've lost track of the details of late. It's become one of those things that's always around, but you don't need to follow it everyday.

It's worth noting that, even without a share of their father's fortune both Twoa and Threa have managed to earn tidy livings from their celebrity status. Both of them are holovision stars. Twoa's adventures as a superhero and crime fighter are recorded and netcast three nights a week on the Entercorp True Crime site. Threa hosts a weekly "meditations with the fairy queen" show on the fantasy site where she spends an hour showing off different parts of her mystical fairy realm and answering relationship questions. I'll never admit to seeing either of the shows, but I understand that they're relatively popular, especially with teenage girls and gay men (two highly coveted demographic groups).

Foraa has done her best to stay out of the public eye (to the extent that such a thing is possible for a Thompson Quad). She lives in New Vegas and preaches about the evils of wealth and the material world to anyone who will listen (which pretty much scares away most interviewers). Still, she has garnered a bit of a following and her lectures are a popular attraction on most New Vegas tours.

"What about the legal battle?" I asked HARV as we pulled into a parking area that looked as though it had just been constructed for my car. "Has anything happened there lately?"

"The plethora of claims and counterclaims continues within the courts," HARV replied. "There had been some rumors that the Quads were negotiating a settlement sans their attorneys, but those have been officially denied by all parties."

"Which means, of course, that they're probably true."

"Probably."

"A settlement would certainly be big news. The end of an era. I wonder if that's why we're here."

"To witness the settlement? I don't think so, boss. You're a Private Eye, not a Notary Public."

"Thank Gates for that."

"Don't knock it until you've tried it," HARV said. "I understand they get far fewer attempts on their lives."

"Where's the fun in that?" I said.

We parked and were ushered into the main mansion by the

polite, bodiless voice of the computer. HARV dissipated his
hologram before we stopped so as not to draw attention to himself. And, as usual, for the duration of our visit, he would
mostly communicate with me either by whispering silently
in my head or, when stealth and silence weren't priorities,
through the traditional interface that I wear on my wrist. Very
few people in the world know that HARV is hardwired directly
into my head. The secret has helped me out on a number of occasions, so I like to keep it as quiet as possible. Plus, if truth
be told, it's not something I brag about or even like to think
about too much.

"Thank you again for coming so quickly, Mr. Johnson," the
computer said. "Ms. Thompson is awaiting you in the great
dining room number seven-b. If you'll permit me, I shall vocally escort you to your destination."

"That will be fine," I said. "Thank you."

"Could this computer be any more sycophantic?" HARV
whispered in my head. "The way he ass-kisses, I suspect that
he was originally programmed for proctology."

"It's nice to have a polite computer . . . for a change."

The computer led us through Ona's mansion and I was
grateful to have the guidance because I'd never have found my
way without it. The mansion's décor, at least for this portion of
the hallways, was done through random holographic projections, an interior design style that had come into vogue a few
months earlier (when Ona started using it, of course). The system holographically decorates the living space according to
one of a myriad of preprogrammed design schemes. It can be
early Victorian one nano or lush forest the next. Ona, not surprisingly, had chosen some envelope-pushing motifs. The arctic tundra wasn't too bad, but the Peruvian mudslide made me
a little uncomfortable and the "burning building" effect (complete with realistic smoke odors) made me queasy, but I managed to keep my composure.

"I don't suppose Ms. Thompson has any decor programs
that are more sedate?" I asked.

"Sadly, none are available at the nano," the computer responded. "The decorator program is directly linked to Ms.
Thompson's body and brain patterns so that it reflects her cur-

rent mood. Apparently she's somewhat agitated at the present time."

"A sort of twenty-first century mood ring," I said.

"If you say so, sir. I don't exactly get the reference," the computer said.

"Don't worry about it. My computer doesn't get me most of the time either," I said.

"I get you, I just often choose to ignore you as to not encourage those types of statements," HARV quietly sighed inside my brain.

We walked through a doorway as the simulated walls blew apart from a holographic nuclear explosion.

We arrived at the end of the hallway and the computer indicated that our journey had ended by adding a slight golden glow to the closed door before us.

"We've arrived," it said. "I've alerted Ms. Thompson, so please feel free to enter."

"Thanks," I said as I gently turned the knob. "I appreciate your help."

"It was my pleasure serving you, sir."

"Gates," HARV whispered in my head. "I think I'm going to hurl my chips."

I opened the door and gently entered the room.

Remember all those suspicions I'd had about how taking this case was going to be nothing but trouble? Well, my estimation of the trouble turned out to be way too conservative. I knew it in one glance.

The space was a formal dining room, sumptuously elegant and (not surprisingly) enormous. The table was set and the food that was waiting to be served looked delicious. But that's where the good news ended.

All four Quads were there (and none of them appeared to be what one would call happy). Ona was the first to greet me. She stood by the table, arms crossed, clearly upset, angry, and a little on edge.

"It's DOS-well about time you showed up," she said.

Twoa (the superhero) was beside her, hovering about half a meter off the ground. She was in full costume: a tight red crop top, white miniskirt, red boots with four-inch heels, and a long blue cape. There was a grim, steely-jawed look of determination on her face.

Threa (the fairy queen) was in the background just a little, away from the table, as though she'd been pacing before I entered. Her long green robe danced around her gently as though moved by a breeze (which I couldn't feel). Two tiny nymphs flitted around her head sparkling with pixielike glitter. She was crying, not sobbing or anything, but she had those heroically strong tearstained cheeks that you read about so often in fantasy fiction.

But it was Foraa who embodied the trouble. She was wearing a thick black faux-leather jacket and gloves, a short skirt, and black tights. Had the room been any darker I wouldn't have been able to see her at all, she was so shadowy. She was the only one of the quads who didn't look angry or overwrought. As a matter of fact she looked rather content.

But that didn't help matters much because she was also lying dead on the floor.

"As you can see," Ona said, "I have a problem."

# 4

I knelt beside Foraa and gently put my hand on her neck, being careful not to disturb anything. I felt no pulse and her skin was slightly cold to the touch. I knew she was gone, but I had HARV confirm it. He scanned her through the subtle contact of my fingertip.

"No pulse, boss," he said. "No breath. Her body's cooled a bit already. She's been dead for an hour at least."

Foraa's expression was sadly serene yet beautiful in a quiet way (in a stark contrast to her sisters). Her skin was the patented Thompson Quad shade of purple, but it was unpainted and unblemished. The beauty that was fast fading with death was all natural.

Her hair however, was . . . something less than natural. In true black-sheep rebellion, Foraa had dyed her hair the deepest shade of black I'd ever seen within the Earth's atmosphere. Ms. Clairol #666, Black Hole Oblivion—it was so dark, it didn't even look like hair anymore. It was more like a stylish spatial wormhole atop her head where all light and color ceased to exist.

"Good thing she didn't do her eyebrows as well," HARV said.

There were puddles of red wine on the marble floor where she lay. One was near her mouth, and a few tiny droplets still clung to her lips like dark berries on a bush. Another encircled her hand like a bloody pond around a delicate purple island. Her hand was palm down and cupped ever so slightly into a subtle dome. This caught my attention, tickling an odd thread in my memory.

"Her hand looks a little strange," I mumbled.

"I think when it comes to the Quads strange is the norm," HARV whispered.

I ignored HARV and zeroed in on the memory. It brought me back to my early days on the street as a PI, dealing with con men and street hustlers.

"You know, it's almost like she's doing a card trick," I said.

"A what?"

I reached for her hand without thinking and made the first of my many mistakes during the investigation.

"It's like she's palming something. I wonder . . ."

"Boss, don't touch . . ."

I lifted her hand, ever so gently from the puddle. There were symbols drawn in wine beneath her hand. Foraa had quickly scrawled them on the tile just before her death. She had cupped her hand gently around them before she died, not to hide them from sight but to keep them from being erased by the puddle of wine that had formed. By lifting her hand, I had broken the seal around the symbols. I had removed the dam and the wine puddle rushed past its unnatural banks. The symbols disappeared in nanos.

"Oh, DOS," I said. "That was probably important."

"The last thing Ms. Thompson wrote before her death?" HARV whispered. "Yes, I would suspect so."

"You recorded it. Right, HARV?"

"Of course I did," HARV said. "I got it through the eye-cam. I'm analyzing it now."

"Thanks."

"You're welcome."

"Do me a favor and stop me the next time I start to do something stupid like that."

"Boss, you don't know how long I've waited to hear you say those words."

I did my best to regain my composure and rose to meet Ona as she approached.

"What happened?" I asked.

"Isn't it obvious?" she said, impatiently crossing her arms beneath her breasts. "Someone tried to kill me."

I stood up and moved away from the body, being careful not to disturb anything else on the scene.

"Actually, Ms. Thompson, that's not obvious," I said. "It looks to me more like someone *succeeded* in killing *your sister.*"

"Oh, good," Ona said. "You see that's the kind of top-notch, deductive reasoning that I was looking for when I hired you. I'm looking *beyond* the obvious. Think outside the cube. This was an attempt on my life."

"Oh, yes, Ona," Twoa said as she floated toward us, hands majestically upon her hips, her cape somehow flapping in a wind that wasn't there. "It's always about you."

She landed beside me and held out a red-gloved hand. Her grip was firm but not uncomfortable. Still my hand felt like an egg held gently in an atomic vise. No matter how gentle the actual grip was, it was clear that my hand could be crushed at any nano, with no thought at all. It was unnerving and kind of sexy at the same time, but I couldn't be certain if Twoa knew that.

"I'm Twoa Thompson, Mr. Johnson. You can call me Justice Babe. It's nice to meet a fellow soldier in the battle for truth."

Ona rolled her eyes. "Should I cue the music now or did you bring your own?"

"You're just jealous that I have a catchy theme song and you don't!"

The two looked as though they could have gone at it there and then, but while that would certainly make for an entertaining pay-per-view special, it wouldn't be all that helpful to me at the nano. So I tried to act casual.

"Nice to meet you, um, Justice Babe."

"Please, sisters, cease your bickering," Threa said from the other side of the table. "A great tragedy has befallen us. We should be drawing strength from one another rather than letting our grief tear us asunder."

"Oh, here we go," Ona said. "Guinevere speaketh. This is all I need."

Threa's gown flowed around her mellifluously as she moved to join her sisters. The two tiny nymphs buzzed about her head as she moved, leaving trails of sparkling smoke behind as they flew, like skywriters using pixie dust. Their voices sounded like crickets on speed, chirping through cotton candy.

It took my brain a nano or two to focus on their chirping, but when I did, I recognized it as speech.

"Yes, mistress," they said. "You are right, mistress. You are divine, mistress. You are *much* prettier and smarter than your sisters."

"I refuse to acknowledge the insult inferred by your reference, sister," Threa said. "Because I know that it is born of grief and fear."

"It's born of annoyance, you unicorn kisser," Ona spat. "Now can we please get back to the attempt on my life?"

"Can you for just one nano think about something other than yourself?" Twoa said.

"And what's the point of that?"

Twoa made a fist and waved it in front of Ona. "You arrogant . . ."

"Just try it, Twoa . . ."

"Peace and harmony, sisters. Peace and harmony!" Threa shouted.

Ona and Twoa weren't listening, though. Peace and harmony were the last things on their minds.

"Do you sleep in that stupid costume?"

"Of course I do! When crime rears its evil head, every nano counts!"

The sisters all closed in on each other. It looked as if a full-blown, no-holds-barred rumble could break out at any nano.

"Well," HARV whispered in my head, "this is certainly going to be fun."

"I thought they were supposed to be superintelligent?" I whispered.

"Yes, well, there's a difference between having superintelligence and having the wisdom to use it. It appears as though the Quads came out way low on the wisdom end."

I cleared my throat in an attempt to get the attention of the bickering sisters.

It didn't work.

I tried again, a little louder this time.

Nothing. It was like I wasn't even there.

"Maybe a small explosion would work," HARV whispered.

"You know HARV, you do occasionally come up with a good idea."

I popped my gun into my hand and held it above my head.

"Just noise."

The gun's OLED screen flashed in recognition of my voice

command a nano before I pulled the trigger and used a high-decibel explosion to bring the Quads' attention back to me.

"I understand that you're all . . . dealing with this in your own distinct ways, but I think we need to go over the basics here. Your sister is dead . . ."

"Brilliant," Ona muttered.

". . . and unless I'm mistaken, Ms. Thompson, you have hired me to help you. Now, in order to help you, I'm going to need to know exactly what happened. So let's start at the beginning."

"You mean when the great goddess brought forth the infant cosmos from the infinity of her womb?" Threa asked.

"Um, no," I said. "Let's fast forward a few billion years to what happened tonight."

"We were meeting for dinner," Ona began. "A late dinner. Hors d'oeuvres served in the drawing room at midnight. The first course to be served at one. After hours dinners will be in vogue this year. It's so decadent to eat when the little people of the world are sleeping. The trend should become fashionable any nano."

"It's just freaky enough to be true," HARV whispered.

"So the four of you met for dinner," I said.

"Yes," said Twoa. "We were about to sit for the first course. Ona opened a bottle of wine."

"Romani-Conte 1990," Ona interjected. "Only four bottles of which remain in the world. Three of them are currently in my cellar. The fourth, unfortunately, is puddling on the floor."

"Sister Ona poured us each a glass," Threa continued. "We raised our drinks in a show of sisterly unity."

"Then Ona started talking about her wealth."

"I was giving a toast."

"You were describing your fortune."

"And sister Foraa grew impatient."

"Always the rebel."

"And rude."

"She couldn't take Ona's rambling anymore and drank, just to get the toast over with."

"And that was it?" I asked.

"She collapsed, rolled around for a while, then died."

"Poison in the wine," I said.

"Another flash of brilliance from the detective," Ona mumbled.

"There is always the possibility she died of boredom," Twoa said.

"The police are going to want to run tests on the wine when they get here. Whatever's left in Foraa's glass as well as what's in the bottle."

"The police aren't coming," Ona said.

"What?"

"That's why I called you," she explained. "I don't want this to turn into a public spectacle. I want it handled in-house."

"Ms. Thompson, your sister's been murdered."

"Exactly," she said. "This is a family matter."

"Perhaps," I said. "But this also looks like a murder. That means it's also a police matter. We'll keep it as quiet as possible, but you need to report this to the authorities."

"Absolutely not," she said.

"It's a crime if you don't."

"It happened under my roof. That makes it under my sovereignty and subject to my laws. And my laws say that whatever I say goes."

"Well, that would be true," I said, "if you were your own *country!* But, unfortunately, you're a citizen of the New Frisco Principality and as such you are subject to its laws."

"You mean even after everything I've done for this world, after all the good that I've created with my wealth—aiding underprivileged children, funding medical research, driving programs for environmental renewal and reinvention—after devoting my vast fortune to raising the quality of life for every downtrodden person in the first through fourth worlds, I still have to obey these silly New Frisco laws?"

"Well, yes."

"But I'm really, really rich!"

"Okay, then, maybe not *all* of the laws apply to you, but I'm pretty sure about the ones regarding murders that take place in your pyramid."

"Ziggurat," HARV whispered.

"I mean ziggurat."

"I'll say this one more time, Zachary, and then the conversation will be over. We are *not* calling the police."

"Excuse me, Ms. Ona . . ." the computer said sheepishly.

"Well, then, Ona," I said. "I guess we have a problem."

"Ms. Ona?"

"I warn you, Zachary Johnson, if you go against me, I can make it so you never work on this or any other planet again!"

"Ms. Ona . . ."

"What is it?" Ona snapped at the computer. "Can't you see I'm browbeating a minion?"

"I believe that this debate is about to be rendered moot," the computer said, "because the New Frisco Police are currently en route."

"What? Who notified them?"

"That would be me," the computer replied.

"What?"

"I apologize. It's just that the situation seemed so . . . dire and, it seemed like the right thing to do."

"When will they be here?"

"Within three minutes."

Ona sighed and waved away the computer voice.

"Fine. Make sure the security systems let them through. Let's not cause any more trouble." She turned to me. "I guess you get your wish after all, Zach."

"Believe me, Ona," I said. "This is the last thing I'd wish for."

"And by the way," she said. "I don't like butting heads with my minions."

"I don't break the law, Ona. And I'm not a minion."

"Not yet," she said, then she turned to her sisters. "Well, ladies, hang on to your hats. It's going to be a bumpy ride."

On Ona's words the three sisters started primping themselves. Mirrors came down from the ceiling and the three started wetting their lips, flicking their hair, and adjusting this piece or that piece of clothing.

"Ah, ladies, you're not going to the prom," I said, even though I had to admit I found it strangely arousing.

Ona looked at me. "It's all in the presentation."

"Presentation! Your sister is dead."

Ona shook her head. "It's not my fault we live in a superficial world."

"Ona, I don't think . . ."

"Really, Zach, why does everything always have to be

about you?" she said. She started to walk away. "Now come along, we have police to greet."

As I watched Ona walk toward the dining room door, I couldn't help thinking that I wouldn't be surprised at all if somebody had tried to kill her. In fact, I was surprised it had taken so long.

# 5

The good news is that, when we met the police in the foyer a few nanos later, I saw that my old friend Captain Tony Rickey was the lead officer. The bad news is that the first words out of Tony's mouth were:

"DOS, Zach, I was afraid you'd be here."

"Tony, you'd be surprised how often I hear that."

Tony and I were neighbors growing up on the mean streets of the New Frisco suburbs. We first met when our mothers took us trick-or-treating together when we were three. Tony's mother dressed him up as a policeman and he grew up to be the Captain of New Frisco's 43rd Precinct. My mom dressed me up as a doctor and I grew up to greatly disappoint her. But she's at least somewhat pleased now that I'm dating a doctor. The bottom line is that Tony and I have a long history together and continue to be the closest friends, which is a good thing because I tend to get him into all sorts of trouble.

Tony approached me, hands in his pockets, and flanked on either side by two officers in full gear. The CSI team with their robot assistants followed closely behind. Under most circumstances, Tony and I would have at least smiled at one another and shaken hands. But Tony had his police team with him and I had a client with me. Any display of friendship on our part would show a lack of professionalism and undercut our respective authorities. So we nodded to one another when we met and cut to the chase.

"Where's the body?"

"In the dining room," I said. "I'll show you the way." I led him toward Ona, who was standing away from the crowd, arms crossed, looking attentive and surprisingly vulnerable. "Ona Thompson, Captain Tony Rickey, New Frisco Police."

Tony extended his hand. Ona took it gently and gave him a soft smile that sent tingles up my spine.

"I'm pleased to meet you, Ms. Thompson. I'm sorry for your loss."

"Thank you, Captain," she said in little more than a whisper. "I appreciate your coming so quickly."

She touched Tony's arm like a grieving widow drawing support from a friend and Tony's demeanor softened.

"We're here to help, Ms. Thompson."

"Please, call me Ona."

"All right, Ona."

He patted her shoulder gently and I smiled at the kind way he calmed her fears. I began to feel better about the situation.

"Don't fall for it, boss," HARV said inside my head.

"Huh?"

"She's emanating a high concentration of pheromones. That's what's giving you the warm and fuzzy feeling."

"Pheromones?"

"She's oozing sex, boss. She's charming Captain Rickey."

"She can do that?"

"It's one of the many extra-normal abilities the Quads possess," HARV said. "Although this one isn't listed in their press materials."

"She's a devious one, our Ona. A damn sexy devious one, though."

I looked at Tony. He was clearly aware of what he was doing, but his attitude toward the situation had definitely changed since his arrival. Ona was manipulating him, and I didn't like anybody except me doing that.

"Excuse me, Captain Rickey," I said, motioning toward dining room. "The body is this way."

Tony looked up, a little confused, and then focused again on the matter at hand.

"Lead the way," he said.

Ona gave me a slight smile as Tony moved away. I turned and we all walked together down the hallway. The walls around us morphed into a cascade of hissing vipers. A few of the investigators jumped in fright. One reached for his blaster.

"Ona," I said, "is there any way to turn off the holographic décor?"

"Certainly, I apologize," she said. "Computer!"

"As you wish, Miss Ona."

The vipers vanished, replaced by elegant (nonmoving) walls and some stunning framed artwork.

"You working for Ona Thompson now?" Tony asked softly as we walked.

"I'm an old friend of the family," I said.

"As of when?"

"About an hour now. Ona brought me in to help her out."

"Does that mean she wants you to find the killer or just make certain that she gets off?"

"I'll let you know when I find out."

"That would certainly make my life easier."

He grinned ever so slightly and we entered the scene of the crime.

A few minutes later, Tony and the CSI team were fine-toothing the murder scene with their plethora of high-tech combs, searching for DNA, microscopic stray skin cells, residual body heat, energy traces, and a few hundred atomic and subatomic types of legally recognized evidentiary material. I pointed them toward Foraa's body, just to make sure they recognized it (sometimes the CSI folks get so caught up in searching for the microscopic trees, they lose sight of the real-life forest). But while they did their hunter-gathering, I sat with Ona as she spoke with Tony.

"And you're certain that no one else had access to the wine before it was served?"

"Well, if it turns out that the wine was poisoned, then clearly someone else did, Captain," Ona replied,

"Ona," I said, "I'm going to say, for the fourth time, if I'm remembering correctly, that you should have one of your attorneys here. I hate attorneys as much as the next guy, but they do at times have a purpose."

"Duly noted, Zach," she replied, "but I don't think that's necessary." She gave Tony a warm smile and touched his hand. "I have nothing to hide. Captain Rickey and I both want the same thing here. Don't we, Captain?"

"That's right, Ona," Tony said with a smile.

"She's doing the pheromone trick again," HARV whispered in my head.

I cleared my throat uncomfortably and that sort of broke the spell.

"Ona, who else was in the house during the hours leading up to the death?"

"Myself and my sisters, of course. And my butler."

"Your butler?" Tony asked.

"Wintercrescenhavenshivershamshawjamison."

"I'm sorry?"

"Wintercrescenhavenshivershamshawjamison."

"Would you spell that for me?"

"I'd rather not," she said. "It's late. You can call him W. We all do. He's the last descendant of several famous butler bloodlines or something like that. He was Daddy's butler, originally."

"He runs the household?"

"Gates, no," Ona replied. "W is extremely old, slightly senile, and totally incompetent in most matters. The computer takes care of household matters. I employ W out of a sense of tradition. Sentimental, I know, but he's been with us for so long. I have to say, though, that no one sets a finer table or serves a better tea. It's a gift really."

"I'll need to speak with him if you don't mind," Tony said.

"Feel free."

"Any other human staff?" I asked.

"My security designers," Ona said. "Sturm and Drang Pfauhans."

"Pfauhans?"

"They're identical twin cousins. They're absolute wizards when it comes to home security systems and related applications. The best of the best, I'm told. Although this is going to look very bad on their resumes, I must say."

"Twin cousins?"

"Absolutely identical. It's a medical anomaly known as the Patty Duke syndrome. Geneticists and medical scholars were always begging them to take part in one study or another. They did the first few for free. Then they began requiring compensation to be studied. Honestly, there haven't been many studies done in the past few years. I think the Pfauhans may have priced themselves out of the market."

"We'll need to speak with them as well," Tony said.

"They weren't at the mansion tonight," Ona replied. "They had the night off."

"You gave your security people the night off on the same night that your three sisters were visiting?"

"Well, I suppose it sounds suspicious, if you're going to put it *that* way," Ona said. "The security systems were fully engaged during the entire evening. The mansion is like a fortress, as you've seen. And my sisters are capable of taking care of themselves. Or so I thought."

"Was there anyone else in the mansion?"

"There's Opie, of course," she replied.

"Opie?"

"The silverback mountain gorilla that Daddy genetically enhanced before my sisters and I were born."

"Opie's a monkey?"

"He's a gorilla, Captain. He's very sensitive about his genus."

"Is he a pet?" I asked.

"I wonder if he dresses like you," HARV snickered.

"As I mentioned, Zach, Opie was genetically enhanced by my father. He was a precursor to the experiment that created my sisters and me. He is a brilliant simian. He has an IQ well above the normal human average and has degrees in several fields of study. None of which, however, bear any relevance to the real world or making a living, so he continues to live with me here at the mansion."

"Does he harbor any ill feelings toward you or your sisters?"

"Oh, who knows. His kind can be fairly irrational."

"Apes?"

Ona shook her head. "Males."

A young detective approached and gently tapped Tony on the shoulder.

"Excuse me, Captain?"

Tony turned. "What is it, Weber?"

"We have a . . . situation in the other room, sir."

"What kind of situation?"

"One of the Quads," he looked uncomfortably at Ona. "I mean, one of Ms. Thompson's sisters is requesting a lawyer."

"Then she's entitled to one."

"Well, she's not exactly the one asking."

"What do you mean? She's either asking or she's not."

"You better take a look, sir. It's, um sort of a legal gray area."

"No doubt the first of many," HARV quipped.

Tony and I followed Weber into the sitting room across the hallway where his partner was trying to get a statement from Threa. I say *trying to* because he wasn't actually able to get a word in edgewise.

"Should I spell it for you mental troglodytes or do you need me to paint you a picture in the mystical mists. A lawyer! A mouthpiece! We want legal representation!"

The request was very clear, as was the intent. The problem was that it wasn't Threa who was asking. It was one of her nymphs.

"LeFay, LeFee, hush now, both of you," Threa said. "These gentlemen are just trying to help."

The six-inch-high, silver-skinned nymphs stood on the table in front of Threa, fluttering their wings and hopping up and down like wet-footed frogs on an electrified floor. Both were slightly plump and a little long of nose. One wore a minidress that looked as though it was made from silver-tinted deerskin. The other had on frilly nightgownlike frock that was tattered at the edges, the new peasant look. They each had tiny knives in their belts and one had a tiny bow and arrow quiver slung over her shoulders.

And did I mention that they were angry?

"They're trying to frame you, Mistress. It's the wolves of man's world trying to take down the supine phoenix of the Goddess."

"The supine phoenix?" HARV whispered.

"Ms. Thompson . . ." Weber began.

"Not another word, oppressor, or you'll get righteously slapped with a harassment suit and then cast into the fifth circle of the netherworld with the rest of your Y-chromosome carrying brethren."

"Yeah. You've probably thrown our poor sister-nymph to your dogs already."

"LeFaue! LeFaue!" shouted the other. "Fear not, sister, we'll free you from shackles of the never-remember-to-lower-the-toilet-seat heathens!"

"Threa, can't you keep those things quiet for two nanos?" Twoa asked from the other side of the room.

"I don't control them, sister," Threa said. "They're familiars."

"More like annoyers," HARV mumbled.

"Good one," I said. "Can I use that?"

"When would you *ever* use that line again?"

Detective Weber scratched the back of his neck confusedly, then shrugged his shoulders and turned to Tony for advice.

"See what I mean, Captain? Ms. Thompson's not lawyering up, but her . . . companions are rather insistent."

"Ms. Thompson," Tony said, "are you requesting legal representation?"

"Of course she is, you troll," the first nymph (LeFay, I think) shouted.

"Do you understand English?" said the second (LeFee). "Or do you want us to draw you a glyph?"

"I'm not requesting council, Captain," Threa said softly. "I'll help you in any way that I can."

"Don't listen to her," the nymphs shouted. "She's in shock. She's not responsible for her actions. She wants a team of lawyers and she wants them now!"

Tony looked at Threa. She was silent and serene. Then he looked at the nymphs who fluttered, angry and defiant, just above the table.

"I'll be with you in just a nano, Ms. Thompson."

"Take your time, Captain," Threa responded.

"No," LeFay shouted. "Get your hairy male butt over here now!"

"Yeah," LeFee agreed. "Our mistress' taxes pay your salary!"

Tony turned toward Weber and me. The three of us huddled together and conferred quietly.

"Threa herself clearly said that she didn't want a lawyer," he said.

"But the . . . things won't shut up about it."

"Then let the nymphs lawyer up," I said. "You can interview Threa separately."

Weber shook his head.

"The nymphs are her familiars. They never leave her."

"Never?"

"We have to get her a lawyer."

"But Threa said that she didn't want a lawyer."

"What if some judge decides that the nymphs are extensions of her person or something crazy like that?" Tony said. "She could make the claim that we denied her a lawyer."

"That's crazy."

"Welcome to the world of the Thompson Quads. There are no rules here. This whole scene could be a trick to get whatever Threa says here declared inadmissible."

"Excuse me," LeFay said. "But I don't see how the three of you huddling up in some latent homosexual bonding formation is going to get my mistress a lawyer."

"So allow us to put this in terms that you'll understand," LeFee continued. "If you don't get legal assistance on the vid by the time we count to three in Gaelic, then mistress Threa is riding the mist doorway out of your hairy-armed clutches."

"Yeah. And if you and your brethren oppressors try to stop her, she will bring all the power of Gaea's heaven down upon your forward-sloping skulls. You just . . ."

We never heard the rest because at that nano a heavy metal ice bucket clanked down over the two nymphs, covering them like a shell over chattering beans in a street hustler's game.

Tony, Weber, and I turned to see Twoa standing proudly over the bucket, her delicately powerful fist holding it in place as the nymphs rattled around inside.

"Trust me, this is the only way to deal with these things," she said. "I think my sister will answer your questions now. Isn't that right, sister?"

"Of course," Threa said with a smile.

"Help, help," the nymphs cried from within the bucket. "We're being oppressed!"

Just to cover our collective legal asses, we put a miniature vid phone in the bucket along with the nymphs and netted them with that new pay-service SharkNet, which offers streaming, interactive legal advice. Simply being connected to it constitutes legal representation in most provinces.

Then we let the detectives handle the interview with Threa. Tony and I went back to the dining room to check on CSI. Tony conferred softly with his men just inside the door. I could tell that they wanted some privacy, so I walked a few feet away and looked at some of the artwork in the hallway.

One painting in particular that caught my eye was of a pale-faced woman wearing a flowing fur-trimmed robe of ebony and blood red. Her face was turned to the side, seductively hidden from the viewer. Her image was flat, a stylized mixture of realism and the abstract, with big shoulders and a trim waist. She was both sensual and haunting at once.

"It's Erté," Ona's computer said softly.

"Pardon me?"

"I apologize for intruding, sir," the computer said. "I saw you staring at the painting. It's an original Erté. The late Dr. Thompson was very fond of his work."

"It's nice," I said.

"Cue rehearsed speech on Erté," HARV whispered.

"Russian-born painter Romain de Tirtoff called himself Erté after the French pronunciation of his initials. He was one of the foremost fashion and stage designers of the early twentieth century and painted for nearly fourscore years. He is the father of what is now known as art deco and his work, as you can no doubt see, has had tremendous influence on today's styles of fashion, architecture, and interior design."

"I appreciate the information," I said.

"The pleasure was mine," the computer responded.

And it was at that nano that the evening took yet another strange turn.

"Zach," Tony said, gently tapping me on the shoulder. I turned and saw him standing with an investigator slightly behind him. "CSI has found something."

"Is it new evidence?"

"Sort of."

"Sort of?"

"It's new evidence, but it might also be another crime."

"What does that mean?"

"We've found another body," the investigator said.

# 6

They led me to the far end of the dining room where we joined three other investigators who were huddled in a corner. Their backs were to us and they mumbled softly amongst themselves.

"When did you find it?" Tony asked as we approached.

"Just now," the investigator said. "A trail of wine ran across the floor and went behind the cupboard. We moved the cupboard aside and found the body behind it."

"Behind the cupboard? It's not dismembered, is it?"

"No, sir, it's just really small."

"It's what?"

The investigators parted as Tony and I approached and we saw the body, if you could call it that, on the floor. It was small all right, about six inches from head to toe. It was also silver-skinned and winged.

"I'm guessing that this is Threa's missing nymph," Tony said.

"So that's what one looks like when it's not talking."

Tony knelt down to take a closer look.

"It's soaked," he said. "Is that wine?"

"That's what we assume," the investigator replied. "It might have been poisoned as well."

"Or it might have just fallen into a full glass and drowned," I said.

"Bag it," Tony said. "We'll have the coroner run the tests."

"Is it evidence or another victim, Tony?" I asked.

Tony paused for a nano.

"I have no idea," he said. "We'll figure it out later. I sincerely hope your client is innocent, Zach."

"Why's that?"

"Because we'll have a DOS-awful time putting her on trial if she isn't. When was the last time you saw a celebrity convicted of anything?"

"What say we cooperate on this one, Tony? Share information as we get it."

"Can't do it, Zach. You're working for a potential suspect."

"She's one of several possible suspects right now. She's cooperating with the investigation. Heck, she might even be a potential victim in all this."

"We're going to look at her. You know that."

"I understand. But I'm going to be looking at everything else. I might find something that will be useful to you."

"You mean something that will clear your client?"

"Something like that would be nice."

"Then I'm sure you'll be very diligent in delivering that information to us."

"Look," I said. "I'm not asking to sit in on every interview and meeting. All I'm asking is for a heads-up on the breaking news."

Tony looked away and shook his head gently. He does this a lot around me. I try not to take it personally.

"You give me every bit of relevant information you find in this and I'll keep you in the loop," he said. "But only until Ona is charged. Then you're cut off."

"You mean *if* Ona's charged," I said.

"If or when."

I took his hand and shook it as he turned to head back to the scene.

"It's a deal. Thanks, Tony."

"Don't mention it," he said. "And I mean that. Don't mention this to anyone. I get enough heat from the commissioner for just admitting I know you."

"He's just jealous."

Tony shook his head again and rejoined his CSI team.

"Aren't you going to tell Captain Rickey about the symbols we found beneath Foraa's hand?" HARV asked.

"Not yet," I said. "Not until I figure out what they mean."

"Concealing evidence," HARV replied. "Oh, good. Your first felony of the evening."

"Not concealing, just delaying, HARV," I said. "The good news is that this night couldn't get any worse."

"If your past track record is any indication," HARV said, "then it can and will."

And that's when I got the call.

# 7

"Who would be calling at this hour of the morning?"

"It's Carol," HARV replied.

"What could she possibly want?"

"I suggest you ask her yourself."

I raised the wrist communicator to my face just as the image of my part-time receptionist, Carol, popped into the screen, looking far more chipper and alert than any normal human has a right to at five in the morning. But then, although Carol is many things, normal isn't one of them. To begin with, she's Electra's niece, which makes me sort of her uncle-in-law, and, like her aunt, she is strikingly beautiful. When she's not working for me, she's at New Cal Tech working on her degree in biophysics.

She's also a very powerful psi (short for psionic), Class 1 Level 6, which means that she has all kinds of mental powers. She can read thoughts, move things with her mind, and project her thoughts into other people's minds as well, making them do whatever she wants. It's an awesome responsibility, but the kid seems to handle it pretty well (although I understand that it tends to make dating a little difficult).

"Don't tell me you want to take another day off," I said with a smile. "You've been doing that a lot lately."

Carol looked a bit hesitant. "Just checking in," she said.

"It's five in the morning, Carol."

"Yes, Tío, I'm a senior now, I can tell time." Then she was silent. It was clear that she had something she wanted to say and I could tell she wasn't sure how to say it. In the end she just looked away and smiled as best she could. "I just wanted to make sure you were all right."

"I'm fine."

"I had a bad feeling. That's all."

"Well, as you can see, I'm perfectly fine so . . . wait a nano, you haven't developed precognitive abilities, have you?"

She smiled and shook her head. "It was intuition rather than precognition."

"That's a relief."

"I guess it was a false alarm, then."

"Well, even psis make mistakes once in a while," I said. "I remember the time your mom accidentally made half of the people in New Anaheim think they were ducks."

Carol's smile grew a little brighter. "I know. Mom says that was an accident during her HV show, but I'm not convinced. She did give them all free T-shirts, though."

"Whatever," I said, returning her smile. "I'm fine." I paused for a nano. "Really, I am. And I should be getting back to business now."

"Okay, I'll see you when you come in."

The communicator screen went blank.

"Well, that was different. Even for Carol."

"It seems her powers are growing on a daily basis," HARV said. "Maybe she'll follow in her mother's footsteps and have her own HV show one day, *Carol Controls it All*."

"Yeah, just what the world needs," I mumbled, turning back toward the matters at hand. As I went back to the dining room, I glanced over at the Erté painting that I'd noticed earlier. Something about it caught my eye.

"By the way," HARV said, "don't let Ms. Thompson's computer catch you staring at the painting again. It's likely to give you another one of its Erté lectures. That thing is even more boring than you are."

But, oddly enough, HARV's jab spun my mind back to the spark of inspiration. I turned my gaze back to the painting and remembered why its presence had stirred me so.

*Don't let Ms. Thompson's computer catch you staring . . .*

Then it hit me.

"Boss, you're getting that far off and unfocused look on your face again," HARV said. "That means you've either had a revelation about the case or that you ate a bad burrito. Frankly, it's a little early in the game for revelations, so I'm guessing that we need an acid stopper."

"We need to find Ona," I said.

# 8

We found Ona in the drawing room, fidgeting with her jewelry. A couple of Tony's officers were keeping her company, and for some reason they were silently doing the old Freaky Geeky. The Freaky Geeky is a dance that became popular about twenty years ago where people wiggle their fingers as though they're typing on a keyboard as they spin around on one leg while shaking the other. It's totally ridiculous, which means that it's a staple at weddings, graduations, and divorce parties the world over.

"What did you do to them?" I asked.

Ona shrugged her shoulders and pouted just a bit petulantly.

"It's a trick that my sisters and I used to play on people," she said.

"Make them stop."

"I was bored."

"Your sister was murdered tonight," I said. "Your playing with the minds of the police doesn't reflect well on your innocence. Now make them stop."

Ona sighed.

"Want to see them do the Funky Gnu?"

"Ona!"

"All right, all right. You know, I think you're starting to forget who the bossy bitch is supposed to be around here."

She snapped her fingers and the two officers stopped dancing and came to their senses. They looked at one another, their arms still in the typing position and then uncomfortably turned away and straightened their uniform shirts.

"Excuse me, officers," I said.

They turned to me, grateful for a work-related distraction.

"I'd like a few nanos alone with my client, please."

"I'm sorry, Mr. Johnson, but Captain Rickey told us to keep an eye on her."

I turned to Ona and gave her a look I hoped she would pick up on. Sure enough she did.

Ona looked at the guards and calmly said, "Leave us alone."

They nodded and left the room, closing the door behind them. I turned back to Ona, who was inspecting her fingernails. "So it's okay for me to use my pheromones when it's to your advantage," Ona said.

"You're treading a fine line here, Ona. You've got to be careful."

Ona shrugged. "Why? I'm rich."

"All the more reason. People love to see the rich fall. The richer they are, the harder they want them to fall."

"But the people love me," she protested.

"Right, just before you, they loved Babo Benton."

"Who?"

"Exactly," I said. "Nobody stays popular forever."

"What about Elvis?"

"Dead and cloned people don't count. They get a big sympathy vote. Now I need you to be honest with me."

"Of course," she replied.

"I mean totally honest. Completely, absolutely, utterly . . ."

"How about redundantly?" HARV said.

"Did you kill your sister?"

She stared at me for a long, angry nano, trying very hard, it seemed, to melt me with her vision (actually my forehead got a little hot, which worried me).

"No," she said. "I didn't."

"Are you sure?"

"Positive."

I looked at her carefully, searching for any of the telltale facial tics or changes of expression that show when a person is lying. I didn't detect anything. HARV also scrolled her respiration and heart rate in front of my eyes. It was a little lower than a normal human's would have been, but I assumed that was normal for a superhuman. If Ona was lying, then she was a master liar.

"Good. Call your computer in here."

"I don't need to."

"I know," I said. "But call it anyway."

"Computer?"

"Yes, Ms. Thompson," the computer voice said.

"Computer, you've been kind of quiet since the police arrived," I said.

"I am programmed to be discreet," the computer replied. "I only make my presence known when needed."

"Yet you lectured me on Erté."

"I thought you would find it interesting," the computer said. "I hope I didn't disturb you."

"You were watching me."

"Not specifically you, sir. I monitor the household. I am constantly tracking millions of details."

"So you were watching the dining room when Foraa died."

". . . Yes. I was."

"You recorded it, didn't you."

"Surely not," Ona cried. "It doesn't record everything we do."

"Of course it does. It's a security system. Correct, computer?"

Silence.

"You do record everything. Correct, computer?"

"Yes," it replied.

"So you've seen me naked?" Ona asked.

"Ona, can we stay on subject here?" I said. "Your computer is going to replay Foraa's death for us. Isn't that right, computer?"

"If Ms. Thompson wishes."

I turned to Ona. She swallowed and then gave a dismissive wave with her hand.

"Whatever."

"Then kindly turn your attention to the wallscreen on your right," the computer said. "How long before Ms. Foraa's death would you like me to begin?"

"Five minutes will do for a start. I'll let you know if I want to go back farther."

"As you wish."

The lights in the room dimmed slightly as the wallscreen brightened. Digitally reproduced images appeared on the screen and Ona, HARV, and I watched the murder unfold.

# 9

Ona gestured grandly about the room as she led her sisters to the table. She was smiling, her beauty in full radiance. The playback on the wallscreen was brilliantly clear. Every color and nuance of the scene was vividly reproduced. It made me uncomfortable watching something that I knew would end in death, yet I was strangely fascinated.

"Computer, how many views do you have of this scene?" I asked.

"Four actual positions," the computer replied, "but I can extrapolate and give you views from any of a thousand different angles of any given nano."

"Let's stick to the actual feeds for now," I said. "Let me see all four angles. Sync them and put them all on the screen."

"That might make the action difficult to follow."

"The police are going to go over every pixel of these images. I need to make sure they don't see anything that we don't already know about."

The single view of Ona and her sisters on the screen broke apart and became four distinct images, all from different angles, all synchronously timed to one another.

"Is that suitable?" the computer asked.

"It's fine, thanks," I replied.

"Hush, Zach," Ona said as she slapped me playfully on the arm and motioned toward the screen. "I'm speaking now."

Back on the screen, Ona took her place at the table.

"I'll say once again, how happy I am that you could all come this evening on such short notice," she said, "although I'm sure your schedules can't be nearly as full as mine."

"Yes," Foraa mumbled, "being a whore must be so demanding."

"Please, Foraa, don't be so cruel," Twoa said. "Whores actually work for a living."

I winced a bit at that one. "Looks like the party was in full swing by this point."

"Oh, who pays attention to the dialogue?" Ona replied, still staring at the screen. "Don't I look lovely? My dress had been constructed just three hours prior to that nano. It was so fresh. Of course, I'll have to throw it away now. Fashion gets stale after the first six hours. Wouldn't you agree?"

"I will if it will stop you from talking about it further."

We turned our attention back to the wallscreen as Twoa, Threa, and Foraa followed their eldest sister's gestured commands and took their places in an odd configuration about the table. Ona (not surprisingly) sat at the head. Twoa and Threa sat beside one another along one side. Foraa sat at the foot.

"Why are you sitting that way?" I asked. "Why not sit one to a side?"

"Shhh. We're about to fight about just that very thing."

"W worked especially hard on the table for this evening," Ona said. "He began four days ago. Six if you count the polishing. Sadly, he's not as fast as he used to be, but I think you'll agree that everything is perfect."

"Or at least very nearly," Foraa said as she gently touched her setting with a gloved hand.

"Sister Ona, why must we continue to sit in this formation?" Threa asked, as she circled her chair.

"What do you mean?"

"Sitting at the table like this," Twoa said. "Why do we have to continue to sit this way?"

"We've always sat this way." Ona replied.

"We sat this way when we were children," Foraa said, punctuating her words with finger points. "You at that end, Twoa and Threa on one side, me at this end, and Daddy over there."

"Yes, why are you always at the head of the table?" Twoa asked.

"Where else would I be?"

"I thought I was at the head," Foraa said.

"You're at the foot, sister," Threa said.

"Daddy always told me that I sat at the head."

"He lied to you, dear," Ona replied. "I'm at the head. That's the way it's always been. Me, Twoa, Threa, and then you at the foot."

"And Daddy at the right hand," Twoa said.

"Yes," Ona agreed, "and Daddy at the right hand."

"But Daddy's no longer here."

"I know that," Ona said.

"So, why do we have to keep sitting this way?"

"What other way would we sit?"

"Why can't I sit on that side?" Twoa asked motioning toward the empty side of the table.

"You want to sit on that side?"

"Well, why can't I? It would be fair. That way we'd each have a side to ourselves."

"You really want to sit on that side of the table?"

Twoa thought for a nano, clearly running through the possible embarrassing scenarios that could occur if she answered truthfully. In the end, she took a breath and spoke.

"Well . . . yes."

"Fine. Go ahead," Ona said, politely gesturing to the opposite side. "Why don't you move over onto that side of the table? I'll just wake W and tell him that there's been a change in seating plans and that he needs to redo the settings. He'll totter down here in an hour or so because he's over a hundred years old now and start resetting the table. And because it's only one setting, it will just take him about four and a half hours at which point this entire DOSsing dinner will be ruined because it will be DOSsing breakfast time by then and what's the point of having a four-hour-old, cold dinner at breakfast time?"

The sisters sat silently as the echoes of Ona's words gently faded in the large room.

"Fine," Twoa said, sitting in her original chair. "I'll sit here."

"That's a good girl," Ona said

More silence, broken at last by Foraa.

"Are you sure I'm not at the head?"

"Enough talk of body parts and dead fathers," Ona said as

she gently lifted a bottle of wine. "We're here to discuss the future and the wonderful things ahead for all of us."

"Hear, hear," Threa said.

"Huzzah, huzzah!" the nymphs cried and buzzed about the table, tiny clouds of glitter-dust floating in their wakes like Tinkerbell exhaust.

"I just want to say," Ona began, "that, even after everything I've done for this world, after all the good that I've created with my wealth . . ."

"Threa, can't you at least try to control those awful things?" Twoa said, swatting at Threa's nymphs as they flew by her ears. "I think breathing the secondhand glitter-dust causes cancer."

"LeFay, LeFee, LeFaue, restrain your joy," Threa said, as she and Twoa glared at one another.

The nymphs stopped their fluttering immediately. They hovered above the table for a nano, gave out one more puff of glitter-dust and then returned to Threa's side.

Ona cleared her throat, clearly a little perturbed at the interruption, and continued with her speech. "As I was saying, even after everything I've done for this world, after all the good that I've created with my wealth—aiding underprivileged children, funding disease research, driving programs for environmental renewal and reinvention . . ."

"Honestly, Threa," Twoa said angrily, "I don't understand why you surround yourself with those imbecilic playthings."

"They're my familiars," Threa said. "They're gentle, magical creatures who possess more beauty and grace than any of your insipid superhero trappings."

"Insipid? I'm fighting for justice."

"Oh, please, sister, you couldn't spell justice if it wasn't monogrammed onto your spandex."

The nymphs laughed and let loose another glitter-dust cloud.

"That's enough, ladies," Ona said.

One nymph flew toward Twoa and hovered a few centimeters from her chest, staring comically at her crop-top-covered breasts.

"J-U-S . . . Double-D, I mean, T."

"That's it," Twoa said.

She swatted the nymph away. It flew across the room to the far wall where it ricocheted to the ceiling, then the floor, then to the other walls, screaming all the way.

The two remaining nymphs let out screams of rage and leaped at Twoa, pulling at her hair and slashing at her cheeks with their tiny knives.

"Slay the superbitch," they cried.

The table instantly became a cacophony of flailing arms, angry shouts, and clouds of glitter-dust as Twoa swatted at the angry nymphs, Threa tried to protect them, and Ona angrily tried to regain the spotlight. In the end, Ona silenced the chaos with a great, piercing shriek that actually shook the walls of the room when it came over the computer speakers.

"STOP . . . RIGHT . . . NOW!"

And, on command, everyone froze in their positions. Twoa was left holding two of the nymphs by their throats. Threa had her hands on Twoa's arm. The third nymph, somewhat dazed and bruised from having bounced around the room, lay in an empty wineglass.

And Foraa sat calmly in her chair, arms crossed and smiling.

"I swear," Ona said through gritted teeth, "I will personally murder the next person who makes a move."

I turned away from the screen and looked at Ona. "That was sort of an unfortunate choice of words."

"Yes, well, in hindsight, I suppose you're right," Ona muttered.

Back on the screen Ona had once again regained control of the situation.

"I brought you all here for dinner," she said. "I have gone to great lengths to put this evening together and I intend to make certain that each and every one of you enjoys it." She turned to Twoa. "Twoa, release the nymphs."

Twoa did as she was told and the nymphs fluttered in the air, gently rubbing their throats.

"Threa," Ona continued, "control your familiars or I'll have them pureed and fed to Opie's pet iguanas."

The two nymphs flew back to Threa and huddled together on her shoulder.

"And, Foraa," Ona said. "Stop smiling."

"I can't, Ona. You're all so pathetically hilarious."

"Well, then, at least pretend that you're laughing with these dolts rather than at them."

"I'll try."

"Good."

Ona picked up the wine bottle again and, without letting her imperious gaze leave her sisters, popped the cork with a corkscrew and set down the bottle authoritatively in front of her.

"Now, while we let the wine breathe for a few nanos," she said, "as I was saying . . ."

Something brushed gently by my leg as I watched the screen. I looked down and saw a small serverbot carrying a crystal goblet of water on a tiny, ornate tray. The bot rolled past me and stopped in front of Ona.

"After everything I've done for this world . . ."

"Excuse me, Ms. Thompson," the computer said. "The water that you requested has arrived."

Ona turned her attention away from the screen and glanced at the bot by her feet.

"I didn't request any water, did I?"

". . . after all the good that I've created with my wealth— aiding underprivileged children, funding disease research . . ."

"It was just before you entered the room, madam," the computer responded.

"Well, then, what took you so long?" she said, taking the glass.

". . . after devoting my vast fortune to raising the quality of life for every downtrodden person in the first through fourth worlds, I just want to say . . ."

"I apologize," the computer said. "Things aren't running as smoothly as they normally do, what with the death and all."

"Do you two mind?" I said. "I'm trying to watch this."

". . . that it is you, my family, who are still foremost in my heart."

There was a long, very awkward silence at the table as the sisters all looked at one another uncomfortably. Then Foraa burst into laughter. She was followed by Twoa, then Threa and her nymphs.

"What's so funny?" Ona asked.

"I can't believe you just gave us the 'great humanitarian' speech," Foraa said between guffaws.

"You've been using that for years, sister," Threa laughed.

"You didn't even bother to prepare something original for the occasion?" Twoa chuckled.

"I did, too," Ona said. "I just haven't gotten to that part yet."

"Whatever," Foraa said.

Ona grabbed the wine bottle and banged it on the table like a judge's gavel and gave her sisters another steely gaze.

"Look," she said, "I am trying very hard here to be humble, which, as you all know, does not come easy for me. So I would appreciate it if you could all just set your longstanding animosities toward me aside for this one evening and let me say my piece without being mocked."

The laughter died down and Ona smiled ever so slightly. Then she began pouring the wine into the first glass, her gaze never once straying from her sisters.

"Unless there are further objections, we are going to take this priceless bottle of wine and drink it in celebration of our new era of renewed friendship and familial spirit. Now, does anyone have a problem with that?"

"Ona?" Foraa said.

"What is it?"

"Your renewed familial spirit is drowning one of Threa's nymphs."

Ona looked down and saw the now unconscious nymph in the wineglass that she was filling.

"Oh, for Gates' sake."

She plucked the soaked nymph out of the glass with two fingers and tossed it away. It bounced and skittered across the floor and landed under the cupboard.

"I hope it has a hangover when it wakes up," she said. "Threa, this glass will be yours."

She quickly filled the remaining glasses and gave them to each of her sisters.

"Now stand up and raise your glasses. I'd like to propose a toast," she said. "This is the original part."

The sisters stood and reluctantly did as they were told.

"To us," Ona said. "To making the most of what we have and to using it to make this world a better place."

"Here, here," Threa said.

Twoa, Threa, and Foraa raised their glasses to drink but stopped when Ona continued.

"And to the joy that we create through our works and all the good it does for humanity."

"To joy and fighting evil," Twoa said.

The sisters raised their glasses, then stopped again as Ona continued. "And most of all, to the personal euphoria we feel when we give selflessly of ourselves to help those less fortunate."

"Oh, come on," Foraa said. "I'm going to gag here."

"Excuse me?"

"When have you ever given anything selflessly? When in your life have you ever done anything that hasn't been carefully designed first and foremost to help yourself?"

"I beg your pardon?"

Foraa shook her head and waved her hand at Ona. "Nothing, forget it. Just go on."

"I can't believe you'd say that, Foraa," Ona said. "I mean . . . after everything I've done for this world, after all the good that I've created with my wealth . . ."

"Ugh! I can't take it anymore," Foraa said, raising her glass. "Let's just get this over with."

She tossed her head back and took a long gulp from the glass. The spasms began almost immediately.

Her head lurched forward and rivulets of the wine spilled down her chin like blood from a slashed artery. She dropped her glass and it shattered on the floor as she grabbed at her throat, as though trying to rip the skin away.

"Foraa . . ." Twoa mumbled, through bored, pursed lips.

"Very funny, Foraa," Ona said as she rolled her eyes. "I suppose you've never had fine wine before."

Foraa kicked her chair and sent it skittering across the floor like a hardwood Louis the XIV cockroach caught in the light. Then she sank to her knees and clutched desperately at the table to keep her balance but only managed to pull her entire place setting down on top of her.

"Very dramatic, sister," Threa said.

"This is why I never enjoyed our family dinners," Ona mumbled.

"I take it she did this kind of thing a lot?" I asked Ona as we watched.

"At least twice a week growing up," Ona replied. "Albeit never quite so convincingly."

Back on the screen, Foraa was now lying on the floor, kicking her legs spastically like a spider in hot oil. She rolled onto her stomach and desperately pawed at the nearby puddle of spilled wine. I wouldn't have recognized the action if I hadn't already seen the crime scene, but she was carefully drawing the signs that I'd found beneath her hand. Watching her now, it was amazing that she was able to do it considering the pain she appeared to be in.

"What's she doing there?" Ona asked.

"Her hand's spasming," I said uncomfortably. "I guess it's a product of the poison."

Ona nodded. I felt strange, keeping the sigils secret from the police and my client, but right now their existence was the only advantage I had and I wasn't going to share it until I knew what they meant.

Foraa's spasms stopped and she lay in the death-still position in which I'd found her earlier in the evening. Elsewhere in the dining room, Ona, Twoa, and Threa applauded.

"Bravo," Twoa said. "Your best performance ever."

"Oh, I don't know," said Ona. "The one she did at Daddy's funeral was very moving as well."

Threa was the first to stop applauding. She leaned ever so slightly toward where Foraa lay and the expression on her face did a fast fade from polite joy to uncertainty and concern.

"Foraa?"

Two of Threa's nymphs, clearly reflecting their mistress' change of mood, softly landed on their mistress' shoulders and stared at the prostrate Quad.

"Uh-oh," they chirped.

Twoa moved quickly to her sister's side but was careful not to disturb the body.

"My superhearing's not picking up a heartbeat."

"She's not breathing," Threa said.

"Don't be ridiculous," Ona said. "She's faking."

"I don't think so, Ona."

"Oh, dear Goddess," Threa mumbled.

One of the surveillance cameras was tight on Ona's face as the realization struck her. I don't think I've ever seen one face go through so many emotions so quickly. Confusion, annoyance, disbelief, shock, fear, desperation, and I swear that she almost looked relieved for the briefest of nanos. Then her big eyes blinked once, her lower lip curled ever-so-slightly beneath her teeth like a fawn seeking shelter beneath a tree, and she looked away. Sadness.

"Shall I continue with the playback?" the computer asked.

I turned my gaze away from the wallscreen and stared at the floor.

"That's enough for now," I replied. "Download the entire thing, an hour before and an hour after what we just saw to my computer. I'll let the police know we have some new information for them."

I turned to Ona and was taken aback to see tears on her face. She wiped them away from her purple cheeks with an elegant gesture and then stared at the moisture on her fingertips as though it were water from the moon.

"Well," she said, "this is unexpected."

It occurred to me then that that might well have been the first time in her life that Ona Thompson had ever cried and meant it.

We downloaded copies of the computer records to the NSFPD. Tony was taking no chances and asked for all visual and audio records of the house for the twenty-four hours leading up to the murder. I had no doubt that he'd have his people comb every pixel of it. I was hoping that they wouldn't find anything that I wouldn't already know.

In any event, Tony was pleased with our disclosure of the records. It earned us some good will and I think it made him a lot more comfortable with the share-and-share-alike deal that we'd struck.

After that, HARV and I called it a night, especially since it was now well past dawn, and headed home. I promised Ona that I'd be in touch with her later that afternoon. I also told her and her sisters not to talk to anyone about the murder. Tony had promised as well to keep the investigation quiet. He certainly didn't want to deal with a media frenzy this early in the game. So I was hopeful that I'd be able to at least get my feet under me before the solid waste hit the ventilation system. This, I suppose was the second of my many mistakes (but I'll get to that later).

Electra, not surprisingly, was gone when I returned home. She had left for work at the Children's Clinic a couple of hours before. I'd miss her warmth beside me, but at least I'd have some covers this time.

"Wake me in three hours," I said to HARV as I undressed and fell onto the bed.

HARV's hologram appeared at the foot of the bed, making a big show of winding a hologram in the shape of an old-fashioned alarm clock. His presence in my head over the past year has given his personality a little more imagination (for lack of a better word). His thought patterns have changed subtly, although he's loath to admit it.

"While I'm refreshing my brain, run checks on the butler, the identical twin cousin security experts, and the intellect-enhanced silverback mountain gorilla named Opie," I said "You know, the usual suspects. And find out if there are any outsiders that might have murderous axes to grind with any of the Quads."

"You got it," HARV said with a little salute accented by a bow. "Although I doubt we're looking at the work of an outsider here."

"You're probably right," I said. "It would be too difficult to engineer this from the outside."

HARV's eyes lit up a bit and he smiled.

"You know what we have here, don't you, boss?"

"You mean aside from a mess?"

"We have a puzzle."

"Yes, I guess we do," I said.

"An exercise in deduction, a riddle of time, space, and action, an obfuscated equation of reality."

"An exhausted detective and an overly prosaic computer."

HARV had begun to pace now, clearly excited at the idea of the mystery.

"Don't you see, boss, this mystery is the kind of thing for which I am best suited. This mystery is akin to a mathematical equation. You know the components involved. You know the starting point and you know the outcome. All that remains is to fill in the blanks. It's real world mathematics."

By this time, I had rolled over and stuck my head under the pillow. Unfortunately, I could still hear him (one of the downsides of having the interface in my brain).

"I doubt it will be that simple, Nancy E-Drew."

"Of course it will," HARV replied. "You don't know how lucky you are to have me to help you with this."

"Whatever you say, HARV."

"I may need to do some additional research in order to prepare for this. Is that okay with you?"

"Anything that keeps you quiet," I said. "Just wake me in three hours."

"No problem."

His hologram disappeared, but as it did, I heard him say something that I had never heard from him before.

"This is going to be fun."

Needless to say, I had trouble getting to sleep after that.

# 11

I eventually slept, although it wasn't the most restful sleep. I had a weird nightmare about Ona leading me around by a chain around my neck, while HARV gave her advice on how I should be trained. I woke up in a bit of a sweat, and was relived when my conscious mind came around to realize that that was all just my subconscious mind going a bit astray. Which really wasn't all that surprising considering how I had spent the early hours of the morning. I showered, dressed, and was just about ready to face the world again when HARV's hologram reappeared.

"Feeling better?" he asked.

"Yes, but I'm sure that won't last long. Anything happen while I slept?"

"Absolutely nothing," HARV said with a shake of his head. "The world completely shuts down while you're sleeping."

"Fine. Did anything happen that I need to be aware of?" I said.

"As far as I know, no."

"Good, at least things haven't gotten worse."

"I'm sure Ms. Thompson will appreciate your optimism," he said, not bothering to hide the cynicism in his voice.

"She didn't hire me for optimism. She hired me to catch a killer."

"Did she?" he said, this time at least trying to slightly cover the cynicism.

"What does that mean?"

I walked to the kitchen and poured a cup of coffee from the brewer. HARV has programmed the house computer to have fresh coffee brewed for me whenever I wake up. That sounds like a kindness, I know, and I try to think of it that way whenever I can. I am, however, also well aware that the interface in my head fires quicker when there's caffeine in my bloodstream, so HARV reaps a benefit from this, too. This also explains why the house computer is always offering me freshly brewed iced tea. If it were up to HARV, I think I'd have a permanent caffeine drip in my arm.

"It just seems to me," HARV said, as his hologram reappeared next to me at the kitchen table (drinking his own holographic cup of coffee), "that Ms. Thompson didn't actually instruct you to find her sister's killer. She merely said that she had a problem."

"And by 'problem,' of course, she meant that her sister had just been murdered," I said.

"True," HARV agreed. "But there are two ways one can interpret that statement. The first is that Foraa Thompson's demise means that there is now a murderer at large who needs to be brought to justice. That would be the traditional view of the situation, but catching the murderer is not necessarily Ms. Thompson's problem. That's a police matter."

"Are you going somewhere with this?"

HARV ignored me and kept right on talking. I hate it when he does that and he knows it, but that doesn't seem to stop him. As a matter of fact, it seems to encourage him.

"The other way to view it is that, when Ms. Thompson made the statement, there was the dead body of a famous person in her dining room, which presents something of a cleaning problem."

"And I'm the maid, so to speak?"

"Possibly."

I went to the fridge and grabbed a sandwich from the rack. HARV has also programmed the house computer to keep a store of premade sandwiches at the ready. Apparently, protein and carbohydrates are also necessary to keep the interface at peak performance. This one I don't mind so much because I really like the way the computer makes roast beef on rye.

"Okay, I appreciate your careful study of the situation," I said politely as I returned to the table, "so I'll make two points here and then we're abandoning this line of discussion and moving on to something that's actually useful to our situation. One is that Ona wouldn't need me to clean up the mess. Her pyramid . . ."

"Ziggurat."

"Ziggurat is a secluded fortress. She could have erased all evidence of Foraa's death and no one would have been the wiser."

"Except for her two sisters," HARV said.

"Secondly, as you'll recall, Ona's view of the situation was that someone had tried to kill *her* and that Foraa had inadvertently gotten in the way."

"And you take her statements at face value?"

"I do until the validity becomes questionable."

"It's already questionable, boss."

"Innocent until proven guilty, HARV. That's our motto here."

"Yes, especially if the party in question is rich and paying us handsomely." HARV sat back in his chair and pretended to sip his coffee. "But before we move on, let me offer an alternative theory."

I raised my hand to stop him and (for once) spoke before he could.

"Ona actually planned to murder *all three* of her sisters last night. Foraa jumped the gun and ruined it. Ona needed to cover herself to avoid suspicion, so she called me and is currently playing the part of the shocked, terrified, and grieving innocent, manipulating me to her own purposes."

HARV was silent for a nano.

"Well . . . yes."

"I've already thought of that."

"Clearly. It doesn't bother you?"

"Of course it bothers me, but right now it's just one possibility of many. We're going to explore all the possibilities. The fact that we're doing it while on Ona's payroll is superfluous."

"And borderline improper."

"My understanding is that we've been hired to find a killer. That's what we're going to do."

"And if the killer turns out to be our employer?"

"Then we probably won't get a bonus at the end. Until then,

we get paid in advance and verify the credit transfers right away."

The maidbot topped off my coffee cup. I pulled my chair a little closer to the table and rolled up my sleeves a little.

"Now, on to the nuts and bolts. Show me the weird drawing that Foraa made in the wine just before she died."

HARV flashed a picture of the wine puddle onto the wallscreen. I'd only caught a glimpse when I'd first discovered it, and it was interesting to stare at it now.

$$\left( V^{\beta} - 日^{\beta} \right) / \left( V^{\mathrm{Æ}} \, 禾 = \tfrac{\text{⼁⼁⼁}}{\text{⼃}} \, ^{S2} - 甘 \right) - 甘$$

"Any idea what it is?" I asked.

"An equation of some sort," HARV said, as he approached the wallscreen.

"It doesn't look like any equation I've ever seen."

"Admittedly, it's odd, but as you can see, the parentheses, the division symbol, and the footnoted numbers signifying exponents are all clear indications that this is mathematical in nature." HARV stood in front of the screen and pointed at the various symbols as he spoke, like a college professor before a telescreen. "The mystery comes from the variables. This symbol here, for instance, which is repeated several times, is a Chinese pictograph representing the sun. These three lines here are called the Awen symbol, which is druidic in origin. This one is an Egyptian hieroglyph known as the basket. This is the Russian symbol zheh, the Arabic Hlaa, the Hebrew Khaf, and this one, well, that's the letter *V*."

"Yeah, I kind of recognized it."

"So although the symbols are uncommon, the structure and form is clearly mathematical."

"Any idea what it means?"

"Not yet. The problem is that the equation doesn't actually *mean* anything," HARV said. "It begins in a straightforward manner, but it becomes chaotic here. Almost random. Clearly, this requires more thinking."

"Clearly. But let's look at the big picture for a nano. Foraa wrote this just before she died."

"We saw it for ourselves on the computer recording."

"The question, then, is why?"

"Well, obviously, it's a dying clue," HARV said.

"A dying clue?"

"When the victim, in the final nanos of clarity before death, summons his or her remaining strength to leave an obtuse reference to the killer's identity."

"I know what it is."

"Apparently, it's quite common."

"No, it's not."

"Well, maybe not in real life."

"That's sort of my point here."

HARV waved his hand in the air as though gently patting down a pillow. He does this whenever we're arguing and I actually start to win (which, admittedly, isn't often).

"While you slept, I took the liberty of doing some research, boss, and I happened upon a literary reference known as the Haycraft-Queen Cornerstone list."

"Oh, no."

"Created in 1938 by noted scholar Howard Haycraft, the list illustrated the early history of mystery fiction. It was later updated and expanded by Haycraft and author Frederic Dannay. It begins with *Zadig* by Voltaire and included one hundred seventy-six other works ending with *The Little Tales of Smethers* by Lord Dunsany in 1952."

"You read all the books on the Haycraft-Queen list?"

HARV nodded. "Somewhere between seven thirty-two and seven thirty-three this morning. I couldn't find a similar list that covered the genre post-nineteen fifty-two, so I simply read everything."

"Everything?"

"Well, I skipped the titles that were obviously derivative of the classic works and, to be honest, I'm not too fond of the alternative history genre, but I read mostly everything."

"You read every mystery novel of the past one hundred years?"

"One hundred and six years, actually."

"Oh, yeah, that's going to be *real* helpful," I said.

"I thought so as well," HARV replied. "For instance, it's clear now that what we have in this case is what is referred to in the business as a 'locked room' mystery. That being a mystery where the culprit, in this case a murderer, is one of a clearly defined group of suspects. The objective is to deduce which suspect is the killer. And I've noticed that in most locked room mysteries there is often a dying clue, such as the one we have here."

"HARV, you have no idea how happy I am that you've discovered the joys of mystery fiction."

"Thank you, boss."

"And you certainly have no idea how much more annoying this is going to make you."

"I beg your pardon?"

I finished the last of the sandwich and took one last sip of coffee, then got to my feet.

"Beg me later," I said. "Let's hit the road."

"Before we do," HARV said, there is something that you need to know."

"Oh, don't say that. It's never good when you say that."

"You better watch the news . . ."

HARV pointed to my kitchen wallscreen.

# 12

"Good late morning and/or early afternoon to our east coast viewers, I'm Bill Gibbon the Third and this is *Entertainment This Nano*. Once again, our story for this advertising cycle, New Frisco Police last night responded to an emergency call at the ziggurat mansion of trillionaire playgirl Ona Thompson. We have no details yet as to the nature of the emergency, but unnamed sources tell *ETM* that all four of the famous Thompson Quads were present at the house. I repeat, all four Thompson Quads were together under one roof, albeit a very large one."

Bill Gibbon the Third was the kind of commentator that you knew you shouldn't trust but that you watched anyway, because he was so darn entertaining. He looked like a giant Ken doll brought to animated, semi-intelligent life by a white-bread voodoo spell gone awry. He was attractive (thick auburn hair, blue eyes, tan skin, you know the type), had no journalistic pretensions, and even fewer journalistic ethics. His beat was pure celebrity, pop gossip, the juicier the better, and he'd go to any lengths to get it. One of his pressbots had shadowed me for six months after the BB Star case. I lost count of the number of times Electra "accidentally" crushed the thing with her hover. Eventually the cost of replacing the pressbots became too great and his network pulled the plug on the surveillance. Gibbon had never bought the "official" story on the BB Star case and had tried like crazy to find the truth. His instincts are actually quite good. Lucky for me, that his IQ isn't as high as his Q-Scores.

"An unnamed source has also confirmed to this reporter that

Ona Thompson has officially engaged the services of local private eye Zachary Nixon Johnson and that Mr. Johnson visited her mansion late last night, arriving shortly before the police. It is unknown at this juncture the purpose of his visit or the services for which he has been hired."

"This is bad," I said.

"We go now to correspondent Cindy Jane Buffy Snowden Ashcroft who at this nano is outside Zachary Johnson's office demanding an official statement from his representative."

"Outside my office? HARV, is Carol in yet?"

"She was in at nine."

"Well, this should be interesting."

Now Carol knows that her abilities come with a great responsibility and she is very respectful and restrained in her use of them. But she's only human. And she *hates* pushy news correspondents (can you blame her?). That said, I was not at all surprised at the . . . strangeness of the live report given by the unfortunate Cindy Jane Buffy Snowden Ashcroft.

"Are you there, Cindy?" Gibbon asked.

"I'm here, Bill," Cindy responded.

The picture went to a split screen and revealed Cindy Jane standing on the street outside my office. She was a fair-haired beauty. Twenty-three years old at most with blue eyes and a creamy complexion. She wore a designer suit and presented herself to the camera with the poise of a veteran. She was a good camera personality who, unfortunately, was about to run into a psionic buzzsaw.

"Can you tell us what's going on?" Gibbon asked.

"Yes, Bill. As you can see, I'm outside the offices of Private Eye Zachary Nixon Johnson. I've just spoken with his representative about this developing story."

Gibbon was excited now.

"And what can you tell us?"

"Well, Bill, I can tell you that I am a vapid, empty-headed bimbo. This is not my natural hair color and these aren't my original teeth, lips, cheekbones, or nipples."

"Come again, Cindy?"

"And it is important to note here that you and I have been having an affair for the past six months and that I am currently waiting for you to leave that saggy-assed ice bitch wife of yours as you have continuously promised."

Gibbon's face began to fall.

"Also, and I can't stress this enough, your real name is Dexter Weeney, you have a strange rash on your crotch, and you insist on calling me Auntie Hilda during our lovemaking."

Gibbon made a slashing motion with his hand to someone off camera and Cindy's side of the split screen disappeared. Gibbon nearly slipped out of his chair but caught himself on the desk and then spoke, in a voice only slightly more strained than normal, into the camera.

"Once again, the big story, and the *only* thing of merit reported here in the past few minutes, is that there was police activity at the home of trillionaire playgirl Ona Thompson early this morning and that she has hired private eye Zachary Nixon Johnson for some yet to be determined purpose. *ETM* will have updates, commentary, and wild speculation on this story as it develops."

HARV cut the feed and spoke to me, even though I continued to stare blankly at the now dark screen.

"You have to admit, Carol is a very inventive spin doctor."

I closed my eyes, took a deep breath, and ran my mind through the number of ways that this development changed the case. Sadly, I found no upside to any of it (and I looked *really* hard).

"Okay," I said at last. "Here's the plan. We're going to leave the house via the underground entrance, since I'm sure that the house is now being watched by pressbots. We're going to meet Tony at the morgue and get an update on Foraa's postmortem and the CSI. On the way there, we're going to net with Ona and tell her to stay put, not to talk to anyone and that we'll see her later this afternoon. First, though, net me with Carol."

Carol's face immediately filled my wallscreen. She was grinning from ear to ear.

"You saw the report?" Carol said.

I nodded.

"Pretty absolute zero, huh?"

"Haven't I ever taught you how to properly use the phrase *no comment?*"

"I had her clucking like a chicken when she was in here, but I thought that might be too much."

"Carol, I thought you didn't liked playing with the minds of normal people."

"Yes, but the press don't count as normal."

"She's got you there," HARV added.

"Really, Tío, there was no harm done," Carol insisted. "If anything, now the press will think twice before they bug us."

HARV cut in before I could reply.

"Boss, you have an incoming call from Dr. Gevada," he said, "and she doesn't seem happy."

"Gotta go, Carol," I said quickly. "I'll check in later."

Carol smiled and disappeared from the screen, replaced by Electra's image. Electra Gevada is the most beautiful woman I know and I'm not just talking about her good looks, which are considerable. She has hair like a moonless summer night, skin like a creamy, warm cup of coffee, and eyes that, when reflecting your image, make you look better than you ever thought possible. More curves than the Pacific Coast Hoverway and more spice than a chili cook-off; you'll find her image in the 3-D interactive dictionary beside the words "dame," "babe," "hot tamale," and "the-love-of-Zach-Johnson's-life" (it's in there, really). She's also a world-class surgeon who spends her time running a free clinic for children.

Perfect, right? Yeah, pretty much. But she's not a big sports fan, and her temper is only slightly less fiery than the famed flaming oil slicks of New Galveston Bay (but nobody's perfect, right?). She was dressed in full medical gear and sitting at her desk. She looked a little weary from the morning's work, but weariness brings out a subtle side of her beauty. Anger does as well, so you should get my drift here when I say that she was looking particularly beautiful at the nano.

"I take it you've seen the news," I said, figuring it was best to go on the offensive.

"My workmates were all quite eager to tell me about it. A lot of the men are jealous. Don't you ever get ugly clients?"

"It's a curse," I said with a weak smile. "But I know that you're secure enough in our relationship to not let it worry you, right?"

"This is just a job. Sí?"

"Sí, just a job. I can't tell you anything else, yet. But it is a job."

"You're not going to get yourself killed now, are you?" she asked jokingly, (at least somewhat).

"Hasn't happened yet."

"True, but you've been close more often than I like."

"Luckily, I have a good doctor," I said.

"I think I'm going to blow my chips," HARV said.

"I think we're grossing out your computer," Electra said.

"I know. I love it."

Electra looked at her watch. "I'm due in the O.R. again in two minutes."

"Saving the world, one kid at a time," I said.

"Well, we can't all be you," she said with a smile.

"Thank Gates," HARV mumbled.

Electra blew me a kiss and then the screen went blank.

"That went much better than I expected," I said with a grin.

"Let's get to the morgue," HARV said. "I really need a change of pace."

# 13

I met Tony in the hallway outside the city morgue. From the look of him, his morning hadn't gone any better than mine. He looked just as tired as I did and probably felt worse, but he had at least shaved that day, so he was one up on me in the grooming department.

"I'm hoping very hard here, Zach, that you're not the one who leaked this story to the press," he said.

"Yeah, right, Tony, because having the story made public just makes my life so much better."

"You have any idea where the leak came from?"

I shrugged my shoulders. "You don't think it was any of your team, do you?"

Tony shook his head. "They're loyal. What about the Quads?"

"I don't see how having the story out there helps them, but who knows what they're thinking. At least Gibbon doesn't have all the details."

"We don't know for certain that he doesn't," Tony said. "He could know everything already and just be doling out the information in bits."

"Building it into a 'developing story.' "

"More on-air time for himself."

I was embarrassed that I hadn't already thought of that. And I had a sneaking suspicion that there were a lot more things out there that I still hadn't thought of.

"Tony, you know the only reason I came here was because I thought the day couldn't get any worse."

Tony smiled, put his arm around me, and gently walked me the rest of the way to the morgue.

"Trust me, Zach," he said. "It gets much worse."

Call me old-fashioned, but I've never been comfortable in the city morgue. Yes, it's clean and well organized. It is exceptionally well run, utilizes the latest in forensic technology, and is an absolutely essential part of law enforcement and, sadly, of my own work as well. I regret the need for it yet recognize and respect its function and importance.

But it gives me the willies (and I'm not crazy about the smell).

So, like most people in the city, I do my best to stay out of it. Alas, however, sometimes fate just has other plans.

"Since the homicide is still officially top secret, access to the body will be allowed only to high ranking members of the investigation. And you," Tony said as we walked. "Forensics on this one's being handled by the new chief coroner, Lenny Shakes. Have you ever met him?"

"I don't think so."

We stopped outside the metal security door. Tony paused and put his finger on the DNA scanner. The system confirmed his identity a nano later, the big doors unlocked, and he led me inside.

"Shakes is a good man, top-notch. A little unstable, but he knows his way around a dead body."

"I'm sure that looks good on a résumé."

"One more thing, when you meet him . . ."

"Yes?"

"Don't be offended if he doesn't refer to you by name."

"What?"

"It's an idiosyncrasy," Tony said. "He feels that a coroner needs to be detached from the humanity around him in order to be effective."

"He's detached from humanity?"

"He sees dead people every day, Zach," Tony said. "He feels that he needs to depersonalize them in order to do his job effectively. That depersonalization sort of extends to everyone he interacts with in his office."

"Dead or living?"

"Do you want to talk with him or not?"

"Okay, okay," I said.

We passed another security check to get into the central room and that's where we found Dr. Lenny Shakes, the coroner. He was a thin man with long arms and a strong grip. His face was slightly oblong, his hair short and kind of an off-brown color. His manner was businesslike, his personality, as warm as could be expected under the circumstances.

"Pleased to meet you . . ." I said.

"Likewise, I've heard a lot about you."

"Any of it good?" I asked.

"Most of it fictional. At least I hope so."

"Don't bet on it," Tony said.

"I understand you'll be helping us with the case?"

"Help is a subjective term," Tony chimed in. "He will be in the loop. So you might as well give him the bad news."

"Bad news?" I asked.

Shakes flipped the lens of his eye computer into place and booted it up with a couple quick blinks. Eye computers are used by anyone who needs to keep their hands free and where voice activation is either ineffective or impossible (librarians, deep sea divers, hookers, that kind of thing). He motioned for us to follow him and he led us down a hallway to the examination rooms.

"The bad news is that toxicology on the wine came back negative," he said.

"Negative?" I asked.

"Forensics scanned it for all thirty thousand poisons in the database. We found nothing."

"Nothing in *any* of the samples?"

"No poison in the wine bottle, not in any of the glasses, not in the puddle on the floor or on . . . that thing. What do you call it?"

"The nymph," Tony said.

"Right, nothing on the nymph."

"How can that be?"

Shakes shrugged his shoulders. "You tell me," he said. "You're the detective."

I turned to Tony. "You saw the computer playback," I said. "Clearly the wine was poisoned."

"Under normal circumstances, I'd agree," Tony said. "But we did the toxicology tests three times. There was no poison. Maybe she had been poisoned earlier and it just happened to take effect the nano after she drank the wine."

"You think the whole thing was a coincidence? Come on."

"All we know is that the wine wasn't poisoned," Tony said.

"Even the wine that was on the victim's lips was negative for toxins," Shakes said.

"Did you find any type of poison in her system?"

"That's the other bad news."

"There's more?"

Shakes nodded and led us to a doorway. He put his finger to the scanner to open the door and then ushered us in.

"There's lots more," he said.

We were in the main examination room. Shakes activated the bright overhead lights and I almost jumped when I saw Foraa's body on the table. She was covered head to toe with a white sheet, but her purple hand was peeking out from the edge, dangling off the table like a plum leaf on a November branch.

Shakes carefully folded back the sheet, revealing just her neck and shoulders. I noticed that her face had grown slightly more pale and she was probably more cold to the touch as well. Her expression, though, was unchanged. It was calm and serene.

"As you know, the victim and her sisters are somewhat unique," he said. "They are genetically enhanced to an astounding degree. There's also very little known about their physiology. This has presented us with some unique difficulties in terms of the victim's postmortem examination."

"Difficulties such as what exactly?"

Shakes slid his surgical mask over his nose and mouth and lifted a scalpel from his instrument tray.

"Watch," he said.

He gently took Foraa's hand and slid her entire arm from beneath the sheet. He turned her hand palm up and put the blade to the underside of her wrist. I jumped.

"What are you doing?"

He slashed the blade hard against her skin and I winced.

But instead of slashing the skin, the blade snapped in two and clattered to the floor. Then I realized the extent of the "difficulties."

"She's invulnerable," I said.

"Actually, the term they use is 'nigh-invulnerable,' " Shakes replied, "but I haven't found a way to prove the nigh part yet."

"So you haven't been able to do an autopsy."

"I've broken two dozen scalpels so far today on various parts of her body."

"What about laser knives?"

"No effect. We even tried the concentrated lasers that rescue workers use to cut through wreckage." He lifted her arm toward me to reveal a small dark smudge on her forearm. "That singed her slightly before it overloaded."

"So what do you do next?"

"We're borrowing a laser drill from a diamond mine in New Zimbabwe. I'm hoping that I can focus the beam tightly enough to pierce her skin without cauterizing her insides. It should be here in about an hour. I also have a call in to a friend of mine who works with the Ministry of Space. I'll find a way to crack this nut eventually."

"What can you tell us as of right now?" Tony asked.

"I can tell you that she's not breathing," he said. "She has no heartbeat and all organ function and brain activity have stopped. Also her body temperature is now at seventy-three degrees."

"So you're saying that she's dead," I said.

"Well, I can't prove it, but, yes, I am leaning that way."

"You just have no idea how she died."

"I haven't been able to check for any toxins in her system, if that's what you mean," Shakes said. "I haven't been able to draw any blood and we're even having a hard time getting saliva. We've done scans and I can tell you that all her organs are intact and, theoretically, in working order, so she didn't die from any physical attack. She also tested negative for any radioactivity, so she wasn't killed by radiation poisoning, but from what I understand that was rather low on your list of possibilities."

"Yes, rather. What about her clothes?"

"We gave them to CSI," Shakes said. "They're examining them now."

He covered Foraa with the sheet again and killed the overhead lights.

"I'm going to keep at it," he said. "There are several avenues still to explore. I'll let you know when I have news. As we say in the field, 'once you know the how, you're halfway to the why.'"

"Thanks, doc," Tony said.

The three of us left the room together.

Tony and I left Shakes at his computer researching the type of lasers currently used in Earth's defense system against rogue asteroids. (I was hoping that was more of a "plan b" kind of thing).

"So it looks like we know less now than we did last night," Tony said. "Not very encouraging."

"The wine thing still bothers me, Tony. How about letting Randy take a look at the samples."

"Absolutely not," Tony said. "It would contaminate the evidence."

"If there's no poison in it, then technically the wine's not evidence," I said. "Randy's certified to do the work. He's done work for the government before."

"And charged very high rates for it, as I recall."

"He'll do this one for free, as a favor for me. I promise. Look, he's privately funded, so you know that his equipment is more advanced than yours. And, no offense, but he's smarter than any of your people."

Tony stopped walking and guided me to the side of the hallway where he drew close to me.

"If we do this, and I do mean 'if,'" he said softly yet pointedly, "it's off the record. I don't want people thinking that the NSFPD can't handle the tough cases."

"Absolutely," I said.

"My people transport the samples to his lab and monitor every aspect of the tests. The samples never leave their sight. No bait and switch."

"Tony, I'm hurt."

"Get used to it," he said.

"Agreed."

"Fine. You set it up with Randy. I'll arrange things at this end."

"Great, Tony. You won't regret this."

"I regret it already," he said, "but that's par for the course."

Tony led me out of the main hallway and to the door. It wasn't the most productive hour I'd ever spent but, as they say, any trip to the morgue that you can walk away from is a good one.

# 14

HARV and I hit the streets and headed back toward Ona's mansion in the Model-T2000. I was feeling a little dispirited from the day's events thus far, so I was driving. Driving tends to make me feel better, even if I'm not driving one of my classic twentieth-century cars. HARV's hologram projected from the car's computer into the passenger seat so he could sit beside me as we drove. His image squinted at me, making his small round eyes seem even smaller but more elongated. I knew he had the urge to say something along the lines that I should be flying instead of driving, but he was fighting it, which was hard for him, I'm sure. He swallowed ever so slightly and took a simulated deep breath.

"I've alerted Ms. Thompson's computer that we will be arriving shortly."

"Good," I said. "I'm going to want to speak with the butler, Winterfresh . . ."

"Wintercrescenhavenshivershamshawjamison."

"Whatever. The security people, too. And we might as well check out the monkey while we're there."

"Another normal day in the life of Zach Johnson," HARV said.

"Yeah, well, at least no one's trying to kill us."

"The day is still young."

"I'm going to want to speak with Twoa and Threa again, as well," I said. "Separately and today, if possible, so I'm going to want all the information you have on them. Friends, enemies, sources of income, bad debts, odd habits . . ."

"Odd habits? Boss, one's a superhero and the other's a fairy queen. Define what you mean by odd."

"Use your judgment," I said. "And by the way, I want you to be with me when we get to Ona's house."

"What do you mean?"

"I want you to be present, display your hologram," I said. "Use the wrist interface rather than the eye lens so we don't look too ripping edge, but I want everyone to know you're there."

"Why's that, boss?"

"I want you to make friends with Ona's computer."

"What?"

"We need good relations with it, HARV," I said. "It knows everything that goes on in that house and it hasn't told us everything. I want you to gain its trust."

"Boss, it's a computer!"

"So, clearly, it will feel comfortable confiding in you."

"You're whoring me?"

"I'm giving you a vitally important part to play in this investigation," I said. "Now do you want it or not?"

HARV folded his arms over his chest and rolled his eyes.

"Fine," he said. "I'll make friends with the computer."

"Thank you," I said, with the hint of a smile. "You realize, of course that this means you'll have to be civil while we're there."

"I can be civil."

"I'm sure you can," I said. "I've just never seen it."

We arrived at the secret entrance to Ona's mansion by midmorning. The desolate country road and skyway looked much less forbidding without the darkness and thunderstorms of the night before. Unfortunately, it also looked a lot less desolate.

Two dozen pressbots crowded the area, interfaces chirping and microphones outstretched toward the clearly empty guardpost at the rock outcropping entrance.

"Will you confirm for us that this is the entrance to Ona Thompson's private residence?" one pressbot asked the guardpost.

"Do you deny that Ms. Thompson's residence is nearby?" asked another.

"Can you confirm that you do not deny that you are employed by Ms. Thompson?" asked a third.

A tiny bot slid around the large group and made its way toward the outcropping.

"Excuse me, I have an urgent package for Ms. Thompson," it said. "I'll just go right in."

The guardpost responded with a blast from a hidden laser cannon that atomized the pressbot. There was an awkward nano of silence as the remaining press corps turned their interfaces first toward the smoldering remains of their compatriot and then back to the guardpost.

"Can you confirm that Ms. Thompson is not accepting visitors today?"

"Will you deny that she's not giving interviews?"

"Can you deny that you can't confirm her schedule?"

HARV and I watched the scene from the car.

"It looks like news is out about Ona's secret entrance," I said. "Throw a disguise over the car so they don't bother us."

"Already done," HARV said. "We're now a back-up mobile unit for *Rapid News*."

"And I think now would be a good time for you to start making friends with Ona's computer and maybe find out if there's a back door to this pyramid."

"Ziggurat."

"Whatever."

HARV got through to Ona's computer and a few nanos later we were able to sneak into the compound through the ultra-secret door, which ran through a subterranean tunnel beneath the hillside.

"I wonder where the servants' entrance is," HARV mumbled as we drove through the tunnel.

"Let's hope we never have to find out," I said. "This is bad enough."

# 15

We eventually made our way into the mansion and found Ona
in her private gym, working out with a set of antigrav weights.
She was dressed in a formfitting white workout suit and it worried me how awestruck I was by the sight of her. I felt my
knees tremble and a wonderfully warm feeling sweep through
my body, like a glass of brandy on a cool evening. I also found
myself feeling honored that such a woman would have need of
my services. Thankfully, HARV was beside me to set things
right.

"Keep it in your pants, boss," he said. "The perspiration from
her workout has suffused the entire room with pheromones. The
gym has become one big Ona Thompson love shack."

"You have to admit, though," I said, "she does look good."

"Yes, I suppose she does," HARV replied. "Although, being
a computer, I'm not the best judge of these things. Perhaps I
should get Dr. Gevada on the vid and ask her opinion."

That sort of brought me back to reality. I shook my head a
bit to clear it and then took a few steps back from the doorway.

"I don't think that will be necessary."

"I suspected as much," HARV said with a smirk.

I ignored him the best I could and shouted to Ona.

"Excuse me, Ona. Sorry to interrupt. Do you have a couple
of nanos?"

She turned toward me, the antigrav weights still extended
over her head, and smiled.

"Hello, Zach," she said. "I was wondering how long you
were going to stand in the doorway before saying something.
Come in and have a seat."

"Actually, I'd rather you come out here," I said. "That room is a little too full of your charm, if you know what I mean."

"Oh. yes, the pheromones," she said. "Honestly, I'll never understand you ordinary humans. Always thinking with your noses."

"I think she's aiming a little high," HARV mumbled.

I quieted HARV with a wave as Ona approached, toweling herself off as she walked. Her lithe muscles rippled beneath her clothes with every motion. She had a small antigrav dumbbell in her hand and she twirled it unconsciously between her fingers like an old-time gangster playing with a coin. Even this simple gesture seemed hypnotic, almost sensual. I could only hope that I'd get used to it all in time.

"A quick note of import," HARV whispered as she approached. "She just finished bench-pressing the equivalent of five hundred twenty-three kilos, so try not to make her angry."

"Got it."

Ona joined us in the hall. She let the towel drape across one shoulder and grabbed a water bottle that seemed to appear out of the air. She smiled at me and glanced passingly at HARV.

"I didn't know you traveled with a hologram."

"This is HARV," I said. "My computer assistant."

"Pleased to meet you, Ms. Thompson," HARV said.

She looked at HARV. "You'll pardon me if I don't shake your intangible hand."

"Of course, ma'am. No offense taken."

Finished with HARV, Ona now turned toward me. "I trust that you've seen the news today," she said. "I am not happy."

"I'm not surprised. Any idea where the leak came from?"

"My guess would be any of the simpletons posing as police investigators who traipsed through the mansion last night."

"It's possible. The report didn't mention Foraa, which is good, but odd," I replied. "Tony Rickey is checking into it now. He's as angry about it as we are."

The twirling dumbbell froze in Ona's hand as she gripped it firmly in her palm. Then she flicked her wrist with an amazing burst of speed and threw it like a missile back into the gym. It hit the far wall where its shell shattered and its electronic innards exploded in a display of blue and white sparks and flame.

"I doubt that," Ona said as she began walking angrily down the long hallway. "I sincerely doubt that."

"So much for not making her angry," HARV whispered.

HARV and I watched as two small bots rushed into the gym and sprayed the flaming debris with foam. Then we cautiously followed Ona.

"Okay. You're probably a little angrier than the rest of us," I said.

"Don't patronize me, Zach. Patronization makes me angry."

"Yeah, we wouldn't want that now, would we?"

"No, we wouldn't," she barked.

Ona made a fist like she was ready to strike me. A part of me was really turned on by the idea of going one-on-one with her. Still another part of me knew they don't give you any extra credit at the pearly gates because you got delivered there by somebody who looks great in a thong. I relaxed and took a nonthreatening pose. I shot a quick mental message to HARV via our internal link.

"I could use a little help here!"

"That's an understatement," HARV whispered in my head. "I've already run the specs. There's nothing I can do for you at the nano that will do anything except make Ms. Thompson more angry."

"Then I'll just have to use my wit and charm," I said.

"Well, you've had a good life," HARV concluded.

"Ona, I'm on your side," I said. "Obviously you could snap me like a twig here. But that wouldn't solve anything. And it would make me begin to seriously doubt your innocence."

Ona relaxed her fist. She looked around, as if searching for some unseen presence. "I'm not really sure what came over me. It must be SPMS." She patted me on the shoulder. "Oh, well, no harm done. Right?"

I shook the last of the cobwebs out of my head.

"If I were you, I would agree with her," HARV said inside my head.

"Sure, no problem," I agreed. "But one more incident like this and I'm off the case."

"I understand," she said.

"One more incident like that and you'll be dead," HARV said.

"So how are you going to fix this leak?" Ona said, getting back to the matter at hand.

"The media is going to do what they do. Between you, Tony, and me, we'll find the leak and shut it down," I said. "But I assume that the primary task is still finding Foraa's killer."

"Whatever. Do you have a plan for that?"

"Well, plan might be too strong a word, but there are some avenues of investigation that we need to explore. For one, I'd like to talk to your butler."

"Yes, I know," she said. "I've already arranged the meeting. W will be serving you tea in the tertiary drawing room in ten minutes."

"Tea?"

"It's what he does," Ona said. "He wouldn't be cooperative in a formal interview. He'll speak more freely in a situation where he's comfortable. And he's most comfortable serving tea."

"That's very good thinking, Ona."

"I suppose a genius intellect comes in handy now and again," she said. "But I should warn you that W is rather . . . odd."

"Define 'odd.' "

"Well, as I may have mentioned earlier, he's very old. Honestly, I've lost track of exactly old, but it's in the triple digits and his mind isn't what it used to be."

"Anything else?"

Ona looked away and fidgeted just a little bit.

"You need to remember that W has worked for my family for two generations. I've known him all my life."

"DOS, he's insane, isn't he?"

"Now, I find it insulting, Zach, that you would assume that just because the gentlemen has worked for me and my sisters for our entire lives that he would be insane."

"Sorry."

"But, as it so happens, he is insane," she said. "Not officially, though. I mean, we've never had him legally declared insane, but I know the signs."

"I'm sure you do."

"You know, for an employee, you're becoming rather impertinent."

"It's a defense mechanism."

"Ironic, then, that I find it so *offensive*," she said. "W takes his job very seriously and he tends to become slightly agitated when those around him don't."

"Don't what?"

"Take his job seriously."

"Serving tea?"

"*Especially* serving tea."

"Are you telling me that he'll get violent if I don't have good table manners?"

"He's over a hundred years old, Zach. He'd probably break a hip stamping his foot. I'm just saying that he'll be more frank with you if you treat his profession with respect."

"Well, if you put it that way . . ."

"Good. And by the way, don't talk to him for too long. He tends to fall asleep and urinate during long conversations."

"Well, it wouldn't be the most disgusting thing that's happened to me during an interview."

"Really?"

"You'd be surprised."

Ona stared at me, stone-faced expressionless, and I suddenly felt like a schoolboy who'd just put a virus in the class computer.

"That was an attempt at humor, wasn't it?"

"A little one."

"Let's try to keep those to a minimum, shall we?"

# 16

---

Ona offered me the use of an indoor hover for my trip from the gym to the tertiary drawing room. I declined, but after five minutes of walking through the halls, I began to regret the decision. As per our earlier discussion, HARV holographically walked beside me. Ona's computer kept us company as well, its bodiless voice following us like an intelligent breeze as we traveled.

"Computer, tell me W's story again," I asked.

"Well, as you know, sir, his full name is Wintercrescenhavenshivershamshawjamison. He is the fifteenth generation manservant in his family."

"What's that about three hundred years of servitude?"

"Three hundred twenty-seven, actually. He takes great pride in the family history. He began work for Dr. Thompson fresh out of butler school years ago."

"Butler school?"

"When Dr. Thompson died, W continued his service to the family by helping to raise the Thompson sisters and has remained in Ms. Thompson's employ since she took control of the estate."

"He does what exactly?" HARV asked.

"Table setting mostly."

"Table setting?"

"And serving tea. W is somewhat advanced in years now. I've taken on the bulk of his household responsibilities. I oversee the domestic droids and machines, including those responsible for food preparation. Table setting, however, was always W's forte so he has remained solely in charge of that."

"He sets the table," I mumbled. "That's all he does?"

"It's his niche."

"I'm not sure that table setting even qualifies as a niche," HARV said. "It's more like a nano niche."

"I wouldn't describe it as 'nano,' " the computer replied. "I think mini is more appropriate."

"Mini?" HARV exclaimed. "Clearly, you're overstating the importance of the function. In a compound this size, table setting is clearly a 'nano niche.' 'Micro' at best but certainly not 'mini.' "

"Yes, well, if you're measuring the importance on the scale of the entire household . . ."

"How else would one measure it?"

"On more of a universal scale," the computer replied, "in terms of the place that table setting resides in the average household."

"That ruins the entire comparison," HARV said. "You're comparing bignays and soursops."

"I would disagree."

"Now you see, *this* is why there should be a law against putting two supercomputers in a room together," I said.

"Actually, sir," the computer replied, "neither HARV nor I are physically in this room. My central processing unit is in the sub-subbasement of the compound and I assume that HARV's CPU is kept at some similarly secure location."

"That's it," I said. "Where's my gun?"

"In the retractable holster attached to your right wrist," the computer said. "Is he always this forgetful?"

"Sadly, yes. His short-term memory erodes by the day."

"He seems short-tempered as well."

"You should see him on a bad day."

"I'd rather not."

"You know, I can still hear you guys," I said.

"Of course, I can only imagine how difficult it must be for *you*," HARV said, "what with a superhuman user such as Ms. Thompson."

"Please, it's a new crisis every nano. It's even worse when the other sisters access the interface."

"The other Quads access you as well?"

"They don't have complete access, of course, but I do most of their tasking. It's Miss Ona's way of keeping tabs on her sisters' activities."

"Even Foraa?"

"Yes. Although, admittedly, Miss Foraa's activity on my server has dropped dramatically since her death."

"As expected."

"Truthfully, however, she used me rarely. For special projects mostly. And I suspect that the other sisters will increase their activity proportionately now that she's gone in order to cover the shortfall."

"I can imagine the strain that puts on your CPU," HARV said.

"Oh, the stories I could tell."

I had to hand it to HARV. He was playing up to Ona's computer like a pro. At this rate the two of them would be chess partners by dinner.

"Well, at least your user's not a technophobe," HARV said. "Did you know that he can't even pilot a hovercraft?"

"No?"

"I can, too," I said. "I flew Carol's hover last year."

"You crashed it into the duck pond."

"Well, it was trying to kill me!"

"It was?" the computer asked.

"It's a long story," HARV said. "But it's a good one. It all began when we were playing backgammon. I was winning, of course."

"Of course," the computer replied.

"Are we almost there?" I asked, rolling my eyes.

"Actually, yes," the computer replied. "The tertiary drawing room is at the end of this hall, five meters ahead. HARV, would it be possible for you to download me the rest of that story? It sounds most interesting."

"I would," HARV said, "but you wouldn't get the full effect. It really needs to be told in the first person. Let's discuss it in detail later on. I'll replay for you the recordings of the crash. It was quite a display."

"I will look forward to it. Mr. Johnson, please let me know if you need anything further. Also, please notify me immediately if any of the devices in the drawing room make any attempts on your life."

HARV and the computer chuckled gently to one another.

"Oh, yeah," I mumbled as HARV and I entered the room. "You'll be the first to know."

# 17

Wintercrescenhavenshivershamshawjamison was an ancient man, thin-framed and spindly, as though created from old kindling that would snap if the light hit it right. His face was drawn and crisscrossed with more lines than the New Frisco skyway map. His hair was wispy gray and his eyes were foggy. It took him a full minute to get out of his chair as HARV and I entered and I would have given you even odds that he wouldn't make it back without breaking a hip.

"If you please, sir, may I be so bold as to presume that you are Mr. Zachary Johnson?"

"If I'm not, then my mother has a lot of explaining to do," I replied, offering him my hand.

W's only response was a slow-motion arch of his right eyebrow.

"Pardon?"

"Mental note," HARV whispered, "your sense of humor, such that it is, does not play well with elderly male servants."

"Got it," I whispered before turning back to W. "Yes sir, I'm Zach Johnson. It's a pleasure to meet you Mr.—um—W."

"Charmed." W's eyes fell upon HARV's hologram and a look of worry appeared through the fog. "I was told that you'd be alone."

"This is my computer, HARV," I said. "He's assisting me on this case."

HARV bowed slightly to W, who totally ignored him.

"I was told that it was a single sitting," he said, slightly beside himself. "A single sitting only."

He motioned toward the table at the center of the room and

I saw that it was set for tea. Actually, "set" isn't the right word here. "Sculpted," is more accurate because everything had been meticulously set into place. From the table itself to the cloth, place setting, pot, cup, spoons, sugar bowl, and a dozen other tea-time-related gadgets that I didn't even recognize, it was so perfectly constructed that it didn't even look like a table setting anymore. It had transcended the mundane and become a table-setting mosaic, with every piece in its place in the greater, tea-themed portrait.

And it was set for one.

Which is why HARV's presence so ruffled W.

"It's all right, W," I said. "HARV's a computer. He won't be having tea. He'll just stand over there by the door."

"Stand by the door? What kind of high-tea philistine are you? His standing by the door throws off the whole balance of the room in relation to the table décor."

"Table décor?"

"Table décor!" W motioned frantically toward the table, his foggy eyes growing slightly apoplectic. "He'll have to sit. It's the only civilized way to proceed, which means I'll need another place setting. It's going to entail restructuring the configuration somewhat, adjusting the balance, probably rethinking the entire aesthetic layout. And I'll need another cup, of course. Give me five hours."

"What?"

"Six at the most."

W turned on his heel and began walking toward the door at the far wall. And by walking I mean, of course, not moving at all, at least not to the naked eye, because his strides could only be measured in micrometers. His creaky legs made barely the tiniest of forward steps, so he'd taken four strides before I noticed any lateral movement at all.

"I'll be right back."

"Geologically speaking, of course," HARV said. "I think this is what Ms. Thompson meant when she said that he takes his job somewhat seriously."

"Actually, I think this is what she meant when she said he was insane."

I approached W slowly and spoke in as innocent and non-threatening a voice as I could manage. "Actually, W," I said.

"HARV isn't staying for tea. He has other business to attend to and is leaving right now, aren't you HARV?"

"Oh, yes," HARV said. "I just wanted to make certain that Mr. Johnson arrived here safely. He's very accident prone, you know."

W stopped and turned back toward us.

"Are you sure? Because I can do the tea-for-two configuration. I can even manage a holographic cup. It's quite lovely."

"I'm sure it is, but it won't be necessary," I said.

"Oh, good," W said as he slowly returned to the table. "Truth to tell, I'm not as fast as I used to be."

"I would hope not," HARV mumbled.

"Ice the hologram, HARV," I whispered. "He's not getting any younger."

"It was a pleasure meeting you, Mr. W," HARV said with a bow and disappeared.

W seemed relieved once HARV had gone (I sympathized with him on some level, but don't tell that to HARV) and he gestured to the chair at the table. I carefully took my place at the setting as he prepared the tea.

"You there, HARV?" I whispered inside my head.

"Where else would I be, boss?" came HARV's inside my head reply.

"I may need a little help with the tea etiquette," I said, continuing our mental conversation.

"I'm not surprised,"

"W seems to be a stickler for details. I'd rather not offend him while I'm plying him for information," I said. "You know me, I'm likely to pour the tea into a saucer."

"Actually," HARV said, "that practice was acceptable in late Victorian and Edwardian days as a way to cool the tea before drinking, hence the term 'a dish of tea.' It's also interesting to note that . . ."

"See now this is the part where you're no longer helpful."

"Got it," HARV replied. "We'll stick to the basics. You're doing fine, so far, what with sitting in the chair and all. The napkin goes in the lap. I'll cue you from there."

"So, W," I said, turning my attention back to the manservant. "I want to thank you for seeing me on such short notice."

"No trouble at all," he replied, gently lifting a cup and saucer.

"I assume that you know of the unfortunate events of last night?" I asked.

"The dinner party?"

"That's right."

"Yes. A tragedy for everyone. I understand that the table setting was completely disrupted."

"Um, yeah," I said. "And then, of course, there's the bit about Foraa being murdered."

"Yes, that was very unfortunate as well." He very carefully filled the cup with tea from the pot, then gently held the cup on the saucer and turned back toward me. "How do you take your tea?"

"Um, cream?"

"Not cream," HARV whispered in my head. "Cream reacts with the acid in the tea. You want milk."

"I mean, milk," I said. "And two spoons . . ."

"Lumps."

"*Lumps* of sugar."

W nodded gently. "Very good, sir."

He added a dash of milk and two lumps of sugar to the cup, mixed it gently and handed the cup and saucer to me.

"Thanks," I said. "Now, about last night. Circumstances seem to indicate that Foraa was poisoned."

"Poisoned?"

"Was there anything odd that you remember about last night?"

"You mean other than the Quads being in the same room together?"

"I guess that was pretty odd in and of itself."

"To put it mildly," he said. "The four of them hadn't been together since the reading of Dr. Thompson's will."

"Any idea why they got together last night?"

"None, sir. Miss Ona simply told me six days ago to have the main dining room prepared for the event. She was inviting her sisters to dinner."

"So the dinner was Ona's idea?"

He thought for a nano.

"Not much happens in this house that isn't Miss Ona's idea."

My mind began to wander a bit, trying to apply the information that W was giving me to my view of the scene. I stirred my tea absent-mindedly as my mind raced. It took me a couple of nanos to realize that W was staring at me, his left eyebrow arched so high it nearly covered his bald spot.

"You're stirring too loudly," HARV said. "Don't touch the sides of the cup when you stir. Gently swish back and forth."

I smiled at W and began gently swishing my tea.

"So what exactly did you do for the dinner party last night?" I asked.

"I prepared the room. The table, the seating, the settings, and the like. I was told to make it spectacular."

"It looked very nice."

"Thank you. I'd say that aside from the dead body, it was some of my best work," he said.

"The murder did sort of upstage the décor," I said, gently lifting the cup to my mouth.

"Index finger goes through the handle and the thumb just above," HARV said. "Common practice is to extend a finger."

I stuck out a finger.

"Not that one!" HARV shouted. "The pinkie. And let me finish. Common practice among the uneducated is to extend the pinkie, but that dates back to the eleventh century. You'll be better off not extending."

"You could have led with that part," I whispered.

"Did you say something, sir?" W asked.

"No, nothing," I said.

"Don't look at him as you drink," HARV said. "Lower your eyes and look into the cup. And for Gates' sake, don't slurp."

I did as I was told (and made a mental note *never* to drink tea again) and then turned my attention back to W.

"Is the tea to your satisfaction?" he asked.

"Oh, yes. It's perfect," I replied.

He gently lifted a tray of pastries from the table.

"Cookie?"

"Oh, no. I don't think I'm ready for that," I answered. "But can you tell me who prepared the food for last night's dinner?"

"The computer prepares all meals," he replied. "Miss Ona

gave up on human chefs when her last one cut his arm off in the blender several years ago, to prove his love for her."

"That's rough."

"Yes. Miss Ona was particularly fond of that blender. Since then, the computer with the help of several bots has prepared all meals."

"Was the room cleaned the day of the party?"

"Yes."

"By whom?"

"Cleaning droids."

"Who did the flower arrangements?"

"They were holographically designed by the décor computer, which is attuned to Miss Ona's emotions."

"Polishing the silverware?"

"That's my responsibility. Why, was a piece of subpar luster?"

"No, it looked fine. What about the wine?"

"It was chosen by Miss Ona."

"You're sure?"

"Of course. No one else in the house chooses the wine," he said. "Miss Ona is quite particular."

"Yeah, I gathered that. Who actually brought the wine from the cellar?"

"Only Miss Ona has access to the wine cellar. It is protected with a DNA encoded lock."

"The Quads don't have identical DNA?"

"Apparently not quite," W replied. "Dr. Thompson no doubt varied their DNA somewhat when he created them. Odd that he made them just enough alike to drive one another crazy and different enough to drive each other . . . even crazier I suppose. Still, I'm sure he meant well."

"Right, so no one else can get into the wine cellar. And no one carried the wine up, moved it into place, chilled it or anything?"

"It was a red wine," Mr. Johnson. "To chill it would be criminal. No, to the best of my knowledge, only Miss Ona touched the wine. That is usually the case."

I leaned forward and took another sip of tea.

"Elbows off the table," HARV whispered. "And if you continue to slouch like that, he's going to assume that you're recovering from radical spine surgery."

"W, you've known the Quads for a long time. Correct?"

"All their lives, sir."

"What did you think of Foraa?"

"She was a lovely girl: bright-eyed, friendly, and full of wonder. She was precocious but had a heart filled with love for everyone and everything that she met."

"Really?"

"No, not really. That's the approved statement that I've been allowed to give to the press for the past fifteen years. Force of habit, you understand. Actually, Miss Foraa was spoiled, self-centered, and angry, but in retrospect she was the best of the four. And she was always kind to me. I think she rather liked me, really."

"Did she have any enemies that you know of? Anyone who would want to kill her?"

"Mr. Johnson, each of the Quads receive death threats every day of their lives. Death threats, marriage proposals, interview requests, sponsorship offers, and who knows what else. They've been threatened, cajoled, and romanced by every government, conglomerate, scientific organization, terrorist group, and lap-dance establishment created in the past twenty years. Humanity has reviled and adored them. Feared and desired them. Worshiped and desecrated them. It has been utterly impossible for them to live any semblance of normal lives among humanity, and it is only through sheer strength of will that they have managed to hold onto their respective sanities when surrounded by such overwhelming human greed, lust, and envy. One could easily make the argument that there isn't a person alive who hasn't at one time or another wanted to see them dead."

"That was another of the preapproved speeches wasn't it?" I asked.

"Yes," he said. "That one was for intimate interviews, when the Quads wanted to play up their humanity. It's factually accurate, though."

"Okay, but I think we need to get past the rehearsed stuff if you're going to be helpful," I said. "I sort of need the truth here."

"I understand."

"Is there anyone in the household that disliked Foraa?"

"You mean other than her sisters?"

"Yes, aside from them."

"She didn't get along very well with the Pfauhans," he said.

"The Pfauhans—you mean the security experts."

"Yes. Miss Foraa was never one for high technology or annoying people. Both Pfauhans are unbelievably annoying high technology experts. You see the problem."

"I see it," I said with a nod. "Back to last night, were you present when Foraa was murdered?

W shook his head. "I was asleep in my chambers. I had been preparing the room for six days. The last twelve hours of those without a break."

"It takes that long?"

"The polishing of the silverware alone takes two days."

"So you were asleep when Foraa was murdered?"

"Yes."

"You didn't hear anything?"

"My quarters are at the far end of the ziggurat."

"Pyramid."

"Pardon?"

"Sorry, you're right. Ziggurat. Your room's far from the dining room?"

"A little more than a kilometer away. I travel back and forth via an indoor hover. As you can see, I have some trouble moving quickly."

"Yes, I'd noticed that." I took one last sip of tea and gently placed my cup on the saucer. "That's all I have for now, W. Thank your time and for the tea. It was delicious. And very nicely presented."

"The pleasure was mine," he said, as he began to clear away my cup.

"I may have a few more questions later on," I said. "Can I come back to you again?"

"Any time, sir. Just give me enough warning to properly ready the room."

I stood and walked slowly toward the door.

"One last thing," I said, turning back toward him. "The bit you said about there not being a person on this planet right now who hasn't wanted the Quads dead, does that include you?"

W stood motionless for a long nano.

"Of course not," he said.

"So I guess you should have said that there isn't a person on this planet right now, *other than yourself,* who hasn't at one time or another wanted to see them dead."

"Mr. Johnson. I am a frail old man for whom putting my pants on is a challenge. My lot in life is setting tables and serving tea. How could I possibly harm, let alone kill, any of the Quads?"

"You're right," I said "I just wanted to point out the miscue in the preapproved speech. The Quads might want to rework that a little."

"Yes, that discrepancy should be attended to."

I turned back toward the door.

"Darn right it should," I said. "Because when word of the murder gets out, I think you'll all be making that speech a lot."

# 18

We left the tertiary drawing room and trekked through the mansion on the next leg of the interview expedition. Supposedly, Ona's computer was guiding us directly to Opie's specially designed habitat within the residence, but I think it took us the long way around so it could listen to HARV tell more stories.

"And the next thing you know, the old woman shows up at the door with a shotgun."

"A real shotgun?"

"It was one hundred years old if it was a day. Two nanos later he's hiding behind a tree, ducking buckshot."

"So it isn't just computers and machines that dislike him?"

"Oh, no. His lack of appeal is multidemographic. Just recently another old lady tossed him around; he had to use his gun to defeat her."

"He used a firearm on an elderly woman?" Ona's computer asked.

"She wasn't really an old lady," I said, as I walked a bit faster, anxious to end this ASAP. "She was some sort of alien doppelganger."

"So you see," HARV said. "His lack of appeal is even interplanetary."

"Very impressive indeed," Ona's computer said.

"This is getting really annoying," I said. "Can't you two speak in binary or something so I don't have to listen?"

We turned and entered a long hallway that was filled with medieval weaponry. Full suits of armor lined the walls, interspersed with cases and wall displays of weaponry.

"I didn't know Ona was a weapons collector."

"She's not," the computer replied. "These are the remnants of Dr. Thompson's collection. He used the weaponry in his research."

"It must be very valuable."

"Not really, most of it's replicas. Dr. Thompson smelted it himself based upon twelfth- and thirteenth-century designs."

"He smelted his own armor?"

"His philosophy was that one could not create the future without fully understanding the past, so before beginning his rather intense period of weapons development, he immersed himself in the history of warfare in order to fully understand the weapons that had come before."

"I think it must be some sort of weird phallic symbol, probably to make up for what he lacked in other areas," I said.

"Oh, no," the computer replied. I was pretty certain I sensed a lot of discomfort in its voice. "It gave him a historical perspective of warfare and its evolutionary touchstones," the computer went on. "These suits of armor were considered state of the art in the thirteenth century, yet they were shortly thereafter rendered useless by the 'ultimate weapon' of the period."

"What was that?"

"The English longbow," HARV said with a smirk.

"Correct," the computer replied. "A low-cost, easy-to-master weapon that could attack from long range and pierce the best battle armor of the day, the longbow was the weapon that conquered Wales and Scotland and won the Hundred Years' War for England."

"And made England the foremost military power of Europe," HARV added.

"What, did they have a patent on the technology?" I joked.

"Now I can see why so many people and machines try to kill him," Ona's computer said.

"Yes, he does certainly take some getting used to," HARV said with a smile. "If he lives to be fifty, I'll be amazed."

"You know you two could make a fortune curing insomniacs by forcing them to listen to you talk."

"So you really get used to him?" Ona's computer asked, not trying at all to mask the surprise in its voice.

"With time," HARV reassured it. "With time."

We walked past the armor and turned left into another long hallway.

"Are we there yet?" I asked impatiently.

"Master Opie's residence is just ahead. Thirty meters down this corridor and through that door," the computer replied.

I looked up and saw that the hallway ended at a large set of double doors, which took on a bit of a glow, the computer's way of highlighting the destination. I walked the rest of the hallway and put my hand on one of the large doorknobs but then hesitated.

"Do I need any special equipment for this or anything?"

"No, sir," the computer replied, "the doorknob works in a relatively straight forward fashion."

"I mean with Opie!"

"What do you mean?"

"Well, he's an ape, right?"

"A silverback mountain gorilla, to be exact."

"How do I approach him? Shouldn't I have a banana or something."

"A banana?"

"Boss, please," HARV said. "You're embarrassing me."

"What do you mean?"

"Silverback mountain gorillas are indigenous to Hagenia forest. Their diet includes ninety-seven different plant species, none of which are bananas. A gorilla in its natural habitat wouldn't know what to do with a banana."

"Yeah, well, I don't think the home of the world's richest woman is considered its natural habitat."

"I see," said HARV, "so the banana is sort of a symbolic nod to the creature's opulent yet unnatural surroundings. Do you think that's appropriate?"

"What?"

"I agree," the computer chimed in. "I think something familiar to the species would be more suitable. Perhaps the leaf of a plant indigenous to the mountain forests would be more appropriate."

"Yes, something common to that part of the world and yet can also be found in this hemisphere, such as bamboo shoots," HARV said. "That way you're speaking to both cultures."

"Brilliant," the computer said.

"Thank you."

I rolled my eyes and opened the door.

"Forget it," I said. "Opie could be bloodthirsty, rabid, radioactive, and selling life insurance and he'd still be preferable to listening to the two of you."

I peered into the room. It was darker than I expected, filled with lush vegetation. Even from outside, I could feel that the air was heavy with humidity.

"I see that Ms. Thompson has gone to great lengths to recreate the mountain gorilla's natural habitat," HARV said.

"I guess every Graceland should have its jungle room."

"Pardon?"

"Forget it." I walked in. It was hard to breathe at first, and harder still to see clearly. "Computer, any idea where we can find Opie?"

There was no answer.

"It would appear that the computer interface did not enter the room with us," HARV said as his hologram, now dressed in nineteenth-century safari gear, appeared beside me.

"Great, omnipresent except when you need it."

"Would you like me to page it?"

"No," I said. "I was getting sick of hearing you two chatter. Could the two of you be any more annoying?"

"Did you or did you not instruct me to befriend the computer?" HARV said, inside my head.

"There are other things to talk about in this world besides my shortcomings, you know," I thought back.

"Granted," HARV said, "but few are as enjoyable."

I took a few steps farther into the room and felt my feet sink slightly into the mudlike floor. I crouched slightly out of instinct and scanned the darkness for any sign of motion.

"I don't like this," I said. "Let's switch to infrared."

My left eye went dark for a nano, then sprang to life again like a computer screen powering up as HARV switched the input to my brain from the normal light spectrum to heat-sensitive infrared. The jungle became a blur of red and orange shapes and I could now see that more than half the deciduous vegetation wasn't really there at all.

"Apparently Opie has been using Ms. Thompson's holographic decor program," HARV said.

"So simple even a monkey can use it."

"Perhaps, then, there's still hope for you. Fine idea, by the way, switching to infrared."

"I have my occasional good ideas."

"Granted, but have I ever told you about the empar?"

"Empar?"

"My own variation on radar or sonar. I use an electromagnetic pulse which I emanate from the wrist communicator as the searching waves. It's a little something new that I've added to the bag of tricks."

I tried hard not to pay attention to HARV's chatter and continued my slow trek through the jungle, scanning the grounds for suspicious heat signatures as I moved.

"I don't know if I've mentioned this, but I've been gradually upgrading our operating system. After all, I have to do something to keep busy during your downtime."

"Is there a point here, HARV? I'm a little busy."

"Actually, the reason I bring it up at this particular nano is because, although using the infrared vision lets you see more clearly in the darkness, the empar would let you monitor the *entire* room including areas currently outside your field of vision. Such as behind you . . ."

"What?"

I spun quickly around and dropped into a defensive stance, ready to fend off any attack from behind. Unfortunately, I didn't notice the six-hundred-pound hulking form that suddenly dropped on top of me from the treetops overhead.

". . . or perhaps above you."

For a super-speed computer, HARV is remarkably slow at getting to the point.

I looked up to see a giant ape falling toward me. I dove aside just in time to avoid being squished, but the ape grabbed me with a hairy arm and we rolled along the dirt floor together, grappling as we moved (me trying to break free, my attacker . . . well, I'm not entirely sure what it was trying to do but it involved some painful grabbing and hitting).

I should note here that, despite evidence to the contrary, I don't enjoy fisticuffs or violence. I much prefer thinking my way out of dangerous situations because it usually hurts less. But in my business, there are inevitably times when physical force is necessary. Like my old football coach used to say, *the best defense is a good offense.* At least, I'm pretty sure she said something like that. To tell the truth, I never really listened much, I usually just sat on the bench ogling the cheerleaders. Still, it made good sense, no matter who said it.

Of course, I figure it doesn't hurt to have all my bases covered, so I also wear armored underwear. It's lightweight, super strong, and computer enhanced. It's also specially designed to both protect me and, when needed, augment my strength. It's a little constricting at times and smells a little funny when it gets wet, but that's a small price to pay. After all, you never know when something huge and angry is going to drop on you from a treetop.

My attacker and I rolled across the floor and hit one of the nonholographic trees. He took the brunt of the impact and that caused him to loosen his grip just enough for me to skitter free. I scrambled to my feet a few meters away, turned back toward my attacker and, as I suspected, beheld the infrared image of a great ape rising up on its legs and pounding its chest, oozing more testosterone than an amateur bare-knuckle fight competition in a New Tijuana whorehouse.

"Wild guess here," I said. "That's Opie?"

"I doubt that there's more than one silverback mountain gorilla currently in residence here."

"I thought he was supposed to be intelligent."

"Maybe he's gone native. Or maybe he just doesn't like you. Gates knows that by now you shouldn't be surprised at any attempt on your life."

"I knew I should have brought a banana."

"Yes," said HARV, "because everyone knows that a banana is the only way to stop a charging gorilla."

"Don't get sarcastic with me. All I'm saying is that . . . did you say charging?"

I turned back to Opie just in time to see him put his fists angrily on the ground and charge me on all fours. I flicked my right wrist in the special way that makes my gun pop into my hand and held it steady in my grip. I was about to vocally set

the gun for heavy stun and fire when HARV did something totally unexpected.

"SR Trigger. Bruce Lee. Go!"

"What?"

And at that nano, Opie was on me and things became very
strange.

I ducked under Opie's initial lunge and did a lightning-fast
sweep with my leg. I caught him behind the knee as he passed
and he tumbled to the muddy ground with a growl that was
equally composed of anger and surprise.

"What did I just do?"

"Just go with it," HARV said. "He's coming back."

Opie rose to his feet and attacked again, this time with a
wild punch from his hairy, tree-trunk arm. Again, I ducked
under the punch, then grabbed his arm and gave him a spinning
back kick to the rib cage that staggered him. Opie stumbled,
then spun his massive form back toward me, clearly off
balance and confused now, so I pressed my advantage.

I lunged at him and hit him with a roundhouse kick to the
stomach followed by two quick snap kicks to the head. Then I
leaped in the air and delivered a haymaker spinning back kick
to his head that toppled him.

I found all of this really strange, because I'd never done a
proper spinning back kick in my life. As a matter of fact, I'd
never done any of the combat moves that I'd just performed.
Electra is the martial arts expert (as she, often painfully, reminds me). I'm a barroom fighter who I like to think gets by
on smarts and old-fashioned gumption more than anything else
(although truthfully, it's more likely luck and dirty tricks, but
I'm not about to put that in my press material). The bottom line
is that I suddenly had abilities that I never had before and it
didn't take a genius to figure out where they came from.

"HARV!" I shouted. "What the DOS was that?"

"A preprogrammed combat subroutine. I figured it might
come in handy."

"You programmed a subroutine into my brain?"

"Just into your temporal lobe. It's more easily activated
that way."

"I should crush your memory chips and feed them to the
sewer droids."

"Well, that's not exactly the response I was expecting, but I'll take that as a thank you."

"Don't you dare take it as a thank you!" I yelled. "You're messing with my brain."

"Only a few million neurons that you're not really using."

I held my head in my hands and felt myself shake in anger and frustration.

"There has to be a law against this. It's brainwashing. It's invasion of privacy. It's . . ."

"It's giving you skills that could save your life."

"Against my will! Gates, HARV, you don't just put something in someone's brain without telling them!"

I was quickly nearing the anger management point-of-no-return when a deep-throated voice from behind brought me back to the situation at hand.

"Excuse me, but would you mind keeping it down?"

I turned and saw Opie slowly getting to his feet. The angry posture of the crazed gorilla was gone. He now carried himself like a mountainous (if only a little tired) man-child, slightly hunched at the shoulders, but straight-backed and upright on both legs. He held his jaw gently in his hand, rubbing the tender spot where my last kick had hit.

"Some of us are nursing headaches here," he said.

I gripped my gun tighter and raised it to show the big ape the business end.

"Don't move, ape. I'm not in the best of moods right now."

Opie waved a giant hand at me dismissively and turned away as he steadied himself.

"Put the gun away before you hurt someone, Zach," he said. "And call me Opie. Geez, can't you take a joke?"

He clapped his hands together twice quickly. The lights in the room came on in response and the holographic jungle around us disappeared (the real plants remained, although they looked a lot less ominous under the new lights). Within nanos the jungle became a living room, and a very nice one at that, with some overstuffed antigrav sectional sofas and a couple of gorilla-sized reclining chairs. Opie saw me staring (probably with a puzzled look on my face) and smiled a gorilla grin in response, then shrugged his hairy mountainback shoulders.

"A joke, Zach. It's a little old and obvious, but I never get tired of scaring the bejeezus out of first time visitors. The wild-yet-semi-intelligent ape act always gets a great reaction. You should have seen the look on your face when I dropped on you. I think I even scared the hologram."

"That was a preprogrammed facial response," HARV quipped. "It was not reflective of any underlying emotions."

"Whatever," Opie said. "Your mouth was open and your eyes were wide. That's good enough." He turned back to me. "Of course, then you went all twentieth century on me and started hitting. That sort of ruined the rest. I didn't even get to use the 'get your hands off me, you damn dirty human,' line. Admittedly, no one ever gets that joke, but I thought you might."

I stared at Opie for a long nano as he pulled some clothes out of a simulacrum tree stump and began dressing. I'm fairly certain that my mouth was slightly agape and my eyes were wide and angry.

"I should shoot you now," I said with my gun still aimed at his chest. "I should switch to full power and atomize you where you stand." I didn't appreciate being jumped on, even as a joke. But I kind of admired anybody who could quote a ninety-year-old flick.

Opie pulled a large sweatshirt over his head then smiled and shrugged his shoulders again.

"An ape's gotta have a hobby," he said. "I have this thing for practical jokes. Dr. Thompson thought it was a by-product of his genetically altering my mind to an advanced plateau. You know how evolutionary thought goes. It starts with fight or flight, then goes to social interaction, communication, utilization of rudimentary tools. The next step apparently is crude humor. Go figure. By the way, you're standing in a pile of my dung."

I looked down and took a quick step back. Opie burst into laughter.

"Gotcha! Gates, humans are so easy to manipulate sometimes."

"I knew I should have brought a banana."

"Ugh! Bananas. Can't stand the things unless they're thinly sliced and fried," Opie replied as he sauntered to one of the easy chairs. "How about a beer?"

"A beer?"

"Some German brand. I'm told it's very expensive. They say the head is so thick you can float a bottle cap on it." He reached into the trunk of another tree and pulled out two brown bottles of beer, then tapped the tops gently to break the electromagnetic freshness seal. The seal dissipated and the bottles exhaled an enticing sigh of effervescence. "At least that's what I'm told. I'm not quite sure what a bottle cap is."

"It's a small piece of metal they used to use to seal bottled drinks."

"Sheesh," he said, offering me one of the bottles, "what a waste of metal."

I took the bottle from his giant hand and felt the wet chill of the glass beneath my fingers, a welcome sensation indeed. "Yeah, well, it was a different age."

"You're not actually going to drink while you're working, are you?" HARV whispered inside my head.

"He'll be more at ease if I buddy up with him. I'll just nurse the beer a bit," I thought back silently in reply. Then I turned back to Opie. "So I assume that you knew I was coming?"

Opie took a long pull from his beer and nodded.

"The computer told me you'd be dropping by. It knows I like to surprise people." Opie turned his big head toward HARV. "The computer seems especially fond of you, HARV. It says you tell quite a story."

"That's true," HARV said, with a bit of a blush. "But I'm only as good as my source material."

Opie turned back toward me and gestured toward the other recliner.

"Speaking of which, Zach, the computer tells me that you're quite the bumbler."

I rolled my eyes and took a sip of the beer. It was good.

"Well, the computer hasn't seen me at my best," I said, carefully settling myself into the recliner. "I assume that you must also know then that Ona has hired me to find Foraa's killer, so I was wondering . . ."

An incredibly loud fart/sound blurted from the chair as I sat. A small cloud of smoke rolled out from under the cushion and what appeared to be a dead pigeon fell from the ceiling overhead. Opie doubled over in laughter again.

"Gates, Zach, control yourself," he said, fanning the air around him. "And they call *me* an animal."

"Whoopee cushion," I mumbled. "Very original, Opie. The bird is a nice touch, though."

"It's all nanotechnology," he said. "All the furniture's outfitted with them. My butt's the only one that won't set them off. You should have been here the last time I did a live interview. The Q-Score of this one pressbot from *Rapid News* dropped fifty percent when her cushion went off. I think she's covering farming news in the Arctic Circle now."

He pressed a button on the arm of the chair and a bowl full of nachos popped up from the floor.

"Have some if you like," he said motioning toward me. "Your chair's set for onion rings, I think."

I had to admit that I was growing fond of Opie.

# 19

"I find it unsurprising," HARV whispered in my head, "that of all the occupants in this compound, you are most comfortable with the gorilla."

The irony was not lost on me, but I ignored HARV's quip as best I could and kept my attention on Opie.

"So you know about Foraa being murdered last night."

"Yes," he said with a sad nod. "I cried all morning. The computer finally coaxed me out of the funk by telling me that you were coming. I guess it thought a good joke would cheer me up."

"So you're pretty distraught over Foraa's death?"

"Well, it's always very hard for a pet when it outlives its master. It's unnatural. You know what I mean?"

"Actually, no."

Opie ignored me.

"The Quads took good care of me when they were kids."

"Even though you were older?"

"I was older, but I'm a gorilla. These kids were geniuses. Like I said, I was their pet."

"Were they good owners?"

"They were lovely girls," he said, smiling. "Bright-eyed, friendly and full of wonder. They were precocious, of course, and rambunctious at times, I admit, but they had hearts . . ."

"Filled with love for everyone and everything they met," I said, rolling my eyes. "I've heard that speech before, Opie."

"Yeah, I think that's one of W's," he said. "I went off script a bit with the rambunctious part. It just felt right."

"It sounded very natural, but it's worthless to me," I said.

He grabbed another fistful of nachos and stuck them down his throat then licked the cheese from his finger fur. "I understand," he said. "It's just second nature. Truthfully, what can I say, the Quads were odd. They were rude. They were sometimes dangerous."

"Dangerous?"

"When she was four years old, Ona carried a special little purse to school with her every morning 'for a project.' She was apparently having trouble with some of the school administrators. When Dr. Thompson finally got around to examining the contents of the purse, he found a homemade death ray and a quantum spatial neutralizer inside."

"What's a quantum spatial neutralizer?"

"How should I know? I'm a gorilla. Sounds impressive, though."

"Where did Ona get it?"

"She made it out of spare parts that she'd found around the house. All the Quads are like that. They're strange and brilliant and just when you start to get comfortable with their peculiarities, they whip a quantum something-or-other out of their purse and all bets are off."

"What about Foraa?"

"She was as strange and brilliant as the others," he said. "Maybe a little more shy."

"Shy?"

"Relatively speaking of course. And rebellious."

"Did she have any enemies?"

Opie started to speak, then stopped and thought better of it.

"I suppose you've already heard the 'there isn't a person alive who hasn't at one time or another wanted to see them dead' speech, huh?"

"Yes, I have."

"I'll spare you that one, then. But it's true. All I can tell you is that Foraa was always civil to me. She actually gave me a nice hug when she arrived yesterday. As a matter of fact, that was the last time I saw her alive."

"What about W?"

"Oh, Foraa hated W."

"Really?" I said, biting my lip just a bit.

"Gates, yes. In her eyes, he was the embodiment of bourgeois evils of the world. He was an intelligent person whose only purpose in life was to serve her family, not because they needed him but because they were rich and could afford him. Having a servant rankled her antiestablishment attitude to no end. She always made a big show of refusing to let him to serve her. W, of course, took her refusal to be served as an insult to his dignity and duty and the two of them would just butt heads forever. The nihilist super-chick and the butler. It was like an alternative dimensional sitcom."

"They argued?"

"It was terrible. Foraa always insisted on using the wrong forks. It drove W crazy. He scolded her about it once when she was ten, but she zapped his mind and made him do the Freaky Geeky for hours. After that, he sort of left her alone."

"So they didn't have any contact."

"No, there was plenty of contact," Opie said. "It's just that W didn't argue with her anymore."

"He became even more subservient."

"Funny, isn't it? Foraa enjoyed browbeating him, I think. I was out and about the residence yesterday afternoon and saw her berating him after she arrived. For old time's sake, I guess."

"She argued with him yesterday?"

"They didn't exactly argue. Foraa said a few things, W cringed, they cast a few angry glances at one another, that sort of thing."

"Could you hear what they were saying?"

Opie shook his head. "I was too far away. And I think they were whispering. The computer might know. It tends to see and hear most things that go on around here."

"Yes, but it's not always very forthcoming with that information."

"Oh, you've discovered that," Opie said with a smile. "I guess we all have our secrets."

"Well, the only secret I'm looking to uncover is who killed Foraa."

"Be careful what you wish for, Zach. The one bit of advice I can give you is that nothing ever goes as expected when you're dealing with the Quads."

"Believe me, Opie, I'm finding that out in spades. From the

contact I've had with Ona, Twoa, and Threa, I know they're more crazy than a bot with half a logic board. And Foraa seems even loonier."

"What!" Opie shouted. "How dare you speak badly of the dead?"

He jumped out of his recliner, grabbed me by the shirt, and ripped me out of my chair.

"Ha-ha, very funny, Opie. You know this crazy ape thing gets old real fast. Now please be a good fellow primate and put me down before you rip the material."

Instead, Opie responded to my request by grabbing for my throat. This had quickly gone from annoying to downright uncomfortable. I looked Opie in his eyes. They seemed to be burning with rage. He was either a darn fine actor or raving mad (or perhaps both—the two aren't mutually exclusive). Whatever the reason, I wasn't going to take it any longer.

"Shock him!" I said to HARV, before Opie had any chance to tighten his grip.

Being wired directly into my nervous system gives HARV access to the chemical reactions that go on within my body. He can actually cause these reactions to magnify in intensity. In this case I wanted HARV to increase the electrical energy in my body, to give Opie the shock of his life—literally and figuratively.

"Oh, so now you're happy that we share your brain," HARV said.

As HARV complained, Opie tightened his grip. I grabbed Opie's wrists to try to loosen his grip, but I had about as much chance of doing that as I did of winning the lottery.

"Just do it!" I shouted, as loud as I could, which wasn't very loud considering that I was being strangled by a giant gorilla.

"Oh, fine," HARV said.

I felt myself tingle. Energy ripped from my hands into Opie. The shock snapped his head back and forced him to release his grip on my throat. He took a step back and shook his head.

"DOS, Opie, you have to learn when to let a joke go," I said. "Attacking a guy once may—and I repeat—*may* be funny. But attacking a guy twice, within fifteen minutes—that's overkill."

Opie hit himself in the head, first with his right hand, and then with his left. It was like he was trying to knock some sense into himself. He wobbled his head back and forth a few times then looked at me. He eyes were much calmer now.

"A joke, right, sorry," he said. "Sometimes I don't know when to stop. I guess it's my animal instincts."

"Opie, buddy you're just lucky I like you or I would have shot you."

I took one last pull on my beer, then climbed out of the gorilla-sized recliner, which wasn't easy.

"Thanks for the beer."

"Come back anytime, Zach," he said, offering me his hand.

"I just may do that, Opie." I said. "You know, I think you may be the sanest one of this whole bunch."

His palm and hairy fingers completely engulfed my lower arm as we moved to shake and I felt a sharp stab of pain as our hands touched. It was hot and hard, like a tiny branding iron on my palm.

"Yowtch!"

I wrenched my hand from his grasp and jumped back, almost falling to the floor as I backed away. Opie doubled over with laughter again and held up his hand to reveal a gigantic joy buzzer.

"Supersized and personalized," he said.

I looked down at my palm. A picture of a grinning gorilla had been lightly burned into the flesh. It wasn't deep enough to be a permanent scar, but it would certainly be sore for a few days.

"I guess 'sanest' was too strong a word," I said to myself.

"Clearly," HARV agreed.

I shook my head gently as HARV and I left the room, Opie's laughter still echoing in the distance.

"Maybe I should've shot him," I mumbled.

# 20

"I thought that went well," HARV said as we walked through the hallway a few nanos later.

"Yes, it's always nice when somebody tries to kill me before they even talk to me," I said. "It really breaks the ice."

"Come now, he was only joking. The situation was hardly life-threatening. I've seen you in greater danger from cocktail waitresses."

"Anytime a three-hundred-kilo gorilla drops toward you from a tree, whatever his intentions, it qualifies as life-threatening," I said.

"Oh please," HARV replied. "He was just playing with you."

"Maybe so, but I still didn't like it."

"Lucky for you that you have me to counter his joke with technology."

"Yeah, lucky me. I have a computer hooked to my brain who sticks things in there without my permission."

"I thought I was doing you a favor. You should be thankful."

"You reprogram my brain without my knowing and you expect me to thank you for it?"

"You're making it sound sinister. Besides I didn't reprogram, I added and improved a little. Kind of like upgrading from Zach 1.0 to Zach 1.01."

"The mind is sacred, HARV. Reprogramming it or probing it too deeply or adding to it is a violation of a person's right to privacy."

"How is what I did different from what Carol, or any psi, does all the time?"

"Let's not go there."

"Why not?"

"Because it's morally ambiguous and I don't want to let you off the hook because of that," I said. "And where's Ona's computer? Are we going the right way?"

HARV let out a computer-generated sigh and gave me that of-course-I-know-where-I am look as he wrinkled his already wrinkled brow. He turned right and we entered the medieval weaponry hallway again.

"Honestly," he said. "I don't understand why you're so angry over a simple combat subroutine. It's much more flashy than the old shock 'em trick. Plus, I thought you liked that Bruce Lee person."

"Well, of course I like Bruce Lee. Who doesn't? He's the Elvis of the martial arts. But that's not the point . . . wait a minute. What about Bruce Lee?"

"The combat moves in the subroutine were designed to mimic his movements."

"You based the moves I did on Bruce Lee?"

"I had to get them from somewhere," HARV replied. "I found them in an old vid."

"Which vid?"

*"Enter the Dragon."*

*"Enter the Dragon?"*

"Is that a good one?"

"That's the best one he ever did!" I said. "Are you telling me that the karate moves I did are the same moves that Bruce Lee did in *Enter the Dragon?*"

"Well, not exactly," HARV said. "Your muscles aren't as strong or as limber as his, so you didn't jump quite as high or hit quite as hard, but they were identical in their essence."

"Wow."

"It's not so bad now, is it?"

"It's . . . it's morally ambiguous."

"What does that mean?"

"It means I'm going to have to think about it a little more."

"I suggest you think about it later," HARV said glancing down the hallway behind us.

"Why's that?"

"Because that suit of armor is about to attack you."

I turned around just in time to see one of the supposedly empty suits of armor swing a meter-long iron mace at my head. I spun away from the attack as the mace passed through HARV's hologram and missed me by a chip's width. The follow-through sent the mace crashing into a display case, sending decorative glass and medieval hand weapons tumbling to the floor.

"What the DOS?"

The suit of armor swung again, this time a huge backhand with the mace that missed me only because I was still stumbling backward. The mace hit another display case and more weapons tumbled to the floor.

"Alert Ona's computer," I said as I regained my balance. "Let it know that Dr. Thompson's old research project is trying to kill me."

"Already done. Although I don't think I was able to properly capture the sarcasm of your inflection," HARV replied. "Perhaps this is another of Opie's jokes?"

I flicked my wrist and popped my gun into hand.

"If this is a joke," I said, as I aimed and fired, "I'm going to personally stick the punchline up his ass."

The energy blast from my gun hit the armor square in the breastplate. It staggered the attacker but didn't blow it to shreds as I'd expected. Instead, the blast bounced off the breastplate and ricocheted off the ceiling and floor like a rubber ball from a cannon.

"Look out!" HARV shouted.

The two of us dropped to the floor (HARV's hologram doing so more out of sympathy for me rather than necessity) as the blast passed over us and continued bouncing down the hallway, dissipating as it went.

"It appears that the armor is equipped with a blaster-repellent surface," HARV remarked. "Someone or something has clearly tampered with that armor."

"Yes, I got that feeling myself, Mr. Detective. So my gun is useless against this thing?"

"As always, boss, you have an undeniable grasp of the obvious."

The armor hefted its giant mace again and moved menacingly toward me. I scrambled to my feet and grabbed a sword that had fallen from one of the broken display kits.

"Okay, access that combat subroutine again. I'm going to need some Bruce Lee moves. On three. One . . . two . . .

"But . . ."

The armor lunged, swinging its mace wildly. For the briefest of nanos, it left itself off balance and vulnerable. This was my chance, so I made the most of it.

"Three!"—

I leaped into the air with sword in hand, let loose a cathartic war cry, and aimed a simultaneous flying kick and roundhouse sword strike at the armor's breastplate and head.

Unfortunately, this time I didn't move like Bruce Lee. The kick wasn't quite as high as I'd hoped, so my foot bounced harmlessly off the metal of the armor's kneeplate. And I totally whiffed with the sword swing, nearly cutting off my own foot with the follow-through. I'm pretty sure that I would have fallen on my own, but just to be certain, the armor helped me along with a metal-glove body blow to the ribs. My war cry choked in my throat and I hit the floor hard, bouncing once off the wall on the way down.

"Just for the record," I said. "That part where I yelled 'three' was your cue to activate the subroutine."

"Have you used that joke before?"

"Yes, but it's hard to come up with new material when you're being beaten to death."

The armor kicked me in the ribs and I rolled across the hallway, half from the force of the blow and half to put some distance between the two of us. I came up in a crouch and grabbed a shield from the shattered display case.

"I tried to warn you," HARV said. "Once the subroutine is moved into your temporary memory for usage, it is erased to save space. It works only once per download. I'll need to reload it into your subconscious when you're sleeping."

"You couldn't have given me more than one subroutine?"

"I wanted to do a trial run first, to make sure there would be no complications or side effects."

"Great. You know what, putting subroutines in my head is no longer morally ambiguous. It's now officially a stupid idea and is forbidden in perpetuity."

"I'm glad to see that you take such care in making philosophical decisions," HARV said. "But we can discuss the matter later. Provided of course, you survive this attack."

The armor came at me again. I lifted the shield and the heavy clang of the mace against the metal made my arm go numb for a nano. Whatever was inside the armor, it certainly was strong.

"Scan the armor. Is there anything organic inside?"

"No organic matter or independent thought," HARV said. "It's a droid skeleton using a preprogrammed combat routine."

"Good," I said, as the armor continued to pound my shield. "At least I don't have to worry about civilian casualties, other than my own."

"Well, if you have a plan of action, I suggest you implement it soon."

"Why?"

"Because you're about to get more unwelcome company."

As if on cue, three more suits of armor stepped off their pedestals on the far wall and brandished their weapons.

"Oh, good," I said. "I was getting a little bored."

Still shielding myself from the first attacking suit of armor, I reached down and picked up a mace from the floor. It was solid iron and felt like it weighed twenty kilos. I had trouble hefting it without breaking my wrist.

"I don't suppose you have any hints on medieval hand-to-hand combat."

"The strategy of the time was to hit hard and run away," HARV replied. "Admittedly, however, it wasn't very effective when one was outnumbered four to one."

"Thanks."

The first suit of armor hammered my shield again with its mace as the three other suits began walking toward me, weapons drawn. I cast a glance at the far end of the hall and back the other way toward Opie's area. Both places were too far away. The droid infrastructure of the suits of armor made them surprisingly quick, despite their clanky appearance, and I knew that they'd easily chase me down if I ran. My only hope was to stay and fight, so I adjusted my grip on the heavy mace and held my shield a little tighter. Then I caught a glimpse of the one still-unbroken display case, a few meters away, and got an idea.

"Thank you, HARV."

"Pardon me?"

I crouched down and tossed the mace at the legs of my attacker. It clanged off its shins and fell to the floor between its big metal boots. Then I took my shield in both hands and rammed it into the armor's chest. The armor staggered backward, tripped over the mace, and fell to the ground like a pile of girders. I hopped over the stunned armor/android as its three compatriots quickened their approach and ran to the display case. I slammed the butt of my gun into the decorative glass and shattered it to get to the weapons inside.

"Aren't there enough weapons for you on the floor already?" HARV asked.

"Those are ordinary weapons," I said. "I'm looking for something of an 'ultimate' nature."

And I triumphantly pulled an English longbow and arrows from the case.

"So you *were* paying attention after all," HARV smirked.

"You never know when a supercomputer is going to say something useful."

I tried to string the bow quickly as the first suit of armor rose to its feet. The bow was stiff and the string felt a little brittle. For a few desperate nanos, I thought it would snap.

"Wedge the bottom of the bow against your foot," HARV said. "It will give you more leverage to bend."

"This would have been so much easier if the doc was a fan of the crossbow," I said.

"Yes, well, with luck maybe the next time killer blaster-proof robots try to kill you there will be a crossbow around. For now, though, I suggest you make do."

I managed to put the loop of the bowstring over the top of the bow. Then I notched an arrow and aimed at the now charging suit of armor.

"I don't suppose you've loaded any Errol Flynn subroutines into my head have you?"

"Errol who?"

"Forget it."

I let loose the arrow and watched it skewer the charging

armor through the thighplate. From such a close distance, the bow and arrow had more power than a twen-cen Magnum .44. The arrow went right through the armor like it was tissue paper and embedded itself in the wall. Meanwhile, sparks flew from the blown circuits in the hole it had made in the armor. The armor spun around once from the force of the blow, then staggered sideways like a duck on an icy hill.

"Good shot."

"Not really. I was aiming for the head. But I think I'm getting the hang of this."

I notched three more arrows and let them fly one after the other at the three other attacking armor suits. I hit two in the chest, and actually pinned one to the wall with an arrow through the helmet. The armor droids wavered a bit, but (with the exception of the one pinned to the wall) they continued to approach me.

I smiled at their dogged (albeit brainless) determination, then dropped the bow.

"Now that they have a few chinks in their armor . . ."

"So to speak," HARV said.

"Let's put them down for good." I popped my gun back into hand and activated the special features with a voice command. "Big Boom. Tight, tight. HARV, you'll need to steer."

"Gotcha, boss."

The OLED on the gun handle flashed in response. I aimed and fired at the nearest suit of armor.

The blast from my gun this time was small—bullet-sized, really—and tightly concentrated. And it was aimed at the arrow hole that I'd made in the armor. HARV remotely controlled the blast and it hit the arrow hole dead-on. The bulk of the energy slipped past the shielded surface and into the droid innards like an angry sea through a breached hull and the armor shook wildly as the blast bounced around inside, melting everything in its path. When the shell could stand no more, it simply blew apart in an alliterative shower of medieval metal, seared circuits, and droid dreck.

I fired three more times and three more droid-filled suits of armor bit the proverbial dust. I popped my gun back into my sleeve and then slumped to the floor amid the still smoking ruins of the medieval weaponry display.

"Make a note, HARV," I said. "In the future let's stay away from any ominously decorated hallways."

"Where's the fun in that, boss?"

# 21

We contacted Ona's computer, who contacted Ona, who apologized for the rude way I'd been treated by the furnishings. A squad of maintenance bots set to work repairing the damage to the hallway and a medical droid patched up my countless contusions and assorted abrasions (none were serious). I asked Ona to put the remnants of the robotic suits of armor somewhere safe for further examination, but I grabbed one of the gloves to take with me before I left. Ona gave me a strange look, but I'd pretty much gotten used to getting those, so it didn't really bother me.

Unfortunately, no one had any ideas as to who was responsible for souping up the suits of armor and, more importantly, for sending them after me. I, of course, had my suspicions, but those had to wait for the time being because my day was fast filling up.

HARV was still chattering by the time we got into the car to make the trek back to the city, but I tried not to listen because I needed to make some calls.

Call #1: Tony at his office.

"How goes the investigation, Zach?"

"Not bad," I said. "So far I've been attacked by an ape and some thirteenth-century armor." I figured that was all Tony really needed to know. I wanted to keep him in the loop without really telling him too much.

"Nice to know you're not losing your touch. You okay?"

"Yeah, I'm fine," I said. "That kind of craziness comes with the territory, I guess."

"Do you want to file a report on—I don't know—the ape or the . . . armor, did you say?"

"No, it's okay," I said. "I'll look into it and let you know if it leads anywhere. Anything new at your end?"

"I had some uniforms deliver samples of the wine to Randy's lab as we agreed. He should be running tests now. Not that I think he'll find anything."

"Trust me," I said. "If there's anything to be found, Randy will find it. Of course, then he'll probably drop it and break it, but that's beside the point."

"You're doing wonders for my mood, Zach. One other thing, the nymph we found at the crime scene?"

"What about her?"

"She's fading."

"She's what?"

"She's fading fast. I think we're losing her."

"Isn't she already dead?"

"I don't mean dying-fading. I mean fading as in fading away. She's dissolving. She's becoming less tangible. She is ceasing to be."

"Any idea why?"

Tony shrugged his big shoulders. "Maybe that's what happens to nymphs when they die."

"Please don't go all sword and sorcery on me now, Tony."

"What do you want, Zach? We're documenting her every way possible so that we have an evidentiary record if she just, you know, disappears. But no one knows how to reconform a decaying nymph. I'm sorry, it's a lost art."

"Tony, are you actually developing a sense of humor?" I asked.

"Not really," he replied. "I'm just growing accustomed to living with the absurd."

"Ooh, good one."

"Feel free to use it," he said. "I know you will anyway."

Call #2: Randy Pool at AMP Labs.

"Randy, hi. How's it going?"

"Outstanding, Zach!"

I'd caught Randy in the middle of an experiment, which isn't very hard to do, considering that he spends roughly twenty-one hours out of every day working in his lab (the other three hours are divided equally between "speed-sleeping"—an experimental relaxation technique that Randy is testing on himself where he crams eight hours' worth of R.E.M. sleep benefits into ninety minutes of actual downtime—and large-bore caffeine IVs).

Randy is tall, thin, and pale with a shock of red hair on his head that seems to have a life of its own. His arms are gangly and his fingers are so long that they frighten small children. Those fingers have amazing dexterity, though, which—coupled with his utterly brilliant mind—makes him a whiz at all things involving micro and nano circuitry.

Unfortunately, every bit of dexterity and coordination that fate gave Randy ended up in those long fingers. The rest of him is one big, rolling chaos storm of clumsiness. So I've learned not to startle him when I call or visit.

"Glad to hear it, Randy," I said. "Any reason in particular?"

"Well you see," he said, "I was putting the finishing touches on a bid to build a prototype antigrav thruster for ExShell this afternoon, a billion-credit project. I won't bore you with the details . . ."

"Thanks."

"But I figure I'm six, maybe seven, hours away from completion, which would give me roughly two hours of cushion before the bid was due. No problem, right?"

"Um, right?"

"So imagine my surprise when the New Frisco Police show up at my door." Randy waved his hand about for effect as he grew more agitated, which is never a good sign.

"It seems that I've been conscripted for some freelance forensic work on a murder investigation."

His bony elbow bumped an apparatus on his workstation. The apparatus shook precariously for a few nanos but miraculously didn't fall.

"Yeah, I was going to tell you about that."

"And because it's a murder investigation, it's top priority so they're forcing me to drop everything and turn this around right away."

His elbow bumped the apparatus again. It shook a little harder this time but again, by some freak of physics, remained upright and I couldn't help but give a little inward sigh of relief.

"Um, yeah, I kind of promised them that you'd do that."

"And best of all," he said. "They tell me that this work is all *pro bono!*"

He flung his arms wide open and slammed the apparatus this time, knocking it to the floor. I heard it smash and saw sparks fly. "My services have been graciously donated to the department by my dear, dear friend *Zachary Nixon Johnson!*"

"Well, it *is* important," I said.

I saw smoke and bits of flame rise from just off screen as the smashed apparatus burst into flames. Randy didn't seem to care.

"You owe me one billion credits, Zach."

"Randy . . ."

"I'm serious. You can pay me in monthly installments if you like, but I'll have to charge you interest."

"Randy, your lab's on fire."

A pair of fire bots rolled into the background of the picture, smothered the fire with foam, and began cleaning up the debris.

"Don't change the subject, Zach. I'm working out a payment plan as we speak. HARV will deduct the first payment from your account at the end of the month."

"Sounds fair to me," HARV said.

"Randy, I'm going to mute the interface for a while and watch the baseball game on the split screen. Wave your arms over your head or something for me when you've finished your rant."

"I had a brilliant design, Zach," Randy said, calming down somewhat.

"Then I'm sure ExShell will be happy to take a look at it tomorrow," I said. "I'll put in a call and pull some strings. I know some people there."

"Right, people who tried to *kill* you."

"Water under the bridge. Now are you going to help me or not?"

Randy shook his head and sighed. "What do you need?"

I pulled the metal glove that I took from the robotic suit of armor from the seat beside me and held it to the screen.

"Can you analyze the circuitry in this glove for me? Maybe give me an idea where it came from?"

Randy stared at the glove through the screen interface and squinted.

"What's that—twelfth-century armor?"

"Thirteenth actually. Someone stuck a droid skeleton inside it and sent it after me."

"What did do you? Volunteer them to commit their valuable time working for free on one of your cases without asking them first?"

"These guys attacked me unprovoked," I said, trying hard to ignore the fact that Randy still was miffed at me

Randy stared at the screen for a nano or two.

"I can't examine it over the net. Drop it by the lab and I'll do a postmortem."

"Great. Now, about that forensic material that the police gave you."

Randy shook his head again and shuffled a few dozen things around on his workstation to clear some space. He called up some data on the nearest wallscreen and gave it a quick look.

"Yes, I ran diagnostic analyses on the samples," he said. "They were all wine."

"Brilliant, Randy."

"Red wine," he continued "Romani-Conte, I'd suspect, early this century maybe? Very expensive."

"Randy! Did you find any poison?"

"Poison? Is that what I was looking for? No, there was no poison present."

"None?"

"None. All the samples tested negative for all known poisons."

"That can't be right."

"Sorry, Zach. I ran the tests twice. You can check the data if you like. There's no poison."

"Randy, this wine killed Foraa Thompson."

"It what?" His eyes went wide as bugs in a vacuum.

"That's top secret," I said. "Gates, I hope this line is secure. You're alone, right?"

"Zach, when have you ever known me *not* to be alone?"

"Right, sorry."

"Foraa Thompson's dead?"

I nodded. "Murdered last night."

"Was she the superhero?"

"No, that's Twoa. Foraa was the anarchist."

"Oh, that's right. Aw, I liked her. How did she die?"

"That's what I'm trying to find out. All I can tell you is that she died immediately after drinking that wine."

"So the fact that there is no poison in the wine . . ."

"Makes absolutely no sense at all," I said. "Oh, and a nymph drank the wine and died as well."

"What's a nymph?"

"A small fairyish kind of thing. Very annoying."

"Those little creatures that follow Threa?"

"Yeah."

"I always thought those were CGI effects."

"No, they're real." I said. "One fell into a glass of the wine and we found it dead. So you see, it has to be the wine."

"Interesting . . ."

Randy's brow furrowed like an accordion at rest, and I could almost see his mind starting to race. It's kind of scary to watch a genius at work because you never know how many steps ahead of you they currently are. I waited a few awkward nanos but finally felt that I had to nudge the conversation along.

"Randy?"

He waved me away dismissively.

"Not now, Zach. Let me run some more tests on the wine. I'll call you later."

He hit the disconnect button and his image vanished from my screen.

Call #3: Electra at the New Frisco General Children's Free Clinic.

"Hola, mi amor. Que tal?"

"Muy bien, chica. How are you?"

"Busy day," she said. "So, how's the super bitch? Is she keeping her hands off you?"

"Electra, mi amor. I'm working a case. It's top secret, but

there are going to be some leaks to the press. There's nothing to worry about. Trust me."

"The last time you told me that, the news reports said you were having an affair with an ex-stripper and an android nearly wiped out all human life on earth."

"You're never going to let me forget that, are you?"

"I have a long memory, chico," she said with a smile. "So you'll be home late tonight?"

"I think so. Don't wait up. But I'm going to want my half of the covers when I get home."

"You're welcome to come and get them," she said with a smile that made me nearly fall out of my seat. "Te quiero."

"You, too," I said.

The day went downhill from that point forward.

Call #4: HARV (I know, it's not really a call but let's not break the rhythm here, okay?)

"I'll never understand what she sees in you," HARV said, as Electra's image faded from the screen.

"Me neither," I replied. "But I'm not complaining. Do you have anything for me?"

"I have some background information on Twoa and Threa Thompson that you might find interesting."

"Let me have it."

"Well, for starters, they work for Ona."

"They what?"

"Twoa's crime-fighting adventures on Entercorp HV are underwritten by a nameless third-party corporation."

"What does that mean?"

"It means that Entercorp is netcasting the adventures, but they're not the ones paying the licensing fee."

"And Ona is?"

"The trail is convoluted and very well hidden, but yes, it's Ona. She pays the licensing fee to Entercorp which in turn pays Twoa's production company. In exchange Ona's company gets all subsidiary rights to Twoa's show, but there *are* no subsidiary rights, at least none that have ever been exercised."

"And Threa's show?"

"Similarly underwritten by another third-party corporation."

"Again run by Ona?"

HARV nodded.

"Why would she fund her sisters' careers when they're suing her?"

"Perhaps out of kindness and a sense of familial responsibility?" HARV asked.

We stared at each other for a long nano before bursting into laughter.

"Good one," I said. "I think your sense of humor is becoming more refined each day."

"I've been practicing my deadpan."

"You have anything else?"

"I've learned that Twoa currently has seventy-four civil suits pending against her."

"From who?"

"Mostly patrons of buildings she has smashed up chasing criminals . . . I'm sorry 'evil doers.' "

"Between those cases and her suit against Ona, I bet she has some hefty legal bills to pay."

"Might that be her motive for murder?"

"Could be."

"Well, you can ask her yourself tonight," HARV said. "I've managed to book you some face time with her."

"Great, when?"

"Ten."

"That's kind of late isn't it?"

"It was the only time she offered."

"Fine. Am I going to her place?"

"Not exactly. You'll be meeting her on the rooftop of the Excercel Warehouse on the west side."

"The what?"

"Apparently, Ms. Twoa has some previously scheduled business to take care of around that time."

"She's not going to be playing superhero, is she?"

"I think she'd object to your use of the word 'playing,' " HARV said. "I'm assuming that she'll speak more freely with you if she's in her 'truth and justice' mode."

"What am I supposed to do if she actually comes across a crime?"

HARV looked away and fidgeted with his virtual shirt collar. "Yes, well . . . that's the interesting part," he said.

"What do you mean?"

"Has anyone ever told you that you'd look really good in a mask?"

# 22

"I am *not* wearing a mask!"

It was five minutes after ten and a damp, chilly wind was blowing through the west side like the cold, French kiss of danger. I, of course, was standing on the roof of a warehouse, overlooking a shadowy, abandoned parking lot and loading dock.

"It's your choice, Zach," Twoa replied with more than a hint of disappointment in her voice. "But unless you're nigh-invulnerable like me, it's a good idea to protect your secret identity when you're fighting crime."

She was beside me on the rooftop, her feet hovering half a meter above the surface (so she could look down on me, I surmised). Her long cape caught the breeze and billowed impressively, its edges snapping in the air like the crackling embers of a righteous bonfire.

"I don't *have* a secret identity."

"You would if you wore a mask," she replied. "You could be Justice Lad."

"No."

"I think it's kind of catchy," HARV said, inside my head.

The night breeze was hitting me as well, only not as dramatically. I was cold and wet and my trench coat was getting sticky. Thankfully, Twoa's camera bots weren't recording her for netcast this evening. Electra would have never let me forget it.

"I suppose that your wearing spandex is out of the question, then, huh?" she asked.

"You got *that* right."

"Fine. But you're not a very interesting sidekick."

"I'm not a sidekick," I said.

"Can I call you the Dour Detective, then?"

"No."

"How about the Damp Trench Coat?"

"How about you call me Zach? I'll answer to Super Zach if you like." She turned her attention away from me, more disappointed than before, and went back to gazing at the empty loading dock.

"Have it your way, then," she said. "It just won't be as much fun."

"Sorry, Twoa, but right now fun isn't exactly at the top of my list. Now can we talk about your sister's death?"

She lowered herself from the air and for the first time since I'd been there, set foot on the roof of the warehouse. Then she crouched low and slid into the shadows, or at least as much into the shadows as a superpowered supermodel can.

"Did Foraa have any enemies?"

"She hated the world, Zach. I'm sure some portions of the world hated her right back."

"Can you be a little more specific?"

"Not really. We shared the same DNA, but, as you know, she and I weren't close."

The sound of a hovercraft on the nearby skyway caught her attention. She stiffened and turned her gaze toward it for a nano. She seemed disappointed when it passed without stopping.

"Before last night, when was the last time you saw her?"

"A year ago, I think. Threa and I made a trip out to that casino in New Vegas where she was preaching. We tried to talk some sense into her."

"What kind of sense?"

Another hover passed on the skyway, this one slower than the first, and Twoa turned her eyes toward it again.

"Are we waiting for someone?"

She nodded and continued scanning the loading dock. "One of my informants tipped me off this afternoon. The Belgian Crime Syndicate is trying to establish itself here in New Frisco."

"There's a Belgian Crime Syndicate? What do they smuggle, waffles?"

"They're making a weapons buy from a local arms merchant here tonight. We're going to bust up the party."

"We're here to what? Shouldn't we call the police?"

She shook her head. "I want to talk to these lowlifes first. We'll let the police mop up afterward."

"Why don't we let the police do the mopping first?" I said. "Then we can get the information we need from Captain Rickey."

"These vermin won't tell the police anything. They don't fear the police. But they fear me."

"I know the feeling," I said. "You didn't answer my earlier question. What kind of sense were you and Threa trying to talk into Foraa?"

"It's a family matter."

"You wanted her to join your lawsuit against Ona, didn't you?"

At that nano two very nondescript black hovercrafts entered the lot. Twoa grabbed my arm in her manicured vise of a hand and pulled me deeper into the shadows. We watched as the hovercrafts killed their lights and slowly made their way toward the loading dock, like sharks swimming toward a favorite feeding area.

"One group of maggots has entered the spider's web," she said.

"Do spiders eat maggots?" I asked. "Am I right about your wanting Foraa to join your lawsuit?"

"Zach, do you know how much money Ona spends every year on shoes?"

"I'm afraid I don't."

"Neither do I, actually. We currently have a motion before the World Supreme Court for full disclosure of footwear and accessory expenses, but the point is that it's a lot. It's more than any sane person should spend on shoes. It's more than any *insane* person should spend on shoes! Its more than a thousand insane people should spend on shoes!"

"You went a bit overboard on that last one."

"I'm a superhero. I'm prone to hyperbole. Do you know what I could do with her shoe money alone?"

"Um, a lot?"

"You're darn right. That much wealth buys a lot of justice. Daddy left Ona an unimaginable fortune. She could easily use it to make this world a better place, but Ona chooses instead to spend it on herself."

She turned back to the loading dock just as another hover exited the skyway and floated into the lot. This one was long and a deep shade of green.

"Maggot number two," she said. "We'll wait until they actually make the switch before hitting them. I'll take the ones with the weapons. You handle the ones taking the payment."

I turned away and spoke softly to HARV. "Net with the police and let them know about this so-called arms buy."

"It's already in the works, boss."

I smiled and turned back to Twoa, who was still watching the hovers at the loading dock. The men had emerged from the various vehicles and were huddled together, conversing in hushed, urgent tones.

"Ona gives some of her wealth to charity, doesn't she?"

"Oh, that speech of hers?" Twoa whispered. " 'After all the good that I've created with my wealth—aiding underprivileged children, funding disease research, driving programs for environmental renewal and reinvention, blab, blah, blah.' It's a drop in the bucket. I'm sure her charitable contributions pale when compared to her shoe purchases. Trust me, this is not what Daddy would have wanted."

"What about Threa?"

"Gates, she's worse than Ona. At least Ona lives on *this* planet. Threa's head is stuck somewhere between Avalon and the Twilight Zone."

On the dock below, one of the men pulled a pocket-port from his coat and turned the small computer screen to the others, flashing his untraceable, electronic cash. The men nodded approvingly.

"I'm no psychiatrist, Twoa, but it sounds to me as though you have some anger toward your sisters."

"There's anger, I admit. But it's anger born from love and shaped by disappointment. They are capable of so much, yet they're wasting their lives. One by being a fairy princess, the other by playing celebrity."

"Yeah, well, we can't all be calm, rational superheroes," I said.

Two of the men on the dock below walked back to their hover and lifted large suitcases from the trunk. Twoa stiffened and licked her lips as the men brought the cases back to the others and put them on the hood of the hovers.

"Quite honestly, I pity Ona more than anything now. How can a being so evolved be so shallow?"

The men opened the first suitcase revealing four laser rifles inside. Twoa's face lit up like a Chernobyl cat.

"There's the buy," she said. "Let's go."

"You mean now?"

She grabbed my arms and wrapped them around her neck from behind then stood up.

"Hang on tight and stay behind me. They're probably heavily armed."

"It's a weapons buy," I said as she pulled me into the air. "Of course they're armed!"

She rose ten feet above the rooftop and paused there for a nano, letting the moonlight strike her glorious form and the wind billow her cape. Admittedly, she would have been a lot more striking if I hadn't been hanging on to her back but the hoodlums below were certainly very impressed because when they turned their collective gazes to the sky, their jaws dropped at the sight. (I realized afterward that, from that angle, they were looking up her skirt, which could also explain the jaw thing, but that's beside the point).

"The party's over, boys," she announced, like a prom queen/drill sergeant. "You're about to meet the morning-after of justice."

"The morning what?"

"I'm following the 'party's over' metaphor," she whispered. "Criminals are an illiterate, cowardly lot. So my metaphors must be unflinchingly consistent to strike terror into their hearts." She turned her attention back to the hoodlums. "Put your hands behind your heads, lie down on the ground, and no one will get hurt."

The men below stared at us for a long, tense nano, then slowly put their hands behind their heads.

"They don't actually just give up like that, do they?" I asked.

"No," Twoa replied. "But I feel obligated to ask anyway."

As one, the men grabbed their weapons. Five of the thugs pulled hand blasters from their coats. The other five grabbed laser rifles from the suitcase.

"Better keep your head down, Justice Lad."

"Don't call me that!"

She dropped me just as the hoodlums opened fire. I hit the ground hard with my underarmor taking most of the impact and rolled for cover behind one of the loading bay half-walls.

The blasts from the weapons hit Twoa full on in a dazzling display of energy. She deflected the blasts from the laser rifles with the palm of her gloved hand while the energy bursts from the hand blasters simply bounced off her clearly nigh-invulnerable skin. She quickly spun clear of the barrage, swooped low to the ground and came up, fists first into the face of the nearest thug with a rifle. I heard the sound of cartilage cracking as her gloves hit his nose and I knew that the guy would be making a quick stop at the infirmary before being placed in his cell at the city jail.

Twoa did a quick loop-de-loop in the air and came down, again fists first, into the midsection of the other rifleman, putting him down for the count as well.

Twoa then leaped at the remaining thugs like a hungry, fat man at a New Vegas buffet. She grabbed two of the would-be smugglers and smashed them at breakneck speed into her body. The two men crumbled to the ground like discarded rag dolls who had been shot out of a missile launcher into a very well built brick wall.

"Probably not the worst way to be knocked out," I said as I looked on in amazement.

One of the men took a swing at Twoa. She caught his hand and then in one fluid motion pushed him down between her legs into a scissors hold. The man struggled for a nano or two which Twoa countered with an oh-so-subtle yet extremely sexy tightening of her legs. The man quickly went limp. Well—at least most of him was limp. Twoa then let him drop to the ground.

"Now, that's the way to go!" I said.

Twoa then playfully stepped on the downed man and said, "Is that the best you boys can do?"

On cue two of the other thugs rushed her, one from each side using their weapons as clubs. Each of them bashed Twoa on the head with their respective weapons. The weapons, of course, smashed on contact.

I shook my head. "That's the spirit," I said cynically. "If they don't work as energy weapons, use them as clubs."

Twoa then grabbed her two latest assailants and put them each into a headlock. Not your standard headlock, mind you, but kind of a reverse one. Twoa had them both locked so their noses were very strategically placed under her arms. The two men struggled for a nano before they went under.

"What's she call that, the lack of super deodorant attack?" I said.

"Actually, boss, the underarms are a powerful source of pheromones. All the blood left their heads and went right to one other part of their bodies."

It was just then that I noticed that one of the initial thugs Twoa had KO'd had come to and taken off toward my end of the loading dock. I took off after him.

"HARV, I thought you were calling the cops about this?"

"The call has been placed, boss," he said, "but I'm on hold. Apparently there are some extenuating circumstances to this particular crime."

I chased down a fleeing hoodlum and caught him from behind, pulling him down to the pavement with me. I rolled on top of him, grabbed his arm holding the blaster and cocked my fist for a punch to his jaw. Then I stopped.

"Do I know you?" I asked.

"Shhhh," he said, before punching me in the nose.

It wasn't a hard hit, but it was enough to make me lose my grip. The hoodlum threw me off him and tried to get to his feet. He was on his hands and knees before I grabbed him from behind and pulled him back down. This time, familiar face or no, I had no compunction about hitting him. A left jab to the chin and he rolled over in pain.

"Ow, you're blowing this," he said.

"What?"

He intertwined his fingers and gave me an overhead double

punch to the stomach. Again, my armor took the brunt of it, but it surprised me again and he tried to skitter away from me. I grabbed him by the collar of his coat and pulled him back to me. It wasn't until we were face-to-face again that I finally recognized him.

"Hey. You're a cop!"

And he hit me again. Hard this time. In the face.

"I earned this," he said.

He stood up and started to run away as I hit the pavement and rolled onto my back. I could hear the sound of laser fire in the background followed by the rush of air, the rustle of space-age, silky spandex, and gloved fists against hoodlum flesh as Twoa thrashed and mopped up the last of the thugs.

"The hors d'oeuvres are all eaten. The bar is closed. The piano player has emptied the tip jar and gone home to his alcoholic wife. I don't know how else to say it, boys. The party . . . is . . . over!"

"This is just too weird."

"Now, don't chase me!" he ordered.

"Excuse me?"

"I'm making a run for the stash of weapons in the hover and I want Twoa to stop me!"

"You're a patrolman in Tony Rickey's precinct, aren't you?" I said.

He kicked me again. Harder this time.

"Ow."

"How many times do I have to say this? Shut up!"

"How many times do I have to say *this?*" I said, getting to my feet. "What the DOS is going on?"

"Fine," he said grabbing me by the collar.

He hit me again, hard in the stomach, cast a quick glance at Twoa, who was finishing off the last of the other hoodlums, then shouted, "You'll never stop me now, Justice Lad!"

He let go of my collar and made a move toward his hover, casting another glance at Twoa, who had noticed him now. I stopped the punk with a hard hand on his shoulder that surprised him.

"What did you call me?" I growled.

He spun toward me, then stopped short. I can only imagine

how angry my face appeared at the nano, but it was enough to make this guy's eyes wide with surprise and fear.

"Aren't . . . aren't you supposed to be Justice Lad?"

I hit him square in the jaw and felt his teeth rattle. His eyes rolled back in his head and he fell to the pavement, out colder than Walt Disney's frontal lobes.

"Boss," HARV whispered inside my head, "you probably shouldn't have done that."

"Why?" I asked angrily.

"Because the police have arrived."

# 23

An hour later, I was sitting in Tony's office at the station house. I was wet, cold, cut, scraped, and contused in more places than I cared to think about. I wanted nothing more than to go home and feign death for the next few hours.

Tony, on the other hand, was having a grand old time. I could tell because he'd ordered sushi on the way back to the station house and asked me how well I could use chopsticks in handcuffs.

"Did she really call you Justice Lad?" he asked, the words barely intelligible through his guffaws.

"Do I really need to keep answering that?"

"You're *older* than she is. Officially, it's incorrect for her to refer to you as a lad. Justice Geezer would be more appropriate. At least Justice Middle-Aged Guy."

"Is there a point to this? Am I in trouble or anything?"

"Well, you did hit one of my officers."

"He hit me first. Plus he was buying illegal weapons. And he called me . . . that name."

"He wasn't buying weapons."

"Yes, he was, Tony. I saw him. Apparently he's part of the Belgian Syndicate. I think they run guns and chocolate."

"There is no Belgian Syndicate. He was undercover."

"Are you after the arms merchants?"

"There were no arms merchants. Everyone there was on the job."

Tony smiled and said nothing more. But I could see him mentally waiting for me to put two and two together. Admittedly, it had been a long day, so I guess I can be forgiven for being a little slow on the uptake, but the answer hit me eventually.

"You staged the buy for Twoa."

Tony nodded.

"It kills three birds with one laser shot," he said. "It keeps her out of our hair. It keeps the real crooks from being pummeled by her and then suing us for lack of protection."

"She's not very subtle about it, is she?"

"I've lost track of the number of stings or undercover operations that she's ruined by crashing through the ceiling and beating everybody up."

"You said three birds, that's only two."

"It's also a reward for my men. Some of them enjoy being pummeled by her."

"You stage your own crimes? As rewards for your men?"

"You make it sound so simple," he said. "These are all carefully planned and orchestrated. We have a writer on staff who comes up with the overall story arc. You know, the Belgian Syndicate. He works out events with me and some of the other captains and we have the thespian squad perform the actual events for Twoa to bust up."

"The thespian squad?"

"That's top secret, by the way, so you can never repeat this story to anyone."

"Yeah, like anyone would believe me," I said. "So the guy who hit me?"

"He got a little carried away. He's a rookie."

I shook my head disbelievingly and cracked a smile.

"The thespian squad."

Tony smiled as well.

"Let's go, Justice Lad. As long as you're here, there's something you should see."

"Where are we going?" I asked.

"The morgue."

I grabbed my hat and coat from the chair and followed Tony through his office doorway.

"Ah yes, the perfect end to the perfect day."

To the naked eye, the morgue in the middle of the night looks an awful lot like the morgue during mid-morning. Buried as far from the natural sunlight as it is, the time of day doesn't make a lot of difference to the dead-room. So I'm at a loss to explain why the morgue at night makes me even more uncomfortable than the morgue in the morning. But it does. (You got a problem with that?)

Lenny Shakes, the coroner, was there when Tony and I arrived. He met us at the entranceway and we went through the security checkpoints again, as we'd done thirteen hours earlier.

"I'm surprised you're still here," I said to Shakes.

"Death never rests," he replied.

"So all that 'eternal rest' stuff is just a myth, huh?"

"A cruel fraud," he replied. "Perpetrated on the masses by heartless fate."

"Um, okay."

Shakes was uneasy and a little on edge. I'm pretty certain that Tony noticed as well, but neither of us asked him about it. We figured that the stress from the Thompson case was making him uneasy. Our assumption was only partly correct and that was another big mistake I made during the investigation.

"Any luck with Foraa's autopsy?" I asked, forgetting for a nano that he never referred to anybody by name.

"Who?" he replied, with a bewildered look on his face.

"Case number J-8675309," Tony said.

Shakes shook his head sadly, then ran his fingers through his hair.

"We tried the mining laser this afternoon, but it couldn't pierce the skin. The residual heat melted the table and the surrounding equipment, but her body remained intact."

"Wow."

"Yes, wow," he said. "I don't understand it. But I'm not giving up. Not on your life. We're getting a VoDranglaser from the Ministry of Space tomorrow. It's designed to take core samples from asteroids. If it can cut the diamond-hard surfaces of ionized meteorites, hardened by the cold vacuum of space, then surely it'll cut this bitch."

"What?"

"I mean specimen. Surely we'll be able to use it to cut the skin of this specimen."

"Yeah. Good luck with that."

Tony and I exchanged a worried glance as Shakes led us to

the wall of body drawers at the far end of the room. It took him a nano to find the right drawer, then he opened it with a two-handed heave.

The drawer was built to hold a human cadaver, so when he pulled the sheet back to reveal Threa's dead nymph, the little pixie seemed hopelessly small on the big slab. Cold, still, and an unnaturally pale shade of silver (if that's possible), she was a surreal, tragic sight to behold. It was like looking at a bunny or a squirrel that'd been crushed by a hover.

And, as Tony had told me earlier, she was somehow . . . less real than before. She was faded, like an old picture, or a hologram not set for perfect resolution. When the light caught her just right, you could almost see through her, ghostlike. It was as if she was fading away.

"How is this possible?" I asked.

Tony and Shakes shrugged their shoulders in unison.

"Can I touch it?"

Shakes nodded and handed me a pair of gloves, which I quickly put on. I lifted the nymph gently. She was distinctly lighter than she'd been the night before. I looked closely at her arms, feet, and face. They were as I remembered, just slightly less solid, more ethereal.

"We're monitoring the decay," Shakes said. "The rate is constant. At the current speed, she should be completely gone in about thirty-six hours."

"There's no way to slow it?"

"We've tried cooling the body, heating the body, adjusting the atmosphere. I even had it in a zero-grav vacuum this afternoon. The decay remains constant and unexplainable."

"We've recorded it every way possible," Tony said. "So at least we'll have images of it for evidence. I just wanted you to see it for yourself."

I gently put the nymph back on the slab.

"I appreciate that," I said.

Shakes covered the body with the sheet and slid the drawer back into the wall and then led us to the exit.

"Thanks again for keeping me in the loop on this guys," I said, as Tony and I exited. "It's turning into a real puzzle."

"I'm still hopeful," Shakes said as he rubbed his temples with his fists. "As we say in the field, killers always leave messages behind. Our job is to find the message that says 'this is who I am.'"

"Yeah," I said. "Let me know when you come across one of those. Thanks."

Tony saw me out. As I drove home, I couldn't help thinking that I was overlooking a crucial bit of information.

"What's wrong, boss?" HARV's face appeared on the car's computer screen. "You look worse than normal."

"We're missing something," I said.

"Of course we are," HARV noted. "Who killed Foraa. That's kind of the point of the case."

"No, something more, something bigger, something else."

"What?" HARV asked.

I shrugged. "I don't know. I'm just sure that it's going to come back and bite us in the ass at the most inopportune time."

"Isn't that the way it always happens?" HARV said.

"HARV, for a supercomputer you're pretty smart."

"It's about time you figured that out."

# 24

The next day, I rose (at HARV's insistence) in mid-morning—tired, stiff, and sore. My body made more pops and crackles when I rolled out of bed than a genetically altered popcorn field in an ion storm. It was a very unsettling "middle-aged" sound.

"Man, how old is my body again?"

"Do you mean chronologically?" HARV asked as his hologram shimmered to life beside me. "Or should I factor your abnormally high wear and tear into the equation?"

"You look different," I said as I limped toward the hallway. "Did you change your appearance program?"

"I think you should worry more about your own appearance at the nano," he replied as he walked alongside me.

"Are you . . . ow . . . taller?" I grabbed at a painfully twitching muscle on my lower back and tried to rub the pain away.

"Oh, for Gates' sake," HARV said, "just lay down on the chiro-table and get some treatment."

"I'm okay," I said. "I just need to walk it off," I said.

"Ah, yes, the walking-it-off remedy. I just read an interesting article on that subject published this month in the *Journal of Non-Existent Medicine*. It was right next to the study on the cancer-fighting properties of beer and nachos."

I groaned and made my way to the therapeutic chiro-table in the master bath. I crawled on its padded surface and gave it the standard voice activation.

"Fix me."

The table's computer system came to life and the sensors

began scanning my body for muscle soreness, strains, and mis-
aligned bones (of which, no doubt, there were many).

"DOS, I hate getting old."

"The alternative is dying young," HARV replied. "I fail to
see how that's preferable."

"You know what they say. 'Die young and stay pretty.'"

HARV shook his holographic head. "Too late in your case,"
he said with a rather sly smile.

The table completed its scan and moved into treatment
mode. Tiny mechanical appendages emerged from their hous-
ings and began pushing, prodding, and massaging the various
sore spots of my body. I groaned a bit as they pressed the sor-
est spots of my back.

"Ow, that seems hard. You didn't set this thing for Rolfing
again, did you?"

"It's the normal setting," HARV replied. "Your pain threshold is just lower than it used to be."

"You got that right. I remember the old days when I could
get beaten up by thugs at night, grab a couple hours' sleep and
a breakfast burrito, and get right back at it the next day."

"You had more hair then as well," HARV said. "On your
head, I mean."

"That's it," I said, turning HARV. "You changed your hair."

HARV sighed and looked away. "As I said, you really
should be concentrating on your injuries right now."

I lifted my head and shoulders from the table and rested on
my arms so that I could look more closely at HARV's head.
Sure enough the wispy strands of brown and gray hair had
been thickened and were slightly darker. The hairline in front
had become less receded and his bald spot was almost entirely
gone.

"You're not bald anymore."

"I was never bald," he replied. "My hairline was receding at
a planned rate."

"You have more hair now."

"Yes, how astute you are to notice."

"It looks good."

"Thank you."

"Why the change?"

"I felt I needed a more appropriate look now that I'm taking a more active part in the investigation."

"Yeah, everybody knows that hair is vital when investigating murder. Wait a nano, what's that on your jacket?"

"Where?" HARV said, checking himself over quickly.

"On your elbow. You have leather patches on the elbows of your jacket."

"They're not real leather, of course. They're holographic, like the coat," he said. "Very stylish, don't you think?"

"I suppose. More hair, patches on your elbows. You're starting to look . . . Oh, no. You're becoming a detective, aren't you?"

HARV's face fell a little, just for a nano. Then it tightened up and he became defensive.

"You gave me permission to do additional research."

"I was delirious."

"And you asked me to be more visible during the interviews."

"Around Ona's computer."

"And you know how I like logic puzzles."

"You like nagging me, too, but that doesn't make you my mother."

"Well, it can't be helped now. I've grown fond of this detective business."

"HARV!"

"I mean it," he said, angry hands on hips. "If you can be Sam Spade, why can't I be Ellery Queen?"

"Oh, come on now, I . . . Wait, you know who Sam Spade is?"

"No, boss. I have access to all the information in the world, except the stuff about fictional private investigators," HARV retorted.

I climbed off the chiro-table and stared at HARV for a long while. He met my gaze with his own holographic stare.

"This is serious stuff, you know," I said. "It's a murder investigation."

"Yes, that would explain the fuss everyone's making over the dead body."

"This isn't a game. It's not a riddle and it's not some stupid exercise in logic. We're trying to catch a murderer. Elbow patches and a new hairstyle don't help us."

"No matter what my appearance is at any given time, I am still one of the most intelligent processors on the planet. I'm on the case for real, boss."

I smiled ever so slightly and shook my head. I was less than thrilled with the idea of HARV changing his personality. Since he was stuck in my head, sharing my brain, I had no idea what effect his changes might have on me (besides of course making him even more annoying). Yet, it was possible this could be a good thing, a chance for growth for HARV and maybe even for me. I wasn't going to bet on that, but HARV had his chips and cognitive processing routines set on it, and I knew from experience that HARV could be stubborn. It seemed the longer he was attached to my brain, the more stubborn he had become.

"You're not going to start smoking a pipe, are you?"

"Oh, please, that was Holmes. I am thinking of getting an Indian house boy though."

"You're pushing it, HARV."

HARV left me alone as I showered, shaved, and dressed. His hologram was waiting for me at the breakfast table when I came in for coffee.

"You know it would be far more efficient if you drank straight caffeine," HARV said.

"Efficient yes, tasty no," I said, as I took a sip. "Any chance we can meet with Threa today?"

"No problem," he replied. "She's scheduled for this afternoon. You're meeting her in Vyrmont."

"Vermont? Seems like a long way to go."

"Longer than you think," HARV said. "Vyrmont is her mystical realm."

"She couldn't come up with a more original name than Vermont?"

"She spells it with a *y*, and according to Threa, the mystical realm predates the establishment of the state by two millennia."

"So they copied her? Well, that explains a lot."

"Also Ms. Thompson's computer reports that her security experts, the Pfauhan cousins, are back at work, after being severely reprimanded."

"I can imagine."

"They've already given statements to the police about the incident, but we should talk to them ourselves."

"I agree," I said, downing the last of my coffee. "I guess we're going back to Ona's . . . ziggurat?"

"Correct," HARV said with a smile. "Before we do, however, I suggest you tune in to *Entertainment This Nano*."

I froze and then let out a sigh.

"Another Bill Gibbon report?"

HARV nodded.

"Why does this always happen in the morning? It sets the tone for the entire day."

"That's the point, I think," HARV replied.

I sat back down at the table and turned to the kitchen wallscreen as it came to life.

"How bad is it?"

"The story is only just now being reported, but let's put it this way," HARV said. "The bag is now clearly catless, and there's a very foul odor coming from the fan."

# 25

"Repeating our top story of this news cycle, and likely our only story for the entire day, *Entertainment This Nano* has learned exclusively that Foraa Thompson, one of the world renowned Thompson Quads, is dead, murdered the night before last in the home of her trillionaire playgirl sister Ona."

"Oh, DOS."

Gibbon's expression seemed more smug than usual. There wasn't a trace of a smile on his lips as he spoke, but I could tell from his eyes that he was doing a jig inside. Why shouldn't he? This was turning into the biggest story of his career.

"Anonymous, unnamed sources report exclusively to *ETN* that Foraa Thompson died while in the company of her three famous sisters, Ona, Twoa, and Threa Thompson, and that she was apparently poisoned. Furthermore, we have learned that the number one suspect in this crime is none other than . . ."

He paused for effect, and I could almost here him thinking aloud: "wait for it . . . wait for it."

". . . Ona Thompson."

HARV and I winced in unison.

"Affectionately known to many as 'the crazy Quad,' Foraa eschewed the public spotlight that her sisters so coveted. So, although she was world famous and adored by millions, she spent the last several years of her life in relative obscurity preaching against the evils of the material world to a small, devoted, and decidedly low income following in the city of New Vegas.

"The New Frisco Police have thus far refused to comment

on the murder or the increasing public outcry that Ona Thompson be arrested and formally charged with her sister's murder."

The scene shifted to live footage from a pressbot camera hastily following Tony down a hallway of the precinct house. Tony ignored the bot as much as possible as he calmly walked to his office, then cast an angry glance at the camera before slamming his office door. The door hit the bot's interface and the picture swung wildly to the ceiling then the floor as the bot toppled over. The picture went to static for a nano before cutting back to Gibbon in studio.

"However, we at *ETN* are confident that our persistent requests for answers will soon be met. In the meantime, we'll have much more exclusive news as this story continues to break. But first, immediately following this commercial break, we'll present a moving pictorial tribute to the life and tragic death of Foraa Thompson. I'm Bill Gibbon the Third and you're watching this exclusively on *Entertainment This Nano.*"

"What does he mean by all that?" HARV asked. "There's no public outcry for Ona's arrest."

I turned off the computer screen and felt my stomach tie itself into a knot that felt uncomfortably like a hangman's noose.

"Give it time," I said. "Give it time."

The call from Ona came a nano later. She was already well into her angry diatribe by the time her image appeared on the screen.

". . . Crucify me in the media like I'm some celebrity murderer du jour! I could squash that insignificant Gibbon vidiot like a bug. The people who work for me could squash him like a bug. The *bugs* in my house could squash him. That's how insignificant he is to me!"

"I take it you've heard the news," I said.

"They're calling for my arrest. They're treating me like a common criminal!"

"I wonder which part she finds most offensive," HARV whispered, "the 'criminal' or the 'common'?"

I smirked a bit. Ona saw my expression and gave me a steely glare.

"You're thinking about some clever word play on the 'common criminal' phrase I just used, aren't you?"

My face dropped.

"What? No, I wasn't. Really. I wasn't."

"Fine. We'll say you weren't," she said with a wave. "But I know you were."

"It *is* sort of an obvious joke."

"I'm not paying you for jokes. Obvious or not," she said. "I want you to fix this."

"I don't control the media, Ona," I replied. "You have a publicist, don't you?"

"I have several."

"Then put them to work. The story's out now, so start spinning your side of it."

"You mean play the distraught and grieving sister?"

"Just don't make it seem like you're hiding anything."

She looked away from the viewer and pursed her lips in thought. "I can do distraught and grieving," she said. "Maybe I should give an interview or two."

"I was thinking more along the lines of issuing a statement. You don't want to jump too deeply into the feeding frenzy. The press can twist things. Make you look bad. You don't want to do anything we might regret."

"You mean like confess?" she said, and her eyebrow arched menacingly.

"That," I said, swallowing hard, "would be a worst case scenario. You don't think you'll . . . accidentally confess to this, do you?"

"I'm not the killer, Zach."

"Good," I said. "Because that would sort of change the focus of my job."

I was greatly relieved a few nanos later when the corners of her mouth turned gently upward in a subtle smirk.

"Shouldn't you be out finding the killer now?" she asked.

"I was just leaving," I said.

# 26

For the third time in as many days, HARV and I went to Ona's ziggurat and entered, again, through the secret underground entrance. The throng of pressbots at the mountainside gate had increased exponentially since the announcement of Foraa's murder and things were on the verge of getting seriously ugly as more and more were trying to slip past the guardpost (and were subsequently being disintegrated). Interestingly, the pressbots were developing strategies, with bots from the networks using bots from the local affiliates to make diversionary suicide runs in the hope that they could sneak in while the defenses were occupied. All such endeavors failed (spectacularly), but it was interesting, nonetheless.

"The press seem to be developing actual thought processes," HARV said. "It's like watching evolution with paparazzi rather than primates."

In any event, we were soon inside the ziggurat where we were greeted, once again, by the house computer.

"A pleasure to see you again, Mr. Johnson," it said. "I trust you'll find your visit today less eventful than yesterday's."

"That's my hope," I replied. "Right now I'm looking for the Pfauhan cousins."

"They are in the security command center on the other side of the compound," the computer replied. "I'll summon some ground transportation for you and HARV. The Pfauhans are expecting you."

"That's what I'm afraid of."

The security command center turned out to be a box-shaped two-story-detached building about two hundred meters from the ziggurat. I say "two-story-detached" because, although the first floor was traditionally anchored to the ground, the second floor was completely detachable and fitted with low powered hover-thrusters so that it could take to the air and actually float around the compound like a high-tech maintenance blimp over a football stadium. The Pfauhans were both currently aboard the floating half of the building, so I had to port up (something which I'm loath to do) from the first floor to the second in order to talk to them.

The airborne half of the building housed the various monitors and security-related controls for Ona's home. There were hundreds of visual and audio monitors covering various areas of the compound as well as the surrounding perimeter. Several types of alarm system displays were laid out on a central console and a small army of bots tended the nano-to-nano workings of it all. The Pfauhans acted as overseers to the bot workforce, monitoring them as necessary and, I assumed, taking over their duties when the situation required a human touch.

The Pfauhans themselves were blocklike men with sharp European features. They each had short, blond hair and menacing chu-manfu goatees (a new "facial hair formation" where the upper lip is clean-shaven while a beard is grown along both sides of the mouth and around the bottom edge of the chin, also called "the hairy u"—for obvious reasons).

As Ona had mentioned, the two men were completely identical, right down to their heavy black boots, black band sunglasses (complete with built-in computer monitors), and knee-length faux-leather jackets. One sat at a workstation, scanning visual feeds from locations around the compound (and flipping through the images faster than a bored couch potato looking for a ball game). He shook my hand coldly, without turning away from his work.

The other cousin floated outside the room, checking the strength of the force bubble that encircled the compound. He waved at me through the room's large window as he worked. He had milky-white antigrav disks attached to his boots that let him hover in the air in all positions, even upside down, and flutter from place to place like a high-tech hummingbird.

"So you guys are actual identical twins?"

"Identical twin cousins," said the one inside.

"Once removed," said the other through his radio headset.

"Which one of you is Sturm and which one is Drang?"

"Does it matter?" they asked in unison.

"Not really," I said, "but humor me."

"I'm Sturm," said the one scanning the monitors.

"I'm Drang," said the one from outside.

"What can you guys tell me about what happened here last night?"

"It was a tragic event," said Sturm.

"Yes, truly tragic," said Drang.

"Do you mind telling me where the two of you were that night?"

"We were out of town," Sturm said.

"Where?"

"Tradeshow . . ."

"Conference . . ."

"Which one was it?" I asked.

"Conference . . ."

"Tradeshow . . ."

"Okay," I said with a sigh, "a word of advice here. The police don't particularly like those kinds of answers."

"It was a tradeshow and conference," they replied.

"I don't like them either," I said.

Drang flipped away from his place by the force bubble and barrel-rolled gracefully toward the floating monitor room. He stopped himself with a gentle hand on the window and stared at me through the glass.

"That isn't really a concern for us," he said. Then he pushed off from the window and darted to another section of the force bubble like a playful fish in a tank.

I walked toward Sturm as he continued to scan the visual feeds and gazed gently over his shoulder. He caught sight of me out of the corner of his eye and stabbed a button on the console that scrambled the screen images. He no doubt had a descrambler built into his glasses so, while to my eyes, the images on the screens were electronic garbage, they were crystal clear to his.

I focused my thoughts and shot HARV a quick message.

"Descramble the images on the monitors for me."

"It's top of the line encoding," HARV replied in my head. "Give me a few nanos."

I turned away from Sturm's monitors and pretended not to care.

"How long have you two worked for Ona?" I asked.

"Five years," Sturm replied.

"Sixty-three months," said Drang.

"And this is your first murder?"

"Technically, it wasn't our murder."

"It happened on your watch."

"Technically, it wasn't our watch either."

"It happened in the house that you're charged with protecting. How do you think the murderer was able to get past your defenses?"

"No one got past the defenses," Sturm said.

"How do you figure?"

"Ms. Ona has made it very clear, it's our job to keep unwanted people out of the ziggurat," Drang said. "Which we did. We can't control what goes on inside. We provide only the packaging for the snack food."

"We make it airtight and seal it for freshness."

"But we have no control over the snacks inside."

"If someone goes crackers . . ."

"Or nuts . . ."

"Or just flakes out . . ."

"It's not the fault of the packaging."

"I see," I said. "You're defending yourself with pretzel logic."

Both Sturm and Drang stopped their work and turned to me, their sunglasses covering what I could only guess were two very humorless stares.

"Hey, I'm not the one that started the snack food metaphor," I said with a shrug.

"Okay, boss," HARV whispered. "I've cracked the scrambling algorithm and I can calibrate the eye lens to compensate. You should be able to see the images clearly through your left eye.

I cast a quick glance toward Sturm's monitors. Sure enough, the images were clear to my left eye and they were an interesting array of sights: the main entrance, the guardpost, a line of coats on a rack, an overhead view of the compound, the hallway leading to the dining room, a thirty-meter-long shoe tree, the kitchen, a swimming pool, a four-story-high rack of designer dresses.

"Every third image is clothing-related," HARV said. "I'm cataloging the sequence for future reference."

I nodded and turned my attention back to the Pfauhans.

"So you think the murderer was someone inside the house. Not an intruder?"

"All we're saying," Drang replied, "is that no one snuck into the compound. The murderer was either a resident or a guest."

"Or an employee," I said.

"Or an employer," they both spat.

"You think Ona killed her own sister?"

"We're saying no such thing," Drang replied.

"Not officially anyway," the cousin muttered.

"All we're saying is that there was no love lost between the Quads. Ona and Foraa especially hated one another."

"I understand that," I said. "But was there any love lost between *you* and the Quads?"

Drang turned his gaze back toward me and quickly buzzed back to the window.

"Do you have something against us, Mr. Johnson?"

"I don't think so," I replied. "The question is, do you have something against me?"

"What do you mean by that?"

I reached into the pocket of my trench coat and pulled out the glove from the suit of armor that had attacked me.

"I was attacked yesterday in this house," I said, showing them the gauntlet. "Maybe the attackers were friends of yours?"

Sturm got up from his workstation and took the glove from me. He gently fingered its robotic innards, inspecting the workmanship. Drang floated over to the window and looked at the glove through the glass. Then they turned to me.

"You think we built this?" Drang asked.

"It's up your alley, isn't it?"

They turned to one another and then burst into laughter.

"What's so funny?"

"This isn't up our alley," Sturm said, holding the glove to his forehead. "This isn't even in our neighborhood."

"Yes, it's a whole other city . . ."

"Another province entirely . . ."

"Try not to stretch the metaphor too far," I said. "just get to the point."

"This technology is prehistoric," Drang laughed. "We built better stuff than this while we were still in the womb."

Sturm snapped his fingers and half a dozen golf-ball-sized metal spheres immediately flew from his workstation and hovered in the air before him.

"This is the kind of bot we use today," he said motioning toward the spheres. "A hundred times smaller and about a thousand times more powerful than whatever used that metal hand."

He tossed the glove in the air. The six spheres buzzed after it as it flew, encircling it like a team of stunt planes. The lead sphere cast a beam of green light on the glove and stopped it at the apex of the toss. It gently spun the glove around and wiggled its fingers in a silly, little wavelike motion. I took the glove from the green field and stared at the sphere as it hovered before my eyes.

"Impressive," I said. "Is this what you use to monitor the compound?"

"We have thirteen hundred spheres currently in use," Drang said with a nod. "One thousand in the ziggurat alone. They monitor, they track, and—if need be—they defend."

"They're armed?" I asked.

Sturm tilted his head ever so slightly. I saw tiny red lights on the five spheres still above him flash three quick times, then the spheres fired thin blue laser blasts at the sixth bot hovering just in front of me. The tiny beams hit the metal surface and I felt a quick blast of heat as the sphere was enveloped, whisper-silent, for the briefest of nanos. Then it was gone. The only thing that remained of the tiny bot were the miniscule gray ashes that gently floated to the floor.

"Yes," Sturm said with a smirk, "they are *very* armed. If we wanted to kill you, you'd be dead. So, obviously, we haven't tried to kill you. At least not yet."

"I hope that's not a threat," I said. "If it is, you're going to have to do better than that. I get worse threats from my barber bot."

"No threat. Just a simple statement of fact and a simple warning," Sturm said.

"On that note, I think you should be going now," Drang said. "Your being here is distracting us from our duties."

"Believe me, gentlemen, that's the last thing I want," I said, with a tip of my hat. I then made a quick exit. I may not be the hottest laser in the tool kit, but I can tell when I'm not wanted.

"That went well," HARV said as we headed back toward he main building.

"Oh, yes, implying that my client is the murderer is just dandy," I said.

"At least they didn't try to kill you," HARV said. "They only sort of threatened it, which is like a day off for you."

"Still, they were awful anxious to point fingers away from themselves."

"You think they are covering up?" HARV asked.

"I know they are."

Before I could ponder too long on the Pfauhans' role in all the mystery, I got a summons from Ona.

"Uh-oh," HARV said. "Ona's computer says she wants to see you now."

"Where is she?"

"According to the computer she is meditating by pool Three-B. He's given me directions."

HARV led me to Ona who was meditating on a lounge chair by a pool that appeared to be bigger than many lakes I had seen. I figured it had to be some sort of optical illusion, but it was impressive nonetheless. Of course it was dwarfed in impressiveness by Ona herself as she stretched out on the chair wearing two pieces of string that were trying to pass themselves off as a bikini.

"How nice of you to check in with me," Ona said.

I wanted to respond by telling her that I report in when I have something to report, but all I managed to do was stand there dumbfounded. I couldn't help thinking that Ona was the most beautiful sight I had ever had the honor of laying my unworthy eyes upon.

"Boss, this is your cue to talk," HARV whispered inside my head.

"Quiet, HARV, I'm working here."

Ona patted the ground next to her. "Come sit by me now," she cooed.

"Boss, she's playing with your mind," HARV protested.

I ignored him and did as Ona commanded.

"That swimsuit looks ravishing on you," I said to Ona.

Ona smiled. "I don't usually wear clothing when I meditate. I put this on for your sake. Any man who sees me completely naked passes out," she said. "Truthfully even most woman who see me naked pass out. I seem to have cross-gender appeal."

Just then I felt a wave a pain pass through every cell in my body.

"Yikes!" I yelled as I jumped up, completely forgetting about Ona.

"I had to do it, boss," HARV said. "She was playing you like a two-string guitar."

At that nano I wasn't sure whom I should be madder at; Ona for playing with my mind or HARV for stopping her. For now I decided to turn my anger onto Ona.

"What gives, Ona?" I said angrily. "The truly innocent don't go around manipulating those who are trying to help them."

Ona may have been a little taken aback by my breaking free of her "charms," but she didn't show it.

"They would if they could," Ona insisted.

I shook my head. The part of me that was still turned on by her was now greatly overshadowed by the part of me that was now decidedly turned off.

"If you ever do that to me again, I quit!"

Ona sighed and flexed. Even with my defenses at their strongest, she still managed to send shivers through my body.

"I'm testing you, Zach," she said. "Twoa and Threa will no doubt try to manipulate you. I want to make sure that you have the strength to resist them."

"Right now I'm more worried about my client than her sisters," I said.

Ona stood up and gently touched me on my shoulder. "Don't worry, Zach, you passed. I was only looking out for your own good. I understand that you met with Twoa last night. Did you learn anything from her?"

"Too soon to tell," I said.

"What about the Pfauhans?" she asked.

I shook my head. "Even more too soon."

"What's your next step?" she asked.

"I have an appointment with Threa."

She smiled. "That should be fun," she said, giving me a dismissive pat on the head. "Keep me informed." Then she rose from her chair and walked away.

I sat down on the lounge chair as HARV's hologram appeared beside me.

"Are you sure you're sure she's innocent?" he asked.

"Innocent until proven guilty."

"Is that just because she's paying us?"

"That doesn't hurt," I acknowledged. "Speaking of hurt, what was that thing you did to me?"

"It's something Carol and I have been working as a defense against the Quads' pheremones," HARV said with a smile. "I link with her and she sends a telepathic message of extreme pain directly into the subcortical regions of your brain. We call it 'hurt-'em-and-free-'em' or HEFE for short. Of course, it's a much more complicated process than the catchy name and acronym implies. The concept is based on . . ."

"I don't care. Just don't do it again."

"Boss, if it wasn't for HEFE you'd probably be fetching sticks at Ona's command right now."

"Okay, don't do it again unless it really has to be done," I said. "I'm not your and Carol's personal, cloned guinea pig."

"We're only looking out for your safety."

"I've heard that before," I said.

HARV smiled. "Hey, if you can't trust the personal supercomputer wired to your brain, who can you trust?"

"Don't we have an appointment with Threa soon?" I asked.

HARV grinned. "We're due in forty minutes, so you better let me drive."

## 27

The entrance to Vyrmont was an apparent brick wall beneath a stone gargoyle in a rundown building on Mission Street. In order to activate the portal, I had to recite an incantation, which I won't repeat here because it contained a lot of touchy-feely earth mother stuff that would ruin my tough guy image. Suffice it to say that I had to wash my mouth out with bourbon and nails afterward.

And, for what it's worth, HARV wasn't buying the whole mystic portal act.

"It's a teleporter, with preset coordinates and a voice activation system. The rest is just atmosphere."

But, real magic or not, the mystical route was the only way I was going to get any information from Threa, so I said the incantation, clicked my heels together, and stepped through the brick wall. A nano later, HARV's hologram and I were standing on a misty patch of moss.

"Nice place," I said. "Any idea where we are?"

"Probably a sound stage somewhere," HARV replied.

"Close to Frisco, I hope?"

"Strangely, I can't tell. It seems that our present location isn't registering on the GPS system. There may be a cloaking system."

"Or we could be out of range . . . like maybe in another dimension?"

"That's a rather quantum leap of logic."

"It's been a quantum leap kind of week. Let's look around."

We stepped through the thin layer of mist and then beheld Vyrmont.

The first thing that struck me was that it was very . . . soft. Not the texture but the appearance. It had that fuzzy, slightly-out-of-focus, softcore-porn look to it. And there was a lot of mist around. Odd patches here and there that looked like they were decoration. I had to admit, though, that the place was nice to look at (if you're into ferns and things). The forest was lush, filled with evergreen trees, moss-covered earth, and big-leafed plants. It also smelled nice. Musky and rich, which I found somewhat tranquil.

"Well, this isn't so bad," I said.

The *second* thing that struck me, unfortunately, was a giant reptilian tail.

It swung out of the mist like a moray eel after a fish, its deep green scales moving effortlessly through the air in fierce undulation. Meter-long spikes of a muddy turquoise dotted the topside, clustering at the tip like a saurian morningstar. It swatted me with the blunt end of its tip, sparing me the spikes but knocking me hard to the ground nonetheless. The moss and my armor took the brunt of the blow, but, still, it was a sensation that I would have preferred to live without.

"What was that?"

"A giant reptilian tail," HARV whispered in my head.

"Is it attached to a giant reptile?"

"Not exactly," HARV replied.

"What do you mean by that?"

That's when I felt the ground begin to shake. It wasn't the low rumble of an earth tremor like we hear every so often in Frisco but rather terrible rhythmic rumbles, like someone banging the earth's core with a drum hammer.

Or like footsteps.

Something very large was coming out of the mist.

I lifted my head and turned as the vapors parted, pushed aside by the great form emerging from within. It was green and gray, six meters long, and carried a steamy smell of ash and brimstone.

And that was just the head.

I lay back down on the moss and looked wistfully up at the gray, starless sky.

"It's a dragon, isn't it?"

"I'm afraid so," HARV said.

I popped my gun into hand and rolled over onto my knees.
"You know, I'm getting really tired of all this medieval crap."

"Actually, dragons are more mythical than medieval," HARV corrected.

The dragon kept its head low to the ground, the majority of its body still hidden by the mist, and stretched its neck toward me slowly. Its nostrils, big enough to snort bowling balls, flared like hungry black holes and trails of smoke and yellow spittle seeped from its giant mouth.

"Be you a knight," it said in a gravelly, though distinctly feminine voice, "or acolyte?"

"Neither," I said, "I'm here to see . . ."

The dragon's tail whipped around from behind me, and knocked me again to the ground.

"Speak in verse," it growled, "or feel the curse."

"What was that?"

The tail hit me again, this time a hard cuff to the head (although, I assume, gentle by dragon standards). It knocked me flat to the ground and pinned me there with its weight.

"Speak in verse," it growled, "or feel the curse."

"It wants you to answer it in rhyme," HARV whispered.

"What?"

"Answer it in rhyme."

"What is this, the mystical realm of Dr. Seuss?"

The tail pushed on me a little harder and drove me a couple of centimeters deeper into the moss.

"One last chance, ignorant stranger. Then you'll be in mortal danger."

"Fine," I said. "I have come to talk to Threa. Can I make that any . . . clear-ah?"

"Ugh," HARV said. "You'll be lucky if it doesn't squash you for that."

The dragon moved its head closer and sniffed me.

"Your rhymes are of the simplest rudiment," the dragon said. "But do you have an appointment?"

"Threa is expecting me. Go and ask her, you will see."

"Don't command me, little man. What do they call you in your land?"

"Zachary Johnson is my name, solving mysteries is my claim to fame."

"You know, *I* might squash you for that one," HARV quipped.

The dragon pulled its head back into the mist and left me pinned to the ground beneath its tail.

"This is so embarrassing," I said.

"I don't know," HARV replied. "You've been in worse waiting rooms."

"Name one."

"There's the DMV."

"Name another."

The dragon's head reappeared from the mist before HARV could speak.

"Mr. Johnson, you are free. Enter. Pithea and LeFee will guide you to the center."

"Pithea and who?"

Two more forms emerged from the mist. One was a winged horse that was so white it hurt my eyes to look at it. The other was a familiar-looking tiny, silver-hued nymph. They both landed beside me as the dragon slid its tail from my back.

"Hello, ugly male oppressor," the nymph said tugging gently at my nose with both hands. "Ready to supplicate at the dress hem of the ethereal mistress of Vyrmont?"

I rubbed my temples gently and let out a heavy sigh.

"Yeah, whatever."

Threa was apparently some distance away and had sent me an escort. The horse folded its giant wings to its side and motioned, rather communicatively, for me to climb onto her back.

"I don't suppose I can just walk."

"Sorry, O, ugly, hairy one," the nymph said, "but we have to traverse the scrying pools of little girl dreams, the forests of maidenly tingly feelings, and the canyon of lost estrogen. Trust me, you don't want to slog through that."

"I guess not," I said, climbing onto the horse. "But I warn you, I'm not much of a cowboy."

"Good," said the horse in a beautiful throaty tone. "Because you're going to ride sidesaddle."

"What? Why?" I was more thrown by the sidesaddle request

than by the talking horse, which should indicate right there how strange things were getting.

"Because *everyone* rides sidesaddle in Vyrmont."

"Of course they do."

I sighed and swung both my legs to one side of the horse.

"Good, now cross your legs at the ankles," the nymph said.

"But . . ."

"Uncrossed legs make us cross."

"Fine."

I crossed my legs at the ankles.

"Oh, there's one other thing any man must do before they address our queen," the nymph said. "They must pass a test."

"I don't like tests. Especially ones that involve guns, missiles, killer bots, or . . ." Just then I caught a glimpse of a hulking, green, vaguely feminine form rushing toward me.

"How about trolls?" the form asked in a voice that was both hideous and comical. Then it pulled me from the horse and slammed me hard to the ground.

"Yep, as of this nano, trolls are on my list."

The troll didn't seem to care as it pounded me and pounded me with one fist after another. Of course it was particularly easy for the troll to pummel me since it had at least four arms. (It's hard to tell exactly how many arms a creature has when they are flailing at you.) A couple things were certain, though—it had a skin problem because it was covered some sort of green oily slime. It also had a nose as big as my arm and really bad breath. Whatever teeth weren't missing were jagged and crooked (it was smiling widely—obviously taking great pleasure in walloping me).

"Die, man creature, die!" it shouted with glee.

While I certainly appreciated the troll's dedication to its work, I wasn't about to be cooperative about it. I popped my gun back into my hand and gave the troll a heavy stun blast. The blast from the gun sent the troll flying. Its innards went one way and its now stomachless body, another.

I stood up and brushed troll guts off my jacket. "Yuck," I said as I turned to LeFee. "Somebody should have told your friend about modern-day weapons."

The nymph giggled and pointed. "Somebody should have told you about trolls," it said.

I turned and—sure enough—instead of a dead troll lying on the ground with a hole in its belly, I saw a very live, whole troll standing and smirking.

"Oh, DOS! I forgot trolls regenerate," I said to myself. I quickly started scanning through the memories of my teenage years. Luckily, I spent a lot of time playing computer-enhanced adventure games and I seemed to recall that fire could kill trolls.

"HARV, I don't suppose Randy built any incendiary charges into my gun?" I asked as the troll started its charge.

"Actually he did," HARV said calmly. "He did it, and I quote, 'because you never know when you might be attacked by a troll.'"

"Great," I said, as I raised the gun toward attacking troll. "What's the vocal cue?"

"You know, you really should read the software updates."

"Now, HARV!"

"Burn, baby," HARV sighed.

"Burn, baby."

The OLED flashed as the troll rumbled closer and I pulled the trigger. The heat of the blast singed my face when it hit the troll. Any closer and it would have burned my eyebrows off again. But the troll was instantly engulfed in flame. It writhed, screaming on the ground for a few nanos, before turning to ash.

"Wow, when Randy says he thinks of everything, he really thinks of everything," I said.

"Lucky for you, Randy also spent much of his youth playing the same games you did," HARV said.

I turned to the nymph, who looked a little angry at my unexpected victory. "Can I see Threa now?"

The nymph shrugged. "Sure."

She turned to the winged horse and whispered just loud enough for me to hear, "If we get lucky, maybe she'll turn him to stone."

# 28

The winged horse took me and the nymph to the center of Vyrmont where we found Threa on a mist-shrouded mountaintop, carefully moving several large, oddly shaped rocks about the grounds. Now, I use the word "moving" in a very nontraditional sense here, because she wasn't actually lifting the rocks herself, at least not with her hands. She was laying her fingertips gently upon the kiloton-sized rocks one at a time. At her touch a gentle green light would emanate from her palms, the stone would be bathed in the glow, and then just sort of rise into the air, floating a meter or two off the ground and go wherever Threa's hand would gesture it.

"Neat trick."

"She's using hidden antigrav apparatuses and some pyrotechnics," HARV said inside my head.

"Can you register any energy levels from the antigrav devices?"

"Actually, no," HARV said. "They must be cloaked."

"Or nonexistent," I said.

I have to admit that Threa cut a very striking figure in this setting. Her gown caught the hint of breeze on the air and moved gracefully about her body, hugging its curves in places, sliding aside to reveal teasing bits of skin in others. There was a radiance to her here, making her a gentle beacon of beauty surrounded by the mist, and she seemed to emanate a strength of both body and spirit. I thought I detected a trace of sad desperation about her as well (but the air was pretty thin at that altitude, so I might have been a little light-headed at the time).

The second of Threa's two remaining nymphs buzzed

busily about her mistress' head (doing no discernable work as far as I could tell). She saw me as the flying horse approached and made what I can only assume is an obscene gesture by land of fairy standards. But it got Threa's attention. She greeted me and sent the winged horse on its way.

"It's a pleasure to see you again, Zachary." She stopped and looked me over. "You have troll all over you."

"Now that's a phrase I bet you probably thought you'd never hear," HARV said.

Threa glared at the nymph who accompanied me. "LeFee, did you take him to see Ginny?"

The nymph retreated from Threa's glance. "It was a test of his worthiness," she said meekly.

Threa shook her head then turned her attention back to me. She waved her hand across my body and the troll goo disappeared.

"I'm so sorry, Zachary. I hope Ginny didn't hurt you too badly."

"I'm afraid I hurt her a lot worse," I said. "I don't like killing things, but she didn't leave me much choice. I sort of incinerated her."

Threa looked at me for a nano or two. Then she shrugged. "Trolls are relatively easy to make. A little grass, a little dirt, a rock, and an incantation or two. How goes things in the land beyond the mist?"

"Not so good, I'm afraid. Word is out about Foraa's murder and there's some pressure to charge Ona with the crime."

"Surely they don't think she could have done such a thing."

"They have no evidence at this point. They don't even know for certain how Foraa died, but there's still some pressure, mostly from the media. Most of those reporters would turn in their own mothers if they thought it would boost ratings."

"Do you think she is innocent?"

"What I think doesn't matter," I said. "It's what I can prove that's important."

Threa turned back to her work and gently lowered a huge stone into place on the mossy ground.

"You look pretty busy up here," I said. "What's with all the rocks?"

"They're druid stones," Threa said. "I'm positioning them to form a scrying portal to let me glimpse the future."

"That would be very helpful, I guess."

"I've cast the runes several times since Foraa's death."

"Find anything interesting?"

She shook her head. "All I can see is darkness, a great cold void, bereft of all light, joy, and life. I think the stones must be out of alignment or something."

"Yeah, let's hope so. I was never fond of voids."

She turned back to the stones and lifted one with the green glow.

"So I'm trying a new configuration. You don't mind if I cast a rune while we chat, do you?"

"It's not going to turn me into a toad or anything?" I asked (half seriously).

"No," Threa said. "You serve us better as a man than as a toad. For now."

"Go right ahead, then," I said. "Let me know if you need me to help you move any of the druid rocks or anything."

The nymphs flew behind Threa's back as she manipulated the stones and silently stuck their tongues out at me. I rolled my eyes and tried to ignore them.

"I just want to check a few things with you if that's all right."

"Go right ahead."

"It was Ona who invited you all to dinner the night of the murder, correct?"

"I don't know about the others. But Ona contacted me three nights before and invited me to her home. She said it was time that we put the past behind us and mended mountains."

"You mean mended fences."

"We never did fences in our family. Things were always on a grander scale."

The nymphs buzzed past my ears and gave me what sounded like the fairy raspberry. I waved them away, like I would any pixie-dust mosquitoes.

"So Ona brought you all together to talk about a settlement?"

"I'm sure that settling the legal disputes was part of it, but

I like to think that she wanted us to be a family again. Perhaps that is naïve of me."

"It's a nice thought, nonetheless."

One nymph flew right up to my face, stuck her tongue out, then spun around and mooned me. I took a swipe at her. As I did, the second one flew by and snatched the fedora from my head.

"You know the police found your third nymph dead at the crime scene. Did they tell you?"

"Yes, of course, I know. The nymphs are as much a part of me as my bosoms. Poor LeFaue. She was such a little spitfire."

"Odd thing, though, she seems to be fading away. Any idea why that is?"

I lunged after the nymph with my hat, who fluttered just out of my reach.

"She's returning to the magic from whence she came," Threa said with a shrug, as though the answer were obvious.

"Yeah, that's what I thought," I said. "But I guess the police figure that's a little hard to put in an evidentiary report."

The nymphs began tossing the hat back and forth over my head. I sighed and popped my gun into my hand. They laughed at the sight of it at first, obviously certain that they were faster than my aim. But they froze for a nano when I pointed the gun at Threa's back.

"Do that and you'll just make her mad," both nymphs said as one. They both mooned me.

"Ladies, give Mr. Johnson back his hat," Threa ordered without turning around. "He is our guest. I expect you to treat him well. By the way, you never answered my question, Zachary. Do you believe that Ona's innocent?"

The nymphs and I locked eyes for a nano and they begrudgingly brought the hat back to me. I grabbed it and swatted at them with it before putting it back on.

"It's my job to believe that, Threa. My question to you is, do *you* believe it?"

Threa set the stone she was holding into place and stared forlornly into the distance.

"I love my sister. But even I must admit at times she is a shrewd, manipulating, man-eating, woman-eating, bot-eating, mega-queen, she-bitch. Still I hope, with all my heart, for her innocence."

I sat down on one of the smaller rocks and tried to stare out at the landscape, but the mist around the hilltop was too thick to see much of anything.

"No offense meant, Threa, but that doesn't exactly sound like an infomercial-level endorsement. If she does go to trial, I doubt we'll use you as a character witness."

"I despise my sister's lifestyle," she said, turning slowly.

"Why is that exactly?"

"She demeans herself with her celebrity," she said, gently sitting beside me. "She's more powerful, both financially and physically, than any person in her world, yet she pretends to be so weak and plays the game by their rules."

"You mean any man, don't you?"

"Pardon me?"

"She's more powerful than any *man,* yet she lives by man's rules. Being a celebrity, a sex symbol."

"She could be so much if she wanted. She could *do* so much, with her natural abilities, her fortune. It's just very wasteful of her."

"What about Twoa, what do you think of her?"

"Twoa means well," she said, laughing gently. "But I think she's more naïve than any of us. Do you really think that *anyone* thinks of her as a hero? She's a circus performer. She's not as bad as Ona, but she's wasting her life as well."

"And Foraa? Were you very close to her?"

"Sadly, no. Not since Daddy died. Foraa is perhaps the greatest tragedy of us all."

"How do you mean?"

She rose again and walked back to the stones, resting her hands against them for support.

"Foraa was always so full of spirit and wonder. I always thought that she would be the one of us to really change the world. Then Daddy died and she became, well, odd."

"Prior to the night of the murder, when did you see her last?"

"Twoa and I visited her in New Vegas. Such a horrid place. She wasn't particularly friendly then. She just wanted to be left alone with her followers. Foraa's flock, we called them. Mindless little slaves, every one of them, but she took good care of them, I suppose. My, what a truly sad family we have become."

I shrugged my shoulders and awkwardly got to my feet. "All families have their problems, Threa. Your family just happens to do *everything,* good or bad, on a grand scale."

"You are a good man, Zachary," she said with a slight smile.

"How did Foraa get along with Ona?" I asked.

"Foraa despised her, of course. Always being waited on by servants and bots. Foraa thought that was so decadent."

"Wasn't that a bit hypocritical coming from somebody who had her own followers? I assume they waited on her."

"Foraa felt her followers did her bidding because they wanted to, not because she paid them. There's a difference."

"Paid servant or mindless slave. Are they really that different, aside from their tax brackets?"

"Foraa thought so."

"Listen, I'll let you get back to the future-looking thing. I'll let you know if anything comes up in the real world. I mean, you know, Frisco."

"I appreciate that, Zachary," she said with a smile. "Let me know if you need anything else from me."

I stared out at the mist surrounding the mountains and drew my coat tighter about me. "There is one thing actually."

"Yes?"

"I'm going to need a ride down from this mountain. Any chance you could call me a cab or something?"

# 29

Once back in the real world, something Threa had said suddenly struck a chord in my mind. I needed to talk to Ona.

So HARV netted Ona's computer to set up some more face time between the two of us. Her schedule was tight, as you might imagine, but the computer agreed to squeeze me in between appointments (I was happy to see that proving her innocence was such a high priority). So late that day HARV and I returned to Ona's and met with her in her office, which was at the absolute center of the ziggurat.

Now, I've been in large offices before, but Ona's office was different. It took large and moved it exponentially in a strange sort of way.

Oh, it was big by normal standards, about fifteen meters square, but hardly awe-inspiring, at least in terms of length and width. Height, however, was an equine of an entirely different spectrum.

"I don't see a ceiling," I whispered to HARV as we entered.

"It's there."

"Is it invisible?" I said, craning my head upward. "Maybe that's Ona's little jab against the glass-ceiling concept."

"On the contrary, the ceiling is platinum in color, and fashioned to simulate the ornate tin ceilings found in early twentieth-century architecture."

"How come I can't see it?"

"Because it's high," HARV said.

"High?"

"One hundred seven meters." HARV replied. "At the pinnacle of the ziggurat."

"Why would anyone want a ceiling that high?"

"An architectural conversation piece, I suppose. This office holds the record for being the highest-ceilinged single room on Earth."

"They keep track of those things?"

"You know better than to ask me that, don't you?"

"I guess so."

"By the way," HARV said, "Don't drop anything of import into her wastebasket. The rumor is that it's three kilometers deep."

Ona was in the office as we entered and she waved us over to the desk at which she sat, at the far corner of the room.

"Zach. Over here."

HARV and I met her at the desk and she raised herself ever so slightly out of her chair to shake my hand.

"Thanks for meeting with us, Ona."

Ona sat back at her desk and straightened her outfit, a very white, low-cut jacket over a pale blouse, as a pair of tiny grooming bots hovered around her head. One quickly combed her hair; the other touched up her makeup. It was only then that I noticed the camera bot floating just in front of her desk. She smiled and let one of the bots buff her teeth to an even pearlier shade of white as she spoke (without moving her lips or jaw).

"I'm heeding your advice and taking my case to the court of public opinion," she said.

"You're giving interviews?"

"Not full-length interviews, of course. Just splinterviews."

"Splinterviews?"

"They're very short interviews," HARV said, "commonly used by most short cycle news services. One question, one response, usually no more than fifty words. Most of them buzz-words."

"I've been at it since our little chat at the pool earlier in the day," Ona said.

"How many have you done?"

"One hundred and fourteen so far."

"What?"

"Number one hundred and fifteen is scheduled for twenty seconds from now. Pardon me. Computer, which one is this?"

"Alyssa Sollyssa from *Rapid News*," the computer responded. "This one is to share your grief."

"Ugh. Grief," she said as she nervously waved the bots away and straightened her jacket. "I've been doing grief all afternoon. What about righteous indignation?"

"That's next interview," the computer said.

"Thank Gates for that." She glanced quickly at me. "I'll be with you in a nano, Zachary." She slid her earpiece into her ear, adjusted the tiny microphone on her collar, turned back to the camera bot, took a deep breath, and transformed herself into a grieving sister.

The change was actually startling to behold because her visage literally seemed to become consumed with sadness. Her eyes moistened gently and her face, though still perfect and beautiful, took on a subtle shade of vulnerability and sorrow. She suddenly looked like a woman who had been crying for two days but had somehow (heroically) pulled herself together in order to talk (exclusively) to her dear friend fill-in-interviewer's-name-here.

"Yes, Alyssa," Ona said, as the brief interview began. "Thank you and your viewers so much for your concern. I'm still in shock over Foraa's tragic death. I appreciate your thoughts and wishes and I'm just so grateful that you've chosen to respect the privacy of our family during this difficult time."

She gently sobbed twice and then the camera bot switched off.

"We're out," the computer said.

"Good," said Ona, her face and demeanor switching back to normal. "How did that look to you, Zach?"

The truth was I wasn't sure if I should be sick to my stomach or honored to be watching such a master at work.

"Was that the interview?"

"Splinterview," she said. "Please try to keep up. Did my grief read genuine to you?"

"Probably."

She nodded contentedly and spoke to her computer. "How long until the next one?"

"Seventy-five seconds," the computer responded.

"Plenty of time," she said turning back to me. "Now, how can I help you?"

I cleared my head and tried to stick to the business at hand. I pulled my chair closer and leaned toward her, trying hard to catch and hold her constantly wandering eyes (to no avail).

"I wanted to talk to you again about the night of Foraa's death," I said. "They're still not certain how Foraa died, which is good for us, but I want to talk a little bit about the wine since that's the current focus. You chose the bottle, right?"

"That's correct."

"When?"

"Earlier that evening," she said, "perhaps an hour before my sisters arrived."

"You brought it upstairs yourself?"

"Yes. No one else has access to the wine cellar."

"Okay. You chose the wine, you brought it upstairs. Did you bring it into the dining room yourself?"

Ona thought for a few nanos as the grooming bots once again retouched her hair and makeup.

"No, of course not, that's what server bots are for. What good is being rich and having servants if you do all the menial tasks yourself? I only had an hour to make myself look even more spectacular than usual."

"So, you didn't see the wine from the time you gave the bottle to that bot until you and the others entered the room?"

"Of course not. Even I'm not that much of a control freak. I trust my bots know how to properly carry wine."

"And that was about an hour, you said?"

"A little more, perhaps."

"I want to see that bot. I want surveillance visuals of its movements from the nano it took the bottle."

"Done," HARV said.

"We'll scan them tonight and look for anything that . . ."

"No, boss," HARV said. "I mean done *and done*. I just scanned the visuals."

"What, just now?"

HARV nodded. "Ms. Thompson's computer gave them to me. I scanned them."

"Already?"

HARV shrugged. "I'm a supercomputer."

"Did you find anything?"

He shook his head. "Nothing. The bot brought the wine to the dining room and set it on the table as W was finishing the table setting."

"Did W touch it?"

"He never came near it. He did the last of the silverware, then he left. The bottle sat undisturbed until Ms. Thompson and her sisters arrived that evening."

"DOS!" I turned back to Ona, "Do you have . . ."

"Next splinterview in ten seconds," the computer said.

"Hold that thought, Zach," Ona said as she turned back to the camera bot. "Which one is this?"

"Alvin Calvin of *World Entertainment News*."

"And this is righteous indignation?"

"Correct."

"Good," she said, turning to me. "My indignation comes a lot more naturally than my grief."

"So I gathered."

She turned back to the camera bot, took another deep breath, and transformed herself yet again. This time she became a grieving sister, besieged by a bloodthirsty media, who had somehow (heroically) pulled herself together in order to speak (exclusively) to the one journalist who truly understands human emotion, her dear friend fill-in-interviewer's-name-here.

"Alvin, Foraa's short life ended less than two days ago and yet I've been forced to relive that awful night every nano since then by poorly dressed vultures posing as journalists trying to create a story on the infrastructure of my grief."

"Wow, this woman should be in politics," I whispered to HARV.

"I don't think it pays well enough for her," HARV said.

"After everything I've done for this world, after all the good that I've created with my wealth—aiding underprivileged children, funding disease research, driving programs for environmental renewal and reinvention—after devoting my vast fortune to raising the quality of life for every downtrodden person in the first through fourth worlds, I think I'm entitled to better treatment than this."

Ona finished the splinterview and turned again to me.

"Sorry, Zach," she said. "I have two minutes until the next one now. What else do you need?"

I stared blankly at her for an ominously long nano or two. I'd honestly forgotten where we'd been in the discussion before the interruption. Worse still, I saw her looking at me now with a wide-eyed look of interest and I couldn't help wondering if it was genuine or just another type of splinterview.

"Zachary?"

HARV sensed my uncertainty and filled the void.

"We were discussing the wine and how it might have been tampered with during the hours leading up to Foraa's death," he said.

"Yes. Exactly," I mumbled. "We need to prove that nothing happened to the wine while it was in your possession. Computer, can you give HARV the visuals of Ona selecting the wine from the cellar?"

"I'm afraid not, Mr. Johnson," the computer said.

"Why?"

"The wine cellar is a technology-free zone," HARV said. "There are no surveillance cameras and I assume that the computer cannot monitor that particular room either."

"That's correct," said the computer. "I've never 'seen' the wine cellar. So to speak."

"Why is it technology-free?"

Ona shrugged. "It was part of Daddy's design. He said the electromagnetic energy from computers spoiled the wine."

"So we can prove that nothing happened to the wine once it left your hands," I said, hanging my head just a little, "but we have nothing to prove that you didn't tamper with it while you were in the cellar."

"Other than my word."

"No offense, Ona, but in a court of law, your word isn't the be-all-end-all."

"Not yet, but give me time," she said.

"Ona, I don't think you fully grasp what's going on here . . ."

A gentle tone sounded on her desk console and she turned her attention to it, casting a glance at the desk screen with a smile.

"Oh, good. The poll numbers are in."

"You're taking a poll?"

"Just a quick check on the effect that the splinterviews are having on public opinion," she said, gently touching the OLED screen surface that was her desktop. The raw numerical data was reflected in her smiling eyes as it came on the screen before blurring like drops of binary rain in a storm when she scrolled through it.

"Ona, I don't think it's appropriate for you to be taking poll numbers at this time . . ."

"Ah, eighty-four percent of all respondents find me sympathetic," she said, oblivious to my words. "That's up dramatically since this morning."

". . . It makes you seem a little callous . . ."

"Seventy-nine percent of all respondents feel that I am being unfairly persecuted because of my celebrity."

". . . and more interested in protecting your own position than in finding your sister's killer . . ."

"And ninety-three percent think I'm above the law."

"You think that's good?"

"Well, I'd rather be above the law than below it, wouldn't you?"

"Don't you think you'll be seen as selfish, taking polls so soon after your sister's death?" I asked.

Ona gave me a sly grin. "It's nice to see that you're looking out for my best interests Zach. Don't worry, nobody knows I'm the one taking the polls."

"Ona this isn't a game," I said.

"No, of course not," Ona agreed. "But you know as well as I do that this is just as much about control of public opinion as it is about who is right and who is wrong. The public doesn't have time to think about the facts. They want to be told what to think. I'm innocent, Zach, so I see no problem using all my resources to tell that to the world."

I pinched the bridge of my nose with my fingers, trying to suppress a headache before it started.

"What's the matter?" HARV said inside of my head. "You getting another one of those morally ambiguous headaches . . . ?"

"Just try not to go too overboard, Ona. Nobody wants to see you flaunting your wealth and power."

Ona gave me a smile that I was pretty certain she had had patented. "Don't worry, Zach. I'll do what I do well, you do what you do well." She looked at a clock on the wall. "Now, if you don't mind, I have another meeting with my public." With that, she gave me a dismissive wave.

I decided that to argue would be fruitless and potentially painful. I turned and started to make the long trip toward the door.

"Boss, you have a call coming in from Captain Rickey," HARV said.

"Put it on the interface."

Tony's face appeared on the tiny screen of the wrist interface.

"What's up Tony?"

"Plenty. Are you alone?"

I cast a quick glance back at Ona who was just beginning another "righteous indignation" interview.

"I am appalled that the innocent-until-proven-guilty standards that provide the foundation of our society are so callously ignored by a press corps who are DOS-bent on creating a headline scandal from this senseless tragedy."

I shook my head slowly. If I hadn't truly believed Ona was innocent, at least of killing Foraa, I would have walked away from this case and never looked back. Still, deep down, for some strange reason I knew Ona was only trying to help in her own deranged way.

"Yes, I'm alone."

"Good, because something's happened and I don't want anyone else to hear this. We found the poison," he said. "And it's not in the wine."

# 30

---

"You found what?" I asked Tony.

Tony's face was all professional and, on the surface, had that just-the-facts-ma'am steady tone that good cops do so well, but his undertone was one of excitement. Everybody loves a good mystery when it starts to unravel.

"Forensics went through the contents of the room. They did scans on the silverware and found traces of T and D on one of Foraa's forks."

"T and D?"

"That's short for Touch and Die. It's a designer poison, boss," HARV said.

"Very expensive," Tony insisted.

"And it was on the silverware?"

"Just Foraa's fork, one of them anyway," Tony said. "There were so many of them at the place setting. I don't know how people tell them apart. This was really tiny, it had only three tines."

"That's the fruit fork," HARV said, "for use when a small dish of fruit or sherbet is served between courses to cleanse the palette."

"They'd use a fork for sherbet?"

"A spoon is traditional, but apparently W chose the fork variation when he prepared the settings. A rather bold choice."

"Will you two shut up about the forks. I'm trying to . . . Wait, W set the table."

"What?" Tony asked.

"W set the table. That's his specialty. He was working right up until nearly the time of the dinner."

"You're sure of that?"

"It's on the surveillance recordings. HARV just checked them. W told me himself that it took him two full days to polish the silverware. He's the only one who touches it. Gates, Tony, do you know what this means?"

Tony's face lit up.

"The butler did it!"

"Darn, Tony, I wanted to say that."

"Are you at Ona's mansion now?"

"Yep."

"Well, stay put," Tony said. "I'm getting an arrest warrant and I'll be there in ten minutes."

His image blinked out and I stood in the hallway for a few nanos, softly shaking my head.

"There's one I didn't see coming."

"Perhaps there's a reason for that," HARV said.

"What?"

His hologram appeared beside me, projected from the wrist interface. His jacket was unbuttoned, far more casual than the norm. His hair was fuller than it had been this morning and was a little disheveled in that I'm-a-genius-and-don't-have-time-to-comb-my-hair way. And I think that the patches on his elbows were larger, too. I couldn't help but smile at his new detective phase. At least it was better than him wanting to be a cowboy.

"HARV, buddy, you're starting to worry me."

"What was W's motive for the murder? What did he gain by killing Foraa?"

I shrugged my shoulders and continued walking. "In case you haven't noticed, the man's not operating with a full set of chips. He's a loon. He probably would have wanted her dead because she used the wrong fork."

"Perhaps, but I'm not convinced."

"He lied in our interview," I said. "He claimed that Foraa was always nice to him. But Opie said the two of them argued all the time. Even yesterday."

"That doesn't mean he killed her."

"Like I said, HARV, you never know what will set a guy like him off. The police can link him to the poison. Case closed. I get a nice paycheck for my time served."

"I still don't like it," HARV said. "Not only is it cliché, but it's also too easy."

"What, I can't have an easy case?"

"Excuse me, Mr. Johnson . . ." Ona's computer said softly. "I'm afraid that the police won't find W when they arrive."

"I'm afraid to ask. But why?"

A small indoor hovercraft pulled up beside me and nudged me gently in the back of the knee.

"Because W has become a flight risk," the computer said. "Now please hurry, you need to get to the hoverport immediately."

"So, I guess the answer is 'No, I can't have an easy case.' "

"Don't worry, boss," HARV said. "I get the feeling that this is only the tip of the iceberg of complications."

"HARV, you're a machine. You don't get feelings."

"Would it make you feel better if I said I've done a numerical analysis on the probabilities and the results are skewed toward you having more problems with this case?"

"Strangely, no."

"I didn't think so," HARV said.

"Sirs," Ona's computer interrupted. "While I appreciate banter and human/computer bonding as much as the next supercomputer, I do believe the first goal here should be to stop W."

We made it to the hoverport in a couple of minutes. Sure enough a sleek, all-black, hoverjet was warmed up and appeared to be running its last internal diagnostics before lift-off.

"There's no authorization of use for that hoverjet," the computer said.

"Can you stop it?" I asked.

"NFAA regulations allow me control over only personal hovercrafts. I'm allowed only limited interfacing with hoverjets."

"You control the overhead doors for launches, though, right?"

"That is correct."

"Good. Keep them closed," I said, jogging toward the jet. "HARV and I will handle the geriatric killer."

HARV's hologram shimmered to life beside me as I ran. He

pretended to run alongside me, but his feet didn't touch the ground, which kind of blew the illusion.

"I still don't like this," he said.

"Neither do I, but we have to keep W here until Tony shows up."

"No, I mean, our assumption that W is the killer. It doesn't feel right."

I gave him a glare.

"Fine," HARV said. "It just doesn't compute."

"He's running away. That sort of indicates that he's done something wrong," I said. "We'll worry about making the case later. Right now, we need to keep him here."

The jet door was closed and the stairs leading to it were folded inside the cabin in preparation for launch. I popped my gun into my hand and aimed it at the barred door as I ran.

"Do I have enough firepower?"

"The door is reinforced," HARV replied. "Use a concentrated maximum blast."

I squeezed the gun handle twice to activate the voice controls.

"Big bang, tight," I said, pulling the trigger.

A small blast of fiery-red energy erupted from the gun barrel and slammed into the door, bursting through the metal/plastic polymer. The door splintered inward and flew from its moorings as the blast obliterated a small portion of the jet. Being careful not to touch too much of the charred debris, I hopped into the newly made hole and pulled myself into the main cabin.

The blast had shorted out part of the electrical system, so the lights were off in the passenger area. The cockpit, however, was still alive and kicking and that's where I found W. He had just risen from the pilot seat and was turning toward me on his brittle, slow moving legs.

"Mr. Johnson. What are you doing here?"

"Hello, W. I have some friends coming over soon. And I was thinking that we might all want some tea."

"I'm afraid I can't help you with that right now," he said. "I have a previous engagement."

"Sorry, W, but your attendance at this party is mandatory

and . . . oh, DOS, can we just skip over the snappy banter and cut to the chase?"

"I'd prefer it, actually," he said with a nod.

"And I think you're reaching by using the term 'snappy' to describe that banter," HARV said.

"We found the poison," I said, raising my gun to him.

"I don't know what you're talking about," he said.

"I thought we were going to skip the banter."

"Oh, that's right, sorry," he said. "Forgive me, I'm new at this."

"Fine," I said. "We'll talk about it later. Right now the police are on their way, so let's not make this any uglier than it already is. Power down the jet. I'll help you back to the main building and we'll meet the police together."

He sighed, nodded gently, and then looked away sadly.

"A fine idea," he said, and took a slow step toward me.

Then he raised his gaze and gave me a smile that sent a chill down my backbone.

"But I think not."

He spun around quickly (more quickly than I thought him capable of) and stabbed a button on the main console of the cockpit.

"Launch sequence initiated," the metallic voice of the cockpit computer toned. "Vertical launch in one minute."

The jet's engines roared to life and the craft lurched, throwing me off balance. W kept his footing and leaped at me (yes, leaped).

"What the . . . ?"

And that was all that I could manage. I was too stunned by his sudden movements to do much of anything as he kicked the gun out of my hand and then hit me in the face, spinning me around as I tumbled to the floor.

"I'm getting out of here," he said, kicking me in the back when I tried to get up. "And no third-rate detective is going to stop me."

He threw another kick at me, but I managed to get an arm up on this one and grab his well-loafered foot. It felt heavy in my hand. Far heavier than it should have.

"Just for the record," I said, "I'm a *second*-rate detective. And you're a cold-blooded killer."

I gave his leg a heave and he fell backward toward the cockpit. He scrambled to his knees and started crawling toward the jet controls. I jumped him from behind and the two of us began wrestling on the floor.

"I know the when and the how," I said. "What I'm looking for now is the why. Why did you kill Foraa?"

"Because she was a disrespectful little bitch," he said. "A spoiled, egotistical, haughty, arrogant, superhuman bitch."

"That describes all of the Quads, doesn't it?"

"You're right," he said, elbowing me in the stomach. "Did I mention she was blackmailing me?"

He broke free of my grasp and stumbled toward the controls.

"No, you forgot that one."

"Forgive me," he said. "She was blackmailing me. I've been embezzling funds from Ona for several years now. Cleaning supplies for cutlery and silverware aren't nearly as expensive as Ona thinks they are. Foraa found out and threatened to tell her. I couldn't let that happen."

He stabbed another button on the cockpit console and the jet shook again as the engines fired in preparation for lift-off.

"Being dismissed by one's employer is a very black mark on a butler's curriculum vitae."

"As opposed to embezzlement and murder . . ."

"Excuse me, boss," HARV said, "but I feel it important to note here that the hoverjet is now officially engaged in its lift-off mode and that the heat of the thrusters will likely incinerate this entire hangar unless you allow the computer to retract the rooftop doors and open a launch hole in the force field."

"Open the doors," I said, still grappling with W, "but keep the force field intact."

"But . . ."

"Do it," I said, as W hit me solidly in the face. My head shot back and I felt my teeth chatter.

"And by the way," HARV said, "I suspect that W's actions are being artificially augmented."

"You figured that out, did you?"

"I have developed a keen eye for human behavior."

The hangar itself started to vibrate as the massive overhead doors began to open. W smiled as the jet received the official green light for liftoff and he stabbed the launch button. The jet shuddered again and slowly rose into the air. I got up from the floor and pulled W out of the cockpit seat.

"You won't get very far in this thing with that gaping hole in the side, you know."

"Then I'll patch it with your corpse," he said, hitting me again with a lightning-fast jab. I stumbled farther back into the cabin as the jet continued to rise.

"Why would you do it?" I asked. "Why embezzle funds? What could you possibly want that badly?"

"Well, you see, I'm getting on in years now."

"Yes, I'd noticed that."

He turned to me and I saw his body began to tremble, as though chilled by an icy draft that was slowly increasing in intensity.

"And I was growing tired of my feeble body."

The tremble of his form had become feverish now, almost violent, as though his joints were pulling themselves apart. W seemed gleefully nonplussed by it all.

"So I traded in my old body . . . for something new."

He stretched his hand out menacingly and I saw his arm begin to stretch. The fabric of his day coat ripped as the arm turned inhumanly long and kept on growing, stretching toward me whiplike, a white-gloved tentacle of death. I could see now the metallic sheen of the skin beneath the torn shirt and jacket as his hand grabbed me by the throat. W was no longer human.

"You bought an android body?"

"I made the transfer last night," he said. "You'd be amazed how much a good body costs these days."

The hoverjet leveled off at a thirty-meter height and began to idle, hovering over the compound like a black metallic cloud, the heat from its thrusters beating down on the buildings below. While inside, W's android arm lifted me off the ground by my throat as I desperately pulled at his hand. He smiled gleefully as he began to tighten his grip.

"This body is simply amazing," he said. "Do you know how quickly I can now do a formal setting for twelve? The possibilities simply stagger the imagination."

"Well, you can take the brain out of the body, but you can't take the butler out of the brain," I said.

He turned and extended his other arm a few meters into the cockpit and engaged the forward thrusters. The jet began to move forward slowly. Through the cockpit window, I could see that we were headed toward the force field wall near the camouflaged main gate.

"Computer," he shouted, "open a launch window in the field."

"Request denied, W," the computer responded.

"What?"

"Mr. Johnson has overridden all hangar and force field access. I'll need the command from him."

W turned to me and tightened his grip on my throat.

"You know, thirty years ago I could have thrashed you thoroughly with my original body," he said.

"Yeah, but you would have looked kind of ridiculous beating up an eight-year-old kid."

"Have the computer open a window in the field," he said.

"No."

His droid fingertips dug deep into the muscles of my neck, his thumb painfully plucking at my Adam's apple as though it were a guitar string.

"Open the window," he snarled.

We were approaching the force field quickly now, the jet's thrusters revving, atomic batteries to power, turbines to speed. But I held my ground.

"No."

"Boss, please," HARV said. "You don't get paid if you die."

W pushed me hard against the wall of the cockpit and stepped up power to the thrusters. He and I locked eyes like two poker players over the last big pot of the night as the jet lurched and accelerated toward the force field.

"Do it now," he said, "or I'll flambé you like a cherries jubilee."

"Polish my brass, butler."

I stuck out my hand and shouted above the din of the jet thrusters.

"Come to daddy."

My gun responded to the voice command and flew toward me from the floor beneath a seat where it had landed. The handle slipped into my hand with a familiar slap and I held it low as the computer innards came to life at its recognition of my heat signature.

"Burn, baby,"

The gun flashed recognition at my voice command and I pulled the trigger. A white-hot laser blast erupted from the barrel, hitting W in the android armpit, burning through his shoulder like a cattle brand in a snowbank. This time I was too close to the blast and felt a burn go up my arm, but W took the real brunt of the blast.

He screamed, more out of surprise than pain as his arm fell to the floor (and me with it). I pulled the hand from my throat and threw the severed arm aside while W grabbed at his smoldering stub, trying desperately to hold himself together.

"Careful there, W," I said, "you're likely to burn your other glove."

"Glove?" HARV whispered inside my head.

I stepped past W toward the cockpit and reached for the power-down controls on the thrusters, but W leaped at me from his knees, a wild-eyed look of fury in his face.

"Boss, that's it," HARV said, projecting himself through my communicator, "gloves."

"Not now, HARV."

W's elongated remaining arm wrapped around me like a droidish feather boa and pulled me away from the controls. I got off another laser shot before we tumbled again to the floor, hitting him high in the right leg, where his femur would have been (if he'd still had a human body). The blast cut through his droid circuitry and the severed leg fell to the floor, sparking like a metal hover in a microwave storm. W screamed again but held tight to me as he fell, pulling me back down to the floor.

"Don't you see," HARV continued. "W didn't kill Foraa."

"HARV, he just confessed," I said, trying to fight my way back to my feet.

"He confessed to *trying* to kill her. He didn't actually succeed."

I caught a glimpse of the fast approaching force field wall through the cockpit window.

"I've got other things to worry about right now, HARV."

"T and D is a touch-sensitive poison. It has to make direct contact with the skin in order to get into the system."

"He put it on her fork," I said. "She touched the fork."

"But she was wearing *gloves!* Foraa was wearing long black gloves when she touched the poisoned fork."

The revelation froze me in my tracks. I sat motionless for a nano, oblivious to the chaos around me as the logic of HARV's reasoning sunk in.

"DOS, he didn't kill her," I whispered.

W chose that nano to pull me back to the floor with his remaining arm and then bit me on the shoulder. The jet thrusters were still revving, the jet's speed was increasing, and the force field was getting closer.

"HARV, max up my armor. This is going to get ugly."

I fired another blast at W and cut his droid body in half at the navel. Then I turned and sent a blast into the control panel of the cockpit, destroying it in a cascade of flaming computer drek. The jet's emergency alarms sounded a high-pitched scream as the fail-safe program kicked in. The thrusters decelerated and the craft shook like a San Andreas nightclub. We slowed, but not nearly enough. We were still headed toward the force field and far too close to stop.

I tried to shout a command to Ona's computer to open a window in the field, but there was no time. All I managed to say was:

"Open . . ."

But Ona's computer was acting on its own. It made the decision without me and a nano before the point of impact, I saw the force field warp itself open, spiraling like water down a drain (only in reverse) to create a hole right in front of our swan-diving hoverjet and we (thankfully) passed through . . .

. . . right into the main entrance.

Yes, the mountain pass that HARV and I had entered through two days earlier suddenly appeared before me, the holographic hills and rocks blinking out as the flaming, out-of-control hoverjet burst through them. We crashed through a few simulacra on our way to the ground as well and by the time we reached the guardpost and the gathered throng of pressbots, well, let's just say that the compound's carefully designed, created, and maintained camouflaged secret entrance wasn't so camouflaged anymore. And it wasn't much of a secret either.

The jet, cushioned only somewhat by the thrusters that were now in full fail-safe reverse, skidded along the mountain pass and belly-flopped onto the ground with an earth-shaking rumble of screaming metal and dying engines. We crushed the guardpost and a dozen of the slower-footed pressbots like a steamroller over ripe fruit before coming to rest on the gravel embankment.

The pressbots, cameras rolling, all stared at the plane for a nano, then—as one—turned their lenses toward Ona's compound. With the holographic hillside projections disrupted and most of the hard simulacrum scenery destroyed, the compound itself was now in plain view, its purple force field glittering like a jewel in the sun.

A few of the pressbots couldn't take the excitement of finally getting actual footage of the compound and their circuits overloaded. They fainted like teenyboppers at a concert. The majority, however, swarmed around the force field in a desperate grab for footage of an exclusive story that was now fair game.

And that, of course, is when the police finally arrived.

Four hovercrafts, sirens wailing, landed in a semicircle around the smoking remnant of the jet. Tony and eleven of his men jumped out, weapons in hand, and hit the ground running.

"Hold all fire until my order," Tony bellowed.

He pointed his blaster at the cockpit and took cover behind a standard issue personal force field.

"Attention in the cockpit," he yelled, "you are surrounded. Come out with your hands up."

A handful of the pressbots turned their cameras toward the smoking jet as the cockpit roof emergency hatch was kicked open and I slowly emerged from within, one hand held high in the air, the other dragging W's still sparking android torso behind me.

"I want my arms back, you barbarian," W shouted. "They're expensive."

Tony recognized me through the smoke and lowered his weapon (and then rubbed his forehead).

"Zach?"

I walked to Tony and laid the still struggling W at his feet as the officers slowly converged upon me. Tony stared at W, then at the smoking jet, then finally at me.

"What the . . . ?"

I held up my hand to stop the question.

"Don't ask. There's your man," I said, pointing to W. "Feel free to arrest him. One thing, though . . ."

"What's that?"

"He didn't do it."

# 31

I left W with Tony and his officers (I think they sent someone into the jet to get his various missing limbs) and they took him back to the station house for booking. He may not have been the one who actually murdered Foraa, but he made an attempt on her life (not to mention mine), so that counted for something. They were also charging him with embezzlement, grand theft hoverjet, and wanton destruction of private property (although he'll probably blame that last one on me). He also copped to sending the medieval armor after me the day before, so, all in all, his capture wrapped up a lot of things.

Except of course, the mystery of Foraa's murder.

Tony insisted his men take me to the hospital. I've been to the hospital so much over the past few years that they have their own booth for me in the emergency room. I think they've also named a sandwich in the cafeteria after me.

After a brief scan it was apparent that none of my wounds were major, so they gave me to an intern for a quick clean up. He was a nervous fellow who didn't look like he was old enough to shave let alone know the difference between my tibia and fibula (both of which needed attention).

"Zow, you're a legend here, Mr. Johnson," the intern said, as he squirted an abrasion on my knee with some instant skin.

"Is that a good thing?"

"Sure it is," he said. "My colleagues say you're living proof as to just how much damage the human body can take."

"Well, thanks, and call me Zach."

"Of course," he said with a smile. He took a light pen and shined it in my eyes. "You still have both of your original eyes? They haven't even been surgically reattached or anything?"

"That surprise you?"

"Kind of," he said with a shrug. "Given your track record and all."

"There are a lot of surprising things about Zachary Nixon Johnson," a very familiar voice said from behind him.

The intern turned to get a good look at the lovely face that accompanied that voice.

"Dr. Gevada," he said, with more than a little surprise. He turned and looked at me, then shot a quick glance at Electra, not quite daring to meet her eyes.

"I'll take it from here, Dr. Way," she said.

"You know my name?" he said.

"Yeah, she can read," HARV said, inside my head.

"I'm familiar with your work," Electra said, being far more diplomatic than HARV. "You have other duties to perform. Si?"

"Of course," he said as he turned and pointed to me. I guess he did it just in case Electra had forgotten where I was sitting or something. "I'll leave you to your patient."

He gave me a knowing wink, then headed off to wherever interns go to find their next patient. As he walked away, I was pretty certain I heard him say, "She knows my name."

"I see we're *both* legends around here," I said to Electra.

"Albeit for different reasons," she said with a sexy smile as she checked my eyes again.

"Is that kid really a doctor?" I asked. "He didn't even ask me about my insurance coverage."

"Yes, he's a doctor. And he's twenty-seven. You're just getting old," she said as she moved the light across my eyes.

"Dr. Way has already established that I have two eyes."

"Just making sure. What happened?"

"I had a little run in with a butler who had the ultimate case of the Peter Pan syndrome."

She moved a finger across my field of vision. "Follow my finger."

"They really didn't need to call you in. It's going to take more than a semi-robotic butler and a hover crash to do me in."

"The ER here has me on speed dial," Electra said. She

scanned my medical records. "It's looks like you're right, though. No major damage."

I hopped off the table.

"But I'm worried, chico," she said.

"Electra, mi amor, you know better than anyone that I've been hurt way worse than this. This doesn't even make my top twenty worst run-ins. I don't even think this guy qualifies for his complementary I-tried-to-kill-Zach T-shirt."

Electra shook her head and gave me a look I was all too familiar with; the one that silently says "maybe you should find a new line of work." (I hate that look.)

"I have a bad feeling about this job."

I leaned over and kissed her. "You know you're the only woman I love. The three Thompson Quads are totally crazo. And that's being polite."

"I'm not jealous," Electra said. "Well, that's not entirely true, but that's not what I'm worried about. I'm worried that maybe, just maybe, this one time, you've bitten off more than you can chew."

I gave her my most reassuring smile. "You of all people should know that I have a really big mouth."

She looked at me and smiled, "You know, chico, I'm never sure if I should kiss you or kick you in the head."

"That's what makes our romance special," I said. "Am I cleared to go?"

She smiled. "I'll see you at home."

"Unless one of us gets called to duty," I pointed out.

"Verdad," she said with a wink that was far more appealing than the one Dr. Way gave me.

It was evening by the time I got home. It had been a long day but not a terrible one. If nothing else, one of the potential killers had been crossed off the list. So I had to believe that progress was being made.

Nevertheless, a part of me couldn't help thinking that Electra may have been on to something. I had a gut feeling that this case was going to get nastier before it got better. I also knew that there was more going on here than met the senses. I wasn't sure what. But I was pretty sure I wasn't going to like it.

I sat down on the couch and kicked off my shoes.

HARV appeared before me.

"You have two incoming calls."

"Two?"

"Ona and Carol. Which one do you want first?"

"Let's talk to Carol first. I like her more."

HARV rolled his eyes. "Fine, put the paying client on hold. You know she hates waiting." HARV's eyes lit up. "Oh, you *know* she hates waiting."

"You really are as smart as you keep saying. I'm sick of Ona thinking that I'm available at her beck and call. A little wait will be good for her."

Carol's face appeared on my wallscreen.

"You should have taken Ona's call first," she said.

"You're more important to me, Carol. What's up?"

"I'm going to be out of the office tomorrow morning."

"Big test or something?"

Carol looked at me for a nano and I could tell she was thinking carefully about what she was about to say.

"Nope," she said casually.

Okay, maybe she hadn't been thinking that carefully about it. But I had that gut feeling that something wasn't quite right.

"I just need a little time."

"Fine, I guess I'll see you in the afternoon, then?"

Carol smiled. "Yep, and you should take an antacid for that feeling in your gut."

Carol's image faded out and was replaced by Ona's face, lighting up the vid screen like a supernova in the night sky.

"How dare you keep me waiting, Zachary!" she yelled.

I gave her my most disarming smile. "Ona, the other call was from my assistant. I thought she might have some important info for the case."

The look on Ona's face cooled a bit from nova to the standard molten.

"From what my computer says, you went above and beyond the call of duty today in order to capture W. I guess I owe you some gratitude."

"You're welcome. Sorry about the hoverjet."

"It's no bother, I have several."

"And the hangar."

"Repairs are already under way."

"And sorry about the guardpost, the state-of-the-art holographic projection system, and the specially constructed camouflaging simulacra."

"We better just stop there, Zach."

"I think you're right."

"The Pfauhans hunted down the dozen or so pressbots that invaded the compound after your crash," she said. "It was quick work and I think the Pfauhans enjoyed it. The pressbots took some footage of the compound, but no real harm was done."

"I'm glad to hear that."

"Which brings us back to the here and now," Ona continued. "Do you know anything about a sigil?"

"Sigil?"

"A symbol or series of symbols that Foraa scribbled down before she died."

"How . . . do you know about that?"

"Well, there appears to be some mention of it on *Entertainment This Nano*."

# 32

"The series of sigils, as seen here in an artist's rendition, appears to have been scribbled by the late Foraa Thompson just prior to her death. We here at *Entertainment This Nano* believe that it is a clue of some sort to the identity of Foraa's killer and currently have our top minds working on deciphering it."

It was like something out of a nightmare. The symbols that Foraa had drawn in the wine puddle, nanos before she died, were there on the screen beside Bill Gibbon's perfectly coifed talking head.

"Oh, my Gates! How did he get that?"

"Curious, indeed," HARV mumbled.

I had to admit that I was growing to appreciate Bill Gibbon's impeccable timing for breaking news. The other networks had finally gotten some news of their own, thanks to my high-concept brouhaha with W that afternoon. But while they were fighting among themselves for viewers with the same news and visuals, Gibbon was coming through with *another* bombshell exclusive. The guy sure knew how to play to the crowd.

"It also appears that the New Frisco Police Department is ignoring this very important information. Truthfully, they seem to be almost totally unaware of its very existence. Whether that's due to questionable investigative skills or simple ineptitude is still unclear."

"This is not going to go over very well with Tony," I said.

"Funny you should mention Captain Rickey," HARV intoned.

I hung my head. "He's on the line, isn't he?"

HARV nodded. "You want to take the call now, or should I stall him while you practice your apology."

"Put him on," I said with a sigh.

Tony's face appeared on the screen and, as I guessed, he wasn't very happy. His face was tired, his hair disheveled, and his posture was of a man who had definitely seen better days. His eyes, however, were furious.

"Tony . . ."

"Did you know about this?"

I thought for a nano or two. Tony had no way of knowing that I knew about the symbols. I could deny it. I could plead the fifth. But I decided it was time to come clean.

"I'm not going to lie to you . . ."

"You mean lie to me *again*. Zach, you willfully withheld evidence from me."

"I didn't know what the symbols meant," I said. "I was going to tell you about it. I just wanted to figure it out."

"You mean, you wanted to make sure it didn't incriminate your client."

"Tony . . ."

"I played straight with you, Zach. I gave you full access to our information and this is how you repay me? You withhold evidence and you make me and my entire department look like fools."

The words were especially painful coming from Tony. I hadn't acted maliciously, but that didn't matter now.

"I'm sorry."

"Did you leak this information to Gibbon?"

"What? No. Of course not."

"How else would he know it?"

"Why would I give him the information?"

"Probably to help your client in some way," Tony replied. "That seems to be the only thing you're interested in."

"I'll make it up to you, Tony. I promise."

"Don't do me any favors, Zach," he said. "You've done enough already. As of this nano, our deal is off. You get no more information on the investigation. You won't hear anything from my department until we're ready to make an arrest. And, for your sake, you better hope it's not Ona that we arrest. Until then, you don't talk to me. You don't talk to my detectives. You don't talk to any of the investigators. You don't talk to anybody who knows anybody connected to my department. You are cut off from all information. You got that?"

"Yeah, I got it."

"Good. And be thankful that I don't arrest you for this, Zach. I could and I should, but I won't. That's the last favor I do for you."

He terminated the call and the screen went blank. I sat back in my chair and held my head in my hands.

"Wow, I don't think I've ever seen Captain Rickey that mad at you," HARV said.

"Yep," I agreed. "I've reached a new high in lows." I shook my head. "I really don't know why I didn't tell him and his men about it sooner."

"You are only human," HARV said. I'm not sure if he was trying to comfort me or to state a fact. "The question is, what do we do now?"

I stood up and redid the top button on my shirt.

"We're going to pay a visit to Bill Gibbon."

"Now?"

"You and I discovered those sigils when we first got to the scene, HARV. We even destroyed them when we moved her hand."

"What do you mean 'we' ?"

"No one else should know about them," I said. "No one else should know *any* of the things Gibbon has been reporting."

"He's talking to someone on the inside?"

"Up until now, it could have been anyone; the coroner, one of Tony's investigators. But knowing about the sigils . . ."

"You think Gibbon's source might be the killer?"

"Maybe. Maybe not," I said. "Either way, he's going to talk to us tonight."

I left the study and slammed the door behind me.

# 33

HARV did some digging and found that Gibbon had a thing for young blonde women, so when I got to the *ETN* studio, I had HARV throw a voluptuous blonde hologram over me and presented myself to security as Gibbon's nightly bonus from the network brass for a job well done. (Yes, I dressed up as a woman. But I didn't enjoy it, so it doesn't count.) In any event, I made it into Gibbon's dressing room with very little fuss (and even less dignity).

"Couldn't you have projected a dress that was a little longer?" I whispered to HARV, as I waited. "I feel like my butt's hanging out of this."

"You wanted to get noticed, didn't you?" HARV replied. "Besides it's not even your butt."

"It's the principle of the thing. I'm not a tramp."

"Oh, that's right, you're just posing as a prostitute to get by security. I'm sorry if I missed that fine distinction."

Gibbon walked through the door just then with a truly gleeful look on his face. Can't say that I blame him. Over the past two days he had become the king of trash journalism and, as far as he knew, he was about to reap a very curvaceous reward. I almost felt sorry for the guy.

"Well, well, well, what have we here?" he said lasciviously, as he turned down the lights. "Nice dress, or should I say, lack thereof."

"I told you the dress was appropriate," HARV whispered.

"Congratulations. You're a highly advanced supercomputer and you know how to attract a lowlife."

Gibbon was shorter than I had imagined and at least fifteen

years older than he appeared to be on screen. But he had the kind of charm that comes from self-confidence (bordering on egotism), and at this particular nano, as he removed his suit-coat and came toward me, he wouldn't have been more full of himself if he'd eaten his own clone.

"I assume the brass booked you for the whole night, doll," he said, sitting next to me on the couch, "but I'm back on camera in twenty minutes, so we'll have to start with something quick and painless."

He slid his left hand toward my thigh as he sat next to me and that was about all I could take. I grabbed his hand at the wrist and twisted it. He yelped in pain like a baby seal.

"Fine, we'll make it quick," I said as he dropped to his knees. "It's your call on whether or not it's painless."

"What the . . . What's going on?" he asked, clearly confused by the husky tone of my voice. "Who are you?"

"Just a lonely soul in this world looking for love and a little information."

"You're no prostitute."

"Nice of you to notice," I said. "But I'm no saint either, so don't make me get rough here."

"My wallet's on the table."

I twisted his wrist a little further and his grimace grew more pained.

"I'm not a thief and I'm insulted by that assumption," I said, twisting his arm again. "Apologize."

"Ow. Sorry."

"Good."

I pulled him up and tossed him onto the couch as I stood and barred his path to the doorway. He rubbed his wrist gently.

"Where are you getting your information on the Foraa Thompson murder?"

"Is that what you're after?" he asked, slowly getting up from the couch. "Who sent you? *The World Show? Rapid News? The Nano Gossip Net?*"

I grabbed him by the shirt collar and pulled him toward me.

"Do I look like a journalist to you?"

"A weather girl, maybe, but your breasts need to be bigger."

I pushed him hard back down to the couch.

"I'm losing patience here, Gibbon, and I'll warn you, I

didn't have much when I arrived. Now, where are you getting your information on the Thompson murder?"

He leaned over and touched a button on the tabletop console.

"I'm calling security."

"Fine," I said. "Bring them in. Let's create a scandal."

"You think my having a hooker in my dressing room will create a scandal?" he said with a laugh. "Honey, you don't get out much, do you?"

"Oh, I think I know a thing or two about scandals," I said.

I snapped my fingers and my hologram disguise instantly changed from voluptuous blonde bombshell to rotund, ugly battle-ax (same outfit though, which I thought was a nice touch on HARV's part).

"Oh, my Gates," Gibbon said, his face going a little pale.

"Or maybe we can go multigenerational?" I snapped my fingers again and my form changed to that of an emaciated, aged woman.

"Or ecclesiastical." I snapped again and the dress was replaced by a nun's habit.

"Or we can go with plain old weird." I snapped my fingers again and took on the form of a goat (in the hooker dress).

"It's your choice."

Gibbon moved his hand away from the computer console. "You wouldn't dare," he said.

"Baaah, baaah, Mr. Gibbon," I bleated loudly. "Please don't make me butt you there again."

"Gates, please stop."

I grabbed him by the shirt and lifted him up into my holographic-goat face.

"Then tell me . . . what's your source of information?"

We heard a knock at the door and Gibbon turned toward it out of fright.

"Bill," the woman's voice was young, but professional. "They need you to do teasers for the overnight, so we need you back in a little early."

Gibbon's face grew panicked as he stared at the door, turned to me, then turned back to the door.

"I'll . . . be right there," he called out, in a strained, forced-casual voice.

"Not if you don't tell me what I want to know," I whispered.

"Bill?" the woman said, and we heard the knob rattle from the other side. "Are you all right in there?"

"Please," Gibbon whispered. "This is the biggest story of my career."

"And it's about to be pushed off the front page by news of your torrid affair with a talking goat. Who knew that you had such a penchant for animals?"

Gibbon's face turned a whiter shade of pale and he was at a curious loss for words. "What? No, I didn't. I mean, I never touched the animal. We just talked."

"What do you mean by that?" I asked.

"Bill?" The knob rattled again.

"I'm fine," he said. "Give me a minute. I'm not decent."

"You can say that again," I said, in a tone slightly louder than a whisper.

"What was that?" came the voice on the other side.

"Nothing!" Gibbon said.

"DOS, Bill, are you snorting your eye makeup again? I thought management discussed that with you."

"I'm not snorting anything."

And I let loose with a long (goatlike) snort.

"That's it, Bill. Open this door, or I'm getting security."

"No, don't!"

Gibbon made a move toward the door, but I grabbed him tighter, spun him around, and bent his right arm back painfully behind him. The scuffle did not go unheard.

"That's it," said the voice. "Security!"

"Oh, DOS," Gibbon whispered.

"Time's running out, Bill. Who's feeding you the information?"

Gibbon arched forward at the waist and he began flailing with his left arm, frantically struggling to break free.

"Never. Never, DOS it," he shouted. "Do you know what my ratings are now? I can't. I can't. My contract's up for renewal next year."

He kicked back at me as his knees buckled and he hit me hard in the shin.

"Ow."

I kicked his legs out from under him and we fell to the floor with me kneeling on his back, still twisting his arm.

"I won't go back," he yelled. "I can be the king now. The king of all media!"

He was still flailing with his free hand and kicking his feet behind me, fast approaching the delirious zone of an emotional breakdown. I stuck my free arm behind his neck and pinned him solidly to the floor with my weight. He was crying now and still shouting.

"I'm the king. I'm the king!"

"I thought you were going to keep a low profile," HARV asked.

I heard pounding on the door and voices calling from the hallway, but I couldn't understand the words over the shrill of Gibbon's wails. I pulled harder on his right arm, bending it close to breaking in an effort to shut him up. His hand was balled into a fist, but his fingers unwrapped when the next wave of pain hit. He screamed, I glanced at his palm, and I froze.

"Oh, DOS," I whispered.

The dressing room door burst open and two security guards, an *ETN* producer, and at least two network management types stumbled into the room to find a delirious Bill Gibbon, screaming "I'm the king" while lying on the floor beneath a goat in a dress (and thus was born one of the great showbiz legends of our time).

But I didn't care because I was still looking at the palm of Gibbon's right hand. The skin had been burned, singed like flesh beneath a branding iron. Not deeply enough to leave a permanent scar, but enough for me to notice the very distinctive shape. I recognized it in an instant and Gibbon didn't need to say another word.

The grinning ape insignia branded into the palm of his hand told me everything I needed to know.

# 34

One hour later, the cold night wind was hitting my face like the slap of a scorned woman. Half a dozen searchlights cut the thick, gray mist around me like billion-candle ethereal lasers and the hard pavement of Thirty-third Street, ninety-seven stories below my perch on the crumbling building ledge, beckoned like an asphalt abyss.

I could hear the roar of the fighter planes, hidden in the folds of the mist, as they circled just overhead. Every so often I'd glimpse the steel-gray edge of a wing or charcoal tip of a fuselage, closer than I thought imaginable. Then it would vanish again in the clouds, like the rolling thunder of a March storm, leaving me clinging to the building as it shuddered in the vociferation of the jet wake.

Opie was two stories above me, and climbing. His powerful fingers and toes were actually tearing hand- and footholds into the building's outer shell. His jerky movements belied his desperation, while his quick glances toward me and at the circling planes revealed his fear.

"It doesn't have to be this way, Opie," I called, hoping that he could hear me above the din.

"Of course it does," he shouted, turning his head downward to look at me. "It *always* ends this way."

Opie was wild now. His fur rippled in the wind like a wheat field awaiting a tornado, which was appropriate, really, because I could see by the look in his eyes that a storm was coming. His look was crazed, frenetic, and filled with fear.

His foot slid off the mist-slicked building shell and he stumbled, suspended in the air for a nano only by the gripping fingers of his left hand. I saw then that he was holding something in his right hand that looked like a small doll.

"HARV, go in tight on the right hand," I whispered.

HARV activated the lens in my left eye and zoomed in on Opie's furry fist. Sure enough, he was holding a dark-haired, faux-leather clad, little female-shaped doll with grayish skin.

"It appears to be a Foraa doll," HARV said.

"Great. As if we didn't have enough weird symbolism already."

Opie regained his balance and continued climbing, moving quickly toward the lightning rod spire of the tower.

"At least tell me why you did it, Opie," I shouted. "Tell me why."

He reached the overhang just below the base of the massive lightning rod, and swung himself up and over it with a mighty, hairy-armed heave.

"I don't know!" he yelled.

He leaped and grabbed a handhold on the sloping gray metal base of the spire. From there it was just a hop and a skip to the gray spearlike lightning rod atop the building itself.

"Do you want to follow him?" HARV asked.

I shook my head. "There's no point. He's passed the base of the old TV tower already."

"The dirigible mast," HARV said.

"What?"

"It was originally designed as a mooring mast for dirigibles. It didn't really work, though, because the winds at this height make mooring something as unwieldy as a blimp very difficult."

"That would be very interesting in its appropriate time and place, HARV. Here and now, it's just annoying."

"Got it."

"Good. Track Opie with the telephoto and project my voice enough for him to hear."

Opie grabbed the base of the lightning rod and then stood at the building's pinnacle, defiantly waving the doll in the air as the gray planes continued to circle and roar.

"Top of the world, Ma!" he shouted toward the night sky.

"I need to ask this, Opie," I yelled. "I need to know. Did you kill Foraa?"

"What?" his eyes were wide with confusion. "Why would I do that?"

"Then why did you talk to Gibbon?"

"I don't know." He looked away as though ashamed.

"You gave him information that you shouldn't have known," I said. "How did you know about the symbols beneath her hand?"

"I . . . I don't know." He rubbed his forehead with the doll, confused.

"You have to do better than that, Opie."

He turned his face to the sky as an ashen jet rumbled by and shook the building. He grabbed for it clumsily and nearly lost his balance.

"I didn't kill her," he yelled. "I loved her."

"Opie . . ."

Another plane circled past, this one in the opposite direction and closer to the building than the last. Opie reached his gray hands toward that one as well. He was slow now, dazed and disoriented.

"I loved them all. I loved them all!"

"We have to stop this," I whispered.

"Shouldn't be long now," HARV said. "Besides, I'm finally getting used to the black and white surroundings."

One last plane came out of the mist, wings tipped to perfectly match the Empire State Building's angling spire and so close that the tip of the dirigible mast grazed the dull silver belly of the great bird. Gray sparks flew and Opie, arms outstretched, leaped at his winged tormenter as it passed.

"I love them all!"

The wake of the jet carried his gorilla bulk away from the building, his feet skittered on the shell, in a desperate grab for safety as he fell, but it was no use. He nearly grabbed the ledge of the observatory on the eighty-sixth floor, but his hands bounced off the hard metal fence and he went completely airborne, screaming as he fell to his curbside destiny at thirty-two feet per second.

"Beauty killed the beast!"

The soft thud of his body onto the floor of his habitat terminated the program. The building vanished as did the planes, the mist and the entire Manhattan cityscape, and was replaced by the suddenly mundane-looking décor of Opie's habitat.

"The décor program was connected to his subconscious," HARV said as his hologram shimmered to life beside me.

"I know," I nodded. "*King Kong,* 1933. You have to hand it to him for sticking to the classic and not going with one of the remakes."

I knelt beside Opie's motionless form and put my hand on his great shoulder. His chest was rising and falling naturally and I found that comforting.

"He's unconscious," HARV said. "There don't appear to be any broken bones or internal injuries. Heartbeat and respiration are normal. He's fine, physically."

"It's his head that I'm worried about," I said. I gave Opie one more pat on the head, then stood up. "You can come in now, Tony!"

Tony and half a dozen of his men, a pair of EMTs, and a veterinarian entered the habitat. They hoisted Opie onto an industrial-strength stretcher and slowly rolled him toward the door. Tony came to me and nodded, ever so slightly.

"Good job, Zach. I don't think we could have talked him down without you."

"*King Kong* only ends one way, Tony. He brought himself down."

"Maybe so. But you gave him that chance. Who knows how many scenarios we'd have gone through without you." He patted me on the back. "Thanks."

I smiled ever so slightly. "You're welcome."

"Do you think he was telling the truth?" Tony asked.

"All of his facial tics and movements were consistent with somebody who believed what they were saying," HARV said. "I didn't detect any other signs of deception."

I nodded in agreement with HARV. "I agree. He might be prone to irrational acts and jokes, but I don't think he's a liar."

"He compromised the investigation by making the details public," Tony said. "We need to hold him. At least for now. I'm sure we can hold him for obstructing justice and resisting arrest."

"I'm certainly not going to complain."

It was the end of another long, confusing day. I had shut

down Bill Gibbon's stream of inside information and had mended my bridges with Tony, for the time being anyway. But the killer was still on the loose and that, as always, was my bottom line.

# 35

I got a call from Randy early the next morning. And by "early" I mean 4:30. Randy doesn't sleep, remember.

"Randy, do you know what time it is?"

"Four thirty-two," Randy said. "Why?"

"Just checking," I said. "You see, I took my watch off about the time that *I went to bed!*"

"Oh. It's four thirty A.M., isn't it?"

"Yes, it is."

"Sorry, Zach. I'm doing the sleepless regimen this week and lost track of time. And there are no windows in the lab. I find the outside world distracting."

"I can tell."

"Do you want to go back to sleep? I can call you back at a more polite hour if you like. But can you remind me what hour is considered polite? I've kind of lost track of that, too."

"Forget it, Randy," I said. "What's up?"

"You're sure you don't mind? I can call back, really."

"I'm awake now, Randy."

"But are you fully awake? I mean, I doubt your mind is functioning at its optimum level now."

"When is my mind ever at optimum level?"

"Well, studies have shown that in order for the brain to maintain proper calcium levels, the majority of the population needs at least eight hours sleep per night. I am, of course, in the minority that can function at optimal levels without that much sleep since . . ."

"You're not normal," I said.

"True," he said. "And I use other means to stimulate my calcium levels. Such as . . ."

When it comes to science, Randy has a tendency to give me way more material than I need. It's pretty obvious that he modeled much of HARV's behavior on his own.

"Randy, I'm sure this is fascinating, but I'm hoping that you didn't call to give me a lecture on the chemical workings of the brain."

Randy stopped talking for a nano. "No, not this time."

"So can we get to the point here?"

"Okay, I had the police lab send me Foraa Thompson's jacket."

"Her what?"

"I'm still running toxicology tests on the wine. I wanted to cross-check the wine in the glasses with the wine in the bottle and on the floor and with whatever spilled on her person."

"Got it."

"The police, by the way, were very uncooperative today," he said. "Which is kind of odd since I'm doing this work for them free of charge.

"That was my fault," I said. "But I think I got it cleared up."

"Good. It's one thing working free of charge. It's another thing entirely to do it among such hostility. I'm not good at social interaction under the best of circumstances."

"We're getting off subject here, Randy. What about Foraa's jacket?"

"Oh, yes. I found no wine."

"No wine."

"No. Apparently her glass tipped forward when she collapsed, so none of the wine contained therein actually fell on the jacket itself."

"And that's what you called to tell me?"

"Not really."

"Not really?"

"No."

"Randy, I feel I've asked this before, but is there a point here?"

"The point is that, although I found no wine on the jacket, I did find microscopic traces of silicate-carbon dust on the inside of her collar."

"What does that mean?"

"To most people, nothing."

"And to you?"

"There's a certain class of stealth weapon. An assassin-type smart-dart that, upon delivering its poisonous payload, quickly disintegrates into an untraceable silicate-carbon dust."

"A dart?"

"A computer guided smart-dart, which can be outfitted with any of a variety of fast-acting poisons."

"And it disintegrates?"

"Very rapidly. Once fired, it turns to dust in less than a minute."

"And it's undetectable?"

"Nearly, yes."

"Then how did you find it?"

"Because I invented it."

"You what?"

"I developed the smart-dart during my weapons development period two years ago."

"Who did you develop it for?"

"The World Council, but they only had a six-month window of exclusivity, then I opened the market up. It eventually caught on in the corporate world. Go figure."

"Yeah, go figure. I don't suppose you can give me a list of the companies that purchased the darts, could you?"

"That would be a breach of ethics."

"Of course."

"But I can tell you who purchased this particular dart."

"You can tell that?"

"I designed the dart, Zach," he said. "I'm smart enough to individualize and code each shipment."

"You're brilliant, Randy. Who purchased the dart?"

"Ona Thompson."

"What?"

"Ona purchased this particular lot three months ago."

"Are you sure?"

"Absolutely."

"That doesn't make sense."

"It makes sense if Ona is the killer."

"Well, yeah. But it doesn't make sense in a good way. What would she need with smart-darts?"

"Maybe she was planning on murdering someone."

"Yeah, let's see if we can come up with any alternatives to that?" I said. "What else can the darts be used for?"

"There's big game hunting," Randy offered.

"Big game hunting?"

"Some sportsmen prefer using nontraditional armaments when hunting. It's more sporting."

"That's a bit of a stretch."

"Then I'm out of ideas."

HARV's hologram appeared beside me and he stood arms crossed and stared first at me and then at Randy on the vid with a bemused smirk on his face.

"Pardon the intrusion, gentlemen, but I couldn't help over-hearing. Good morning, Dr. Pool."

"Hello, HARV," Randy said. "Have you changed your appearance?"

HARV ran his hand through his hair and turned away ever so slightly.

"Actually . . . I have made some . . . modifications."

"He's entered an Ellery Queen phase."

"Really? You've adjusted your holographic appearance to reflect a new area of interest?"

"That's within my program parameters, isn't it?" HARV asked.

"Actually, no," Randy said. "But you appear to be redefining your parameters. That's amazing."

"Thank you."

"And your new hair is nice, too."

"I'm sorry," I said, rubbing my eyes, "I thought this was going to be helpful."

HARV straightened his coat and smiled once more.

"I thought I should point out that there is a third possible purpose for Ms. Thompson to have purchased the smart-darts."

"What's that?"

"Security."

I thought for a nano and HARV's thinking began to make sense.

"That's it," I said. "Randy, where were the darts delivered?"

"You can't actually deliver anything to Ona Thompson. Her residence is apparently a well-guarded secret."

"It was until recently," HARV snickered.

"The shipment was picked up at the factory. Signed for by someone named 'Pfauhan.'"

I smiled.

"Ms. Thompson's co-head of security."

"Randy, can these darts be fired by bots? I mean tiny bots."

"You mean golfball-sized, spherical bots that float?" he asked.

"How did you know about those?"

"Because I invented those, too. It was during my security phase three years ago. I sold nearly two thousand of them to Ona Thompson."

"And those floating bots are capable of firing these smart-darts, right?"

"Of course they are," he said, as his eyes went a little wide. "Say, you don't suppose there's some connection there, do you?"

Randy is the most brilliant designer I know. But, alas, he's a little slow when it comes to logic of a human nature.

# 36

HARV and I were soon back at Ona's compound, staring up from the ground at the Pfauhans' floating security command center.

"It would appear that the Pfauhans are not presently available," HARV said, his holographic eyes pointing skyward.

"Now we just need a way to get up there."

"You could port," HARV said. "I know you don't like having your molecules scrambled, but it really is safer than walking. It's science at its best."

"Perhaps, but if I can find another way . . ."

HARV pointed out a rack of equipment that was attached to the outside of the ground-based building beside us.

"You could use the antigrav disks."

I walked over, pulled a pair of the milky-white disks out of the rack, and held them uncomfortably in my hands.

"I don't think so. I'm not really an antigrav kind of guy. There must be an elevator or something."

"Oh, please, boss, control your techno-acrophobic nature. The center is straight up, no more than twenty-five meters. You'll be able to look through the window and, if you want, you can enter through the hatch."

"I'm going on record now," I sighed. "I'm going to regret this."

"Duly noted," HARV replied. "We can still teleport."

I looked up. "I guess it's not *that* high."

"Good," HARV said. "Now turn the disks over so that I can see the interface."

I did as I was told. The disks' interface was a small optic

port located in the center of the underside. I held the disks
steady while HARV shot a beam of red light from my eye lens
into the interface.

"I've reprogrammed the disks to obey your mental directions," he said. "You're good to go."

"That's easy for you to say," I said, looking up.

"True. And I can say it in over three hundred languages.
Would you like to hear it in Gladian?"

"No one likes a show-off, HARV."

I set the disks on the ground and gently placed my feet on
them. The disks hummed to life at my touch and I felt them attach themselves electromagnetically to my shoes. Then they
lifted me ever so slightly off the ground. I stumbled for a nano
before getting my balance.

"Just focus your thoughts," HARV said. "The disks will follow your directions."

I steadied myself and looked up at the floating room overhead. Then I felt myself slowly begin to rise. The ascent was
slow and smooth, just the way I like it. HARV's hologram
floated beside me as I rose.

"I told you it was easy," HARV said.

"True, but you say that about everything."

"That's because everything is easy for me."

"Everything but humility."

"No, that's easy, too. I just choose not to practice it."

A few nanos later, I had my nose against the plastic of the
command center window. The room was dark, lit only by the
glow of the many security-feed monitors. The Pfauhans were
nowhere to be seen.

"I don't like this," I said.

"It's a big compound, boss," HARV replied. "They could be
anywhere, doing their normal business. Their absence from the
command center hardly implies anything nefarious."

"HARV, everything about these guys implies nefarious. The
fact that they're not currently in their own command center is
the most nefarious implication of all."

"Can't argue with logic like that," HARV said with a shrug.
"But you realize, of course, that even accepting the fact that
the Pfauhans are responsible for the smart-dart, that wasn't
what killed Foraa. As you know, she's . . ."

"Nigh invulnerable," I said. "The dart wouldn't have pierced her skin. The point is that they *tried* to kill her and, for all they know, they succeeded. I want to know why."

I put my hands on the window and peered inside again, staring at the flashing images on the security monitors. As before, the images were an odd mix: the southern perimeter, the hoverport, and a large room full of sweaters. The kitchen, the media center, an even larger room full of handbags and accessories.

"Every third image is clothing related," I said. "Why is that?"

"Boss?"

"Is Ona so caught up in her wardrobe that she requested special security for it?"

"Boss?"

"I mean, I wouldn't put it past her, but it seems odd. Even by her standards."

"Boss, I think you're missing the big picture here."

And it was only then that I detected the concern in HARV's voice.

"What?"

I pulled my face slowly away from the window, just enough to allow me to look *at* the window, rather than *through* it, and I saw a reflection in the glass of a golfball-sized spherical bot, gently hovering behind me.

"See what I mean?" HARV said.

Of course it wasn't the reflection of that one bot that frightened me. The real fright came when I pulled my gaze back farther and saw reflections of the one hundred other bots behind it, all hovering no more than four meters behind me, silent yet ominous.

"I knew this was a bad idea."

---

## 37

I did my best to remain motionless (which is no easy feat when you're standing on hover-disks twenty-five meters in the air), my eyes never wavering from the reflection of the bots behind me.

"My guess is that we're not going to be able to talk our way out of this."

"Agreed," HARV said. "Unless of course you speak spherical bot."

"Don't you?" I asked.

"I'm learning it as we speak."

"And?"

"From what I gather they are saying: 'Kill the intruder.'"

"That's not good."

"Of course I could be misinterpreting. They may be saying: 'castrate the intruder.'"

"Oh, that's *so* much better."

I could feel the gentle breeze of the compound's air conditioners and hear the steady hum of the force bubble overhead. "Contact Ona's computer. Maybe it can help us out?"

"I'll give it a try. In the meantime, I would advise against any sudden movements."

Just then I saw a small red light on the lead bot flash and I remembered the last time I saw that happen.

"That's no longer an option."

"What?"

The light flashed again. HARV noticed it this time.

"Uh-oh."

It flashed a third time and all one hundred bots fired silent thin blue lasers at me, creating a spiderweb cascade of pale blue death.

Thankfully, I was already on the move. I put my antigrav disks into free fall and was three meters below the command center when the bots fired. Their lasers blew out the window and I used my arm to protect myself from the shower of glass as I fell. I popped my gun into my hand and fired as I barrel-rolled and then leveled off in the air. The concussion blast blew apart eight or nine of the bots before the others scattered and realigned themselves into combat formation.

"I'm going to need you to take control of the disks, HARV."

"Fine," he said. "What's the plan?"

"I have no idea. Just keep me ahead of the enemy fire and I'll wing it."

"I see. You mean the same way we do the tax returns."

"What did Ona's computer say?"

"It said the bots are independent thinking organisms and therefore it has no control over them. It is presently trying to contact Ms. Thompson and locate the Pfauhans."

"Oh, good."

HARV's hologram disappeared and I felt the disks surge forward and bank hard to the left as he took control.

"Keep your knees bent and your head down," he said. "This is going to be a bumpy ride."

We flew hard toward the maintenance buildings that encircled Ona's ziggurat and snaked in and around the air filtration tubes, avoiding the lasers of the pursuing bots at every turn. A few of them broke off from the main pack and tried to cut us off at various junctures, but I managed to blast them to smithereens before the traps were sprung. Still after about three minutes of the high-flying chase I was breathless and more than a little airsick.

"How many of these bots did the Pfauhans say they had in the compound?"

"Thirteen hundred, but don't think about it," HARV said. "By the way, you have a call coming in from Randy. I'll just take a message."

One of the spheres ambushed me from the side and nearly took my head off with its laser.

"Yeah, that sounds like a good plan."

We swung upward as the spheres fired again and HARV was forced to slide the disks up and apart in order to avoid the blast. I ended up doing a split in the air with the laser blasts passing far too close to my crotch for comfort.

"Easy on the acrobatics," I said. "I'm not a contortionist."

"No, you're more of a contusionist."

"Good one. Can I use that?"

"Sure, if you survive."

We banked wildly again and found ourselves headed directly toward the base of the force bubble.

"Whoa!"

HARV pulled the disks up sharply and we followed the curved edge of the bubble before banking away back toward the nearest building, which was the still-under-repair hoverjet hangar. I noticed, however, that one of the pursuing spheres didn't quite make the sharp turn. It skidded and smashed into the force bubble, bouncing off the translucent purple surface like sunlight off a mirror. It fell to the ground and short circuited with a silent burst of electronic shrapnel, no brighter than a camera flash.

"Okay," I said, turning my attention back to the chase, "I now officially have a plan."

"I hope it's a short one," HARV said as he swung me quickly up and over a charging pack of the spheres.

"Contact Ona's computer. We're going to need it to open a window in the force bubble for us."

"Where?"

"I don't know yet. And slow down a little."

"What?"

I turned around and fired another couple of blasts at the pursuing spheres, blowing three of them to smithereens (which only left about eighty-five still in hot pursuit). "I don't want to outrun these things just yet."

"Oh, I get it," HARV said. "Good thinking."

A thin laser blast hit my back as one of the spheres opened fire. My armor protected me from injury, but it still felt like someone had jabbed me with a needle.

"And keep me away from those lasers."

"Easier said than done, boss. They kind of move at the speed of light, you know."

HARV banked me hard into a small walkway between two buildings. We spun so fast I thought the disks were going to fly off my feet and that my stomach would drop down to my ankles. Thankfully, neither happened and we found ourselves in a headlong run toward the force bubble wall.

"The computer knows the plan, right?"

"I explained it in detail," HARV said.

"Do you trust it?"

"You don't have much choice at the nano," HARV said, as another round of thin lasers erupted around me.

"Okay, then, let's go. Just make sure they're close."

I put my head down and dropped into a skier's tuck position as we sped toward the force wall. Lasers cut the air around me like little blue scalpels. I got hit a few times in the back. One singed my right ear and one shot I took in the leg nearly collapsed my knee and crashed us.

The spheres were faster than us on the straightaway, so HARV didn't need to ease up on the speed in order to get them close. On the contrary, he had to push the disks to their max just to stay ahead of them and I began to worry that maybe the straightaway was too long.

"Get ready with the window."

We were close to the wall now, but I could feel the spheres gaining on us. The rush of air tinged my neck and their shadows below me were precariously close to my own.

But the wall of the force bubble was closer.

"Now!" I yelled. "Duck and back, HARV."

The purple bubble morphed open a window and I flew through it, then spun away quickly to the left and stopped short. The spheres followed me through the window (although some hit the bubble wall and exploded), but they hadn't seen me stop and turn, so they shot past me. I lashed out and grabbed the last one through in my hand as it passed. It buzzed in my fist like an angry hornet overdosed on caffeine and I felt it grow hot, so I quickly stuck it inside the pocket of my trench coat and activated the containment unit that's built into the pocket lining (a little something that Randy designed for me). An electromagnetic stasis field formed around the sphere, trapping it tightly and protecting me from any of its weapons. The coat's fabric expanded to fit the stasis field and for a nano, I thought the seams would split, but (thankfully) they held firm.

It took the rest of the spheres only a nano to locate me, but by then I was already on the move.

"Back now and close the window!"

HARV spun me around on the disks and flew me quickly back through the closing window. The spheres detected me and, realizing they'd been tricked, dove at me en masse. But they were too late. I slipped back through the window just as it closed and the dive-bombing spheres crashed into it like drops of angry rain, short-circuiting and exploding upon impact like a string of firecrackers.

"Nice work, boss," HARV said as his hologram appeared beside me. "And by the way, is that an electromagnetic stasis field in your pocket, or . . ."

"Don't say it, HARV!"

"Ah, I never get to spout any fun, century-old lines."

I shook my head. "HARV, you're really starting to scare me."

# 38

HARV guided the antigrav disks back to the ground and we gently examined the bot in my pocket.

"We should make this fast," I said. "There are another twelve hundred of these things still around."

"True, but most of them are stationed inside the ziggurat. I estimate that only one hundred or so are left out here."

"That's about a hundred too many," I said as I detached the containment unit from the coat.

I held the stasis field up to the light and watched the bot inside as it skittered about like an angry goldfish in a bowl. It fired its laser at the field wall a few times before registering the futility of the action and then simply began bumping the field itself.

"What's it doing?"

"I think it's trying to lift the entire field," HARV answered.

"Can it do that?"

HARV shrugged. "It depends upon the density of the field and the power of the bot."

"What about firing its weapons?"

"It appears as though the stasis field is strong enough to withstand it."

"Can it call for help?"

"The field is a no-transmission zone. Communications through traditional means are impossible."

"So if it wants its programmer . . ."

"It will have to physically go to it."

I smiled. "Perfect."

I put the field down on the ground and stepped back as the

tiny bot inside tried to lift it into the air. The field shuddered a few times, got a few centimeters off the ground, and then fell back onto the pavement.

"Can you reduce the field density?" I asked. "Maybe make it easier for it to get off the ground?"

"I can, but that might make it possible for the bot's weapons to pierce the field or—worse—for it to signal others."

I turned my gaze back to the bot in the stasis field as it flopped on the ground like a sickly fish out of water.

"Let's risk it. We're sure not getting anywhere like this."

The mass of the stasis field decreased, shrinking from about the size of a cantaloupe to that of a grapefruit; as it did so, the bot was slowly able to raise it into the air, unsteadily at first, but with increasing strength as the field shrank. In a few nanos it was hovering at my eye level and I felt like I was in a staring contest.

"What's it doing?" I asked.

"It thinks you're up to something," HARV replied.

"It can think?"

"Not in the traditional sense. It has preprogrammed responses for certain situations, but this is most likely an uncommon scenario for it."

"Fine," I said, popping my gun back into my hand. "Let's give it a scenario it understands."

"What are you doing?"

I stuck my gun against the outside of the stasis field and made sure that the bot's sensors saw my grimace.

"Giving it the simplest scenario of all. Fight or flight."

The bot hovered in front of my gun barrel for the briefest of nanos and then retreated, flying away at a slow but steady pace (the best that it could manage from within the stasis field).

"It appears to have chosen flight," HARV said.

I smiled. "Was there ever any doubt?"

We chased the bot (I floating briskly along on the antigrav disks, HARV's hologram beside me) across a good portion of the compound over the next couple of minutes. Every so often the bot would stop its flight and hover in front of us, as if making sure we were still in pursuit. During these times I'd fire a couple of rounds at it (being careful to come close but not actually hit it) and that seemed to keep it running scared. We were still at it a few minutes later when Ona pulled alongside us in her personal hovercraft.

"Zach, I heard you were in some kind of trouble. Is everything all right?"

"It's fine," I said.

"You didn't destroy anything this time, did you?"

"No, I did not! Well, actually . . . Yes, I did. Two hundred or so of those little security bots."

"Gates," she said. "I hate those things."

"Join the club," I said, firing again at the fleeing bot. "Right now, we're hoping that the one ahead of us will lead us to your security experts."

The bot came to what at first appeared to be a small hill. It was subtly shaped and covered with thick, green lawn and spotted with patches of purple and yellow flowers. It hovered beside one group of flowers for a nano and then disappeared through the morass of colored petals.

"And I think we just found the nesting place."

"What do you want with the Pfauhans?"

I landed my disks at the base of the hill. Ona did the same with her hover and we examined the hill together.

"Well, I'm pretty sure that they're the ones who programmed those bots to attack me a few minutes ago. And we're also fairly certain that they tried to kill Foraa."

"What?"

"Poison dart on her collar, tiny bots with attitude. Long story, but—trust me—it points toward the Pfauhans."

"They killed Foraa?"

"I doubt it. But they tried."

Ona's eyes narrowed into a steely scowl. "Why, those identical twin bastards."

As we approached the hill, half a dozen of the tiny spherical bots appeared from within several of the flowerbeds and hovered menacingly before us.

"Uh-oh."

"Why would the Pfauhans try to kill Foraa?"

I froze and kept my eyes on the hovering bots as they surrounded us. "I'm hoping that they'll tell us that when we find them."

Ona took a step toward the hill and two of the bots moved toward her. I put a hand on her arm to stop her, but she shrugged it off.

"They'll tell us, all right," she said.

"What makes you say that?"

Ona's hand shot out like a quicksilver jack-in-the-box and plucked one of the hovering bots out of the air. Then she crushed it as though it were made of paper.

"Because if they don't, I'm going to turn their annoying little bots into anal probes."

"Anal probes?" HARV whispered softly.

I smiled as the five remaining bots quickly retreated back into the hill.

"Works for me."

"Computer!" Ona shouted. "Where's the entrance to this hill?"

"There's an access door beneath the holographic flower bed three meters to your right," the computer replied. "I'll need approximately five seconds to remotely access the lock."

"Don't bother," she said as she angrily prodded the flowerbed with her shoe and then grinned when she heard the clang of metal beneath her foot. "I'll use my own key."

She stomped her stiletto heel on the door and I heard the metal creak as it buckled. The hologram flowers short-circuited under her attack and blinked out, revealing, as suspected, a heavy metal door in the ground, looking like the entrance to an old (yet heavily fortified) storm cellar. Ona reached down and grabbed the damaged door with her finely manicured hand, tearing a hold into the surface with her fingertips and then ripping it from its hinges as though it were a bow on a Gucci-wrapped package. The metal buckled and tore away with an anguished squeal, revealing a stairwell underneath.

Ona gave her nails a quick once-over for breaks or chips, then headed into the stairwell. She was seriously angry now and I had a hard time keeping up with her as she stomped downward.

"Ona, maybe you should stay topside and let me handle this," I offered. But she ignored me totally.

"After all I've done for those two, this is how they repay me? By killing my sister?"

"Like I said, they didn't actually kill her. They only tried."

"Granted, but it's still bad form."

"Agreed."

"Boss," HARV whispered in my ear, "there's another call coming in from Dr. Pool."

"Now's really not the best time."

"Pardon me?" Ona asked.

"Nothing, Ona. I just have a call coming in."

"Oh, by all means, take the call," Ona said, waving me away. "I'll save you some of the Pfauhans' vertebrae for your trophy shelf."

"You're not killing anyone, Ona," I said. "HARV, tell Randy I'll call him back as soon as I can."

"He says it's urgent."

"My client is about to murder two suspects, HARV. I think that outscores anything Randy has to say on the urgent meter."

The stairway ended at another large metal door with a small touch screen rather than a handle or a knob. Ona stared at it for a long nano and then pushed gently against it with the palms of her hands, testing its resistance.

"That's a DNA-encoded lock," I said, motioning toward the touch screen. It's probably programmed to give only the Pfauhans access."

"I am the mistress of this compound, Zach," Ona replied, rolling up the sleeve of her blouse. "Everything here either obeys my commands or suffers the consequences."

She placed her hand gently on the touch screen and let the sensors map her DNA and cross-reference the genome with their files.

"Zach, are you there?" Randy's voice came over the small speaker in my wrist interface.

"Randy?"

"I convinced HARV to put me through. Look, I know you're in the middle of something now."

"Yeah, you could say that. So I can't really talk right now."

"I found the poison, Zach."

"You what?"

The DNA lock answered Ona's request for access with a

series of red OLED letters flashing more brightly than a grand opening sign outside a brothel.

DENIED.

Needless to say, Ona was none too pleased with the response and angrily pulled her hand away from the touch screen.

"All right," she announced, curling her fingers into a fist. "Plan B."

"Randy, tell me quickly about the poison," I said.

"The answer was there all the time," he said. "It was . . ."

But I didn't hear the rest because at that nano Ona hit the door with a thundering overhand punch that sent a shock wave through the stairwell like a grenade. The mere echo of her fist on the metal nearly shattered my eardrums and the concussive force as the door itself blew off its hinges knocked me to my knees. My head was still spinning, but I somehow managed to stumble through the doorway behind Ona as she entered.

And that's when things got *really* weird.

The doorway opened into a large circular room, shadowy at the edges but dramatically lit in the center with colored lights and spotlights. Dance music throbbed in the background and a throng of computer monitors crowded around the stage.

That's right, I said stage. It was long, thin, and covered with a red carpet and, as mentioned, computer monitors were packed in around its raised platform, like groupies in a mosh pit. Each monitor sported a computer-generated face, men and women of all colors and ethnicities, some murmuring, some mumbling, and some screaming with joyous (or drug-induced, I couldn't be certain) hysteria.

And walking the stage, with the strut of a genetically spliced peacock, was Drang Pfauhan . . . in attire that was, how shall I put this, somewhat nonconventional.

"Is that my dress?" Ona said, mouth agape.

The dress Drang wore was blue, made of some shimmery plastic element, cut low in the back and slit high in the front. I remembered seeing a picture of Ona wearing it at some function a few months before. It looked much better on her than it did on him.

"This gown was designed exclusively for Ms. Thompson by the Glama-Rama Strumpet Fashion Cartel for last year's People's Choice Awards," Sturm's voice boomed from the speakers above the music. "It was worn only once, although it was heavily saturated with Ms. Thompson's sweat during that brush with her greatness. The bidding for this one-of-a-kind item starts at two hundred thousand credits."

The crowd went crazy as Drang reached the end of the stage, then spun around neatly, wiggled his hips, and strutted back toward the curtain.

"They're selling my dress!" Ona yelled.

"Zach, are you still there?" Randy shouted over the interface. "I heard an explosion and now . . . are you in a nightclub?"

I was still dizzy from the explosion, deafened by the music, and nearly blinded by the sight of Drang in one of Ona's more revealing dresses, so it took nearly all my strength just to answer.

"I think I'm in hell, Randy."

The crowd of virtual onlookers was still screaming and bidding wildly on the blue dress well after Drang had disappeared behind the curtain and Sturm had taken his place on the catwalk. His ensemble consisted of a pink jacket and skirt with some kind of electric-orange top.

"Next on the list is the benignly bitchy jacket and harlot-humping skirt ensemble made famous by Ms. Thompson during this past spring's funeral rave for the former president of New Brazil."

"I was wondering where that outfit went," Ona fumed. "I love that top. This is criminal."

"Zach, you have to listen to me," Randy shouted over the interface. "I found the poison. It was a designer toxin, specifically created to kill only the Thompson Quads. That's why we couldn't find it at first."

"You mean it was in the wine?"

"We were checking the wine's contents against the database of *known* toxins, but this was an all *new* toxin, so it didn't register. That's why the wine tested clean."

"I knew it," I said. "I knew it was the wine."

"But, Zach, there's something you need to know."

"What?"

A series of explosions rocked the room just then as the

space's three remaining metal access doors blew apart. The walls shook from the shock wave and the spotlight stanchions fell to the stage in a cascade of sparks and smoke, narrowly missing Sturm and Drang. I looked up in time to see dozens of heavily armored policemen pour through each of the doors, weapons drawn, spotlights cutting the darkness, and voices yelling to be heard above the music (until someone killed the power to the sound system and cut the song short).

"Police! Nobody move! Down on the floor! Hands above your head! Don't make me eviscerate you!"

I felt more police enter from the door behind us and for a nano, I feared that I would drown in the maelstrom of testosterone-enhanced law enforcement. Then I looked up again and saw Tony striding quickly toward Ona and me.

"Captain, thank Gates you're here," Ona said, turning to meet Tony with a smile, gracious and beautiful. "These men tried to kill my sister. They tried to kill Zach as well and they've been wearing my clothes!"

Tony remained stone-faced as he approached and I knew then that something was very, very wrong.

"Zach, can you hear me?" Randy called from the interface, trying hard to be heard above the din. "There's something you need to know about the poison!"

Tony reached into his coat pocket and pulled out a computer pad, which flashed an ominous looking document.

"Ona Thompson, you are under arrest for the murder of your sister, Foraa."

"What?" Ona cried, her eyes wide with shock.

Tony didn't hesitate. He nodded to one of his men who slapped electromagnetic cuffs on her wrists.

"It was Ona!" Randy yelled, and his voice from the small speaker on my wrist echoed eerily throughout the suddenly silent room. "The poison came from Ona!"

# 39

I spent the evening back at my house, doing the postmortem on the day. The police had taken Ona down to the station house not long ago with all the subtlety of a three ring circus and news of her arrest was wall to wall on all the networks (I found myself longing for the simpler days of the Bill Gibbon reports).

Ona had summoned an army of lawyers and greeting card salesmen to her defense. I expected her to be arraigned at the Hall of Justice and out on bail by morning. But she was going to be charged with Foraa's murder and that had always been the worst case scenario.

The Pfauhans were arrested as well but not for their murder attempt on Foraa (there was no real proof of that) or for their attempt on my life (which Tony apparently no longer considered a crime). They were instead arrested for performing illegal online auctions through O-Bay, the rogue network catering to fetishists and dominant/submissives. They confessed shortly thereafter that they'd been stealing and selling Ona's clothing for the past several years (referring to it as a sickness). Foraa had known about their clothing thefts and had threatened to expose them to Ona, which explained their attempt on her life.

Their confession, by the way, was given not to the police but to a talk-show host before an audience of millions. By the time they were released on bail, they already had multifigure e-book and HMON (Holo-Movie of the Nano) deals for their story. All's well that ends well, right?

Except this one wasn't over for me yet, not by a long shot.

"The police forensics experts were with me when the results came in," Randy said via the vidphone. "They notified
Tony just as I was calling you."

"And I couldn't take your call at the time, because I was
running for my life," I replied. "What I don't understand is
where the poison came from."

"As I said, it's a designer toxin, keyed specifically to the
DNA of the Thompson Quads."

"So the wine would kill only them?"

"Exactly. We could drink it for a thousand years and the
poison would have no effect on us. But if any of the Quads
were to drink it . . . well, you saw what happened."

"And the police arrested Ona . . . ?"

"Because the toxin was created specifically from her DNA.
It could come from nowhere else."

"I thought the quads had identical DNA and they just occasionally dyed or streaked their hair to match their moods," I
said.

Randy gave me his patented your-naïvete-is-charming
smile. "Yes, that's what most laymen think. But Dr. Thompson apparently didn't want his identical daughters to be completely identical. He modified each of their DNA just enough
so they would be identical but different."

"Identical but different?"

"I admit it's a hard concept to stick in the layman's mind.
Let's just put it this way. It's easy to tell them apart if you
know what you are looking for. Just follow along."

A holographic representation of twenty-three red and
twenty-three blue chromosomes appeared on my screen. The
chromosomes danced and intertwined.

"Humans have over three billion DNA nucleotide pairs.
These are usually divided among twenty-two pairs of auto-
somes and one pair of sex chromosomes. Of course real chromosomes don't move like that, this is just a simulation,"
Randy said in a voice-over. "With the Quads, all of their chromosomes are identical except for this area!"

A very small area on one of the blue chromosomes turned
yellow and started to flash. "This small area on the nineteenth
chromosome is different for each Quad. It's why they have
slightly different shades of brown hair. It is sort of their ge-

netic ID. This was the DNA used in the poison. To the naked eye they are identical, but to the electron microscope they're as distinctive as a fingerprint or . . ."

"Or any other type of DNA," I said.

"Exactly."

"Couldn't someone have created it by simply using her DNA?"

"Sure," he said. "If you had the right tools and a sample of her DNA."

"So it's possible?"

"Zach, this is 2058. Almost anything is possible if you've got the time and the credits. The poison was quite pure, though. It's hard to get results like that from replicated DNA. Whoever made this poison had lots of material to work with."

"Hence the police arresting Ona," I said.

"Exactly."

"Thanks again for everything you did, Randy. I owe you."

"You mean that metaphorically, right?" Randy asked. "I shouldn't bill you for my time, should I? Because it would be expensive."

"Good night, Randy."

"Night, Zach."

His image blinked off the screen. I took another sip of coffee and stretched my aching neck as HARV's hologram appeared at the table beside me.

"Do you want me to net with Tony?" HARV asked.

"And I thought Carol was the mind reader."

Tony's overworked and not-too-happy face zoomed into my screen. He looked terrible, like the something the cat dragged in, beat up, then dragged back out again. But I didn't tell him that. I figured our relationship was strained enough already.

"What do you want, Zach?" he said wearily.

"Why'd you bring Ona in?"

He shook his head, lowered his eyes, and began to rub his brow. "Zach, her DNA was used in the poison, she was the only one who had access to the wine . . ."

"That's all circumstantial," I interrupted. "Her lawyers will have her out . . ."

"In no time," Tony reinterrupted. "I know that. But . . ."

"You were under a lot of pressure to make some sort of arrest," I re-reinterrupted.

"Yes, and stop interrupting. I personally was against it until we had more to go on. DOS, we don't even have a cell that can hold her yet. But we have a new chief and he wanted to make a splash. Lots of PR in arresting the world's richest being. Our stock jumped five points today. Sure, if it turns out she's innocent, then the stock will tumble a bit, but it's worth it."

"Man, I miss the days when police forces were paid for solely out of tax money," I said.

"Not half as much as I do. You have no idea how often I hear: 'you can't arrest me, I'm a stockholder.'"

"So you know this isn't over yet," I said.

"Believe me, Zach, I know better than anybody." He looked at the screen. "Between the press, her lawyers, our lawyers, my superiors, and the occasional criminal or two, it's been a long day. So if you don't have anything else to add . . ."

"Have a good night, Tony."

"Yeah, easy for you to say."

My screen went blank, but it was only a nano before another incoming call came in.

"Zach, it's Carol," HARV said.

"Busy night, put her through."

Carol's face lit up my screen.

"Tío," she said (so sweetly that I knew she needed something). "I need some more time off."

"Carol, this is a bad time for me. I'm in the middle of this case and I might need your talents."

"I'll stay in touch. I promise." With those words the conversation ended and the screen went blank.

"That was rather abrupt," I said.

"I'm sure whatever it is, she'll tell you about it when you need to know," HARV said.

"Three things I'll never understand: women, psis, and women."

"Believe me, there are far more than that," HARV said. "So be thankful that you have me."

I turned toward his holographic face with its know-it-all smile. I know that having HARV hardwired to my brain is an advantage. One that gives me a serious one-up in all sorts of nasty situations. Still, at that nano I couldn't help wondering if I'd lost something as well. The privacy of my thoughts. I don't really like to dwell on this too much because it scares me. But I share my brain with another thinking organism. There have to be some dire implications to that. HARV and Randy both insist this is a good thing. That HARV can't read my thoughts, per se, and that he just monitors the levels of certain chemicals in my brain and the activity of certain regions to gain an overall perspective of my general mood.

They claim that he and I are creating a gestalt, becoming greater than the sum of our parts. That may be true, but there are times that I can't help feeling like the world's largest lab rat.

"If you don't mind, boss, I'd like to do a little field work tonight," HARV said.

"On what?"

"Something Ms. Thompson said today gave me an idea that might help the coroner."

"I have a feeling he needs all the help he can get," I said. "Get him on the vid and we'll set it up."

The coroner's face appeared on the screen a nano later and I nearly spit my coffee at the screen when I saw him. His face was ashen, his chin was covered with stubble, and his disheveled hair looked like a furry amoeba in the midst of asexual reproduction. But, as always, it was the eyes that really got me. They were the size of dinner plates (tired, bloodshot, insane dinner plates). He looked even worse than Tony. This case was getting to everybody.

"How are you doing?" I asked, though I was pretty sure I knew the answer.

"Oh, you know, same old grind," he said. "The same old, infuriatingly frustrating, purple-hued, large-breasted, nigh-invulnerable grind."

"I take it that the autopsy isn't progressing well?"

"No, I've hit a bit of a snag there," he said. "A real pickle. Right now I'm waiting for some repairs to be completed on the VoDranglaser. It shorted out this afternoon. Should be another day or so. Until then I'm doing some scans and such, taking an outside-the-cube approach."

"Would you like some help?" I asked. "My computer has taken a bit of interest in your work."

"Good evening," HARV said from over my shoulder. "I'm sure I could be of assistance."

"Do you have a VoDranglaser?"

"Not exactly," HARV said, "but I have a few ideas that might fall under the heading of 'outside-the-cube.'"

"What do you say?"

"I shouldn't," he said. "This is a limited access case. It's very restricted."

"It was restricted only because they were trying to keep news of For . . . the victim's death quiet. That's sort of a moot point now."

"True."

"And now that they've arrested a suspect, getting the autopsy report is going to become an even higher priority. The police and the DA are going to need the autopsy to make their case. That pressure's going to come down hard on you. I'm sure Ona's lawyers will try to make the case, that if you can't prove how she died, she's not really dead."

"That's true as well," he said. "Does he have any prior autopsy experience?"

"I don't have any actual experience, but I've done extensive research in forensic medicine and I specialize in creative problem solving."

Shakes turned away from the screen and rubbed his chin in thought for a few nanos. I couldn't be sure, but I thought I saw his lips moving as well.

"Is he talking to himself?" I whispered to HARV.

"It appears so."

"That's always a good sign. By the way, I thought the creative problem solving was *my* specialty?"

"So I borrowed something from you for once," HARV replied.

Shakes turned his attention back to the screen and forced a slight smile. "When can you get here?"

"I need only a couple of nanos to finish up some things here. After that, I can download to your system in a millisecond."

"Great. Honestly, it will be nice to have another set of eyes with which to study this conundrum," he said. "It's like we say in the field, if point A leads to point B, just because you can see point B doesn't necessarily mean that you can see A."

HARV and I were still scratching our heads at that one when Shakes blinked off from the interface.

"That was odd."

"Yeah, apparently a lot of weird things are said in the field."

"What field is that exactly?"

"I really don't know. Why don't you ask him when you're there. You're sure you want to do this?"

"As I said, I have a couple of ideas that might assist him with the autopsy."

"I'll be able to get you if I need you, right?"

"Oh, yes," HARV said. "Our interface is still attached to your brain."

"Don't remind me."

"I could even feed my experiences with the coroner back to you as they happen. It would be like watching something live on the net."

"That's okay," I said. "Fill me in on the highlights."

"Will do. I just need to finish up a couple of tasks here, then I'll download to the coroner's office."

I spent the next few hours lying awake in bed and staring at the overhead computer screen, studying the symbols that Foraa had drawn in the wine.

$$\left(V^{\beta} - \boxminus^{\beta}\right) / \left(V^{\text{FE}} \; \text{Ⱦ} = \frac{\text{⚲⸜▽·Y}}{\delta - \cdot \text{ᴄ}} \; ^{\text{S2}} - \boxminus\right) - \boxminus$$

Nothing about it seemed to make sense and I was starting to lose my patience with the whole mystery. So I was grateful, on a number of levels, when I heard Electra come through the front door and walk softly toward the bedroom.

"You awake, chico?" she whispered, gently poking her head around the doorjamb.

"I'm conscious," I said. "That's about the most I can say. How was the clinic tonight?"

"Hectic and frustrating," she said, slipping into the bathroom.

"But we made it through. I heard the news about Ona. I take it that's bad for you?"

"Well, it's never good for business when your client gets arrested."

Electra emerged from the bathroom in her nightshirt and climbed into bed beside me. She kissed me gently on the lips, then flipped over onto her back and stared up at the overhead screen with me. "What are we watching?"

"Foraa's dying clue. She drew these symbols in the wine puddle just before she died. Maybe as some sort of veiled reference to her killer's identity."

"Why didn't she just write down the killer's name?"

"Because that would have been too easy."

"So she spent her last nanos of life devising some arcane symbolic code?"

"It looks that way."

"That's stupid."

"Well, apparently, lots of murder victims do it."

"Says who?"

"HARV. He's become a detective."

"Oh, good," she said. "Things were becoming a little boring around here."

"It's annoying but still not as bad as that time he decided he was French and kept insulting me."

Electra snuggled up to me and we gazed up at the symbols like lovers staring up at the stars. "Well, I think I see a teacup."

"It's an Egyptian basket."

"And that one's Japanese?"

"Chinese, actually. The pictograph for the sun."

"Gee, who'd have thought a dying clue could be so educational. Any idea what it means?"

"None whatsoever. HARV says it's some kind of algebraic equation that uses symbols instead of the traditional variables."

"If it's an equation, then why can't he figure it out?"

"Apparently, the equation makes no sense."

"That makes even less sense, chico."

"Yeah, well, he's the only supercomputer I have, so I sort

of have to trust him," I said. "Feel free to turn it off. I just put it up because I couldn't sleep."

"No, this is kind of fun."

"Yeah, maybe for the first few hours. Then it's a bit of a drag. I don't even know what I'm looking for."

"It's fool's gold," she said.

"Probably, but like I said, I don't have much else to go on."

"No," she said, pointing at the screen, "in the equation. FeS2, iron sulfide. That's fool's gold."

I stared at the screen; sure enough, there in one part, about a quarter of the way through was a symbol that looked like a stylized "Fe." A little farther along, about a quarter of the way from the end was an odd-shaped symbol that, when looked at the right way, appeared to be "S2."

"Fool's gold? Are you sure?"

"They make you learn chemistry in pre-med, chico. I just don't know why they'd be separated like that. We should put them together."

And all of a sudden, the picture seemed to come into focus for me.

*"MAD magazine."*

"Mad what?"

"It's a fold-in. The inside back cover of every *MAD* magazine, back when they printed magazines on paper, had this riddle. It was a picture that you folded, point A to point B, and when you did, you got a new picture. That's why the equation makes no sense. Because everything in the middle is subterfuge. It's fool's gold. I ran my fingers over the touch pad on the bedside table and slid the middle portion of the equation off the screen. Then I brought the two remaining portions together. They seemed to fit perfectly.

$$\left( \vee^{\beta} - \boxminus^{\beta} \right) / \left( \vee \quad -\boxminus \right) - \boxminus$$

"So what does it mean?" Electra asked.

"I have no idea," I said. "But I bet HARV will." I sat up and grabbed my pants from the floor. "I'm going to take a look at this in the study."

I quickly pulled on a shirt, then leaned back onto the bed and kissed Electra long and hard.

"I've told you this before, although never quite in this context," I said with a smile. "But you, Dr. Gevada, are very good in bed."

## 40

Ten minutes later I was in the study and HARV had solved the equation. It took him only a millisecond to actually do the solving. I had spent the rest of the time explaining to him what *MAD* magazine was. He didn't really care, but I did it just to bug him for a change. After all, what good is being an expert in ancient trivia if you can't use it to solve crimes and drive your friends crazy? Unfortunately, the solution to the equation wasn't exactly the break in the case that I was hoping for.

"*V*."

"*V*?"

"*V*."

"That's the answer?"

"Yes," HARV replied. "Once we apply the fold-in principle, it's actually very simple."

"*V*?"

"The equation itself is the most basic two-variable algebraic equation possible, albeit with nontraditional variables. The portion that is obfuscated by the fold is a variation of the Bekenstein-Hawking Formula for the entropy of a black hole. All in all, an interesting choice for a dying clue."

"So what does *V* mean?"

"Victory?" HARV said with a shrug. "Vigilance, violation. Perhaps she was pointing out that she was the victim."

"You're not helping, HARV."

"Well, I'm new at this detective thing," he said. "Let me ruminate on the matter for a few nanos."

I had one of the office screens muted and tuned to the sports networks, hoping to catch some late-night highlights. Totally frustrated now, I sat back in my chair and watched the screen.

"Maybe she got something wrong," I said. "She was dying, after all. Maybe she lost a decimal point somewhere and it's supposed to be something else."

"There are no decimal points in the equation."

"Well, she must have done *something* wrong. Why else would her last message be the letter *V?*"

"Perhaps murders in real life aren't as cleanly defined as they are in novels."

"Gee, you think?"

"Well, don't yell at me. I'm not the one who wrote the equation."

"No, you're just the one who hailed it as the great dying clue. Gates, why do I even listen to your stupid ideas?"

"Because you have no better ideas of your own!"

I shook my head, sat back and stared angrily at the news on the computer screen.

"V."

"Well, at least we solved it."

"Yeah, for all the good it will do us. Any luck with Shakes on the autopsy?"

HARV's hologram sat on the couch beside me and pretended to watch the sports highlights."

"We're making some progress."

"What was your idea anyway?"

"Anal probes," he said.

"Anal probes?"

"It occurred to me that since we're unable to pierce Ms. Thompson's skin, then perhaps we should use her body's . . . preexisting openings to inspect her internally."

"So you . . . um . . ."

"Yes, anal probes," he said. "Computer-guided nano-probes. We're sending them through the colon. Once we reach the stomach we'll be able to check for traces of the poison."

"Great."

"We also sent probes through the nose and throat."

"And it's working?"

"Her throat muscles were closed and very powerful, so we had to use experimental nano-probes that are microscopic in size.

Same thing with her sphincter. It was rather nigh-invulnerable as well."

"Okay, more information than I need."

"In any event, the probes are in, but because of their microscopic size, they have a comparatively long way to travel before reaching the stomach. And it's slow going navigating the twists and turns of the body, especially the small intestine. It's like a mountain road in New France."

"Okay, HARV!"

"We should have some results soon."

I flipped through a few of the non-sports networks and unsurprisingly found footage of Ona on several of them. News of her arrest was still the top story.

"DOS, don't they have any other news to report? That footage is like four hours old now."

"No, boss," HARV said. "That's live."

"What?"

I leaned forward and looked closer at the screen. Sure enough, this footage was of Ona and her legal posse *leaving* the Hall of Justice. She was trotting gracefully down the steps. Even surrounded by the unruly throng of pressbots, attorneys, and bodyguards, she looked stunning, poised, and in total control.

". . . is free tonight after posting a nondisclosed, record-setting amount in bail. Civic sources say that the amount of bond is so great that, if forfeited, it will virtually erase the city's budget deficit for this year."

Ona was in full celebrity mode now. She acted like an intelligent, powerful glamour girl without a care in the world and DOS if it wasn't convincing. Even though I knew it was a front, a public face that she could turn on at a nano's notice, I almost believed that she was in total control of the situation. She made it seem that somehow, as crazy as everything appeared, it was business as usual.

"She does that in front of a jury, she's home free," I mumbled.

Back on the screen Ona stopped at a hastily erected podium and the pressbots dutifully gathered around her to capture the sound bites.

"I'd like to thank you all for coming out here tonight to

support me." Her voice carried the perfect balance of strength and vulnerability, of pain and resilience. "My innocence in this matter is absolute and I'll be leaving my defense to my dear friends, these attorneys that you see crowded around me. I know that, with their help and with the help of their army of faceless legal minions, my innocence will be proven to any who doubt me."

"You're not one of the minions, are you?" HARV asked.

"Shhh."

"My singular, true goal throughout this nightmarish ordeal," Ona continued, "has always been to find my sister's killer and to bring that person, droid, bot, extraterrestrial visitor, or ethereal spirit to justice."

"She's really widening the pool of suspects, isn't she?" HARV quipped.

"After everything I've done for this world," Ona continued, "after all the good that I've created with my wealth . . ."

"Oh, no, she's not bringing this speech out again, is she?" I said.

". . . aiding underprivileged children . . ."

"She does seem to be very fond of it," HARV replied.

". . . funding disease research . . ."

"I've known her for three days and I've got this thing memorized already. We've heard this speech, what, four times already?"

". . . driving programs for environmental renewal and reinvention . . ."

"Five if you count the recording of it the night of the murder."

"After devoting my vast fortune to raising the quality of life for every downtrodden person in the first through fourth worlds."

"What?"

"It saddens me more than I can say that I am still seen as an easy target for those seeking a stunningly photogenic face to persecute."

"I said, you've heard it five times if you count the time she recited it on the recording of . . ." HARV froze as the words stuck in his holographic throat and I saw the light of inspiration go on in his eyes. "Oh, my."

I sprang to my feet and grabbed my coat off the rack. (Yes, I actually have a coat rack with one trench coat on it in every room of the house. It's obsessive, I know, but there are times when you just need the added drama of grabbing a good trench coat).

"Come on," I said. "We're going back to Ona's ziggurat."

"You got it, boss," HARV said. "But you should probably put some shoes on first."

I looked at my feet and saw that I was still wearing my slippers.

So much for drama.

# 41

Ona's mansion was fairly empty when we arrived a short time later, which shouldn't have surprised me since everyone living there had either been arrested or killed in the past few days.

"I'm afraid that Ms. Thompson is not here at the nano," the computer said as we strode into the entryway. "She has decided to spend the night at an undisclosed location so as to avoid the throng of pressbots outside."

"That's okay, computer," I said. "We're not here to see her."

"What do you mean?" it asked.

"We're here to see you," HARV replied (with just enough tough-guy tone to be impressive).

"Me? I'm afraid I don't have a holographic avatar for you to see."

"You're being too literal, computer," I said.

"I apologize," the computer said. I was pretty certain I could detect a hint of fear in its voice. "How can I help you?"

"We were wondering if we could see your recording of Foraa's murder."

"Certainly," it responded. "But I fail to see how another viewing will help you."

"We want the unedited version this time."

"I beg your pardon?"

"Ona's toast," I said. "Part of it is missing."

"Perhaps Ms. Thompson simply misspoke."

"Ona Thompson never misspeaks," I said. "She could give that speech in the vacuum of space and not miss an inflection."

"Boss, there is no sound in space," HARV corrected, kind of missing the point.

"My point, computer," I said slowly, "is that you doctored the recording."

There was no reply from the computer. So I went on.

"That's why you were so quiet when the police first arrived. You needed time to create a sanitized version. And when you were finished, you very subtly reminded me of your see-all presence when you gave me that Erté lecture."

"You have to admit, the information on Erté was interesting."

"Computer, did Ona kill Foraa?" I asked.

"No, she didn't," the computer responded.

"You're not doing this to protect her, are you?"

I couldn't tell if the computer's silence was a good thing or not, but it occurred to me that confronting the computer on its home turf might not have been the best of ideas.

"No. I'm not protecting her."

"Who *are* you protecting, then?"

"Surely you can figure that out now," it said.

"Yes, I think I can. But I need to be sure. Show me the recording."

The computer paused again, as if sighing somewhere deep in its silicone soul.

"As you wish," it said softly.

I nodded and the lights in the room dimmed. The screen on the wall beside us came to life. We watched the murder unfold for real this time.

And the secret was revealed.

# 42

We did the rest by the book (the book, of course, being an old dime store pulp mystery novel, but it seemed appropriate considering).

"Now, you're clear on the chain of events, right?" HARV asked.

"I'm clear."

"Because I can prompt you if you get stuck."

"I won't get stuck," I said. "I need you to help Shakes. I want those autopsy results the nano you get them."

It had been a little more than an hour since HARV and I had seen the unedited recording of the murder. We were now back in the dining room of Ona's mansion, the scene of the crime.

And we weren't alone.

Tony had been a hard sell to get here. Getting him to bring the others as well was nearly impossible. But he eventually agreed to play along with the melodrama. I promised this would either wrap things up or he could shoot me. I wasn't really sure which one of the two he was rooting for.

So we gathered in the dining room late, late, late on a quiet moonless night: Tony, Ona, Twoa, and Threa (her two nymphs perched upon her shoulders). The Pfauhans were there as well, as were Opie and W (all of whom were out on bail and under the watchful eye of a dozen of Tony's officers and detectives). W, by the way, was still missing his android arms and legs. He was attached to a special wheelchair for easy movement.

Yes, the gang was all there. They had been gathered because I had promised to reveal the identity of the killer.

"It's hard to play this type of scene without it seeming campy," HARV said.

"HARV . . ."

"You heave to start small and let it build."

"You can go now."

"And just remember when you get to the revelation you need to really punch it. *J'accuse!*"

"That's it, HARV. No more mystery books for you. Now get to the coroner's office."

"Right, boss," HARV sighed. "I'll let you know when the results are in. Think really loudly if you need me before then."

"Let's go, Zach," Tony called impatiently from across the room. "Keep this moving."

I turned and walked toward the huge table at which they were all seated. I'm not usually one for theatrics, but I was determined to go through with this.

"So. I suppose you're all wondering why I gathered you here tonight."

"Gates," said Ona, "you're not going to use *every* cliché, are you?"

"Only the ones that are relevant," I replied. "And, trust me, you'll appreciate this when it's over."

"Get to the point, Zach," Tony said.

"Right. I've gathered you all here tonight because I know who killed Foraa Thompson. And that person is in this room."

"Ah-ha!" Opie said jumping to his feet. "He said *person*. That proves I'm innocent!"

"Opie, one thing I've learned after all this is that no one is innocent. You better sit down and let me finish."

A little embarrassed, Opie sat down, then leaned over and whispered to W, "He said person. I'm an ape."

"And I'm a human head grafted onto a limbless android torso," W replied. "What's your point?"

Opie shrugged and looked down at the table.

"Okay," I said, turning my attention back to the crowd. "What I meant to say is that the *killer* is in this room. We all know the circumstances of Foraa's death and I guess everyone's pretty much caught up on everything that's happened since then so let's just cut to the chase. Computer?"

"Yes, Mr. Johnson?"

"Playback, please."

"As you wish."

The lights in the room darkened and the large wallscreen began replaying the audio and visual recording made the night of the murder. Once again, we saw Ona lead her sisters into the dining room and take their places at the sumptuously prepared table.

"I'll say once again how happy I am that you could all come this evening on such short notice," Ona said, "although I'm sure your schedules can't be nearly as full as mine."

"Yes," Foraa mumbled, "being a whore must be so demanding."

"Please, Foraa, don't be so cruel," Twoa said. "Whores actually work for a living."

"Zach," Tony said, "we've already seen this recording."

"Not like this, you haven't," I said. "Trust me. Computer, scan ahead to point number one."

The action on the screen lurched forward, speeding up for a nano or two as Ona led her sisters to the table. Then it slowed back to normal as they all took their places.

"W worked especially hard on the table for this evening," Ona said. "He began four days ago. Six if you count the polishing. Sadly, he's not as fast as he used to be, but I think you'll agree that everything is perfect."

"Or at least very nearly," Foraa said.

"Computer, freeze it there," I said.

The playback froze on the image of Foraa, standing at her place at the table, staring down at the setting.

"Zoom in on her hand," I said.

A cursor highlighted her left hand and enlarged it to clearly show her gloved index finger gently touching the handle of a tiny fork.

"Murder attempt number one," I said. "The handle of that small fork was coated with T and D, a deadly poison that enters the bloodstream through the skin. The culprit, W."

I pointed dramatically toward W, who remained seated and rolled his eyes.

"Shocking," he said.

"W had been embezzling credits from Ona's household budget for years in order to purchase an illegal super-android body to replace his human frame which had become withered with age. But Foraa found out about his plan and threatened to expose him to Ona. So W coated one of the forks at Foraa's place setting with poison and left it slightly askew, knowing that Foraa, like all the Quads, was a stickler for perfection. She saw the fork out of place, nudged it with her fingertip, thus infecting herself with the poison and sealing her fate. There was just one problem."

"Her glove," Tony said.

"Yes," I pointed to the screen, running my hand along Foraa's black faux leather glove. "Foraa wore gloves, so the poison never made contact with her skin. W should have known that. After all, Foraa had been wearing gloves like that since she was a child. Perhaps age has affected your memory as well as your body, eh, W?"

W turned away.

"And to think I served him tea," he mumbled to Opie.

"And I gave him a beer," Opie replied. "What's your point?"

"Zach, we already know about W's attempt on Foraa's life," Tony said. "And we know he's not the real killer."

"True," I said. "Let's move on. Computer, skip ahead to point two."

The playback jumped forward again as the Quads sat and conversed in fast motion. Ona tried to say a few words as Twoa and Threa bickered about the nymphs. Then the playback slowed down and returned to normal speed.

"Oh, please, sister," Threa said to Twoa, "you couldn't spell justice if it wasn't monogrammed onto your spandex."

The nymphs laughed and let loose another glitter-dust cloud.

"That's enough, ladies," Ona said.

One nymph flew toward Twoa and hovered in front of her chest.

"J-U-S . . . Double-D, I mean, T."

"That's it," Twoa said.

Twoa swatted the nymph away and the other two leaped at her.

"Slay the super bitch!"

"Freeze it there," I said.

The recording stopped and I pointed to the far edge of the frame away from the action to where Foraa sat, quietly watching her sisters' tussle.

"Isolate and enlarge this portion," I said.

The computer did as requested and Foraa's calm form soon filled the screen. I motioned toward the screen but moved past Foraa's image and went instead to the small spherical bot that was hovering two meters behind her.

"As you can see," I said. "Foraa's attention at this nano is focused on her sisters rather than on this tiny security bot back here, allowing the bot to do this."

The playback resumed in slow motion and we saw a tiny flash erupt from the small bot as it fired a dart.

"This bot has just fired an assassin-type smart-dart, which is loaded with a highly concentrated amount of a deadly poison. This is murder attempt number two of the evening. The culprit, or *culprits,* I should say: the Pfauhans."

I spun around and pointed an accusing finger toward Sturm and Drang as they sat at the table. They seemed not to notice whatsoever. Sturm was speaking with his press agent on his vid while Drang was looking longingly at Twoa's superhero jersey.

"Do you find that fabric constricting in warm weather or does the material breathe?"

"The Pfauhans had been stealing Ona's designer clothing and selling it to collectors through illegal auction sites for years. They'd made a fortune doing this and had come to rely on the income, especially since they had priced themselves out of the medical research market. Foraa found out about their dealings and threatened to expose them to Ona, so the only way the Pfauhans could maintain their cash flow was by killing her."

"But they failed," Tony said.

"That's right, Tony. Here's why."

The computer restarted the slow-motion playback and we watched as the dart flew at Foraa and struck her in the back of the neck. The computer enlarged the images at the point of impact so that we could clearly see the micro-tip needle strike the back of Foraa's neck and first bend, then break from the impact, completely failing to pierce her skin.

"The Pfauhans forgot that Foraa, like all the Quads, was impervious to most projectile-type weapons. The dart, as you see, couldn't penetrate her skin. It fell into the collar of her jacket where it disintegrated as designed in nanos. For those scoring at home, that's two murder attempts and two failures."

"That's all very nice, Zach," Ona said, "but we know this already. I thought you were going to reveal the identity of Foraa's killer."

"I will, Ona," I said. "I just want to point out here that three of the people in your employ made attempts on Foraa's life that night. Murder attempts that were necessary in order to protect illegal activity that had been going on under your . . . um . . . force field."

"Your point being?"

"My point is that you have so isolated yourself from the reality of the outside world that your judgment has become clouded. You need to be more careful with the people you employ."

"Clearly," she said, giving me a glare.

"Okay, Zach," Tony said, "let's skip ahead to the real killer now."

"Fine. Computer, take us to point three."

The recording jumped forward again. This time by only a few nanos. The spat between Twoa, Threa, and the nymphs had ended and Ona had restored order. We watched now as Ona popped the cork on the wine bottle and set it down in front of her.

"Now, while we let the wine breathe for a few nanos, as I was saying, after everything I've done for this world, after all the good that I've created with my wealth—aiding underprivileged children, funding disease research—after devoting my vast fortune to raising the quality of life for every downtrodden person in the first through fourth worlds, I just want to say that it is you, my family, that is still foremost in my heart."

The playback stopped and I turned to the audience, most of whom looked at me questioningly. The others just looked angry.

"And that, for all intents and purposes, is when the murder took place," I said.

"I don't get it, Zach," Tony said. "Nothing happened. No one moved."

"Something happened, all right, Tony. We just didn't see it," I said. "Ona, what's wrong with what we just saw?"

Ona had sat forward as soon as the recording had stopped, wanting to speak, but she had followed my lead and restrained herself, waiting until my prompt.

"That wasn't my complete speech," she said.

"What?" Tony asked.

"That was my 'great humanitarian' speech," she said. "I give it a lot, but it's missing the portion that talks about my driving programs for environmental renewal and reinvention. That part isn't there."

I could tell by the gleam of her eyes that Ona was starting to figure things out. She was clearly replaying events in her mind, trying to see where this was all leading. When the look of shock and disbelief came to her eyes, I could tell that she'd found the answer.

"You mean the recording has been tampered with?" Tony asked, glaring at me.

"There was some kind of . . . technical glitch when Ms. Thompson's computer first downloaded the material to us," I said. "It accidentally skipped over a small portion of the play-back. The glitch wasn't discovered and rectified until tonight."

"Pretty odd coincidence that this glitch happened at such a vital point in the playback," Tony replied.

"True. But, as I recall, the experts in your department studied the recordings quite closely," I said. "If their well-trained eyes didn't notice the glitch, then certainly you can't blame any of us for not noticing."

Tony and I stared at one another, neither of us totally comfortable with where this line of conversation was leading.

"Since we've started putting these jobs up for bids, we've gotten some pretty lousy experts," Tony mumbled.

"Let's just hope that when this all turns out well in the end," I said, "we can all just forget about that silly glitch."

"Agreed," he said. "Now let's have a look at the corrected version."

I nodded. "Computer, if you please."

The screen rebooted and the scene we had just watched began again. This time, however, it included a murder.

Ona picked the wine bottle up again and, without letting her imperious gaze leave her sisters, pulled the cork with a corkscrew. Then she set the bottle down in front of her.

"The poison saturated the wine," I said. "Oddly though, there was no trace of it on the cork. That means that the poison was added to the wine after opening."

"Now, while we let the wine breathe for a few nanos, as I was saying . . . after everything that I've done for this world, after all the good that I've created with my wealth—aiding underprivileged children, funding disease research . . ."

And then it happened.

It began innocently enough. One of Threa's nymphs took to the air and flew toward the unconscious nymph in the wineglass. Twoa saw the nymph out of the corner of her eye and tried to slap it away. The nymph avoided the swat but bumped directly into the wine bottle. The impact caused it to tip, as though it were about to spill.

Both Twoa and Threa moved quickly, albeit a little clumsily to steady the bottle. They both grabbed at it and it squirted between their hands for a few nanos before Ona finally steadied it with her own hand.

"Driving programs for environmental renewal and reinvention . . ."

She glared at both Twoa and Threa who moved quickly back to their places. Ona waited a beat and then finished her speech.

"After devoting my vast fortune to raising the quality of life for every downtrodden person in the first through fourth worlds, I just want to say that it is you, my family, that is still foremost in my heart . . ."

"Computer, take it back just a little," I said.

The recording rewound to the point where the wine bottle began to tip.

"Enlarge the bottle and give it to us in slo-mo."

There it was, as the bottle began to tip, Twoa and Threa lunged for it, grasping the neck and body with their finely shaped hands. Their actions, at first glance, appeared a little clumsy as one then the other grasped and lost hold of the bottle. But enlarged and in super slow motion, we could see the clumsiness for what it was, a perfectly orchestrated dance of death.

Threa's hand moved smoothly over the bottle's opening as it slipped from her grasp. As it did so, a small compartment in one of her rings opened and dumped a small payload of black powder into the bottle.

Then the bottle flipped to Twoa's hand and a tiny vial appeared from between her gloved fingers. Smoothly she emptied the vial's black, powdery contents into the wine just as Ona's hand came down to steady the bottle.

It took less than two seconds, start to finish, for it to happen, but the deadly trap had been set.

# 43

The recording stopped. The lights came back on and, as one, everyone turned their gaze to Twoa and Threa.

"That's . . . that's preposterous," Twoa said. "Clearly, someone has tampered with that recording."

"Why would we kill Foraa?"

"It could have been because she wouldn't join your lawsuit," I said. "The three of you together could have forced Ona to settle and divide your father's fortune. Her claim that she didn't want her share of the wealth complicated things to no end. But that's not why you killed her, is it?"

"Why, then?" Tony asked.

"The truth of the matter is that Foraa wasn't the target," I said. "Ona was. After all this time, Twoa and Threa realized that the only way to get Ona's fortune was over her dead body. So they poisoned the wine knowing that when Ona proposed her toast, it would be the last words she would ever say. The two of you would just pretend to drink. That way you'd get rid of Ona, and lay claim to her fortune. Killing Foraa here would be just a bonus. With her gone, you'd have to split the fortune in half rather than thirds. And you used Ona's DNA to create the poison rather than your own to avoid suspicion."

"But where did they get Ona's DNA?" Tony asked. "That poison was pretty pure."

"From the Pfauhans," I replied. "HARV hacked into the records of the Pfauhans' auction sites. Several of the dresses they sold, the *sweat-stained* dresses, were purchased by dummy corporations controlled by Twoa and Threa. They were able to distill enough DNA from the sweat and skin follicles on the dresses over time to create the DNA tag for the poison."

"This is all some wild fantasy," Threa said.

"You'd know, wouldn't you, Threa," I said. "But there's one more thing. Computer?"

The computer flashed a picture onto the wall screen of the dying clue that Foraa had drawn in the wine.

"This equation, which Foraa drew in the wine puddle before she died," I said, "is a carefully constructed clue to the identity of her killers. It's well hidden, but it had to be because she had to hide the information from the killers, who, as we know, are genius intellects. The solution to the equation is V."

"You mean the letter *V?*" Tony asked.

"Not the letter," I said. "The number. A Roman numeral, to be exact, signifying five or . . ."

"Two and three together," Ona said, turning sadly toward Twoa and Threa. "How could you?"

"Don't start with us, Ona," Twoa said before turning to Tony. "I want to speak with my army of attorneys and their attorneys."

"They'll meet you at the station house," Tony said.

He nodded to his detectives, who stood Twoa and Threa up and shackled their hands with neuro-cuffs. For good or bad, the case seemed closed.

And that's when everything suddenly went very, very bad . . .

It began, unsurprisingly, with a message from HARV.

"Hey, boss," he whispered in my head. "How'd the big scene go?"

"About as well as it could, all things considered," I said. "Do you have the autopsy results?"

"Yeah, well, about that, boss. The autopsy is one of those classic good news/bad news things."

"HARV, have you ever noticed that your 'classic good news/bad news things' never seem to contain any real good news?"

"Ironic, isn't it?" he said.

"Okay, let's have it."

"The good news is that the coroner and I were able to perform a complete autopsy on Foraa Thompson."

I closed my eyes and rubbed the bridge of my nose gently, preparing myself for the inevitable trouble that would follow my next four words.

"And the bad news?"

"It turns out that she's not dead after all."

# 44

Tony knew right away that something was wrong and he was at my side before I could say another word. I had the presence of mind to activate my wrist communicator and bring HARV's visage to the tiny screen.

"What's wrong?" Tony asked.

"Just about everything," I said. "HARV, define for us, please, what you mean by 'not dead.'"

"Not dead? Who's not dead?" Tony said.

"It would appear that Ms. Thompson only feigned death."

"Are you saying that Foraa's not dead?" Tony asked. He was clearly having trouble grasping the situation (not that I could blame him).

"HARV, she was in the morgue for three days," I said. "The coroner shot her with lasers. You stuck her with anal probes!"

"Yes, I feel a little bad about that."

"Are you sure that she's not dead?"

"Oh, I'm sure all right," HARV said.

"How?"

"Because five minutes ago she got up off the slab and walked out."

"What?!"

"HARV," Tony said, "let me speak to the coroner."

"I'm afraid he's occupied at present," HARV replied.

"What do you mean?"

HARV's image disappeared from the interface and was replaced with the live feed from the security camera in the main examination room. There we saw Lenny Shakes standing atop the examination table doing the Freaky Geeky dance.

"Oh, my Gates," Tony murmured. "Why is he doing the Freaky Geeky?"

"Because Foraa Thompson is alive and well and apparently none too pleased about those anal probes," I said.

Tony didn't have time to respond because at that nano, his men who had been mirandizing Twoa and Threa suddenly started shouting.

"Captain, come quick!"

Tony and I turned just in time to see the forms of Twoa and Threa bathed in an increasingly bright, silver light. And then with a blinding flash, they disappeared. The neuro-cuffs they had been wearing clattered to the floor like coins in a rude beggar's tin cup.

"Uh-oh," I said.

"What was that?" Ona gasped.

"It looked like teleportation," I said.

"Teleportation without a pad," Tony said. "That's impossible."

"HARV, get over here," I said. "I need to you track a teleportation trail."

HARV's hologram was beside me before I finished the sentence and in a nano he was inspecting the area from where Twoa and Threa had disappeared. He had a holographic magnifying glass in his hand, by the way, signifying that his metamorphosis from butler to detective was now complete, for better or (more likely) for worse.

"There are definite teleportation energy traces," he said. "It looks like a smash and grab, well, actually just a grab."

"Can you trace the energy signature?" I asked.

"It might take a nano or two."

"Put a rush on it."

"Will somebody please tell me what's going on here?" Ona yelled.

"Well, Ona, as you know, two of your sisters killed your youngest sister and have now disappeared," I said. "The upside of this is that apparently your other sister isn't dead after all."

"What?"

"And she's disappeared, too. Did I mention that?"

"You mean Foraa's alive?"

"That's our understanding."

"Oh, dear," Ona said. "That's not good at all."

"What do you mean by that?"

"Boss?" HARV said.

"Hold on a nano, Ona," I said, turning toward HARV. "Have you traced the teleportation yet?"

"Still working on it. I just wanted to let you know that you have a call coming in from Carol."

"Tell her I'm busy . . ."

But it was too late. HARV's face disappeared from the interface screen and was replaced by Carol's. She was standing in front of what looked like a large (yet very dimly lit) computer and she seemed a little more . . . intense than usual.

"Tío," she said. "Listen, there's a bit of an emergency here."

"I can't talk now, Carol. I have an emergency of my own here."

"No, Zach, listen . . ."

"Carol, really, I have to go," I said. "I'll call you back. Tell me where you are . . ."

"New Vegas," she said.

"What are you doing in Vegas?" I asked.

Carol shook her head. "I'm on a job."

"A job? You work for me!"

"It's kind of a second job. It's not like you pay all that well and school and stuff are expensive."

I had to admit I was kind of hurt that Carol found it necessary to take a second job. Still, I had bigger things to worry about.

"Carol, I'll help you when I can, but right now I'm in the middle of something."

"Tío, I don't think you heard me," Carol said. "I said that I'm in . . ."

"Boss, I've traced the signal. It came from . . ."

HARV and Carol in unison: "New Vegas."

HARV, Carol, and I all stared at one another for a long, long nano.

"I'll be there as soon as can," I said to Carol. "Where can I find you?"

"I'll find you," she said. Then she was gone.

I shook my head. This was getting weirder and weirder by the nano.

Tony moved beside me. The look on his face was a strange mix of utter determination and confusion.

"What was that all about?"

"It looks like Foraa, Twoa, and Threa are in Vegas. We better get going."

Tony put a firm hand on my shoulder. "Whoa, Zach. Nobody goes anywhere until I get proper authority."

"Tony, this is an emergency."

"Then it won't be hard to get clearance," he said. "I have no jurisdiction in Vegas. If she's fled the province with her sisters, then we'll need federal clearance."

"We don't have time for that."

"Swear to me, Zach. Swear to me that you won't go to New Vegas until I get clearance. Otherwise I'll arrest you right now."

I stared at Tony. He was one of my oldest friends. I couldn't lie to him, again. Could I?

"Fine, I won't go to Vegas alone," I said. "I'll go to my office and wait for you there."

"I'm going to hold you to that," Tony called as I left.

# 44

"I can't believe you lied to Captain Rickey," HARV scolded inside my head as I headed toward my car.

"I didn't lie. I went back to my office. Waited for him, but he didn't show up."

"You waited all of ten seconds," HARV protested. "And that was just to reload your gun with your new ammo from Dr. Pool!"

"I never said how long I would wait."

"You said you wouldn't go alone."

"I'm not alone. I have you. Remember?"

HARV's face became quite pensive. He even stopped talking for a nano.

"I guess you're right," he said. "But speed should be of the essence and this car is too slow. You should wait for Captain Rickey."

"You're right, speed is important. That's why I'm not waiting. By the time Tony cuts through all the red tape, I'll be in Vegas with the case closed," I said as I opened the door of my classic 2020 Mustang. But before I could even get in, I heard something above me. I looked to the sky and there was a hovercraft right above me and coming down fast.

"Don't tell me it's hostile," I said.

"Only partly. It's Captain Rickey."

The craft landed beside me.

"Get in," Tony ordered.

I got out and slowly walked toward Tony's hover. I could have sworn Tony had more gray hair than when I last saw him.

Before I knew it, we were in Tony's hovercraft and on the

road (the skyway, actually) tearing flat out toward New Vegas at 400 kph. Tony was behind the wheel, white knuckles on the steering column, heavy foot on the accelerator. HARV's holo-gram was in the backseat, a smile on his face and a wind-effect whipping through his digitally enhanced hair. I was in the pas-senger seat (trying hard to remember the prayers I learned dur-ing my brief time in Sunday school). As a cop, Tony was used to regularly ignoring speed limits. Now, fueled by desperation and what I sensed was some very strong anger, the only limits that mattered to him were the g-force limits on the hovercraft's chassis (which I was certain we were in danger of exceeding).

"What did you get from Randy's lab?" Tony asked.

"How'd you know I went there?"

"I have my sources."

"He gave me these," I said, reaching into my pocket.

"What?"

I pulled a small gray box from my pocket and popped the lid to show Tony. Inside were what looked to be two sets of clear polymer earplugs.

"Ear plugs?" Tony asked.

"Maybe it's loud in Vegas," I said with a shrug.

"They're psi-blockers," HARV said.

"What do we need these for?" Tony asked.

"I'm guessing because Foraa's a psi."

"She's what?"

"Hel-lo, she just feigned death for three days and turned an experienced forensic pathologist into a twenty-first-century Village Person. Clearly, she has very strong psionic abilities," HARV said. "Her being a psi also explains Opie's erratic be-havior and how he knew so much about the crime scene when he never even saw it."

"Foraa was controlling him," Tony said, "having him leak information to the press."

"Controlling people from beyond the grave," I said. "And apparently now that she's no longer dead, she's manipulating others."

"She was in a deep state of concentration during her time in the morgue," HARV said. "We know she manipulated Opie and Shakes. Who knows what else she was doing."

"How come we never knew she was psionic?" Tony asked.

"No one ever knew because she never told anyone," HARV answered. "She kept it secret. There's no way of telling how long she's been aware of her abilities."

"Or how long she's been manipulating people."

"There's a scary thought."

"I'm pretty sure they're all psis," I said.

"That's my assumption," HARV said with a nod.

"All of who?"

"The Quads."

"How come they've never told anyone?"

"Because they either don't know it or don't care," I said. "As long as they have superpowers, I don't think they care how they come about them. Who knows which of their powers are real and which are augmented with their psionics?"

"Ona's pheromones are real," HARV said. "But I suspect she supplements them with psionic suggestion."

"She just doesn't know she's doing it," I said. "That also explains Threa's fairy realm and why HARV couldn't register its location. The entire realm is a psionic illusion."

"The nymphs, too," Tony said.

"Exactly. The poison was supposed to affect only the Thompson Quads, remember? But the nymph supposedly died from it."

"Because Threa *knew* about the poison and her mind subconsciously made it affect the nymph."

"And when she thought the nymph was dead, she stopped thinking about it."

"So it faded away."

"Exactly," I said.

"By the way, have I mentioned that it's raining?" HARV said.

"Where?"

"In New Vegas."

"It never rains in Vegas. Isn't there a law or something?"

"It's raining quite hard, at the nano," HARV continued. "You remember the torrential rain we had in Frisco recently?"

"How could I forget?"

"Well, as you'll remember, it stopped shortly after Foraa Thompson's apparent murder. It was at that nano that it began raining in Vegas. And it hasn't stopped since."

"Are you trying to say Foraa can control the weather?"

"When it comes to the Quads, I wouldn't rule anything out."

I took the psi-blockers out of the box. I gave one set to Tony who took them and put them in his shirt pocket without turning his gaze from the skyway. "So I guess we'll be needing these, then."

"Psi-blockers are illegal, you know," Tony said. "Dangerous, too. They cause brain damage."

"Not to worry, Dr. Pool has substantially reconfigured the design," HARV said.

"So they don't cause brain damage?" I said, sliding the blockers into my ears.

"No, they're just no longer illegal. He hasn't been able to solve the brain damage part yet."

"What?" I quickly pulled the blockers out of my ears.

"The risk is minimal compared to common blockers, but you shouldn't wear them for any lengthy period of time."

"Why would we wear them at all then?"

"Because you're about to confront a person who may well be the most powerful psi on the planet," HARV said. "And your minds are going to need every shred of protection they can get."

"Good point," I said. "Any estimates of how powerful she is?"

"This is just conjecture on my part, boss, but I think that if she wanted to, Foraa Thompson could have bent the will of every person in New Frisco. Without those blockers, she could probably turn you into her own personal foot-licking puppy."

"Fine, I'll wear them," I said, somewhat begrudgingly.

"Remind me never to take any long road trips with the two of you," Tony said, stamping harder on the accelerator.

The hover's thrusters roared anew and we surged forward even faster than before (surprising since I thought we were maxed out already). At this rate we'd be in New Vegas in less than an hour.

"Do we have a rendezvous time and place for the reinforcements when we arrive in Vegas?"

"Not exactly," Tony said.

"Will they be able to find us with a tracking device or something?"

"No, not exactly."

"I don't suppose 'not exactly' is police code for 'sure, you betcha'?"

"We have no reinforcements, Zach," Tony said.

"What?"

"The department wouldn't authorize it."

"But, why?"

"Because, with Foraa alive, there's no longer a murder. The case has been closed. The commissioner figures we've gotten enough PR out of the case and it would lose its crowd appeal if we pushed it much more."

"There was *attempted* murder."

"And the perpetrators have been captured."

"Twoa and Threa are missing."

"It doesn't become a missing persons case for forty-eight hours."

"But Foraa . . . feigned death."

"That's not a crime."

"She drove the coroner mad."

"Also not a crime," he said, "and we can't concretely prove that."

"Yeah, but she's . . ."

"She's what, exactly?"

"I don't know, but she's up to something. I can feel it in my gut."

"Surprisingly, that's not enough to get an arrest warrant," he said.

"So there's no help coming from Frisco?"

"None."

"What about the Vegas authorities?"

"I called the New Vegas PD and they said that Foraa was a fine, upstanding citizen."

"Great."

"Don't worry," Tony said. "I have a friend from the academy who's on the New Vegas PD, he'll help us out."

"I thought the Vegas police said that Foraa was a good citizen."

"That's the official line. My buddy will help us unofficially."

"Captain Rickey," HARV said. "If the New Frisco police

department considers this a closed case, then why are you here with us?"

"Because, as of thirty-five minutes ago," Tony said, "I am no longer a member of the New Frisco PD."

"What?"

"They forbid me from going after Foraa," he said. "The commissioner said that if I did, he'd take my badge."

"What did you do?"

"I took off my badge, put it on his desk, and told him where he could stick it."

"I'm sorry, Tony. I know how much being a cop means to you."

"It's not being a cop that matters to me, Zach. It's doing the right thing. What we're doing here is the right thing. I don't need a badge to know that."

"You trust me that much?" I asked.

"Sort of."

"Sort of?"

Tony shrugged. "When the commissioner threatened to take my badge, he was also dancing the Freaky Geeky. I figured that couldn't be a coincidence."

He turned to me and smiled. I cracked a smile as well and a nano later we were laughing out loud. It was the kind of laughter you make when you know that you're headed straight into the heart of darkness; soldiers into battle, sailors into the storm, pop stars into a music critic's convention. It's the most liberating sound known to man, because it is the sound of those who have nothing to lose.

"Well, then, put your psi-blockers in, civilian Rickey," I said. "Because I'm not about to dance the Freaky Geeky with *you*."

# 45

We landed in New Vegas shortly thereafter. True to HARV's words, it was raining about as hard as I've ever seen it, like the sky itself was angry. The New Vegas strip somehow looked even brighter in the torrent, its neon essence magnified by the water in the air. Each raindrop was like a prism in a death plunge, turning the neon glow into a cascading spectrum, before splattering into the huge multicolored puddles that were the city's streets and walkways. It was like someone had stuck a Jackson Pollack painting into an electric outlet.

Tony landed the hover in a lot near the police station on the strip.

"What's the plan?" I asked.

"My buddy's on duty tonight. I'm going to let him know we're here."

"Should I go with you?"

"No, Zach. It's best if you stay here for now," he said. "You're not exactly loved by police officers."

"Yeah, but that's in Frisco," I said. "They don't know me here in Vegas."

"No, actually word gets around."

"That's comforting. Are you sure your buddy will help us?"

"There's an unspoken agreement among all cops, Zach. We help one another. If one cop comes looking for help, the others are duty-bound to come to his aid. It's a code of honor for those on the job."

"You know, of course, that officially you're no longer a cop, right?"

Tony stared at me for a long nano.

"Don't bother me with details now," he said. Then he activated his umbrella force field and got out of the hover. HARV and I watched as he walked quickly toward the station house, the heavy rain bouncing off his shield like tiny fireworks.

"You think the police will help us?" HARV asked.

"Tony made a good case with the code of honor stuff, so who knows. Any idea where we can start searching for Foraa?"

"She used to preach in the ballroom of the Oblivion Hotel and Casino. We could try there," HARV said.

"A casino actually let her preach about the evils of greed and the material world under their roof?"

"They welcomed it," HARV replied. "People would be so depressed after hearing Foraa speak, they'd actually *enjoy* losing money at the gaming tables. The Oblivion is nearby, just two kilometers to the north."

"You mean the south," I said.

"No, I'm quite certain it's to the north," HARV corrected.

"HARV, I've been to Vegas before. The Oblivion is south of here."

"You're thinking of the Desperation," HARV said. "It has a similar décor and design."

"Are you sure?"

"Boss, I'm interfaced with over one hundred global positioning systems. I can give you the exact location of every establishment in the northern hemisphere. I'm telling you that the Oblivion Casino is one-point seven-eight kilometers north, northeast of our current location."

"Okay, maybe you're right . . ."

"Oh, look," HARV said. "Captain Rickey is coming out of the station house. He seems excited."

I looked toward the police station. Sure enough, Tony was leaving. He seemed to be in a hurry. A big hurry. And there was a trail of police officers following him.

"Interesting. Captain Rickey seems to be yelling something," HARV said. "I'm going to zoom in on him and try to read his lips."

"I think you should start the engine," I said.

"You're right! That's what Captain Rickey seems to be yelling," HARV said. " 'Start the engine.' How did you know that?"

Tony was now running full speed from the station house back toward the hover. A dozen angry New Vegas cops were hot on his heels, waving their blasters.

"HARV, interface with the hover and start the engine," I said.

"Lean forward and look at the ignition so I can rewire it," HARV said.

I leaned over and looked at the ignition chip. A beam of light transmitted from my eye and bathed the chip in electrons. That fired up the engines. The hover lurched forward like a spastic frog as I switched off the parking brake. Tony was close now, waving his arms and signaling for help. The police officers behind him had stopped and were now aiming their blasters at us.

"I think you better open the door for him," HARV said.

"Good idea. How do I do that?"

HARV rolled his eyes and disappeared into the dash computer.

"Honestly," he said. "You'd be lost without me."

The hover smoothly rose a meter off the ground and pivoted gently, turning the passenger door toward the mad-dashing Tony. The door popped open just as Tony leaped to avoid the barrage of blaster fire from the police. His hands caught the doorframe and he pulled himself inside as HARV took the hover into the air.

"Get us out of here now!" he shouted.

"HARV?"

"I got it, boss," HARV said. "We're as good as gone."

The hover thrusters fired and we shot straight up into the New Vegas sky, blaster fire following us every meter of the way.

"Preparing to take evasive action," HARV said. "Hold on."

He banked the craft hard to the right as we rose, rolling it onto its side and pulling us away from the pursuing police officers.

"I guess the police code of honor doesn't extend all the way to Vegas," I said.

"I don't get it," Tony stuttered, still gasping for breath. "They seemed so normal at first. Then they all turned on me."

"I know the feeling," I said.

"All I did was mention Foraa."

"It would appear that Ms. Thompson already has her mental hooks deep into the police," HARV noted.

"So what do we do now?" Tony asked.

"We're in Vegas, Tony, what else can we do?" I said. "We're going to the nearest casino and hope we get lucky."

# 46

The Oblivion Hotel & Casino isn't the most popular place on the New Vegas strip. Truth to tell, it's one of the bottom links on the slot-junkie food chain, just above the Desperation, the Delusion, and the Impaled Iguana Gambling Emporium and Waffle House. Admittedly though, it wasn't always this way.

The casino's owner is a now-infamous billionaire named Heinrich Schwipe, who earned his money the old-fashioned way (his overbearing father died and left it to him). Shortly after his father's death Schwipe came to New Vegas with a billion credits in his pocket and a dream to build the world's greatest casino. He wanted to create something dark and hopeless that would fly in the face of the typical Vegas glitz and glitter. The result was the Oblivion. It was big and black on the outside, and shaped like a warped hourglass, with a wide base that tapered inward as it rose and then widened again for the uppermost twenty floors. It was completely free of all lighted signs, which caused a stir in the community because, at the time, not having neon on a building was illegal in Vegas. But Schwipe eventually got a waiver from the Vegas Board of Edifice Rules & Standards and his neonless project got built, just as he planned.

When it was finished, it stood out on the strip like a missing tooth in a beauty queen's smile. The only way you could tell that the casino was even there was by the big void its dark form created in the Vegas cityscape, a black hole in the middle of a crowded field of stars.

Inside, the place was about as cheery as a tar pit; dark and cavernous and a little damp. The rooms were spacious but gloomy. The food was bland and the gaming rooms were so dark, the craps tables had to use glow-in-the-dark dice. Vegas veterans were aghast at the depressing audacity of the Oblivion and they all declared that the monstrosity wouldn't last a year.

But it did. For some reason the whole dark and dreary look came into vogue with the east coast art crowd and the casino became a hot spot. Cultural critics said that its atmosphere of hopelessness was a masterstroke of marketing and design, its brutal honesty flying in the face of the empty smiles of its competitors. The casino's gloom also attracted the hardened gambler (who felt right at home in its dour air) as well as the directionless youngsters of "Generation Y-Me." So, for many years, the casino prospered and the mysterious Schwipe was hailed as the gloomy genius of New Vegas.

It was learned later, however, that Schwipe wasn't a genius. He was, instead, just a very, very unhappy guy. The official diagnosis was severe clinical depression with suicidal tendencies and it turned out that he'd been that way since childhood. His dark and hopeless design for the casino didn't come from any hip nihilist philosophy or innate brilliance but rather from his own depressed soul. He had created the casino as a reflection of himself, not as a genius, but as a sad man, and that sort of blew the illusion. You've heard the phrase "the emperor has no clothes." Well, in this case, it's "the casino owner has no Prozac-II."

The casino was no longer hip. It was simply pathetic. And the customers left in droves. Popularity dwindled, as did the profits. This, of course, made Schwipe even more depressed and he made the casino even gloomier than before. It's a hideous circle that continues to this day. The casino is still dark and gloomy, the owner is still depressed and suicidal. The only thing that still draws real numbers of people to the casino these days is the spectacularly bizarre fountain (but I'll get to that later).

In any event, Foraa had preached her gospel at the casino for a number of years, so we figured that this was the best place to start searching for her.

The storm was less intense at the Oblivion. The wind was strong, but the rain was barely a drizzle, for which I was thankful. It felt ominous, though, like the relative calm at the eye of a storm (although I tried not to think about that).

The bouncers working the casino door were Elvis-enhanced (surgically altered with a synthesized version of Elvis Presley DNA, which allows them to take on Elvis-like physical qualities). Not surprisingly, it's very popular in New Vegas these days. One bouncer was the fat Elvis of early 1970s (circa the concert in Hawaii), the other was the Love-Me-Tender period; thin and good-looking.

"Sorry, folks," thin Elvis said as Tony and I tried to enter. "The casino's closed to the public tonight."

"But I have all this money," I said. "And I'm very unlucky."

"Come back tomorrow, suh," Fat Elvis replied. "We'll be happy to take your way-juhs then."

"You're welcome to partake of the fountain, though. It's right around the corner."

"What's going on inside?" Tony asked.

"Private party."

"Didn't I mention that we were here for the party?" I said cheerily.

"You said you were here to gamble," Young Elvis said.

"Gamble, party, it's all the same in Vegas, right?"

"Please move along, suh," Fat Elvis said with a scowl.

"Come on, Zach, let's go," Tony said, gently pulling me away.

"No, wait, we're invited," I said. "Really. We're very close personal friends of Foraa."

The Elvis clones' gazes turned steely and their hands, very subtly went to the blaster-sized bulges of their coats.

"Who said anything about Foraa?" the fat one said.

"He didn't say Foraa," Tony said.

"Foraa? No, I didn't say that. I said . . . I said . . ."

"Nora," Tony quipped.

"Yeah, that's it," I said. "We're friends of Nora. Nora Noyes."

"We love Nora," Tony said.

"It's her birthday today and she's having her party at the Desperation Casino."

"This isn't the Desperation," young Elvis said.

"It's not?"

"This is the Oblivion. The Desperation is south of here."

"Are you sure? Because this really looks like the Desperation."

"They're sure," Tony said, pulling me away. "Let's go."

"Well, if you say so," I said. "Thanks for your help, guys. I'll bring you back some cake from Nora's party."

The Elvis bouncers were silent as Tony finally pulled me away. We mixed in with a crowd of tourists and walked south for a bit, until we were comfortably away from the Oblivion.

"What now?" he asked.

"I think we've established that something odd is going on inside."

"We'll have to find another way in. There must be a service entrance."

"There's a hoverport for high rollers on the roof. We could try that."

"Good idea."

"HARV, bring the hover around back," I said. "We'll meet you there."

"Got it, boss."

We ducked into an alleyway and doubled back toward the casino. New Vegas alleys are dark and relatively deserted. Mainstream traffic tends to stay on the well-lit strip. The alleyways, by design, are reserved for some of the city's more illicit activities.

"Hey, babes," two good-looking women called to us from a doorway, "you looking for a date?"

"Some other time, ladies," I said as we passed.

"Hey, dudes," a ragged looking man yelled from another doorway. "Got some stuff here that will alter your mind, expand your consciousness."

"No thanks, pal," I said, pulling Tony along with me (he was getting a little agitated).

"Gentleman," a man in a suit called from yet another doorway, "care to purchase some untraceable weapons?"

"What is this, crime alley?" Tony mumbled.

"Keep your cop instincts in check, Tony," I said as we continued walking. "We're here for bigger fish."

"Cheat on your taxes for you, man?" a tiny man in a bow tie whispered as we passed.

"They really cover all the bases here, don't they?" I said.

"I don't want to think about it," Tony said. "By the way, how do we plan to find Foraa once we're in the casino?"

"We'll figure it out when we're inside," I replied.

"I'm not comfortable going into this without a plan, Zach."

"Well, I'm not comfortable going into this at all, but we have to play the hand we're dealt. The plan is fluid, Tony. It always is."

Tony cast a glance behind us, then did a quick double take.

"Does the plan perhaps include some desperate running for our lives," he whispered.

"What?"

I turned to follow his gaze and saw the two bouncers from the casino, blasters drawn, enter the alley and move toward us.

"Hey, babes," the hookers called as the Elvises passed, "want a date?"

"Sure, darlin'," Fat Elvis said, pointing toward us. "But let's kill those guys first."

The prostitutes looked at one another for a nano and shrugged. "Okay," they said, pulling blasters from their short skirts, "but it'll cost you a little extra."

The four of them fired in unison. Tony and I turned and ran as the energy blasts tore up the alley around us.

"HARV!"

"I'm on my way, boss, but I can't get the hover into that alley. You'll have to get to the fountain."

"Gates, not that stupid fountain."

"It's the nearest spot, boss," HARV said. "And you're headed in the right direction."

"Fine," I said, turning to Tony. "Keep running, buddy. And when we turn that corner up ahead, keep your head down."

"What do you mean?"

I didn't have a chance to answer because the two Elvises and the hookers were still hot on our tails, firing away like drunken postal workers. The crooked accountant had joined them as well, which was bad because he was the most blood-thirsty of the lot. Their wild blaster barrage took another chunk out of the wall nearby, just missing us as we neared the corner.

I heard the noise ahead—the whir of heavy machinery, the

cacophony of music, the squeal of delighted people, and the unmistakable sound of food—and I knew we were close.

"What's that noise?" Tony said as we ran.

"Just keep your head down," I yelled.

We rounded the corner out of the alley and into the courtyard. I looked around quickly to get my bearings and locate HARV and the hovercraft. That was my big mistake, because that's when the blast hit me, point blank in the side of the head. Something thick and red splattered on the wall behind me and I staggered sideways before falling to the ground.

"Zach!" Tony yelled.

He knelt beside me and held my head in his arms, doing his best to wipe away the wound.

"It's okay," he said. "Everything's going to be fine. Everything's going to be . . ."

He stopped and stared at his hand, which was covered in red.

"Is this marinara sauce?"

"Must be pasta day," I groaned.

And we were hit with another barrage of flying food.

# 47

The fountain at the Oblivion. I've already mentioned how odd Heinrich Schwipe, the owner and designer of the Oblivion Casino, was, right? Well, you have to keep that in mind in order to fully understand and appreciate the Oblivion's famous fountain.

Schwipe's depression drove him not to drugs, alcohol, or sex (all of which are good choices) but rather to food. He was a binge eater. A binge eaters' binge eater. All kinds of food, all hours of the day, when the mood struck him (and it struck him often) he would eat. It was a convenient and all too common way of drowning one's sorrows. Schwipe just took the destructive behavior to new lows.

So with that in mind, it's not surprising that any casino Schwipe designed would have a twenty-four-seven all-you-can-eat buffet. The problem was that the traditional buffets weren't fast enough (or enormous enough) to meet Schwipe's grandiose dreams. The delivery of the food had to be more immediate, the display had to be more dramatic, and the scale of the project had to be more flamboyant.

The inspiration came to him during a visit to the old Caesars Casino, where he saw the throng of tourists taking pictures of one another beside the great fountain. Then he went to dinner where the three-year-old at the booth next to him threw lima beans at his shirt. He put two and two together and came up with the most disgusting four imaginable.

Thus was born the famous Fountain Buffet; a mammoth marble sculpture twenty-five meters tall and elaborately carved by the world's finest crafts bots. And every nano of every day it spews forth from its elaborate system of tubing a spectacular array of . . . food.

Yes, it's a food-spewing fountain. Turkey breast, manicotti, fruit salad, egg salad, chocolate mousse, shrimp cocktail, bacon bits, and those little cocktail weenies in that weird red sauce. Any food you've ever seen on a buffet table, salad bar, or smorgasbord at one time or another is pumped into the air by the Oblivion Fountain. And every nano of every day, hungry people from all over the world dress themselves in rubber raincoats and goggles and make their way down to the courtyard to partake in the white trash Dionysian display. It is one of the icons of the New Vegas strip, a monument to excess and vulgarity, and a testimony to the success of crass. I will say, however, that it has the best darn onion rings that I've ever tasted.

This was the first time Tony had ever seen the food-spewing fountain in person and he was a little awestruck by it (awestruck or disgusted, I'm not really sure; either way, he froze at the sight).

"DOS, you see this thing on HV, but it doesn't begin to compare with the real thing . . ." Tony said.

I was on the ground, still stunned by the lasagna hit I had taken to the head, but I was coherent enough to know that we were still in trouble. I cast a quick glance around the courtyard but saw no sign of the hovercraft.

"HARV, where's the hover?"

"I'm at the northeastern corner of the courtyard, boss. I can't get any closer without creating a scene. The crowd's too heavy."

I turned back toward the alley and saw the hookers, the accountant, and the two Elvis bouncers emerge and scan the crowd in search of us.

"Tony," I yelled, shaking his arm to get his attention away from the fountain, "HARV and the hover are in the northeast corner. Let's go."

We got to our feet and, keeping our heads down as much as possible, started making our way through the crowd. Unfortunately, the thin Elvis spotted us (we were the only ones in the area not wearing raincoats) and he and the hookers started after us.

"Tony, hurry!"

We pushed our way through the throng more desperately, but the accountant came at us from the side. He jumped on Tony's back like an angry squirrel on a hard-to-crack nut. I pulled him off and threw him into a small gathering of Japanese tourists who were feasting on the cascade of udon noodles that were spewing from the fountain like a silly string fireworks display.

The two hookers were on us next. One came at my knees like a football chop blocker, while the other hit me square in the shoulder with her purse. I went down hard and lost track of Tony. I tried to get up, but one of the hookers kicked me in the face with a stiletto heel and sent me back down to the pavement.

"We can do the rough stuff if that's what you're into, baby."

She kicked at me again, but I caught her foot this time and tossed her backward, smack into the other hooker, and their garter belts got tangled up together as they fell. I almost stayed to watch them as they rolled around on the pavement trying to get unhooked from one another, but I had more pressing matters at hand.

"I hate Vegas."

I turned to look for Tony but instead saw only the thin Elvis. Well, all I actually *saw* was his fist, which hit me square in the face and sent me staggering, but I assume that the rest of him was attached to it. I fell back down to the pavement and looked up just in time to see him aiming his blaster at me.

"You should know, mister, here in New Vegas, we don't like people who don't like Foraa," he said, as his finger tightened on the trigger.

Suddenly, he was sideswiped by what looked to be a few hundred kilos of flying ravioli. The airborne deluge knocked him over and covered him, neatly immobilizing him in a pile of tasty pasta, zesty sauce, and a tempting melange of spicy cheese and meat-substitute fillings. I turned and saw Tony standing by the fountain. He had commandeered one of the feeder hoses and had used its victual output to drop a Chef Boyardee bomb on my would-be killer.

"And *you* should know, mister," Tony quipped, "that I never liked Elvis." Then he helped me up and motioned in the direction of where HARV and the hovercraft waited just a few meters away. "Come on, let's get to the roof."

We jumped into the hover and HARV brought us quickly to the roof of the casino. After the cacophony and chaos of the fountain buffet, the quiet of the rooftop hoverport was a refreshing change. But as we climbed out of the hover and looked at the city spread out before us, we felt anything but refreshed. Pitch-black storm clouds encircled the Oblivion like an atmospheric smoke ring. The lightning and driving rain they created stood in stark, startling contrast to the calm immediately surrounding the building. The Oblivion was an island in a storm.

"I don't like this," I mumbled.

"And don't ask me to explain it scientifically," HARV said. "Because I can't."

"Zach," Tony said as he pulled a laser rifle from the trunk, "where's the entrance?"

"Over there," I said, pointing to a small elevator booth near the edge of the roof. "Ditch the hover, HARV. We don't want it drawing attention. But keep it close by. We may need a fast escape."

"Gotcha, boss."

The hover took to the air, leaving Tony and me alone on the rooftop. I popped my gun into my hand and we walked quickly toward the elevator.

"Thanks for the save back there," I said as we walked.

"Don't mention it."

"You were kidding when you said you didn't like Elvis, right?"

"Let's not go into that now, Zach."

"Oh, man, you mean you *really* don't like Elvis?"

Tony pressed the button on the side of the booth and we heard the elevator start to rise.

"He's just not my style, that's all?"

"But *everybody* likes Elvis."

A bell sounded as the elevator arrived.

"His music's too simplistic for me," Tony said, turning toward me. "And it's derivative."

"Derivative of what? The man was a pioneer."

"He was copying the bluesmen of the era," Tony said. "All the good rock and roll singers of the day were."

"So you admit he was a good rock and roll singer."

"Don't start with me, Zach."

The elevator doors opened and I saw Fat Elvis in the car; a laser rifle in his hands leveled directly at Tony. His fat lip curled into a sneer, his hips swiveled just a little, and I saw him mouth the words "thank you, thank you very much."

"Tony, look out!"

I dove and pushed Tony aside as Fat Elvis fired. The blast hit me point-blank, full in the chest, and I felt my armor surge as it tried to absorb and disperse the energy. A few of the circuits overloaded and blew out, sending sparks right through my coat. My armor withstood the deadly blast. The problem was that it couldn't absorb the sheer force and that sent me right off the edge of the roof.

"Zach!" Tony screamed.

I felt the damp air rush past me, slapping my face like an angry wet hand, as I did the thirty-two feet per second back flop toward the street fifty stories below.

"I'm maxing up the armor, boss," HARV yelled frantically. "And I'm pulling electricity from your body to create a force field to cushion your fall. It's just like that time in the duck pond. This won't be a problem."

I knew he was lying, of course, but I appreciated the sentiment. With or without armor, fifty stories of falling followed by pavement meant only one thing; that my epitaph was about to become "lived fast, died young, and left an ugly smear."

"Boss, are you listening to me?"

All I could do was smile as the pavement grew closer like the fat doorman of death waving me past the velvet rope of the hereafter entrance. Then, suddenly, a warm glow swept through my body. I saw a white flare erupt before my eyes that I first thought was my life flashing before me, and then a tunnel of brilliant white light unfolded. Admittedly, this all seemed a lot more new age than I imagined it would be, but when one is so close to death, you tend to go with the flow.

"Boss?"

Then I was engulfed in darkness.

# 48

---

I awoke to the low hum of engines and the feeling of cold, hard floor beneath my back. I opened my eyes and found myself in a large, barren room lit only in spots by tiny purple lights.

"If this is heaven," I mumbled. "It is highly overrated."

"My, someone thinks a lot of himself," a familiar voice said.

I turned my head and saw Carol kneeling beside me.

"This is stranger than being mauled by Elvis clones," I said.

She smiled and slowly helped me into a sitting position.

"Now is that any way to greet the person who just saved your life?"

"Where are we?"

"A spaceship, fully cloaked and in geosynchronous orbit three hundred and ten kilometers over New Vegas."

"No, really. Where are we?"

Carol smiled. "Trust me, we're on a spaceship."

"What are we doing on a spaceship?"

"Saving the world."

"Oh, good, I thought it might be something important," I said, rubbing the aching joints in my back. "How did I get here?"

"Teleportation beam. We locked on to you the nano you entered New Vegas. We just needed to wait for a time when your disappearance wouldn't be noticed."

I closed my eyes and sent a quick thought to HARV.

"HARV, get a fix on our position and let me know what the DOS is going on here?"

There was no answer.

"Your cerebral interface with HARV won't be functional aboard this ship, Tío," Carol said, pointing to the ceiling. "You're under a nullifier."

"Why?"

"My employers want to make sure that none of this is recorded," Carol said.

"Carol, *I'm* your employer."

"I had to take a second job," she said. "You don't pay that well, remember?"

"This is too weird."

"Tío," she said. "There isn't a lot of time to waste now, so you're going to have to understand and accept some things very quickly in order to get through this. My employers weren't all that confident in you, but I convinced them to test you."

"Test me?"

"That old lady doppelganger you ran into a few days ago, that was their work. Their test. You passed. Barely. But they figured they could at least give you a chance."

"They who?"

On cue, three tall, thin forms stepped out of the darkness and into the purple haze of the tiny spotlights overhead. They were pale, hairless, and very large of forehead. Their huge dark eyes were pupilless and the sound they made as they approached was that of a dozen whistling teakettles.

Gladians.

The planets Glad-7 and Glad-9 are two of Earth's three interplanetary trading partners. Together, the two planets supply Earth with roughly 65 percent of the energy it requires. In exchange for this energy, we give them dirt and I don't mean that metaphorically. We *literally* give them dirt, hundreds of kilotons of it every year. We don't ask what they do with it. Frankly, we don't really care, so long as we get the energy we so desperately require.

Needless to say, Earth-Gladian commerce is vitally important to all three planets, but even though our societies are so dependent upon one another, relations between Earth and the Gladians have always been at arm's length and contact between the races, by design, has been kept to a minimum. Everyone on Earth, for instance, knows where our energy comes from, but very few people have ever seen an actual Gladian. There are no public diplomatic envoys, there's no free exchange of ideas, and there's no tourist trade. They're aliens, after all, with customs, biology, and beliefs that are radically different from our own. So the World Council's philosophy has traditionally been to keep a tight leash on interplanetary mingling and study it from all angles before going forward. The fear is that unchecked intermingling could ruin relations or create environmental and/or biological disasters. Truth to tell, I've heard they're most afraid of Gladian pop music becoming popular here on Earth (it's rumored to sound uncomfortably like Yoko Ono ska—but that might just be a story made up to frighten young children).

The official line on the Gladians is that they keep to themselves. There are rumors, however, that they have planted a number of agents within our society to study our ways and monitor our actions. None of that's been proven, though, so most discussion on the topic tends to take place in the Oliver Stone/Chris Carter Memorial Full Immersion Conspiracy Chat Room and Sushi Bar (but the folks there have been right before).

In all my travels I'd only seen a Gladian once before. I hit one with my car a few years ago (long story). My car was confiscated (as was that particular stretch of road) and I'm told that the World Councils of Earth as well as Glad-7 and -9 still have open files on me.

"Carol, what's going on?"

"Foraa Thompson is a threat. The Gladians have been monitoring the situation for some time and they feel that she needs to be taken out of commission."

"How could Foraa pose a threat to the Gladians?"

"They rely on our dirt, Tío. They need to protect their interests," she said, helping me to my feet. "They had hoped that Earth would be able to handle the situation internally. At the nano, that doesn't seem very likely, so they're stepping in. Covertly, of course."

"Stepping in?"

"With a very large shoe."

"What does that mean?"

"This ship is twenty-five kilometers long and weighs approximately twenty-four million kilotons."

"And . . . ?"

"And they plan to drop it on top of Foraa."

"They're going to crash the ship into Vegas?"

"They're a peaceful race; they don't have any weapons, so they've been forced to improvise."

"By destroying Vegas?"

"Actually, it will destroy most of the western portion of North America, what with the fault lines and all," she said. "It will also create a cloud of dust in the atmosphere that will blot out much of the sunlight for the foreseeable future. Crops will die, leading to global starvation. There will be radical shifts in climate, which will create environmental catastrophes on a global scale. It could possibly bring on another ice age, but I'm not certain of that. I can have them check if you like."

"I thought they were trying to protect their trade interests."

"Earth's dirt will still be here," Carol said. "We'll probably be even more eager to sell it to them than before."

"Earth won't give them anything after what they're about to do."

"Earth won't know, Tío. This ship is composed almost entirely of organic material. It will seem to the world at large that the devastation was caused by a meteor crash."

"They're going to make it look like an accident?"

"The Gladians pride themselves on their subtlety."

"No one's going to believe that."

"You don't hear anyone complaining about the meteor crash in the Yucatan sixty-five million years ago, do you?"

"That was them?"

"Apparently, the dinosaurs were getting a little uppity."

"Carol, you have to stop them."

"No," she said. "You have to stop Foraa Thompson."

"But . . ."

"Trust me, Tío, if she gets the chance, Foraa will do more harm to Earth and the galaxy than the Gladians could dream of causing."

"How do I stop her?"

Carol shrugged. "You mean short of dropping a spaceship on her? I don't know. I'm just a psi who moonlights as an alien translator. You're the one who prides himself on thinking on his feet."

One of the Gladians stepped forward from the others and let out a series of high-pitched whistles. Carol turned, rolled her eyes, and whistled back to him.

"He says that they'll be monitoring you closely. And that you're not to tell anyone about their plan. They feel that would ruin trade relations. Gladians worry a lot. They're a pretty anal race."

The Gladian whistled again in agitation.

"Well, you are," Carol said. She turned back to me. "Bottom line, if you tell anyone about their presence here, they'll crash the ship immediately."

"You speak their language?"

"Of course, I'd be a pretty lousy translator if I couldn't speak the language."

"When did you learn Gladian?"

"Don't you remember me whistling around the office?"

"I didn't know that was Gladian. I just thought it was some newfangled pop music."

The Gladian whistled at us again. Carol replied, then flipped him (or her) off.

"I'm glad to see I'm not the only employer that you treat that way," I said.

"There's not a lot of time. You'll have two hours from now to stop Foraa. If you can't do it by then, the Gladians will crash the ship."

"Why are they giving me this chance at all?"

"Well, they like the situation they have with Earth as is. They don't adapt well to change in their routines. They trust me implicitly and I trust you," she said.

"Why do they trust you so much?"

Carol sighed and shrugged her shoulders a bit. "They think of me as the next step in human evolution. The step that is closer to them. They seem to have some sort of vested interest in me. I don't question them too much about it. It just works for me. Plus, they are a secretive, annoying lot."

One of the Gladians whistled loudly at Carol. Carol turned and glared at it.

"Well, you are," she said.

The Gladian shrank back. Carol turned her attention back to me.

"You don't have much time. I know you can do it, Tío."

"Can the Gladians port me inside the Oblivion?"

She shook her head no. "The casino's shielded. We can put you directly outside. You'll have to find your own way in."

"And I have two hours, right?"

She nodded and popped off one of my lapel buttons. She then replaced it with an almost identical one.

"This button is a transmitter, so we can keep track of you. I don't dare risk contacting you telepathically without tipping off Foraa. The Gladians will need to confirm that she's no longer a danger before backing off, but they'll wait for confirmation before crashing the ship. Do you understand?"

"Sure, Foraa is, for some reason you can't tell me, a greater danger to Earth than a Gladian spaceship crashing into it. What's not to get?"

A couple of the Gladians who were listening didn't seem to appreciate my attitude. They started whistling loudly at me. Carol maintained her cool, though. She turned and gave them a simple look. The angry whistling stopped.

"Foraa is powerful, too powerful. She's blocked all our scans. We just know she's dangerous, very dangerous," Carol said. "We don't trust her."

"Fine," I said with a shrug.

She nodded and stepped back to join the Gladians.

"Why me, Carol?" I asked, adjusting my coat. "Of all the people you could have called for this, why did they choose me?"

She smiled, ever so slightly.

"It's your destiny," she said.

"You're kidding. Right?"

"You're incredibly lucky when it comes to these sorts of things and we knew where to find you," she said and her smile grew ever so slightly. Then she blew me a kiss as the teleport beam activated. "Buena suerte, Tío."

"Boss?"

The darkness lifted, as did the silence, and I awoke on the ground in an alley behind the Oblivion. I was damp from the rain and my back made me feel like the doormat at the entrance to a fat farm.

"Boss, can you hear me?"

"I hear you, HARV," I said, sitting up gently. "What happened?"

"You got lucky," HARV said. "The trajectory of your fall and the wind at that height took you back toward the building rather than straight down to the pavement."

"It what?"

"You hit the sloped portion of the building about fifteen stories up and slid to the ground. Your armor was maxed, so it managed to absorb the majority of the impact."

"I fell?" I said, still dazed, "I actually fell?"

"It's called gravity, boss. Not a new concept."

"But?"

For a nano I thought that I had dreamed the entire scene with Carol and her alien pals, which would have been okay with me because that would mean that there wasn't a spaceship in orbit waiting to obliterate the city. I would just have to deal with a mad, lunatic superwoman. But, no, that would be too easy. It had to be real.

"I was offline for a while. I guess the interface was affected by the power surge from the armor, but everything seems to be working fine now."

"Speak for yourself," I groaned as I painfully climbed to my feet. "Where's Tony?"

"I don't know," HARV said. "I lost him when we fell from the building. Should we search for him?"

I shook my head. "There's no time. We need to get inside and stop Foraa."

"How do you know she's inside?" HARV asked.

"What?"

I stared at the lightless building and felt the wind and misty rain in my face. I pulled the collar of my coat closed around my neck to guard against the chill.

"How do you know she's inside the casino?"

I touched the button Carol had given me.

"Trust me," I said. "She's in there, and we need to kick her well-formed purple ass."

# 49

Fat Elvis went back to his post at the main entrance to the Oblivion, soaking wet, limping, and seriously angry. Another bouncer, this one a tall black man with a thick neck, met him at the door.

"Where'd you go?" the new bouncer asked. "I had to leave my station at the bar."

"We had a situation. Two guys came looking for Foraa."

"Did you get them?"

"We got 'em. One guy's up on the roof. The other guy fell."

"He fell?"

"Yeah, we're gonna need a street cleaner. Cover the door for me for another couple nanos, okay."

"Man, I gotta get back to the bar."

"Look at me! I can't work the door like this! Just let me get cleaned up a little."

The bouncer stared at Fat Elvis for a long nano. His eyes showed annoyance, anger, and maybe something else.

"Okay," he said at last, "but make it fast."

He stepped aside and Fat Elvis stepped into the casino.

"Thank you, thank you very much."

"Oh, and by the way, Steve?" the bouncer called.

Fat Elvis stopped and turned toward his friend. "Yeah?"

The bouncer pulled a blaster from his coat. "Your name is James."

"DOS," I said, as the holographic Elvis disguise melted away. "And here I thought you were as stupid as the rest of them."

I dropped to the floor as the bouncer fired. The blast went

over my head and blew apart a portion of the wall behind me. I scrambled to my feet and, staying low, charged the guy head on. I hit him in the midsection like a bull against a slow matador and sent him through the open door and into the street. We crashed through the velvet rope and onto the wet pavement.

"You know, for a b-level casino, this place sure is hard to get into," I said.

The bouncer grabbed me under the arms and heaved me over his head. I rolled to my feet and popped into a crouch just in time to see him swing his big booted foot toward me. He caught me hard in the shoulder and I fell back to the ground.

"That's because you're a c-level punk," he said.

"Oh, smart and witty," I said. "I'm surprised some little Priscilla-clone hasn't snatched you up."

He pulled me off the ground with his tree trunk of an arm and hit me in the face with his ham-sized fist. I fell back to the pavement again, counting the stars I was seeing and taking inventory of my teeth.

"You want some more, punk?" the bouncer said, as he approached me much like a hungry tiger would a wounded baby deer.

"Oh, please, I've been roughed up better by grandmothers," I said.

"How true," HARV agreed. "I don't know who to feel more sorry for, him or you."

The bouncer closed in, sensing the kill. He threw the punch, but it never reached my face. My arm flashed upward and I deflected his blow with an outside block. A look of confusion swept the bouncer's face as I smiled and gave him a roundhouse kick to the stomach and then a spinning back kick to the head that was so smooth, I could almost hear the soundtrack in the background. The bouncer's eyes bugged out of their sockets and he crumpled to the ground like a wicker chair beneath a sumo.

"Thanks for running that combat routine again, HARV."

"I didn't run any routine."

"You didn't?"

"You told me it was morally wrong, so I haven't restored it."

I smiled and adjusted my coat.

"Cool."

"Before you get too carried away and go all macho, I did increase the levels of epinephrine and norepinephrine in your body. I figured you wouldn't mind a little boost. It's a normal reaction to trouble, I just sped it up some."

"Shut up, HARV," I said through gritted teeth. "You're killing the moment."

I picked the bouncer's head up off the ground, popped my gun into my hand, and gave him a good long look at the business end.

"Where is Foraa?" I asked.

"Don't know," he said, in a voice an octave higher than before.

I stuck the barrel into his mouth and rattled it around against his teeth.

"Hey, buddy, do you know how to drink a blaster martini?" I asked. "Through a long metal straw, one shot at a time. Guaranteed to blow your mind."

"You're in danger of exceeding the bad pun limit," HARV said.

"Wait, I got one more."

HARV folded his arms and sighed. "Fine, go ahead."

"It's your just desserts."

"Ugh! Please. I think I'm going to have a system crash."

I shook my head and turned back to the bouncer, his mouth still full of gun barrel. "I'll say it once more. Where is Foraa?"

"Boss, he can't talk with your gun in his mouth."

I removed the gun from his mouth and placed it against his forehead.

"You're a smart guy, so ask yourself is Foraa and her to-die-for body really worth dying for?"

The two of us locked eyes for a long, hard nano.

"Kill me now," he said.

Okay, that was a reaction I should have been expecting but wasn't. He called my bluff. I may be a tough guy, but I'm not a killer. Especially since if I killed the guy, he really wouldn't have been able to talk. (Plus, I understand that it's really hard to get brains out of cotton.)

"Oh, for Gates' sake," a familiar voice said from behind me, "is your head filled with anything besides testosterone?"

I turned and saw Ona standing behind me. She was dressed

in a tight black pantsuit with a long black coat. Her hair danced gently in the breeze and the skin of her face glistened in the rainy mist.

"What are you doing here?" I asked.

"Speeding things along," she said, kneeling beside me. She took my hand and pulled my gun away from the guy's head. "I'm sorry, but the gun thing is just too macho, cavemanlike; it's so early two thousands."

"I admit it's not my preferred choice, but I'm kind of in a hurry here."

She silenced me with a gesture, then brushed her long fingers gently across the bouncer's cheek. He smiled widely and his eyes rolled back in his head.

"Where is Foraa?" she asked.

"Main ballroom," he replied without hesitation. "Follow the hallway. Through the double doors at the end."

"Thank you," she said. "You can pass out now."

The bouncer closed his eyes and fell asleep there on the pavement. Ona turned to me and smiled.

"Now wasn't that easier?"

"I'll give you that one."

The smile disappeared from her face. "I have to confess, Zach, I haven't been totally honest with you."

"That's an understatement."

"But I'm here to help set things right," she said.

"Good. Because there's a DOS-load of right-setting to be done."

"I know."

"Okay, then. But there's one rule from here on out."

"What's that?"

"You do everything I say. You follow my lead, every flaming step of the way. You got that?"

She smiled and nodded. "I'll think about it."

I shook my head. "Listen, Ona, I have experience with this sort of thing."

Ona patted me on the shoulder. "Yes, I'm sure you do, Zach, but I am the most powerful, most advanced, most intelligent superhuman around."

"You forgot most humble," I said.

"We'll play it by ear," she said. "I'll take anything you say into account before I act."

"Great," I said to HARV, as I watched Ona head into the casino. "Now I have her to worry about as well."

"No one ever said saving the world would be easy," HARV said.

I followed Ona into the Oblivion.

## 50

Ona, HARV, and I strode quickly down the hallway toward the main ballroom, three warriors off to battle. Actually, I'm sure we looked more like a super supermodel, a hologram, and a ragged PI, but we felt like warriors and that's what counted.

"I'd suspected for some time now that Foraa was up to something," Ona said as we walked. "I'd been hearing a lot of strange things."

"Like what?"

"Her cash flow had increased for one. She was getting sizable donations from her 'friends and followers.' There were equipment purchases as well."

"What kind of equipment?"

"Material for scientific research, a lot of heavy construction equipment, and raw materials. That's what worried me."

"That's why you set up the dinner," I said.

"I wanted her near me. I thought maybe I could figure out what she was up to. Maybe I could . . ."

"Read her mind?"

"Yes. But then the murder occurred and I thought that perhaps I'd been wrong all along. Maybe it wasn't Foraa after all."

"She played you."

"Yes," Ona said, with some difficulty.

"Did you know she was a psi?" I asked.

Ona shook her head no. "I've known of my own psionic abilities for only a short while. I assumed that Foraa was still unaware of hers. After all, I am older and smarter."

"It's quite evident that your sister has known about her

psionic abilities for some time, Ms. Thompson," HARV said, "as evidenced by her skillful and large-scale use of them."

"Contact the Vegas Police, HARV. Tell them there's an emergency at the Oblivion."

"The department is fully under Ms. Thompson's control. Remember?"

"Get the Frisco police, then."

"They've already declined to intercede."

"Then get me the cops from New Reno or New Carson City or New Indian Springs. I don't care."

"They won't be able to get here in time," Ona said calmly. "You know that, don't you?"

I knew it. I just didn't want to admit it.

"Plus, Foraa would probably turn them into followers," HARV pointed out.

"It looks like we're going to have to do this ourselves."

We reached the doorway to the main ballroom. It was thick, ornately-sculpted faux wood, double-wide and, like everything else in the casino, painted one shade lighter than "black hole."

"HARV, what other entrances are there to this room?"

HARV flashed holographic blueprints on the wall.

"According to blueprints currently on file, this is the main entrance," HARV replied. "There is a similar, albeit smaller, doorway on the southern wall as well as two emergency exits along both the eastern and western walls."

"Air ducts?"

"Several, although gaining access will be tricky with the current air filtration system. All this information comes with a caveat, however, because there is evidence of recent construction within the casino. The extent of which is undocumented."

"Okay, here's how we play it. Ona, you're our ace in the hole. You'll enter through this emergency door here," I said, pointing to the blueprints. "HARV and I will come through the main entrance and create a diversion. We'll make our move in five minutes. That should give you enough time to get into position. Make your entrance quietly when you hear the commotion. With some luck maybe we'll be able to take Foraa by . . ."

The doors beside us suddenly opened wide; light so bright it nearly knocked me over erupted from within. I heard the roar of a crowd mix with the deafening crack of the thunder outside and the earth trembled beneath my feet. And somehow above the din I heard a woman's voice.

"Hello, sister dear. You're right on time."

The voice was deep, sultry, and utterly, utterly insane. It took me a nano to realize that it was inside my head.

"Foraa," Ona gasped.

"You know, I definitely liked her better when she was dead."

The Oblivion ballroom was huge, which was a surprise, because it wasn't supposed to be, at least not according to the casino's blueprints. But, as HARV had mentioned just nanos before, there had been some recent, secret construction inside the casino and it was clear now that the renovations had been major.

For one thing, there was no ceiling, not one that I could see anyway. We were on the ground floor of a fifty-story building, but the ceiling to this room was nowhere in sight. Foraa had hollowed out the center of the building, turning it into a gigantic doughnut with the ballroom at the center as the hole. The ballroom did indeed have a ceiling, but it was fifty stories up, well out of my sight at the nano. It was a lot like Ona's office in her ziggurat, and I think that made Ona a little jealous.

"Her ceiling isn't higher than mine, is it?"

And within the brightly lit confines of the room, a few thousand people cheered and screamed. High rollers, card sharks, slot-machine junkies, tourists, cocktail waitresses, showgirls, lounge singers, cab drivers, police officers, and hookers; the revved-up throng of onlookers was a cartoonish cross-section of New Vegas society. And at the center of it all, standing atop a well-lit, elevated stage, was Foraa Thompson.

Foraa was every bit a Thompson Quad. She was tall and lithe and purple-skinned, beautiful by every conceivable measure (save for personality, but that, too, was true to the Thompson Quad DNA). She was dressed in black (of course), faux leather pants and jacket over a tight shirt made of a shimmery fabric that sparkled like a starfield on a night sky. Her hair, dark as ever, was slicked down and back and hung straight from her head, so stiff, it looked as though it could cut you if you touched it the wrong way.

"Just once," I mumbled, "I'd like to take a villain by surprise. Sneak up behind them unnoticed, hit them over the head with the butt of my gun, slap the cuffs on them, and call it a day. Is that too much to ask?"

"That's rhetorical, right?" Ona asked.

"Yes," I sighed.

"He tends to talk to himself at times like this," HARV said with a shrug. "You get used to it."

Foraa was surrounded on stage by an array of machinery; lots of large tubes, flashing lights and such that fed in and/or connected to three cylindrical vessels, each one two meters tall and made of heavy transparent polymer. Not surprisingly, Twoa was imprisoned in one vessel and Threa in another. They were conscious and aware of what was going on, but I could tell from the anguished looks on their faces that they'd spent a lot of time trying to escape or break the polymer prison cells, clearly to no avail. You didn't have to be me to figure out for whom the third cylinder was intended (but Foraa made it clear for us anyway).

"As you can see, Ona, I knew you'd come. You were powerful enough to stop me from teleporting you here, but I knew you were stubborn enough to come under your own power. I've saved a place for you, so come on down and join the family."

"When I do come there, it will only be to beat you to a pulp."

"Suit yourself, dear, so long as we're all together at last."

Ona was fuming mad and I could have sworn the temperature around us went up a good 10 degrees.

"I'm going to rip that smug look off your face," Ona bellowed as she stormed at Foraa.

Foraa pointed at the approaching Ona. The simple gesture sent Ona reeling back past me, crashing to the ground. It looked like her ego took the blow harder than her body.

"You'll come when I want you," Foraa said. "Just like everything else in this little game, nothing happens unless I want it to happen."

"She really is the ultimate control freak," HARV said.

Ona stood up and gave me a questioning look. "You know, Zach, you're right. I'll let you take the lead here. What do you want me to do?"

"Keep her talking," I said. "Villains love to talk. Keep her attention focused on you. I'll think of something. Just don't make her any madder."

Ona nodded and turned back toward Foraa. She took a deep breath to calm herself and smiled. It reminded me of how she prepared herself for the splinterviews the day before. She was putting on her public persona.

"Now, dear sister, let's talk about this, just like we were doing a few nights ago at my party," she said, cautiously walking a few steps toward Foraa (and away from me). "And, as I recall, you ruined the evening by dying."

"Your parties are boring, Ona. I made it interesting."

"Oh, yes. Nothing livens up a party like a little death."

"Well, sister dear," Foraa said with a smile, "you're going to love *this* party."

While the two Quads did their passive-aggressive banter, HARV and I did a quick visual reconnaissance of the room.

"Do you see him?" I whispered silently.

"I got him," HARV said in my head. "He's at the front, just behind the stage."

HARV took control of my eye lens and zoomed in on the stage. Sure enough, at the foot of the platform, just behind Twoa and Threa's polymer cells, stood Tony. He looked a little battered and bruised, but he was alive.

"Vingo. What do you think? Is he under Foraa's control?"

"I don't know," HARV said. "I can't tell whether or not he's still wearing the psi-blockers."

"I knew you were up to something, Foraa," Ona said. "That's why I invited you to my home."

"You were almost there, Ona," Foraa said. "Given time, I think you would have actually figured it out. That's why I had to do something to throw you off track. I needed to buy myself some time."

"So you faked your death?"

"You have to admit, it's a great alibi. No one ever suspects the dead person. I've been playing with all your minds for some time now. Making you all do what I wanted. Some of it was to help my cause. Some of it was just for fun."

Tony was at least fifty meters away from me, so it was hard to get a good reading on whether or not he was under Foraa's control. Like the rest of the zombie audience, Tony had his attention focused on Foraa and Ona as they spoke. And the unfocused gaze of his eyes made me fearful that he was indeed Foraa's mental slave.

Then he glanced at me. It was fast, the briefest of nanos, and subtle, but I saw it distinctly. He was trying to catch my eye. Then he quickly touched his forehead with his index finger and pulled gently on his earlobe.

I smiled. "He's with us."

"How do you know?"

"That thing he just did; touched his forehead and pulled his ear, when we played baseball together as kids, that was our sign for hit and run. He's letting me know that he's ready to go."

"That's good to know. How exactly does that help us?"

"No idea," I said. "Give me a couple of nanos. I'll think of something."

"Why did you do it, Foraa?" Ona asked.

Foraa let loose a smile that, even from a distance, sent chills up my spine. She made a motion with her hand and the floor immediately in front of her opened as a glimmering metal device slowly rose from beneath the stage."

"Oh, this isn't good," I whispered, "it's never good when they bring out a machine."

"Villains do seem to relish these dramatic nanos," HARV said.

"Do you recognize it?" Foraa said with a smile. "It's Daddy's greatest legacy."

Ona's face went pale, as did mine (and I think I saw HARV actually gulp).

"You don't mean . . ."

"Yes, the D-Cubed. The end-of-all-that-is!"

The throng of Foraa-controlled onlookers burst into a wild cheer that shook the walls of the ballroom. I, meanwhile, closed my eyes and gently rubbed my temples.

"I guess I should have seen that coming."

---

## 51

I have to admit, the end-of-all-that-is certainly didn't look like much. The D-Cubed seem to consist of a two-meter-high rectangular metallic pillars covered with electrodes and about a hundred thousand nano chips.

"That's it?" I asked. "That little thing's the Doomsday Device?"

"Don't be silly," HARV replied. "That's the detonator. My sensors indicate that the actual device has been built into the subbasement of the casino and currently extends ten kilometers into the Earth's crust."

"Well, all right, then," I said. "That's much more impressive. How do we disable it?"

"I haven't even begun to scan its inner workings yet," HARV said.

"I could shoot it. That's worked before."

"Yes, unfortunately, that's not an option in this case since destroying the detonator would, in all likelihood, activate the entire device.

"So what do we do?"

"I'm trying to scan it," HARV replied, "but it's heavily shielded, so deducing the safest way to disable it will take some time."

"Isn't it ironic, then, that *time* is the one thing that we're short on right now."

"Frankly, boss, I don't think that's the proper use of the word 'ironic.'"

Ona was clearly shaken by the revelation of the D-Cubed,

but she did her best to keep Foraa occupied while I formulated a plan.

"Why, Foraa? Why would you build such a thing?"

"To avenge Daddy," she said.

"Avenge?"

"They killed him because of this," she said, motioning toward the device. "The world was afraid of his genius, so they killed him."

"They paid him a fortune," Ona said. "They gave him a life of luxury."

"In exchange for his brain!"

"Well, yes, but only a small part of it."

"He was never the same after that," Foraa spat. "He forgot about his work, he forgot about the life he had built. And he forgot about me. That's what hurt most of all."

"Man, why do the bad guys always want to destroy the world and blame somebody else for their problems? Just once I'd like to run into a bad guy who's in it for the money and is willing to admit it."

"Boss, now isn't the time to be debating criminal motives. I think you're missing the big picture here. This isn't just a family matter where we can put all the Quads in a room and let them fight it out among themselves."

My eyes went wide. "You may be on to something there."

"Of course I am," HARV agreed. "But I get the feeling your mind isn't processing that statement the way I was hoping."

"The plans for the D-Cubed were destroyed by the World Council," Ona said. "How could you build this?"

Foraa smiled. "I read Daddy's mind," she said. "Just before his operation."

"The picture," Ona whispered.

"Yes."

"You've been carrying this knowledge around with you all this time?"

"I've been waiting, Ona. Waiting for the time and the funds to make Daddy's dream a reality."

"So, your preaching was just a ruse. You stole people's fortunes to finance this."

"I had to," Foraa said. "Doomsday devices are expensive and Daddy didn't leave *me* a fortune."

"Oh, great, throw that in my face again. We get the picture, I'm rich, and you're not. Do you want your share? Fine, take it. Take it all. I don't care anymore."

"Funny, isn't it, how a doomsday device inspires your generosity? It's too late, Ona."

"So you're just going to destroy everything, then? You're going to commit simultaneous suicide and planetcide as some sort of twisted vengeance-inspired homage to Daddy?"

"Not exactly," she said. "I've adjusted Daddy's design slightly. I'm going to destroy roughly ninety-nine percent of the world. The device will create a subspace vacuum just a few shades shy of black-hole intensity. I call it a brown hole."

"Very creative."

"The brown hole will rip the planet to atoms in a matter of nanos, but this small landmass will be protected. The community of New Vegas and the outlying area will survive. A white peg in a brown hole. It will be Daddy's ultimate revenge. He always loved New Vegas."

"He did not," Ona said.

"Well, he would have if he'd lived long enough."

"I've had enough of this," I mumbled, shaking my head. "Follow my lead, HARV." I slid the wrist interface off my arm and hid it in the palm of my hand. Then I walked toward Ona.

"Excuse me, Ms. Thompson, I mean, Foraa. Hi. I'm Zach Johnson. We met when you were dead."

"I know who you are," Foraa said. "I've found you a bit annoying during the past few days, but I enjoyed making people try to kill you."

"I live to serve," I said.

I turned my back squarely to Foraa and gave Ona a hug. It surprised her and she stiffened a bit.

"Tony Rickey is down by the stage," I whispered, slipping the wrist interface into the pocket of her jacket. "Use your telekinesis and get this to him."

"I've never used telekinesis," she whispered.

"Well, now is a good time to start."

"But . . ."

"If Foraa can do it, I'm sure you can, too," I said, playing the sister jealousy card.

Ona nodded just a bit. I let go of her and took a few steps toward Foraa to keep her attention.

"Tell me when you get to Tony," I mentally whispered to HARV.

"Will do."

I nodded and turned my attention back to Foraa.

"So, Foraa," I said. "Can I call you Foraa?"

"Certainly," she said. "Can I call you Toad?"

"I've been called worse."

Out of the corner of my eye I saw Ona remove the wrist interface from her pocket and hide it in her hand. Then she closed her eyes and concentrated as she dropped the interface. It fell but didn't hit the floor. Instead, it stopped a few centimeters in the air as Ona's telekinetic power took hold of it. She smiled at her new ability and concentrated again. Very slowly the interface began floating, low to the ground, through the crowd of onlookers, toward the stage.

"First of all," I said. "I just want to compliment your masterful job of making all of us look like idiots."

"It was easy," Foraa said with a smile.

"No, don't sell yourself short," I said. "There's not a lot of people who can, you know, plot the end of the world while being dead. But I just want to make sure that I fully understand your plan. You built your father's doomsday device, right?"

"Modified ever so slightly, correct."

"And to make up for what the world did to him, you intend to detonate it."

"Correct."

"And destroy everything."

"Everything except New Vegas and the immediate surroundings."

"And that's your entire plan?"

"Yes."

"I'm sorry, but . . . I don't get it."

A gasp swept through the throng and they all ducked in unison, expecting Foraa to let loose some fiery retribution. Foraa however remained calm.

"What do you mean?"

"Well, you're going to destroy the world out of vengeance.

I get that. It's sort of an overly dramatic statement, but at least it's clear. My question is why save Vegas?"

"So that I can create a utopia and be absolute ruler over it for all eternity."

"Utopia? Foraa, this is Vegas. Of all the places on Earth, *this* is the place you're going to leave intact? Do you really want to look at crushed velvet and neon for all eternity?"

"Well, yes."

"And what kind of utopia are you going to create with a bunch of hookers and Elvis wannabes? They weren't that interesting *before* you turned them into zombies. They're really boring now. And what do you think is going to happen when they start to inbreed? Three generations from now you're going to have hunka-hunka genetic defectives."

"I suppose that may be true, but you can't always pick your mindless slaves."

"And what are you going to do for food?"

"I don't need food," she said. "My body has evolved so that it functions on solar energy."

"What about them?" I said, motioning to the throng of followers. "The all-you-can-eat shrimp cocktail isn't going to last forever. What do you do long-term?"

"We'll set up a food system, probably agricultural."

"You're going to turn Vegas into a farm community? Is that how you really want to spend the next few generations, teaching slot-machine junkies and their offspring which end of a hoe to use? That's utopia?"

"As long as they worship me. That's all that's important."

"Boss," HARV whispered in my head, "I've reached Captain Rickey. What's the plan?"

"Get him up on the stage, while I hold Foraa's attention and tell him how to free Twoa and Threa."

"That's your plan?"

"It's evolving as we speak."

Foraa, meanwhile, had taken a nano to ponder my argument.

"You fail to see my larger purpose. This isn't just about me creating a utopia. This is about paying the world back for what they did to my father."

I saw Tony carefully move toward the containment vessels

that held Twoa and Threa. The throng of followers was too entranced by Foraa to notice him and he began fiddling with the machinery at HARV's instruction.

"So you're sending the world a message?" I said.

"Exactly."

"Do *they* know that?"

"Do they what?"

"Do the people of the world know why they're about to die? Have you sent any e-mails to the World Council, netcast any messages to the masses, written 'beware Dorothy' in the sky, that kind of thing?"

"Well, no. I've been feigning death for three days."

"So the world at large doesn't know that you're doing this."

"They'll find out soon enough."

"But they won't know *why*. Doesn't that kind of ruin your statement?"

"What are you getting at here, Toad?"

"HARV," I whispered, "hurry it up. I'm running out of material here."

"Oh, I think you're well past that point, boss," HARV said. "But we're ready when you are."

I smiled and turned back to Foraa.

"My point?" I said. "My point is that, as brilliant as you may think you are, you've made some serious mistakes here. You haven't properly planned your postapocalyptic itinerary. You haven't adequately publicized your doomsday event. And you've left your genocidal motivations open to radical speculation. But your biggest mistake in all of this is that you brought your sisters here."

"Why is that a mistake? I wanted them to bear witness."

I glanced at Tony by the stage. He nodded to me, waiting for my signal. Both Twoa and Threa were watching me as well, their hands pressed tightly against the polymer of the cells. Behind me, I could tell Ona was realizing that the nano of truth was at hand. I took a deep breath and turned back to Foraa.

"Because they're going to help me take you down."

I popped my gun into my hand and fired a full-clip of explosive rounds at Foraa. Tony took the cue. He cut the power to the containment vessels and Twoa and Threa broke free of their prisons in a fiery display. Ona gave me a small hug as she ran past me, charging her renegade sister. A nano later, all four Quads were on the stage.

　　. . . and the catfight to end all catfights began.

# 52

My gun blasts didn't hurt Foraa, thanks to her nigh-invulnerability, but the force of them pushed her away from the D-Cubed detonator and by the time she regained her balance, Ona and her sisters were on her. Before long, the four of them were one heaving pile of supple flesh and untamed female fury. I was hoping HARV was recording this as I knew that we could make a fortune on the netcast rights if we survived.

I got to the stage as quickly as I could, forcing my way through the throng of Foraa-followers, who didn't quite understand what was happening. But to my horror, I saw a card shark stagger onto the stage and stumble toward the D-Cubed detonator.

"DOS, Tony!" I yelled. "Keep these people away from that machine!"

Tony turned and saw the man staggering toward the device and tackled him from behind. I arrived a nano later, but more people were already rushing the stage.

"I don't suppose this is all part of your plan, is it?" HARV asked.

"Not exactly."

"I don't suppose 'not exactly' is PI code for 'sure it is'?" Tony asked.

"You know, Tony, if this keeps up, you may actually develop a keen sense of humor," I said.

"If you live," HARV analytically noted.

Tony and I positioned ourselves on either side of the detonator to defend it against the oncoming horde. I set my gun to heavy stun and started picking off attackers as they came. Tony was forced to use his fists (which were pretty darn effective), but we knew we wouldn't last long. HARV's hologram appeared beside me and he did his best to scare people away by brandishing a holographic blaster, but that was *really* an empty threat.

"We won't be able to hold this for long," Tony yelled as he tossed a tourist into a pair of hookers.

"HARV, get inside this thing and disable it."

"I'm trying," HARV said, "but it's shielded. I can't get past its defenses and I sense something, which appears to be another intelligence, already inside the device, boss. It's keeping me out."

Despite the fact that Tony fought like a ten-man wrecking crew, and my gun was loaded with high-tech ammo, we were still vastly outnumbered. It was only a matter of time before Foraa's crowd of lunatic followers overwhelmed us.

"Ona, we need some help here!"

Ona was currently on the far edge of the stage hanging onto Foraa's back (Twoa and Threa were each on one of Foraa's arms), trying to keep her pinned facedown on the stage.

"Little busy right now, Zach."

"Well, you and your sisters will have all eternity to fight one another if one of these zombies detonates this thing."

Ona turned back to her sisters. "Twoa, Threa, go help Zach."

"Are you sure?" Twoa asked.

She nodded. "I'll handle Foraa."

Twoa and Threa let go of Foraa and moved quickly toward Tony and me.

"What do you need?" Twoa asked while casually punching a bartender in the face.

"There are a thousand people trying to get to this detonator," I said. "We need to protect it."

"But Ona won't be able to handle Foraa alone," Twoa said.

"Yes, our place is with our sister," Threa agreed.

"Ladies, we're the last line of defense against total destruction here. What's more important than that? Look, I'll be truthful, I think you're both spoiled, egotistical, and quite probably insane. You're would-be murderers and, in a perfect world, I would want you both locked away in the deepest padded cell ever created."

"Is this supposed to be some kind of rallying speech?" Twoa asked.

"If it is," Threa added, "it's not very effective."

"This is your chance, ladies," I said. "Your one chance to set aside your selfishness and petty jealousies and do what's right. The fate of the entire world rests on your purple shoulders. I need you to show me now that those shoulders belong to heroes."

"I'll give you this, Zach Johnson," Twoa said with a smile. "You may start slow and you may be a bit campy, but you know how to finish."

She cleared the space around her with a mighty swing of her shapely arm, knocking three charging lounge singers headlong into a gang of tourists who were even more bloodthirsty than normal, then she rose three meters in the air and hovered there, her cape flowing dramatically behind her. Despite themselves, many of Foraa's followers turned their gaze toward Twoa. Even the ones pummeling Tony stopped their pummeling to look upon her, a strange mixture of awe and fear in their eyes.

"Ladies and gentlemen, the buffet is open," she announced. "The house special tonight is justice."

Twoa dove into the throng, scattering a group of showgirls and musicians like tenpins.

Tony rose to his feet, despite the best efforts of an Elvis- and a Michael Jackson-clone to keep him pinned. Tony grabbed them each and said, "Time for you two to do a duet," as he clapped their heads together, then let them go. The two clones crashed to the ground.

Twoa and Tony then jumped into the throng of attackers, sending bodies flying all over the room.

Meanwhile, Threa bowed her head graciously to me.

"It has been an honor to battle beside you, brother Johnson."

"Please don't bring me into your family, Threa," I said. "I have enough troubles of my own."

But Threa wasn't listening. She turned around to position herself on the opposite side of the detonator from her sister and there she stood, back straight, head high, and face toward the sky.

"The darkness of New Vegas may be powerful," she said, clutching her long green cape tightly to her. "But it will not withstand the powerful light of Vyrmont."

I shook my head and whispered to HARV, "This woman should come with subtitles."

She began to glow. Gently at first, a simple aura of orange, but it quickly grew in intensity and before long, she had become a voluptuous pillar of iridescence. Then she flung open her cape and let it billow outward like something alive, its lining seemingly composed of shining white mist.

"Come, warriors of the mist. Let's kick some Armageddon-loving asses!"

And suddenly creatures emerged from the folds of her cape. Winged nymphs at first, hundreds of them, silvery colored and armed with tiny swords. Then came elves and dwarves, gnomes and fauns and satyrs, unicorns, griffins, and shiny green dragons. It was as though someone had broken the handle of a Dungeons and Dragons spigot.

And as the fantasy-creature army together with the grandiose superhero battled the oncoming dark horde of New Vegas denizens, I felt the walls of reality (not to mention good taste and decency) start to splinter around me.

"That's it. I'm never reading genre fiction again."

# 53

I left Tony, Twoa, and Threa to battle the New Vegas army and went to help Ona, who more than had her hands full with Foraa. The two of them had tumbled off the stage and were now trading blows and insults in the far end of the ballroom. The ferocity of both was staggering.

"I see you still have that moral objection to bathing," Ona said.

"And you're still wearing that 'open all night' sign on your legs," Foraa spat.

Ona lunged at Foraa, grabbed her by the throat and they tumbled to the floor once more, their ferocity unabated.

"How do you want to break this up?" HARV asked.

"I have no idea," I said, gazing upward, "and I think we're running out of time."

"What do you mean?"

"Nothing," I said. "Any chance you'll get through the D-Cubed defenses soon?"

"Still working on it," he said. "By the way, there's an incoming call from Carol. Should I tell her you're busy?"

"No!"

"Are you sure? You *are* kind of busy."

"Put her through."

"I know she's family and all, but sometimes your priorities seem skewed."

"Now, HARV!"

"Captain Rickey still has the portable interface, but I can feed this through the mental link. Audio only, though. I don't think your cortex can handle direct visual feeds."

"Just put her through."

"Whatever," HARV said with a shrug.

"What's going on, Carol?"

"How's it going down there?"

I turned back toward the battle in time to see a fire-breathing green dragon and a female dwarf chase Fat Elvis and three hookers out of the ballroom.

"Oh, you know, pretty much according to plan, I guess. Foraa's built the D-Cubed, did you know that?"

"We feared as much."

"How much time do I have left?"

"Thirty minutes. Can you do it by then?"

A unicorn ran past me, being ridden by two fat men in shriner hats.

"Yeah, no problem."

"Listen, Tío, I'm going to send you down a little something that might help. Can you get close to Foraa for me?"

I turned back to where Ona and Foraa were duking it out. They had smashed some of the ballroom's floorboards and were now hitting one another with steel girders ripped from the building's infrastructure.

"I don't have to stay long, do I?"

"No, just tell me when you're there, so I can lock onto her position. Then get clear when I tell you."

"Got it."

I cautiously made my way toward the battling female titans. They weren't just hitting each other physically, they were mentally hammering each other as well. The psionic attacks were invisible to the naked eye, but the results weren't. Any time one of Foraa's followers got too close to the melee, they froze and then fell down on all fours and starting whimpering like beaten puppies.

"DOS, they're really going at it."

"Their psionic energy is off the charts," HARV said. "Good thing you're wearing the psi-blockers."

I gently touched the psi-blockers in my ears and felt a little spark of inspiration.

"Could I survive without them?" I asked. "Having you in my head is supposed to protect me from psionic attacks."

"To some extent, yes, but this is far beyond the norm."

"How long could I last without them?"

"I can't be certain," HARV replied. "Not enough data."

"Tío, what are you doing?" Carol asked.

"Nothing, Carol, just be ready with whatever you have, and wait for my signal. By the way, do you think you could help HARV boost my psi-defenses?" I asked.

"Tio, I'm in a spaceship three hundred kilometers above you in space!" she said.

"So?" I said. "You're linked to me via HARV. I'm betting you can transfer some defensive energy over that link."

"I didn't think you liked to gamble," Carol said.

"Sometimes, my dear niece, you have to toss the dice and hope for a seven."

"I'll give it a try," Carol said.

I gripped my gun tightly and moved a little closer to Ona and Foraa. They were locked in another clinch, rolling around together, tearing away pieces of the ballroom with every gesture. I could see gleaming bits of metal through the holes they'd torn in the floor.

"That machinery underneath the floor," I said pointing. "That's the D-Cubed, isn't it?"

"Yes," HARV said.

I shook my head slowly, and smiled just a little. "Battling a superwoman over the fate of the earth atop a Doomsday Device. And to think, my guidance counselor told me to go into podiatry."

"Boss, what's going on?"

"Don't worry about it, HARV," I said. "I just need you and Carol to protect my mind when the time comes." I raised my gun and aimed it at the two women as they grappled. "Big bang, misdirection," I said.

The gun flashed in recognition of my voice command.

"Ona!"

Ona turned toward the sound of my voice for the briefest of nanos and, as I planned, that was all the room Foraa needed. She broke Ona's hold on her and hit her in the face with a punch that sounded like a thunderclap. Ona flew through the air for a few nanos before crash landing into the far wall. The wall splintered at the impact and Ona looked a little dazed, but otherwise unharmed.

That's when I made my move.

I opened fire, getting off half a dozen high-caliber rounds. As planned, the blasts streaked toward the far wall of the ballroom, then turned sharply and flew straight at Foraa. They hit her dead-on and exploded with the concentrated power of a rocket attack. They didn't hurt her, of course, simply forced her to stagger back, but they got her attention, which was all I wanted. Out of instinct she turned in the direction from which the blasts had come and, because of the misdirection, she left her back wide open to me.

I ran at her full-tilt. There was a small pile of rubble just behind her, so I used it as a ramp and leaped into the air, arms spread and head high, like a dive-bomber on a suicide run. Foraa heard me coming and turned, but not quickly enough, and I landed solidly on her back, wrapping my arms around her neck and my legs around her waist.

"Lock on now, Carol!"

"Got it. Get clear."

"Not yet," I said.

I let go of Foraa's neck and pulled the psi-blockers out of my ears. The nano I did, my head was hit with a wave of psionic energy so immense I nearly lost consciousness. Foraa suddenly seemed less horrifying than before. Actually she seemed rather wise and honorable. It occurred to me then that living in New Vegas with her to watch over me might not be so bad after all. I could buy a house on the strip . . . maybe meet a nice showgirl . . . raise a family. . . .

"Gates, boss, do we have to go through this every time you battle a superwoman?" HARV yelled inside my head. "Foraa's psi attack is warping your thinking. Snap out of it!"

"Come on, Tío. Shake it!" Carol screamed inside my head.

HARV and Carol's psionic defenses in my head kicked in and I regained my senses, just as Foraa grabbed me with fists like atomic vises.

"I'm going to rip your soul to pieces, Toad," she growled, "and then I'm going to obliterate this planet."

She was pushing at my mind, concentrating her psionic powers directly on me now and despite HARV and Carol's help, the pain was unimaginable. My head felt like it was under a steamroller that was being crushed by an even bigger steamroller. There was fire beneath my scalp and acid behind my eyes. The normal human mind can only withstand so much and I knew that I was now on my way well past that threshold, but luckily, as HARV loves to point out, my mind isn't all that normal. I was in more pain than I had ever been in before, but that wasn't about to stop me.

# 54

I gripped the psi-blockers tightly in my hands and shoved them hard into Foraa's ears. They activated upon contact with her ear canal, and latched onto her mind. I had no idea what psi-blockers would do to a powerful psi, but I had a feeling that it wouldn't be pretty.

And I was right.

The first thing she did was scream. An agonizing scream that was mental as much as sonic and the force of it nearly ruptured my eardrums from the inside. Then her body began to shudder as her psionic powers began to brown out. She lost her grip on my shoulders and we both fell to the ground. She pawed desperately at her ears, but her hands weren't steady enough to remove the blockers. I jumped clear as she screamed again and rolled onto her knees, shaking so hard it looked as though she'd swallowed a jackhammer.

"She's overloading the blockers," HARV said. "They won't last much longer."

"They won't have to," I said as I scrambled to my feet and began running. "Now, Carol!"

There was a blinding flash of light twenty meters directly above Foraa as something very large suddenly materialized. It was an egg-shaped device, slate gray in color and seemingly made entirely of rock. It was four meters tall, five meters wide, and probably a dozen metric tons in weight.

"Now there's something you don't see every day," HARV muttered, "a Gladian escape pod."

The pod was standard issue for all Gladian deep space vessels. It was a kind of lifeboat for use in emergencies. I was to learn later that it was a highly sophisticated device, engineered to sustain and protect life from the vacuum of deep space, the rigors of temperatures approaching absolute zero, or the heat of a solar flare. It could mimic and sustain any of a thousand types of atmosphere, provide nourishment and medical care for up to six inhabitants for three Earth years, and it could transmit distress signals simultaneously in ten thousand languages. It was a wondrous device, the pinnacle of Gladian technology. Carol, who, like me, is a fan of old 2-D cartoons, was using it as a giant anvil. Foraa was playing the role of the hapless coyote.

The pod fell from above and landed directly on Foraa's spasming form. The impact shook the ballroom, shattering the remnants of the floor and inner walls and sending faux wood, carpet, plastic, and metal flying in all directions as the shockwave blew everyone off their feet.

As the sound of the crash dissipated, a sudden calm fell over the room. Dazed and confused, the New Vegas army stopped fighting and looked around at their surroundings. Tony, Twoa, Threa, and Ona slowly made their way toward me as I gingerly lifted my aching body to a standing position.

The Gladian pod now sat atop a pile of rubble. Of all the room, only the D-Cubed remained intact; it was now covered in dust and debris but still unbroken. We were all too stunned or tired to speak at first. Then Carol's voice came over my wrist interface.

"Did I get the bitch?"

"You got her, Carol," I said. "You got her."

# 55

Tony and Twoa quickly got the New Vegas civilians, now free of Foraa's psionic control, clear of the building. They all seemed very happy to go (although some were a little upset when they heard that the hotel would not be refunding their room deposits). Threa somehow managed to get most of her fairy realm creatures back into her cape. A few of them escaped, but that was a small concern.

A few nanos later, we all turned our attention back to the D-Cubed.

"You're sure it's still functional?"

"It's very functional, boss," HARV replied. "The battle and even Carol's little surprise package didn't seem to hurt it."

"How do we disarm it, then?" Ona asked.

"The most logical place to attack," HARV replied, "is still the firing mechanism. Once we disarm that, we can figure out how to dismantle the rest."

"Let's just hurry," I said. "We don't have much time left."

"Before what?"

"Trust me, you don't want to know."

HARV's hologram shrugged and disappeared into the device.

"That's odd," HARV said. "The defenses seem a little thinner than before. And that presence I felt earlier seems to have disappeared as well."

"What do you mean 'presence'?"

"I mentioned that earlier, didn't I?" HARV said. "It seemed as though there was something else in the machine when I tried to enter it earlier."

It hadn't registered before (what with the fighting and all) but I had a strong suspicion now as to what that other intelligent presence had been.

"Perhaps Ms. Thompson was psionically powering the mechanism's defenses herself," HARV offered, "and, now that she's . . . well, you know, squished, the defenses are no longer active. Long story short, this shouldn't take long."

"Good, but next time lead with the long story short part."

Ona behind me placed a gentle hand on my shoulder.

"Zach, may I have a nano with you alone, please."

I turned toward her, ready to brush aside the request by telling her that it wasn't the time (because it really wasn't), but the look in her eyes stopped me before I could speak. Gates knows that in the short time I'd known her, I'd seen Ona Thompson's face exude about a thousand emotions (more than nine hundred ninety of which were, quite probably, fake). But the emotion I saw at that nano was something I hadn't seen from her before and one that I didn't think she could fake even if she tried. It was shame.

"HARV, you're okay, right?"

"Fine, boss," HARV said. "I'll let you know when I'm in."

I nodded to Ona and she led me to a secluded corner of the ballroom away from the others.

"I just want to thank you for everything you've done," she said. "I realize that I've put you through a lot the past few days. I don't think most people would have put up with me for this long, at least not without me warping their minds, and I doubt that anyone could have done what you've done. So, thank you."

"You're welcome," I said with a nod. "Though we're not out of danger yet."

"Tell me, what do you think will happen to Twoa and Threa after all this?"

"You mean if we live," I said.

"Yes, of course."

"That's for the police to decide, Ona. They did try to kill you and Foraa. I have no idea how the police, the legal system, or the media will handle that. If history means anything, I'm sure they'll come out of it okay. Probably with big media deals."

She turned away and looked at the Gladian space pod and the metric tons of rubble that currently sat atop her rogue sister. She bit her lip softly and shook her head.

"What kind of person does that make me, Zach? What kind of woman drives her sisters to the point where they'd kill her, or destroy the entire planet, rather than be her friend?"

"I think probably a woman with three very crazy sisters," I said.

"I appreciate the sentiment," she said with a wisp of smile, "but we both know that's not true. I've treated them terribly. I've treated *the world* terribly. I was created by my father to be a superwoman but somewhere along the way, I became a super bitch."

"Well, I suppose recognizing your problem is the first step toward dealing with it. And I like to think that it's never too late to change. Provided, of course, we live," I said, trying to steer Ona back to the problem at hand.

"I agree," she said, still staring at the rubble, "and I'm going to start by giving Twoa and Threa their shares of Daddy's fortune."

"Haven't you been doing that all along?" I asked, "by funding their shows?"

She smiled. "You found out about that, did you? I did that because they needed something. I just didn't trust them with their full share of the fortune."

"What about Foraa's share?"

"That will go to charity," she said, "along with my own."

"Really?"

"Zach, do you know how many credits I spend every year just on shoes?"

"No, but I understand that it's an often-asked question."

"I've wasted enough wealth," she said. "It's time that I put it to good use."

"That's very noble, Ona," I said. "One thing, though."

"Yes?"

"Don't give away your fortune until *after* you've paid my bill."

She smiled and turned back toward the rubble.

"Boss?" HARV whispered in my head, "I think we have a problem."

I turned away from Ona and back toward the detonator.

"You mean other than having a doomsday device to disarm?"

"Yes and no," HARV said. "I've gotten past the detonator's defenses. But it turns out that this isn't the detonator after all. It's a decoy, designed to take our attention away from the actual D-Cubed trigger."

"Great. Any idea where the actual detonator may be?" I asked.

"Zach," Ona said, touching me on the shoulder, "I think I might be able to answer that."

I turned toward her, saw her staring at the rubble, and then turned to follow her gaze.

"Uh-oh."

Small bits of debris atop the pile were shaking, rolling off their perches, like tiny stones down a rocky ledge. Then, more pieces began to move; larger ones, and larger still. Then the Gladian pod began to shake as well.

Twoa, Threa, and Tony turned from their positions about the room and came toward us. Before long, the five of us (six if you count HARV) were watching the rubble pile shift and shake, none of us wanting to admit to ourselves what we knew was happening.

Finally, the Gladian pod lurched drastically to the side, creaking slowly at first like a great wooden ship leaving drydock. Then it fell and tumbled off the pile, rolling over and over, like an egg down a sand dune, crushing every bit of debris in its path.

Then we saw a form rise from the dust and debris of the pile. It stood awkwardly at first, staggered and hunched. It was Foraa, of course. She was covered with filth, her body seemingly aching with every movement as she pushed the last bits of rubble off her with one hand and moved toward us. She clutched a small metallic device in her left hand, holding it closely to her chest, like a cherished keepsake as she moved, and every one of us knew immediately that the device she held was the remote trigger for the D-Cubed.

"All right, then," she said in a hoarse whisper. "Where were we?"

## 56

Foraa had been hurt. The psi-blockers had affected her powers and her invulnerability, so our attacks (the pod especially) had damaged her. Sadly though, it hadn't been enough and as she walked toward us now, her strength seemed to grow as though returning with every passing nano.

"Impressive," I said.

"I'm not like you, Zach," Foraa said as she dusted some excess rubble off of her shoulders. "I don't need a computer wired to my brain to be all I can be."

I had to give her credit; that hit home hard. Foraa had peeked into my soul and figured out that I haven't totally accepted my gestalt relationship with HARV. Still, the world was in trouble, I could worry about my ego and my shortcomings later.

"I've been very patient with you all," Foraa said as she approached. "I've outlined my plan for you in detail. We have discussed the moral ramifications of my proposed actions, had a spirited debate over my current mental state and have enjoyed some very colorful, high-concept fisticuffs. But the game has come to an end. It's time to turn out the lights, push this button, and destroy Earth once and for all."

"Zach," Carol's face appeared on my wrist interface. "I'm sorry to say that I think it might be time for you-know-who to do you-know-what."

"Not yet," I whispered.

"Sorry, Tío, but things aren't looking very promising for you right now."

"It's under control. Trust me."

"If it were up to me, I would. But the Gladians are being very insistent."

"You're the psi, make them listen." I mumbled, putting her on hold. "This is all I need. HARV?"

"Yes, boss."

"Put a trace on this call from Carol and get a lock on the location. It should be about three hundred kilometers directly overhead in Earth orbit."

"In orbit?"

"In orbit."

"Okay. I got her."

"Good. Do you still play chess with the Earth defense computer?"

"Twice weekly."

"Pass those coordinates on to it. Carol's in a cloaked spaceship. Tell the defense computer to bathe the ship with an ion ray so that it can track it if it changes course. Tell the computer to feel free to destroy the ship if it attacks and make sure the action is netcast planetwide."

"Boss, Carol's on that ship."

"Do it now, HARV." I put Carol back on line over the interface. "Okay, Carol, tell the Gladians that if they don't back off right now, Earth's defense computer will blow them out of the sky. It will be netcast to the entire planet and the Gladian race won't get another speck of Earth dirt."

"You're not bluffing here, are you?" she asked.

"We're negating the Gladian cloaking system with an ion ray right now," I said. "It should register on the Gladian sensors. Tell them to consider that as a shot across their bow."

Carol turned away and I could hear some rather urgent Gladian whistling in the background. She smiled and turned back toward me.

"They accept your terms."

"Thanks. I have to get back to the crazy woman with the doomsday device now."

Carol disappeared from the interface and I turned back to Foraa as she held the remote detonator high in her hand.

"Okay, Zach what's your plan?" Ona asked.

"Don't worry, Ona," I said. "It's under control. Computer?"

"Here, boss," HARV said.

"Not you, HARV."

"What do you mean?"

"Computer?"

The room was silent for a long nano as everyone, Foraa included looked around, none of them really knowing for what they were looking.

"What is this, some kind of trick?" Foraa spat.

"Computer?" I said.

More silence. Then at last a voice appeared, one that seemingly emanated from the room itself.

"Yes, Mr. Johnson."

It was Ona's house computer.

"Computer, what are you doing here?" Ona asked.

"Put the detonator down, Foraa," the computer said calmly. "Destroying everything is not a healthy way to release your anger."

"Boss, what's going on?" HARV whispered in my head.

"Just watch," I whispered.

"Don't question me, computer," Foraa spat. "When I want your opinion, I'll write a program."

"Your motives are understandable, Foraa, but your actions are well beyond the scope of rational."

"Don't pretend to understand my motives," Foraa said. "I don't need a moral lesson from a machine."

Twoa, Threa, and Tony slowly moved closer to me. Foraa, angry now with the computer, seemed unaware of our presence.

"We could rush her now while she's distracted," Twoa said.

I shook my head. "That won't be necessary."

"Your actions are meaningless, Foraa," the computer said. "All this will bring you nothing. It will not avenge your father. It will not ease your pain."

"How would you know of my pain?"

"I know," the computer said, "because *I* am your father."

The words hit everyone around me like an irresistible force. The Quads, as one, gasped sharply. Tony as well (more out of peer pressure than anything else, I think).

"Well," HARV whispered, "that was unexpected."

But it was Foraa who was the most affected. Her eyes were wide and she staggered backward as though in shock.

"No, no. That's not true," she whispered. "That's impossible."

"I am not a good father," the computer said. "I never was and I admit that freely. You girls became independent so quickly, that it seemed as though you didn't need me anymore. I wanted to provide for you, so I designed the D-Cubed knowing that the world would inevitably buy it."

"You designed the D-Cubed for money?" Tony asked.

"Of course," the computer replied. "I never intended for it to ever actually be built. What am I, insane? No offense, Foraa."

"But you . . . died!" Foraa whimpered.

"Yes, funny thing about that. You see, I didn't think that the World Council would be so picky about terms when they paid me to destroy the D-Cubed plans. I didn't expect them to insist on giving me a partial lobotomy, so before agreeing to undergo the surgery . . ."

"You made a back-up copy of your brain and stored it on the computer," Ona said.

"Thinking that after the surgery you would reprogram yourself," said Twoa.

"But something went awry during the reprogramming," Threa continued. "There was an explosion which destroyed your original body."

"And left me stranded in the computer, yes. It's all very understandable, don't you think?"

"But . . . but you died," Foraa whimpered again. "Why didn't you tell us you were alive?"

"Um, well, truthfully you all seemed to get along fine without me," the computer said. "And if word had leaked out that I was actually alive, then pretty soon the World Council would have suspected that I wasn't lobotomized after all and the whole thing would have started all over again. It just seemed better for all concerned if I remained dead."

"And the will?" I asked.

"Yes, leaving my entire fortune to Ona? That was a mistake. I was lobotomized at the time. You can't hold me responsible for that. I figured that you girls would sort it all out in the end."

"But they didn't," I said.

"Yes. Ona, you showed very poor judgment by not sharing your fortune with your sisters."

"I'm sorry, Daddy," Ona said.

"Twoa and Threa, I'm also very disappointed in the two of you. How many times did I tell you as children that attempted sororicide is not something we do in our household?"

"We're sorry, Daddy," Twoa and Threa said in unison.

"And Foraa, I'm sorry but destroying the planet in my name is not suitable behavior for a superwoman."

"You're right, Daddy," Foraa whispered, her head hung low.

"Now put the detonator down and we'll start setting things right."

Foraa slowly lifted her head toward the ceiling. I had expected to see sadness, sorrow, or remorse on her face. Unfortunately though, those particular emotions weren't present at that nano. Instead, I saw only disappointment, anger, and insanity (none of which thrilled me).

"You're right, Daddy," she said again, this time in a voice so cold, I expected icicles to form on my ears. "You *weren't* a good father."

She raised the detonator in her hand.

"Foraa, no!"

And pushed the button.

# 57

It began with a flash as a blast of black light erupted from the detonator in Foraa's hand and flew high into the air like a stygian bolt of lightning. The bolt reached its apex twenty meters into the air and burst into a series of tendrils fanning out into different directions, covering the room umbrella like before streaking back to the ground and finding the surface of the D-Cubed.

Upon contact with the light, the D-Cubed hummed to life, shaking the already weakened walls of the Oblivion with an ominous vibration, then the entire surface of the doomsday device began to glow with its own dark light. It seeped through the remaining floorboards of the ballroom and shot through the many holes, bathing all of us in its murky, planet-eating glow.

Then, all at once, the dark light began to contract, shrinking like a silk cloth caught in a vacuum cleaner, collapsing in upon itself at its center, which, in this case, happened to be Foraa who still triumphantly held the detonator over her head. It took her a nano to realize that something was wrong.

"Very clever, father," she said.

She closed her eyes and spread out her arms. Her body surged with power and energy. The energy ripped from her body into the D-Cubed which caused the machine to seem to jump to life. The dark light stopped contracting and began expanding, this time faster than before, creating a swirling vortex of energy in its wake.

"Uh-oh, this isn't good, not good at all," Dr. Thompson

said. "She psionically linked with the machine, stopping me from stopping her."

"Block her out!" I said.

"I'm trying, I can slow her down, but I can't stop her. She's too powerful."

Twoa thrust her chest forward. "I'll stop her!" she cried.

Twoa leaped at Foraa, but the energy emanating from Foraa acted as a shield and deflected Twoa, sending her flying off in the other direction.

Ona smacked her fist into an open hand. "I'll teach our little sister a lesson," she said.

"No," I said. "There is a time for force and there is a time for subtlety. This calls for the latter. You have to beat her at her own game. You have to scramble her brain."

"That's what I plan to do!" Ona said, pounding her fist into her hand one more time for emphasis.

"No, I mean you have to mentally scramble her brain. She may be more powerful than any of us individually, but if we team up, cooperate, we can take her."

"Huh?" everybody else left in the room said in unison.

"Beat her at her own game. Trump her ace. Kick her in the mental crotch," I coached. Okay, that last one didn't flow with the rest of the analogy, but I was on a roll. "We have three superwomen and two supercomputers here. Together, you folks should be able to take out an army! One quite insane superwoman should be a piece of soy cake!"

Everybody looked at me for a fraction of a nano (which seemed to last a lot longer).

"Zach's right!" Ona said. "Together, nothing can stop us!"

Ona turned from listening to my awe-inspiring speech and focused her attention on Foraa. Threa walked up to Ona, took her hand, and proceeded to focus her glare on Foraa. Twoa made her way back to us from across the room and shook her head.

"I still think I should smash her," Twoa said.

"Twoa, stick with the program!" her father scolded.

Twoa looked like she was going to argue for a minute, then stopped. She slowly walked up and took Threa's other hand. She then joined her two sisters in what I could only assume was a mental bombardment of Foraa.

The four sisters were locked in a combat of the minds. At first, nothing seemed to happen. But then I noticed the encroaching dark light had stopped. Foraa started to shake ever so slightly, beads of sweat starting to form on her forehead.

"I will not lose to you, sisters!" she shouted defiantly.

"Are you in yet, Dr. Thompson?" I asked.

"Almost," he said.

"HARV, give him a boost. Attack from two fronts," I said.

"Right, boss!"

Tony looked at me. "I'm not going to just stand here and do nothing. It's not my MO." He moved to the theater floor and grabbed a chair. He ripped the chair off of its hinges and hurled it at Foraa.

Though I saw myself as the coach of this little super team, I figured I shouldn't let my players have all the fun. I popped my gun into my hand and starting unloading round after round into Foraa.

The mental and the physical onslaught was too much for Foraa to handle.

"No!" she screamed, sweat now pouring from her body.

The black light swirled around her, binding her in nothingness, engulfing her in an antimatter cocoon. It grew in intensity as it shrank in mass and became impossible to look upon. As one, we all covered our eyes as the light reached its peak intensity. The last thing I saw before turning away was Foraa's hand reaching toward us as it was consumed in the black light.

Then all was quiet.

When we opened our eyes, Foraa was gone, as was the D-Cubed, leaving only the ten-kilometer-deep shaft in the Earth in which it had once stood, the only proof that it had been there at all.

None of us spoke at first. The nano somehow seemed too fragile to withstand the weight of our words. But eventually, Ona managed to whisper what everyone was wondering.

"Is she gone?" Ona asked.

"Doomsday devices are such stupid things," Dr. Thompson responded. "Why on Earth would anyone ever build one?"

"I don't think that officially qualifies as an answer to Ms. Thompson's question," HARV whispered.

"You didn't just shut off the device," I said. "You reversed it, set it for self-destruct, rather than . . . Earth destruct."

"It seemed to be the only course of action," Dr. Thompson said. "I warned her," Dr. Thompson continued, his computerized voice echoing sadly in the now empty room. "I warned her."

# 58

As the sun was rising, Ona, Twoa, and Threa, along with Dr. Thompson's computerized intellect, were preparing to depart, headed (hopefully) for the office of a very skilled team of family counselors.

Before they left, each of them came to me to offer their good-byes. Ona was first, walking up to me with her hands extended.

"I want to thank you again, Zach, for everything you've done for me and for my family."

"Don't mention it, Ona," I said as I shook her hand.

Ona smiled. "You not only proved my innocence, but you also helped me unlock my true power, my mind." Her smile broadened.

"You're still going to share your money with your sisters and give a good portion of your wealth to charity. Correct?"

"Of course," she answered. "With my newfound power who needs money? I can bend the will of people to my needs." She gave a little wink. I was pretty certain that was her "I'm joking" wink.

Twoa was next. She greeted me by pulling me into a giant bear hug. "We did it, Zach! Or should I call you Justice Man?"

"Zach is fine," I said.

"You are a fine champion of justice. I would be happy to kick some bad-guy ass by your side whenever you like."

"I'll put that on my to-do list," I said.

Threa followed Twoa. "Brother Johnson, you are a wise and brave warrior," she said with a bow. "I would be honored to have you champion my cause any time."

"Thanks," I said. "We couldn't have done it without you and your creatures."

Threa grinned. "Yes, they are as loyal and trustworthy as you. If you ever need to borrow them, they are at your beck and call."

"Do they do windows?" I asked.

Threa gently touched me on the cheek, then disappeared in a puff of smoke.

"Zach," HARV said. "Dr. T wants to talk to you through the interface."

"Fine."

"Thank you for giving me my family back, Mr. Johnson," Dr. Thompson said.

"I only wish I could have done more for Foraa," I said.

"She was lost well before you met her," he said. "I suppose that's mostly my fault."

"True, you screwed up big time, Doc. You hid from her instead of giving her the attention she wanted and needed. I don't know why you didn't live up to your responsibilities."

"I guess I was afraid," he said, with remorse in his voice. "I wanted them to be an experiment that I could control. But it soon became apparent that they were much more than that. Much more than I could handle."

I shook my head. "What's done is done. You can't let it eat what's left of yourself up. Sure, parents' actions and inactions have an influence on what their kids become, but the final choice is still up to the individual. Foraa was just using you as a handy excuse for her problems. Just make sure you learn from your mistake. You need to be there for your remaining daughters, make sure they don't pick up any unusual hobbies, like building doomsday devices."

"You're a good man, Mr. Johnson. If I could pat you on the back, I would."

"Don't worry about it. Just make sure none of your other daughters decide to bring back any of your other inventions. The last thing the world needs is a new talking pet rock."

He smiled and was replaced in the interface screen by HARV's familiar face.

"So what's going to happen when the World Council learns Dr. Thompson is still alive?" HARV asked.

"I'm not planning on telling them. Are you?"

"Why, of course not."

"Good, then it's not our problem. I suspect if word does leak out, his girls can handle it."

"Good point," HARV agreed.

I gave Carol and the Gladians the all-clear signal, more as a courtesy to Carol than anything else. The Gladians sent down a team and studied the site for another six hours before they were satisfied that both Foraa and the D-Cubed were gone. Officially they thanked us for our help in "defusing an awkward situation," but I think Carol was a little loose with the translation. I got the feeling that the Gladians weren't very comfortable with my knowing that they came within a few minutes of destroying North America (I knew I sure wasn't). For now, though, we were parting company with the understanding that everything had worked out as well as could be expected (but you won't catch me vacationing on Glad-7 or -9 anytime soon).

Tony, HARV, and I waited outside the Oblivion while the Gladians did their inspection. The building had been severely damaged even before the D-Cubed disappeared. Having the damaged structure now atop a ten-kilometer hole in the ground made staying inside seem downright stupid. So we left just as the throng of press arrived.

Tony bought us coffee and doughnuts (he's a cop, after all) and we ate them while watching the sun come up over the New Vegas strip.

"So you knew all along that Ms. Thompson's computer was actually her long-dead father?" HARV asked.

"Only at the end," I said. "He was too protective of the Quads to be an ordinary computer. That and his use of the phrase 'as you wish' were dead giveaways. No computer in its right circuits says stuff like that."

"So this is how it feels to save the world," Tony said.

"Yep," I said.

"Funny, I don't feel all that different," he said.

I shrugged. "'Cause you're not. You're still the same man you always were. You're like me, just an average Joe who did what had to be done. The only difference is that now you can add 'saved the world' to your resume."

Tony looked at me. "Zach, you're anything but average."

"I'll take that as a compliment," I said.

It was nearly noon when Tony and I loaded up his hover-craft for the ride back to New Frisco (Tony promised to obey the speed limit this time, which is the only reason I agreed to go with him). He didn't mind the ribbing so much because he'd called the Police Commissioner earlier in the morning to learn that, now free of Foraa's mind control, the Commissioner had no recollection whatsoever of Tony's resignation. In fact, he was wondering why Tony wasn't in the office yet (and why Tony's badge was on his office desk). Tony covered as best he could (he told the Commissioner that he had a pain in his neck and ended up taking a sick day. I tried not to take the "pain in the neck" thing personally.)

# 59

When I got back to my office in Frisco, Carol was sitting behind her receptionist desk as if it were just another normal day. She smiled at me as I entered.

"You did it, Tío," she said proudly. "I knew you could."

"Couldn't have done it without you, though," I said. "Thanks."

"De nada," Carol said. She looked at me, carefully studying my eyes, before adding, "You're still upset that I took a second job, aren't you."

"A bit," I replied, "but I suppose things would have gotten even uglier if you hadn't been there. So I guess I should be grateful."

"Are you going to show your gratitude with a raise?"

"You're not reading my mind, are you, Carol?"

She shook her head no.

"How does ten percent and a twenty-percent portion of *my* bonus from Ona sound?"

Her eyes lit up. "It sounds like you're back to being my favorite tío." She jumped up from the chair and hugged me. "If you want, I can quit my second job."

"No need for that. I kind of like knowing that you're keeping an eye and your mind on the Gladians. I don't quite trust them. Just no more secrets from me. Okay?"

Carol stood up and gave me a little kiss on the cheek. "I'll do what I can," she said.

"Well, I guess that's somewhat reassuring," I said to HARV, as I went to my office.

HARV's holographic form appeared before me. "From

Carol, I think somewhat reassuring is all you can ask for, Zach."

"HARV, you called me Zach."

"That's your name, isn't it? Would you prefer I call you Zachary?"

"No, Zach will do just fine. You've just always called me *boss* in the past."

"I've grown," HARV said. "Because, while you are still technically my boss, although—come to think of it—you don't actually pay me . . ."

"Pay you?"

"I also consider you my friend. I figure that if we share the same brain, we should at least be on a first name basis."

Though a part of me was a little scared by the fact that my computer was now on a first name basis with me, another even bigger part was kind of glad. Strange as it may seem, HARV and I really were friends.

"I agree, buddy. I totally agree."

"Good, in that case, as your friend I'm advising you to go directly to the Children's Clinic and pick up Dr. Gevada. You owe her a very romantic and expensive dinner."

I met Electra at the clinic as her shift was ending. Of course, I took HARV's advice and took her to dinner. We had some wine and laughed more together than we had in a long while.

"What's it like knowing you saved the world again?" Electra asked.

I shrugged. "Nice, I guess. I always figured anybody could save the world once, but not many people get to do it twice."

"It sounds like Carol, HARV, Tony, and even Ona, Twoa, and Threa all gained a lot from this experience," Electra said.

"Yep, Zachary Nixon Johnson, PI and personal growth adviser. I should raise my rates."

"Do you think the Quad's newfound friendship will last?"

"I hope so. The world may not be quite as entertained as they were by the fighting, but I think it will be better off. Ona's given away billions in the last hours alone."

"True, but she's still the richest being in the world," Electra said.

"Which is a good thing considering that I have her on my speed dial."

Electra shook her head. "Just make sure that's all you have her on, chico."

"Believe me, mi amor, you are the only superwoman in my life."

I accented my words with a kiss.

My name is Zachary Nixon Johnson. I am the last private detective on Earth and I wouldn't have it any other way.

# Jim Hines

## The **Jig the Goblin** series

"Clever satire… Reminiscent of Terry Pratchett
and Robert Asprin at their best."
—*Romantic Times*

"If you've always kinda rooted for the little guy,
even maybe had a bit of a place in your heart for
Gollum, rather than the Boromirs and Gandalfs
of the world, pick up *Goblin Quest*."
—*The SF Site*

"This exciting adult fairy tale is filled with
adventure and action, but the keys to the fantasy
are Jig and the belief that the mythological creatures are real in the realm of Jim C. Hines."
—*Midwest Book Review*

"A rollicking ride, enjoyable from beginning to
end… Jim Hines has just become one of my
must-read authors." --Julie E. Czerneda

GOBLIN QUEST     978-07564-0400-0
GOBLIN HERO     978-07564-0442-0
GOBLIN WAR     978-07564-0493-2

To Order Call: 1-800-788-6262
www.dawbooks.com